Born in London in 1874, **Mau** a scion of a family long prom. the British Empire. The son director of the Bank of Englan ....i at Baring Bros.) he was educated at Eton ...u at Cambridge, and joined the diplomatic service in 1898. In 1904 he became a journalist and reported the Russo–Japanese War in Manchuria; later he was a correspondent in Russia and Constantinople. He is credited with having discovered Chekhov's work in Moscow and helping to introduce it to the West. Baring is remembered as a versatile, prolific and highly successful writer, who produced articles, plays, biographies, criticism, poetry, translations, stories and novels. He is regarded as a representative of the social culture that flourished in England before World War I, his work highly regarded to this day for the acute and intimate portraits of the time.

# MAURICE
# Baring

## *Cat's Cradle*

HOUSE OF
STRATUS

This edition published in 2001 by House of Stratus, an imprint of
Stratus Holdings plc, 24c Old Burlington Street, London, W1X 1RL, UK.

www.houseofstratus.com

Typeset, printed and bound by House of Stratus.

A catalogue record for this book is available from the British Library.


ISBN 0-7551-0090-5

# DEDICATION

*To Hilary Belloc*

MY DEAR HILARY,

I dedicate this book to you, although perhaps you may never read it. You would probably say, before reading it, "It is one of those..."; but I will not say *what*, for the reviewers would seize the phrase and talk of nothing else. You and I have both of us reviewed books, and we know how it is done. You have described the process accurately in a handbook to literature – *Caliban's Guide to Letters* – which I hope young journalists study; read, mark, learn, and inwardly digest, as the Collect says.

I dedicate this book to you, partly as a little act, a small sign of friendship; partly because you have dedicated three books to me, whereas I have only dedicated one to you – and that is out of print; and partly because, *if* you read it, you would see what I meant: you would agree.

It is a story. It is a true story. The main facts, strange facts, improbable facts, are all true; even the frame, the setting, is near the truth, although I invented it. You can find the story in the old files of a newspaper; but, in turning the true story into fiction, I had to attenuate the facts, to foreshorten, to lessen, to

i

diminish, to tone down; because what is true in life is not necessarily true in art – the old tag about *le vrai et le vraisemblable* – and to give to fiction the appearance of reality, to make the reader swallow it, you must needs temper the powder of fact with the jam of (relative) probability. The reader could not have swallowed the crude improbable facts of this tale neat and undiluted from the glass of fiction – he would have said they were impossible; so I have toned down the truth, and in a way spoilt the story and made another.

The story has a moral.

You will perceive what that moral is should you read it, but, in case you don't read the book, I will tell you what that moral is presently. Before I do that I want to digress for a moment. You will remember that years ago, when we were young, merry, and very, very wise, people used to talk a good deal about "Art for Art's sake," and maintain that a work of art with a moral was a contradiction in terms. Strangely enough, they used to regard as their masters men who not only practised, but even preached the direct opposite: Baudelaire, for instance.

Strangely enough, too, sometimes the fruit of their theories was poor as a work of art, but powerful as a sermon: instances will leap readily to your mind. But it always seemed to me that if life has a moral (which it seems never to be without), and if art be the reflection of life, art must have a moral too. And so it has. *Hamlet* has a moral. *Faust* has a moral. *Madame Bovary* has a moral; the novels of Henry James, as well as *The Diary of a Nobody* – in fact, they have the same moral:

"Be good, sweet maid, and let who can be clever;"

And it always seemed, and it still seems to me, that those who jibbed at the thought of a *moral* in art were merely muddle-headed; they really meant one of two things: either it is bad art to *point* the moral, to nudge the reader's elbow – that the moral should be self-evident and proceed from the nature of the work

(Maupassant writes about this somewhere at length) – or they meant something else which I will explain presently.

Now *trente ans après* the shibboleths have changed outwardly, but the foolishness underlying them remains the same. The world of the precious is just as foolish as it was in the days of Molière or in the " 'nineties," in spite of streams of light irony being poured on it by Max Beerbohm and thunderbolts of satire hurled at it by others (such as Mr Shaw, Mr Wells, and yourself).

Last year, so I am told, in one of those houses, near the Zoo, where the lions of Chelsea and the tigers of Bloomsbury are fed at luncheon-time, and roar gently as any sucking dove to the semi-intelligent, and sometimes to the wholly beautiful, a certain author was mentioned whose work is well known for its rapidity and vigour, its force, its crude stark power, its colour, noise, and life. One of the lions – so I am told – said the work of this author was *immoral*. Had you made that remark you would have been justified, because you regard morality or immorality as factors of cardinal importance, art or no art; but the lion in question did not. He was an art-for-art's sake lion – a Paulopostproustian lion – a post-Freudian lion, a post-expressionist lion, a post-Pirandellian lion, a post-Dadaist lion, a baroque lion, a broadbasedbellbeige-trousered, narrow-necked-rainbow-coloured-jumpered lion, a post-cubist-neomilaneseSalvatorRosaCarloDolci anti-classical yet anti-Ruskinian anti-(all except-the-early-operas)-Wagnerian, – neo-early-nineteenth-century neo-romantic-quasirelativist-pseudo-Lamartinian lion. And, as some other person present (so I am told) pointed out, had any one said to his lion that the latest find from the dung-heap on sex and psycho-analysis was immoral, he would at once have said that morality had nothing to do with the matter. As was pointed out, the lion disliked the work of the author in question, but knowing that as art it was too obviously effective to deride or to ignore, and so being cornered, he said it was immoral.

And how often do we meet with the converse? When readers and critics say that Mr Jones (the poet) writes badly, or that Mr Smith (the essayist), who used at least once upon a time to write well, has now begun to write *bad English*, what they really mean is they disagree with Mr Jones' aesthetics and with Mr Smith's politics and religion. So when people now say that they do not care whether a book has a moral or not, I for one do not believe them.

To go on to the moral of this book.

It has been expressed by Cervantes in Spanish. Here are his words. I read them long before I ever thought of writing the book, and, I may say, to satisfy the lions, that I wrote the book first and deduced the moral afterwards.

"Solo se vence la pasion amorosa con huilla, y que nadie se ha poner á brazos con tan poderoso enemigo, porque es menester fuerzas divinas para vencer las suyas humanas." ("Love is too strong to be overcome by anything except flight, no mortal creature ought to be so presumptuous as to stand the encounter, since there is need of something more than human, and indeed a heavenly force, to confront and vanquish that human passion.")

It has also been admirably expressed, partly in English and partly in French, in a poem by yourself, composed at my table, and in my presence:

"The Love of God which leads to realms above
Is *contre-carréd* by the god of Love."

"*Contre-carréd*": yes. That is to say, met, counteracted, assailed, undermined, thwarted, checked at every turn, but not necessarily *defeated*, not necessarily *checkmated*, by the god of Love...in this case...but, if you want to know how this applies to my story, you must read it; and if you do, don't tell your friends what happened before they have read the book. I hope the reviewers won't either; but that, as I know, is asking a great deal.

The scene of the story begins in Rome, and Roman places and people, as they were a long time ago, play a part in the tale. A few months ago I revisited Rome. I had not been there, save for a day during the War, for twenty-three years, and I found many changes. I was surprised to find that many things had disappeared, and I was still more surprised to find so much that I had known was still there... Beautiful things had been destroyed and ugly things had been built – but that is not all. Nature as well as art had in those twenty-three years suffered at the hand of man: the divinely elegant waterfall of Tivoli – Horace's Tibur (*ille terrarum mihi præter omnes*) is no more. I recommend you to sing that waterfall in a dirge; it is now among the good things that have come to an end.

One day I was walking down a side street and I came across what in my dreamland and my limbo-world had been the original of my "Palazzo Fabrini.".... It is now an hotel. I walked into it and asked for an imaginary friend, for one of the characters of my book: "Is Mr Clifford in?" I asked. No; there was no such person staying in the hotel. The stately rooms I observed had retained their shape, but they had been redecorated by a Munich firm in what used to be called *modern style*... What was once the big reception room on the first floor was now an Oriental lounge tiled and palmed, where *thés dansants* take place... The pictures and the furniture were of course all sold years ago; Prince Roccapalumba's *salotto* is now the *vestiaire* where you pay to have your coat and hat looked after, and Princess Blanche's sitting-room, which looks out on the street, is the American bar...a Jazz band plays every afternoon during dinner, and after dinner as well...

It was playing hard as I left the hotel, but the street was unchanged; it was just as dark and as narrow as ever. A wine-cart passed me drawn by a mule, and the hood of the cart sprawled on one side like a sail, the shiny outside made of black oil-cloth and stamped with a pattern of red roses, and lined inside with green cretonne...and on one of the barrels lay a dog, and the driver sitting on one side made hoarse noises, and in the street some one somewhere was playing a violin and some one else was singing, and the music they made was not jazz, no; but something much older, and something Roman...as old as anything I tell of in my story. Blanche might have heard that tune from her sitting-room on a certain evening in May...and a little farther up the street against the massive corner of the "Palazzo Fabrini" – now *l'Hôtel de l'Enfer* (at least that is what it ought to be called) – there was a flower-stall.

You remember what a Roman flower-stall looks like? It faces you upright like the back-cloth of a stage scene, a flat bank, or a bookcase or a shrine...over it is spread an immense white sunshade. It has ranks and rows of flowers. The first row of the serried stalls (*fauteuils d'orchestre*, as it were) is full of roses, red and white, crimson and pink, then come red and pink carnations; tulips – large wild tulips, and red and white anemones; the windflower wet (you remember Rufinus' epigram νοτερή τ᾽ ἀνεμώνη – and red peonies. Then another and a sharper note – orange marigolds, colossal, pale yellow daisies and white daisies, purple irises, and pale mauve stocks, mauve pinks, purple cyclamens; every shade of mauve and lilac:

"Men che di rose e più che di vïole,
  Colore aprendo,"

("That's out of your class, you great Swede").

And then at the top in the gallery of that divine audience – lilies, lilies of the valley, arum lilies, and great branches of white blossom and green leaves. That is where Princess Roccapalumba bought flowers to send for Bernard after his fall; that is where Titian chose a pink for *La Bella*; that is where

Antony perhaps bought a rose for Cleopatra; that is where
Sextus, the false, who did the deed of shame, bought a
tempting token to send to Lucretia; where Numa Pompilius
bought a discreet nosegay for Egeria; and possibly where
Rufinus himself (although a civil servant in new Rome) chose
his garland (he may have been on leave).

The flower-stall was, is, and shall be, Rome. Do what you
will, restorers, destroyers, renovators, improvers, classicists,
futurists, cubists, relativists, artists, architects, builders,
speculators, prehistoric investigators, municipalities,
companies, syndicates, syndics, corporations, committees,
bankers, professors, politicians, lunatics, vandals ancient and
vandals modern, pull down this Palazzo, destroy that street, dig
here for the bones of the Dinosaur, build a picture palace more
colossal than the Colosseum, and barracks and banks larger
than the baths of Caracalla, a tower higher than Eiffel's, a sky-
scraper five times as high as St Peter's, pull down these
baroque or those Byzantine churches (according to the fashion
of the moment) – ("Credette Cimabue nella pintura tener lo
campo, ed ora ha *Dolci* il grido,") – change this, and alter that,
burn what others have adored, and adore what others have
burnt, put a tram on every available piece of empty pathway.
Make the fountain of Trevi into a powerhouse; drain the lake of
Nemi; canalise the fountain of Bandusia; switch off the
waterfalls of Tivoli...it doesn't matter. Call it progress, or big
thinking, or new building, or fast living, or success, or
evolution, or the triumph of the fittest, or of the idea of Rome
for the Romans; call it what you like, you will never conquer
Rome. Rome will conquer you; and when you have done your
best, and your worst, through your labyrinth of sky-scrapers,
through your Babel of towers, steel and iron, through your
acres of barracks, through the noise and stench of your wheels
and your cars and your engines, and your cylinders; through
your overhead wires and ground rails, your electric sparks, and
your forest of aerials, through the fumes of petrol and the

smoke of your chimneys, and the roar of your furnaces, there still will come the hoarse notes of a peasant on a wine-cart laden with barrels drawn by mules, bringing to the city the *vino dei castelli*, the fire-opal wine of Frascati or the produce of the land; some one will still put up that booth of flowers, those tiers of roses, peonies, pinks, and marigolds, lilies and greenery under the spreading white sunshade; and in the hoarse ejaculations of the peasant on his wine-cart, or the song of some sad or light-hearted son of the street, or in that array of colour and fragrance which strike the heart of the wayfarer with rapture like a chord of music, Rome will rise again and assume her lawful rights, recover her old domain and be clothed once more with her ancient dominion, – immortal, indestructible, imperishable Rome.

3 Gray's Inn Square
*June* 17, 1925

# BOOK I

# CHAPTER I

Henry Clifford was born the year Byron died. He was the younger son of the younger son of a peer – the last of an old Whig family. He had inherited neither titles nor estates. His father was a diplomatist of some distinction, and Henry at one time was destined to follow his father's profession. He spent two years, as an attaché, at Berlin, and a year in Portugal. But he was determined not to spend all his life abroad, and as his motives and the mainspring of his character were mainly unashamedly selfish, without qualification or compromise, his purposes acquired in this way a steel-like quality.

His determination to do as he liked and to live as he wished was complicated neither by ambition nor by a call to civic duty. It was tempered by a worldly and slightly cynical philosophy. Politics bored him; he disbelieved in responsibility; he had no estates to look after.

After his brief experience of diplomacy he came back to England, and was for three or four years private secretary to a leading Whig politician. Through the good offices of his chief he obtained a comfortable billet in the House of Lords.

He had now got what he wanted. He was fond of travel in reasonable doses – travel restricted to the nearer capitals of Europe – and, in moderation, of racing, shooting, and yachting. He enjoyed visits to certain country houses, and he was fond of dining out where he knew for certain that the food would be excellent and the company agreeable.

He married an unobtrusive, ladylike, gentle wife, who had exquisite manners, never said anything silly, and knew how to order dinner. She was a martyr to headaches and neuralgia, but she never complained, and (without any adventitious aids, save sal volatile) she concealed constant and excruciating suffering behind a diffident manner, apologising for such foolish ailments.

Henry Clifford's little dinners in Curzon Street were famous. It was considered a rare privilege and the hallmark of a certain distinction to be asked to them. Bores had to abandon hope, not as they entered, but of ever entering his door.

Sometimes there would be a little music after dinner. Mario would sing, perhaps, and Grisi, or M Fechter and Mademoiselle Colas would act a French proverb, or Parry would sing his inimitable songs at the pianoforte. But never an inferior artist.

Henry Clifford had carved for himself exactly the mode of life that he wished, although it is probable that he did so without much forethought or calculation, but naturally and almost unconsciously. He was known as a connoisseur in the art and the arts of life. His opinion was sought and taken on all questions that concerned the amenities and the elegances of living; art, letters, music, and the drama. By literature you must understand French memoirs, which he devoured (and an occasional novel from Cawthorn & Hutt, the circulating library); by art, a temperate, respectful, and bored acquaintance with the Old Masters (like the relation between a courtier and an authentic but too well known royal personage); a cultivated taste in prints and plate; a *flair* for bric-à-brac, French furniture, and china; by music, the Italian Opera at Covent Garden; and by the drama, the French play, the Wigans, Sam Sothern, and Marie Wilton.

He did not touch the Bohemian world at any point. He found his circle of friends and acquaintances readymade, and he found it in Mayfair and St James's. He belonged to several Clubs, and he was looked upon as an authority in Clubland, not only in the matters I have just mentioned, but also in more important things – the things that really mattered, such as racehorses, claret, French cooks, boots, dogs, tobacco, and women. He often went racing, but he was a prudent gambler, and he seldom betted, and never played any card game except whist, and that rarely. He was not well off, and had small hope of ever being better off, and he knew that the secret of comfort was to live just a little below your income; if he did not succeed in doing that, he never exceeded it.

He had many friends among the rich, who helped with his investments. They envied but could not emulate his dinners, so exquisitely cooked by a Frenchwoman, and his parties, where the greatest Italian singers sang, or the best actors of the day were delighted to act, for nothing.

He was recognised as an *arbiter elegantiarum* – people said, "Henry Clifford has such good taste," but he never paraded his knowledge, nor ever boasted. He sought tact and ensued it, and managed his constant infidelities and love affairs with discretion. He played with fire without singeing himself. In his youth he made love to women older than himself, on principle, and he was never unkind nor uncivil to his wife. She, however, with the lucidity of those who are supposed to be completely stupid and utterly null, read her husband like an open book, and was always aware of his most carefully concealed intrigues, and when, not long after their marriage, his roving affections were definitely centred in a person who was the wife of a Russian diplomatist, Princess Solski, a woman of immense cleverness and understanding, handsome and distinguished as well (*"Irina tue tout le monde par sa distinction,"* a French lady said of her), Constance Clifford accepted the fact without a murmur. Henry Clifford saw Irina Solski every day of his life, and took no step without her advice.

In 1851, not till three years after their marriage, Mrs Clifford gave birth to a daughter, and nearly died. The doctor said she could never have any more children. The daughter was called Blanche. Constance Clifford had no more children, and she died when Blanche was thirteen years old. Blanche was looked after by a Swiss governess, a large and comfortable creature called Mademoiselle Zeulen, who spoke a hybrid French and was nicknamed "Lud," nobody knew why.

The advent of Blanche introduced a new element into Henry Clifford's life. He worshipped his daughter from the moment she was born, and an unsuspected vein of tenderness in his nature was brought into play.

Blanche was a precocious child with adorable ways, and she soon became her father's companion and playmate. When she was twelve years old he talked to her exactly as he would have done to a grown-up person.

Blanche did not take after her mother, who had been fair and pale, with the look of a sick doll about her. Nor was she like her father, who was handsome, but in another way. He was tall, and not so dark as his daughter, bearded, with pronounced features, and sharp, steel-blue eyes that saw everything that was to be seen on the surface, and which gave him the look of a well-bred bird, a distinguished, rare peregrine falcon.

Blanche was said to be like her grandmother, Henry Clifford's mother, who was always talked of as a person of great beauty and charm, and it was said that when she stayed in a country house the guests at breakfast usually gravitated to the end of the table where she was sitting.

As a little child Blanche was pronounced exquisite, but the wise shook their heads and said it was too good to last. When she reached the schoolroom age it seemed for a time as if they might be right – she was too small. But when she was sixteen she shot up, and grew sufficiently tall. When her hair was done up there was, so Mademoiselle Zeulen said, no more doubt about it, and relations and friends admitted that she had *looks*.

Blanche was perhaps going to be a beauty. *"Elle a une jolie coupe de figure,"* Mademoiselle Zeulen added, "and I have taught her to sit up."

Blanche's complexion was white, without looking unhealthy – it was white as the petal of a flower, almost as white as a camellia, and quite as soft; her hair was dark, and her eyes soft and dark, with very long lashes. There was something southern about her, something a little exotic, and yet at the same time entirely English, as if she had been a flower grown in one of the warmer southern or western counties.

She was not supposed to have any foreign relations or foreign blood, but it was said that her grandmother had been gay in her youth, and one could not be surprised at anything.

Blanche came out when she was seventeen, and was taken out by her aunt, Henry Clifford's sister, the widow of a distinguished soldier, who was like her brother, only a little more pronounced and more exaggerated, and where Henry hinted, Caroline Somner *asserted*. If Henry Clifford looked like a noble species of bird, his sister had something rapacious in her expression.

Blanche was considered to be an exceptionally pretty girl. Her father sought the best advice as to her clothes, and took trouble about their every detail; they were made in Paris.

Towards the end of her first season she fell in love with a distant cousin, a penniless boy, who had just passed into the Army. He was in a line regiment and had little beyond his pay to live on. His name was Sydney Hope; he was good-looking, engaging, and full of spirits. He proposed to Blanche, and she accepted him. She told her father the news, confident that he would be overjoyed, and without a shadow of doubt but that he would share her joy.

She was not disappointed in his sympathy. Henry Clifford thought there was nothing to find fault with in the boy; he had every quality one would like to have in a son-in-law, save the one, the indispensable: means. Henry Clifford talked over

7

the matter with his sister and with Princess Solski, and they both agreed with him that the marriage was, and would always be, impossible. There was no money and no prospects. There was one distant relation, it is true, who was well off, but he had heirs in plenty. Henry Clifford himself was not well off. He needed what he had got, every penny of it, to live (this really meant for his amusements, his entertainments, and his little dinners). And then Blanche's education had been so expensive – her music lessons, and her strange fad for learning Italian… taxation was worse than ever, one did not know where to turn…that last thing he had been put on to in the City had not turned out as well as he had expected; not badly, but not what you expect when you get advice from the best authorities. It was ridiculous to think that Blanche with her looks could not do better. He was ambitious for her; he earnestly wished for her happiness, but the idea of her happiness was inseparable in his mind from worldly advantage.

"Blanche is not only going to be pretty, but she will be a real beauty," Princess Solski said, and Caroline Somner thought that girls always began by an engagement that didn't count. It was a thing like measles that had to be got through.

Henry Clifford made inquiries and paid a few visits. The first person he went to see was old General Hope, Sydney's father, who said it was clearly impossible that his son should marry, and said it was doubtful whether Sydney could afford to go on living in his regiment. Then Henry Clifford went to the War Office and to the India Office, where he had friends. He learnt, among other news, that Jack Ilford was going out to India as Governor of Bombay. He would, of course, be wanting an ADC. Henry Clifford ran into Ilford on the steps of the India Office. They were old friends. They had a short talk on the topics of the day. It was characteristic of Henry Clifford that, although there was only one topic which he wished to discuss with Lord Ilford, he did not mention it on this occasion. He had a horror of being buttonholed, of pressing a point at the wrong moment, of being inopportune, and he never did to others what he hated having done to himself, not from unselfishness, but from the feeling that he might be protecting himself for the future. He asked instead after her Ladyship, and Ilford asked him to take pot-luck and dine with them at their house in Portland Place that night.

Henry Clifford accepted. He was the only guest at dinner, and he had plenty of time after dinner for conversation over the port.

The next day Sydney Hope received a letter from Lord Ilford asking him to call at Portland Place, and in the course of the week it was arranged that Sydney should go out to Bombay as the Governor's ADC.

So far from thinking that this was the end of their romance, both Blanche and Sydney thought it might be the foundation of their fortunes. It was perhaps, they thought, the first step in the ladder of Sydney's career.

They had each of them been told by their respective fathers that no public or formal engagement could be thought of, that marriage in the near future was impossible, short of a miracle. They both declared that they were prepared to wait for years. They cited cases where people had waited for years. They confidently expected that the miracle would happen, and that the sudden intervention of Providence would smooth out all their difficulties and make the fulfilment of their hearts' desire possible.

Sydney sailed for India in October.

Blanche, as was only natural, took his departure badly, and Henry Clifford said she needed change of air and change of scene. He arranged that his daughter should spend the end of the winter and the spring at Rome with her Aunt Caroline, who had an *appartement* in that city. The change would do her good, they said, and it was a pity to get into a groove. She had been learning Italian, so what could be more timely than a visit to Italy? It would be a pity if the lessons were wasted, and she were to forget all she had learnt. She would, moreover, enjoy the picture galleries and the sights, and there were always charming people at Rome. He would have liked to take her out at once, only he was unable to leave England just at that moment, owing to the political situation. The Government had just resigned, and Mr Gladstone had formed a new Administration. Parliament met in December, but both houses adjourned till February.

Henry Clifford settled to take Blanche to Italy directly after Christmas, and to stay there till Parliament met once more. He would then go home, but would come back and fetch her at Easter.

Blanche accepted these arrangements with apathy. Now that Sydney had actually left the country, her hopes were dashed, and her faith in a miracle happening was somewhat dimmed. But she showed a brave face to the world, and she did not wish her father to be sad on her account. Her devotion for him exceeded, if such a thing were possible, his devotion for her.

Nothing could have surpassed Henry Clifford's solicitude for his daughter during these difficult days. He did everything he could to brighten and to please her. He and Blanche left England directly after Christmas, and passed through Paris on the way out, and stayed three nights at the Hôtel Westminster. Henry Clifford took Blanche to the Théâtre Français and to the Odéon, where a promising actress, Mademoiselle Sarah Bernhardt, had made a hit in a little play by one of the younger poets, a M. Coppée.

They dined one night at the British Embassy and one night at the Tuileries, where she was much admired, and received beautifully turned compliments from Frenchmen young and old.

Henry Clifford was an accomplished linguist, and spoke French idiomatically and unaffectedly, and his daughter had inherited his gift. It was easy for her to get on with foreigners, who were only too eager to pay attentions to so beautiful a girl.

They started for Rome towards the end of December, and travelled to Nice, whence they posted by the Cornice to Genoa, and then went by railway to Florence, where they stayed a night.

Blanche was enchanted with her first glimpses of the south and with the beauty of Florence (in spite of the cold). Her father said the city, which was now the capital of Italy, was much improved. He made the most admirable of cicerones, and he enjoyed initiating Blanche into the beauties of the place. The approach to Rome (they posted the last lap of the journey from Orte, and went by Civita Castellana, Nepi, and Baccano) delighted Blanche still more, and she experienced no disappointment when from the southern edge of the crater of Baccano she looked for the first time at the sudden panorama: the Umbrian and Sabine Apennines covered with snow, the Tiber, Mount Lucretilis, in the far distance Tivoli, the Alban Hills, and the dome of St Peter's itself over the cypresses of Monte Mario, in the dazzling clearness of an Italian winter's day.

Mrs Somner's apartment was in the southern quarter of the town, the second floor of a spacious palazzo not far from the Farnese. The Romans said this was the healthiest part of the city. She had, of course, many intimate friends among the Romans, as well as in the foreign and English colonies, and she entertained with economy and discretion.

Blanche was introduced to several charming Italians, but her heart was in India with Sydney, and superficially she was busy gathering fresh impressions, so that she did not give herself time to think about the people. Her father thought she was looking better, and she seemed to grow prettier every day.

He was well satisfied that he had done the right thing in bringing her to Italy. He did his utmost to distract and to amuse her. This meant a great deal, as there was no more delightful companion in the world when he chose than Henry Clifford. He was gay, light in hand, and had a vein of quick, dry irony, a kind

11

of humorous weariness that made his descriptions and comments unexpected and amusing. He was exceedingly appreciative; he knew how to extract the essence of a situation, and where interest and amusement was likely to be found. He had a nose for anything that had point. He took Blanche to see all sorts of out-of-the-way sights, private collections, and picturesque spots.

He introduced her to the most agreeable people, he kept her from the bores (whom he was a past master in warding off), and he was always ready to talk over things with her, to compare notes and impressions, and to laugh over any little incidents of the day.

Henry Clifford had to be back in London for the opening of Parliament on 15th February. He decided to leave Blanche with her aunt. But before he left, an incident occurred which turned out to be of immense importance to Blanche.

Blanche and her father were invited to dinner one night by the French Ambassador to the Vatican, and it was there that they made the acquaintance of the Prince Roccapalumba. Blanche sat next to him at dinner. He had inherited the title at his father's death some years previously, and he was now, although only thirty, the head of the family. His mother, who was an Englishwoman, came from one of the old English Catholic families. His Christian name was Guido. He was short, thin, and sallow, with a head too big for his body and a nose too long for his face. His hair was thinning rapidly, and he had rather cold, large, penetrating, grey eyes and well-shaped hands with long, tapering fingers. He was immensely rich, and owned a magnificent palace in Rome, full of the kind of pictures that bored Henry Clifford most acutely, estates not far from Rome, a villa in Florence, and some property in England. He had been to school for two or three years at Stonyhurst College, and had studied for a year at the University of Fribourg in Switzerland. In spite of his excellent education (his teachers had for the most part been men of European reputation, each in his speciality), he had absorbed little knowledge, nor did he care greatly for arts or letters. In spite of this, he gave the impression of culture, or rather of an immemorial civilisation and of an uncanny intelligence. He was more intelligent – one felt – than he had a right to be. He talked English like an Englishman.

His intelligence, acute as it was, paled beside that of his mother. She had been dazzling rather than beautiful in her youth, but after the age of thirty-five she changed but little, and became imposing. She was majestic, but she never grew too large, always picturesque and artistically arranged, she preserved her freshness, her activity, and the keenness of her interests unabated. The first epithet applied to her by Italians was "*artistica*," and by English people "handsome," and sometimes "*simpatica.*" She was naturally amiable and agreeable, but self-centred and exacting, and she would take trouble to be more than civil and pleasant to all with whom she might be thrown together, as long as they acknowledged her supremacy and submitted unconditionally to her sway. Her manner was gentle and caressing, but showy, her methods insinuating and soft, but this superficial softness concealed a will of iron and an inflexible determination. She was, in spite of an exemplary piety – which was genuine – fundamentally non-moral, and one felt that she belonged more to the Renaissance than to the nineteenth century.

She had become so acclimatised by her long sojourn in Italy that few people took her for anything but an Italian. Italy and Rome more especially had absorbed her, and her very looks seemed Italian; her hair might have been painted by Titian; it had red lights in its silken gold, and there was something about her, something in her opulent lines and the soft languorous brown eyes and white skin, that suggested a Giorgione.

She was devoted to her son, her only son (she had one daughter as well, at this moment twenty-two years old and still unmarried, whom she disliked), and she was determined to find him a wife after her own heart – if possible, an Englishwoman. That night at dinner she sat next to Henry Clifford and opposite Blanche and her son, and there was little that escaped her. She had known Henry Clifford a long time, and they got on admirably.

"I congratulate you," she said, "on Blanche. She is already enchanting, but she will grow into a real beauty. She looks so un-English, too." And the Princess rapidly reviewed Blanche's genealogy. "And how well she speaks French."

"Oh, I think the girl will be passably pretty!" said Henry.

"How long has she been out?"

"Only one season."

"And I am sure there must have been many *soupirants* already."

"Oh, plenty of sighs, but no bridge! – only boy-and-girl affairs – nothing that counts."

"She has plenty of time. She is so young – only seventeen?"

"Eighteen this month."

"She takes after your mother."

"So people say."

"*Tant mieux.*"

The Prince took trouble to make himself pleasant to Blanche, and his mother noted the fact with satisfaction.

He offered to help her to see the sights of Rome. He promised an audience with the Pope, a seat for a ceremony in the Sistine Chapel; many other favours and privileges; he would lend her a horse should she wish to hunt in the Campagna; she and her father must, of course, come and dine at his Palazzo at once and see his pictures – the famous Titian – and the Moroni. It was a convenient house to dance in. He would try and arrange something. Was she fond of dancing?

"Yes, indeed."

Excitement, the freshness of everything, gave Blanche vivacity, and at the mention of the word dancing she thought of Sydney and the rapturous excitement of her dances with him, especially the night he had proposed to her, and she blushed. The effect of this fitful colour in her white skin was enchanting, as of the dawn on snow. At that moment the old Princess looked at her, and she decided that Blanche was to be her daughter-in-law. She did not anticipate any opposition or trouble on her son's part, but, if by any chance there should be any, it would have to be got over.

# CHAPTER II

The Prince lost no time in asking Blanche and her father and her aunt to dinner at the Palazzo Fabrini, where he lived, and in which his mother and his sister occupied an apartment on the second floor.

There Blanche met the principal notabilities of the Roman world and several well-known English people, and there, too, she made the acquaintance of Guido's sister, who, unlike her brother, was gaunt, dark, shy, and silent.

This was the beginning of a gay life for Blanche. She was invited everywhere. Expeditions to Tivoli, to Frascati, to Nemi were made, to the Prince's Estates, or to his Castello near Subiaco. She hunted in the Campagna. She went for drives in the Prince's drag. She visited the Colosseum by moonlight, and she heard the Pope say Mass at St Peter's and the Papal choir sing Mass in the Sistine Chapel.

Time passed quickly. But Blanche had not forgotten Sydney; she wrote to him long descriptions of her doings and impressions, and every now and then she heard from him – touching and slightly illiterate protestations of his eternal fidelity, with a few allusions to the excellent sport he was having. The gaiety of Rome increased as the first touch of spring was felt, and culminated in the carnival.

The night before her father, who had to be back in England for the opening of Parliament, left, a large ball was given at the Palazzo Fabrini – a striking entertainment: the outer reception rooms full of Cardinals in scarlet; pine torches flaring on the staircase; a blaze of historic jewels everywhere. Throughout the evening Blanche received the attentions of one cavalier in particular – Prince Roccapalumba. This did not surprise her; he was the person she knew best. Later he conducted her to supper. After supper he led her to the end of a long corridor, where there hung, brilliantly lit with candles, the portrait of one of his ancestors, rather a sinister nobleman in black velvet with a white ruff, to whom he bore an unmistakable resemblance.

They sat down at right angles to the picture on two tall, stiff chairs covered with faded red velvet. The sound of music came from the distance, the swish of skirts, the laughter and talk of the guests. There were masses of candles everywhere, and men in splendid but faded liveries at every door.

Blanche looked pensive, but prettier and fresher than ever against the background of sombre splendour, the marbles, the tapestries, the gildings, the brocades, the dark portraits. She, who used to appear exotic in England, in Italy seemed deliciously English, in spite of her dark eyes and white skin, dressed all in white, with white roses in her hair and light blue ribbons. She was like the white jessamine that grows on an English terrace. She was thinking of India, and whether she and Sydney would ever dance together again. She became suddenly aware that the Prince had been talking to her for some time, and that she had been answering without paying attention. Her mind had for the moment been miles away, and she was abruptly brought back to reality and to the present by some remark he made. He alluded to something he had said earlier in the evening, and she did not follow. She did not at first understand…and then suddenly, in a flash, she understood. He was asking her to be his wife… She blushed scarlet; she had never thought of the Prince in such a light, nor had she for a moment dreamt that he would ever regard such a thing as possible. She thought he being an Italian and a Catholic, she being English and a Protestant – and nobody in particular, as she thought – put all such things out of the question. It was a shock to her. She still could not believe that he meant it. He made himself plainer. He poured out a torrent of passionate, persuasive eloquence – in English, breaking every now and then into Italian.

"But, Prince," she said, "I am engaged to be married."

She told him about Sydney. He listened with deference, and then he said:

"Forgive me; I didn't know."

She caught sight of her father coming towards them.

"There's papa," she cried. "He has come for me."

"I'm quite ready, papa," she said to her father. "The Prince has been showing me this interesting picture."

She smiled at the Prince, said good night, took her father's arm, and said:

"Aunt Carrie's longing to go home. I'm quite ready."

Her father saw at once by her manner that something unusual had happened, and he guessed, more or less, what, but he asked her no questions. The next day he left for England. He promised to come back as soon as the Easter recess began.

And now a new life began for Blanche. The balls and the entertainments were all over, but nevertheless she was fully occupied, and the Prince still managed to organise expeditions and amusements for her, although since the evening of the dance at his palace he never obtruded himself on her society, and was never alone in her company. He kept in the background. He saw her none the less, as his mother often asked her to *déjeuner* or to dinner when they were alone, or when there were only a few English friends.

Blanche missed her father greatly. Mrs Somner had none of his gaiety, and sight-seeing bored her. She knew the sights all too well. She liked spending hours in the curiosity shops and driving a hard bargain over an object she did not really want.

Blanche spent almost all her time with her aunt and a great deal of time with Guido's mother, who took her for long drives. After her father had been absent about a fortnight the Prince left for his country estate, where his mother said he had affairs. Her son had told her what had occurred between him and Blanche, and had declared that if he could not marry her he would marry no one, but would go into the Church. The Princess had no intention that he should do any such thing, but before taking any definite step she wanted to make quite certain whether Blanche was exactly what she needed for a daughter-in-law, so she sent her son away to the country with orders not to return till Henry Clifford came back from England, and she, in the meanwhile, subjected Blanche to a searching examination which was carried on without Blanche being aware of it, although she felt that she was being paid a great deal of attention. The Princess only mentioned her son in an impersonal way, but she frequently laid stress on his great devotion to his mother and on her great devotion to him. Attention, too, was often called to his good qualities, when occasion arose for it, naturally, and in the course of conversation, but the Princess never overdid matters. She was a past master in the art of stopping at the right moment and of leaving things unsaid.

The scrutiny and period of observation to which she subjected Blanche satisfied her that she was exactly the wife that was needed for Guido: beautiful, cultivated, intelligent, kind, amiable. She had always wished him to marry an Englishwoman of good family and honourable lineage. She was a Protestant, but it was only a matter of time, thought the Princess, before that difficulty would be got over. In the Princess' eyes she had no religion at all. Henry Clifford had several Catholic relations, and he, she knew all too well, would agree that to be Princess Roccapalumba *"vaudrait bien une*

*Messe.*" As to the girl's feelings and her engagement to Sydney Hope, the Princess did not give them a thought, so completely certain she was that she would have her way.

As to the religious question, the Princess thought there was no hurry about it. No need to fuss. The girl would be converted in time, of course. The girl was a sensible person, and common sense in the long run would necessitate conversion. A sensible person naturally became a Catholic when faced with the facts. But the Princess had no great zeal for making converts. She was intensely Catholic, but politically only platonically Papal; she shared both the Italian and the English genius for compromise, and she made up her mind that it would be wiser in the long run for her son to be *Italian* rather than Papal, and she brought him up accordingly and committed him to nothing. She was, to a certain extent, anti-clerical, and she never allowed a priest to interfere in her private affairs.

As soon as Henry Clifford returned to Rome to spend his Easter holiday there, the Princess sent for him and acquainted him with the situation. Her son was desperately in love with Blanche, and was being driven to despair because Blanche had refused him, alleging that she was engaged to some one else. Guido was really serious. He had taken this refusal most seriously. He had never been really in love before. It was making him ill. She had had to send him away from Rome. He was a man who, when he was possessed by an idea, was possessed by it entirely. If he could not marry Blanche he said he would enter the Church, and his mother knew that if he said a thing like that he meant it.

She had, during Henry Clifford's absence, got to know his daughter well, and she considered that she would make a perfect wife for Guido. What did he think?

Henry Clifford said that nothing of course would please him better than an alliance between his daughter and the son of his old friend. He was sure he could not have a more admirable son-in-law than Guido, who was intelligent, distinguished, capable in every way...so serious and so *rangé*.

As for Blanche, she was a good girl, and there was no doubt she was good-looking and would probably become still more so in the course of time. There was the religious question. He had no prejudice in such matters; several of his cousins, one of his brothers (Charles, who had made the unsatisfactory marriage), and a sister who had died, Cornelia, whom the Princess remembered, were Catholics. Of course he could not press Blanche on the point. She must be free to keep her own religion. She had been brought up as a Protestant.

"Not a 'ritualist'?" asked the Princess.

"I never went into that," said Henry. "I took her to the Chapel Royal on Sundays or to St Paul's. I never encouraged fads."

"I see – just ordinary Church of England."

"But, of course, the girl must be free to choose."

"Of course."

"She can't marry that boy. He hasn't a penny, nor will he ever have a penny. Besides that, it would be a great waste. He isn't worthy of her. But I can't make her marry Guido if she doesn't want to."

"Blanche is such a devoted girl," said the Princess.

"She is devoted to her father, and she will in the long run do anything you want."

"She's a loyal child, too."

"I dare say the young man is occupied. India is so far, and the change of climate and habits make such a difference, and men, young men especially, are so fickle."

"You don't think Guido will change his mind, or would regret it?"

"Guido has never looked at any one yet in that way, with the idea of marrying... I was in despair."

Henry, before he left the Princess, promised to do what he could. She knew that he would do nothing foolish, and she felt that the matter could not possibly be in safer hands.

21

The next day he took Blanche for a drive in the Campagna. It was a grey day. It had rained a little in the morning. But as they drove along the Appian Way the charm of the Campagna seemed greater and more powerful than ever. When they had driven for some way past the tomb of Caecilia Metella, the coachman was told to stop and they got out and walked.

It was then that Henry Clifford gently approached the topic for the first time. He began by talking of Sydney Hope, and he pointed out to Blanche how absolutely out of the question it was for her to think of marrying him. How could it happen? What could they possibly expect to live on? What were his prospects? Supposing he were to marry, how could he go on living in the Army? He could barely afford to do so now, as it was, now that everything was provided for him. Things being so, was it fair on him to keep him bound by an engagement that could not possibly result in anything tangible?

He would never like to ask her to release him from the bond, She would have to take the first step.

"We're both ready to wait," Blanche broke in here. "We neither of us mind how long we wait."

"But it would be no use waiting," her father explained. "In ten years' or in fifteen years' time the situation would not be greatly different from what it is now. The boy would still not be able to afford to marry. All waiting would mean is that you may prevent him marrying some one who would be well enough off for him to marry."

And then gently Henry Clifford went on to talk about the Prince. He knew what had happened. She did not probably realise the effect her refusal had had on the young Prince. Italians were sensitive. The Latin race were so far more sensitive than Anglo-Saxons. His mother was seriously alarmed. She doubted whether he would ever recover if Blanche's decision proved to be final. Even if he were to recover his health, he would most certainly retire from the world. He would go into the Church, he would become a monk.

Italians were quite indifferent till they cared, but when they cared they cared violently. It would mean the ruin of his life.

"Yes, but, papa, I don't love him," she said.

And then Henry Clifford expounded his philosophy.

First love was a temporary thing that everybody went through. When it happened, you thought it would last for ever, but it didn't. She must take his word for that. He had experienced the same thing at her age. He had been engaged to be married when he was nineteen. He had sworn eternal love and eternal fidelity to a girl. The marriage had been prevented by the girl's parents, and he had thanked Heaven for it ever since. A year later she had married a Member of Parliament. And her parents had been perfectly right. First love was not really love at all, and marriage was marriage. That sort of love – first love – was nice, but it lasted, at the most, a few months. But marriage lasted one's whole life; that was why, in order to marry, something else was needed...not only a boy-and-girl flirtation. Marriage must be built on solid foundations, not only on rainbow dreams.

Now a man like the Prince had been through those early fevers and tremors, and had got over them. When a man of his age – and he was just the right age, not too young, but not too old – thought seriously of marriage, and liked some one well enough to *want* to marry her, it was serious, and Guido not only liked her...it was not only *reason* on his part, he loved her furiously, he loved her like a boy of twenty. He had the fire of youth and the good sense and the reason of a grown-up mature man.

And then he had the right to marry. Think of his position. His family was one of the very oldest in Italy. He was respected throughout Europe. It was not like marrying a man who was entirely foreign. His mother was English. He had been brought up in England – he spoke English like an Englishman – he had property in England; he would live a great deal in England. It was no hardship to spend the winters in Rome! What a relief it was to be back here after the bitter cold they had just been experiencing in London! That was the English spring! People had died like flies of bronchitis. Every one had colds. It was terrible out of doors, but worse indoors, in the damp and draughty houses, while here one basked in the sun, and never felt cold, even in these huge palaces. One hardly wanted a small wood fire in the evening. And then the Prince's villa in Florence – it was a dream. She might think him mercenary to talk of these things, but they did make a difference to life.

"You see, dearest," he said, "love in a cottage is all very well *in theory*, but in practice nine times out of ten it kills love. Men are so selfish. Women endure everything, but men put up with nothing, and then they lay the blame on the woman. You see I know your character, and I feel certain you need the companionship of some one who is your equal in intelligence – on the same level as you, who has the same tastes, and of some one who can make life interesting for you. Guido will be able to give you and to show you everything that makes life interesting and enjoyable. He will be able to show you all the most interesting places in the world and to introduce you to all the most interesting people under the very best conditions. He knows every one who is worth knowing all over Europe. He and his mother have friends in every capital of Europe – in Paris, in Vienna, in St Petersburg – and they know the nicest people in England as well."

"He's a Roman Catholic, isn't he?"

"Yes; but, of course, he would respect your religion. Nobody would expect you to change unless you wanted to. I told his mother that you had been brought up with entire freedom in these matters. And, after all, the difference is negligible. It's not as if you were asked to marry a Mussulman or a Hindoo. The Creeds we say in church and the Creeds they say in church are identically the same. Compared with agreement on such large questions, disagreement on lesser matters, such as the Pope and Saints, or whether to fast on Friday or put up candles to

St Anthony, are, I can't help thinking, trifling. '*Querelle de moine*,' Leo X said when he heard of the Reformation. I think he was right. Sensible man."

"But if we had children they would have to be Roman Catholics."

"I'm not quite sure even about that. The sons must, I think, be brought up in the same religion as their father. I don't know about the daughters; they are sometimes brought up in their mother's religion. At least that used to be so in England."

"Would you really want me to marry a man I don't love – a man I feel I could never love?" Blanche repeated.

"I want you to believe me when I say that in this matter I think I really do know better, that I am a better judge than you are yourself. You know how fond I am of you. You know that I would sooner die than let you do something which I thought would lead to your unhappiness. I think you don't really understand, that you can't understand, you can't *know*, what marriage means, nor what real love means. I think you think you couldn't love Guido now, but I am sure you will love him. I believe he would make you happy. I believe he is the husband you need, who could make for you the life you deserve, and the life you are suited to. It is useless to tell me that you would be happy as the wife of a subaltern in a line regiment, living on nothing a year, in garrison towns, and *in India!* – especially when the glamour had worn off and you saw him as he really is, a no doubt estimable but quite commonplace young man, rather selfish, used to having his own way, incapable of giving up anything, with no career before him, and interested only in hunting and shooting and soldiering, and not able to talk about anything else. At any rate, even if you don't agree, even if you don't think I am right, I want you to trust me in this matter. I want you to rely on my experience, and on my love of you, and my understanding of you, and my knowledge of life and of the world. I ask you to marry Guido *for my sake*. I should not ask you to do this unless I was quite sure that it was the best thing

25

you could possibly do. Don't say 'yes' or 'no' now, but think it over. Take plenty of time and remember how unhappy you will make that poor man if you say 'no,' and how unhappy you will make your poor old father! And don't think you are being disloyal to that boy in India. He knows perfectly well that there is no chance of his ever marrying you. His father was quite frank about it with me, and he had it all out with the boy before he started for India. By keeping him to his word all you will do is *to wreck his life*. He is far too young to marry now, even if it was possible, and it's *not* possible. And he knows it."

That was all Henry Clifford said. They walked on in silence. To the left of them there was the broken arch of an aqueduct. A brown-faced shepherd dressed in skins was minding some sheep and fluting a plaintive tune on his pipe.

The clouds lifted slightly to the north-west over the dome of St Peter's.

Blanche turned round and looked at the church, which was now plain in the watery silver rift of the clouds. The scene moved her; she felt it was the stage and the setting of something momentous in her life, and she knew that whatever she thought she would end by doing what her father wanted her to do. She loved him too much not to; although it was only the last argument that affected her. If she gave up Sydney it would be not to risk spoiling *his* life.

This, she thought, looking at the melancholy Campagna, the grey sky, and the silvery rift over the distant church, will be my life and my fate. The die is cast.

She was not far wrong.

# CHAPTER III

After spending Easter at Rome and witnessing not only the Easter festivities but those which celebrated the jubilee of Pope Pius IX as a priest, Blanche returned to England with her father. The Prince followed them shortly, and, towards the end of May, Blanche wrote a letter to India breaking off her engagement. She refused to take any further step till she received an answer from Sydney Hope.

The answer came towards the end of July. It was pathetic, inarticulate, and badly spelt. He had always known, he said, that it was too good to be true. He knew that he was not worthy of her and that he would never have been able to give her the life she deserved, but, he ended, "you will always be my godess" (spelt with one "d"). Blanche cried a good deal when she received this letter. Two days later her engagement was announced in the *Morning Post*, and letters and congratulations began to pour in.

The wedding was to be in London in September at the Brompton Oratory. The night before, Blanche had a last talk with her father. She told him that she loved the Prince no more than when she first knew him. Did he think she was right in marrying a man whom she felt she could never love? Her father brushed aside her arguments and repeated all that he had said before. He was more persuasive than ever. He pointed out, too, how difficult it would be to break off the engagement at the eleventh hour,

"But that is just the beauty of the eleventh hour. That's what it's there for, surely," she said.

"If the decision concerned yourself only, it would be different," her father said.

After this Blanche felt there was no help for it. She must go through with it. The next day she was married.

They went for their honeymoon first of all to Paris, where they saw the end of the Exhibition, and then to Venice, and then to the Prince's villa at Florence.

In December they settled down for the winter at Rome at the Palazzo Fabrini. Blanche's life as a married woman and as an Italian Princess had begun.

Her father was right: she had not realised what marriage meant, in spite of his tactful warnings. It was worse than anything she had imagined... She made another discovery; not the usual one – that she had married *someone else* – but the contrary. Guido was what she had suspected, only worse: marriage was what she had not expected, and beyond all nightmares.

The second discovery (which she did not make till she came to Rome) was that her mother-in-law was to be a daily factor in their lives. She had no intention of leaving the palace (nor indeed, since she lived in a separate apartment, could she be expected to), and Guido was afraid of her and consulted her about everything.

She was amiability itself to Blanche, and yet Blanche began to fear her.

Blanche was not happy: those two little bald words express the whole thing, and tell the whole story, but on to what vast vistas they opened!

It was only gradually that she realised what the kind and degree of the unhappiness of her married life was to be in the future; her heart was still in India.

Providence is kind to mortals in this respect; however far-sighted they may be, they see little ahead; if they could see the whole future as on the unrolled canvas of a panorama, there would be few who could go on living after having faced the sight. Certainly not Blanche, who was by nature gentle, sensitive, and essentially feminine.

As it was, she was for the moment greatly envied. People said she was indeed fortunate. She had everything the heart could desire. St James said that everything in the world was vanity except a carriage – and in Rome Blanche had several.

Her father rubbed his hands when he thought of how wise and fortunate he had been in having contributed to bring about such a marriage.

Blanche's letters so far were the only fly in the ointment. He would not admit it to himself, but they did make him a tiny shade uneasy, not by what they said but by what they left unsaid.

He found a thousand plausible reasons to account for anything that might be lacking.

One must allow, he said to himself, for so many things – for youth, for the change, for the new surroundings.

Blanche wrote to him enthusiastic letters about their travels, about the Paris Exhibition, the sunsets at Venice, the pictures at Florence…and the great beauty and comfort of the palace at Rome, the kindness of Guido's mother… Guido's infinite attentions and forethought…and yet in all this there was just something missing. It would come, thought Henry Clifford; he must remember she was still a child.

Blanche begged her father to come and spend Christmas or Easter with them at Rome, but Princess Solski advised him not to go – not yet. She advised him to urge Blanche to spend the summer in England as soon as Italy became too hot, at Guido's country place, which consisted of a spacious house and a certain amount of property in Berkshire, not far from London.

The winter in Rome – the last winter of Papal Rome – was a brilliant one, and Blanche enjoyed the outside surface life; the spectacles, the colour; as to her domestic life, she soon realised that it was Guido's mother and not she who was the ruling spirit in her household.

The Princess made her influence felt gradually and subtly. It was as if a screw were being turned slowly but surely on to the liberty of her daughter-in-law. The Princess seemed to be effacing herself, but Blanche gradually realised that any plan she made herself or any suggestion she made to Guido was put before his mother and received her sanction before it was adopted. If his mother disapproved of it, it was shelved. Guido would find some pretext, and would explain that for this or that reason it was difficult. He always used the word "difficult" – sometimes in Italian, *"difficile."*

One night at the opera where the Prince had a box, a young Englishman, a certain Dennis Lowe, a youthful Member of Parliament, whom Blanche had known in London, came and talked to them during the *entr'acte.* He stayed rather a long time in their box. Blanche was glad to see him and to hear the latest news from London. He had been one of her partners; he had seen her father and knew several of her friends. She asked him to *déjeuner* the next day and he came. They met again the same evening at a musical evening at one of the Embassies.

The next day Blanche was talking over with Guido a dinner-party that it was arranged they should give. They needed another man, and Blanche suggested Dennis Lowe.

Guido hesitated, and then said he was not quite sure whether he would do because of his politics.

"What are his politics?" asked Blanche.

"Well, it appears his father is very violent," said the Prince, "and a friend of Garibaldi's. Besides, we shall now be fourteen without him. I've asked that new French attaché."

Later on in the morning Blanche asked Guido for the list of guests. He was busy writing a letter when she asked him, and he answered absent-mindedly:

"It's there, on the little table."

She took it and looked through it, and she noticed that Dennis Lowe's name had been scratched out in pencil and the name of the French attaché had been substituted for it, but the handwriting in which this amendment had been made was not that of Guido but the still more decided script of his mother.

Dennis Lowe left Rome shortly after this incident.

When they were alone, Guido's mother nearly always dined with them, and after dinner they sat in one of the large, high drawing-rooms until eleven: Guido, Blanche, the Princess, and her daughter. Blanche did needlework; the Princess talked or did a patience, and Donna Teresa looked on and helped, and said nothing, and answered questions that were put to her in monosyllables.

On Monday night they received after dinner, and on Wednesday night Princess Julia, as she was now called, received in her apartment.

People began to arrive at ten and went on coming till eleven or later; they stayed till one, sometimes later, and drank tea.

On these occasions Guido's mother, Princess Julia, sat in a chair near the fireplace and held a little court, as though she were a queen. Blanche played, it seemed, a secondary part, but if any one paid attention to Blanche somehow or other in the course of the evening they would be drawn into Princess Julia's circle and there they would remain.

Princess Julia had a ready, rapid, and effective brightness of conversation – in three languages – the power of nailing any topic to the *tapis*, exhausting its possibilities, and then changing it for another one, before it was a moment too late – before there was the slightest danger of tedium, that most people rightly called brilliance, and which Blanche found profoundly paralysing and impossible not only to emulate, but even to take part in and to play up to. It had the effect of making her speechless. And the more cleverly Princess Julia would rope her into the conversation, as with the dexterity of a cowboy lassoing a steer, the more dumb and void of ideas Blanche felt herself become, when she was conscious that the lasso had caught her.

Another little episode was a great eye-opener to her. In one of her letters to her father she had said that she disliked very much a certain Russian, Dimitri Ossipov, who attended her Mondays and Princess Julia's Wednesdays without exception. He was a special favourite of her mother-in-law. He was easy and superficial, and had a skin-deep acquaintance with almost every subject under the sun, but his tastes lay in the direction of the French literature of the eighteenth century and Italian pictures: he was musical, too, and played and sang.

Blanche could not endure him. He had a slightly contemptuous attitude that got on her nerves. She described him at some length to her father, and said, among other things, that he seemed always to be mutely condoling with her mother-in-law for her daughter-in-law's want of culture, when it suddenly became plain that she had never read Ariosto and did not care about the Italian Ballet.

The day after she had written this letter, Ossipov's name cropped up at *déjeuner* as to whether he should or should not be asked to join some expedition that was being planned. Upon which the Princess said to Guido: "Do ask him. I want Blanche to get to know him. She doesn't know him yet. She will like him so much when she does know him. She'll find him so interesting about Ariosto and the Italian Ballet."

As she said this in a tone of matter-of-fact disinterestedness, she gave Blanche a swift, searching look, so swift that Blanche was hardly aware it had happened, and so sharp that she knew it was meant for her.

Blanche felt herself turning cold as she heard the Princess say this and experienced that look, and she remembered that she had left her letter half written in the open blotting-book in the large *salone* for a little time while she had been writing it the day before, as she had been called out of the room for a moment. She knew that Princess Julia had read the letter, and she also knew that her mother-in-law wanted her to know that she had read the letter. She was not in the least ashamed of the fact.

Blanche had as yet no friends. She tried to make friends with Donna Teresa, but she met in her the attitude of a dog which has been so much beaten that it dare not try to be friendly – a kind of shy trepidation lest it should be discovered in the act of being patted. And yet Blanche felt drawn towards her, and longed to make friends. She might have done so but for a change in the family circumstances which came about then. There was another important personage in the Roccapalumba household, and that was the Conte Mario Guerrini. He visited the house almost every day of his life, coming either to *déjeuner*, to dinner, or after dinner, at Guido's apartment or at the Princess Julia's. He was, so Guido explained to Blanche, an institution – an *enfant de la maison*.

"You will adore him," he added. "We all adore him."

He had been in his youth extremely good-looking – dark, with regular features and light grey eyes. Now his hair was grey and in parts white, but still thick and curly. There was something slightly Assyrian about him. He looked older than his age, and was prematurely wrinkled. He was not yet fifty, but he had persistently, so people said, burnt the candle at both ends. He had spent several fortunes, had been a gambler, a traveller, and a cosmopolitan, and he belonged to the Papal *Guardia nobile*. He had married a rich wife, and he had been a widower for the last ten years. He had known Princess Julia intimately for the last twenty-five years.

She consulted him on all social questions, just as she consulted Ossipov on all questions connected with literature, art or music, pictures and bric-à-brac, but on these two latter

33

categories she checked Ossipov's opinions by those of Count Guerrini. For experience had taught her that in such matters the opinion of a man of the world, who was a man of the world and nothing else, was necessary as well as that of a professional connoisseur whom a too artistic temperament might lead astray. Now, whether Princess Julia had become a little uneasy during the last year about the Count, whether she thought that he showed signs of restiveness, and appeared to be a shade less assiduous and a shade less attentive, or whether it was from her innate love of tidying and tying up things, of never leaving frayed edges about – shortly after Blanche and Guido's return to Rome, the Roman world was suddenly informed that the Count was engaged to be married to Donna Teresa. The announcement was made soon after Christmas.

Blanche was perhaps the only person in Rome who was surprised, and this was not from want of observation on her part, but from insufficient opportunities for observation. The matter had been settled during her honeymoon, and she had not lived quite long enough in Rome to focus her moral perspective.

She found that this engagement made it more difficult than ever to get into touch with Donna Teresa, who seemed to shrink from her advances more than before, and to go about like a guilty person with an apologetic expression, as much as to say, "Don't blame me for doing this. It is not really my fault." The truth of the matter was that Donna Teresa did not dare make friends with Blanche. As it was, her mother's cross-examinations were searching enough. She dreaded any intimacy with any one so greatly that she deliberately made it impossible, because she knew that once intimate with any one the relation would be used by her mother as an instrument or a means of getting information. And Teresa was too loyal to submit to such a thing. She took after her father, the late Prince.

Blanche, knowing that in her immediate surroundings there was no chance of friendship, cast her eyes round the outer circle of their acquaintance; there were the Italians, the English and foreign colonies, the passing tourists, and the Embassies.

It was in the Russian colony that the most promising elements seemed to be. There was a Princess Olenev who had an apartment in the Palazzo Orlandi; she lived there with two charming daughters. Princess Olenev was handsome and picturesque, cultivated and musical. The daughters, Nelly and Ira, were neither of them pretty, but they had charm and were full of fun. Ira was tall and dark and rather pale. Nelly was short and fair, with twinkling grey eyes. You felt that both were the salt of the earth. They were always at home after dinner, but Blanche found it was impossible for her to go there without her husband, and then only on the day which he considered to be their formal day of reception, although the Princess had told her again and again that she was at home to her every evening, and hoped she would often drop in. She did manage to meet them in the daytime, and she used to enjoy even their formal evenings, their Tuesdays, which she attended with her husband, and often with her mother-in-law as well.

It was at their house she met a young man who was half Russian and half Spaniard, called Alexander Valesky, known in general as Sasha. He wrote verse in Russian and in English, and was full of original ideas. He spent the winter at Rome for his health, as his lungs were weak. Blanche made his acquaintance at one of the Princess' Tuesdays, and they made friends at once. The next day they met casually at the Capitol, and they talked of art, pictures, and books. Alexander Valesky promised to send her a book he had told her of, a book of poems by a Mr Browning, which had been out a few years, but was quite unknown. He sent her the book the next day. It was called *Men and Women*, and she enjoyed it greatly. They met soon again at the house of Princess Olenev. That night her husband had a chill and did not accompany her, nor did her mother-in-law, who had gone to the opera with her daughter and Count Mario. Blanche had suggested remaining at home, but Guido had rather peevishly urged her to go, as he wished, he said, to be left alone. So she went. There were few people that night at the Princess', as it was the first night of a new opera, and all Rome was going to hear it, except Blanche, who had made an excuse of Guido's health for not going.

Blanche was delighted to find Sasha Valesky at the Olenevs'. They had an amusing talk all together at first. Later on, a few people looked in, and among others Dimitri Ossipov, but he paid little attention to Blanche, and devoted himself to the Princess. Blanche and Sasha had a long discussion about the Browning poems, then about poetry and books in general, and finally about people at Rome and elsewhere. The time went quickly, and Blanche noticed that when she said goodbye it was half-past twelve.

Two days later, at *déjeuner*, Guido mentioned the name of Sasha Valesky. He had seen him at the Club.

"He's looking iller than ever," he said. "We ought to ask him to something. Blanche doesn't know him."

"She would like him," said his mother. "They would have so much in common"; and she added, with just a slight touch of icy irony in her voice, "Those difficult poems by that extraordinary Mr Browning, for instance."

"Who's he?" asked Guido.

"I don't know much about him," said his mother, looking at Blanche, "except that he's rather a revolutionary and a *mangeur de prêtres*, and writes very" – here again she put the word in the inverted commas of irony – " 'difficult' poems. They are too high-flown for me."

Blanche blushed, and she realised that her mother-in-law had informers in every camp.

A little later Sasha Valesky's aunt asked her to tea. She was staying with her nephew. The Olenevs were coming and others. Blanche felt that, if she went, it would somehow or other be reported to her mother-in-law. But why not? Why should she not go out to tea? Her situation with regard to her mother-in-law would have to be cleared up some day. What did it mean? What did she really want? Was she, Blanche, never to take a step without asking her mother-in-law's leave? Were there certain people that her mother-in-law disapproved of? Or did she disapprove of everybody as far as Blanche was concerned? Blanche, after thinking over the matter, resolved to go, and if necessary to have it out.

So when the day came she fully expected the Princess to ask her at *déjeuner* whether she would like to drive with her in the afternoon, which she frequently did, and more especially, Blanche thought, if she wanted to prevent her doing something else. But to her surprise the Princess said nothing, and did not even ask her what she was going to do. Guido was busy. He always went to the Club between five and seven.

At half-past four Blanche went to Valesky's apartment. It was a pretty apartment not far from the Palazzo Venezia on the third floor. There she found the Olenevs and some pleasant Italians and English people whom she knew. They had just settled down to an amusing talk when Ossipov was announced.

"I have brought you a friend, as a surprise," he said, laughing, and after him, imposing and handsome in black and pearls, with a large bunch of crimson roses at her waist, walked the Princess.

# CHAPTER IV

Blanche was more puzzled than ever after this. She felt she must establish and follow a definite policy towards her mother-in-law, but what was it to be?

The winter was coming to an end, and Rome was beginning to fill up with visitors. Some friends of her father's were arriving. Some of these she knew already; others arrived with letters of introduction. She was asked one day to take part in an expedition to Hadrian's Villa by a young Lord Kiltarlity, whom she had known in London and whose family were all of them great friends of her father. They had a shooting lodge in the Highlands, where her father used to shoot every year. Blanche on this occasion thought she would try a new policy. She went straight to the Princess and put the matter before her, and asked her advice. She found her mother-in-law all sympathy and smiles. Of course she must go. No objection was made. The Princess went so far as to find an occupation for Guido which made it impossible for him to go as well. There was no interference and no questions asked afterwards. Blanche spent an enjoyable day.

"She likes to be consulted," thought Blanche. "Well, why not consult her whenever I can, and then, if I really don't want to on some given point, I needn't, and she won't mind, as she will think it was an accident." So Blanche took the line of consulting her mother-in-law about every trivial thing which didn't matter – what new books to read; whom to leave cards on; whose day to go to; what guests to ask to dinner and whom not to ask; what sights to show to which foreigners. It seemed to answer admirably. About none of these things did Blanche happen to care a brass farthing.

To the outside world it cannot have appeared that Blanche had anything to complain of. Her mother-in-law lived in the house, it was true, but her apartment was quite separate, on another floor, with its own front door. It might just as well have been in another street. She would see her mother-in-law no more than if that had been the case. Again, the whole world agreed that Princess Julia was a fountain of tact. She never went to see Blanche; she never had a meal with the married couple unless Guido or Blanche asked her. It is true that she nearly always spent the evenings with them, or asked them to her apartment when they were alone, but that was because Guido asked her to. He preferred it. He was used to it.

Blanche, too, admitted that, even realising all that she realised, she had little that was tangible to complain of. The Princess never interfered in so many words, never cross-examined her, never asked a question which it would embarrass her to answer, was quite perfect in her dealings with Guido, helped her in every way with the Romans and the foreign residents, told her all she wanted to know, made things easy for her – and then she was so generous she would load her with presents.

"Princess Julia is so generous that she would give the clothes off her back to any one who asked her for them," some of her admirers would say, and on Blanche's wedding-day her mother-in-law gave her the beautiful *point d'Alençon* veil she had been married in herself, and also a magnificent necklace of emeralds and diamonds. When Blanche had protested, the Princess had said, "Take them, my dearest; I am far too old to want them, and you will look lovely in them."

But, in spite of these manifestations of generosity and the seeming effacement and the obvious tact on her mother-in-law's part, Blanche felt, nevertheless, as though she were surrounded by an invisible web, as if her every action, her every word, and almost her every thought were known to the Princess. How it was done, she had no idea. There was no system of spies, but the Princess had a knack of always knowing some one everywhere, and knowing that some one well enough to find out from them exactly what she wanted to know, without seeming to ask them. Blanche saw that it would be quite hopeless ever to try and conceal anything from her in Rome, and difficult to persist in any line of conduct that was not approved of by her mother-in-law. She felt that Guido had all his life been in the same situation, and was now, at the age of thirty, as much afraid of his mother as he had been at the age of ten.

A striking proof of what Blanche suspected was soon to be afforded her.

Sasha Valesky had left Rome for Florence soon after his tea-party. He was away about three weeks, and then Blanche one day received a note from him saying that he had come back, that he would much like to see her. Could they not meet at the Olenevs'? He was going to spend the evening at their house the next day. It was not their regular day, and they would be able to talk. The Olenevs would be delighted, he knew.

Blanche thought to herself, this is a test-case. Circumstances were favourable. Guido was absent from Rome; he had gone to his Castello to see his agent. Donna Teresa and her fiancé were dining in, and an English friend of the Princess, a Mr Cawthorne, an art critic, who had the most extensive knowledge of the picture galleries and who was a devoted slave of the Princess. After dinner the Princess settled down to patience. Cawthorne sat beside the card-table and gave her advice. Donna Teresa and Mario played bezique at the other end of the room.

"I promised," said Blanche, "I would look in for a moment at the Olenevs'."

She said good night to everybody.

Her mother-in-law smiled sweetly and made no comment. Blanche went round to the Palazzo Orlandi, and there she spent a most enjoyable evening alone with Nelly and Ira Olenev, Valesky, and a young, good-looking Italian called Ubaldo Agostini, who played the mandoline. Blanche stayed rather late.

Guido came back the next day.

They were giving a dinner-party for their English friends and discussing the matter in the Princess' apartment just after *déjeuner*. Once again Guido suggested inviting Valesky.

"I don't think he would do," said the Princess. "And that reminds me – " she said, and broke off.

They went on discussing various people who would do or not do for the dinner-party, and presently Guido went out. This occurred in the week of the Carnival.

"What I remembered I wanted to say just now, dearest Blanche," said the Princess, as soon as Guido had gone out, "was this: Don't you think it a tiny bit of a mistake to see so much of Sasha Valesky? Of course, I know that there is nothing in it – that it means nothing, and that it is perfectly harmless, but one must remember that Rome isn't London. People here are so different, and they do talk so."

"But I have hardly set eyes on him," said Blanche, getting red.

"You see," said the Princess, taking no notice of Blanche's interruption, "everybody knows everything at Rome. The whole of Rome knows that you stayed so late at the Olenevs' the other night, quite alone with those two young men, without the Princess even."

"She did come," said Blanche.

"Yes, after the opera was over, in time to say goodnight to you. You mustn't think I have got anything against Sasha

Valesky. I think he is *charming.* So cultivated and clever, and musical. But I do not think he is a good friend for a young married woman in Rome. In the first place, he has no principles. In the second place, he has had so many affairs. He's always being engaged and breaking it off at the last minute in the most disgraceful, outrageous way. In the third place, he is at this moment spending mints of money on that dancer, the Zanelli. One can't have people in Rome saying that you have the Zanelli for a rival."

"I have only seen Prince Valesky three times," said Blanche, "and he is ill, and I don't think he will live very long."

"If that is so, the sooner he changes his present mode of life the better," said the Princess; "but you owe it to Guido and to the name you bear now not to be talked about; and if you go on seeing so much of Sasha Valesky you will be talked about, that is quite inevitable, and I must ask you, Blanche dearest, for all our sakes, NOT to do it. You see, all sorts of things that are in themselves quite harmless and which you can do quite well in London are impossible in *Rome.* You must remember that you are here a public personage and that you are living in public. It is not fair on Guido, and he would be quite miserable if he knew."

"I promise you," said Blanche, "that Guido shall never have cause to complain of me."

"I knew you would understand, dearest," said the Princess; "you are such a sensible child," and she walked towards her and gave her a kiss.

Two days later Blanche, without any effort or action on her part, met Sasha at a dinner-party at one of the Embassies, and sat next to him at dinner. Fortunately her mother-in-law was not present.

He proposed various plans and meetings. Blanche told him it was impossible.

"I see," he said. "Princess Julia has taken action."

Blanche smiled sadly, but said nothing.

42

"I thought we might be going to be friends," he went on.

"I mustn't have friends – not here."

The tone of her voice was sincere and absolutely final.

"I thought she would stop it," said Sasha. "You know she hates me because I don't swallow her – whole. The whole secret of Princess Julia is this. If you admit her, if you acknowledge her claim to be legitimate queen, queen of everything – life, art, people, letters, music, taste, politics – then she will eat out of your hand and never interfere with you. But if she suspects opposition and disloyalty in you as a subject, or, still worse, covert sedition or open rebellion, then she will oppose and fight you tooth and nail, and in the end thwart you."

"I believe you are right," said Blanche pensively.

"You see, she knows I don't believe in her. I think she is not exactly a sham, but everything about her is artificial – her piety, her intelligence, her culture, her political interests, her artistic tastes, her conversation, her knowledge, her complexion, her hair."

"I think she is a very clever woman," said Blanche.

"She is a remarkable woman, a *great* personage in the *grand* manner; a talent even," said Sasha. "Unfortunately, I can't bow my knee to her. She can't tolerate equality; she must be surrounded by inferiors or people who admit her superiority – slaves who accept *everything* she does *unconditionally* and *unreservedly* without any *arrière-pensée*. I can't, and the result is she hates me, and never loses an opportunity of giving me some little pinprick. Up to now I haven't minded. Our paths crossed so little. I kept out of her way as much as I could – only now it is a bore… She will prevent our being friends. She will have her opportunity of annoying me."

"It's just as well," said Blanche. "I have understood one thing – one mustn't have friends, here – at least, I mustn't."

"I suppose Princess Julia would be shocked at the thought," said Sasha ironically.

"I think she would, honestly."

"And yet after having lived with Mario Guerrini for twenty-five years she is now marrying him to her daughter!"

"Sh!" said Blanche. They talked of other things. Blanche enjoyed her talk, sadly knowing it as the last she would have with him.

Towards the end of dinner he again asked her: "Can't we really be friends?"

"Not here, not really," said Blanche. "I wish we could."

"Then it's goodbye."

"Yes; I'm afraid it is goodbye."

"I shan't stay another day in Rome. I shall go back to Florence and stay there. I only came back to see you. You must know that. You must have guessed it. I know you know it. I abominate Rome. I detest every one here except the Olenevs. I came to see you and to see you only... "

"I thought you had many friends."

"The Princess told you that. I suppose she told you I was living with the Zanelli. I was in love with her once, five years ago, when I was a boy, and I created a scandal by giving her a family emerald – an heirloom. Such a lovely thing! What fun it was to give away! But I haven't set eyes on her for over a year, and she is living now with Ubaldo Agostini. I have been in love once or twice, but never really till now…every one says that, you will say…this time it's true. I didn't think it could happen, and now it has happened, and it's too late…well, it doesn't much matter, because I shall in any case be no bother to you. I shall go tomorrow, and I shall stay at Florence till it gets too hot…and then I shall go home to Russia to my estate and stay there till…till the end, and that won't be long. The doctors only give about a year or two, and then only on condition that I live in impossible places – places that I hate, like Madeira or Cannes. I hate the Riviera. Now, let us talk of other things – Patti and *la Grande Duchesse…* "

The conversation became general at Blanche's end of the table. After dinner, Guido remained for a little time in the smoking-room. Then there was music, followed by a dance. Sasha Valesky went away early. Just before he went he gave Blanche a look. It was the last time she ever saw him. He went to Florence the next day, as he said he would, and she had no further opportunity of saying goodbye to him.

Blanche pondered over what he had said about her mother-in-law, and came to the conclusion that he was right. It was opposition, suspected covert opposition, that the Princess could not bear.

"She shall not have it from me, at any rate," thought Blanche. "If ever I have to oppose her, it shall be in the open."

Thus it was that Blanche decided on what her policy was to be in all her future relations with her mother-in-law. She decided to accept her unconditionally; only, if ever she felt that their wills clashed on any one point where she, Blanche, felt that she was in the right, then if it should come to a fight she would fight, even if foredoomed to defeat; only the fight should be an open one.

Her mother-in-law seemed to realise this, for from the moment Sasha Valesky left Rome she was like honey to her daughter-in-law, and never tried to interfere with her in any way. On the contrary, she went out of her way to amuse her, and to arrange amusing things for her to do.

Blanche welcomed the advent of Lent. It meant less entertainment. Although foreigners still came to luncheon and dinner, for the most part they formed a court round her mother-in-law; Blanche was profoundly grateful for this. Her life flowed on uneventfully in its usual rut all through Lent and Easter, when again she witnessed the magnificent ceremonies of the Church. Here was another point in which she was grateful to her mother-in-law. Princess Julia never discussed the religious question with her. Sometimes they would visit churches together. Princess Julia would explain the pictures, comment on the sculpture, but rarely say anything about the religion which these things represented. On one occasion she said to Blanche:

"It's all so beautiful; it all *means* something."

And on another occasion, one morning when they were visiting the Church of St Cecilia in Trastevere, and the church happened to be full of children who were running in and out, although a Mass was being said in one of the side chapels, Princess Julia said, as if answering an unspoken question: "They are allowed to, in our church. You see, they feel quite at home."

Once, too, Blanche admired a silver crucifix in Princess Julia's apartment, and her mother-in-law insisted on giving it to her, but apart from this she never approached the subject, and never showed any sign of wanting to discuss it with Blanche. She seemed to think it natural, too, that Blanche should go to the English Church on Sundays.

After Easter, Donna Teresa was married to Mario Guerrini, and they left Rome to spend their honeymoon in Paris. At the beginning of May, Blanche and Guido left Rome for London, and established themselves at Princess Julia's country house, Norton Park, which was in Berkshire, about an hour's journey from London. Princess Julia did not accompany her daughter-in-law to England. She said nothing of her plans, but she hinted vaguely that she might join them later.

# CHAPTER V

Norton Park was a large, grey stone house, situated on sandy soil in a stretch of country that was a mixture of fir-woods and heather. It was a cheerless building, originally built in the seventeenth century, burnt down at the beginning of the nineteenth century, and entirely rebuilt at the end of the thirties. It was surrounded by laurels, and had shrubberies and rhododendron bushes in plenty, but no garden. It had been left to Princess Julia by her uncle, Edmund Holmhurst. Inside there was a long corridor on the ground floor, which opened on a series of living-rooms, which had no doors. Along the other side of the corridor there were marble busts of celebrated men, beginning with Cicero and ending with the Duke of Wellington.

Princess Julia had done nothing to the house. She was used to beautiful backgrounds; she had knowledge and taste, but a glance at Norton Park had satisfied her that you must either reform it altogether or not at all, so she left the house as it was. The living-rooms were decorated in yellow satin, save one room, which was done up with red plush stamped with gold fleur-de-lis.

The house was full of uninteresting pictures and religious and legal books: treatises of law, sermons in many volumes, and other volumes of piety. Large plate-glass windows looked out on to a shelving lawn. Blanche's heart sank as she entered the house. It was pouring with rain the day they arrived, and the house and the grounds were looking their worst.

The day after their arrival her father came down from London late in the afternoon and stayed the night. Blanche was delighted to see him. He looked at her narrowly. She had improved in looks, but she was rather paler than usual. Henry Clifford thought there must be a good – the most satisfactory of all reasons for this, and he was right. Guido informed him that they were expecting her baby in the autumn – September or October. Blanche was anxious that the baby should be born in England, but Guido was strongly opposed to this. His mother, too, thought it would be better that Blanche should be back in Rome some time before. He was sure his father-in-law would agree and use his influence with Blanche. Henry Clifford nodded assent. They had an animated dinner. Henry Clifford surpassed himself in keeping the ball rolling. He told them all the news; he made them laugh. He suggested all sorts of plans for the future. Guido must, of course, come up to London. The journey was so short and convenient. He would put him up as an honorary member to the St James's Club. It was pleasant, however, at this time of year to be sleeping in the country. London was hot and dusty. He thought they were going to have a really hot summer.

He did not have any opportunity of talking to Blanche till the next morning. Guido never came down to breakfast, but had a cup of black coffee in his bedroom. Blanche, on the other hand, liked having breakfast downstairs, and she made on this occasion a special assignation with her father.

Blanche wanted to see her father alone; at the same time, she slightly dreaded the interview. She did not want her father to guess that she was wearing a mask. So when he suggested the plan before going to bed, she accepted it with alacrity.

They met the next morning at half-past nine in the heavily ornamented stucco dining-room; it had large mahogany sideboards and a complicated chandelier.

"Well, tell me all about Rome," her father said, after he had kissed her and helped himself to a boiled egg at the sideboard.

"They are all so kind, especially Princess Julia. There is nothing she won't do for me. She had all my apartment done up for me, a marble bath put in – a real Roman bath. It looks lovely now. The bedroom is done up in faded pink brocade. She gave me a lovely white silk quilt embroidered with silver that she had inherited. I believe it belonged to Henriette d'Angleterre. She is a wonderful woman. She has a genius for arranging things."

"Yes, she's taste – taste – rather exotic, perhaps, but there's no harm in that in Italy. I suppose one doesn't see so much of her now. Does she still live in the Palace?"

"Yes, of course. She has her own apartment, but she might as well be at the other end of the town as far as we are concerned. She never comes near us unless Guido asks her."

"I suppose you see her in the evenings?"

"Of course, when we're alone – she often looks in, or we go up to her."

"And the daughter is going to be married?"

"Yes – to Count Mario."

"You know him?"

"Oh yes; I've known him for years."

There was a pause.

"I dare say that will answer," Henry Clifford said, disposing of the subject.

"I expect so."

There was another pause.

"Guido is looking well. He hasn't been to England for some time?"

"Not since he left school."

"He tells me you are anxious to stay on here until – "

"Yes, I am anxious."

"But, my darling child, you know it would entail all sorts of bother."

"Surely one can arrange that."

"I suppose one could, but Guido seemed to wish – "

"I suppose his – " Blanche caught herself up; she was going to say, "I suppose his mother insists" – instead of which she said, "I suppose he doesn't want to stay on so long."

Henry Clifford noticed the hiatus.

"I should think he would have to be back. He has a lot to do, hasn't he?"

"Guido is always busy."

Blanche changed the subject. She asked after various people in London. She asked her father what he had been doing, whom he had been seeing. Why didn't he come to Rome for Easter?

"Impossible, my dear child – impossible this year to get away. I ran over to Paris for a day or two at Easter, but I managed that with difficulty. Next year I'll come if we're all alive."

There was another pause.

"I suppose you and Guido entertain a great deal?"

"We are at home every Monday evening. We have dinner-parties sometimes."

"Very pleasant they must be, I'm sure. Guido had an excellent cook. Italians make the best cooks in the world when they are good. Better than the French. Charming people the Romans, ain't they?"

"Charming," said Blanche. There was for a second a listless note in her voice.

Henry Clifford looked up.

"Yes, quite charming," said Blanche hurriedly. "They are all so kind to me – "

"I suppose you've made hosts of friends? – the hare with many friends."

"Oh yes – lots."

"You know Baroness Tresdorf?"

"Yes, papa; I've been to her day."

"And Donna Maria Monteleone?"

"Yes; just – "

"And Princess Dolly Chereny?"

"She's been away most of the time."

"And the Linskys?"

"Guido doesn't care much for the diplomatic world."

"No? He's right, but she's a charming woman – *simpatica*, handsome, intelligent. But who are your principal friends?"

"I like Princess Olenev and her daughters."

"Ah yes. The Russians. And who else?"

"I saw a great many English people in the spring. We used to take them to see the sights. Lord Kiltarlity was at Rome with his sister."

"Yes, yes. Oh, I forgot! – you know my old friend, Donna Elena Genzaro, of course?"

"Yes, I know her, but I can't get on with her; she frightens me."

"You must get to know her; such a pleasant woman, so clever, so gay – brilliant – "

"That's just it; she's too brilliant for me, papa."

"Nonsense, child. And the climate agrees with you? You're careful not to go out at sunset, I hope?"

"I love the climate, and the Campagna. In spring it is so lovely – the Pincio, the Borghese Gardens, and Tivoli, and Nemi." Blanche tried to put a note of real enthusiasm into her voice. "Of course," she continued, "one never has time to see half what one wants to see. I feel if I live all my life in Rome I shall never see half of what there is to be seen."

"And I suppose you attended some of the ceremonies?"

"Oh yes; the Pope's Jubilee and the services at St Peter's."

"Interesting, aren't they?"

"Yes; most impressive," she said, without conviction.

"She's not been converted," thought her father. Their conversation was interrupted by the arrival of Guido, who had come down rather earlier than usual.

Henry Clifford was not altogether satisfied with the state of things. She seemed happy enough, he thought, with her husband. But their talk about her life at Rome had not satisfied him. She seemed to know so few people, to have no real friends. What did it all mean? He had another talk with Guido before he left for London. He told him he was sure Blanche would not insist on staying in England. Before he left he arranged that Guido and Blanche were to come to London in the course of the week. He could put them up in his house if they would like to stay the night.

Guido would come up the next day, for the day; he had some business to attend to. Blanche would probably come with him, but he would have to leave her to herself. That would be all right. She could go to her father's. They could all have luncheon together somewhere.

Henry Clifford said he would arrange it.

Blanche was relieved when her father went. This first conversation had been an ordeal, and she was glad it was over. The next time she saw her father they would not have to discuss Rome so much. She felt she had come out of it well as far as Guido and her mother-in-law were concerned. She knew she had made her father easy on those two importantt points, but she felt she had done less well about her life at Rome and her friends. This was indeed true.

Henry Clifford thought there was something amiss. It seemed incredible to him, knowing Rome and the Italians and the foreign colonies at Rome as he did, that Blanche should not be the centre of a circle of fun and life and gaiety. She was enchanting to look at, striking and uncommon, and delightfully easy to talk to, full of fun and gaiety – at least she had been – an adorable companion; and yet he had the impression that she had been leading a lonely life. "Perhaps she is not feeling well," he thought, and he put it down to that. "It is only natural, and then, after that long journey, one can't expect anything else."

But the impression did not wear off.

He discussed the matter with Princess Solski, who expressed a great wish to see Blanche and to judge for herself. Henry Clifford said he was arranging a little dinner for Blanche and for his son-in-law – just one or two pleasant people; she must come, of course. The dinner came off the following week. Blanche and Guido stayed that night at her father's.

Princess Solski and her husband came, and a young diplomatist, Hedworth Lawless, who had just been appointed a paid attaché to the Legation at Florence. He had already been for two years an unpaid attaché at Washington. Henry Clifford, who knew his father, had asked him, so that he might make Blanche's acquaintance. There were also present a young and good-looking couple, Lord and Lady Hengrave; Lady Harriet Clive, who was amusing as well as pretty; and Henry Clifford's sister, Mrs Somner.

Blanche seemed to blossom in her native air. She was doing hostess. She sat at the head of the table opposite her father, between Solski and Lord Hengrave. Solski talked to her about Rome, and Lord Hengrave talked to her about the opera – Patti, Hortense Schneider, the Paris Exhibition, the Grand Prix, racing, and hunting. "I've hunted in the Campagna," he said, "and damned good sport it was." Blanche liked him. He was amazingly good-looking – like an old picture, she thought.

She was looking well herself, dressed all in pink, a confection of Worth's, with soft flounces, and in which rainbow-like tints melted and blended, and a pink rose in her hair.

Lord Hengrave evidently admired her, and Lady Hengrave shared his views about Blanche's looks, for she said to Henry Clifford, on whose left-hand side she was sitting

"Rome suits Blanche; she is looking well – very well," she added, in another tone of voice, with a meaning look at Henry Clifford, which meant, "very well, considering."

Lady Hengrave herself was a good judge, as she was recognised as one of the smartest of the young married women in London.

She respected Henry Clifford for having brought off such an obviously good marriage. Lady Harriet Clive, on the other hand, who was already a widow, thought that it was positively tragic that Blanche should be married to a waxen foreigner who lived in Italy. Italy was a nice place to go and stay in for a few weeks at Easter, or in September – but to live there for ever!

"You must be glad to be back," she said to Blanche after dinner, as they went upstairs. "I know Rome – full of old women who gossip. Cats, ain't they? I know your mother-in-law, too," and she sighed. "However, you will be able to come to England every year. You must, for your father's sake; and then Italy is unhealthy in the summer, isn't it?"

Princess Solski a little later talked to Blanche, too, and compared notes. She knew the Olenevs. Sasha Valesky was mentioned.

"He's clever," said Princess Solski, "and writes well, but I'm afraid he is delicate."

Blanche asked the Princess what his history had been, and she said that he had always lived abroad from the age of fifteen in the winter, and sometimes in the summer, owing to his health. He had published two books of poems in Russian, one of which showed extraordinary promise, and the other which was in itself a performance. He wrote verse in English, too, which was good enough to be accepted and published by English literary reviews.

"I wish I knew Russian," said Blanche.

"It's a difficult language for a foreigner," said the Princess.

They talked of Rome; of Princess Julia, whom Princess Solski knew well; of Donna Teresa and Mario Guerrini.

"I wasn't surprised at all. I think it is a good thing that the poor girl should have an independent life of her own. Such a nice girl. So well brought up."

They talked of Rome, of the political situation in France, and then the men interrupted them.

They were all re-grouped, and Henry Clifford arranged that Hedworth Lawless should talk to Blanche. He was anxious that they should make friends.

They did so easily. Blanche found him particularly agreeable, easy, and natural. He seemed to be looking forward to going to Florence, and she wondered how diplomatic life in general would suit him in the long run. He seemed sanguine, and she felt a twinge of pity for him, for she felt somehow that he had as yet little idea of what the life really meant.

They settled down into groups, into just the opposite grouping to that of the dinner-table; that is to say, Henry Clifford went into the little back drawing-room with Lady Harriet, Lady Hengrave annexed Guido, Princess Solski talked to Lord Hengrave, and Solski to Mrs Somner.

A little after eleven the party broke up. Henry Clifford was satisfied with his evening. Blanche said she had enjoyed herself.

Guido said that Princess Solski was looking very handsome. "So *simpatica*. Such a clever woman, too, so wise."

Henry Clifford nodded approvingly.

"I liked that young man I talked to after dinner," said Blanche. "He's coming out to Italy."

"To Florence," said Guido, with a shade of rectification in his voice.

"He's in love with a very pretty girl," said Henry Clifford.

"Oh, really," said Guido, with relief, it struck Blanche.

"Is he jealous, already jealous of *everybody*?" she thought.

The same thought flashed through her father's brain.

"Yes, a very pretty girl," Henry Clifford went on – "a Miss Woodville. They say she's got a little money, so they will be able to marry – if she consents, that is to say; he's not well off, but he has got something."

As Lord and Lady Hengrave were driving home in their brougham, Lord Hengrave said to his wife:

"That girl of Henry Clifford's is damned good-looking, a damned good-looking young woman, and a great deal too good for that pasty-looking foreign Prince. I don't like the looks of him, and I'm not at all sure he's to be trusted. In fact, I wouldn't trust him – not a yard."

"He is well off, very well off indeed, with a palace in Rome and houses everywhere, and his family is very old – one of the oldest in Italy. His mother is English, too – one of the Pevenseys."

"I don't say he isn't well off, and he may date back to Romulus for all I care, but I repeat, he's not good enough for that girl. She's a first-rate girl."

"Girls are lucky to marry at all nowadays, considering their manners," said Lady Hengrave, although it was only a few years ago that she had been a girl herself. "I'm thankful we've no girls." A rash statement, for although Lady Hengrave had as yet no girls, but only two boys, she was destined to give birth to a girl before the end of the year.

# CHAPTER VI

The next evening Henry Clifford called on Princess Solski about five o'clock. He was anxious to glean her impressions of the situation.

The Princess poured out tea and lit a little thin cigarette.

"Blanche has come on a great deal," she said. "She is no longer a child, and she is improving in looks. She will be more beautiful next year. Of course she looks a little tired now. I find her charming, so simple. Italy will suit her. It ought to suit her."

There was a pause.

"Yes, it ought to suit her," he repeated.

"You think it doesn't?"

"She seems to have so few friends. She knows none of my old friends."

"They are too old for her, your old friends. You forget she belongs to another generation. She must make friends in her own generation."

"She doesn't seem to have done that."

"Perhaps it will come in time. She has made one friend."

"Who is that?"

"Sasha Valesky."

"Ah, he is delicate, isn't he?"

"Yes; he won't live long, I'm afraid. He was sure to fall in love with Blanche."

"You think he's in love with her?"

"Yes; even if I hadn't seen this poem in a Russian review."

She handed him a review in a pink paper cover, with a very long cryptic name – "Russkoe" something.

"Shall I translate it for you?"

"Yes, please."

She read out, translating the poem as she read the Russian to herself: "The winter is dead and the snows have melted, the fields are flooded, and here and there the bare trees seems to float upon the silvery waters, the floods vanish suddenly – then come the white flowers, the anemones, the narcissus, and the lilies of the valley. But you are whiter than all these. You remind me of the white lilac that grows in my garden – not in this southern garden of cypresses and roses and Judas trees, but my garden far away in the north were the nightingales sing gladly all day. There only the lilac grows – the white lilac, so sweet, so simple, so without pomp, and so altogether like you."

"You think that is meant for Blanche?"

"I should think so even if it were not called 'To B.' It's a good thing Guido doesn't understand Russian."

"You think he would be jealous?"

"Horribly jealous – jealous as a miser is jealous of gold."

"But this will not be serious. I don't think Blanche would fall in love with him."

"Perhaps not, poor boy, but he is ill, very ill, I know. They wrote to me, his cousins did. But if it was not so, Blanche is just the person who would make him go quite mad."

"But I thought he had so many affairs."

"Oh yes; there was the Zanelli and Madame Ischia, and plenty of *Anges gardiens*, but nothing serious, really serious, not now. This would be, I'm sure. And I'm sure she likes him."

"*Likes* him, possibly. Do you think I have made a mistake?"

"Who knows? We can't do anything without making mistakes. Anything else might have been worse. Certainly if she had married that young soldier it would have been *much* worse. There are advantages. And then Blanche is *très raisonnable*. You can rely on her absolutely. It would need something really big and important to make her lose her balance, something with a much greater calibre than poor Sasha has. One does not take him seriously."

"But supposing she did?"

"She won't."

"He so ill – *un condamné*."

"That might make things worse. Pity. He might live for years."

"I hope he may. I hope he may get well. I like him enormously. But you can set your mind at rest. It will not be her *grande passion*, and if it is his, he will die of it."

"Poor boy."

"Yes, poor boy."

"Blanche and Guido have gone back to the country?"

"Yes, this morning. At least she went back, he stayed behind. He says he has business, but what he does I don't know."

"He's mysterious – mysterious about nothing, I think."

"But you do think that Blanche is fond of Guido?" interrupted Henry.

"I think she is fond of her husband."

Henry noticed the distinction.

"Then all is well."

"Yes, all is well. And she seems to like her mother-in-law."

"That is good," said the Princess Solski, as if relieved.

"Princess Julia," she added, "can be nice, exceptionally nice, to people if she likes them. And of course she loves her son ferociously."

"I think Blanche looks happy. I thought she looked so well last night."

"What will he do all the summer?"

"I don't know; we must help her to amuse him."

"Is he fond of racing?"

"Apparently not."

"I'm afraid he will miss the Italian talk, the daily gossip in the clubs, that long, long conversation without beginning or end, which is Italian life. Here it is so different. Vasili" (Princess Solski's husband) "minded it at first, but now he quite likes it. England is all right when you get used to it, and when people accept you. Then it is better than any other place in the world. But it takes a long time sometimes for that to happen, and there are foreigners to whom it never happens."

"People are being civil to Guido. Blanche and he will be asked to everything."

"But will she be able to go out if she lives in the country?"

"Not much; and I don't think she feels up to a lot of big entertainments, but he ought to go to some of the big houses. I am going to take him to the Derby. He will enjoy the opera, too."

Some one was announced: the Second Secretary at the French Embassy.

"On the whole, you think all is going well?" Henry said, before the new arrival came in.

"Yes, I'm sure of it; you can set your mind at rest."

In the meanwhile Blanche, the subject of all this speculation, was back at Norton Park. Her father had promised to come and spend Saturday and Sunday with her, and to stay till Monday morning. She wanted to see some of her girl friends, but this was more difficult. One of her friends, Maud Locksley, was engaged to be married to Sir Ralph Dallington; her cousins, Millicent and Amy Stewart, were being taken out by their aunt, who would not let them go anywhere alone; and the girl who had been her greatest and indeed her only intimate friend, Rose Leigh, had been married while Blanche was in Rome, and was still on her honeymoon abroad.

Among the young married women, of whom Lady Hengrave was the centre, she had not many friends, as when she had been out they had looked upon her as still belonging to the schoolroom, and had taken no notice of her. Her other girl friends were still unmarried and occupied with their own affairs.

Blanche realised before she had been many days at Norton Park that Guido not only missed Italy, but was intensely bored in England. He frankly could not endure English country life, and Blanche made it easy for him to go up to London. But London did not amuse him much. He had nothing to do, although he talked of mysterious appointments, and matters that had to be seen to, and business that had to be dispatched, important questions that had to be settled without delay, lawyers that had to be interviewed. What they could be Blanche had no idea, nor did she ask. She was only too delighted that he should have some excuse for getting away and for obtaining a little comparative amusement.

Boredom was making him restless, fidgety, and critical. He complained of the English climate, English cooking, and, above all, of English conversation, or the lack of it.

During their second week at Norton Park, Lady Hengrave invited them to dinner at their house in Portman Square, and Blanche's father said that she had better come up for this dinner. Guido would meet some people he ought to know.

They went up to London for the dinner and stayed the night.

It was a large formal dinner-party, and Guido had sat between Lady Hengrave and a dowager with ringlets, rather prominent teeth, and a huge tiara.

He complained afterwards of the intense dreariness of the conversation after dinner, when the men were left alone. He said it was unimaginable. Henry had taken him on after dinner to a large party that was being given at Sussex House – a political party, orthodox and conservative. But Guido complained of the heat and the crowd, and he told Blanche that there was no doubt her countrymen were in social matters totally uncivilised – barbarians, in fact.

Blanche was at her wits' end as to what to do. She suggested asking the Solskis down to spend Sunday. But Guido suddenly said that he did not like Russians – Russian men, that is to say. He liked Princess Solski. He thought she was agreeable. Blanche went up to London and consulted her father.

"Guido is bored with England. He talks of going back at once. You must find something for him to do," she said.

"But what does he do at Rome?" her father asked.

"I don't know, but he is always busy. You see, he's at home there, and has his own affairs to look after, and then he has his Club, his estates, and his property in Tuscany, and his farm, and a quantity of things, and there are always people who want to see him. And he takes an interest in Italian politics. He's busy at home, very busy, but here there is nothing for him to do. He's not fond of sport, and he rightly says that here nobody really cares for anything else."

"There is a ball at Arlington House," said her father.

"He really doesn't care for those large entertainments, and I do agree that it isn't amusing for him. He knows nobody – he's no friends, that is to say. People are civil, of course, but that's different. And then they send him down to supper with the most important person, which means the oldest and the most tiresome, as a rule. He enjoys seeing you. He enjoyed going to the opera with you the other night. I think that's what he liked best. It reminded him of Italy."

"Yes, yes," said her father; "we must think. Hengrave told me yesterday he wants you to go and spend Whitsuntide at Bramsley."

"I don't think Guido will like that."

"It's a comfortable house. And Giorgiana Hengrave is good - looking, agreeable, and, after all, quite knowledgeable. I expect she will have asked a few quite pleasant people."

"Would you come too?"

"Of course."

"I suppose we shall have to?"

"I think it would be as well."

"We should have to go there some time."

"Yes, I think so; and then we will try and think of something amusing for him to do. It's a pity he doesn't care for racing. I think he likes going to the St James's Club."

"Yes; he said he enjoyed that, and the House of Lords interested him. You see, papa, Guido is interested in serious things – foreign politics, literature, and art. He thinks every one here is so uneducated."

"So they are, thank God!" said her father. "That's what makes them bearable."

Henry Clifford took Guido to the Derby, which he found impressive, and Blanche went too; but he complained first of the heat and the dust, and then of the rain. They drove down in a coach which belonged to a cousin of Henry Clifford's, Cecil Law, who backed the winner, Kingcraft, and advised Guido to, but he obstinately backed Macgregor.

They were asked out to many dinners and parties, but Blanche did not feel strong enough to go to the big parties, and Guido refused to go to the small dinners. He was bored – bored to tears – but he did not suggest going home, and the reason was, Blanche thought, that his mother had written to her and to him saying that of course they would stay in England till the middle of July. She suggested meeting them then at Cadenabbia, where they might stay for a little on the way to Florence. Guido had a little villa – really a farmhouse – at Cadenabbia, on the lake.

The Sunday after the Derby they went to Bramsley. Guido made no difficulties about going. He regarded it as a duty, and Blanche realised that directly he had made up his mind that something was a duty, the more disagreeable it was, the more he enjoyed doing it.

Bramsley was in Easthamptonshire, a little farther from London than Norton Park. They found several guests: the Solskis; Henry Clifford himself and his young cousin, Cecil Law; a Countess Felseck, a pretty and attractive Swedish lady; Lady Hengrave's eldest sister, Louisa, and her husband, Algy

Fenton, who was on the Stock Exchange; and Lady Harriet Clive. Blanche wondered how Guido would bear it, as she considered that Bramsley was a dish that only an English palate could appreciate. He got on well with Lady Hengrave; he admired her, and said she reminded him of the Empress Eugénie; he admired her more than her sister Louisa, whom Blanche considered the better-looking and the more attractive of the two. She had all Lady Hengrave's dazzle, the bright skin, the fine shoulders, and the opulent silken hair, without any of the stiffness and severity of line and expression.

The first evening went off well. Lord Hengrave, Guido, and Henry Clifford played whist after dinner, and Lord Hengrave with difficulty restrained himself from an access of violent temper when Guido, his partner, took no notice of his call for trumps. He contented himself with burying his head in his hands and sighing.

On Whitsunday, Guido drove in a fly to a church in the town, which was three miles off. Lord Hengrave never let his horses go out on Sunday. Blanche went to church with the family, and listened to a long sermon from the parson, who took off his surplice before he went into the pulpit, and refreshed himself with a glass of port before beginning to preach.

Luncheon on Whitsunday was rather a long meal. Some neighbours came – a young Captain Calhoun, with a pretty wife. At the end of luncheon the children appeared – a little boy aged four, called Edward, and a baby aged two, called Gilbert. Gilbert, having upset Lord Hengrave's glass of sherry, had to be sent back in tears, and not without kicks, to the nursery. After luncheon they went for a Sunday walk and inspected the stables, the farm, the dairy, the garden, the kitchen-garden, the hothouses, and the croquet ground.

On Monday they drove into Barminster to see the Cathedral, and had luncheon with the local member who lived there.

Both Lord Hengrave and Cecil White made up to Blanche whenever either of them had an opportunity.

On Tuesday they had a croquet party in the afternoon, and on Wednesday they had luncheon and spent the afternoon at Captain Calhoun's, and on Thursday Guido said he had pressing business in London, so he and Blanche left. The remaining guests stayed till Saturday, and some of them over Sunday.

Guido was gloomy and morose on the return journey; he made no comment on the visit. He left Blanche when they arrived in London to go back to Norton Park by herself, saying he would come by a later train.

When Blanche got back to Norton Park she found awaiting her a parcel forwarded from Rome. It contained a Russian review. She turned over the pages, understanding not a word, and wondering who could have sent her such a thing. Nothing was written on it. She was looking at it and turning the pages over listlessly, wondering what they were all about, when Guido came back from London. He at once asked her what it was she was reading from Rome.

"It's a Russian review some one has sent me from Rome. I can't think who, unless it is one of the Olenevs; only they know that I can't understand Russian."

"Let me see it," said Guido.

He took the review and looked through it and put it down again.

"It's time you dressed for dinner," he said.

Blanche went up to dress.

She was the first to be down.

Guido was silent at dinner, and only answered in monosyllables. He asked Blanche if she had had any letters from Rome. She had not heard from any one.

"Every one seems to be away – all the people I know."

"On the contrary, from what I hear, Rome appears to be very full," said Guido. "We shall have to go back soon. It would be a pity to miss the next Session." Guido was alluding to the

Session of the Ecumenical Council, which did not interest Blanche. She did not know what it was all about.

The next morning a letter reached her from Florence, enclosing a printed cutting from a newspaper, headed:

## TRANSLATION FROM THE RUSSIAN INTO ENGLISH DOGGEREL, WRITTEN IN FLORENCE

"Out there the winter dies, the snows take flight,
And in the flood-bound fields the withered trees
Are all a-floating upon silvery seas;
And now the floods have vanished in the night.

Now bloom the white flowers, white anemones,
Narcissus and the lily of the vale;
They carpet the woods green with pattern frail;
But you, white flower, are whiter than all these.

You are the flower that in my garden grows,
Not here with cypress, Judas-tree, and rose,
But in a northern garden far away;
There gladsome nightingales sing loud all day,
There the sweet lilac grows, so white in hue,
So lovely and so simple; so like you."

The poem was not signed, or, if it had been, the signature was cut away, and underneath it was written, "See," and then two Russian words, and after them, in brackets, "*Russian Review*, page 91."

Blanche looked at the Russian review, and she saw that page 91 had been torn out.

# CHAPTER VII

As the summer went on and grew hotter and hotter, Guido became more and more bored. He seemed to grow into a different man than he had been in Rome; or rather at Rome, he had been living, so it struck Blanche, behind a mask, with a soft pedal pressed as it were upon him. The soft pedal was, she thought, his mother's influence. He was showing himself now in his true colours, and this was no surprise to Blanche, for he was exactly what she had supposed him to be. There was no disillusion and no disappointment where there had been no illusion and no hope.

She saw him as he was: meticulous, narrow, tortuous, self-centred, jealous – so she suspected – insanely jealous. Ambitious, yes; but of what? What were his aims? He was intensely secretive – secretive even about the smallest things. He never said where he was going, what he was going to do, nor what he had done, and whom he had seen. Even if he bought a pair of gloves he made a mystery about it.

Blanche wrote to her father and said that she thought Guido felt lonely at Wood Norton. On the other hand, he refused all invitations, so what was to be done? Henry Clifford arranged to take Guido and Blanche one Saturday afternoon to a small party (music was mentioned) given by a friend of his, Mrs Roden. They were asked to come when they liked in the afternoon and stay for dinner. They lived quite close to London, at a place called Little Warlop, and it was less than an hour's drive from Norton Park. Francis Roden was a Member of Parliament, and also of a well-known firm in the City. He was well off. Rachael Roden, his wife, was Lord Hengrave's sister. She was cultivated, picturesque as well as beautiful, and enthusiastic. Gabriel Carteret, the young painter, had made a name by his portrait of her. She looked particularly striking that afternoon, dressed in mauve silk with broad flounces and a camellia in her hair. Their house was the centre of everything that was most agreeable in London. There was a slightly foreign element in it and something not Bohemian, but in touch, nevertheless, with the world of art, letters, and music. There you might meet a painter or a sculptor, and almost certainly a musician, but no lion-hunters and no lions. If a celebrity was there, it meant he or she was not only a friend but a great friend. Henry Clifford was a great friend of the Rodens.

The afternoon Guido and Blanche drove there in a hired open landau was hot and lovely, but the roads were dusty. It was a great relief to arrive at the cool house with its panelled-oak rooms full of flowers, its chintz chairs, cool verandahs and shady lawns. Many of Blanche's friends were there: her father to begin with; a cousin or two; the Hengraves; Maud Locksley, who it was said had a more beautiful figure than any one, and trod the ground like a goddess, and her fiancé, Ralph Dallington, a dark and much bewhiskered dragoon; the most intimate friend of her girlhood, Rose Leigh, who had now come back from her honeymoon, and was now no longer Rose Leigh but Rose Latimer – a little fair, pink-and-white, laughing creature, as pretty as a kitten; Cecil Law, smart in grey, with his long, reddish whiskers and purposely pre- (Franco-Prussian) war trousers; the Solskis, Lady Harriet Clive, and Hedworth Lawless, whose engagement to his fiancée, Elsie Woodville, was announced. She was present herself, a lovely thin girl with great, dark, lustrous eyes, a small white face and masses of dark hair; a vision in lace flounces and pink ribbons, with a tiny little ribboned bonnet poised on the top of her head, and in the middle of its brim, hanging over her forehead, one pink rose. There, the centre of a group of fervent admirers, was tall Lady Vanbrugh in the first bloom of her dazzling beauty. There, too, was Countess Felseck, whose rippling little high nervous laugh and foreign lisp seemed to be the exact accompaniment to her light blue eyes, her dazzling skin, and fair, frizzled hair, the centre of another group in which were Gabriel Carteret, the painter, Adrian Tyne, the diplomatist, who had translated Musset into English and wrote original verse, too; and a little way off, talking to Madame Frantz, the pianist, was young Lord Stonehenge, the Parliamentary Under-Secretary for Foreign Affairs.

Princess Solski at once annexed Guido and took him on past the lower terrace to a summer-house near the croquet ground, which she said was the prettiest part of the garden. Adrian Tyne noticed Blanche directly she arrived, and asked Henry Clifford to introduce him to her, which her father did at once. She had never seen him before, although she had often heard of him. He was nearly always abroad. He was still unmarried, although there were rumours of an engagement. He was at present *en poste* at Vienna, and over in London on leave. He was thought to be good-looking; his hair and his whiskers were dark and curly, his eyes a curious grey-blue, and there was something gay and radiant about him, infinite warmth and infinite refinement.

"I'm going to take you to the Dairy," he said to Blanche. "I know the way; there are a lot of chairs under a tree there, and it is the coolest place – perhaps the only cool place. But I suppose you don't feel the heat after Italy."

"Oh yes, I do," said Blanche. "I don't think one ever is hot in Italy."

They talked a little of Italy and compared notes about living abroad. Was there any chance of his coming to Florence or to

Rome? He thought not – none at all; they would most probably send him to Buenos Aires or to some other remote spot. But he knew Italy well, she discovered. He was musical and loved the opera.

"We may probably hear some good music this afternoon."

"Really?"

"Yes; Madame Frantz may play and Waller perhaps will sing. I saw both of them on the lawn just now."

"How delicious!"

"Yes; the nicest of all ways of hearing music is when it happens by accident, with nothing prearranged."

They discussed musicians, and somehow this led them to talk of the Olenevs, and, through them, of Sasha Valesky. Adrian Tyne knew him well; he had met him in Paris.

"Poor chap, I'm afraid he won't live long," he said, "*now*."

"Why *now* particularly?"

"He's had so much unhappiness lately."

"How?"

"Don't you know his whole history?"

"No; do tell it me."

Adrian Tyne told Blanche the whole story of Valesky's career as he knew it. How for a time he had been in love with a ballet dancer, but that had been of no importance. After that, however, he had been engaged to be married to a Polish cousin of his. This marriage had been more or less arranged for him by his mother, who adored him, and by the parents of the girl. They had been publicly engaged, and then, just when the time for the wedding was approaching and everything was ready, he felt he couldn't marry her, and he broke it off.

"Did the girl mind?" Blanche asked.

"Yes; she minded very much, so did the parents, and so did his mother."

"What was the girl like?"

"She was charming. But Sasha had never been in love with her. He had never pretended to be. He had only given in to his mother. He was in love with some one else."

"Who was that?" asked Blanche.

"It was a Russian girl called Olga Varin."

"And did she love him?"

"No, she didn't, and it was that, I think, which made him ill. When I first knew him he was just as well as any one else. His lungs were a little weak, but instead of taking care when he knew that Olga Varin wouldn't marry him, he did desperately foolish things on purpose. He made himself ill, in fact, and now what was at first a sort of sham has become a tragic reality. He really is ill, so I'm told, but you must know better, as you have seen him since I have."

"Did he know the Russian girl after or before he was engaged to his cousin?"

"I don't know when he first knew her – first met her, that is to say – but he certainly didn't fall in love with her till after he was engaged. That is why he broke the engagement off. If he hadn't met her I think he would have married his cousin."

"But why did you say that you did not think he would live long now?"

"Because I heard yesterday that Olga Varin has just married a Prince Peter Zamensky."

"And you think he still loves her?"

"Yes; unless he loves some one else – some one he has met since."

"When did that happen?… I mean the breaking off?"

"Two years ago."

There was a pause, and then Adrian Tyne said: "Do you think it was awful of him?"

"What – to break off the engagement?"

"Yes."

"No, not a bit; I admire him for it. I think it's a difficult thing to do, but really, in those circumstances, the only thing to do. He would have made his cousin miserable."

"Of course, *now* the parents are delighted – her parents, not his mother, of course. They wouldn't allow their daughter to marry him in the state he is now – at least I hope they wouldn't. One can never be sure, parents are so extraordinary, and Sasha, you know, is immensely rich, in spite of all the money he has spent and the follies he has committed. But I'm glad you don't think it was awful of him, because... "

There was a pause.

"Why?"

"Because I intend... I have definitely made up my mind to do just the same thing."

"Are you engaged?" asked Blanche. She was genuinely surprised.

"Yes. It hasn't been announced, but it is just the same as if it had been, so far as the girl is concerned. She's not a cousin. She is a nice, a wonderfully nice girl – far too good for me. But I know *now* I can't marry her."

There was a long pause.

"Do her parents know about it?"

"Yes; that is the worst of it. They approve, and they are such nice people. It was to be announced next week, but I am going to write about it tonight. There are none of them here today."

"Perhaps if you waited you might change your mind."

"It would be no good. I didn't *know*, you see. Exactly the same thing happened to me as what happened to Sasha. My mother put it into my head; said I ought to marry; said this girl was exactly the right person, and I agreed, but I was never in love with her, never for a moment. I thought I was, but then I met some one else and suddenly my eyes were opened; in one blinding flash I knew – "

At that moment Henry Clifford and Lady Harriet Clive walked on to the lawn, and Henry said:

"If you walk through into the house, through that door, you will find yourselves in a long passage, and that will take you straight into the dining-room. If you go there now you will find one or two people, and Madame Frantz is going to play. Don't say a word, but just go there. I thought you would like to know."

"Thank you so much," said Blanche; "but aren't you coming too?"

"Yes; we are coming in a moment, but we are looking for my sister Caroline, who will never forgive me if I let her miss the music."

Blanche and Adrian walked through the passage into the dining-room. It was a long, low room with the dining table at the end of it (this had been pushed into the window, and chairs were dotted about), where they went in, and what looked like a smoking-room at the other end. There were sofas and chairs and a grand pianoforte. Princess Marie of Halberstadt was sitting on the sofa: appreciative and rather large. The dining-room looked out on to a verandah, but the guests in the garden were hidden from sight by the Venetian blinds, which were down. Madame Frantz, a dignified lady with grey hair, was sitting at the pianoforte. She looked at the little audience and smiled. Gabriel Carteret was there, and Mrs Roden and Lady Stonehenge, Waller, and a few others.

She played a Chopin prelude, and then a Beethoven Sonata, Op. 112. A few more people, attracted by the sound, came as she played, and sat silently in the verandah. Blanche and Adrian Tyne sat right at the farther end. When she had finished, there was no formal applause, but a spontaneous pouring out of thanks and appreciation. After a slight pause, Mrs Roden said something to Waller, the baritone, and he came forward with some music. He sang the "Erl König" first, in German, and then Schubert's "Leiermann." By the time he had finished there was a crowd in the verandah, and they asked for an encore, and he sang Gounod's "Maid of Athens."

After that, Mrs Roden thought the artists had been generous enough, and said that everybody must come and have tea – they must all be so thirsty. Tea was in a large tent outside on the lawn: tea, iced coffee, and strawberries and cream; and a band began to play – not a brass band, but a Hungarian band which played Strauss' valses in so intoxicating a manner that some one suggested a dance, and presently couple after couple began dancing on the lawn.

Cecil White and Lord Hengrave both asked Blanche to dance with them at the same moment. But Adrian Tyne interposed and said: "The Princess is dancing this with me."

"Then I must have the next one – if there's a next one," said Lord Hengrave.

"No; I must have it," said Cecil White.

He made a lot of noise when he talked, and he was sulky if people did not do as he wished, so Blanche promised him the next dance and Lord Hengrave the one after.

The band played valses by Strauss and Waldteufel with intoxicating lilt and rhythm – "The Blue Danube," and others. Blanche danced the one dance she had promised, and then she said she was tired and would look on. Adrian Tyne never left her side, but she was not allowed to enjoy his conversation uninterruptedly, as Cecil White came every now and then and sat on the other side of her and joined in the conversation.

He told her long stories about his sporting and other adventures, told with great liveliness in racy English and a certain amount of noise, gesture, and linen shooting, and a good deal of facial expression. Lord Hengrave looked on jealously, and Lady Hengrave, who was dancing with Lord Stonehenge, gave the group a sharp look. Presently Guido and Princess Solski arrived on the scene and went into the tea-tent. Henry Clifford there detached Princess Solski from Guido, and he was taken in tow by Lady Harriet Clive.

They watched the dancers. Guido danced with Lady Harriet and a little later with Countess Felseck, who had been up till then Lord Hengrave's chief partner. Dancing went on like this until seven. Every one had been bidden to stay for dinner. Guido said he thought they must go home, but Henry Clifford, with the aid of Princess Solski, overruled this. They were expected; it would spoil the table and throw out the numbers; Mrs Roden would have to rearrange everything. It would be extremely rude – in fact, impossible – to go.

Before dinner they went indoors to tidy themselves up, to the bedrooms. Twenty people sat down to dinner. Blanche sat between Francis Roden (on his left – Princess Marie was on his right) and Lord Hengrave.

Francis Roden was cultivated, inquisitive, and alert; he piped rather than talked, like a bullfinch. He was an extremely kind-hearted, rather quaint, happy host, with pointed features and a wise, twinkling eye, long black whiskers, and hair a little long at the back, who liked seeing a lot of people round him, and liked to see them enjoying themselves. He was glad, he told Blanche, that the music was over. "Thank God it didn't last too long!"

"But she plays so beautifully," said Blanche.

"I know she does, my dear," he said, with a slight squeak; "but I can't abide it."

"But the singing?" she said.

"I don't mind when he sings in a civilised tongue," he said, "but when he sings German, I can't stand it."

"That's what I like best," said Blanche, laughing.

"I know you're right, and I'm wrong; but I leave music to Rachel; she likes it," he said, as if aggrieved.

A little later on she told him she was going to ask him a great favour.

"Well, I hope it's not something too difficult, my dear Blanche," he said, with a twinkle in his eye, "because, whatever it is... I should certainly do it. Nobody could refuse you anything."

"I want you to get me a seat in the House of Commons, in the Strangers' Gallery, for my husband next week, the day of the debate."

"Is that all? Well, I think that can be managed," he said, with a little dry smile. "I'll ask Stonehenge; only it's lucky the Ladies' Gallery has a grille, otherwise you would distract the members." Blanche laughed and blushed. "It's true," he said. "Rachel told me before dinner that you would break everybody's heart here, and I don't wonder."

It was in a sense true. Blanche seemed to be the centre of attraction that evening; everybody was talking about her. People seemed to have discovered her for the first time. There were many beautiful people there. Nothing could have exceeded Lady Vanbrugh's beauty – beauty beyond definition, beauty absolute; nobody could be more attractive than Countess Felseck; more distinguished than Princess Solski; more handsome than Princess Marie; more glittering than Lady Hengrave; but Blanche seemed somehow to suit that evening, and to have blossomed out as never before. Perhaps it was the admiration which she could not but feel she was being surrounded with. It was not that she was more beautiful than all those other women – perhaps she was not as beautiful – but her charm, her delicacy, was like the fragrance of an exquisite flower, as aromatic as verbena, as sweet as a tea-rose.

She was dressed (Worth was the artist) in soft black Chantilly laces, with pale yellow ribbons and flounces, a pale tea-rose in her hair and a cluster of tea-roses at her waist. Adrian Tyne was sitting opposite her, and he never took his eyes off her during dinner.

Lord Stonehenge asked Lady Hengrave, his neighbour, whether she did not think Blanche was lovely.

"She certainly has looks," Lady Hengrave said. "I always have said she had looks, but it's a pity she overtires herself. She will spoil her looks if she's not careful."

Gabriel Carteret, asked by his neighbour, Lady Harriet Clive, whether he did not admire Blanche, said he would rather paint her than almost any one.

"Then why don't you?" she said. "It will be quite easy, I'm sure. How would you paint her? As she is?"

"Yes; as she is."

"But, if you were to paint her in any fancy way, what would you choose for her?"

"I think in that case I would paint her as the heroine of some fairy-tale – something like the Marsh King's Daughter."

"What's that about?"

"I've rather forgotten. It's Hans Andersen. It's the story, I think, of a beautiful Egyptian Princess who flew disguised as a swan to the northern marshes of the Marsh King, who marries her, and there is a daughter. And then I forget what happens, but I remember the description of the beautiful Southern Princess with long black hair and her soft swan's plumage falling off her. Afterwards the daughter is turned into a lotus, I think. I don't know whether it's the daughter or the mother this Princess is like, or both. At any rate, it's a beautiful story, and the name suits her – the Marsh King's Daughter. Or, if you want a classical subject, I would choose Eurydice in a Renaissance masque, or possibly Proserpine, Queen of the Fairies, with music by Purcell. But I think what she is really like in the Limbo of history and fiction is one of those unhappy crowned or uncrowned or discrowned Queens – like Marie de Neubourg (was that her name?) in Victor Hugo's *Ruy Blas*, or Henriette d'Angleterre, or that Princess of Hanover, Sofie Dorothea, whom Königsmark loved, or her great-granddaughter, Caroline Matilda, the heroine and victim of the Struensee tragedy; but really I see her as a *modern* subject, and I shall paint her as that, or not at all – portrait of 'Princess X,' or 'Madame Trois Etoiles' (such a nice name). Only two days ago I was reading Grammont's *Memoirs*, and I remember he talks of one of the Restoration beauties as having *'la peau d'une blancheur éblouissante'* and *'les mains jolies'*; and *'La Dame aux Camélias'* would be a good name, if the name were to remind one of the flower. She does remind me of a camellia; the extraordinary whiteness and delicacy of her texture. Princess Roccapalumba! What a name! What better name could you have for a portrait, after all? Anything else would spoil it."

"She's so young still," said Lady Harriet. "Poor child! I can't help thinking she will suffer the tortures of the damned."

As soon as dinner was over they went out into the garden again. It was a beautiful, breathless night. The moon had risen while they had been having dinner, and silvered the terraces, the garden, and the further hay-fields. The hay harvest was at its height, and the hay was stacked in haycocks in the field beyond the terrace. There was a warm, intensely delicious smell of hay in the air. On the verandah the air was fragrant, too, with verbena, honeysuckle, jessamine, rosemary, sweet geranium, and *Gloire de Dijon* roses. On the lawn the band was playing in a tent, and the guests had left the rooms and the verandah, and most of them had begun to dance once more.

Blanche sat in a high wicker chair which had red cushions inside it. On a chair next her Adrian Tyne was smoking a cigarette. Guido had been piloted by Countess Felseck to a seat at the farther end of one of the garden walks.

The band was playing a valse, *"O schöner Mai."* The women in their muslins and light clothes, some of them with lace veils on their heads, looked like elegant ghosts. The dancers made no noise as they danced on the lawn.

There were pauses in the conversation between Adrian Tyne and Blanche. They were both rather pale – she from fatigue and excitement, he from suppressed emotion. The summer night was going to his head. He began pouring out incoherent words, whispered exclamations, swift, soft, meaningless nothings – a cascade of warm words of hinted endearment, unexpressed, unexpressive admiration, adjuration, praise, and ecstasy – to Blanche, when some one approached them, to her immense relief. She was, she knew, too tired to protest; she felt too weak for any resistance, and although there was nothing in her at the moment that responded to Adrian Tyne's wave of passion – on the contrary, she felt millions of leagues away, almost in another planet; she felt it was intoxicating to listen to words that were like music – it was balm to her sore spirit, if only for a moment; and, if only for a moment, to let yourself float on the tide of a summer dream: to hear yourself praised, admired – however little it might mean – to be looked at with wonder – even if that were only civility... It was Mr Roden who came up to them. He was smoking a cigar. He approached Blanche.

"Would you like a little music?" he said in a piping whisper.

"Oh, above all things!" she said. Then she stopped short. "But you don't like it."

"*I* don't signify. I shan't listen to it, either. But if you like it, you shall have it – and German music, too."

"Oh, please don't bother for me!"

But Mr Roden was already off like an arrow.

Presently the band stopped, and just behind Blanche and Adrian Tyne in the verandah, they heard Waller's voice singing Schubert's "Serenade."

That was just what was needed to make the night perfect. Blanche felt all her tiredness vanish. Her spirit seemed to be lifted as on wings, and to be made one with the darkness, the smell of the hay-fields and the climbing flowers, the music and the glimmer of the moon on the trees and the fields.

Why could one not stay like that for ever?

She was brought back to earth by the song coming to an end, and then the silence too deep for applause was suddenly broken by the voice of Lord Hengrave saying very firmly:

"I'm not going to let Master Adrian monopolise you the whole evening. It's my turn now. You promised me this dance."

"I'm afraid I'm too tired to dance, Lord Hengrave."

She smiled at him encouragingly. He was, she felt, safe.

"Then I'll sit down here," he said.

Adrian Tyne, too angry to speak, got up, and saying, "Au revoir, Princess," in a strained voice, went away.

Lord Hengrave was not left long to enjoy Blanche's society in peace, and just as he was on the verge of a declaration, Cecil Law appeared on the scene and took the stage and began talking to Blanche in the loudest of voices, taking no notice whatsoever of Lord Hengrave, who, however, refused to budge from his chair, but sat on in sulky silence in spite of the still sulkier hints and voice and attitude of Cecil Law, who said it was his dance. The scene was put to an end by the arrival of Lady Hengrave; she said, in an icy voice, looking at Blanche with no good eye, that it was time for them to go home. And at that moment Guido arrived, too, and gave the scene a scrutinising look and said the same thing to Blanche.

The guests began to go. Some of them were driving to London in carriages and cabs, and others went in flies to catch the last train. As Blanche and Guido left, she caught the far-away strains of Strauss' "*O schöner Mai*," which had been asked for as final dance, and she saw staring at her under the ivy-mantled *porte-cochère*, with wildly bright eyes, the handsome face of Adrian Tyne.

Guido said scarcely a word during all the drive home.

# CHAPTER VIII

The next day, which was Sunday, Guido, after he had walked to Mass – there was a church quite close – spent the morning in writing letters. He seemed preoccupied and absent-minded. Every now and then he looked at Blanche thoughtfully and inquiringly, in a manner that made her feel uncomfortable. Her father came down to see them in the afternoon, stayed for dinner, and went back afterwards. He seemed in high spirits. Blanche, he told Guido, had been the success of the Rodens' party. All London would be raving about her. He had been driven back after the party by the Stonehenges in their carriage, and both of them – Lord and Lady Stonehenge – agreed that Blanche was the most attractive person there.

"We're all very proud of you, aren't we?" he said, looking at Blanche and turning to Guido. "Lady Stonehenge said you did credit to England and to Italy, and that Rome had given you a *cachet* that English women didn't have as a rule. She is a good judge, too – Lady Stonehenge. Her mother was French and belonged to the old régime."

Guido nodded and looked on approvingly.

They discussed the party at length. It had been pretty. What was so attractive about the Rodens' parties was there was no fuss about them; everything happened on the spur of the moment, spontaneously. Blanche must see more of them. They had a house in Green Street.

They sometimes had musical parties in London. Mrs Roden, too, had been delighted with Blanche, and as for Francis Roden, he was frankly in love with her.

The next two days Guido spent in London, and slept there; he had, he said, important business. Blanche began to receive a quantity of letters and invitations; not just cards, of which she had already a quantity, but notes from people: from the Stonehenges, asking them to spend Cowes week on their yacht; from Lady Kiltarlity, asking them to Scotland in August; from Countess Felseck, begging them to come and play croquet at her little house near London; from Cecil White, asking them to stay at his house for the Goodwood Races; from Lady Hengrave, asking them to Bramsley for the partridge shooting; from Lady Vanbrugh, begging them to dine for a dance she was giving; from the Permanent Under-Secretary for Foreign Affairs, asking them to luncheon; and many other letters of the same kind. Blanche kept them till Guido came back from London, and then she asked him what she was to answer.

"It's a pity we cannot accept any of these invitations except that luncheon at Sir James Wilbraham's" – this was a large political luncheon they had been asked to – "as we shall not be here. It is very civil," he said, with a slight tinge of irony in his voice, "of them to ask us to so many things. However, we shall be able to take advantage of their hospitality another year, or, better still, to return it to them should they visit us in Italy."

"When do you mean to start?" asked Blanche.

"I must be at Rome on the 12th of July, and I must stop at Florence on the way. I want to take the journey easily, and to stop at Paris for a night or two. So we shall have to start soon – at the beginning of next week. Tuesday – no, not Tuesday; it's unlucky, but Wednesday."

Blanche said nothing. That evening she wrote to her father and implored him to make one final effort to persuade Guido to let her stay in England until her baby should be born. But she felt as she wrote the letter that it was useless. Guido was to go to the House of Commons the next day to hear Mr Gladstone speak on the Education Bill. The day after they were having luncheon with Sir James Wilbraham.

She saw her father at this luncheon, which proved to be solemn, official, and dreary, and he took her aside afterwards and told her that he could do nothing. Guido would not leave her in England, could not stay there himself, even if he wanted to, and, moreover, did not wish his child to be born in a foreign country.

"I must say I understand that," said Henry Clifford. "There is nothing to be said against that. I'm afraid there is no help for it."

"We go tomorrow. I probably shan't see you again," said Blanche.

"Nonsense, my child. Don't talk such nonsense. I shall come out to Rome in the autumn. I shall be with you at the time. You'll see all will be for the best."

The next day they left for Paris. Henry Clifford came to see them off. He was surprised at their departure, which he thought sudden, but Guido explained to him that he wished to be back in Rome for the next public session of the Ecumenical Council, which was to be held in July.

As it was, they did wisely, for they arrived in Paris just in time to witness the first flash of lightning, the first far-off rumble of thunder which heralded the storm of the Franco-Prussian War.

Events then began to move with headlong rapidity, as they do when a real catastrophe is about to happen. Nobody seems able to do anything except either to watch the advancing flames or to take some step which seems to fan them, and yet every one is supposed to be, and probably is, desirous of putting out the fire.

Guido thought it would be unwise to stop in Paris, and he left that city, which was already in a state of agitation, on the

7th July. They stayed two nights at their villa in Florence, and then found themselves back once more at the Palazzo Fabrini, which Guido said was the pleasantest spot in which to spend the summer.

Princess Julia was there to meet them, and she received Blanche with great warmth, and did not seem to be curious about her time in London, but every now and then she asked just the question which seemed to probe the most vital spot – just the question which was the most difficult to answer, although it seemed so ordinary.

Rome was full, and at the same time empty; full of people and empty of friends. The Olenevs had gone to Berchtesgaden. There were no other people that Blanche was particularly anxious to see. The town was full of ominous rumours, and both morally and physically there was thunder in the air.

War was thought to be certain. Wild rumours were abroad – rumours that contradicted one another from hour to hour.

Donna Teresa and her husband were in Switzerland. They were expected back soon.

And now, after the excitement of the last days in England, of her brief stay in Paris, with its feverish atmosphere and clouds charged with lightning and impending calamity, culminating on 18th July with the declaration in St Peter's of the Decree of Papal Infallibility and of war between France and Germany, Blanche fell a prey to a reaction of inexpressible depression which swung like a pendulum between the extremes of violent revolt and stagnant apathy. She paid no heed to these tremendous events, more than to the violent storm which broke over the City on the night of the 17th, and thundered and lightened, while the Decree was being read in St Peter's and the French crowds were shouting "*à Berlin*" in the boulevards of Paris.

She felt that such things could not touch her; that she was imprisoned for life; doomed to a life sentence; for better, for worse; to be Princess Roccapalumba, and that there was no escape. She felt, like Hamlet, that henceforth the whole world must be a prison; that she was the victim of a mistake. She saw nothing ahead but infinite misery and unending dreariness. She looked down the long dreary avenue of a life without love. She could still, she thought, at a pinch, respect her husband, but love him, never. Even this attitude was destined soon to undergo a sudden and violent change for the worse.

It was two or three days after they had come back to Rome. Blanche had been out for a walk by herself late in the evening, which she often did. She had wandered in the narrow, dark streets near the Pantheon, which she was fond of, and she had sat for some time in a cool church. She did not even know its name. On the way home she was caught in a storm.

When she came in she glanced at the letters on the large marble table in the hail, and on the top of them she thought she saw one in a handwriting which seemed familiar to her, with a foreign stamp and postmark, although for the moment she didn't place it. But she didn't stop to pick them up; she was in a hurry to change, as she was wet. She went to take off her hat and change in her bedroom, which was on the same floor as the hall, and on the first floor of the palace. To get to her bedroom she passed through the *salotto*, a small, high room in which Guido sometimes sat and read – although it was not his own private room – and where they had tea in the afternoon, He asked her whether there were any letters.

"Some for me, and I think one for you," she said, and she went to her bedroom to take off her hat and to change her shoes and her gown, which were wet. When she came back, Guido handed her a packet and said: "There are your letters."

She looked through them; they were circulars from dressmakers, one begging letter, and a note from her father, who always wrote to her every day.

"Is that all?" she asked.

The letter with the Russian postmark was not there.

"Yes; were you expecting any more?"

"I thought I noticed another one with a Russian postmark. I thought it might have been from the Olenevs."

"I think you must have been mistaken," said Guido. "I gave you all the letters that were on the table."

He rang the bell. Presently Alfredo, his servant, came into the room.

"Were there any other letters for the Princess besides the three on the hall table?" he asked.

"No others, Eccellenza."

"You see," he said, and he went on reading the newspaper.

Tea was brought in presently, and they had a short, desultory conversation. Guido talked of the war news. It was not, it appeared, good, but then the newspapers told such lies; they always exaggerated.

At six, Guido said he must go out to the Club. He left Blanche by herself.

"Teresa and Mario come back tomorrow," he said as he went out.

When he had gone, Blanche sat by herself in the *salotto* till the sun set. She held a book in her hand, but she did not read. She sat looking into the large empty fireplace, and at times she looked up at the sombre portrait above it of one of Guido's ancestors, pale as wax, with grey eyes just like his. Then she caught sight of something in the fireplace in front of the unlit logs. It was a little heap of burnt paper. Some one had been burning something, only the work had not been done quite thoroughly. A little scrap of paper had been left unburnt. It was a stamp and a postmark torn from an envelope; the postmark and the stamp she saw, as she picked them up, were Russian. It was as if this piece had been left unburnt on purpose, as none of its edge was burnt. Blanche threw it back on to the fireplace. She felt cold inside. She felt that her feelings for Guido had turned from respectful indifference to a cold, calm hatred. And there she was, married to him for ever, for better, for worse. There was no escape. Till death us do part.

But she was too heartbroken for tears. Her grief was hopeless, and therefore, as the poetess said, passionless. The letter was, she felt certain, from Sasha Valesky. She remembered now where she had seen the handwriting before. She had seen it on the envelope of the letter enclosing the English poem; also on the wrapper of the Russian review that had been sent her.

Then she said to herself: "I have been punished; I had no right to hear from him." Then again: "Why have I no right? Why shouldn't he write to me? Mayn't I receive and read my own letters? Am I to be spied upon and censored all my life?" Then another voice said within her: "You have no right to receive the kind of letters he writes to you, and you know it." "But, how do I know he would write that kind of letter? Hitherto he has never written at all." "No, but he has done worse."

This dialogue went on in a vicious circle buzzing in her head.

She did not see Guido again till he came into the *salotto* just before dinner. They were to dine with his mother in her apartment. They walked up the long steps to the second floor in silence.

Although Princess Julia's apartment was so high up, the rooms were as lofty as those on the first floor, and all of them spacious. They were furnished with tact. Princess Julia knew how a Roman house should be arranged. The cooking, too, in her apartment was better, Blanche sadly recognised, than on the first floor. The reason was simple. Princess Julia had taken the excellent cook who had been with Guido's father for herself as soon as her husband died.

Princess Julia was affable. A French priest, the Abbé Fromentin, was the only guest, and they sat down in the large dining-room, hung with faded red silk and decorated with a few pictures – one beautiful Guardi and a Fragonard.

Princess Julia asked if there was any news.

No news, only rumours. One really didn't know what to believe. It was a shame, taking the Prince Imperial to the front.

He was too young. Guido thought it a good thing. Princess Julia said she was so sorry for the Empress.

"She is a very high-souled lady," said the Abbé – "immensely courageous." And he told an anecdote of her behaviour on the night of the attempt made by Orsini to blow up the Emperor. "*Elle a montré un grand sangfroid. Avant la fin de la soirée elle a pu sourire,*" he said.

"It is monstrous," said Guido, "of the English to harbour all these Nihilists. They prepare these crimes at their leisure in England, where nobody touches them, and they commit them abroad. The English don't care, because they know that if they treat them well the Nihilists will not commit any outrages in England, but save up all their exploits for us."

Blanche said nothing.

Then the Abbé tried to change the subject by saying that every country had its *mauvais sujets,* and that the Irish Fenians were a thorn to the English.

Apropos of news Guido said suddenly: "There is one bit of news I heard at the Club." He paused. "Sasha Valesky is dead. He died at his country estate in Russia."

Blanche felt as if she had known this already, and it was with cool, calm, pretended naturalness that she said: "Oh! I'm so sorry. I was afraid he was seriously ill. The Olenevs will miss him dreadfully."

"Yes," said Princess Julia; "he went there a great deal. Did you know him, Monsieur l'Abbé?"

"Yes; I had the honour of knowing him a little. He was a good Catholic, and intelligent. *Très instruit.*"

"I knew him well at one time," said Princess Julia. "In fact, I think I was his oldest friend in Rome. Do you know, Blanche, I once nearly gave him the Guardi! He was a charming companion when he liked, and it's a great pity he made so little of his life."

"He published one or two books," said the Abbé.

"Yes; books of poetry, in Russian," said Princess Julia.

"Of course, I couldn't read any of that, but Mania Olenev tells me they are very good. I have read some of his verse in *English*, though. He used to send them to the *Academic Review* sometimes. They were quite nice. Pretty, but one could see he was a foreigner; couldn't one, Blanche?"

"I don't know that I have seen any of his English poetry," said Blanche. "Ira Olenev read me out something of his once, but I think it was a translation from the Russian."

"Russian is a difficult language," said the Abbé, "but fortunately the Russians are wonderful linguists; they talk all languages, and talk them well. But it is remarkable and rare for some one to write verse in a language that is not his own."

"Yes – remarkable," said Princess Julia, "and sometimes convenient."

After dinner, Princess Julia played patience, and Guido and the Abbé played a game of backgammon. Blanche did some sewing. Every now and then Princess Julia made a remark to her, and the conversation ran in this fashion:

"Yes; I think that was wise. Ten on the nine and that frees the knave. So it's not coming out this time. Sasha Valesky will be very much missed next winter – in Rome. Ah! there's the seven. *Dans tous les mondes.* He knew everybody. *N'est-ce pas*, Monsieur l'Abbé? Did you see Mr Roberts at the Club, Guido? No? What a pity, that blocks the row. He'd such good taste. Three, four, and five upon six, colour upon colour. I thought he might have some French news. Ask him to dinner if you do see him. I suppose – now I don't know what to do. I suppose there will be a Requiem for Sasha Valesky. You must find out. We must *all* go. I suppose you've got a black gown, Blanche? I suppose they'll have something at the Russian church, too. *Panichida*, it's called, isn't it, Monsieur l'Abbé? Knave, Queen, King. It will probably be the day after tomorrow. You must put off going to Florence a night, if necessary. Yes; I think so. He was a *very* old friend of mine. I know his mother, too, extremely well – the old Princess – and she will be very hurt if

we don't all go. It's the least one can do. Yes; she's in Russia –
in the country, I think. Another Ace. I believe it *is* coming out.
I really do believe it's coming out, after all. *C'est bon signe.* It
will probably be tomorrow. We won't go to the Russian
church. That's not necessary, and that will probably be at the
same time. Yes; they last longer than ours. You can find out at
the Club tomorrow. There! it is really out. Come and look,
Guido. *Venez voir, Monsieur l'Abbé.* Come and look, Blanche.
It really has come out this time. That must mean good luck.
Now we must try again, but, of course, it won't come out
twice running. They say Marie Antoinette did her *Réussite*
thirteen times running in the *Conciergerie*, and that it did not
come out *once.* I think I won't try *Metternich* again; it's too
difficult. I will do *La Belle Lucie*, and if the Kings come out on
the top I will make what I call the 'Royal Nursery.' "

Princess Julia did *La Belle Lucie*, and, thanks to the "Royal
Nursery" – in other words, to a little bit of cheating – it came
out; and at eleven punctually she got up, and everybody knew
it was time to go. Monsieur l'Abbé said good night, and Guido
and Blanche kissed Princess Julia and went downstairs.

Blanche was convinced now that Sasha Valesky had written
to say goodbye to her and that Guido had destroyed the letter.
She did not suspect him of having read it. She felt that she
could never forgive him, never feel the same towards him as
long as she lived. The incident brought to light a whole train of
other little incidents, deeds, words, and looks that she had
forgotten, and she realised that she must have been hating
Guido for some time.

"What a way," she thought bitterly, "to start married life!"

The next morning there was a Requiem Mass at Santa Maria
in Via. A great many people attended it, and a great many ladies
in black. "*Ses anges gardiens*," some one said. But there was
no one there whom Blanche remembered as having been a
special friend of his. Blanche was listless throughout the
service. She did not attempt to follow what was happening.

The rites of the Roman Church were a sealed book to her, although she had attended several of the more important ceremonies. These had impressed her as spectacles, and she had enjoyed them as such. Guido had explained various items...what this meant, what was happening at a given moment; but, as usually happens on those occasions when one has not within one the clue to what is happening, she found it difficult, if not impossible, to listen to what she was being told.

She thought of Sasha, and wondered whether he was aware of this ceremony, and whether the soul went on living after the death and decay of the body. Perhaps he was here in this church. She had liked him; had been fond of him. They might, she knew, have been great friends, and Guido had known this and had prevented it, or would have prevented it. In some curious, unreasonable way she thought that Guido was responsible for Sasha's death. And yet she knew this was absurd.

Princess Julia cried a great deal during the Requiem – gentle, discreet tears, which were not violent enough to disturb her appearance, but sufficient to soften her expression, to moisten her eyelashes, and to make her look interesting.

Blanche looked at Guido and thought – was it her imagination? – that there was an expression of triumph on his face. Was there any one in the whole of that church, she thought, who had cared, or who now cared, a fig for Sasha? Were they not all performing a social duty just in the same spirit as they would leave cards on each other on New Year's Day? "Have they really any religion?" she wondered. And this led her to the thought – had *she* any religion? "I don't suppose I have," she said to herself. She thought of what she had been taught as a child, first by her mother and then by "Lud." She had never questioned it. She now felt too tired morally even to think of it. "I only know one thing," she thought – "it's no help to me."

At that moment a chant that was being recited ascended the scale and reached a note of piteous anguish on the words:

"Qui Mariam absolvisti,
Et latronem exaudisti,
Mihi quoque spem dedisti."

Guido pointed to the English translation in the book which he had provided her with. It was extremely unlikely, Blanche thought, that anything could give her *hope*. But how wonderful if that could one day happen. She didn't ask for *happiness*. That, she thought, was out of the question, but if she might one day have *hope* – the little coloured gem that lay at the bottom of Pandora's fatal box.

She brooded over this, and when she came to from her reverie, she realised that the Requiem was over.

They were to start for Florence the next day. They had put off going because of the Requiem, but Blanche felt that Guido was glad of the excuse for staying another day in Rome, which he preferred so infinitely to any other place in the world. He left her to herself that day. She spent the whole afternoon wandering about the streets on foot. She went to the fountain of Trevi.

"Shall I throw in a penny?" she said to herself. "Do I want to come back here? No, I don't, and I shall probably have to come back all too often without the aid of any pennies."

She left the fountain. She walked through a network of little streets till she reached the Pantheon. From there she walked to the Palazzo Alfieri, through the Piazza di Gesù, to the Via delle Boteghe Oscure.

It was getting late. She would not be back for tea. Perhaps she would catch Roman fever. Not yet, and not in this quarter of the city, but little did she care if she did. She asked a *contadino* who was passing what time it was. He gave her a charming smile and said, *"Saran le Ventiquattro."*

92

She was in a little, long, narrow street which was sheltered from the low rays of the setting sun. "I am not far from home," she thought. But she had no wish to go indoors. In the street in front of her a man was walking behind a donkey which was laden with vegetables. He was carrying a large, green, open sunshade and making encouraging noises. Further on, from the windows of an upper storey, came the sound of some one playing on a clattering pianoforte an air with a multitude of flourishes and trills – the drinking song from Donizetti's *Lucrezia Borgia*. It was divinely gay. The tune for a moment brought back to her mind her father's drawing-room in Curzon Street...a party she had been allowed to "come down to" when she was quite a little girl, so that she might say in after-life she had heard Mario.

A loaded wine-cart came rumbling by. A dignified-looking peasant was sitting sideways on the edge of it, near the shut hood which sprawled over the side like a sail, with its pattern of pink roses, like those on a Pompeian mosaic, and lining of green cretonne. He opened his throat and sang the phrase of a song:

"Oh Rosa delle rose, O Rosa bella,
Per te non dormo ne notte ne giorno – o – o – o – o – o."

The contrast with the gay music of the pianoforte – which had now stopped – was sharp. This phrase seemed to come from another century, from another world... It seemed to Blanche like the fragment of a chant, but, oh! so old and so far away. Proserpine might have listened to just such a snatch of song when she was picking flowers in the vale of Enna.

The singer prolonged the last note of his phrase till his breath failed him, and the song died away in a discordant, blurred chromatic. It was deafeningly loud, nasal, and, at the same time, hoarse, and piercingly sad. A dog that was sprawling over one of the barrels barked.

The cart rumbled down the street, and when it had turned the corner and was out of sight, Blanche heard the same phrase being sung once more. This time distance softened the harshness of the sound, and the song became mysterious and magical, one with the hour and the place; and then silence for one brief second seemed to descend upon the city and the street, but only to be broken immediately.

All at once the church bells began to ring. She seemed to be in a crystal kingdom of ringing sound. The man behind the donkey stopped and took off his hat. It was the *Ave Maria*. Small groups of men and women who were sitting and standing at the doorways talking in a loud chatter, some of them singing, some of them knitting, all stopped doing what they were doing and were silent. Hardly had the Angelus ceased ringing when Blanche heard the sound of another bell. In the distance of the dark street she saw lighted torches waving and coming towards her, as if in a hurry. And then the sound of many voices – that peculiar, rhythmical, almost mechanical unison of voices praying. A great hush descended upon that street, which was swarming with so intense, vivid, coloured, and loud a life. Blanche heard the people crying: "*Il Santissimo! Il Santissimo!*" Those who were indoors snatched lamps from the table – lamps as old in shape as those of the Vestal Virgins, or the Wise and the Foolish Virgins – and the whole Street was bright with a sudden spontaneous illumination.

It was a priest bearing the Blessed Sacrament to a sick man to give him the Viaticum. Beside him was a boy ringing a bell and bearing a tall lighted taper. A carriage came clattering down the street at that moment. When the coachman reached the procession he stopped, and a lady, dressed in black, got out and knelt down while the little procession passed. It passed swiftly by, and Blanche followed in the crowd. They turned up another little street; on each side of them was a kneeling crowd. There the house of the sick man was reached; a few members of the crowd followed the priest into the house; the others stayed outside. They knelt down, and some of them said the Rosary and some of them the Litany for the Dying. The ceremony seemed to be swiftly over, for soon the priest appeared again, and again the little procession was formed. The crowd thickened. They sang the *Te Deum*. The lamps were once more held out of the windows, and the street was illuminated. Blanche let the procession pass her this time, and then she turned into the street that led her home to the Palazzo Fabrini. Guido was not at home. He had gone to the Club.

# CHAPTER IX

Blanche and Guido left for Florence the next evening. The doctor said that the climate of Rome was trying for Blanche in her present condition, and a great deal too hot. At Florence their villa was high up on the hill, on the Fiesole side, and she would have plenty of air.

A passionless, stagnant melancholy, a starless depression, settled down on her once more, and she hoped with all her heart that when her baby was born she would not recover. They had not been long in Florence before they received the news of the capitulation of Sedan. Princess Julia had already joined them when this news arrived. Guido said this meant the end of the Pope's temporal power: the end of the oldest monarchy in Europe.

Shortly after the entry of Victor Emmanuel into Rome they were joined by Mario Guerrini and Donna Teresa, who arrived from Switzerland.

Life for Blanche proceeded in much the same rut as it did when she was in Rome. In the morning she sat in the garden of the villa, and sometimes she drove to the town and visited a church or a gallery, and in the afternoon she went for a drive to the Cascine with her mother-in-law or with Donna Teresa. Princess Julia demanded just as much of Mario Guerrini's time and attention as she had done before his marriage.

Donna Teresa was just as shy and as shrinking. Towards the evening there would sometimes be visitors, although there were not many Italians in Florence at that moment, nor, that year, many tourists on account of the war.

Their evenings were just the same as before. Guido and Mario played backgammon and sometimes chess; Princess Julia did her patience; Donna Teresa looked on and helped her; and Blanche sewed.

From time to time Blanche heard from her father, but the post was irregular and uncertain. He sent her a great deal of political news and told her all the gossip of the London Clubs. She was, he said, much missed, and he was perpetually being asked whether she was coming back next year – what a pity it was she had left England so soon.

At the end of November her baby was born. It was a boy, and he was baptized Giovanni Guido Antonio Julio Enrico. Blanche was extremely ill, and her life was feared for. Guido had prayers offered for her in many of the churches of Florence.

But she weathered the crisis and gradually floated back to life in a state of intense weakness. She was passionately fond of her little boy, who had black eyes, but who was, so Princess Julia said, nevertheless the image of his father.

Henry Clifford was not able to get to Florence in time for the birth of the baby, and now he was being kept in London. But his sister, Mrs Somner, had come out, and Blanche was glad to see her Aunt Caroline. She stayed with them at the villa.

It was a cold winter, and in Florence you felt the cold more keenly perhaps than anywhere. The doctor, so Guido said, recommended a return to Rome, where it certainly was warmer.

Blanche did not much mind whether she was at Rome or Florence. She was entirely wrapped up in her baby. Guido seemed to take a condescending interest in the infant as well. But here, again, Blanche felt to her intense irritation that she was not a free agent. The nurse was chosen nominally by

Guido, but in fact by his mother. His mother's opinion was sought and taken in preference to hers. She was always consulted, it was true, with the utmost courtesy; and if her opinion coincided with that of her mother-in-law, with which it was at once compared, and by which it was checked, it was allowed to pass, but if there was a divergence, then her opinion counted for nothing, and that of her mother-in-law was accepted. Blanche had not minded this, or had learnt to put up with it, so long as it concerned trivial matters – social questions and the routine of the household – but now when it affected her baby she felt it was intolerable.

She asked Guido if they could not go abroad or to England. Guido said this was difficult. It was impossible for him to leave Italy. Blanche had wished to have an English nurse for her baby. She thought this was reasonable, as the child could thus learn English in the easiest possible way. It was not from British prejudice or from any anti-Italian feeling. She was nursing the baby herself. But Princess Julia not only settled that the little Giovanni was to have an Italian nurse, but chose one herself. She was a nice homely woman called Assunta, and Blanche liked her, but she was careless, and held peculiar but decided opinions on medicine – that is to say, on what were the best remedies for certain diseases.

Blanche hardly went out at all that winter. She was engrossed in her child. She thought of nothing else, and the monotony of her life, the pressure exerted by Princess Julia, the feeling that she was never out of reach of perpetual surveillance, were for the time quite indifferent to her.

Her Aunt Caroline was at Rome, the Olenevs, and one or two other friends. Her father wrote to her constantly, but his letters arrived irregularly. He hoped to come out at Easter, but when Easter came he was not able to. Blanche would no doubt come to England for the summer. But Easter passed, and Guido showed no signs of wanting to go to England. Blanche did not much care. She was happy with her child. The baby, Guido said, was too young to travel. They would spend the summer at Cadenabbia. They did not leave Rome till the end of May.

Guido established Blanche and her baby at Cadenabbia, but he frequently went to Rome himself, and Blanche was left to herself. This she did not mind. She read a great deal, she practised the pianoforte, she was happy with her baby. In September they went to Florence, and there they were met by Princess Julia, Mario, and Donna Teresa. There was not room for them at Cadenabbia, for Princess Julia would not travel without her little court. She had to be amused. She needed company. She used from time to time to make Blanche feel that her daughter-in-law's education had indeed been neglected in matters such as the painters of the Renaissance and Roman history.

The little Giovanni was just a year old when one evening he seemed to be feverish. It was thought to be nothing, but as the next day Blanche was not satisfied with his looks she sent for the doctor. The baby had a slight rash. The doctor said it was nothing, not even chicken-pox, but he gave certain definite precise instructions about what was and what was not to be done.

Assunta, the nurse, thought she knew better, and she procured an ointment which she said was a sovran remedy for a rash, and she also concocted a brew from certain herbs which could not fail to be a help. Without telling Blanche anything about it, and without Blanche being aware of it, she rubbed the baby's face with the ointment and gave him the brew to drink at bedtime. The next day the rash seemed to have gone, and Assunta was triumphant and told Blanche what she had done – at least she mentioned the ointment, but not the brew. Blanche was annoyed, and said she must do nothing without consulting the doctor, but she did not at first imagine any harm had been done. In the course of the morning the baby got worse and his temperature went up rapidly. The doctor was sent for and was puzzled. Blanche told him what Assunta had done, and he asked to see the ointment. When he saw it he was angry. He said that she had done wrong to use such stuff. It had driven the rash in. He prescribed some medicine, and said he would call again later. The baby got no better. When the doctor called again in the evening he was distinctly worse, and the doctor did not know what could be done. Assunta was in tears. Blanche was distraught, but outwardly terribly calm. The doctor stayed with them, but nothing which they did or tried abated the baby's fever. He cried. He had fits of convulsions, and finally towards three in the morning he died. Blanche was at first stunned and then demented, and then stunned once more.

And then she fell ill herself. Perhaps this was a mercy. She had typhoid fever. Whether the baby had typhoid and she caught it from him was not known. The doctor said not. She was seriously ill for six weeks, and it was not until after Christmas that she was convalescent. The doctor ordered her a warm climate and complete change of scene, and Guido took her to Cairo for a few weeks. Her father came out at Easter and met her at Rome when she and Guido came back from Egypt.

Blanche was now a different woman. She seemed to herself a hundred years older. But her illness and her sorrow had increased rather than diminished her beauty. She was beautiful in a different way now. At first, for a time, her illness seemed to take away the bloom of her youth, but the bloom came back later. She had come of age. That phrase seemed to have, a special meaning applied to her now. Up to now she had been a deliciously fresh vision of grace, of youthful promise, an enchanting blossom of spring. Now there was dignity about her – the dignity of sorrow, and the majesty of stricken motherhood. There was a meaning in her eyes, which seemed to have become larger and certainly deeper.

She could no longer keep her father in the dark about the true nature of her married life. Indeed, although she admitted nothing to him when he told her that he knew she was unhappy, her disclaimers carried no conviction. He took the blame entirely. He said: "I was wrong and I admit it, and never again will I attempt to interfere in human affairs." He burst into tears one day when they were alone, and she sobbed in his arms and tried to comfort him, saying: "You mustn't be unhappy about me, beloved papa. It isn't your fault. We must make the best of it, and I promise you I will."

Henry Clifford thought it would do Blanche good to spend the summer in England, and he sounded Guido on the subject, but Guido said that the doctors considered the English climate would at present be too damp for her. He proposed to remain in Rome until the end of May and then to take Blanche to Switzerland for a change.

When the end of May came, Princess Julia suggested that Blanche and Guido should stay with her in a little house she bought at Posilipo, and over which she was greatly excited. They could bathe – it would be very agreeable, nicer than Switzerland, and more convenient for Guido, who would be able to get to Rome when he wanted to. Guido thought this an excellent idea; and Blanche, who since the death of her child had been in a state of apathy, was indifferent. So they went to Naples and stayed there till the end of September: Guido, Blanche, Princess Julia, Mario Guerrini, and Donna Teresa. The Abbé came for part of the time, and an Englishman called Howard de Lisle, who was one of Princess Julia's greatest and most useful friends. He was an apparently ageless person, who was not old, but who gave one the impression of never having been young; one could not visualise him as young. He had once been an architect, and still carried about a leather case with twenty-four well-cut cedar pencils of various shades from HHH to BBB, and made a sketch with a few lines when asked to. He had a picturesque beard, talked several languages fluently, was well off, and seemed to have nothing particular to do except to travel to various parts of Europe and to stay with friends at country houses. He had written a novel which had been published under a pseudonym years before, and had enjoyed a certain amount of success. It had been pronounced clever but disappointing. He was without any ambition, and he made no further attempts in the field of literature. He enjoyed helping his friends to furnish their houses, and giving advice and opinions on questions of architecture, decoration, landscape gardening, and the merits, faults, and limitations of contemporary artists. Princess Julia found him useful, as he had knowledge and experience, and he admired her, looked up to her, believed in her, and played the part of an adoring, willing slave. Blanche thought him well-meaning, but tedious. Guido liked him, and he was kind to Teresa.

Life at Posilipo was an exact replica of their life at Florence, except that Guido went to Rome perhaps a little more often than when he lived at Florence, and Blanche enjoyed the climate, the sea-bathing, the blazing noon, and the wonderful nights when the sea was phosphorescent and Vesuvius a transparent vision of rosy fire.

"I ought not to be dissatisfied," she thought, "in the midst of so much beauty."

But, however much she repeated this formula to herself, she could not help feeling lonely.

Towards the end of September they all went back to Rome, and Blanche went out into the world once more and resumed her normal life.

She had to bear a fresh trial in the shape of an infatuation that Guido was suddenly seized with for the wife of one of the Secretaries of the American Legation. She was a Mrs Winslope. She came from one of the old Virginian families. She was young, distinguished looking, and handsome rather than beautiful – that is to say, she had fair hair, light blue eyes, a dazzling clear complexion, but rather hard and sharply cut features.

She made friends with Blanche and with Princess Julia. She was intelligent, well-read – rather too well-read – cultivated, and musical. Princess Julia approved of her thoroughly, although she did not like Americans as a rule. Through Blanche she made friends with Guido, and gradually, and by slow degrees, she made Guido her own. He placed her on a high pedestal; her word became law.

If she were mentioned or an opinion of hers quoted, he became as serious as if he were talking politics. Grace Winslope was a Catholic, and had been educated in a convent in France. She was beautifully educated. She was a mine of information on many subjects, and especially on Italian art and history, but she was never tedious. She had fine social instincts and training, and she was an accomplished linguist. She could hold her own in any company and in any conversation, and you had to know her fairly well, and it needed rare penetration and sharp discrimination to grasp the fact that she pretended to know more than she knew, and that she was less clever than she appeared to be. Her goods were in a carefully dressed shop window. The shop was not so well stocked as one would have thought. But this did not detract from her amiability, her freshness, and her agreeable presence. Yet when people talked of her great originality, those who knew her really well reflected that what people took for originality was the skilful presentation of second-hand impressions carefully noted and garnered and successfully assimilated.

Blanche found it peculiarly trying when Guido talked of Grace Winslope's *illuminating* comments on this or that, when Blanche could tell in an instant whence Grace had gathered them. Grace had an infallible instinct for profitable soil in this respect, and she knew a Rome – many Romes – into which most foreigners rarely penetrated. She had friends in various camps, and especially in the literary, artistic, and archaeological worlds. But she never mixed her friends, but kept them in watertight compartments, so that the inhabitants of each compartment were dazzled by her versatility and her many-sidedness; each little group being unaware that it was helping to contribute to the entertainment of some other and totally different group.

Guido quoted her at all moments, and never let a day pass without seeing her. He was offended with Blanche if she did not respond to his appreciation, or if she did not show alacrity in asking Grace to their house, or in accepting invitations to her house. Grace had placed herself on the footing of being one of Blanche's best friends, and Blanche had to listen all day to paeans of praise, not only of her cleverness and of her goodness, but also of her practical ability – how well she managed her household, and ordered dinner, while Blanche knew quite well that Mr Winslope did all that himself – and she found this frankly trying. On the other hand, she delighted in the company of Grace's husband, Charlemagne Winslope, who was good natured, a little long winded and ponderous, and given to rather elaborate phraseology, especially if he paid a compliment. Blanche, not without malice, enjoyed carrying on an innocent flirtation with him.

One afternoon in October, Blanche was walking in the garden of the Palatine and enjoying the sunshine, when she nearly ran into a stranger, and realised that it was not a stranger at all, but the diplomatist whose acquaintance she had made at the Rodens' party – Adrian Tyne.

He was by himself. He took off his hat and said, laughing: "I was wondering if we should perhaps meet."

"Are you staying here?"

"I'm here for good. I've been appointed to the Embassy."

"Oh!"

There was a pause.

Blanche wondered whether he was married.

"May I pay my respects some time?"

"Of course. On Monday nights we are always at home after dinner. It is my 'evening.' Guido would be delighted if you came, but I warn you that you will not find it amusing."

"I saw Mrs Somner yesterday. She very kindly asked me to dinner next Tuesday."

"We are going that night."

"Well, we shall meet there; that will be delightful."

They walked together a little way, and then Blanche said she must go home.

They did meet on the following Tuesday, and Blanche found out that Adrian Tyne was still unmarried. So, if he had really been engaged, he had broken off his engagement. Adrian Tyne, so she learnt, had the reputation of a breaker of hearts. He was thought to be attractive, extremely fickle as well, and there was a story that he had lately behaved badly to a charming girl, that he had been engaged to be married and then had wriggled out of the engagement just as it was about to be announced. He was a man of fastidious taste in all things: art, literature, landscape, architecture, comfort, food, wine, tobacco; but, above all things, in people and in looks. He abhorred the second best, and his instinct, which always and everywhere led him to what was outstanding and pre-eminent, now at this moment led him straight to Blanche. He had admired her from the first moment he set eyes on her at the Rodens' party. It had then been, he thought, a *coup de tête* – he had tried to think – of the most transitory kind, a tribute to a summer night. But Adrian now felt he knew better; it was the *coup de foudre*. A real case of love at first sight. He felt that he would only have to see more of her to be madly in love with her. He had never met any one who pleased him so much, from every point of view. She was the incarnation of what he had dreamt he might one day meet. That night at Mrs Somner's his first impression was confirmed. He and Blanche talked without effort. They sat next to each other at dinner.

Blanche liked him, thought him agreeable, amusing, clever, and good-looking, but that was all. She knew that would always be all for her. For her, he just missed having charm, or she was blind and impervious to what every one else seemed to feel.

He was, she thought, made for her mother-in-law, and had she, Princess Julia, been twenty years younger, he would, she was convinced, have been the passion of her life. For her, Blanche, he was just a shade too artificial, and although with her he really was sincere, more sincere than he had ever been before, as sincere as he could be, she could not help noticing the slight presence, not of effort, but of *art*, of *technique*:

"*So fühlt man Absicht, und man ist verstimmt.*"

That would be putting it too strongly, because in his company Blanche talked without effort or pause. She enjoyed his society, but there is a gulf between that and the possibility of other feelings.

Mrs Somner asked Adrian Tyne to play the pianoforte after dinner. He played by ear all sorts of French, English, and even Italian songs.

Adrian Tyne was careful that evening – careful in his behaviour to Blanche, knowing that Guido would notice everything, and he took pains not to neglect Guido. He observed him, and he realised all the difficulties and danger that there might be in that quarter. He was a man of quick intuitions. From what he had heard from others as well as from what he had himself observed, he instantly and fully realised Blanche's situation. He resolved to reconnoitre the *terrain* thoroughly before beginning operations. He decided that the key of the position, the most important factor, more important even than Guido, was Princess Julia, and before taking any further step he decided to deal with that factor. His mother, Lady Mount-Stratton, was a friend of Princess Julia's, and he asked his mother to write to her and ask her to be kind to him. In the meantime, he kept himself in the background and contented himself with leaving cards at the Palazzo Fabrini. His mother, who was devoted to him, wrote an effusive letter to Princess Julia, who asked him to dinner. Blanche and Guido were not present, but only a few English people and the Abbé.

Adrian took pains to be nice to the Princess, and, sharp as she was, she suspected no ulterior motive. She had no grounds for suspicion. Blanche's name was mentioned, and Adrian said he had met her and the Prince at Mrs Somner's, that his mother was a friend of Henry Clifford's. The next week he attended Princess Julia's Wednesday evening, and the following Monday it seemed quite natural to everybody concerned to see him again at the Palazzo Fabrini, on the lower floor this time. That evening he paid a great deal of attention to Princess Julia; she admitted that she found him charming.

Blanche was right. Princess Julia and Adrian Tyne were well suited to each other. But at present he was not giving her a thought. He found her agreeable, but from his present point of view she was merely an important piece in a larger and different game.

Blanche was his objective. He meant to make a determined effort to win her.

Blanche was up to now unaware of this. She thought he had outlived the mood he had shown signs of at the Rodens' party in England. That was, after all, a long time ago. He had seemed different at her aunt's – reasonable, friendly, pleased, but nothing more; and when at her evening he asked if he might come and see her some day in the afternoon she said, "Certainly."

"Can I come tomorrow?" he had asked.

"Certainly," she said again, but she was sure he was just being civil, so remote had he seemed to her both this evening and at her aunt's, in spite of superficial ease and civilities, so much so that she never thought for one moment he would come, and she never dreamt of staying at home on the chance; so that when she came back late the next evening, after paying several visits, she was surprised to find his visiting card on the hall table.

Two or three days later Princess Julia asked him to *déjeuner* to meet Blanche, her husband, and some others.

Adrian had arranged an expedition to Ninfa. He had asked the Olenevs, Princess Julia, and an English friend who was staying at Rome, and they had all accepted.

He chose this opportunity to ask Blanche whether she and Guido could not come.

Guido said, to the surprise of Blanche and of Adrian, that he was unfortunately engaged those two days – they were to stay the night in a villa – but he was sure that Blanche would like to go if she were free, and he would be delighted for her to do so.

This answer took Adrian by surprise. He was off his guard. He could not help showing by his expression a flash of relief and of unexpected pleasure. Blanche was looking at him and she saw his look, and in one second she realised the meaning of his behaviour, of his tactics, of the whole plan of campaign, which he had so painstakingly carried on and, as he thought, so carefully concealed, ever since the day they had met on the Palatine. She also understood that Guido would never be jealous of Adrian, for his instinct told him that Blanche did not, and never would, love Adrian. She also felt, although she was not looking at her, that Princess Julia was looking at Adrian. She felt that she too had seen this self-revealing flash and had understood.

So with a calm presence of mind, and without a flicker of hesitation, she said:

"I wish I could go. I think it would be very great fun; unfortunately just on those two days I am selling at my aunt's bazaar."

The next day, when Adrian went again to see Blanche in the afternoon, she was again not at home. He went upstairs to Princess Julia's apartment. She was at home, and there was no sign that the smallest grain of sand had crept into the well-oiled machinery of their relations.

He stayed and talked to her a long time, and when he left her he felt that he had not been ill-rewarded for the trouble he had taken, and he was convinced that he had accurately gauged the key of the position.

# CHAPTER X

Although it seemed to Blanche that she had divined Adrian's tactics, she did not take them seriously. He might be intending to make up to her, but then he made up to dozens of others. It was nothing more than a game on his part – a game which he couldn't help playing, but which she did not intend to let him play as far as she was concerned.

But she soon realised that, game or no game, he was not behaving now as he usually did. He went nowhere where he was not likely to meet her, and he paid no attention to any one else. He attended her mother-in-law's evenings regularly, and went out of his way to pay her any little attention or render her any little service he could.

He left off coming to Blanche's evenings, and when she said something about it to him one day when they met at the American Legation, he said: "I see you don't wish to see me. You are always 'not at home' when I come to see you. I don't wish to force myself upon you."

Blanche said she would always be delighted to see him. She was often in after five, but she made no rules about that. One fixed day was enough.

"Oh, your evenings!" he said – "that is worse than anything. You are there and not there; one is close to you, but a thousand

110

miles away. I thought at one time we were going to be friends
– real friends."

"You've so many friends," Blanche said, laughing.

"You have been listening to lies. People tell lies about me. If
you only knew. If you only had an idea what I feel about you."
Blanche interrupted him.

"If you want to be friends – and there is no reason why we
shouldn't be friends – you must drop all the nonsense," she
said, laughing, and she roped some one else into the
conversation.

He came to see Blanche the next day. Again she happened to
be out, but without any intention on her part. She had some
visits to pay.

Two or three days later, Princess Julia, who was sitting in
Blanche's *salotto* after dinner, doing her patience with the aid
of Teresa, said to Blanche

"Why are you so unkind to Adrian Tyne?"

"Unkind! I'm sure I don't mean to be," said Blanche.

"His mother wrote to me," Princess Julia went on, "and
asked us to be civil to him, so I feel we ought to do something
for him. I think he is so particularly agreeable."

"Yes," said Blanche. "I think so, too."

"But you never ask him inside the house."

"I thought dinners and things bored him. But we've got a
dinner next week. Shall I ask him, Guido, on Thursday? It's
nearly all English people – the Winslopes and that Lady Jane
Somebody who's staying at the Hôtel de Russie."

"Yes," said Guido, who was playing at backgammon with
Mario. "By all means, ask him."

He came to dinner. He was deferent, rather subdued,
irreproachable, and kept off all dangerous topics. He was civil,
and played up and scarcely spoke to Blanche.

She did not see him or hear of him after that for a week, and
then her mother-in-law again returned to the charge. "Why was
she so persistently unkind to poor Adrian Tyne?" and Blanche

suddenly realised that Princess Julia was, for some hidden reason of her own, encouraging the affair, making it easy for him, "because she knows," thought Blanche, "that I can never be fond of him."

He met Guido, Donna Teresa, and herself out riding one day in the Campagna, and they rode together for a time. Adrian complained of her great unkindness. Blanche laughed at him, and they talked gaily for a little while on all sorts of topics. Blanche suddenly felt comfortable with him. "If he drops all the nonsense, we can be friends," she thought, and she hoped he now understood, when she had told him that the only way for them to be friends was for him to drop the nonsense, that she had really meant what she was saying. Her impression was confirmed by his manner when they met at Princess Julia's house, and, later, at her own evening. He now came naturally, as a matter of course. "He is reasonable now," thought Blanche. "He has understood, and now I can really like him."

But just before Christmas there was a ball at the Russian Embassy. It was the first large entertainment Blanche had been to since the death of her child. It was a picturesque entertainment. Many of the Roman notabilities were there, and all the leading foreigners and diplomatists.

Princess Julia looked picturesque and regal in green velvet and a large string of pearls. But Blanche had blossomed once more into her old freshness and something more than her first beauty. She was all the more striking now for the new seriousness in her eyes and the increased dignity of her carriage. She was surrounded by partners directly she arrived. For the first time Rome really took notice of her. She had now lost all the indecision but none of the freshness of extreme youth. She was dressed in grey satin, and she wore all Guido's family jewels, very deftly arranged – large emerald ear-rings and emeralds in her hair, and straps of diamonds on her shoulders.

She danced with Adrian twice. He certainly was an excellent dancer. He was inerrant in rhythm. He took her after one dance to a large, long marble corridor which was banked with flowers. She was flushed after dancing, and there was the faintest tinge on her very white skin. They were sitting in a secluded spot.

"This reminds me of the first time we met," he said.

She smiled at him and thought, "He's not going to begin again."

He read her thought, and said rather savagely: "Well, yes. I've had enough of all this pretence and all this farce. Yes; I do love you, and always have loved you from the first moment I set eyes on you. Yes; I was engaged – it is true. I broke off my engagement after seeing you." (This was possibly true, thought Blanche, but he would have done so in any case.) "I have never been like this before. You have changed my whole life. It is no use trying to stop me. I will have my say out. I am suffering, really suffering; I shall die of it. Any one can see that I am a different being – I go nowhere; I can't bear the sight of any one or anything else. I can think of nothing else; I can't sleep. It is making me ill. You are killing me. Yes; I want you to run away with me. I don't care one scrap for my career. I never meant to stay in diplomacy. I have quite enough for us both to live on. We would go and live in England, which is obviously the only place for you to live in. You are not meant to live abroad here in Italy, where you haven't a friend, with a husband you loathe, for, you can say what you like, I am quite sure I know you loathe your husband."

He poured out all this in a torrent of passion. He was white; he was trembling all over; his eyes were blazing, and he seemed on the verge of tears.

She tried to reason with him. She was gentle; she said "I don't love – I can never love – you. You must face that once for all. As to running away, you are really insane to think of such a thing. Even if I were devoted to you, I would never do that. It would ruin your life. However, we needn't discuss that. That is not a thing I can discuss for a moment, even as a joke. You don't understand me nor my life. You don't really know me. You are making a gigantic mistake. It is not me at all you love, but an imaginary Blanche of your own creation. If you really knew me, you would find – I am quite sure of this – that you wouldn't love me. We were not meant for each other – not suited to each other in any way. It is a *coup de tête* – a piece of imagination on your part – and it won't last."

"But think of the time it has lasted – ever since I saw you that day at the Rodens'," he said.

"That's because you didn't see *me*," she said.

"Oh, but it's been much worse here since I have seen you!"

And he began all over again.

Blanche wrestled with him.

"It isn't kind of you to go on like that. It puts me in such an impossible position. I told you from the first that we could only be friends if you put all that nonsense out of your head."

"Nonsense! Don't you see," he said, "that it's a matter of life and death? Don't you see that you are killing me – that you will kill me if you go on like that?"

Blanche saw that every word she was saying was making it worse.

"I must go back," she said. "I promised to go down to supper after this dance with the Ambassador."

"One moment; one word more," he begged, but to Blanche's great relief they were interrupted by the arrival of another couple, and he was obliged to lead Blanche back to the ballroom.

Directly after supper she asked Guido to take her home. She was, she said, rather tired. Guido did so, but was surprised that she should want to go away so soon, as she appeared to be having such a success.

"I've got a splitting headache," she said.

The next day she received a letter of eight sides from Adrian – an incoherent outpouring and repetition of all he had said the night before. She didn't answer it. The next time she saw him was at Princess Julia's evening. He did look worn and pale. She managed to exchange a few words with him, and begged him not to write. She would not read any letters. She was in great perplexity. She realised now that it was not one of Adrian's ordinary affairs, of which she had been told on all sides that he had so many. It was, she believed, really serious this time. Her conscience was clear. She had given him no encouragement. The only thing she could blame herself for in the slightest was for having listened to him the first time they met at the Rodens'. She had listened to him with pleasure that night, but she had looked upon that incident as something as unreal as a dream, and she was so convinced at the time that it meant nothing. How could she guess? How could she foresee?

And now, what was to be done? If she saw him, things were impossible; if she didn't see him, it made him worse.

Rome was intolerable; the new régime seemed to have attracted swarms of tourists from everywhere; everything was in a state of chaos; a new and vulgar Rome, an international parvenu Rome, was growing up like a hideous mushroom.

She begged Guido to take her to Florence; but Princess Julia got wind of this and put a veto on the plan. She seemed, Blanche thought, to have divined what was happening, and to be enjoying the situation – enjoying the difficult position in which Blanche found herself. This was her revenge for the manoeuvring that Adrian had practised on her; only, she visited her revenge on Blanche instead of on him. She went on being charming to him, and kept on twitting Blanche with her unkindness towards him, and even asking them to meet at meals at her house.

Blanche was at her wits' end as to what to do.

She could not avoid seeing him, as both her mother-in-law and Guido urged him to come and see them. She avoided seeing him alone, but this was not always possible. For instance, Guido would ask him to luncheon and then go away afterwards and leave him with Blanche. Then he would make a scene and threaten to kill himself.

She said to herself that people never did these things, and often talked like that, yet she could not help feeling a little bit uneasy. One never knew. She felt that she was entangled in a net through no choice or fault of her own. Once or twice she thought to herself, "What if I took him at his word and *did* run away with him? I should be free of this Roman life, free from Guido, free from Princess Julia, whatever happened. But then," she reflected, "it would ruin his life, and besides, what is the good of thinking about such a thing? I know perfectly well I shall never do it. But they really would deserve it," she said to herself, as she thought of Guido and her mother-in-law – Guido always asking him to the house, and Princess Julia blaming her for being, as she said, so unfriendly to him, and so inhospitable to this friendless Englishman, who was so lonely in Rome and so much in need of friends.

As time went on, the situation became more and more difficult. Adrian lost no opportunity of going to the places where he knew he would meet Blanche, and there was no means of avoiding him without looking silly; nor did she want him to think she attached any importance to the matter. Princess Julia looked on with a kind of honeysweet malignity. What did she want? thought Blanche – for her to disgrace herself? For her to have a lover? What was it? As for Guido, he was impenetrable, and she had no idea whether he noticed what was happening or whether he was enjoying a double pleasure in watching Adrian Tyne's torment, and in experiencing a self-satisfied superiority in the thought that Blanche belonged to him, and that he was secure.

Blanche seemed to feel this, and she felt at times that she would like to shake his serene self-confidence; she would like to frighten him, only not now, not so long as Adrian was entangled in the situation. She had come to grow too genuinely sorry for him to venture to play any tricks.

Matters went on like this until Easter.

Guido had decided to spend Easter at Florence, and he talked of inviting some friends to their villa. His mother was coming, and Henry Clifford had been asked.

They were discussing the matter, as usual, with Princess Julia, after dinner in the Princess' apartment. There were all the usual appendages – patience, backgammon, the Abbé, and even Howard de Lisle.

"You must ask Howard," said Princess Julia.

"Of course, he is expected," said Guido.

Howard de Lisle declined the invitation with a courtly bow, as he was already engaged to spend Easter at Porto Fino, and pointed out to Princess Julia that she was missing an opportunity of putting a four on a five.

"And who else?" asked Guido.

"Won't that be a nice party as it is?"

"You must remember that Teresa and Mario can't come," said the Princess.

"What about Adrian Tyne?" said Guido quietly, without looking at Blanche.

"That would do admirably, because his mother, Lady Mount-Stratton, is coming to Florence, and we could ask her," said Princess Julia. "I heard from her this morning."

"Will he be able to get away from the Embassy?" asked Blanche.

"Why not? They can always have leave," said the Princess.

"Yes; but then they like going to England."

"When they stay in the same country it doesn't count as leave," said Guido.

"One can but ask the poor boy. It's a pity Blanche doesn't like him better. He's one of the few agreeable foreigners in Rome," said Princess Julia.

"I think him extremely agreeable," said Blanche.

As they walked back to their apartment that evening, she said to Guido: "Do you really want me to ask Mr Tyne to Florence?"

"Why not?" said Guido. "It's true what my mother says, that you dislike him."

"I don't dislike him at all, but I would much rather he didn't come."

"I've asked the Winslopes," said Guido, "and they are coming, so I thought we wanted another man. And then, as my mother has asked Lady Mount-Stratton, who is an old friend, it would seem odd – she would think it odd of us – not to ask her son."

"Has she asked Lady Mount-Stratton already?"

"I have asked her to do it."

Blanche felt there was nothing more to be said, so she said to him:

"You'll see him at the Club, won't you? – so you can ask him then."

"It would be more civil for you to write," said Guido.

Blanche said nothing.

The next day at *déjeuner* she and Guido were at their own house, and a few Italian friends of Guido were there. He asked Blanche whether she had remembered to write to Adrian Tyne.

"I quite forgot," she said, in a voice that was not meant to carry conviction. She was determined not to do it.

Guido said nothing. The next day she got a note from the British Embassy.

"Your husband" – it ran – "whom I saw last night at the Club, has very kindly asked me to spend Easter at Florence with my mother, who is coming out there – she is coming to Rome later.

118

I am so extremely sorry not to be able to accept, but the Ambassador is going on leave and I shall be left in charge. It is too unlucky."

Blanche nearly cried from relief when she read this. She dreaded his visit unspeakably.

Guido showed no sign of further interest in the matter, and when his mother pointed out that they were a man short, he asked the Abbé to spend Easter with them.

# CHAPTER XI

They went to Florence, and Lady Mount-Stratton and Henry
Clifford arrived a day later – in the evening, just in time for
dinner.

Lady Mount-Stratton still looked young for her age. She was
over sixty, and in spite of that, and in spite of her grey hairs and
the many little lines on her ivory face, pretty was still the
epithet you felt inclined to apply to her. She had a radiant smile,
which lit up her face and made it look young. But her grey-
green eyes were full of wisdom, and she had a way of prettily
shrugging her shoulders, which seemed to say, "Well, what can
you expect?" She had had a life full of movement and
adventure. She was a widow. Her husband had served on the
staff of the Duke of Wellington, and afterwards was appointed
British Envoy to the King of Naples. Later on he migrated to
Florence and Berlin, and then to St Petersburg, as Secretary of
the Legation. And he died two years later, in the prime of a
brilliant career. Lady Mount-Stratton had known every one of
importance in Europe. She had been the centre of agreeable
and cultivated society, and had established a sort of
Continental Holland House wherever she had been, and she
had been the friend of Talleyrand, Prince Metternich, Prince
Paul Esterhazy, Meyerbeer, and Mendelssohn. She knew Henry
Clifford well, and was delighted to meet his daughter, all the

more so as she had received constant and accurate bulletins from several reliable friends about her son's state of mind, whose infatuation for Blanche had by no means escaped notice. She was passionately devoted to her son, but she had no illusions about the difficulties and drawbacks of his peculiar nature and temperament.

On the evening of Lady Mount-Stratton's and Henry Clifford's arrival, they were a party of eight – Princess Julia, the Winslopes, Henry Clifford, the Abbé, and Lady Mount-Stratton, who looked extraordinarily well and unbelievably young, dressed in black, with artificial pansies on her gown and real cherry-pie pinned over a fichu of lace. They dined at a round table in an enclosed loggia, from whence you had a lovely view.

"It's so nice to be back at Florence. I haven't been here for years – not since we were here *en poste*, thirty years ago."

"I suppose, Lady Mount-Stratton, you find it greatly altered and considerably spoilt?" said Mr Winslope.

"I can't judge yet. I haven't explored my old haunts. Nothing can prevent its being lovely."

"Yes," said Mrs Winslope. "I always think that at Naples you *look*, at Rome you *pray*, and at Florence you *think*."

"And at Venice you smell," said Mr Winslope.

"*Il faut beaucoup aimer Florence*," said the Abbé. "*Cela a souvent été dit, mais on ne peut pas le dire trop souvent.*"

"I think Florence the most enchanting of all the places in Italy," said Princess Julia. "Blanche is like Guido – she likes *Rome* best; it's impossible to tear her away from *Rome*."

"You can't wonder at that," said Mr Winslope. "The Princess has so many admirers at Rome that she would break their hearts if she stayed away too long at one time. The city would suffer a total eclipse. They feel at Rome that the Princess belongs to them, and that she has no right to go and shine on any other rival cities – not that they don't want to have her there. Now, only the other day, Lady Mount-Stratton, your son, Adrian, was saying to me – and I regard your son, Adrian, as the best all-round judge of all that is best in society in Europe – he was saying to me that he considered Princess Blanche to be the most exquisite and elegant hostess in Europe."

Henry Clifford felt his daughter's discomfort at this remark as acutely as if it had been an electric shock.

"It's such a pity Mr Adrian couldn't come here," said Princess Julia. "*Guido* asked him," she said, stressing the "Guido," "but, as you know, he is in charge, and you know what that means. I am hoping he may be able to get away before you go, but, if not, you will be able to see him in Rome, won't you?"

"He'll probably see much more of me than he wants to in Rome," said Lady Mount-Stratton. And then, abruptly changing the subject, she said to Guido, "I do hope – we all hope – that you are both coming to London this year. You haven't been to London for such a long time – have they, Henry?"

"No," he said. "They must come, and you must come, too, Princess Julia."

After this the conversation remained in safe waters.

Blanche was anxious to have a talk with her father as soon as possible on the subject of Adrian Tyne. Before going to bed she asked Lady Mount-Stratton and the Winslopes what they would like to do the next morning. Lady Mount-Stratton said she did not feel inclined to do anything energetic at once – that she would stay at home or sit in the loggia and write letters. Mrs Winslope said she thought she would see how she felt in the morning.

Just before going to bed, Blanche said to her father: "We will go to the town in the morning, and even if the others come, we can always manage to have a talk."

The next morning nobody came down early except the Abbé. Blanche arranged with Guido that she should drive down in the little carriage with her father, and that, if the others wanted to come down later, they could have the big carriage. She did not think they wanted to come.

At eleven o'clock, to her surprise, the large carriage with two horses drove up to the door. Her father was ready.

"I didn't order the large carriage," she said. "They must have made a mistake. However, it doesn't matter."

At that moment Guido walked into the hall, followed by the Winslopes and his mother.

"I have persuaded them to come, after all, Blanche," he said. "So perhaps you won't mind," he said to Henry Clifford, "driving my mother down in the victoria and meeting us in the town. She has a few things she wants to do. We had better meet in the Piazza della Signoria. We'll go in the barouche, Blanche, and the victoria will be round in a moment."

So Guido, the Winslopes, and Blanche drove off in the barouche, and Henry Clifford was left to escort Princess Julia.

"I'm not going to hamper you or be in the way, darling," said Princess Julia, as the others started. "I only want to be dropped. I've got a little shopping to do."

A few minutes after the barouche had started, the victoria came round to the door.

Princess Julia and Henry Clifford got into it.

"Do you mind if we stop at the Palazzo Alberti on the way?" asked Princess Julia. "I've a note to leave."

Henry Clifford said that the longer the drive the better. They talked about Blanche at once. She was looking well.

"It was difficult to get her anywhere for a long time after… " said the Princess. "It was a tragic thing, poor child; she was quite distraught, quite prostrate, but now she's looking better. I have never seen her look better. I always thought she was pretty," said Princess Julia, "but now she is a real beauty. I need hardly tell you she's greatly admired. Of course," Princess Julia went on, as if she were answering Henry Clifford's unexpressed speculations, "a sensitive creature like Blanche was bound to feel a shock like that more deeply than any one, and after the tragedy," – she hushed her voice, and talked as if she were afraid of being overheard – "you mustn't forget she was *seriously* ill. You've no idea how ill she was; how frightened we all were. And all that was bound for a time to sadden her life. I was in despair. I thought she was going to be permanently unhappy." Henry noticed the word "unhappy," not "ill." "However, she has wonderful powers of recuperation; wonderful elasticity of spirits; and I think she looks better now than she ever did, and is really happier in every way – happier than she has ever been since they first married. People like her so much in Rome. Every one – Italians, Englishmen, foreigners, Russians – they are all in love with her."

"Safety in numbers," said Henry.

"You needn't be uneasy. You can trust Blanche absolutely. After the baby died, she wouldn't go out at all for a long time. It was almost a year before she went anywhere, and then only by degrees. Really, people hadn't discovered her; then all at once they did. I shall never forget how beautiful she looked at a ball given by the Russians. She surprised us all. It was like a new birth suddenly."

"I suppose she has broken several hearts."

"They all rave about her, especially that naughty boy of Lady Mount-Stratton's."

"Adrian Tyne? I thought he was engaged to be married."

"So he was, to Fanny Morton, Lady Castlebridge's girl. He broke it off. It was never announced. He broke it off the summer Blanche was in London."

"Had she met him?"

"Only just, I think. She didn't know him till he came here."

"Is he really in love with her?"

"Quite desperately, poor boy. And if it weren't Blanche, and if one didn't feel so *sure*, so utterly safe, I really should be a little uneasy. Because he *is* attractive, and I am afraid unscrupulous. I don't think he has *any* principles, but one can't help liking him all the same – at least I can't; but that's because he's civil to me, and an old woman like myself cannot resist being pleased when a young man like Adrian Tyne is civil and nice."

"But Blanche... "

"Blanche doesn't encourage him at all. It's not *her* fault that he's always in the house and monopolises her at calls and parties everywhere, and follows her about out hunting in the Campagna. It's Guido who doesn't see and who *will* ask him. He asked him here for Easter, and it *is* such a pity. It is only making him unhappy, and it may end by making her unhappy, although, of course, she never thinks that anything like that could happen. Guido doesn't understand. He knows, quite rightly, that Blanche never would give a man like Adrian a thought, but he doesn't understand that adoration in the long run is an intoxicating and dangerous thing. He doesn't see that Blanche is unconscious of her power. I assure you nobody could have behaved more sensibly than she has done. She doesn't encourage him at all, but the fact of her not encouraging him, of her really avoiding him, makes it worse; it is as effective as the supremest *coquetterie*; in fact, I am often obliged to ask the boy, so as to ease the situation, to make it seem natural...because, you see, if Blanche never asks him and takes no notice of him, and Guido always asks him...and Guido simply likes him, finds him amusing, agreeable, and so much easier for an Italian to get on with than most Englishmen... I was going to say that, if Blanche never asks him, and Guido does, it makes the situation look so odd...look as if...now what one wants is to make it seem natural and normal."

"But does Blanche like him?"

"I wish she liked him more. She is *angry*, and a little *unfair* with him, which is the worst of all policies, and she either *never* talks to him at all, or she talks *more* than she is aware of. She will not pay the slightest attention to him for two or three weeks, and then, at a ball, dance with hardly any one else. The worst of it is that she feels, I think, what so many of us feel about him: that she dislikes him in theory; she is angry, furious with him in theory, but likes him in practice. Fortunately Blanche is thoroughly, fundamentally sensible, clear-headed, honest, and *straight*, and she would never dream of doing or thinking anything that could give Guido a moment's anxiety or pain. But if it were any one else but Blanche I should feel uneasy. I'm afraid she's annoyed with me. She thinks I'm encouraging Adrian. She thinks, rightly, that Adrian couldn't possibly be civil to an old woman like myself for *mes beaux yeux*. It must irritate her; I so understand it. But, if she only knew, without me he would be far worse and the situation would be *far* more difficult. I do manage to keep him in order a little, and to make the whole thing appear more or less natural."

"And Guido?"

"Guido is delighted that some one should admire Blanche. He is so *bon enfant*. And he likes the boy, and thinks it all great fun. He thinks that Blanche, too, is rather hard on him, and *that* amuses him. She *is*, from Adrian's point of view, hard on him; because, you see, she, without knowing it, is more enchanting to him when she is angry, in her superficial *dépit*, than anything you can imagine. And then, every now and then she relents... one can't help it, with Adrian. It is impossible to be angry with him. I should be just the same. Any woman would."

The Princess then changed the subject, and presently they arrived at the Palazzo Alberti, where the Princess dropped a note, and they then met the others in the Piazza. Princess Julia took Winslope shopping with her; Guido took charge of Mrs Winslope, and Blanche was left with her father. She was longing to talk to him, and felt grateful to her mother-in-law for having made this *tête-à-tête* possible.

She at once began to tell him about Adrian Tyne. She told him the whole story from her point of view and the exact situation. She said nothing about any motives that she suspected might actuate either Guido or her mother-in-law, but merely that they both liked Adrian, and put her in an awkward situation unconsciously by continually asking him to the house, and they evidently were surprised at her lack of alacrity and enthusiasm when there was any question of asking him.

"And you know, papa, quite, quite honestly, I could never *care* for him. I like his company; I think he is agreeable, but I don't really feel his charm – not like other people do. Not like my mother-in-law does, for instance."

"Ah!" thought Henry Clifford, "the Princess is right. That's just what I thought. She is unconsciously jealous." But he said: "Of course, he's had affairs in every capital of Europe."

"I know," said Blanche, a little impatiently, "although all that is exaggerated" (again Henry thought he detected that note of jealousy), "and at first I took no notice of it. I never gave the matter a thought. I didn't even take the trouble to stay in when he said he was coming to see me. I never dreamt he would come. For a long time I thought it was nothing. At one moment I thought it was all right, that he understood, and just when I thought it was safe and comfortable, he broke out, and since then, nothing but threats of killing himself and scenes whenever he has had the chance. Of course, I never do give him the chance if I can help it. I have done my best not to see him, but they do make it *so* difficult. It's so difficult not to look silly; not to look as if I thought it was more than it is. Of course, I know it's nonsense – all nonsense, really; only it is tiresome just now."

Henry Clifford thought this almost the classic form of the avowal and narration of an incipient love affair.

"But do you see him often?"

"I never make the slightest effort to see him, but I can't help meeting him; we meet everywhere, constantly. He goes everywhere. I can't shut myself up like a hermit just to avoid him, and then it seems so silly to look as if I were avoiding him."

"My dear child, you needn't mind telling me everything."

"But, papa, there is nothing to tell, or, rather, I *have* told you *everything*. I like him, but that's all. I don't really feel his charm – really not."

As she said this, Henry Clifford was quite convinced that what she meant was that she minded *any one else feeling* his charm, and, above all, her mother-in-law.

"I know, I know," he said. "Well, well, my dear child, there's nothing to be done. We all know you won't do anything foolish. But do remember one thing – that all this has happened to this youth several times before. Not long ago he was engaged...*engaged*, mind you, to be married, to Lady Fanny Morton, a charming girl and an heiress. He broke this off at a moment's notice for the *beaux yeux* of whom? Of that pretty little French actress who sang in the last Offenbach. And that, of course, didn't last a month. And then he was madly in love for a time with Lady Vanbrugh – madly in love with her...swore he would kill himself, that he'd become a monk, and Heaven knows she never looked at him – laughed at him, and the result was, he soon recovered. He'll always be like that all his life. He won't be able to live without having not only some love, but some *unhappy* love affair – something to worry and fret about."

"But you don't really think it's my fault, papa?"

"I think that probably without knowing it you do everything you can to make it worse, to aggravate his feelings."

"But, papa, what am I to do? What do you want me to do?"

"Just to treat him like an ordinary person. To see him like you would see any one else."

"But you've no idea how impossible he becomes directly one is the least bit nice to him."

"Ah! that's just it. Sometimes you are just the least bit nice to him, and sometimes you are horrible to him, and that's the result. Of course, it drives the boy mad. Don't think, my dear child, that I'm blaming you for one moment; I thoroughly understand."

"Oh, papa, you *don't* understand. I believe you really do believe I'm in love with him."

"Just a teeny little bit more than you think. Just enough to make life a little bit exciting, and who can blame you?"

"But, oh, papa, I'm not. I'm not; I *swear* I'm not," and the sincerity and vehemence of Blanche's tone convinced her father that, although she wasn't conscious of it, the opposite of this was true. "I really can't bear the sight of him – that's to say, when he's tiresome. I get on with him. I can't help getting on with people when they are nice to me, and amusing…and kind. But I do really promise you that is all there is, all there *ever* has been, and that I never thought, never dreamt… "

"I don't think you know yourself. I know you think that all that is true, but I think there is more that you don't realise. And I really do believe the best remedy is to see as much of the boy as you like, quite openly and quite publicly. Don't let him feel you are annoyed with him. Don't let there be any mystery, any barrier. And then I believe the whole thing will pass over. It's of no consequence."

Blanche realised that it was no use her saying anything; that between her and her father there was a barrier raised by his conviction lately taken root; that it was as much her fault as Adrian's; that she was more in love than she knew, and that, although it was not a serious love affair, she at least was enjoying it; she was being a coquette, perhaps an unconscious one (which was worse), and she knew now that, with her father's worldly nature, temperament, creed, and theories, once such an idea had taken root in his mind, nothing would drive it out. She saw, too, that her mother-in-law had sown the seed of the idea, and she realised, too, that if she accused her mother-in-law to her father of having done this, it would be worse than useless: firstly, because her mother-in-law could do what she liked with Henry Clifford; and, secondly, because he would merely think she was being jealous. He thought that, she felt, already.

# CHAPTER XII

EASTER came and went. The party at the Villa Moroni spent the days in sight-seeing and expeditions. Occasionally they paid a few visits. Sometimes Italian or English friends came to luncheon or to dinner. Florence was overfull of visitors. Blanche did not return to the topic of Adrian Tyne with her father. She saw it would he useless. His mind had been skilfully coloured once and for all with one definite dye.

She faced the prospect of Roman life with dread. She thought that Lady Mount-Stratton would understand the situation, but she hardly dared to broach the topic with her. It was so difficult for her to discuss this with his mother, and yet she felt that the only possibility of any help lay in that quarter.

She made up her mind to try, if the opportunity presented itself. It was not easy to find an opportunity. Princess Julia marshalled the guests and made arrangements for them. Blanche never found herself alone with anybody, and even if she wanted to speak to her father she had to arrange it beforehand, to make an appointment, which even then was not always kept.

Guido spent nearly all his time with Mrs Winslope, but in such a way that it did not seem as if he were doing so. She seemed to be taking part in the general life, always to be suggesting plans in which they could all take part, but they resulted as a rule in dividing the party into two groups, one consisting of herself and Guido, and the other of the remaining guests.

The days passed, and never once did a favourable opportunity present itself until the last day of their stay in Florence. On that day it had been arranged the night before that they should spend the morning in seeing those sights which they had not yet been able to see.

There were several things that Mrs Winslope was desperately anxious to see and which she had not seen so far: the Perugino Crucifixion in Santa Maria Maddalena dei Pazzi, and the Benozzo Gozzoli frescoes in the Palazzo Riccardi.

They were all to drive to Florence in the morning in two parties: the Winslopes, Guido, and Princess Julia; Blanche, Lady Mount-Stratton, Henry Clifford, and the Abbé. Guido's party started first, and later – a good deal later – as Lady Mount-Stratton not only got up late, but was always unpunctual, the second party assembled in the hall and had been waiting some time when Lady Mount-Stratton arrived, full of apologies, but not dressed for going out, and – taking Blanche aside – said to her: "I am so dreadfully sorry, but I have just remembered that there is one letter I must write for today's mail, and if I don't write it this morning it will miss the post, so I must ask you to go without me." And then she added in a whisper:

"Stay with me, if you can."

"Of course you must stay," said Blanche. "I will stay and keep you company."

"I rather wish you would," said Lady Mount-Stratton. "We can have a little talk later. I've never been able to talk to you yet, dear."

Blanche went to her father and told him that he must take the Abbé and join the others. She wanted to stay behind. He could always get rid of the Abbé if he wanted to.

Henry Clifford understood, and he and the Abbé went off by themselves, and Blanche said to Lady Mount-Stratton:

"I will take you to my sitting-room. You will be able to write your letters there in peace, and no one will disturb you."

Lady Mount-Stratton laughed.

"I've no letters to write," she said – "not one. I wanted to talk to you."

"Let's go out," said Blanche. "One never knows who won't disturb one here. There is no peace in this house."

"I should love a little walk," said Lady Mount-Stratton. "I'll just get my hat."

A little later they strolled through the garden into the *Podere* at the back. They walked along the edge of the green corn under the olive trees. It was a wonderful Florentine morning. When they had first arrived, the spring had hardly begun; the almond trees had been in full blossom; now they were all green. The Judas tree at the back of the square white villa was in full bloom. It looked like a piece of compact pink mosaic against the intense blue of the sky, which seemed as solid as marble.

The city beneath them looked so fresh, so miraculously flower-like, as if it had been conjured up for them by a magician.

They turned round and looked at it.

"It certainly *is* a beautiful view, isn't it?" said Blanche.

"Quite beautiful," said Lady Mount-Stratton, to whom it brought back many memories.

"One would have to be thoroughly ungrateful and stupid to mind living here," said Blanche, "not to like it – "

"One is not master of one's likes," said Lady Mount-Stratton sadly. "There have been moments in my life when I have hated the sight of beautiful views. But I don't want to talk of myself. Let us sit down under this little brick wall. Sit on my dust-cloak – there. I want to talk to you. I haven't had a word with you since I've been here, and I've been longing to, all the time. I've been watching you, all the same, my dear child, and admiring you so much – very much indeed. You do it all beautifully."

"I've nothing to do."

"That's the most difficult thing of all to do well, isn't it? Let me think; how long have you been married? Four years – five years this autumn. That's a long time when one is as young as you are. I was telling Guido he must bring you to England this year."

"He talks of going to England at the end of July."

"That's too late. Everybody will have left London."

"Guido doesn't much care for London."

"Won't he be bored in the country in England still more?"

"Yes; but he will have friends. The Winslopes have been appointed to London, and they are going there quite soon. They say they are going to take a house in the country, and they have asked us to stay with them. That will be a resource for Guido. And now there is a great friend of his at the Italian Embassy, Alfredo Castrovillari. Guido knows him and his wife."

"Will you be glad to get back to Rome, or do you like Florence better?"

"I like Florence as a place, but I have more friends in Rome. I have no friends here at all."

"But a great many in Rome, of course?"

"A great many acquaintances – not many friends."

"My son tells me everybody adores you."

"He exaggerates. He doesn't know me as I am really. He sees an imaginary *me*. I expect he always idealises people, doesn't he?"

"No – not as a rule. When he admires, he admires extravagantly; but, as you have probably noticed, he *is* clear-sighted – he has few illusions."

"I think he is full of illusions," said Blanche, laughing.

"Full of one idea, which you call an illusion, but which he doesn't. I know, dear Blanche, of course, what has happened."

"I thought you did. I hope you know the truth. I don't want to say anything in self-defence, or to excuse myself. I am quite

133

ready to take any blame there is to be taken, but I told him from the first that I didn't love him, never could love him, and that if he wanted to be friends he must drop that idea. I thought he had for a time, and then I saw that he hadn't. Even then, I think I could have managed; only, both Guido and my mother-in-law persisted in throwing him in my path, asking him to the house on every possible occasion, and making things impossible for me. They asked him here. Of course I should love him to come here, for him to be here for you, if it were not for that. I do beg you to believe, Lady Mount-Stratton, that I have done nothing to lead him on. I have never seen him except when I couldn't help it. Of course we meet everywhere, and then Guido and my mother-in-law make it impossible for us not to meet. And I really think it is dreadfully tiresome of them; why they do it I cannot conceive. They like him, I know, but I am sure my mother-in-law must understand the situation. She is far too clever not to, or perhaps, as is most natural, she just likes his company and does not intend to give it up. Perhaps I am being uncharitable. Only, the result is that he is making himself miserable. I thought at first it was only a temporary affair, almost a joke, a game; but now, unless I am completely deceived, I don't think it is. I know people say it is always the woman's fault, that the woman can always stop this kind of thing, if she likes, but that she never does like. I think that is often true, but in this case I think I could stop it if it wasn't for Guido and my mother-in-law, and for the extraordinary way they are behaving about it all, which I confess I don't understand. And now, to crown it all, when I told my father about it and begged him to help me, I saw that he, after a talk with my mother-in-law, thought it *was* my fault, and that I was in love with your son, and nothing that I could say could make any difference. So now I beg you to believe me and to help me. If you don't and can't, nobody else will or can, and I shall despair – "

"I do believe you, Blanche," said Lady Mount-Stratton. "I am devoted to my boy, and I have tried to be a good mother to him, but I would not be his mother if I, too, were not clear-sighted. I know him so well, and I have followed his career so far, step by step, and know all about his affairs – and, as you know, there have been a great many. Two years ago he was engaged – you know all that. He broke it off, and perhaps it was just as well, as I know he wasn't in the least in love then, and it was perhaps too soon for him to marry, and so all is for the best. But none of those other affairs were real. This one *is* – as real as it will ever be. He loves you. You are quite right. He loves you in a way he has never loved any one before, in a way – if you forgive me – you haven't yet loved any one; and I don't know whether to pray that you may or may not do so in the future." She sighed. "At the same time, I don't want you to think things are worse than they are – he will get over it. It will not be his last affair. Adrian isn't the kind of person to die of a broken heart – he will recover; but while the illness lasts it will be bad, and he will never have it so badly as this time. And you don't love him at all; he doesn't even attract you. I don't believe that you even appreciate him fully – appreciate certain things in him that others would appreciate – all that there is; and there is a lot. He is wonderfully gifted. But the reason he doesn't attract you, the reason you don't love him, Blanche, is the same reason why he will get over it – and you feel this instinctively, although you don't know it – it is that, much as he loves you, *he loves himself better.* I believe I am the only person he loves better than himself, I – his old mother – it is strange and odd, but it is true. Now I know him through and through, and I know you well enough to see that everything you have told me is true. I believe every word you have said. I know it isn't your fault. I don't understand your husband – at least I do, to a certain extent. I think, perhaps, I understand him better than you do. I think you are, my dear, perhaps too young to understand him, certainly too young to be *sorry* for him. One day, perhaps, you will be

135

sorry for him. I know you are good to him, an admirable wife and all that – but that is different. It's not your fault. You married too young... However, his conduct is to me the proof that what you have told your father and what you have just told me is true. It proves that he is not jealous, not a scrap jealous of Adrian, and he is capable of great jealousy. Well, if he is not jealous, he knows you don't care for Adrian, and never will care for him. As for Julia, I think she likes Adrian, and likes power, and likes domination, and likes having a hold on people, and altogether I expect her motives are mixed. Well, the question is, what is to be done? Adrian has only been here six months. But, apart from everything else, this climate is not good for him. He's delicate, you know. The doctors say warmth is good for him. But Rome isn't, I'm sure. I feel that if he stays here he will get Roman fever. I said so when he was appointed, but he was so obstinate."

"I don't think he does look well."

"Well, directly I get back to London I will do my best to get him moved. I think Paris would be the best place for him at present. And then I must try and get him cured. It won't be easy, my dear child, because you have, through no fault of your own, just by being your lovely, adorable self, done him such serious mischief, given him Roman fever."

"I'm so sorry," said Blanche; "I really did nothing."

"I know you didn't; but listen to me, Blanche. I know exactly what you feel about Adrian. I have been through just the same thing when I was your age, and when I first married. There was a man who was fond of me. Every one thought him charming. He was good-looking; he was clever; he was amusing; he was a *mauvais sujet*; he had all the vices, that is to say, all the attractions, and I got on with him, was amused by him, appreciated him, but I could never have cared for him, was never charmed by him, never carried away the least little bit. He had a hundred affairs, and he made up to me, and I treated it as a joke, and I think I wasn't like you, I encouraged him a little, not much, but a little, till I saw it was serious, then I left off. I was afraid of playing with fire, and circumstances separated us. My husband was sent to another post, the man was left behind. He was unhappy – for a time – and he got over it. But what I wanted to tell you was this: when that happened it gave me the idea that I was proof, immune to all that kind of thing, that I should never be carried off my feet by a sudden involuntary passion, that I should continue all my life to lead a perfectly humdrum life with my husband, and that I would never have a *grande passion* for any one else. But oh! how wrong I was! and from what unexpected quarters and at what an unexpected moment the attack came! I couldn't believe it was true when I first realised it! and how different it was from anything that had happened to me before... I married young, knowing nothing, and because I was told to...and the misery it entailed and the happiness too – but in the end the misery! Great happiness and great misery! I sometimes wonder whether, if I had my life to live over again, I should face it, whether I would choose to have it the same or not – and I'm not sure. I believe that, in spite of all, I would not have things different, that I would have it, with all the pain and misery, but the suffering was so great that I really don't know...and this is saying a great deal, if you knew how great, how wonderful, the happiness was at one moment...only, the price! May you be spared that! But what I want to tell you is this...don't ever for one moment think that *you are immune* – one is *never* immune... It is never too late to be foolish. One never learns any better. '*On arrive novice à tous les âges*,' La Rochefoucauld said, and oh! how true that is! You must be as old as I am to know how true that is...and I am sure that you one day – I don't know how or when – will have to go through all that, and, remember, however wonderful it is, however one prepares, one has some day to pay for it all...to the uttermost farthing. The Papists talk of Purgatory, but a lot of us have our Purgatory here in this world, or at least some of it, and I pray that you won't. But one pays, I'm sure, for all one has made other people suffer in the suffering one has oneself. And, if you have made Adrian suffer, if you are making him suffer now, through no fault of your own, I am sorrier for you than I am for him, for I know, from my own experience, that once in one's life one has that particular bill to settle, and the payment is torture.

"It only happens once in one's lifetime – one may have other affairs. I did – many, and I own quite frankly I enjoyed them, but there was one which made up for all the pleasure by the pain it caused me, as well as the joy. The pain was as strong as the joy; so strong, that I could hardly bear it. But one does bear it. Human life is *almost* intolerable, but not quite. At least most people find it *just* tolerable. I did; but then I am strong in a way, and tough, but you, my dear, I am not sure you will bear it; if ever such a thing happens to you, I am afraid it will kill you."

Blanche smiled sadly. "I find life difficult enough as it is," she said, and she burst into tears. Lady Mount-Stratton took her in her arms and they both cried.

"I know, I know," said the older woman, comforting her. "I know how difficult it is, and how lonely one is, and how little one knew, and how little one realised, and the prospect looks so long, so long, and so dreary, so appallingly long as it stretches out in front of one, but it isn't really as long as it looks; it all goes by so quickly, really, and everything, one finds, as one grows older, matters so much less than one thought at first…and, in the end, one knows there is rest and sleep, and that nobody will wake and disturb one. You mustn't worry more than you can help; and, as to Adrian, I promise you that will be all right. I will get him away from Rome, and we will find a nice wife for him. He is bound to marry, and he will make his wife miserable, but she must be a nice woman and go through with it all the same. We all have to; that is what we are here for. I don't understand why it is so, but it is, and it's no good bothering! We shall know in the next world, but not in this. And remember this, if ever you want the help or advice of an old woman, you can always have mine. But one never listens to advice, and I think it is just as well one doesn't. It is difficult to help any one – perhaps impossible – but what one can do sometimes is to help those whom one loves to know what they are thinking themselves, to find out and to realise what they really want. And if ever you want any such help, you will always find mine ready. But, really, the only way we can help people is by loving them. There's a platitude for you!

"Now it's getting late. I think we had better walk slowly back."

When the others came back from Florence, they found Lady Mount-Stratton and Blanche sitting in the loggia and discussing the topics of the day in the most serene and detached manner.

The next day the whole party returned to Rome.

Lady Mount-Stratton went to stay at her son's apartment, and Princess Julia told Blanche that she must organise some expeditions and entertainments in which both Lady Mount-Stratton and her son could take part. Blanche wrote the suggestions she was asked to make to Lady Mount-Stratton in such a way that the latter understood their source and their exact weight, and she skilfully and tactfully eluded them. She had made the discovery that the Roman climate was bad for Adrian. She wrote this to Blanche in confidence, and said that he must not be encouraged to do too much. Blanche showed the letter to her mother-in-law. At the beginning of May, Lady Mount-Stratton went back to London, and she took her son with her. His leave had fallen due. He had no wish to go to London at all, but his mother had hinted that Guido and Blanche were likely to be coming to London in the month of June, and, as he thought there would be far better opportunities of his seeing Blanche in London than in Rome, he took his leave and went back with his mother to London.

The Winslopes left Rome shortly afterwards. Charlemagne Winslope had been appointed First Secretary to the American Legation in London. They invited Guido and Blanche to come and stay with them in September, as they expected by then to be thoroughly settled in the country house they had taken near Windsor. Guido and Blanche stayed on in Rome all through the month of June, and they then spent three weeks at Vichy, where Guido, who had not been well, had been recommended to take the waters, and after that they went to Gérardmer for a *Nachkur.* After staying a few days in Paris on the way, they arrived in London at the beginning of August.

They went straight to Wood Norton, where they found Princess Julia, who had preceded them. She was already established there, with Howard de Lisle (who had been invited to stay for a month), her daughter, her son-in-law, her patience-table, and the Abbé. She had turned Wood Norton upside down, and the gaudy Early Victorian rooms had been lent a shadow of Roman dignity. The uglier pictures had been relegated to the lumber-room, handsome brocades had been put on the walls and flung carelessly on screens, and new chintz had been chosen for the chairs. The house was full of flowers in Oriental vases. Her own bedroom had been repapered. There were white silk curtains in it, a picturesque four-posted bed, and a beautiful looking-glass on the dressing-table.

"Dear Guido and Blanche are so thoughtful," she said. "They told me to have everything done that I thought should be done; they said I was to be sure to get anything I thought necessary, so I have just got a few little things... "

# CHAPTER XIII

Blanche found that Wood Norton had been transformed into a miniature Palazzo Fabrini – that is to say, the routine of life, thanks to the presence and the arrangements of her mother-in-law, was the same here as in Rome.

Princess Julia had established the same little court; and the same idle courtiers – her son-in-law, Howard de Lisle, and the hard-worked slaves, Teresa and the Abbé (who did all the fetching and carrying) – were revolving in their appointed orbits around her central authority.

Guido now went up to London every day and returned late in the evening. He said that London was so far more pleasant in August than during the season...he enjoyed it far more, now that it was said to be "empty." Princess Julia went up to London every now and then to do the round of the furniture shops, and she took Teresa and the Abbé with her, and always came back laden with parcels. Blanche felt that she herself was a negligible quantity in the household; she was there for show, like a screen or a lamp.

She was thrown back upon herself and forced to look into herself. No words could describe her loneliness.

None of her English friends were available. Her father had met them at the station when they arrived, but he was full up

141

with engagements, and started for Scotland the day they had arrived in London.

Blanche heard from Lady Mount-Stratton. Adrian Tyne had been appointed to the British Embassy at Paris, and he had proceeded to his new post as soon as his leave was over at the end of June. Lady Mount-Stratton had added a few obscure phrases and hints which meant, so Blanche thought, that all was going well and that she need not be uneasy. She understood the meaning of these hints when, a few days after receiving the letter, she read in the columns of the *Morning Post* that a marriage had been arranged between Lady Fanny Morton, the second daughter of the Earl of Castlebridge, and the second brother of Lord Mount-Stratton, the Honourable Adrian Tyne, who had recently been attached to the British Embassy in Paris.

Blanche wrote to Lady Mount-Stratton to congratulate her, and received an effusive letter in answer. Adrian, she really did hope, was going to settle down at last. She was glad he was going to marry Fanny Morton, as she was a charming girl in every way, and would make an admirable diplomat's wife, a perfect ambassadress. She spoke French so well and was so well dressed. Apparently Lady Mount-Stratton felt certain that Adrian would one day be an ambassador.

The marriage was to take place in London in November. Adrian had cut short his leave in the spring owing to the Paris appointment, and would be allowed two months in the autumn for his marriage and his honeymoon.

Blanche felt relieved. There was one difficulty settled. At the same time she realised that, if she were honest, she would have to admit to herself that she was experiencing not a disappointment, not a shadow of jealousy, but a slight sensation of blankness. Life seemed emptier than ever now that it was shorn of this complication, of this element of excitement. Of course it was a relief, a solution, but the vista which opened out before her and stretched out on to infinity seemed now more dreary, more unrelieved than ever.

She had the satisfaction of telling the news to Princess Julia. "I always knew," said the Princess, "that he would end by marrying Fanny. She will make him a good wife. I always thought, by what he told me, that he regretted having broken off the engagement."

"Oh, he *was* engaged?"

"Yes," said the Princess; "and it was broken off just before you and Guido went to England. It is just as well; he has had time to think well over it, and living abroad has made him realise, probably, that there is, after all, nothing so nice as an English girl."

Blanche received a little note from Adrian saying he was engaged to be married, and after the word "married" there was an exclamation mark.

Blanche wrote to him her sincerest congratulations.

Blanche had several aunts besides her father's sister, Mrs Somner, but the only two who played any part in her life were, firstly, a younger sister of her mother's, Lady Wenbury, who lived with her family almost permanently in the country, in the north of Wales, and, secondly, the widow of her father's younger brother, Mrs Walter Clifford, whose husband had been for many years a Member of Parliament; he was a classical scholar, a member of the Athenaeum, and a contributor to the *Edinburgh Review*. She had spent most of her life either in London or in her husband's constituency in Northumberland, but when he died she migrated in search of a warmer climate to the Isle of Wight. Her eldest daughter, Mary, was six years younger than Blanche. Mary had just come out, and Mrs Clifford had taken a house in London for the season.

Mrs Clifford had been considered almost a beauty in her day, and was still thought handsome. She had gentle manners and an amiable disposition, but her suavity concealed inflexible opinions on politics, religion, and social affairs. At one time she had come under the influence of Dr Pusey, and she held strong High Church views.

Hearing that Blanche was in England, and having started on a round of visits at the end of July, she wrote to Blanche and asked whether she might stay a night or two at Wood Norton on her way back to the Isle of Wight.

Blanche discussed the matter with Guido, and said that, if they asked Mrs Clifford (Aunt Cecilia), Lady Wenbury (Aunt Harriet) would be offended if they did not ask her. It was, she pointed out, a duty to ask both of them, and it would be as well to get both the duties done at the same time...and Guido and Princess Julia agreed with her. So Lady Wenbury was asked, and she said she would be delighted to stay for a few days on her way to the west, where she was going to meet her husband (who had been yachting with the children) at a cousin's house in Cornwall. So the two aunts were asked to meet each other, and they arrived at Wood Norton towards the end of August. Aunt Harriet, whom Blanche had not seen for eight years, reminded her a little of her mother; she was small, pale, unobtrusive, with fair hair and grey eyes, and a gentle, deprecatory manner, only she was more conventional than her mother had been; her opinions had become crystallised in stiffer moulds and narrower grooves, and her views on life and conduct were decently hidden behind a veil of irreproachable orthodoxy, which she could not bear any one to ruffle, let alone to lift.

Princess Julia received the two aunts with an excess of honeyed sweetness, which showed Blanche that her mother-in-law disliked them both. But Guido and Teresa got on well with them, and said they were both amiable.

Each of the aunts on separate occasions approached Blanche on the subject of religion.

"I hope, Blanche darling," said Aunt Harriet one morning, when she had asked Blanche to show her the "grounds," "that living abroad hasn't shaken your Faith."

"I don't think so," said Blanche – "I hope not; although I do think it is difficult sometimes to know exactly what one's Faith is." She had not meant to add this comment. She had been thinking aloud, and she repented her words as soon as she had uttered them; at the same time she felt, "If I can't confide in Aunt Harriet, I can confide in no one. She is the nearest relation I have in the world, except papa, and papa doesn't understand that sort of thing." She felt, too, a certain tenderness for her Aunt Harriet, as she alone of her relations reminded her of her childhood, her nursery days, and her mother's gentleness.

"But surely you go to church on Sundays?"

"Yes, Aunt Harriet, I do."

Aunt Harriet gave a sigh of relief. That settled the matter; as long as one went to church on Sundays that was all that was necessary. One needn't go into anything else. She didn't want to. It made her uncomfortable. She turned to a different and safer side of the topic.

"Although I suppose in Rome it is difficult to find a *real* Church among so much that is theatrical and superstitious."

"There's an English church."

"Ah yes, but what sort of church? One never quite knows abroad what one may not have to put up with. In the country, too, it's sometimes difficult. In London it's different. There used to be such a good clergyman at the church we used to go to, at St Jude's. He preaches most beautifully, and doesn't do anything *odd*. At some of the country churches – in Bournemouth, for instance, where we spent a Sunday last year – they did such odd things," and she added, with bated breath, "almost *profane*."

"The clergyman at Rome is just an ordinary clergyman," Blanche said reassuringly.

"I hope they don't try to undermine your Faith?"

"Who?" asked Blanche, although she knew quite well what her aunt meant.

"I mean Princess Julia and all of them."

145

"Oh no; they never interfere with me."

"Well, I'm glad to hear it. I know how sly they can be. You see, we have had too many perverts in the family as it is. There is your poor Uncle Charles" (a younger brother of Henry Clifford's, who had startled his family by becoming a Catholic) – "he was got hold of by your Aunt Mercedes; she is a foreigner, and one can't be surprised; and there is Edmund Lely, your father's first cousin once removed, he became a monk, and goes about barefoot, abroad too; and then there was your poor Aunt Cornelia. That was a great shock to us all when it happened. Of course we were all very nice to her; in fact, I'm afraid that we were *too* nice to her. Because we were nice to her she forgot that we knew her to be mistaken."

"I hardly remember Aunt Cornelia," said Blanche. "How old was she when she was converted?"

"It was some years after her marriage that she was perverted. It was Dr Newman's doing. He's a dangerous man – so plausible."

"Did it make her happy?"

"If they like to call it happiness to give up all responsibility and to have everything settled for you they can; but I think it wrong to call anything happiness that involves all that."

Blanche changed the subject.

On Sunday morning the Italians walked to Mass at ten. The Abbé had already said Mass early. Howard de Lisle stayed at home. Blanche suggested to her aunts that they should walk to church at eleven. The church was within easy walking distance.

Punctually at a quarter before eleven, Mrs Clifford was ready in the hall for church, dressed in magenta with a velvet bonnet and carrying a large Prayer Book.

Lady Wenbury had decided not to come. She had a bad headache, and thought that she might feel faint in church. She would lie down and read the lessons in her bedroom.

"I was afraid at first," Blanche said, as they were walking to church, "that Aunt Harriet was not coming to church because she thought it might be 'odd.' Her maid is Low Church, she told me, and she has been telling Aunt Harriet dreadful things about our poor harmless Vicar, Mr Soothby, but I reassured her. She really has got a bad headache."

"Harriet knows *nothing* about church matters," said Mrs Clifford. "I said to her yesterday when we were talking about churches that they were thinking of adding a Lady Chapel to our church at Ryde, and what do you think she said? Would you believe it! She said she did not approve of men and women being separated in church. She thought it Romish!"

Just at that moment they passed a little tin tabernacle.

"That is where Guido goes to church," said Blanche, pointing to it.

"Oh, that's where the Romans go. How extraordinary foreigners are about some things! The Abbé, for instance, was surprised when I told him I was a Catholic! He said he thought I was a Protestant. Fancy thinking *me* a *Protestant* of all people! Then he said he presumed I would go to Mass with them. I had to explain that, although I was not a Roman, I belonged to the older branch of the Catholic Church, which, while it did not accept all the intolerable claims of Rome, and especially the utterly indefensible modern pretensions of Pius IX, was gradually getting back to what it had been in England before the Reformation. But, after all, it is not astonishing foreigners should know little about our Church when many English people know nothing about it."

By this time they had reached the church.

It was a red brick building. There were no signs of anything ritualistic about it. There were some flowers in the brass vases above the altar and two unlighted candles and a red altar cloth. The clergyman did not wear a cassock, and the choir consisted of boys in surplices, but without cassocks. There was an anthem and three hymns. The clergyman turned to the east when he said the Creed, and in his sermon he made a sympathetic allusion to the separated Brethren of the Universal Church in Moscow, Constantinople, and Rome.

Mrs Clifford grudgingly approved the service. The sermon she thought excellent. She returned to the subject of religion with Blanche as they walked home.

"I do hope, dear Blanche, that because you live in Rome you will never cease to be a Catholic."

"To become a Roman Catholic?" asked Blanche.

"Yes; to go over to Rome. Nobody has a right to do that, least of all English Catholics. In old days one could understand it, when the Church was choked with Protestant weeds, but now – "

"Guido and my mother-in-law say that it is impossible to find out what English people do believe; that the English Church is split up into sects, and that it is only the State part, the national part, that holds together, and that that is an institution like the House of Commons."

"Of course they would say that."

"But I find I know so little about it that I can't discuss the matter with them – not that they ever bother me about it. But I should like to know what one ought to say. I find I know so little about my own Church."

"I will send you a most interesting book written by a friend of mine, Father Anselm; it is called *How to Refute the Errors of Rome*. You will find it exactly what you want."

"I suppose that it would not, after all, be odd if one day I were to become a Roman Catholic, considering my husband is one," and she was going to say "considering my children would be," but she had given up all hope of ever having another baby.

"You owe it to your Church, to your father, and to all of us *not* to change," said Mrs Clifford. "You can find all you need in your own Church, which is far older and more apostolic, besides which the Roman Church is full of corrupt doctrine which it has forced upon everybody in a cruel and unscrupulous way. Until the Church of Rome mends her ways and becomes more truthful and more *open*, less grasping, less superstitious, and less *pandering*, there can be no question of reunion or of our submitting to Rome. And in saying all this to you, my dear Blanche, I am merely quoting Dr Newman's very words, as far as I can remember them – what he wrote before he went over."

"I sometimes wonder" – Blanche was urged by a sudden imperative impulse to cry out the truth somehow, somewhere – "whether I really have any religious faith at all. I mean, whether I believe anything, feel anything. Do you know, Aunt Cecilia, that a service just like that one which we have been sitting through doesn't seem to reach me. It means nothing to me."

"These trials are sent to us to test our Faith. It is a pity that you can't hear Mr Ludgate preach. He has a church in the north of London, and I go to hear him every Sunday when I am in London. He is a refreshing preacher. He reads his sermons in the morning and he preaches extempore in the evening; and I am sure if you were to hear him he would set your doubts at rest. If ever you are in London, do not fail to go to his church – St Olaf's, Windermere Terrace, Regent's Park."

"Is he High Church?"

"He is a *sound* churchman, but it is difficult for him, owing to his mixed congregation, to make any innovations as to ritual at present. He hopes later on to be able to do something. He says we must not be impatient, we must let the seed grow, and I think he is right. Some people do more harm than good by being over-hasty. As long as one knows that a priest is not *sloppy* on the important points, we must leave the rest to him."

"All these clergymen seem to me to be teaching different things," said Blanche, "and I can't help thinking that there is some truth in what Guido says – that this is the result of the original separation at the time of the Reformation."

"But we don't recognise the Reformation."

"No; but Aunt Harriet does, and so does Aunt Caroline, and so does papa."

"You must remember that it is only a short time ago that interest in Church matters has been revived. The Church was choked with Protestant weeds."

"But," said Blanche, "most English people, and nearly all the people I know and like and respect, don't call them weeds, Aunt Cecilia; they think Protestantism is a fine thing; they are intensely proud of it. One has only to read the *Times* newspaper to see that this is true. They are always attacking what they call the ritualists, and you know what a cry of Papal Aggression was raised by Cardinal Wiseman. Nothing is more popular than a cry of 'No Popery.' "

"But, my dear Blanche, I have just told you we have nothing to do with the Church of Rome."

Blanche sighed; she felt too tired to argue.

"The English Church," her aunt continued, "is a part of the original pure stream of the *Early* Church; it has got separated from the main river because the main river has become contaminated and choked with refuse. It has had, it is quite true, its own weeds, but they are gradually being cleared away."

"But, Aunt Cecilia, what you call the *weeds* are the very things most Anglicans are *most* proud of."

"Protestants, my dear – not Anglicans."

"Well – Protestants; but Aunt Harriet and papa *are* Protestants. 1 was brought up as a Protestant. I suppose I am a Protestant – "

"Nonsense, my dear! You are an Anglican and a Catholic. You say, 'I believe in the Holy Catholic Church,' every Sunday; you don't say, 'I believe in the Protestant Church.' But I will send you the little book I spoke to you about. I see you have already been tainted by Roman casuistry. Only, I do solemnly beg one thing of you: if ever you feel tempted to go over to Rome, pause and remember that, as Dr Newman said in the days before his eyes were sealed, the Roman Church is everywhere associated with the lowest and worst democrats, and is always pandering to the spirit of *rebellion*. It is everywhere encouraging the *undeserving* poor and the needy. Its most prominent theologians – and I'm again quoting Newman before he fell – have been guilty of something very like perjury. Dr Newman says, and rightly, Look everywhere and you will see that its leaders are in close alliance with political parties notorious all over the world for *liberalism* and infidelity – yes, *liberalism*." (Mrs Clifford was a staunch Tory, and knew that Henry Clifford was a Whig.) "I don't say Rome hasn't made converts among us – alas! she has made all too many – but how? By misrepresenting her doctrines, by being *plausible*, by appealing to the weakness of human nature, to our frivolities (in the case of your poor Aunt Cornelia), to our weakness (in the case of your misguided Uncle Charles), to our eccentricities, as in the case of that silly cousin of ours, Edmund Lely...the agents of Rome are everywhere, worse here than in Italy; they try to attract our attention with their nursery tales and pretty pictures and tinsel, but remember, my dear Blanche, that underneath all that sweet jam there is a bitter powder, and until the Church of Rome ceases to be what she practically is, a union between her and England is *impossible*, and that it is sinful for an English Catholic to go over to her fold; it is more than a sin, it is *treachery* – the act of a renegade."

By this time they had reached home.

# CHAPTER XIV

The aunts stayed a short time at Wood Norton, and each of them before leaving wrote to Henry Clifford.

Lady Wenbury wrote as follows:

"WOOD NORTON, *Friday.*

"My DEAR HENRY, – Before leaving Wood Norton I must write you one line to tell you what a pleasure it has been to stay under the same roof as dear Blanche once again. It has been a real joy to see her again after *so many years*. I was almost despairing about ever seeing her as the children make it impossible for one to go abroad now in the holidays, and Wenbury says we can't afford it, although he can always afford to yacht!!! So you can imagine how delighted I was when Blanche *pressed* me to come. She is in very good case, and such a dear! Of course I hardly recognised her, not having set eyes on her for so many years! She is a real beauty, and, what is still better, she is so ladylike. Looks without that are, after all, nothing, and it is getting rare!

"She reminds me more and more of your dear mother. And Princess Julia saw it, too. What a charming woman, and how clever! Guido, too, was most kind to us. His sister is there, too, and clever with her embroidering. I found her a help with my work.

"Cecilia was there, too (without the girls). I believe she proposed herself. I know, of course, that Cecilia is *clever*, and that I am *not*, but I can't help thinking it a pity that she should encourage Blanche with her High Church views to play with Romish ideas – I call it playing with fire – when it must be so difficult for her as it is to resist all her present surroundings. We know that Roman Catholics always try to pervert English Protestants; they *have* to. But I am happy to say that Blanche's faith – let us pray it may remain so – seems still to be unshaken. I go to London tomorrow for a night on my way home. The boys are enjoying their yachting, and I do hope you are having the same glorious weather as we have been having here. – Your affectionate

"HARRIET WENBURY.

"PS – Blanche was delighted at getting the grouse. We hear good accounts from Scotland."

By the same post Henry Clifford received a letter from Mrs Clifford:

"WOOD NORTON, *17th August.*

"My DEAR HENRY, – Blanche very kindly asked me to stay here on my way home. I meet Mary tomorrow in London. She is to travel up with her cousins from Brockley, where she had a pleasant visit. I enjoyed my visit here greatly. Blanche is beautiful, and she has a look of Desclée, only she is far *prettier*. She has *charm* and *intelligence* as well as beauty. It is a pity she has given up her playing. I don't think her mother-in-law is musical. Italians seldom are *really* musical; they only care for *their*

*music.* Blanche has so far resisted *all* temptation to go
over to Rome, but I really think this is a *wonder*,
considering the Erastian principles which she has been,
and still is, exposed to, through no fault of yours, I am
sure, my dear Henry. But you must realise that it is *far*
easier for the Romans to influence a girl who has not
been taught anything, not the A B C, about her *own*
Church, and who does not even know that she belongs to
the *Catholic Church*, than if she were properly instructed
and grounded. I think, however, I was able to be of some
help. It was a little unfortunate that Harriet should have
been here just now. She is *far* from being a help, as she
knows *nothing* about Church matters, and is just the
wrong person for Blanche *at this moment*. Blanche says,
it is only fair to say, that Guido and the Princess do *not* try
to influence her. I don't think they do *directly*; they would
be too clever to do that, but of course indirect influence
goes on the *whole time*, and that slow, silent pressure
which we know so well; but if she should ever yield to it,
and go over, I, for one, shall blame that Lutheran
governess of hers (recommended by Harriet),
Mademoiselle Zeulen; and people like dear Harriet, who
are so well meaning, but who say and do just the wrong
things! However, we must not meet troubles half-way! I
hope you have been having good sport in Scotland and
catching fish and shooting well. They were delighted here
with the grouse. It is a pity that the Italians do not care for
game! The weather has been perfect. – Your affectionate
                              "CECILIA CLIFFORD.

"PS – How I wish I could manage to run over to Rome in
the winter. They kindly asked me to, but the girls make it
impossible, and now that Mary is out!!"

Towards the end of the month Blanche and Guido went on a
visit to the Winslopes at a house they had taken on a five years'
lease near Windsor – a large, low, Palladian building, decorated
inside by Adam and situated in a spacious park.

Charlemagne Winslope gave them a warm welcome. Mrs
Winslope welcomed Blanche with effusive expressions that
seemed to give out light rather than warmth. There were
several other guests staying in the house: a Mr Ridgeway, who
had been a lawyer in America and who was now the
correspondent of an important journal in Paris, and his wife –
he was enjoying a holiday; a Mr Francis Bretherton, who was
said to be a scholar, and was engaged at present on an edition
of Propertius; Lady Harriet Clive; and a banker from New
Orleans who was paying his first visit to England, John J
Geach, and his wife, Dolores. Blanche greatly enjoyed the
change of atmosphere. She suddenly felt as if she could breathe
more easily.

Grace Winslope faintly provoked her; she felt there was
something about her which every now and then did not ring
quite true; on the other hand, she liked her host and she found
all the other guests likeable.

Ridgeway was interesting, but a little serious; his wife was
good-looking, crystal clear, and kind. John Geach had a dark,
olive complexion, black hair, and twinkling eyes, and a serious
way of expressing incongruous ideas. His wife was dark, too –
a creole – with a white skin and soft eyes. She was engagingly
frank, and she said straight out what she thought without
putting any brake on her vocabulary; at the same time, there
was nothing rough about her. She never hurt nor wounded.

Blanche liked her immensely.

Francis Bretherton was a scholar between thirty and forty.
He had light blue eyes, and there was a sense of coolness,
equipoise, and detachment about him. You felt as if he were
looking at you through the wrong end of a telescope. He wore
gold-rimmed spectacles, and there was a slight twinkle in his

eye, except when he said something funny – then he became grave. Blanche had been told somewhat vaguely about his having shot lions and being fond of alpine climbing, as well as of the classics.

She sat next to him at dinner the first night she arrived at Longford Park, and he won her heart when she asked him which he thought the most exciting sport by saying, after a moment's pause, with grave deliberation, "Botany."

"I believe," she said then, "I should be a botanist if I had the chance. I was brought up as a Cockney. We always lived in London, and I only *stayed* in the country with relations, aunts and cousins. We had no country home of our own. In spite of that, I had wonderful days and sometimes months in the country, and my favourite sport is bird's-nesting, but I haven't seen a bird's nest since I was married."

They talked of places foreign and English. As they went on talking, Blanche became gradually aware that she was talking to this stranger as if she had known him for years. She was conscious of an unwonted ease, as if she were swimming without effort in a sea of intimacy.

She said out loud: "I can't help feeling that we must have met before, and yet I know we haven't."

"We have, although I don't think you remember it. We have met twice, I think; once on the Capitol – you were showing the 'Dying Gladiator' to some friends and once in the Campagna, a hot day towards the end of May – you were picking flowers."

"I remember," she said, laughing, "and you must have been the man with your back turned to us, who was sketching. I was with my sister-in-law."

"Yes; I was trying to sketch an aqueduct. It was a failure."

"Do you often come to Rome?"

"I have been there once or twice, but I shall come often now. I want to consult some books in the Vatican. I am editing some Latin texts. I shall probably stay there all next winter."

"In an hotel?"

"I think not; in a flat. Or, perhaps, I may stay with friends."

"I hope we shall see a lot of you. I live in Rome always."

"Really? You must find that trying, don't you?" Blanche laughed.

"Most people would think it is a privilege," she said.

"Nothing makes up for exile, though, does it?"

"Nothing," she said, with profound conviction.

There was a pause. Blanche not only wondered at herself, and at the ease with which she found herself talking to Bretherton, but she felt alarmed; for a second she had lifted the mask she was accustomed to wear. She knew quite well that she and Bretherton might be friends – nothing more than friends, but great friends.

"Have you lived much abroad?" she asked.

"I was twenty years in business in South America," he said. "Then, partly from what I had made, and partly because I inherited a little money, I had enough to retire."

"You didn't like business?"

"No; I had no vocation. I went into it for fun originally, and then, owing to circumstances, had to stay."

"But how lucky it came to an end."

"Yes; but it used up all the best years – the only years worth living."

"Some people say," Blanche said pensively, "that you get happier as you get older – that you only begin to be happy as you get past middle age."

"That's because they've stopped *living. Life* is over when one's forty, but something else goes on – retrospect dreams, contemplation, memories. Just when one reaches forty is the dangerous moment. I once heard some one talk of *'le néant d'avoir quarante ans.'* Didn't Horace Walpole, or Robert Walpole, or Lord Chesterfield say that at the age of forty every man was tired of being honest and every woman of being *honnête*? If one can get past that bar – the bar of the forties – one reaches a safe, calm harbour beyond it. Forty is, I think, *l'âge difficile.* I have almost reached it. It is an astonishing thing to look back suddenly on the road and realise that one's youth is dead. To you, I suppose, it seems so far away that you can't visualise it. You can't imagine it."

"I feel as if I had passed it already," and again Blanche was conscious of having dropped the mask.

She turned to her other neighbour, her host, who, she saw, was not talking. One word was enough to turn on the tap of his genial address and his frank admiration.

"Lady Harriet and I were just agreeing," he said, "that the Roman climate has a peculiar effect on British women. It makes the plain handsome and interesting, and it makes the beautiful more beautiful still. Now what Grace and I miss most now that we have quitted Rome are the kind British friends we made there, not but what the Italians were hospitable and kind to us, but blood is thicker than water, whatever one may say, and it is our British friends we miss most. Somehow the British are easier to get on with abroad, when they are living abroad, than they are in their own country. Although I will say that for newcomers we are getting on mighty fast, and Grace has the house so full of English celebrities sometimes that you can't see to eat. The British are all right when you know them, but you've got to know them first."

"I'm afraid they're terribly rude and inhospitable to foreigners, and when one thinks what you all do for us – "

"No, Princess, you've no right to say that. I won't have you say it; I remember when I was a youngster… " – and the tide of reminiscence flowed easily on till they reached dessert.

Lady Harriet Clive, who was sitting on the other side of Winslope, and who was getting a little tired of Ridgeway's conversation, which was less racy and far more serious than that of Winslope – Ridgeway was erudite and well versed in the literature of four languages – claimed her host's attention once more, and Blanche, after a pause of isolation that lasted a moment or two, looked towards Bretherton.

Mrs Ridgeway abandoned him gracefully, and Blanche asked him what particular work he would be engaged on in Rome.

"I'm editing Propertius," he said.

"I'm afraid I don't know the difference between one Latin writer and another; but I did enjoy some translations from Latin poets made by some one who was an English diplomat at Rome – a Mr Adrian Tyne. I saw them in some newspaper."

"I know his translations – they are good."

"Did you know Mr Tyne?"

"Only by name. I rarely went into the diplomatic, or, indeed, into any other world, when I was at Rome."

"You were right. It is *tiresome*," she said, with great vehemence, and then she realised that for a moment she had dropped the mask altogether. She blushed pink, quite faintly. A soft tinge spread over her extremely white skin.

Bretherton looked at her gravely and impartially. He thought to himself: "If I had met her twenty years ago I would have seized her and taken her to the ends of the earth, and nothing could have prevented me from doing it."

Blanche felt uncomfortable. She felt that Bretherton was seeing through her, had seen through her, once and for all – that henceforth the mask would be useless; no mask would be of any use. And at that moment Guido, who was sitting between Mrs Winslope and Mrs Ridgeway, at the other end of the table, gave her a look – one piercing, swift, cold look – that embraced both her and Bretherton, and every one, and everything, and that seemed to penetrate right to the depth of her, through all masks, and through all covering layers, disguises, and defences. She felt with intuitive presage that just as Guido had never minded her intimacy with Adrian Tyne, so he *would* mind any kind of intimacy with Francis Bretherton, however harmless. She abruptly changed the subject to something more impersonal.

"Will you go to other places in Italy besides Rome?"

They talked of places in Italy and Greece. Bretherton spoke of the classical writers.

"Is it true," Blanche asked, "that Greek and Latin writers are really the best?"

"Greek writers are as much better than modern writers as Greek architecture is better than modern architecture. Of course that does not prevent, say, Chartres Cathedral or Seville Cathedral from being magnificent, any more than Homer makes Shakespeare or Dante less great... Gothic architecture and all modern literature obey the same rules as the Greeks followed, and aim at the same goal – they are the rules and goals of common sense – and nobody has ever invented another standard, or, according to that standard, done better. There has never been anything better than Homer or Paestum –"

"Paestum. We went there from Amalfi. I'm afraid I didn't enjoy it at the time, but then I was so, so... " – she was going to say "unhappy," but she corrected herself in time, and said, "tired, and not well."

"You must go there again."

"We must all go there. You must come with us."

Who "all" meant was left undefined.

"Yes; I shall want to go to Naples to consult the Francheschini Library."

"Is that a good one?"

"For my purposes it is the best in the world, except the library at Ambleside House, in London."

"Who does *that* belong to?"

"It used to belong to Lord Mayfield. He was an old man nearly ninety when he died, not long ago. His estate and his London house, and everything, went to a nephew, as he had no children. No sooner had he died than the nephew who inherited the property died too. He was not a young man, and an invalid into the bargain, I think. He was about sixty. The property went to his son, a man of about thirty-five, and he was drowned, almost as soon as he inherited the title, about a fortnight ago, at Shanklin, in the Isle of Wight. You must have seen it in the newspaper. And now the property has gone to a distant cousin who never thought he had the remotest chance of inheriting anything."

"What was his name?" Blanche asked, without really wanting to know.

"He was the son of a soldier, and he is a soldier himself – a young, penniless, line officer. He had just come home on leave, after doing five years in India. His name is Hope, or, rather, was Hope – Sydney Hope. Now, of course, it is Lord Mayfield, and he is one of the richest men in England."

Blanche repeated the words slowly and absently:

"One of the richest men in England."

She made an immense effort of self-control, but, in spite of that, she felt she must have betrayed some emotion, as she felt cold all over, and it was as if her heart had stopped beating.

"I mustn't faint – I mustn't faint," she said.

She repeated once more, in a voice which seemed to her to come from the end of space:

"One of the richest men in England."

She had turned white, whiter and of a different whiteness than that of her usual complexion. She was wan now, not white. There was a hunted look, too, in her eyes and the marks of suffering on her face.

"It's quite a romance," she forced herself to say, and she even brought out some ghost of a smile, some pretence of a laugh.

Bretherton thought at first she was feeling ill: then he saw it was pain of soul, not of body.

Blanche saw that Guido's eye was on her, and mercifully at the same moment Mrs Winslope gave the signal for the move, and Blanche was able to sweep out of the room, which she did as if nothing had happened, and Bretherton and Winslope, both of them, admired her carriage and her swift, graceful walk – an almost musical walk.

"There goes a beautiful and charming woman," Winslope said in an undertone to Bretherton, as he moved up to the other end of the table.

Guido had noticed the change which had come over Blanche at the end of dinner, and she had told him that she had felt a little faint. She knew he had not guessed the cause. He was out of earshot of their conversation, and even his uncanny second-sight could hardly have helped him to divine what she had been talking about. But when Guido went up to bed he found Blanche brushing her hair in front of a looking-glass and laughing – shaking with laughter.

"What is the joke?" he asked.

"It's only their expressions make me laugh sometimes," she said. "Mr Geach, he said the Pope was a 'nobby boy.'" She laughed again at intervals till she went to bed.

She slept little that night – she thought about nothing but Sydney Hope, and she went on thinking about him the next day. She kept on saying to herself: "You must be sensible; you must not imagine that you have got a broken heart, or that you are like a heroine of romance. You may have a broken heart, but it is not that which has broken it... Besides which, it was your fault...your fault and no one else's. Did you love him? Yes. You did, as far as one can love at that age, but your father was right – all too right; you did not know what love meant, but what did that matter? Why couldn't they let you marry him? Why couldn't I have married him?" she said. "We would have been poor, but what did that matter, and it just shows what can happen. Why didn't they know that he had some prospects? Perhaps they did know, but thought it was too improbable...at least he was an Englishman, and I would have lived among Englishmen had I married him. Oh, it wasn't fair! it wasn't fair! But the irony of it!" And every now and then she would break out once more in hysterical laughter.

"Then," she would say to herself, "it was *your own* fault, your *own* fault, and no one else's. You might have waited. If marriage was impossible for the moment, with Sydney, there was no earthly reason why you should have married Guido. You did think it would be rather fun to live in Rome, in the Palazzo Fabrini, and to have a villa at Florence. You were not true to yourself nor to Sydney. If you had refused to marry Guido, nobody could have made you." Then she said to herself: "All that is true, but, oh, my God, surely I am being punished, and my punishment goes on day after day, and I see no chance of its *ever* coming to an end."

All this happened on a Saturday evening; the next day they spent sitting in the garden and walking in the park. Guido went with Mrs Winslope and Mrs Geach to church. Blanche said she would not go to church. She had a headache.

Bretherton spent the whole morning in the library, which, he said, was an interesting one.

Blanche was left in company with Winslope, the Ridgeways, and Lady Harriet Chive.

Lady Harriet asked her many questions about Rome, and brought into her talk the name of Adrian Tyne. Blanche was able to answer with calm. She said with transparent sincerity that she thought it such a good thing that he was going to be married, and that she was convinced he would be happy.

Lady Harriet, who had heard about Adrian's infatuation, did not know what to think – whether Blanche was an accomplished coquette or simplicity itself.

Blanche talked to her of Rome, with enthusiasm; so much so that Lady Harriet wondered. She felt in her bones that Blanche did not love Guido. There must be, she thought, some one else.

Blanche liked all the guests. Ridgeway was really interesting, and not merely erudite. He told you interesting things, in an interesting way, and not in such a way that you could not listen. Mrs Ridgeway was full of the sparkling waters of human kindness.

Bretherton, she felt, she could make a real friend of, but ever since the conversation they had had the first night at dinner he had retired into a shell. Was it instinct? Did his antennae warn him of danger? Whether or not this was so, he was wise to go, for had he not done so, there is no doubt that Guido would have left the house the next day.

Guido, Blanche thought, was obviously happy. He enjoyed being with Grace Winslope, and she treated him frankly as a piece of personal property; at the same time, her conduct and her manners were perfectly decent.

Blanche did not dislike her, but she could not help feeling faintly irritated, and she became aware that she had the capacity of being jealous – jealous even where Guido was concerned. And then it is always irritating to see people being taken in, especially when they are being taken in by a particular type of person. Blanche would not have minded nearly so much had Grace Winslope been an unmixed siren, but being what she was, a person about whom everybody said, "Grace is so *really* good, so sincere," or "so clever and so unselfish, and so devoted," she felt that she had no right to descend to the arts and to use the weapons of the Chloes and the Lesbias and the *Celimènes* of this world. But she did so, none the less, and it was peculiarly irritating for Blanche when she heard Grace saying to Guido phrases, whose source she knew, such as: "Greek writers are as much better than modern writers as Greek architecture is better than modern architecture." Or, "Nothing *better* than Paestum has ever been done in the way of building." And Guido would murmur to himself: "*Vero, vero,*" and afterwards say to Blanche: "It is extraordinary what a *rich* mind Mrs Winslope has. She has such an all-round culture."

Lady Harriet Clive's appreciation of Mrs Winslope was different. She thought it extraordinary that Grace should know how to behave! and she kept on saying to Blanche: "You know she really has got manners," which amused Blanche immensely, as if one would have expected her to behave like a savage.

That evening Blanche sat next to Geach at dinner, and she found him delightful. He was as quick as lightning, and every word he said came straight from his own mint. After they had been talking for a little while he said to Blanche: "Princess, I guess we have met before." Blanche looked a little bit puzzled. "Not here," he continued, "but in some other pack."

He did a lot of business in China, and apparently he had a house in Hong-Kong. He asked Blanche to come and stay with him.

"You would like the Chinese, Princess," he said; "they are good judges of the best, and they have no use for the second best. Cute? Why, they make the ordinary European seem beside them like turtles among two-year-olds."

After dinner they played a round game.

The next day Mrs Winslope and Bretherton had to go up to London for the day, but the other guests stayed on. Blanche received from her aunt the little pamphlet she had been promised, called *How to Refute the Errors of Rome*. It was rather an inconvenient gift to possess just at the moment, as she did not wish Guido to see it. She knew it would annoy him.

She talked a little to Mrs Geach about her religion. They were walking in the kitchen garden.

"I suppose you were born a Catholic?" said Blanche.

"Yes," she said, "I was born a Catholic, and I've had a good deal of experience since my first birthday, and I've knocked around and nosed around a good deal, and I believe that if you want a religion, it's the best there is…it's the only one that can understand the wants of a person like I am, and I'm just an ordinary person. Or, take a man like John. John isn't a saint, and I suppose no better than most, and I suppose he's broken most of the rules in the book; I don't mean he's gone about with four aces up his sleeve, but he's no plaster saint; well, John just swears by his religion. And what's good enough for him is good enough for me. You're different; you've been born into something else, and I quite understand your not wanting to move, but you won't mind my saying that whenever I go into one of your churches I feel it is kind of cold and empty, even when it is full; it feels more to me like a Board Meeting than a religious service. In our churches I feel at home, and comfortable. Perhaps you feel the same about yours."

"I expect I ought to," said Blanche, "but I don't. To tell you the honest truth, in our churches what I feel is either acute misery or else I'm bored, and that must be wrong. I'm sure it's my fault, but it's true, none the less. And what I like about your church is the natural way with which it deals with religious things. There is no false shame about it. You take it all *naturally*, as a matter of course. But it must be fearfully difficult to believe all you have to believe."

"Well I guess, Princess, that a human being that can say the Creed and believe it, don't find it difficult to believe the Church is right in telling you to go to Mass on Sundays and to quit eating meat on Fridays."

"No, that's quite true, but it's all so complicated and difficult."

"It sometimes seems to me that you people are like people who are looking at the wrong side of a piece of needlework. They can't make out what it's all about. But if you look at it from the right side it's all clear."

"Yes," said Blanche. "I suppose so. I've had a great many relations who were Catholics, besides my husband," she said, laughing; "but the truth of the matter is, that I don't think I have any religious faith. It all means nothing to me. I believe I'm a heathen, or a pagan, or a savage. I wish I wasn't like that, as I know what a comfort religion is to people, but I am like that."

"Well," said Mrs Geach, "you can take it from me, my dear, that we're all of us changing the whole time, but there's one thing that don't change any, and that's the old Church, the

Catholic Church. It was there yesterday, it's there today, and it will be there tomorrow, and I guess that Our Blessed Lord was right when He said that He had built it on a rock, because if it had been built on anything else, why, there wouldn't be a brick of it left by now, considering how busy people have gotten trying to knock it down."

"There's no doubt about it," said Blanche, "that your religion means more to you than ours does to us. Ours means going to church on Sunday, and to a church that is shut every other day of the week; but your religion is part of your everyday life; your churches are open to all always. But you know, Mrs Geach, I don't always *like* Catholics."

"I agree with you. There are some mighty bad ones going around, but I dare say they'd be worse if they weren't Catholics; and if they aren't good, at least they know what they ought to be."

They were joined by Mrs Ridgeway and Lady Harriet, and the conversation was shunted into another groove.

They stayed till Friday at Longford Park, but Bretherton left on Tuesday morning, and Blanche had no further opportunity of any talk with him.

# CHAPTER XV

It was only when Blanche got back to Wood Norton that she began to feel the full effect of the blow that Bretherton had unwittingly dealt her by telling her the news of the sudden fortune that had come to Sydney Hope. It hurt her in two different and distinct ways: firstly, she was conscious of having been punished for not having been true to herself and to him, for her want of faith, for doing, in fact, what she knew was wrong – wrong to and for herself, however right it might appear and be; and, secondly, she experienced a wild feeling of revolt at having been trapped unnecessarily…her marriage appeared to her now to have been farcically unnecessary, and yet there it was – inevitable and never to end till Death them did part…she had made her bed, she must lie in it; she had chosen a part, she must play it, and play it to the best of her ability. She must do her best by Guido…she had, however she might like to look at the matter, definite and binding obligations towards him.

She blamed herself and herself only, and she felt sorry for her father, who must, she felt, know the news. "But papa," she thought, "would probably have advised me to marry Guido even if all this had happened to Sydney at the time they both proposed to me…but now he knows… " So Blanche was more than ever thrown back upon herself. She felt like some one imprisoned in a dungeon from whence there was no escape and into which no ray of light penetrated from the outside world.

In the middle of September her father came south from Scotland, and spent a few days at Wood Norton.

Blanche saw at once that he had heard about Sydney Hope, although they neither of them mentioned it.

One day when they were alone together, Blanche said to her father: "Why did Uncle Charles become a Roman Catholic?"

"My dear, his wife was a Spaniard, and so, of course, a Catholic. She did it."

"And Aunt Cornelia?"

"Cornelia was unhappy," said Henry Clifford, brushing away the question, "and she lived a great deal abroad. It suited her. Catholic Churches suited her. They understood her."

Who "they" were remained undefined.

"But couldn't she have found consolation in the religion she had been brought up in?" asked Blanche.

"You see, my dear child, the Roman priests are so much more human than our clergymen; they study human nature, and they are trained to understand people and to allow for the weaknesses and vanity of human nature. No clergyman would have been of any use to poor Cornelia. She was a woman of the world, and impatient with fools, but of course the priests understood her. They are men of the world."

"You think, then, she was what is called 'got hold of' by the priests?"

Henry Clifford hesitated. He suspected from the nature and trend of Blanche's questions that she was contemplating a change. He had foreseen from the first that this might happen, and had discounted the fact. He had resolved, if it did happen, not only not to make any objection, but to behave towards Blanche as if it were the most natural thing in the world.

I wouldn't say that. She lived abroad, especially in Paris, and her friends and her *entourage* were Catholic – Catholics of the educated, cultivated kind... There was an Abbé she knew,

Charlet his name was, I think – a charming man and a gentleman – and then she was unhappy."

"But supposing I were to become a Catholic, papa, would you say that I had been got hold of by the priests?"

From this moment Henry Clifford began to suspect Blanche was thinking of it.

"No, of course not, my dear child; but are you thinking of it?"

"No, no, I'm not dreaming of it; but I mean all things are possible…and I think it's only fair to them to say *now* that they never seem to me to be trying to get hold of me. The Abbé *never* talks about religion, as you know – and even if he did, he wouldn't, I think, be particularly inspiring. The Princess sighs sometimes over the beauty of the Catholic Church, and Guido answers questions, if you ask him, but they seem to look on me as a hopeless case… 'invincibly ignorant' – that's what they call it, I believe."

Henry Clifford was now, from this moment, convinced once and for all and in such a way that no argument would have shaken, that Blanche intended to become a Roman Catholic. He was neither surprised nor shocked; on the contrary, he was slightly relieved. He knew she was unhappy, and he felt that he was to blame for her unhappiness. He realised fully, too, that had Blanche had children, or were she to have children in the future, he would have felt doubly responsible for any unpleasantness that might arise from the difference of religion between Blanche and her husband; firstly, because he had made the marriage and, secondly, because he had encouraged her to think that the difference of religion was not a serious drawback.

It was impossible for him now to make any objection or to let her think he minded, even if he did.

He talked to her in the most soothing, reasonable way, just as if he had in no way read what he guessed to be her intention.

"If you ever feel it necessary to change your religion, you may rely on me, my dear child, to understand your motives.

You may rely on me not to misunderstand you, but, unless you feel it imperatively *necessary* to make a change, I should advise you to remain where you are. It's not that I don't admire the remarkable qualities of the Roman Church. It's a sensible religion, and they preach and practise sense, there's no doubt about it. But you were not born in it, after all, and so why bother? If you are happy as you are – stay where you are."

But he knew, as he said this, that she was *not* happy where she was, and that that sad fact lay at the root of the whole affair. But so as to make Blanche feel completely comfortable, and so as not to let her think she had committed herself in any way, nor that he had read any intentions which she might wish to keep – and he was convinced she was doing this – he continued to talk in the same soothing, reasonable, impartial tone of the much travelled wise man of the world, and he even went so far as to make her feel – as he thought – quite secure that he was not prying on her secret thoughts by putting up a lukewarm defence for Protestantism, which, although he hated parsons, was by no means insincere; for, in his heart of hearts, he thought that whereas all churches were women's business, and not things that men need bother about, the Church of England was of all religious institutions the least harmful.

"I know our Church hasn't much to show either in its work or in the efficiency of its ministers, but that, to me, is its *great* advantage. Its teeth have been drawn. It may have less capacity for good, but that cuts both ways, and it has less capacity for harm as well, less influence, and, therefore, less possibilities of persecution, fanaticism, and all that… "

"But, papa, Americans don't seem to feel all that fear English people have of Catholics. When we were staying at Longford, Mrs Winslope was a Catholic and so were the Geaches, but the Ridgeways weren't, nor is Mr Winslope, and they all of them talked to me about religion in the most ordinary way; they seem to think our fear of Catholics almost funny – almost

171

comic – almost as funny as the way we regard money, which Mr Geach told me was a 'scream.' "

"Ah, but Americans have no history, you see, no traditions."

"But would it make you unhappy if I became a Roman Catholic?"

"Nothing that made you happy would make me unhappy, my dear child, and I know that if you became a Roman Catholic you would do so for good reasons and you would be a *good* one. It's absurd to say there aren't good Catholics in the world. I have known plenty. I won't even say I'd rather you didn't. All I would say is this: don't do it unless you feel you *must*. If you feel you must, well and good, and nobody will understand it better than I do, but I think unless one feels one can't do otherwise, it's better to remain in the religion in which one has been born and brought up. Of course it's tempting to think one has shelved responsibility once and for all, and that one can begin again with a clean slate."

"But Guido and my mother-in-law say that all that is nonsense, and that, so far from abandoning responsibility, Catholics are the only people who know what moral responsibility means."

"Yes, yes. Does the Abbé discuss these things with you?"

"The only things the Abbé discusses with me are bees, and abstruse questions of botany and Early Church History. He has written about fifteen books on the Early Church, but I am too ignorant for him to discuss that with me. I don't think the Abbé would ever bother to make converts. He seems to think that we are in one rut, and so firmly embedded in it that we can't get out…that we're not like the heathen or pagans, or even Jews, liable to conversion, but that we are in a rut which we can't get out of because we think that *they* are in the rut, and that our rut is the middle of the road; it is not like people who have never heard of the road; it's the dispute as to which is the road, the main road, the old, straight road – the only road – that being so, he thinks we are right according to our lights, and that if we act up to our lights we will go to heaven. That's what he thinks, as far as I can make out, when I have talked to him about such things, but it has always been *I* who have talked to him, and never he who has talked to me. He is so logical, and it all seems so easy when he answers a question – too easy for me."

"Yes, they are logical, certainly – too logical sometimes. And then, the French put things so well – so clearly. They are not afraid of platitude."

Henry Clifford gently let the conversation diverge into other channels. He was no longer so sure of his ground. Blanche had perhaps gone further than he knew, and he thought it would be wiser to say nothing more. By saying too much he might urge her in the wrong direction; by saying too little he might hurt her feelings. It was safest to say nothing.

This conversation led Blanche to think over the matter.

First of all, she read the book which her aunt sent her. She opened the book and came upon this sentence: "At once then it is plain that a Roman Catholic is *less* likely than an English Churchman to know God's Will and Word, so far as they are set down in the Bible." That one sentence was in a sense enough for her. It caused her to make up her mind on the nature of the book. On the one hand, she had too great an experience of people who held this kind of view in England, and living abroad had thrown up this particular form of insularity in bold relief. On the other hand, her father's influence had from earliest youth tended to make her aware of this insularity, and not only to condemn it, but to hold it up to ridicule, to eschew it utterly.

She continued to read the book, but she alighted on nothing that she thought convincing. It seemed to consist of a series of disconnected assertions based on the views of one highly prejudiced and not extremely well-informed parson. He complained of want of certainty in the dogmas of the Roman Church, and if complaints of this nature were well founded, other complaints she had frequently heard made in other quarters or seen in books could not be true. The complaints contradicted one another.

Again, she could not help feeling that in demolishing the claims of Rome, the primacy of St Peter, the authority of the Pope, etc., the Anglican Church, as thus expounded, was questioning the validity of her own orders, cutting down the branch on which she was sitting herself, and sapping her own foundations. In fact, the book led Blanche to the conclusion that, if the claims of Rome were false, the claims of all the other separated Churches must be *more* false...but was the claim, the unique claim, of Rome false? For the first time in her life she began to think it might be true. If it were true, what a difference it would make! What would all the rest matter?

It was not, she was now convinced, a question of accepting this doctrine or that practice, but of believing or disbelieving in the Church's claim to authority. If the Church is of divine origin, and teaches with divine authority – if she is, in fact, the representative of the divine on earth – well, then, the rest would be simple...

It was in the middle of September; Henry Clifford had gone back to London, and Guido suddenly informed Blanche, in a manner which had the outward form of consulting her opinion, but which in reality was the notification of a decision that had been irrevocably taken, that he thought of staying in London until the end of November. He had heard of a nice little house in Hill Street belonging to a friend of his mother's, which was to let. It would he a change for her. Teresa and Mario would have to go back to Italy, but he thought he could persuade his mother to stay on.

That meant, thought Blanche, that she had decided to stay on. Blanche thought that Mrs Winslope must be at the bottom of this plan. She accepted it with seeming readiness. Indeed, she would have preferred London to Rome, but London with her mother-in-law in the house, in a small London house, was more like Rome than Rome. She realised that the plan had been

174

made; the matter was settled, and she merely said to Guido: "When shall we move?"

"Whenever you like – of course, it depends on you. If you think it is a good plan, we shall be able to get the house at the end of the month."

"I think it would be an excellent plan," said Blanche, and she felt the iron enter her soul more sharply than ever before.

Blanche went to bed early that night. She said she had a headache, but it was heartache from which she was suffering. She could not sleep; she was too sad for tears; she was conscious only of infinite blackness – around her, beneath her, and above her.

"I cannot go on living like this," she said to herself. "I am too unhappy."

And then, like many unhappy people, she turned for consolation to that text-book of sorrow, the *Imitation*. "But neither this nor anything else can be of any comfort or help to me," she thought, "for I am utterly abandoned. I can't even pray, I can't even cry – my heart is dry, my soul is shrivelled – it is like a husk, and I feel that God is farther from me than thought can imagine, and that I am alone in nothingness, the darkness, and the cold...outside in the cold." She shivered and shuddered.

She opened the book at random, and came upon this passage: "Believe in Me and put thy trust in My mercy. When thou thinkest that thou art far from Me, I am often nearest to thee. When thou judgest that almost all is lost, then oftentimes a great reward of thy desert is at hand." And again, a little farther on, she read: "Think not thyself wholly forsaken, although for a time I have sent thee some tribulation or withdrawn from thee the comfort thou desirest; for this is the way to the Kingdom of Heaven."

She felt as if a voice were speaking to her, personally and directly – a voice that she knew, but yet something more than a voice, although soundless, and at the end of the darkness there was a glimmer of light; she felt as if between her and the

175

abyss one tiny drop of shining dew had fallen and had gradually become magnified and immense, and expanded into a bridge, a bridge over the gulf; all of a sudden she felt safe and secure, and she heard the voice of Truth speaking within her without noise of words.

She remained awake, happily awake, till four, and then she fell into a dreamless sleep. When she woke up the next morning she felt as if she had returned from a long journey or had recovered from a protracted illness, weeks and weeks of devastating fever.

And then she said to herself: "What ought I to do next? Ought I to become a Catholic or ought I to remain in the Church I was brought up in? Isn't it presumptuous of me to want to change?" And at once a host of difficulties and drawbacks presented themselves to her mind. How would she explain it to her aunts? What line would her mother-in-law take? Wouldn't the Abbé be always interfering with her? Wouldn't it be like living in a school under the eye of a schoolmaster? Goodness knows, she had little enough liberty already. Why, after all, should she take any step at all? She could go to Catholic churches, if she preferred them. She could have all the advantages of them without any of the disadvantages. She need not tell a soul she thought the Catholic religion true. Was it true? And if true, why should it be the only true religion? She belonged, after all, to a branch of the Church...they believed the same things in essentials...they repeated the same Creed in church every Sunday... "I believe in one Holy Catholic and Apostolic Church." But when Aunt Harriet and Aunt Cecilia said those words, did they mean the same thing? No; they didn't; whereas Teresa, the Abbé, Guido, her mother-in-law, Valesky, her Aunt Cornelia did mean, had meant, the same thing when they said it.

Guido and her mother-in-law and Mario had all gone up to London. The Abbé had gone to France. It was one of those days towards the end of September which are in a way more beautiful than the most beautiful summer days. The leaves have not yet fallen from the trees; there has been as yet no frost to nip or blight the roses on the wall – the *Gloire de Dijon* and the *Rosa Devoniensis*. But enchanting gossamer threads hang from leaf to leaf; the acrobatic spider weaves her fantastically ingenious web and waits for her prey.

Blanche was left alone in the house with Teresa. She was fond of Teresa, although she had never as yet exchanged one confidence with her. They were both of them standing in the verandah, looking out on to the too-closely shaven lawn. Guido and the others had just left for the station. There was a feeling of utter peace in the air.

"It's nice of you to stay with me," said Blanche.

"I love staying with you, *Cara*, but you look, oh! so tired today."

It was true: possibly the night was the last straw after months of wear and tear – the last drop. Blanche had aged in the night; she looked ten years older. The bloom of her beauty seemed to have gone; on the other hand, there was a new light in her eyes.

Blanche sat down in a basket-chair.

"Yes," she said; "I do feel a little bit tired."

Teresa sat down in the chair next to hers.

How still it was! How mellow! And yet, in the beauty and the stillness of the full-foliaged trees, of the overripe fruits on the distant wall, of the golden haze and the cloudless blue sky; in the sparkling dew on the grass – the heavy dew that is the precursor of the first frost; in the gleaming threads of the gossamer on the creepers and the full-blown roses, which one touch of frost, one felt, must dishevel and irretrievably ruin…there was a presage of doom, and more than a hint of advancing winter.

"I know," said Teresa gently; "life is so difficult, isn't it? And you, *Cara*, are so brave."

The sentiment and especially the epithet were so unexpected, so startling to Blanche, that she broke down altogether and she cried, she cried her heart out. It was the first time she had been able to cry for months. She had forgotten how to. And Teresa cried; they both cried together. After a little while, when the passion of tears had spent itself, Blanche said to Teresa:

"I want you to take me to your church one morning early, one morning when... "

"When we can go by ourselves," said Teresa. "Of course I will."

"I should like to be a Catholic, only... "

"I know. But you know, *Cara, they* don't matter...they none of them matter; nothing matters...it is bigger than all that... "

"Yes, I'm sure – only – "

Blanche was amazed at Teresa's understanding, and she realised now, for the first time, fully to what an extent Teresa must have been crushed by her mother. It was as if a steam-roller had passed over her soul.

She told her of her doubts and fears and half-formed, unfledged aspirations and desires...she didn't say definitely that she wanted to become a Catholic, but merely that, having for a long time felt that all belief was out of the question for her, that her soul was as arid as a desert, her heart as hard as a rock, she now no longer felt that, and she wondered whether this would lead to anything else; ought she to take another step?

"You must do nothing in a hurry," said Teresa, "and nothing unless you feel you *can't* help it. From what you tell me, I am sure that God has given you *Grace*, and it won't remain at that. Do not worry. Read the *Imitation*."

Guido and his mother returned later on in the day, and the next days were taken up with making arrangements for the new London house. Guido wanted Blanche to come up and see it, but Blanche, delighted to leave the matter in her mother-in-law's hands, pleaded headaches and fatigue, and said that she would far rather that his mother did everything; she understood those things so much better than she did; and it would be a surprise...she had found the right word...a surprise; that was just the word that Guido needed, and he went on arranging the house with the direct aid of his mother, and the indirect aid of Mrs Winslope, through whom he had got the house.

As the house was furnished, there was no question of doing much, but, in spite of that, Princess Julia managed to effect a transformation in a short time and in a confined space.

At last the house, was ready. Guido suggested that he and his mother should go up and spend the night in it and leave Mario and Blanche and Teresa to come up the next day. Teresa and Mario were only going to spend the day in London, as there was no room in the house for them, and Mario wanted to get back to Rome.

Blanche and Teresa spent their last day at Wood Norton. Teresa took Blanche the next morning to early Mass in the little tin tabernacle in the village.

Blanche had never been to Low Mass before in her life. It was only since she married that she had known such a thing existed. Her Aunt Harriet, in fact, had often informed her that Catholics were not allowed to receive Holy Communion at Mass.

It was a divinely still morning. There was a touch of cold in the morning air, and the first frost – a slight one – had left white traces on the grass.

But the stillness of nature, great as it was, was less great, so Blanche thought, than the inexpressible stillness inside that little, unpretentious church with its paper flowers and tinsel ornaments, while, with swift ritual, businesslike gestures, blessed murmur and tinkling bell, the divine Drama proceeded and was played to a satisfying end; and greatest of all was the stillness on the faces of those – a worn and bent old woman of the village, a middle-aged man who looked like a shopman, and a young woman (a servant, Blanche thought) – who had received Holy Communion.

# CHAPTER XVI

Blanche found life in London in October more pleasant than she expected. First of all, she saw her father, but only at intervals and for brief spaces of time, as he was engaged to several country houses for the shooting. They were almost neighbours. But her whole life was now changed by the new interest that lay at the back of it. Not that she thought of it constantly at first. She decided to put the matter away from her for the present, and not even to enter a Roman Catholic church, but to give her own church a chance; to see whether she could not remain where she was, and go to any church she fancied, when and where she felt inclined, thereby retaining her independence. But, do what she would, the thought was ever there, and kept on cropping up, and every little incident seemed to conspire to bring back her thoughts to one object and to keep them in one channel.

She went on Sundays to St Paul's Cathedral and to Westminster Abbey. "After all," she said to herself, "what could be more dignified and more impressive than this?" And yet to her there was something wanting. "I can feel patriotic here," she thought to herself, "but not *religious* – that is to say, not more religious than I feel anywhere else."

She went to the High Churches, to St Olaf's, that her Aunt Cecilia had recommended to her, and to another church,

181

St Anselm's (also recommended by her aunt), where the service seemed to be outwardly indistinguishable from a Roman Catholic service. And yet Blanche felt there was a profound unreality about the whole thing; not that she doubted the sincerity either of the ministers or of the congregation. She felt, however, that it was all wrong, and it was while sitting in this dim High Church, during a sung "Mass," where on the altar six candles were burning and where the air was thick with the smell of incense, that she realised that she did not feel face to face with *reality* here; not only that, but she knew where she had felt reality, and that was when in the dark side street she had witnessed the procession of the Viaticum being taken to the sick man, the kneeling crowd, the lamps, the boy ringing the bell...

"That was real; this isn't," she said. Then a voice whispered, "Isn't that your love of the foreign, the picturesque, the Roman, the *pagan* practically, that is leading you astray and blinding you?"

"No," she answered; "I felt the same thing, and more strongly still, in the tin tabernacle at Wood Norton. I felt there that I might be in the Catacombs, and yet what could be less picturesque? A tiny church, pitch-pine benches, cheap Stations of the Cross, the only music a squeaky harmonium and two school-girls' voices, and, for stained glass, transparent coloured paper, statuettes of Our Lady and St Joseph that were certainly anything but artistic...nothing to delight the eye...and yet, how real"...and in a flash a series of pictures passed before Blanche's eyes. She heard once more the halberds of the Papal Guard clash with one single thunderous rap on the marble pavement of St Peter's, as the soldiers with perfect precision knelt on one knee at the Elevation of the Host, and then the silver trumpets singing in the Dome...that and the tin tabernacle at Wood Norton were one and the same, and why? The pictures in her mind and the echoes in her memory blended and melted like dissolving views till they left one picture. And that was the inscription round the Dome of St Peter's. She remembered looking up at that while one of the great ceremonies of the Church was being carried out with every form of pomp and splendour, in the old Papal days soon after she was married, and she remembered thinking: "It is so magnificent, the assertion is so uncompromising, and the expression of it so glorious and so solid, and has lasted so long, that it ought to be true – even if it *isn't*...and yet in those days," she said to herself, "I used to add, 'What a pity it is that they should be mistaken!' but now I understand that it is *we* who are blind to a great solid real fact, not *they* who are mistaken. The scales have fallen from my eyes.

"I may put off the hour, but I *know* now that whatever happens to me, if I am honest with myself, I shall have to be a Catholic some day, whatever drawbacks it may entail, however inconvenient it may be; but what a miserable creature I am to talk of drawbacks and inconveniences face to face with such a privilege, so superhuman an adventure!

"I may put it off, but an invisible rope is pulling me surely to my destination."

Thus it was that at St Anselm's, her Aunt Cecilia's favourite church, Blanche found her road to Damascus. But even now she took no further step. She knew no one in the world whom she could talk with about it. Teresa had gone. She did not want to tell Guido till she had definitely made up her mind.

She dreaded telling her mother-in-law. It would seem to tighten their relations. She knew no priest here; the only priest she knew well was at Rome – she had never yet talked of religion with him, and she couldn't begin to by letter. She dared not go to Farm Street Church for fear of meeting her mother-in-law, who went there often and at odd times. And yet she wanted to take the step. She knew now it was irrevocable; the question was how and when?

These few moments in an Anglican High Church constituted the most momentous experience of her life, and she realised this and smiled when she thought how little anybody knew what had happened to her, and how the great experiences of life happen at odd moments and in unexpected ways, and are completely unguessed at by the outside world…

A few days later she was walking through Leicester Square. She wasn't thinking much of what she was doing, and she turned up a side street. She was thinking that Leicester Square was the only democratic square in London, just as the conclusion followed quite naturally, if unexpectedly – the Catholic Churches are the only churches that are Catholic, the only churches where the poor are allowed to feel at home.

She found herself at that moment opposite the French Church; she walked in. The church was empty and dark. It reminded her a little of Rome, although she could not have said why, but there was something vaguely familiar to her in the atmosphere, especially when from a dark corner a woman dressed in black emerged from a Confessional at the end of the aisle and went to put up a candle in the chapel of Our Lady, beneath her image. Blanche sat down at the end of a bench in the side aisle. She felt extraordinarily peaceful. She did not kneel, but she remained seated, looking towards the altar. On her right was an altar and an image of Our Lady. She did not know whether she had been there a long time or a short time, when a man walked into the church. She paid no particular attention to him; he seemed just an ordinary well-dressed man, but presently she noticed that he seemed to be slightly disconcerted, not at his ease, as if what he had found was not what he had expected… He walked up the side aisle, forwards a few steps, then backwards, then forwards again. In the meantime the priest had left the Confessional at the east end of the side aisle and walked back towards the door. As he passed Blanche, who was sitting at the end of the bench, he met the newcomer. The latter looked at him inquiringly, and hesitated. The priest asked him in French whether he wanted anything.

The newcomer mumbled something in French which Blanche could not hear, but she caught the word "*Non.*"

"*Vous êtes Catholique?*" the priest said distinctly.

"*Non,*" the stranger said, in a slightly defiant tone of voice; "*mais je suis Chrétien.*"

"*C'est la même chose,*" said the priest, and then, with a slight bow, he walked past Blanche down the aisle and disappeared up a little spiral staircase that led to another floor.

Presently the newcomer gave a final look round the church and then left it.

This stray remark which Blanche had overheard in this fashion had the effect of a pistol-shot on her.

"Yes," she thought, "that is it – '*C'est la même chose.*' Christianity is Catholic, and all Christians *are* Catholics, whether they know it or not – although many never find it out."

It was one of those casual remarks that sometimes have the effect of a flash of lightning. All other Christian people, she thought, may be branches or leaves, living, or dead, but there can only be *one tree.* But, she reasoned, if I think this – and I do – *I* can't remain where I am; otherwise *I shall be a dead twig.*

"Others can be separated and live because *they are unconscious of the separation,* but I am conscious of it, and so there is not a moment to lose."

That day at luncheon her mother-in-law said she was going out driving with old Lady Hurstmonceux, who was the head of one of the most prominent Catholic families in London. Blanche felt that she could go anywhere safely. She said she had some shopping to do, which was true, but she had also something else to do. She drove to the Brompton Oratory and, sending in her card, she asked to see a priest. She did not mind who it was.

She was shown into a little waiting-room on the ground floor in which there was an Arundel Print. Presently a tall man arrived. He was between thirty and forty.

"He looks more like a soldier than priest," thought Blanche.

He was upright, dark, and had penetrating eyes.

Blanche went straight to the matter.

"I want to be a Catholic," she said.

He looked at her with tenderness, with a kind of awestruck respect, she thought, and he said gravely and gently:

"God bless you, my child," and then he added, "What brought you to it?"

Blanche's eyes filled with tears. "I really don't know. It came gradually – "

She told him who she was and he told her his name – Father Adrian Byrne.

He asked whether she had told her husband.

"I don't want to tell him till I have been actually received – not until it is a *fait accompli*."

She felt Father Byrne was surprised.

"It will be a great surprise to him" – Blanche knew she was putting this rather lamely. "Of course if he had been a Protestant I should have told him, but as he's a Catholic he is sure to be pleased. He has no idea I am thinking of it, and I don't want him to think he has influenced me."

"But he would only be too proud of that."

"Yes; but I don't want my Protestant relations to think that I have been 'got hold of,' forced into it by *his* relations – by his mother and his sister, for instance. His mother lives with us."

"She is an Englishwoman, isn't she? Let me think – a daughter of Lord Pevensey?"

"Yes. In Rome she lives on the floor above us, and now in London she is staying with us."

Father Byrne pondered a little. He understood the situation.

"I think I should tell them, all the same," he said gently. "You will find they will understand – "

"I couldn't really…don't ask me – not till it's done. I know it's foolish… I don't want to tell anybody about it, even after it *is* done, till I get back to Rome. Is that possible? I don't go back till the end of next month."

"Quite possible, only, if you are received into the Church before you go back, you would have to go to Mass on Sundays and to abstain on Fridays – if your health can stand it."

"I shall tell Guido and my mother-in-law directly it is done, of course – but not the rest of the world... You see, I have a lot of relations...they hold strong views...some of them do...on Church matters... I'm sure you think I'm a miserable coward, but my life is complicated."

"And your father?"

"Oh, papa! He won't mind; he's already made up his mind that it will happen: he made up his mind before I had thought of it."

Father Byrne arranged that Blanche should come to him for instruction. She paid these visits to the Oratory like a thief in the night.

"I am a kind of female Nicodemus," she said to Father Byrne, laughing.

The October days passed swiftly for Blanche. She enjoyed her London life now. They saw few people. Her father was away. Guido saw Mrs Winslope constantly, and she and her husband sometimes came to dinner. Princess Julia sometimes invited a friend of hers. She led her own life in London, where she seemed to have many interests.

Blanche went to see Father Byrne three times a week. She was anxious to be received, she said, as soon as possible.

"You are taking the Kingdom of Heaven by storm," he said, laughing.

"I want to be received here and not abroad," she said. "I know I am impatient, exacting, and unreasonable."

"No, no, no; that's all to the good."

He was surprised to find she had read few books about religious questions. She had reached her conclusions from life and not from literature.

It was on a Wednesday in the fourth week of November that she made her General Confession in Father Byrne's room in the Church of the Oratory.

It was after she had done this and received Absolution that Blanche felt what it meant to be a Catholic and how and why it was different from anything else – a difference of kind and not of degree. It was the act of bowing the head, of making an act of contrition, and receiving the Sacrament of Penance that made her feel she was bowing the head under the low and humble porch that opened on to spaces of infinite freedom.

"And this," she thought to herself, "is what people call surrendering their responsibility to a priest!"

She promised Father Byrne to tell Guido at once. Her father, as it happened, was coming to dinner. He had just come back from a ten-days' stay in the country for the shooting in the west of England, so as to see Blanche and say goodbye to her before she left England.

Blanche was dressed early, and she waylaid Guido on their way down to dinner and told him that she had been received into the Church that day.

"Give me an opportunity of telling papa after dinner," she said, "and you tell your mother."

Guido seemed to be thunderstruck, but he had no time to express his surprise, or, indeed, to say a word, for at that moment Henry Clifford was announced.

After dinner, Guido took his mother into the back drawing-room where the card-table and the patience cards were ready, and he shut the door, and there he communicated the news to his mother, while Blanche told her father.

Henry Clifford did not raise an eyelash in surprise.

"I knew it must come," he said, "and under the circumstances I honestly think, my darling child, that it is the best thing that you could have done... Of course you know I'm not a Churchman, and you know what I feel about those things... " (Blanche didn't quite) "...but, in spite of that, I can't help feeling a little bit sorry that there should be any even superficial and formal division between us; I mean, I'm sorry we shall be *not* going to the same Church, or that if I suddenly felt I wanted to go to church I couldn't see *you* there too."

"Perhaps you'll come to mine," said Blanche.

"No, darling; I'm too old to change, and I must get on as I am. I'm afraid it all means little to me, but that's no reason why it shouldn't mean a great deal to other people; and, in fact, I know it does, and I'm sure it does to you, and all I can say is that I hope with all my heart it will make you happy."

"I'm afraid Aunt Cecilia will be annoyed."

"That can't be helped," said Henry. "I've no patience with the ritualists."

It was a relief to Henry Clifford; firstly, he hoped it was an indication that there might be hope of another child being born; and, secondly, it salved his conscience a little; he thought that some kind of amends was being made for the unhappiness he had caused Blanche in encouraging the marriage.

When her father left, Princess Julia was sympathetic, affable, and interested.

"I have never been more surprised," she said; "although I sometimes hoped and, of course, *always* prayed it might happen."

They talked of Father Byrne. Princess Julia knew him a little and liked him.

"A charming man," she said – "such a gentleman."

The next morning early Blanche and Guido went to Mass at Farm Street, and Blanche made her first Holy Communion in a Catholic Church. Her mother-in-law was following a treatment and not allowed to get up early. When Blanche had talked about this with Father Byrne, he had said to her:

"Of course you can go to Mass at Farm Street and make your First Communion there," and she had said, "I would rather not go to Farm Street; I don't like it. I would rather go somewhere else."

"You will be surprised to find how little you will mind what church you go to soon. You will find it doesn't matter."

Now Blanche realised that this was true. She had at Farm Street on that November morning the same sense of being in the Catacombs, of witnessing something infinitely old and completely real, as she had experienced in the little tin tabernacle at Wood Norton; the same feeling that she had experienced more dimly in the side Street at Rome that evening when she had seen the procession of the Viaticum to the sick man. Now she felt the bell was ringing for her soul, and that she was being welcomed to a place of refreshment, light, and peace, and to one of the many mansions of the House not made with hands.

"And this," she thought to herself again, "is what people call 'sinning against the light!' 'Selling their soul!' If they only knew!" The beauty of that First Mass she went to as a Catholic was to shine before her like a lamp for the rest of her life. She realised how impossible it was to explain this to people on the other side of the door. If you spoke of the *beauty* of Mass they thought you meant architecture, stained glass, candles, incense, music, or flowers. It was not aesthetic beauty; it was the satisfaction of the soul in the presence of reality – the only reality; the eternal, the everlasting, the supernatural...

Blanche, Guido, and the Princess left London on the last day of November, and they stopped two nights in Paris and then travelled to Florence. Just before they left London they attended Adrian Tyne's wedding. He was married at St Paul's, Knightsbridge, and both he and his bride seemed to be radiantly happy. Lady Mount-Stratton gave Blanche a handshake full of meaning, and whispered to her afterwards, in the house where the presents were shown and the wedding breakfast was being held – the wedding had been in the morning – "I am grateful to you, my dear Blanche, for this – without you it wouldn't have happened."

As Blanche watched Mr and Mrs Adrian Tyne drive away in a brougham under a shower of rice from Upper Brook Street to the station, she felt that a little piece of her life had slipped away; just as in a child's kaleidoscope a slight shake varies the pattern, and one little bit of glass falls away from the main design never to come back in exactly the same place. In this case, the piece of glass was Adrian Tyne. Blanche felt that she was turning over a new leaf of life, and she made many new resolutions.

She wrote to her aunts and informed them of her change of religion.

They both of them received the news with resignation. Aunt Harriet wrote as follows:

*"Tuesday.*

"MY DEAREST BLANCHE, – It was indeed *dear* of you to think of writing to your poor old aunt! Your letter coming as it did so soon after my visit to Wood Norton, where I had thought you still so *settled,* and when I wasn't expecting anything, was just a little bit of a surprise! I am sure you have meant to act for the best, and have acted for the best from your point of view, and that you are not to blame. If any one is to blame, it is your father, for having exposed you to such temptations and *snares,* but then, how could it be helped? Your poor dear mother always said that Henry was so *rash* and apt to be taken in by *foreigners.* However, there it is, and it can't be helped, and, although I can't help feeling a little grieved that you should have been taken away from us, it cannot, of course, make any *breach* between us, and I shall always feel what I have felt for you. One can't help feeling thankful that your dear mother was spared such a trial. But, after all, we must always remember that all trials are sent us for our *good.* Every cloud has a silver lining, and the darkest hour is that before the dawn, and that is why

I feel that *some day all* those who are mistaken and who have been led astray will be led back to the true fold once more.

"The children send their best love. We have been having wretched weather and envying you in your beautiful hot Rome! I send you my very warmest and dearest love, and, although I can't help feeling rather sad, it will never make any difference to my deep love and affection. – Your affectionate

"AUNT HARRIET."

Aunt Cecilia wrote, too:

"*November* 10, 187 – .

"MY DEAREST BLANCHE, – It was kind of you to write to me so *promptly.* I need hardly say that after my visit to you at Wood Norton your letter was not a *surprise.* Although I did not, I confess, think that anything would happen so *soon,* I was afraid it would be only a question of time before you went over. It would have been unreasonable to expect you to *resist,* when one considered the pressure that was being brought to bear on you, and all the circumstances. You know my views. I don't blame you, my dearest Blanche, in any way, but I do blame all those who had anything to do with your upbringing for not giving you a sound *Catholic* education. However, I don't wish to dwell on the *dark* side of the question. What is done is done, and it's no good crying over spilt milk. But there is a brighter side, too – a side of *hope.* I pray for the day when Rome may see the folly of many of her claims and be persuaded to listen to the voice of *good sense* and *Truth* and to renounce those which are indefensible, and then I, for one, shall be the first to work with all my heart for *reunion*; and, should that happy day come, we should all belong to one fold once more under One Shepherd. May we all live to see that day! If you had been properly educated in Church matters and brought up as a Catholic – your influence on Guido might have been instrumental in bringing this about, and, who knows, in unsealing the eyes of those who are now blind?

"Of course, my dearest Blanche, I shall never cease to be fond of you, or be in any way *less* fond of you, however *mistaken* I may think you to be. But it is more a case of being *misled* than mistaken, and I do not think you are in any way to blame.

"Mary and Jane send you their very best love. I told them the news. Please remember me to Guido and to Princess Julia. – Your affectionate aunt,

"CECILIA."

# CHAPTER XVII

Guido and Blanche stayed only a night in Florence. Guido was in a hurry to get back to the Palazzo Fabrini. By this time everybody had heard of Blanche's change of religion, and she no longer had any desire to conceal it. The Italians took it as a matter of course; the English Catholics applauded; the English non-Catholics showed no surprise.

Blanche herself soon felt that she had been a Catholic all her life. She took it as a matter of course. Nor was she worried by people discussing it with her. They all took it for granted, from the Pope – she was given a special audience – down to the servants at the Palazzo Fabrini.

She had not been long in Rome when one day, as she was walking towards St Peter's, she met Francis Bretherton. He had arrived, he told her, for the winter, and was working in the Vatican. He had taken a small apartment.

"You must come and see us," she said.

"I don't go out much – not at all, in fact."

"You don't know many people?"

"Hardly any one; a few painters, a German professor, and Madame Svensen, the wife of the Swedish archaeologist."

"You must meet some friends of mine called Olenev. They are just the kind of people you would like."

"I'm not much use in society."

"They are not people you would mind...they are comfortable, easy people, and great fun...musical, and fond of books."

"How shall I meet them?"

"I will manage that." Blanche did not ask him to her house because she felt she must be careful with Guido and her mother-in-law. She wrote down Francis Bretherton's address.

"They know Madame Svensen," were her parting words.

She saw the Olenevs that evening and told them about Bretherton, and they asked Madame Svensen to introduce him to them. In a week's time the meeting was effected, and Bretherton soon became a friend of the Olenevs and a regular visitor at their house. Blanche asked him to one of her Monday evenings, at which he put in a brief appearance, but she met him at the Olenevs' often, and she began to venture in other, wider artistic circles, where she met him too. There was Aldini, the sculptor, who received in his studio, and Madame de Laurens, at whose salon one met the whole of artistic Rome, and Princess Baltzoff, who liked literary people. Blanche began to go to all these houses. She had known these hostesses before just a little, but she had not often attended their entertainments. But now she knew she would meet, or might meet, Bretherton there, she began to go. For in Bretherton, for the first time in her life, she saw the making of a possible friend, some one she could be friends with and who would not make love to her, who was aloof and indifferent and detached, and who lived in a world of his own. She cherished this idea as a dream, as a hidden treat, as a castle in Spain, for so far she had hardly talked to him at all, although she had met him several times, and, beyond asking him to her evenings, she had not invited him to the Palazzo Fabrini. She was guarding her treat jealously and prudently, like a dog who, when he sees his dinner being brought in, is so afraid, by any premature manifestation of joy, of losing it, that when it is first put before him pretends not to want it, and looks away, indifferent and even disdainful, and only when he feels quite sure that it cannot be taken away, begins to devour and gulp.

Blanche, knowing how easily things upset and annoyed Guido, how unaccountable were his likes and dislikes, resolved to say nothing in particular about Bretherton, but to treat his existence as a matter of course. But although they met on several occasions, Blanche never had an opportunity of talking to him. Then, one afternoon, they met by accident at the Protestant Cemetery. He began to talk to her, not as if he were beginning a conversation, but as if they were going on with one which had been interrupted on some other occasion.

They talked a little of Shelley and Keats. Bretherton did not care for either of them. He thought Shelley too vague and thin, and Keats too luscious, like treacle.

"I like things in black and white," he said – "outlines, friezes – line better than colour."

"You are austere…and severe. I couldn't live up to a standard like that. I think I am sentimental. I like fairy-tales! – Hans Andersen, Grimm, Undine, and *easy* poetry, Heinrich Heine and Herrick and 'The Ancient Mariner' – things that are homely and cosy and familiar. It is something you meet with quite unexpectedly sometimes. Milton's *L'Allegro* seems to me cosy, for instance, or is it because I learnt that by heart when I was a child?"

"No, I think I know what you mean – the quality of German songs – Schubert, for instance."

"Oh, Schubert!" said Blanche, thinking of that summer evening at the Rodens', when Waller sang the "Ständchen." "You are a musician, aren't you?"

"I think," said Bretherton, "that music is the greatest of the arts. It can *say* more. I don't know much about it, but I know enough to know that."

"And yet," said Blanche, "you so often find cultivated and artistic people who are quite unmusical. My mother-in-law, for instance, appreciates art and literature, pictures, sculpture, paints well herself, and knows Dante and Tasso by heart and all the English poets…and yet music is pain to her. But my husband is musical – he is fond of Italian music, that is to say – and his sister plays the pianoforte beautifully."

"Do you play?"

"Oh, I have no accomplishments, and, if I had, I shouldn't have time!"

"You do too much."

"Do I look very old and tired?" asked Blanche.

"Not old!"

"You may just as well be honest, because even if you are not, other people are. Maria, Guido's old nurse, told me, with that complete frankness of the poor and that great naturalness of Italians, when I arrived this time, that I was so changed she hardly recognised me."

Bretherton laughed. "You don't look a month older," he said. "But you do look as if you were recovering from a severe illness."

"So I am," she said. "I am convalescent and I shall soon be quite well."

Blanche looked at her watch. "I promised to be home at five punctually. I am expecting all sorts of people. We will meet again soon." She smiled at him and went. But she made no appointment and gave him no invitation.

Francis Bretherton stayed behind and pondered. She was un-English, he thought – more like an Italian – she had the simplicity of an Italian. Did that come from living in Italy? Yes; she looked different from when he had last seen her at the Winslopes', but even then she had looked different from what he remembered her to be when he had first caught sight of her one day in the Capitol. Then she had been something softly radiant and fresh, like a branch of white blossom…now she was beautiful, but with the pale beauty of some one who has visited the shadows for too long.

He thought of her living in that immense, gaunt, and gloomy Palazzo Fabrini, presiding at those stiff evenings, accompanied always by that sallow-faced, melancholy-looking patrician, with his long features and his long hands.

What a life, he thought!…and she must still be so young, and some lines came into his head:

> "Why should only I
> Of all the other princes of the world
> Be cas'd up, like a holy relic? I have youth,
> And a little beauty."

That was it. She had youth and a little beauty. What wonders the poets effected by economy of phrase! he thought. That phrase, "a little beauty," gave a sharper, a more overwhelming impression of beauty – of rare and absolute beauty – than a thousand superlatives or than any array of sumptuous epithets.

He had heard she had recently changed her religion. That must, he thought, be the result and not the cause of any crisis she had gone through. He walked up and down the little cemetery and mused and wondered. She reminded him of some one – the only woman he had loved, and who was now dead. She had, he thought, the same insinuating grace, the same subtle aroma, the same absence of embarrassment.

"Am I falling in love again?" he said. But he smiled sadly to himself and wished it might be true. "But it's just as well," he added to himself, "that it is not true."

He went home to his books, and buried himself in his work, and no distracting image danced in his brain. He had been all through that; he had had the illness too badly to have it again. He had been through the long tunnel and come out the other side.

From time to time Blanche and Bretherton met, and every time they did so, they added a link to the invisible chain of intimacy that bound them. They generally met in a crowd – at the Olenevs' or at Madame Svensen's or at Princess Julia's. He had got to know Princess Julia. He had given up coming to Blanche's evenings. It was tacitly understood between them that this was an act better left undone. Blanche did not think of him much, and yet the glimpses she had of him, the snatches of talk with him, were a source of untold happiness to her. It was the first time for years – since her marriage, in fact – she had had a friend. Valesky would have been just such a friend, she thought, but then he would have spoilt it by making love to her... Adrian Tyne was, of course, impossible...but Francis – the more she saw of him, the more detached he became. The more, too, she saw him, the less intimately they talked, and the greater the intimacy became...it was as if they could communicate with each other without words.

They liked the same places and the same people. Blanche was fond of a little church called Santa Maria in Cosmedin, with its uneven floor and its pale, coloured marbles. Francis liked this church, and they met there more than once by accident. They were both fond of walking on the Janiculum. They both liked going to St Peter's in the early morning.

About religion they never exchanged a word, but Francis, Blanche knew, was not a Catholic. He was a pagan, she thought, of the Stoic school.

He would often spend his evening at the Olenevs', and if Blanche were there he would make no great effort to speak to her, but he would sit on a sofa at the other end of the room, next to one of the Olenev girls, while the others made music, and listen in silence, drinking in every note.

He was passionately fond of classical, and especially of chamber, music. The thin thread of sound that heralded the opening of a Beethoven Quartet, exquisitely played, was the greatest of all treats to him.

The Olenevs were devoted to him, and regarded him as the quaintest of quaint animals, and laughed at whatever he said. His quiet manner tickled them.

Matters went on like this till Christmas, and Blanche felt safe. She thought she had made a friend for life, and just the friend that she needed.

Gradually she began to see more of him. He dined once or twice with Princess Julia, but he did not pay her as much attention as she could have wished, and she pronounced a verdict that he was less intelligent than he seemed. He seldom came to the Palazzo Fabrini, and never unless he were asked.

Blanche asked him to one of their larger dinner-parties, but that was only natural, especially as she often asked a sprinkling of Roman *savants* to her house, and Francis knew most of these.

The Abbé liked him and pronounced him to be, for an Englishman, singularly well informed.

They spent Christmas in Rome, and on Christmas Eve, Blanche, Princess Julia, and Guido went to Midnight Mass at their Parish Church – a little church quite close to the Palazzo. The church was crowded, and Blanche was surprised to see Francis standing in the crowd. The next time she saw him at the Olenevs' she asked him whether he had enjoyed the service, and he said, "Yes; all those chants and sayings and the whole story that Saint Luke tells us is the softest cradle-song, as Renan well said, that has ever been sung to soothe poor ailing mortality. It is the loveliest of all fairy-tales and fables."

"Supposing it is true?"

"Pray that I may come to believe it is true," he said. "I should like to."

"I will."

Early in January the Olenevs gave a musical evening. Blanche and Guido were invited, but Guido told Blanche that the music at the Olenevs' bored him and that she must go by herself.

Blanche went, and enjoyed it immensely. Some Bohemian artists, who were passing through Rome, played a Quartet by Beethoven in B Flat; a world-famous *Liedersängerin* sang a cradle-song of Bach's, and a Russian pianist played the "Moonlight Sonata"; and then there was an interval when everybody drank tea. The second part of the programme consisted of a Saraband for the violin, a Quintet in A Major by Schubert, and two Schubert songs – "An die Freude" and "Die Forelle." Blanche sat next to Francis Bretherton, and she felt how he responded to the music with every fibre of his being. They talked little in between, but Blanche seemed, from that evening, to have got through her period of convalescence. The old radiance had come back to her eyes, the faint warmth, which was hardly colour, to her skin, the note of happiness to her laugh. She looked more beautiful than ever, and the music seemed to act on her like a charm. Everybody present noticed it, and Princess Olenev complimented her during the interval in the programme when the guests drank tea.

"We thought you were looking peaky when you first arrived, but now we have got back our *real* Blanche. Oh, my dear, you are a real *star*! *Une vraie étoile, n'est-ce-pas?*" she said, appealing to the group round them.

To Blanche's astonishment Guido arrived in the interval, in time to see her complimented, and he sat through the Saraband, the songs, including an encore ("Der Leiermann"), and the Quintet. When the concert was over, Princess Olenev went up to him and told him that she must congratulate him on Blanche's looks. "Never had she been so much *en beauté*. When she had first arrived from England everybody had thought she was looking so pulled down, but now Rome had evidently worked a miracle – a month, two months, in the sun and she was a transformed being. Never had she looked so well."

Guido smiled wanly.

He drove home with Blanche. She was still sparkling with excitement. Rarely had she enjoyed an evening so much. She felt she had looked well, and she had enjoyed the praise she had received and which she knew she had deserved.

But more than anything she had enjoyed sharing the music with Francis Bretherton: all that he had said, still more all that he had left unsaid. For the first time since her marriage she had felt happy at Rome, had felt that life was worth living and full of possibilities, that the future was a thing you could actually look forward to with happy expectation. She felt what she looked – a transformed being.

"There is one thing I want to say to you, Blanche," said Guido in a toneless voice.

Blanche suddenly felt cold with apprehension, cold with the fear of some nameless possibility.

"Yes, Guido?"

"I think it is a mistake for you to see so much of that Mr Bretherton."

There was a silence. Blanche felt that she was blushing, and she was glad of the darkness of the carriage. She felt her life was tumbling about her like a pack of cards. She felt exactly as a schoolboy feels who has, in company with the other boys, devised some treat, some amusing and harmless occupation, some craze, some adventure that has hitherto escaped the notice of the masters and then is suddenly discovered and promptly forbidden.

The boys on such occasions are resigned enough. They felt the whole time it was too good to last.

"I hardly ever see him," she said at last. "He never comes to our house. I only meet him at that kind of party."

"That's just it."

Was Guido suspicious, she wondered? Did he think that this publicity, these meetings in broad daylight, in public, were intentional and deliberate and hid something else?

Guido seemed to read her thoughts.

"Rome isn't London," he said. "Some things are impossible here. That is one. People understand things so differently here."

"But surely they wouldn't think – "

"Yes; that is just what they would think."

"What do you want me to do?"

"To give him up – not to see anything of him."

"I see nothing of him at all as it is; you can't expect me to say to him suddenly, 'You are not to meet me anywhere.' I can't help meeting him – Rome is so tiny."

"You know what I want you to do, and how to do it. Any woman can always do what I want you to do, and any woman knows exactly how to do it. You say you never see him. You know quite well your life, your whole mode of life, has quite changed since we came back this time. You see quite different people...people like the Svensens and all those musicians and archaeologists... *La Haute Bohème*... You never went near them before."

"Madame Svensen is a great friend of the Olenevs – I have always known her."

"There are others. I don't know all their names – Aldini – "

"But you don't call Mr Bretherton a Bohemian...and that's not what you mind."

"No; that's not what I mind."

"You mind my having friends."

"Not friends – that friend."

"You... " She stopped.

"Well?"

"Nothing; only I was going to say that it seems rather unfair and unnecessary that I should have to turn my life into a desert."

"I don't want you to turn your life into a desert. I object to *that* oasis."

"It is not as if he were like... "

"That is exactly why I object. I object to such friendships. That is why I want you to stop it *now* before it has gone further... I would rather you had a lover and hid it from me than an open friendship of this kind. If you had a lover and concealed it, I should either not find it out and be easy in my

203

mind, or find it out and kill your lover, and be still easier in my mind."

"I don't believe it."

"I know, you see, you never would have a lover."

"Take care, Guido – be careful. People sometimes do such unexpected things."

"People! But you are not *people*; you forget who you are. You are" – he smiled a little bitterly – "my wife… You are…apart, separate; and the world must and shall know it and feel it; and that is why I don't choose you to have such a 'friendship' tagged on to your name."

He spoke with icy vehemence, so much so that Blanche wondered. He was certainly in earnest, but she did not understand him.

"I suppose," she thought, "I never have understood him."

Again he expressed her unspoken thoughts.

"You don't understand," he said, with a slightly bitter laugh. "Don't you see? Can't you understand? No, you can't. All I ask is for you to believe me. But what's the use? Understand or not, as you like, I won't have it. It" – he rapped out the words slowly and they fell like icicles – "must stop."

They had arrived at the house, and they walked slowly up the gloomy staircase. It was dark, save for the light of a candle in the hall.

Guido lit two candles and gave one to Blanche ceremoniously. She felt like a prisoner being brought back to prison, from which she had escaped for a little, by an inexorable gaoler.

"Good night," he said, as he led her to her bedroom.

And as he looked at her she noticed – she thought she noticed – for a second, for a flash, a look of sadness in his grey eyes, as if he had lifted his mask. Blanche felt that perhaps the moment had come for an explanation that might alter their whole lives…

"Guido," she said, and there was an accent of piteous appeal in her voice.

But that look in Guido's eyes lasted only for the flash of a second. Directly she spoke, he let the mask fall once more.

"Yes," he said icily.

"Nothing... I only – I only wanted to say 'Good night.' "

"Good night, Blanche – sleep well."

When Blanche got to her room, she felt at first excited. Her brain was in a whirl. She was wild with suppressed anger – fury. She felt inclined to rebel, to scream, to beat, to bite – and then she said to herself, "What's the use?" and her rage subsided in a flood of tears. She had thought a new life was beginning for her. *Vita Nuova* – a springtide. Something harmless and solid...she felt so safe with her newly found religion in the background...and now...perhaps that was the reason she had been sent this trial, to show her that things were not so easy as she thought...but, oh! it wasn't fair! Might she not have one friend? Guido had friends in plenty, in Florence and in Rome, in England even – friends she knew and friends she knew nothing of...

How devilish of him to find out so soon, in spite of all the care she had taken... Who had put him on the scent? Princess Julia, no doubt; she didn't like Bretherton because he did not flatter her, did not play up to her. She had said something, Blanche remembered, about the Olenevs' party to her the day before – something in a slighting tone about there being too many of those rather tiresome, learned, English would-be scholars there, and too many Bohemians... She had not paid attention to it at the time, but she remembered now that her mother-in-law had given her one of her swift looks, one of those particular looks which meant, "This is meant for you, and I want you to know it." But what was she to do? Should she obey Guido, or should she defy him?

Had he the right to insist on it? What right had he? For, after all, there was no harm, no possible harm in meeting a man sometimes at dinner-parties or in Museums at Rome.

If there was, then why was she obliged to see *any one?* Why was it wrong to talk to some one you got on with and understood, and right to talk to any one who bored you? Surely that wasn't right? Surely, just because a thing was tiresome or annoying or disagreeable, that was not a *proof* that it was a duty…surely not…she would consult a priest on the subject. Father Michael, the priest to whom she went to Confession as a rule, he was understanding and experienced; he would be able to tell her. At any rate, if it was so, those were not the precepts that Guido and his mother practised…they did what they liked…but perhaps she was not being fair… How complicated life was…altogether too difficult for her to deal with…and thus, after tossing restlessly about until the daylight began to creep through the curtains of the tall windows, she at last fell into a heavy sleep.

# CHAPTER XVIII

The next afternoon she called on Father Michael Gardiner. He lived not far from the Palazzo Farnese. He was between forty and forty-five – a large, well-built, active-looking man with a high forehead, a clear skin, and bright and penetrating eyes. He came from an old English family which was distinguished by its piety; one of his brothers was a monk, and two of his sisters were nuns. He had been certain of his vocation even in his schooldays.

He was a relation of Blanche's mother-in-law, Princess Julia. Although she liked him as an acquaintance and approved of him as a Catholic and a priest, she was careful to have no professional dealings with him. He was too near home for her taste, and too discerning.

He was not a man of great culture or learning, but he had all the intelligence of the heart, if not of the head, and it would have been difficult to deceive him. The poor and the unhappy loved him instinctively. He was sometimes misunderstood by the proud – by *all* the proud, whether social, intellectual, or spiritual.

Blanche had met him in the early days of her marriage at her mother-in-law's evenings; she had always liked him, but each had respected the other's difference in religion, and this had kept them apart. After her conversion, he had welcomed her warmly, and had told her, and made her feel that he meant it, that his friendship, experience, and advice were always ready should ever she wish to take advantage of them. Blanche took him at his word.

He welcomed her on this occasion. He did not appear surprised to see her, and offered her a cup of coffee. "I can't offer you tea," he said; "the old woman who looks after me, Maddalena, can't make it!"

His rooms were bare, except for a bookshelf, in which there were some books of piety. He was not a great reader; he carried on all his work by word of mouth. He was an effectual preacher, but he was still more effectual in personal intercourse.

They talked of various matters, and presently they drank coffee. Father Michael asked after Guido and Princess Julia and Father Byrne, who, he knew, had received Blanche into the Church.

"I want to ask you something, Father Michael," Blanche said, after a little pause.

Father Michael nodded.

"Must one always be sure that because a thing is disagreeable, it is one's duty?"

Father Michael laughed.

"Certainly not," he said. "You would get into a sad tangle if you think that."

"It nearly always works out like that, all the same. At least, directly a thing *is* pleasant, one has to give it up, however harmless it is."

"You had better tell me what is worrying you." Blanche told him the whole story. Father Michael looked grave and sighed. "And what are you going to do?" he asked.

"Isn't it very unreasonable of Guido?"

"I think it shows he is far-seeing and fond of you."

"Fond of me!"

"I am sorriest for him. You are too young to be sorry for him. But let us leave him out of the question for the moment. Supposing you went on with this friendship. Such a relation begins almost imperceptibly, but it grows quickly, and it soon becomes a chain. You would soon, each of you, reach a point when neither of you could do without the other. And then what would be the result? Misery to him and to you."

"But, Father Michael, you don't realise that he, Mr Bretherton, has, I am quite sure, never given the matter a thought in that kind of way. He just looks upon me as a nice acquaintance, some one with whom he can be comfortable."

"Thank God it's gone no further!"

"But, Father Michael, the only reason why I liked – why I knew we could be friends, is because I knew he would never make love to me."

"I know Mr Bretherton better than you think I do."

"Don't you agree with me that he is detached…impersonal?"

"Intellectually – yes."

"I feel him to be so serene, so indifferent."

"Appearances are deceptive."

"Then you don't agree with me?"

"Not entirely… I think he has the characteristics you speak of…but I think he has had, and may still have, other tendencies. I think he has been a man of strong passions. If that is so, you never know when passion may burst out again. He may be like a dormant volcano, and there is all the difference between a dormant and an extinct volcano. You want me to think he is extinct. It may be so – I don't know."

"But we should never – there would never be any question… "

"No; you think that now, but you don't know how rapidly these situations develop, when once you let them begin. They take the bit in their teeth…they take charge. Remember the Greek proverb that Lord Byron was fond of quoting, that

209

the blind god's approaches are made walking, but his retreat is on wings."

"There is no question of the blind god, I promise; but all this simply means I can't have a friend. Guido has as many friends as he likes. He used to see, and does still see, his friends every day of his life."

"Perhaps if you had let him know you minded, that wouldn't have happened and wouldn't happen."

"Of course I know I am being punished. I suppose I ought never to have married – an Italian. It is all *my* fault – nobody else's."

"Apart from anything else, your marriage has had one inestimable result, that of bringing you into the Church, and you should bear that in mind and be thankful. But now, stop thinking of yourself, and think for a moment of this Mr Bretherton. Why should you make him unhappy?"

"I might make him happy" – the words escaped her.

"That would be worse."

"I didn't mean that; I mean, why couldn't we just be friends?"

"You know it would be more than that…a friendship of the soul, if nothing more; there is nothing more intimate than that. It might make him extremely unhappy."

"Then it is true I must make my life into a desert?"

"Humanly speaking, yes; and it is then you will find that there are wells of water in it that nothing can excel."

"Oh, Father Michael, don't say that to me; I don't find that; I don't feel that; I haven't enough Faith – not nearly enough… You talk to me as if I were a saint… You are expecting me to live up to too high a standard. I can't; you are asking too much of me."

"All I am asking of you is not to prepare a Purgatory for yourself and for him in this life. You will make three people unhappy – Bretherton, yourself, and Guido."

"You want me to give up thinking of people?"

"Yes, in that kind of way... You read the *Imitation*, don't you? You remember the saying: 'Unless a man be detached from all creatures he cannot freely attend to things divine.' "

"But I've got to live in the world, after all. I'm not a nun. I wish I were. I would far rather not live in the world. But I've got to. And, what a world! A world that I hate and abominate! In exile, too! I don't really like Italy nor Rome. I hate Rome! I – "

"Hush, hush! You mustn't talk like that. Besides, we are all of us in exile, whoever we are and wherever we are."

"But, Father Michael, it is *so* unfair. When Adrian Tyne made love to me – violent, passionate love with the worst motives, every day and all day, on every possible occasion – Guido did not raise a finger. He seemed to encourage it."

"He knew it was safe."

"That would be *abominable*! I think one day he will find he has made a mistake. I will take him at his word."

"You are seeing things in the wrong perspective. There never was a word to be taken at. Guido knows you better than you know yourself. He knew quite well that there was no danger from that quarter, but every possible chance of danger from this new quarter."

"That's just where I know he is so wrong – so *utterly* wrong."

"But I agree with him, and so do you, if you are honest with yourself. Can you deny that the thought of this friend of yours has not been the main object in the back of your mind for the last two months?"

"Yes, in a way, but quite harmlessly..."

"You can't treat that kind of thing like a toy... It is not a toy, but an explosive. It looks harmless, but it may go off."

"I don't feel strong enough, well equipped enough, to deal with life."

"We none of us feel that, because we none of us are... Have patience, and remember that comfort will come in its proper season. God will not abandon you. You have already been given exceptional grace; you mustn't throw it away."

"The fact of the matter is, I haven't enough Faith... I haven't... "

"That is enough," Father Michael said, with authority. "We have talked enough about it now."

They talked of other things, and Blanche, though she did not feel particularly convinced, when she went away, felt better for seeing Father Michael.

"It isn't so much what he says, but what he is," she thought, "that does me good."

She felt, too, that when he spoke of human passions he knew what he was talking about. But when she left him he remained plunged in thought for a little, then he went to his *prie-Dieu*.

Blanche ultimately decided to do what Guido wished. He was right, she knew, about one thing; it was at the present stage easy for her to do it in regard to the outward aspect of the affair, without anybody being aware of it. She gradually shifted her orbit. She no longer went to the Olenevs'; she made them come to her. She avoided the houses where she knew she would meet Bretherton, and she went to other houses where she knew she would not meet him.

For the first time, really, since the death of her child, with one brief exception when her appearance had so forcibly struck Adrian Tyne at the Russian Embassy, Blanche had the appearance of being *mondaine*, of going out into the world, of taking part in things, of enjoying herself. She was playing a part, but she played it well. She knew she had recovered her looks, and she took a malicious joy in making the most of them, in making an effect. She took trouble – trouble that was no trouble to her – about her clothes. She had unerring instincts in such matters. She was one of those who never imitate, but whom others imitate and envy. She eschewed the commonplace and the common and alighted quite naturally on the exceptional, the rare; but never on the eccentric. In other words, she had good taste. She had all her father's taste, and

mixed with it her mother's femininity. She was in such matters
inimitable. She was, too, rich enough to allow herself the
luxury, the supreme luxury of simplicity. So, try hard as her
acquaintances did, they found it hard to imitate her.

Given Blanche's looks, her character, her ways, her
position...the total of what she was, it was impossible that this
total should not, in a place like Rome, produce an effect, a
response. It did. People for the first time – for although her
beauty had always been noticed, it had never until now
received the seal of universal public opinion – began to talk of
nothing but the *beautiful* Princess Roccapalumba. She was
quoted to strangers as one of the sights of Rome. The Italians
forgot she had ever been an Englishwoman. They claimed her
as an Italian, perhaps not altogether without reason; but even if
there were no Italian strain in her blood (which could be
argued), her years in Rome had given her an undeniable Italian
stamp.

She played up to this now.

She said to herself: "All right, Guido, since you wanted it,
you shall have it. Don't be surprised, don't be shocked, don't
wonder if things turn out in an unexpected manner."

After that last interview, she did not go near Father Michael.
If she went to Confession, she went to any priest – anywhere.

It was a gay season that winter in Rome, and Blanche threw
herself into the whirl of things.

It can't be said that she enjoyed – a moment of it, but she
enjoyed doing it, just as an artist, an actor, enjoys doing a thing
well, however sick at heart she or he may be feeling at the time.

Among the infinite vibrations and responses that her new
line of conduct caused, there were two which stood out pre-
eminently. The first was a negative one – Francis Bretherton.
He noticed at once and acutely the change that had come
about. He felt no grain of bitterness. He had, in a way, half
expected it. He had felt that something out of the way had been
happening, something that was not as it should be. He had also

213

felt, "If this goes on, it may well develop into something else. I may lose my head." Then, when the subtle breach occurred, he knew that nothing worldly had prompted Blanche... She might enjoy such things – why not? But Bretherton knew that in Rome, at this moment, worldly success was not Blanche's main object. There was something else behind it.

He played up to her instinctively, shielding the situation, or rather helping her to shield the situation. He buried himself in his work and no longer went to the houses where formerly he had felt sure of meeting her, so he helped to veil the breach. He guessed that she did not wish the world to notice anything, and acted accordingly. He guessed right. The Olenevs upbraided him by letter for his desertion. He was too busy, he said, to go out at present anywhere.

His publisher was clamouring for proofs.

Blanche divined his tactics, and was devoutly thankful; only all this made her more and more angry with every one.

"What fools they are!" she said. "What perfect fools they are! – all of them, and especially the clever ones!"

The second response was positive. It affected an Italian friend of Guido's, whom she had known ever since she had been married, but who had hitherto taken but little notice of her, partly because he had been otherwise occupied, and partly because he thought it was waste of time to pay attentions to Englishwomen.

They were, he used to say, either impossibly good or impossibly bad.

His name was Alfredo Chiaromonte. He was a contemporary of Guido's – short, dark, and square, distinguished looking, well-made, hard, and athletic, a good rider and a reckless gambler. He had no particular profession. That month of January, not long after Guido's ultimatum about Bretherton, he began to pay attention to Blanche and to make up to her.

At first she paid no heed to this, knowing that he had the reputation for that kind of thing, and that more often it meant nothing. He was supposed to be more or less permanently tied to a well-known singer.

As a matter of fact, this cord was already frayed, and its strongest strand was on the verge of a final snap, but nobody knew this.

To Blanche's surprise he persisted. She made assignations with him at public occasions and entertainments, such as her mother-in-law's evenings, which she never dreamt he would keep and which she, on her part, deliberately did not keep, and to her surprise he kept them meekly. A mischievous demon entered into Blanche. She said to herself, "Why not? It is, after all, Guido's fault; he has brought this upon himself." And she set out to play up to Alfredo, to captivate him by a thousand little coquetries. She did it skilfully, almost imperceptibly – quite so to him. She feigned indifference, but she led him on nevertheless. And as his admiration increased, and the flame of passion began to blaze within him, so did her beauty increase, for Blanche was a person who responded to attention, love, praise, warmth, as a flower does to the sun.

Whether Guido noticed what was going on, she did not know, and did not care. He seemed to notice nothing, and, indeed, to any one without Guido's uncanny intuitions and powers of observation and divination, it would have been difficult to notice anything. On the surface there was nothing to notice. Beneath the surface, and in reality, there were a thousand little things almost daily.

Blanche was taking part in an elaborate game, and the game was called "playing with fire."

For Alfredo it was soon no longer a game; he was now seriously and passionately in love with Blanche, and prepared to go to all lengths, with all the fire of his ardent southern temperament.

So things went on without any visible ripple on the surface of Blanche's life until the great historic fancy-dress ball at the Palazzo Sori, which was to take place on the Thursday before

215

Ash Wednesday, the 12th of February. Rome had talked of little else for a long time. The Palazzo Sori was one of the finest and most typically Roman houses in Rome. Prince Sori was as Roman as his palace, and delightful and easy into the bargain. Princess Sori, although by birth an Austrian, looked Roman; she was a beauty – stately, dark, with sad grey eyes and an ivory complexion.

Fancy dress was not confined to any one period, and Blanche, knowing that she could not vie with any of the Italian beauties if she went in a Renaissance or mediaeval costume, and knowing, too, that nothing was more effective than a dark person when *poudrée*, went as a lady of the Court of Louis XV. Her hair was powdered; her dress was copied from a picture of Madame de Pompadour by Boucher. The wide overdress and train were made of silk, a shade lighter than the colour of a dead leaf; the under-dress of taffeta, a shade deeper than the tint of an apricot. It was all trimmed with silver lace, with bows of silver ribbon down the front of the body and on the sleeves, which ended in wide lace flounces. She wore no jewels, save a small circle of pearls in her powdered hair and four rows of pearls round each wrist. One yellow-pink rose nestled at the corner of her body against her dazzling skin, and round her neck there was a small ruff of silver lace.

It was a symphony in russet and silver.

The whiteness of her skin seemed more dazzling than ever, and as for her eyes, they were like stars; their brightness and, indeed, the brightness of her whole person was intensified a hundred times by the powder on her hair and on her skin, and by the rouge on her cheeks, which had been applied in artfully negligent dabs as in the days of Madame de Pompadour. She also wore a cunningly placed *mouche*. She seemed, not like a person dressed up, but like a ghost from another world…if she was touched, she would vanish, one felt – and there was an air about her.

Blanche insisted on Princess Julia wearing the jewels which she (Princess Julia) had given her (Blanche) when she married. She did it with effect. Princess Julia's dress was copied from a picture of a Venetian lady by Bartolommeo Veneziano which hung in the Palazzo Fabrini. It was of old-rose velvet with elaborately designed embroideries and cunningly inserted emeralds and pearls, so well arranged that they looked like shining trimmings in their proper place, and not like ornaments put there for show. She was one of the most impressive figures at the ball. Nobody understood how to dress up better than she.

Guido, too, looked well. He was dressed in a black velvet costume copied from a Moroni, of one of his own ancestors, in the Palazzo Fabrini, and he wore the Order of the Golden Fleece (in which there were large rubies) that had been given by Charles the Fifth to that ancestor, and a sword whose hilt, inlaid with emeralds, had been chiselled by Benvenuto Cellini. His complexion, his grey eyes, his long thin hands, all seemed to have the *patine* of a genuine old master.

Alfredo Chiaromonte went as a Venetian noble, in a dress copied from a picture at the Pitti Palace, of white satin embossed with a close pattern of black velvet and a large collar of diamonds.

There was a dazzling crowd of Byzantine figures that seemed to have been torn from enamels or mosaics, and figures by Titian, Van Dyck, Velasquez, and Giorgione, who looked as if they had stepped out of the frames whence their doubles looked down, impassive, from the high walls – there was a Van Dyck from the Borgniola Palace at Genoa, with a long stomacher of diamonds and a large ruby in her head-dress plaited with pearls, and there was the famous "La Bella di Tiziano"; Olivares, the Minister of Philip II; and a whole cluster of Venetians in white satin, gold, blue velvet, sable, and pearls. But among the crowd of Princesses stiff as idols with jewels, and others beautiful with a more simple picturesqueness, evoking all the Renaissance with tints of stuff or glints of hair, or all the Middle Ages with a head-dress and a quaint jewel, or the Louvre (Anne d'Autriche with shoulder-straps of gems) – amidst all that memorable crowd, there was no one who made a greater effect than Blanche.

It was the night of nights for her looks, and her eyes put out the jewels of the others. When she passed there was a slight murmur, and people stopped to look at her.

As for Alfredo Chiaromonte, he was like a man mortally stricken. He looked at no one else. She danced with him twice and accepted his invitation to supper...the supper was perhaps the finest sight of the whole fantastic evening...in that dining-room where the gorgeous ceiling (painted by Guido Reni) and the tapestries diverted the attention even from the chiselled gold plate and the crystal and emeralds of Benvenuto Cellini.

After supper, he led her through the long rooms on the ground floor, where a bank of flowers screened an orchestra playing, on to a platform that was built into the street.

And it was there he spoke out; the restraint of his manner and of his expressions veiled a volcanic vehemence of intention, and Blanche, instead of putting him off and checking or stopping him, looked at him boldly and shamelessly, straight in the eyes as much as to say "Yes."

When he noticed this he turned white. He was shaking all over. He asked her to run away with him in matter-of-fact tones. And she in an equally matter-of-fact tone said she would.

They discussed the how and the when as if they were making arrangements for sightseeing. Everything was settled. Blanche said she would meet him at such and such a time and at such and such a place, and they would leave Rome together for Naples first, and then who knows.

She felt light-headed, as if a heavy burden had been removed from her; she had no doubts, no remorse, no hesitation, no regret, just a calm determination. She was longing for the hour when her boats would be definitely burnt, when she could actually see the conflagration.

A little later, when they had made all arrangements and gone upstairs, her mother-in-law met her and said to her:

"Guido has a bad headache; he has gone home by himself, and is sending back the carriage for us."

Blanche thought this was unlike Guido.

Presently she went home with her mother-in-law. Guido had gone to bed and had left a message that he did not wish to be disturbed.

Blanche sat up a long time writing a letter – a short letter, not of explanation, but of *severance* – of final, definite, and everlasting severance – to Guido.

She wrote it several times; each time it became shorter.

"He will get this tomorrow evening after I am gone." She was intending to leave Rome the next evening, and to meet Alfredo at the station.

She finished her letter and locked it up in her dispatch box, and then she went to bed and slept soundly till she was called as usual at half-past eight.

But hardly had she been called than her maid came in with a scared, terrified expression on her face and said that the Prince had had a seizure and was seriously ill.

Blanche put on a dressing-gown and rushed to his room. Guido was lying pale as death and motionless on his bed, like a wax figure with staring eyes. The doctor was sent for. Princess Julia arrived; the whole household was in commotion. The doctor was puzzled, took a grave view of the case, but did not regard it as hopeless. Blanche sent Alfredo Chiaromonte a short note cancelling their arrangements definitely, and she found time to burn the letter she had written the night before and locked up in her dispatch-box. Towards the evening Guido was a little better.

# BOOK II

# CHAPTER I

Fourteen years after the events narrated in the last chapter, Bernard Lacy and his friend, Walter Troumestre, were spending their leave at Easter-time in Paris.

They were both in the same regiment – the Coldstream Guards – and they had been both of them educated at the same school – Beaumont College. They both came from old Catholic families. Bernard's mother was still alive; he had only one younger brother, and no sisters. His uncle, Sir Christopher Lacy, Bart., owned a large estate and an extremely beautiful old house in Fenmouthshire, called Alton-Leigh.

Walter Troumestre was three years the elder, and at the date of which I am writing he was twenty-five years old and his friend was twenty-two.

Although they had been at the same time at the same school, they had overlapped, and it was only when they both left school that they made friends. They were widely different, both in appearance and character.

Walter Troumestre was small, fair, a little short-sighted, untidy, impulsive, chivalrous, and enthusiastic – a romantic. Bernard Lacy was a realist; he was dark, with slow, grey eyes which were sad for their age. He was finely cut rather than built, as out of some hard substance, like granite; square and large at this time, although still undeveloped and immature;

extremely good-looking, with nobility of feature; there was something a little steely about him; he was orderly, methodical, and energetic, with strong prejudices, likes, and dislikes, and a great deal of shyness and reserve and immense sensitiveness. He took a good deal of knowing, hut those who took the trouble to break through the defences of his reserve were rewarded. He had a generous disposition and was full of unexpected gentleness and soft surprises.

They had been ten days in Paris, and they were each of them (although neither of them admitted it to the other) beginning to feel a little bored, and to wish for England once more. They had been to several plays which they had found tedious, and done a certain amount of sightseeing; they had driven to the Bois, visited the principal cafés, had *déjeuner* at the Café Anglais, dined at Bignon's and the Ambassadeurs, entertained two local Trilbys at supper, supped at Montmartre, and attended a dinner-party at the British Embassy. They were sitting in the courtyard of the hotel. It was their last evening. They were discussing what to do.

"No more plays," said Bernard, who was a John Bull; "they talk so fast."

At that moment the hall porter brought them a note which had been sent by hand. It was from one of the secretaries at the Embassy. He enclosed two *fauteuils d'orchestre* for the opera, in case they would like to have them. He had been going, he explained, with his wife, but was now unable to go.

"I suppose we must go," said Bernard.

"It's worth while seeing the house, and tonight is the good night, and we shouldn't be able to get good seats ourselves."

"I wonder what opera it is," said Bernard as he sat down to the writing-table. "I suppose I must write and say we shall be delighted to use the tickets."

"Yes," said Walter; "we must go; they will know if we don't," and, taking up Galignani's newspaper, he said, "It's *Le Prophète*, with Jean de Reske."

"It doesn't make much difference to me," said Bernard, "what the music is. I think all operas are equally silly, but I dare say we shall enjoy going there."

"Jean de Reske is a good singer. He's a Pole. And I believe it's well put on – splendid scenery."

They dined early, and arrived at the opera about nine.

Their places were at the end of the fourth row, just underneath a *baignoir*, which was empty when they arrived. In the course of the act its occupants arrived. These were two ladies and three men; two of the men looked like Frenchmen; the third, an older man, over sixty, was an Englishman. One of the ladies, who was evidently the hostess, and showed the other one into the visitor's place of honour, was dressed in white satin. She (the hostess) was tall and fair, with a little head such as Velasquez paints, poised on a lovely, long neck and magnificent shoulders, round which, over her bare arms, a piece of tulle seemed to have been negligently flung. She was beautiful; but for the moment nobody noticed her, so entirely eclipsed was she by a dark companion dressed in cream-coloured shimmering satin and black lace, with a face like a flower and eyes like sad stars. Although darker, she was more radiant; not so gay, but brighter, more graceful, more exquisite, and more fascinating – in a word, more lovely than her companion, with something more than the ordinary attributes of beauty – a fourth dimension of charm, mystery, and wistful majesty. She looked like some one strayed from a fairy-tale – an exotic, bewitching Princess – and the hostess beside her looked like a distinguished lady-in-waiting.

Bernard Lacy noticed her at once.

"I wonder who that is," he said.

"Which one?"

"The dark one, of course."

"A foreigner, I should think, but she doesn't look French."

Bernard did not say so, but he thought the dark lady was the most beautiful person he had ever seen.

Her face had just that still magic that some pictures have…you look and look at them as into a clear stream – you can't stop looking – and the more you look, the more enigmatic and mysterious the transparent depths become.

This person, Bernard thought, made every one else seem either common or commonplace. She was like an authentic old master among paintings of the second rank, a fairy princess among mere mortals; and yet the person she was with was not only distinguished, but lovely, and younger – a great deal younger (nine years, in fact) – than her dark companion; Bernard, nevertheless, felt he couldn't look at her, so endlessly fascinating were the looks, the line, the colour, that is to say, the radiance, the shape, the ways, and the expression of the dark lady; and the fair lady's skin, her weak point (it was a little rough), looked coarse beside, and was shown up in startling contrast by, the flower-like texture of her companion's neck, face, and shoulders.

Walter Troumestre voiced his thoughts when he said: "I admire the dark one most; the fair one is all right, but the dark one is unlike any one I've ever seen. I wonder who she can be."

In the entr'acte they walked in the foyer, and met a friend, Harold Locke, who was an unpaid attaché at the Embassy. He led them back to the front of the house and told them who all the people were in the boxes. Harold Locke was, in spite of his youth, a man who knew most things about most people.

The fair lady in the *baignoir* was a Madame d'Aurillac, accompanied by her husband and a famous academician who was an authority on Greek vases and coins; the other lady was a Princess Roccapalumba, who had had rather a romantic history.

"She was a Miss Clifford," said Locke, "a daughter of Henry Clifford; that's the oldest of the three men sitting in the box. She married a Roman Prince when she was quite young, one of the richest men in Italy, but reasonable, and not one of those *black* nobles, a liberal, with an English mother, the daughter of

226

Lord Pevensey... They rallied to the Quirinal when Victor Emmanuel took over...they used to entertain, and then, one fine day, the Prince was stricken by a mysterious illness, and since then he has been an invalid and never goes anywhere."

"What is the matter with him?" asked Bernard.

"Nobody knows. It's a mysterious nervous disease. Sometimes for weeks – I believe when it first began it was sometimes for *months* – he can't move. He has to lie on a sofa... "

"And see nobody?"

"No; that's the funny part. You can see him, and he can talk to you, but you are not allowed to talk to him – it hurts him after you're gone. Every doctor in the world has been consulted, and they can do nothing."

"Is he here?"

"Oh no! He can't move; he has not left Rome once for fourteen years. The Princess hardly ever leaves him alone for more than two days. She comes here once a year to meet her father – if he can't go to Rome. She just stays a night; she is going back tomorrow."

"How awful for her!" said Walter.

"She has behaved extraordinarily well," said Locke. "She is devoted to her husband, and nurses him, and looks after him every moment of the day, and gives up everything else. His mother is alive, and he has a married sister; they help, too, of course."

"What a fate!" said Bernard, "and for such a good-looking woman!"

"Yes," said Locke; "but you should have seen her ten years ago" (Harold Locke was only just twenty-seven at the moment, but the tone of his voice, as he said this, suggested the reminiscent accent of a man of fifty). "She was beautiful...a vision."

"I can't personally imagine her much *more* beautiful than she is now," said Walter pensively. "The more one looks at her, the more fascinating she seems. She has got such speaking eyes, and what a wonderful dazzling white skin. She's like a...she's like...one of those flowers that come out in the evening – what is it?" A phrase of a song of Schumann's came into his head. He hummed:

"Die Lotosblume ängstigt
    Sich vor der Sonne Pracht."

"Walter is getting quite poetical," said Bernard, with a laugh that had something forced in it.

At that moment – they were standing in the gangway – a young Frenchman came up to Harold Locke and poured out a volume of talk.

"I must leave you," said Harold to Bernard and Walter. "I will see you later."

He left them, and presently they saw him in the *baignoir* talking to Madame d'Aurillac and the Italian Princess.

Neither Bernard nor Walter enjoyed the opera. Bernard thought it silly, and Walter thought it missed fire both as music and drama.

During the next entr'acte Harold Locke appeared again in the stalls and told Bernard and Walter that Madame d'Aurillac wished to make their acquaintance, that Princess Roccapalumba knew their relations – so did her father, who was a friend of both their families.

They walked round to the *baignoir*, where they were introduced to Madame d'Aurillac, Princess Roccapalumba, Monsieur Théodore Saverny of the Académie des Inscriptions, and to Henry Clifford. Madame d'Aurillac's husband had left the box. Madame d'Aurillac spoke English fluently; Saverny not a word; Bernard was a halting French scholar; but Walter knew no fear in any language, and was ready to talk with a Chinaman with a vocabulary of four or five words.

After the preliminary openings: "How long are you staying? How are your parents? Where are you staying? Have you enjoyed yourselves?" – Madame d'Aurillac addressed herself to Walter and roped him into a French conversation with the professor as soon as she saw (which she did in a minute) that he was comfortable in French and that Bernard was not. Bernard joined into the talk of Henry Clifford, the Princess, and Harold Locke.

Henry Clifford talked of the opera. "Reske looks the part, but of course he isn't a *real* tenor. You should have heard Mario in the part – Mario, and Viardot as Fides – that was worth hearing."

The Princess talked amiably to Bernard, but she seemed to him to be worlds away.

How long was he staying? Paris was so gay, but so crowded; it was a pity it was so cold.

Henry Clifford asked after Bernard's uncle and mother. He had stayed with his uncle last autumn at Alton-Leigh. It looked more beautiful than ever; he always thought it the most beautiful place, and the most beautiful *house* in England. "It is quite unspoilt."

"Yes," said Bernard; "it is a beautiful place."

"And what is more," thought Henry Clifford, "it will soon belong to you, young man; for anything more decrepit than old Sir Christopher looked the other day I have seldom seen."

Sir Christopher Lacy was a widower, and had no children.

The entr'acte came to an end, and that was the last chance Bernard and Walter had of speaking to the people in the box.

The next day they went back to London. They travelled in the same boat with Henry Clifford, who talked a great deal to Bernard – asked where his mother was living; said he would come and see her at once – and altogether made himself agreeable.

229

Bernard lived with his mother. They shared a little house in Ovington Square. He had a younger brother called Stephen, ten years younger than himself, who was now at a private school.

Mrs Lacy was just forty-four. She was small, with twinkling brown eyes that were sometimes full of fun. She was more intelligent and more cultivated than her son, and she learnt things without any effort. She was sensible and worldly-wise without being worldly; a good, practising Catholic, but not bigoted; given to a multitude of hobbies and occupations. In the country they lived in a small Dower House which belonged to Alton-Leigh. Sir Christopher lent it to her.

She came to London during the winter, but she generally went abroad for a month or so if she could. She was fond of gardening and music; she read Dante and St Thomas; she spoke Spanish and Italian, and a beautiful old-fashioned French; but the main interest of her life was her son. She was not well off, and she could just manage to give him enough to live on in the Army; but then there were expectations. Sir Christopher liked his nephew, and he would certainly inherit Alton-Leigh, which, after her son, was what Mrs Lacy loved best in the world.

Bernard was devoted to his mother and enjoyed her society immensely; he told her everything.

He described Paris and the meeting at the opera with Henry Clifford.

"And he says he's coming to see you directly."

"He won't, though," said Mrs Lacy, with a twinkle in her brown eyes. "However, I am always grateful to people for making themselves agreeable, even when I know they don't mean a word of what they are saying."

"Is he such a humbug as all that?"

"He's a *faux bonhomme*. He's always civil to me if we meet, but we hardly ever do meet except possibly at your uncle's; he goes to the shooting parties there, and I met him there one year. It was the year you were at Sandhurst."

"And the daughter – do you know her?"

"Blanche? I haven't seen her for years. She never comes to England now. I remember her coming out so well. It was before you were born. She was a lovely girl. Everybody liked her, and everybody was sorry for her when she married that Italian."

"Why? Didn't she like him?"

"He was and is, I suppose, immensely rich, and it was what is called an excellent marriage. But I don't think she ever can have been fond of him. I am convinced that Henry Clifford made the marriage. It didn't turn out so badly as we all expected; but then came this awful catastrophe, and ever since then she has led the life of a nurse. I must say she has behaved beautifully."

"I thought her beautiful."

"You should have seen her as a girl. I shouldn't like to see her now. It would be a shock."

"A shock? Mother, you've no idea what she looks like; she's a young woman."

"It's always a shock to see some one one has known as a girl years afterwards. Let me see! She married in 'sixty-nine – four years after you were born; she must be nearly forty."

"Nonsense."

"Thirty-seven at least."

"Well, she certainly doesn't look it. I should have thought she was hardly thirty."

Mrs Lacy laughed.

"That would please her."

"I suppose she's a Protestant?"

"No; she became a Catholic some time after her marriage."

"Were lots of people in love with her?"

"There was one young man who wanted to marry her – what was his name? – the man who inherited in such an unexpected way, and became Lord Mayfield – Sydney Hope... Henry Clifford wouldn't hear of that *then*, because the young man was penniless and didn't seem to have any expectations. He is immensely rich now. She married almost directly she came out.

231

And since then I don't know; all I know is that ever since her husband has had this extraordinary illness, nobody has ever breathed a word against her, even in Rome, which is a hotbed of gossip."

"Did you see her when you went to Rome three years ago?"

"No; I didn't. She never went out, and I hardly at all. I lived a real tourist's life. But I heard about her and heard how well she behaved."

"She must be a wonderful woman… "

"Yes," said Mrs Lacy pensively.

"You don't think so?"

"I think that, although *all* women are, of course, wonderful in a way, in a way *none* of them are; and that there is no such thing as a 'wonderful' woman. But men think there are, and that's just as well."

"I always say you're a cynic, mother, and that it's a wonder you haven't corrupted me."

Mrs Lacy laughed and said nothing. She wondered, as she always wondered, what sort of woman her son would marry. Would she like him to marry a woman like Blanche Clifford? Yes; if he could have known Blanche Clifford twenty years ago. She would have done beautifully. Now she was so desperately afraid he would come across the wrong person, and at the same time she knew too well the folly and futility of trying to influence people in these matters, and, above all, in trying to *prevent*.

"I suppose that a marriage like Mr Clifford's daughter made is just the sort of marriage you would like me to make," Bernard said suddenly.

"God forbid!… "

"But, mother, be honest and admit that you would like me to marry a rich woman – a really rich woman."

"I want you to have enough to live on, of course. One can't live on air if one is married."

"I shall try and marry an American heiress from Chicago."

Mrs Lacy laughed, but she never felt easy on the subject; she was always afraid of a possible entanglement. Bernard told her everything, but there was one door, as in the castle of Bluebeard, that she did not dare to ask the key of.

# CHAPTER II

Mrs Lacy felt uneasy about Bernard, not because anything was happening, but, on the contrary, because nothing was happening. Bernard appeared to be fancy-free. He had had last year a passing adoration for a well-known actress, which Mrs Lacy had cleverly encouraged. It was an infatuation born of the footlights, and the adored person laughed him lightly out of it. She was thirty years older than he was, and used to these young adorations. Mrs Lacy was uneasy because she felt something was bound to happen soon, and whether this uneasiness was caused by the shadow of coming events or not, her fears were realised all too soon. Bernard had not been back in England a fortnight before he fell in love.

It happened at a ball, a *bal blanc*, given at Whitehall House. He came, and saw, and was conquered. It was a girl who had been out one year who achieved this. She was eighteen; her name was Rose Middlemore. She was a younger daughter in a large family. Her father was a squire who lived in Northumberland; her mother had been a beauty. Her eldest sister was married; she had one sister older than herself who was out already, and three more sisters still in the schoolroom. She was extremely pretty and fresh looking – a small oval face charmingly cut, fair hair, and soft black eyes, a springing walk, and a beautifully straight figure; it was obvious that she liked outdoor life. She did; she was a fine rider, a good swimmer, an excellent lawn-tennis player. Bernard fell in love with her at first sight, and his mother was conscious of the fact directly it occurred.

Rose Middlemore was just such a girl as she would have chosen for Bernard, only there were drawbacks. She was poor, but that did not much matter, as Bernard would have enough for both of them; she was a Protestant, but Mrs Lacy had faced the fact that it was more likely that her son would marry a Protestant than not. In fact, one ought to be thankful, so Mrs Lacy thought. The weeks went by. It was a gay season. Bernard, who didn't care, or who hadn't hitherto cared, for balls, went to every ball now. Parties, too, were organised – expeditions on the river. His cousins, who lived near London, were asked to ask So-and-so to play lawn-tennis, and why not Mrs Middlemore and her daughter?

Then one evening later in the summer – it was during Lord's week – Bernard proposed to her. She seemed astonished, really astonished. Somehow or other she had never thought there could be a question of marriage, yet; and then she realised that if ever such a question should arise, and should it arise now, it could never be Bernard. She liked him; yes, that was why she had been able to enjoy dancing with him; the expeditions on the river, the lawn-tennis, the rides in the park, all that they had done together; but she had looked on Bernard as part of the accessories of this gay outdoor life, as a tennis-racket, a nice pony, or a faithful dog; she could never imagine being fond of him in any other way. She told him so, and Bernard's dream was suddenly and rudely shattered. He couldn't believe it at first; at least, he thought there must still be a grain of hope that she might change her mind. But she was quite definite, firm and kind and sensible, and he realised it was true.

The next day his mother read the story in his face and in his silence.

Mrs Middlemore, whom she knew a little, came to see her, and told her the story which she had heard from her daughter. She would, she said, have liked the marriage. The difference of religion would have been, as she said, "a pity, but one can't have everything." That he would one day be the owner of Alton-Leigh was a consideration that remained unexpressed. It was undoubtedly one of the "things one *would* have"; and Mrs Middlemore knew from experience how difficult it is to bring up a large family on a small income and with the help or hindrance of an unbusiness-like husband.

She was a kindly, vague, plaintive woman, who had spent years not actually in regretting but in realising the drawbacks of a somewhat rash, hasty marriage, and she would have welcomed a solid prospect for her daughter. But she knew her daughter well, and "Rose," she said, "never changes her mind when once it was made up about that sort of thing." It sounded as if "that sort of thing" were a matter of daily occurrence, but she presently qualified the statement by saying that only last week Rose refused to go to a course of lectures on French literature given at the house of one of her cousins, although all her friends were going and her father wished her to go, saying it would be so good for her French.

"We implored her to go, and she speaks French so nicely when she chooses. But nothing would make her, and I had to explain to Sarah Sylvestre that Rose couldn't go after all – after I had originally accepted, which was so tiresome, and Sarah was put about. But nothing would move Rose. So I feel about this there is nothing that will make her change."

Mrs Lacy agreed. She said that she, too, was sorry, and they parted amicably.

But Mrs Lacy was saddened, for she knew that her son would take it hardly. He did. He was miserable and gave himself up to his unhappiness. The taste seemed to have gone from life for him. He no longer took an interest in anything; he refused to go to Scotland, where he was asked, nor to his uncle's shooting in October, saying he couldn't get leave. He refused to go anywhere, and the only person in whose society he seemed to find any pleasure was Walter Troumestre.

He never mentioned Rose's name to his mother, nor did he ever say a word about the whole affair, although he knew, of course, that she knew, and she knew that he knew that she knew.

Mrs Lacy did not know what to do. Bernard possibly nursed a spark of hope that Rose might still one day change her mind, but he would certainly not have admitted this, and if he did, the spark was soon to be extinguished, for one day in August, Mrs Lacy read in the *Morning Post* the announcement of an engagement between Rose Middlemore and a certain Lionel Hughes, who was the younger son of a neighbouring country squire and had some employment in the city.

"Well," thought Mrs Lacy, "that at any rate puts an end to it; and it is just as well perhaps that it should have happened so soon."

Bernard spent most of the autumn in London. From time to time he went to the Dower House, but he never stayed for more than a day or two.

Mrs Lacy began to be alarmed; he seemed to get no better – the wound seemed to be just as fresh as the day on which it had been inflicted – and he had grown into a different person; when he was with his mother he didn't seem to be there, and, with others, he was unlike his usual self.

Mrs Lacy was at her wits' end. There was, she thought, nothing to be done. People talked of the healing influence of time, but time seemed to be going extremely slowly. "No; things will go on like this," she thought, "till something else, some new factor, replaces the old, but who knows what this new factor will be?"

In November, Mrs Lacy came back to London for the winter. She found Bernard no better; he was hidden behind a thin, intangible curtain of depression. It made her sick at heart.

She could get him to go nowhere, and he treated human beings now as if they were ghosts; they did not seem to exist for him. She wished she could get him to go abroad; she suggested Paris, but he wouldn't hear of the suggestion.

Then Providence intervened in the shape of a certain friend of Mrs Lacy called Mrs Crowe, who always spent the winter in Rome with her husband. Mr Crowe was an invalid without an illness. They had a house in Rome, that is to say, a comfortable apartment on the first floor in the Via Gregoriana – *Casa Crowe*. This year Mr Crowe took it into his head that the Roman climate would not suit him, although it had suited him admirably hitherto, and he determined to spend the winter in Tangier. The Crowes were well off, and they had no wish to let their house; at the same time, they wished to keep the establishment going, so Mrs Crowe came round to see her old friend, Mrs Lacy, and offered to lend her the apartment for three or four months, or longer if she wished.

Mrs Lacy thought this would be a Heaven-sent opportunity of getting Bernard away from England for a little, if only she could persuade him to go. She feared it would be difficult.

The first thing she did was to enlist the help of Walter Troumestre. She explained to him the situation and begged him to help her.

"He will go," said Walter, "if he thinks you want to go and won't go without him."

"Well, you must dine with us tonight and help me."

That night during dinner Mrs Lacy casually mentioned that the silly doctor, whom she had been to see to give her a gargle for her throat, which had been a little troublesome, told her that she ought to spend the winter abroad.

"Why don't you?" said Bernard.

"It's out of the question," she said, and as proof of the impossibility she told him about Mrs Crowe's offer.

"But why not jump at it? – you must."

"I only told you that to show you how completely out of the question I regard it, that even with all these facilities, and a charming apartment offered me for nothing, and the servants there, and everything ready, I still couldn't dream of it. Because, my dear boy, I can't leave England this year."

"But why in the world *not*?"

Mrs Lacy gave a long string of totally unconvincing reasons, none of which Bernard accepted.

Finally she said: "I couldn't be all that time away from you, and nothing would induce you to go to Rome – in fact, I should never *dream* of letting you come."

"It is the one place I have always longed to see," said Bernard.

Walter here chipped in, and said this was true; only the other day Bernard had said that he wished he might one day have an opportunity of seeing Rome.

"My dear child," said Mrs Lacy, "Rome would bore you to death. Besides, you would have to give up all your hunting, and your uncle promised to mount you this year."

"I don't want to hunt," said Bernard; "besides which, there is excellent hunting in the Campagna. I believe it's the greatest fun – marvellous jumps."

"You would be bored to death in a week."

"I know I am not clever," said Bernard in an offended tone, "but I'm not such an absolute Philistine and barbarian as you and Walter think. I might be capable of appreciating *some* of the things in Rome. I mean, I suppose I could admire the ruins, the Forum, St Peter's, and all that."

"Of course I know you would like all that part of it, but you would get *so bored*."

"But, mother darling, I shouldn't have to stay there years. Can't I come out and keep you company for a month? You can send me away whenever you get bored with me. I *do* want to go."

"You're only saying that for my sake now. I don't want you to come. I shall have lots of friends, and I shall be perfectly happy."

"Mother darling, I want to come; that's just what I should like to do. I'm sick to death of London; I don't want to go to Uncle Christopher's – not this year, please; it will be so dreary. Please let me come with you; we should have such fun, and you shall educate me, and show me the sights, and we will make a lot of new friends, and you will find me a nice American heiress to marry. You know, they all of them go to Rome."

Mrs Lacy laughed; this was the first time that Bernard had spoken like that for months. He had suddenly for a moment become his old self.

"And Walter can come with us – won't you, Walter?" Bernard added.

"Yes; there is nothing I should like so much, and we might explore some of those small places in the environs of Rome, and we might go to Naples and Amalfi. I'm longing to see Amalfi."

"Well, that's settled," said Bernard.

"We must think it over carefully," said Mrs Lacy.

They did. The thinking over took the shape of talking of nothing else that evening, and Bernard made Mrs Lacy write a letter – she refused to post it that night, and insisted on "sleeping on it" – to Mrs Crowe accepting the offer and saying that she would be delighted to take possession of the apartment from the 1st of December for three months.

Bernard had a clear six weeks' leave, and was entitled to more, and would be able to stay at least two months, he said.

Mrs Lacy did sleep over it. Much as she wanted to take Bernard away from London, she was fearful now of doing anything rash, or committing a mistake. "If," she thought, "he should hate Rome, it would be worse than if he stayed here."

To tell the truth, she was alarmed by the success of her scheme, by the ease and rapidity with which things had fallen out. "All this is too easy, and too good to be true," she thought to herself. "There must be some bad thing coming behind." Nevertheless, she didn't change her mind, and nothing occurred to make the plan impossible or even difficult. Bernard arranged for his leave. Walter was to come out later and spend Christmas with them. She and Bernard were to start for Rome via Paris and Florence at the end of November.

It seemed to Mrs Lacy to be too good to be true. Ever since the plan had been made, Bernard had been a changed man. He was almost, not quite, but almost his old self. What was the secret of this? The joy of getting away from old surroundings and associations? Of making a break? Perhaps. Bernard could not have told you, and the last reason he would have given was that possibly in some corner of his brain there floated, like a subtle scent, the memory of the face that he had looked at with so much interest in the *baignoir* of the Opera House at Paris, last Easter – a face which he thought he would be certain to see again in Rome. But that of all reasons was the last which he would have admitted was the true one. Whatever the mainspring of his conduct, there was no doubt, since this journey had been decided on, his spirits had improved; he was a different man than the Bernard of the end of the summer. Every one noticed it, and even the wedding of Miss Rose Middlemore, which took place in London at St Peter's, Eaton Square, in the month of November, did not appear to damp his half-regained spirits.

And yet Mrs Lacy was uneasy. She felt it was unreasonable. She kept on saying to herself that she had every reason not only to be pleased, but to be heartily grateful. She had got what she wanted, what she had prayed for; but she was one of those people who are frightened when their prayers are granted, and looked forward with dread to the price they may have to pay…for herself she cared nothing, but she was frightened for her son. She wanted him so desperately to be happy; she was so afraid that he might miss happiness, and what she was most afraid of was, he might miss it through some fault of hers, some piece of mismanagement, some mistake on her part.

The night before they left for Rome she was unable to sleep.

That afternoon she had spent on her knees in the Oratory, and she had heard Benediction. She had put up a candle to Our Lady and to St Anthony of Padua, and had prayed with all her soul for her son.

"Let me," she had prayed, "have any misfortune that may have to be endured, but let him be spared. There is nothing I cannot endure, but he is so little versed in the grammar of grief and sorrow; he is such a novice, such a beginner. I know he must go through the harsh school of life, but don't let the lessons be too hard for him."

And yet she knew, as she said words like these over and over again, not that the prayer would be unheeded, but that she was asking for the impossible.

He would have to go to the school of life like every one else. There was no escape – no escape from life, no escape from sorrow, misery, and pain; or, rather, man confined in those dungeons is forced to make his own rope-ladder, to climb the spiked walls, and with scarred hands and bleeding feet to reach "lasting freedoms."

# CHAPTER III

The change of mood that seemed to have happened to Bernard ever since the mention of the Roman project, not only persisted, but increased when he left England and travelled south with his mother.

He was not yet himself, his mother thought, but he was better; convalescent, if not well. He had never yet been to Italy, and the first glimpse of the south enchanted him, although he said nothing about it. Bernard was not a man who expressed enthusiasms easily; you had to dig them out of him, and this could only be done with a sympathetic spade. His mother knew this, and was careful not to look as if she thought he was enjoying himself. On the contrary, she adopted a slightly critical attitude about everything, which made him take up the cudgels for the Government, as it were.

She would say, for instance: "I always think that the first glimpse of Italy is a tiny bit disappointing," knowing full well that Bernard, so far from being disappointed, had been startled out of his wits. Or again: "I always think it is rather nonsense people talk of the blue sky in Italy, when it is no bluer than anywhere else."

It happened that year, contrary to Mrs Lacy's fears, to be of an azure that beggared description, a real solid cerulean like the sky in an Alma Tadema picture – everything one could

243

desire or dream, and they had left London in a thick, yellow, inspissated fog. When she said this, Bernard answered hotly: "Well, really, I don't know what more you want. You must at least admit this is better than a London fog."

When they arrived, Mrs Lacy pursued the same tactics. She advised him not to go to St Peter's at first.

"You will be disappointed," she said; "you had better get used to Roman architecture first. If you go straight to St Peter's you will only think it a slightly vulgarised Brompton Oratory and not so big. I mean it *is* big, we know, but it doesn't *look* big, at first."

Bernard went straight to St Peter's. He went there by himself without telling anybody. He knelt in front of the *Pietà*, and there his wound seemed to open afresh and the old sorrow came back, only there was now less of bitterness in it, although just as much grief.

He prayed for Rose, and prayed that she might be happy, and the vastness of the space seemed to embrace his spirit. And in that airy, empty space he felt as if his tired spirit was being uncrumpled, soothed, and released from a long, painful cramp.

He didn't tell his mother that he had been to St Peter's, and in the same surreptitious way he visited the Colosseum.

But far more hazardous and difficult than the question of sightseeing was, Mrs Lacy knew well, the social question. Mrs Lacy wanted him to meet people. When they arrived, one of the first things Bernard had said was that he hoped they wouldn't be drawn into the English Colony. Mrs Lacy had heartily agreed with him. She did not know many English people in Rome just at that moment. There was a new ambassador who had just been appointed, Sir Hedworth Lawless. He came from Washington. Mrs Lacy did not know him, but she wrote her name and Bernard's at the Embassy, and they were asked to dinner.

It was not a large dinner-party – only ten people. There was a dignified Russian lady, Princess Mania Olenev, who was picturesque-looking, with white hair and black pearls, and evidently artistic; Colonel Laurent, the French military attaché; Count Mario Guerrini and his wife, Donna Teresa; and an Englishwoman, Lady Ralph Dallington, who was young, gay, and handsome, and effectively dressed in black with yellow chrysanthemums; and Herbert Napier (easy and light in hand), one of the Secretaries. Bernard took in Lady Ralph; it was a round table; on the other side of him was Donna Teresa Guerrini. Bernard found out in the conversation that she was the sister-in-law of the interesting-looking lady whom he had seen in Paris, and this gave her, to him, a reflected interest.

She told him her brother was a little better. He loved seeing visitors, especially English people, and it would be an act of great unselfishness on his part if one day when he had nothing to do he would call at the Palazzo Fabrini, or, if he preferred it, at her house, the Palazzo Guerrini, and she would take him. He always saw visitors every day from half-past four till six. One must not talk much to him.

"It tires him dreadfully to be talked to, of course."

Bernard wondered at the "of course."

"But it does him good to talk *to* people."

Bernard could not help reflecting that as a rule it was the other way round. Most invalids found it less tiring to listen than to talk, but then one never knew.

He made an arrangement to pick up Donna Teresa on the following Thursday at five o'clock.

"I will tell my sister-in-law you are coming. She will be delighted; she is always so pleased to see English people."

This was Bernard's first glimpse of diplomatic life. He liked the Ambassador. Lady Lawless he thought delightful. In the first place, she was extremely good-looking, and then there was nothing official about her; she was easy, comfortable, and full of fun. She laughed at herself.

After dinner there was a little music. A Miss Sims had been asked in to sing.

Lady Lawless explained at dinner that she hated music and knew nothing about it, but that she had been asked as a favour to give this young lady a trial (a chance), and as she knew that Princess Olenev was a great *connoisseur*, and Donna Teresa an admirable pianist – as good as a professional – she had asked her to come that evening.

"But she shan't sing *too* much," Lady Lawless explained quietly, with gentle intonation and twinkling eye; "you need not be afraid."

They went into a large, long, empty room – the ballroom – where there was a grand pianoforte, and presently Miss Sims arrived with a female accompanist. She was a healthy-looking damsel, and neither shy nor embarrassed.

"*Elle est sûre de son fait*," said Colonel Laurent.

Her first song was in French. It was Tosti's "Ninon." The voice was pure and well trained, but as soon as she sang the word *fais* in the phrase – "*Que fais-tu de l'amour?*" the English, not to say the *London*, intonation of her speech hit you hard. Colonel Laurent winced, and Lady Lawless looked solemn. Napier's face crinkled up in effort to suppress budding smiles.

Scarcely had the hurried applause died down before Miss Sims said, "I will now sing an Italian song." Lady Lawless gasped.

"*Voi che sapete*," she announced, "by Mozart."

Nearly every one present, with the exception of Bernard, had heard Patti sing the same song.

The accent of Middlesex came out unmixed and strong on the word *sapete*, especially on the second syllable – she pronounced it *pay* – and as soon as the song was over Sir Hedworth asked for something English. He was not musical, but he had instincts. Miss Sims obliged with "The Devout Lover," and when this was over, before she could announce a further item, Lady Lawless was by her side, at the pianoforte, pouring out compliments and thanks to her.

"I like that one best of *all*," she said, "and *how* kind of you to have been able to spare us a moment tonight, and to have given us *all such* a treat, and to have sung so many songs. I do hope it hasn't *tired* you; you must take *great* care of that *precious* throat. The Ambassador has so enjoyed it; we *all* have, and you must come to tea and sing another song very soon." And as she talked she took Miss Sims' music from the pianoforte, and rolled it up neatly into a *rouleau*, and tied it up with a little piece of pink ribbon, and presented it to her with a charming but completely final bow, and an equally charming and final "Thank you," and calling Herbert Napier, she said to him, "Mr Napier, will you take Miss Sims to have a cup of tea or some lemonade?" and, so saying, she led the guests back into the drawing-room, and Napier conducted Miss Sims to a small buffet on the top of the staircase, where there were refreshments, whence she was ultimately "shown out."

"She may do for concerts in England," said Lady Lawless; "one never knows what English people will like."

"She has a nice voice," said Donna Teresa, "but she has not much artistic feeling, I fear."

The party, for a Roman party, broke up early.

Lady Lawless, as she said goodbye to Bernard, made eyes at him, and said plaintively that he must come and see them often, although she knew full well how tedious it was for a young man to go to an Embassy.

As they drove to their apartment Bernard was silent, and yet his mother felt that he was pleased with his evening.

"Sir Hedworth is much the nicest ambassador I have ever seen," she said, "and she's amusing."

"Good-looking woman," Bernard said. And then, after a pause, "That French military attaché is a good fellow. He told me some interesting things about Tonquin. I should like to go there."

Mrs Lacy was hopeful after Bernard's first glimpse of Roman society.

On the following Thursday, Bernard kept his appointment with Donna Teresa at the Palazzo Guerrini. He was there at a quarter to five, and she drove him in her carriage to the Palazzo Fabrini.

On the way she explained to him that he need not keep silent.

"Guido likes hearing other people talk to each other a little. That does not tire him so much. But it tires him to be talked to. If it is a good day, he will talk."

"I can't speak a word of Italian," said Bernard.

"Guido speaks English like an Englishman. He was brought up in England."

"Of course."

When they reached the Palazzo, which was in a narrow, dingy street and not impressive outside, they walked up a long flight of stairs to the front door, on the first floor, and they were ushered from the high, gloomy hail along a corridor, through the several rooms where there were some fine old pictures, which impressed Bernard more by their gloom than by their beauty – they were nearly all family portraits – to Guido's room.

It was a high, square room, dimly lit with oil lamps. It struck a chill, although in the high fireplace a small wood fire was crackling. Guido was lying on a sofa near the fire. On one side of his sofa a large arm-chair was occupied by a handsome, fair-haired lady dressed in black. She had an air of importance about her.

In a group round the sofa there were three more Italian ladies, all of them elegant and talkative; one was dark and handsome, and reminded one of a Renaissance picture; she had rather a deep, hoarse voice; the other was dark, too, but small, with a high, curly, fuzzy coiffure; she was gay and animated, and had the ways of a bird.

At the other side of the fireplace Princess Roccapalumba was presiding over another group of people who were talking in an undertone. This group consisted of two bearded Italians and an old French Abbé.

Bernard was introduced to the Princess. She welcomed him gracefully.

"I remember meeting you so well," she said, "that night at Paris in Thérèse d'Aurillac's box. My father used to be such a friend of your mother's. I want you to know my husband."

She led him up to the sofa where Guido was lying. He could see Guido better now. He was dressed in ordinary dark clothes, and had a light rug round his feet, which went up to his waist. He looked pale, certainly, like a man who has been too long indoors. There was something slightly waxen, but no visible marks of suffering or pain in his face.

Bernard was introduced.

Guido bowed and smiled faintly, and stretched out a long, bony hand, which Bernard shook carefully.

A chair was brought up for him. He was presented to the fair lady, who was Mrs Winslope, the American Ambassadress, and to the two dark ladies, one of whom – the taller – was Donna Laura Bartolini; and the other – the small, twittering lady – was Donna Maria Alberti.

Guido asked Bernard a few questions – when he had arrived, how long he was going to stay, whether this was the first time he had been to Rome – and the conversation soon became general.

That is to say, Guido delivered a flowing monologue in English, with a word or a phrase every now and then in Italian, and the Italian ladies punctuated it with adroit comment, without ever interrupting it.

If any one ventured on too long a comment or on anything which threatened to be a serious interruption, Guido put out a long, silencing hand with the gesture of a conductor who is moderating a too emphatic crescendo.

Guido discoursed on politics, the German Emperor, Crispi, Bismarck, the Egyptian question, the difference between Lord

Salisbury and Mr Gladstone, the question of Anglican orders,
the impossibility of getting on with the French Government, a
recent speech in the Chamber of Deputies, the general failure
of parliaments everywhere.

For a permanent invalid, Bernard thought that Guido was an
energetic monologist.

After he had been sitting there a little while, taking part in
the conversation by nodding and an occasional "Yes," "No," or
"Really, how interesting!" the door opened and an imposing
figure entered the room – a tall lady with grey hair and an
opulent figure, dressed in green velvet and sable, with a long
enamel chain round her neck, a lot of jingling trinkets, and a
picturesque head-dress.

Every one got up to make obeisance to her, and Bernard was
presented to Princess Julia.

"My mother," Guido murmured.

She greeted Bernard affably, and said: "I remember your
mother when she was a little girl. You must bring her to see
me."

She asked with a tender seriousness after Guido, greeted her
daughter-in-law and kissed her with unconvincing effusion, and
greeted every one else in turn. She then established herself in
the place of honour and dominated the conversation. She was
the only person whom Guido neither interrupted nor tried to
silence. He listened to her meekly.

Bernard watched the young Princess while this was going
on. He had wondered whether the fleeting impression he had
received in Paris of great beauty and rare interest would be
confirmed, or whether he had been led astray by something
accidental.

The impression he received now was even stronger. He
watched her while she talked Italian to the two Italians and the
Abbé. She was dressed simply in black; her hair seemed to be
done negligently, the waving curls over her forehead and at

the back seemed to have been twisted and finished in a *tour de main.*

"She *must* be younger than mother thinks," thought Bernard. "She can never have been better-looking than she is now. But then some women improve as they grow older – that is a known fact."

Her skin was so extraordinarily white, the line of her throat so taking. Bernard thought he had never seen any one so attractive in his life; nor, he thought, so remote, so aloof, so indifferent. "She does not *really* notice one is in the room," he thought, "in spite of her civility and her unflagging talk."

After the old Princess had been in the room about five minutes, he thought he had been there long enough, and he rather shyly rose to his feet, and said something about having to go.

Donna Teresa helped him out, and Guido said goodbye to him plaintively, and the Princess Julia asked him to bring his mother to her Wednesday evening after dinner without fail. The young Princess smiled an aloof goodbye, and he left the palace with a slight sense of relief. It was all rather oppressive, he thought, as he walked home.

"They are all very nice and all that – charming," he said to his mother, as he described the visit to her, "but I could, of course, never really get to know them – never *be friends* with any of them."

# CHAPTER IV

The following Wednesday, Bernard and Mrs Lacy went to Princess Julia's apartment after dinner, where they met many people. Princess Julia received them with affability; she was almost gushing to Mrs Lacy, and took pains to be charming to Bernard. But the young Princess was not there; it was said she was tired, and that the Prince had had a bad day. This was the beginning of a new phase of Bernard's stay in Rome; he gradually exchanged the world of tourists for the Roman world. He discovered by degrees that Roman society consisted of a number of small circles that were separate and independent of each other, but each of these circles touched some one or other or others of the circles at one point, or at more than one point.

There was a group of people who were international, who belonged to one fold that had sheep in London, Paris, St Petersburg, Nice, Cannes, Monte Carlo, and Vienna. This was a small group; one characteristic of it was that all its members spoke English, and none of them, either in Rome or in St Petersburg, were English, although it numbered a few Americans. Then separate from it, but touching it through individuals at certain points, there were the diplomats, some of whom kept to themselves and associated only with other diplomats; others – Sir Hedworth, for instance, and Herbert

Napier – belonged to and mixed with the international world. Then there was the Roman purely black society; and the Roman white society, embracing men of note, English statesmen, and French academicians: liberal, accessible to foreigners, and yet distinct from the diplomatic world and only touching it at certain points. In close touch with this world there was the artistic and literary world, the world of savants, archaeologists, scholars, men of letters, Dante students, palaeologists of every nation; and in touch with this artistic and literary world, and counting among its units a famous novelist, a talented sculptor, and a conscientious archaeologist, was the permanent American colony. There was an English Catholic colony, in close touch with the Roman black world, and an English ultra-Protestant colony, which ignored the Papacy and looked upon the whole vast, long, and ancient Catholic tradition as the erratic whim of a small, misguided, lapsed Protestant sect, which would one day come to its senses; the Russian colony, touching the diplomatic world at certain points, but otherwise separate from it; and last, there were just the Romans, ordinary Roman society, men who went to the club, women who drove on the Pincio, and who spoke Italian and did little else; and then there was the Italian political world, the deputies, who touched the white society at certain points, but who also were separate.

Bernard touched the fringe of the diplomatic society, and the fringes of both the black and white societies: the black through Princess Julia and some of her friends as well as through the ecclesiastics who were friends of his mother, and the white also through Princess Julia and another group of her friends; the Russian colony through the Olenevs, whom he had met at Princess Julia's and at the British Embassy, and more than the fringe – the heart and centre – of the international Roman world through Princess Roccapalumba, or rather through the people whom he met at her house, who were relations of men whom he met at the Club, of which he had been made an honorary member, and whom he met out hunting in the Campagna.

Belonging to this latter group were Donna Laura Bartolini and Donna Maria Alberti. The former was a widow and lived in a small flat; the latter had married a man much older than herself, who was prominent in the political world. Bernard, after meeting them for the first time at Princess Roccapalumba's house, kept on coming across them at various other houses, at the British Embassy, out hunting, at the Opera.

One day Donna Laura asked him to dinner. His mother was dining elsewhere, and he went by himself, and found nobody but Donna Maria, and a middle-aged man called Alfredo Chiaromonte, who for years had been her *cavaliere serviente*, a young man called Carlo Altamara, and, to his great surprise, Princess Roccapalumba.

He sat next to Princess Roccapalumba at dinner. She seemed pleased to meet an Englishman, and he no longer had the impression that she was so remote and aloof as to be unreachable.

She asked him to come and see her.

"I am at home every day of my life from half-past four till six, and it does Guido good to see people."

Bernard wondered whether she was ever at home any other time.

They talked about England and London. She had not been to London for fourteen years.

"England comes to me," she said. "There are so many English people here, and new ones every year, and one sees many old friends. Living in Rome makes one lazy; one does not care to go anywhere else; one is quite happy where one is – at least that is what I feel."

"But don't you go sometimes to other places in Italy?"

"Yes; to Florence for a night or two sometimes; sometimes to Naples."

"And do you stay here all the summer?"

"Yes; that is the time in Rome I like best of all."

"You don't mind the heat?"

"One stays in all day, and the Palazzo Fabrini is so cool."

Bernard looked at her and wondered, and then the conversation became general, and they talked about hunting and about Giraldi, the new soprano.

After dinner many young men looked in, till the little apartment was crowded, and they stayed talking and smoking cigarettes until one in the morning.

As Bernard walked home he thought of Princess Roccapalumba and the extraordinary life she led with this invalid husband, and he wondered what she really felt about it all; whether she had friends, had or had had lovers or a lover possibly?...whether she was used to exile.

The next day he and his mother had *déjeuner* with the Olenevs (which they did nearly every other day). The two girls, still unmarried, Princess Nelly and Princess Ira, were there. They were now over thirty, both of them. Bernard liked them immensely, and had got to be on intimate, friendly, easy terms with both of them. They were so sensible and so natural. After luncheon he and Ira went into her sitting-room and talked. Bernard talked about Princess Roccapalumba.

"She is my greatest friend here," Princess Ira said. "She is a wonderful woman. I have never seen anybody *si peu égoïste*."

"And what is he like – the Prince?"

"You have seen him?"

"Yes."

"Well, that is all, but *il est très lucide*. Italians are; they have such centuries of tradition behind them. I always feel when I am with Italians, and with English people as to that, that *nous sommes des barbares*. Yes, all of us Russians, the most civilised of us."

"You are much cleverer than English people, I think. You take my breath away sometimes."

"We are cultivated – too cultivated; we have made a fetish of culture in Russia, but unfortunately we absorbed all our culture before we were civilised. English people seem to me to be a thousand times more civilised than we are, and Italians a thousand times more – more, I don't know what – *intellectually* civilised, if you understand."

"Then the Prince is clever?"

"No, not at all, and yes, very much. He does not care for art and books."

"No more do I – much; at least, I know nothing about them."

"But at the same time he understands everything that is happening. He knows what one is thinking. It is uncanny; he frightens me; I find him uncomfortable."

"And she is devoted to him?"

"She is marvellous to him. Think of receiving like that every day! A woman, too, who finds society a bore."

"But will he never get better?"

"I don't think so."

"Do they know what is the matter with him?"

"I really don't think they do. Westerling, the Austrian doctor, says there is nothing the matter with him – that it is all imagination and nerves; but, then, what are nerves? It is just as bad, isn't it, as if there was really something? If I think I am ill, it is the same, I find, as if I were ill."

"Yes; and if one still thinks so, after fourteen years, it ends by being true."

"Of course."

"But does he see different doctors?"

"He has seen all the best doctors in Europe."

"And they can do nothing?"

"Nothing."

"And does he never move from that sofa?"

"He is lifted into bed at night, but he has never walked since he has been ill; that is to say – nobody knows that he has except… "

"Except what?"

"I was going to say 'except me.' I don't think I ought to tell you that story. Nobody knows it but Nelly, but I will tell it you because I know you will not repeat it. Well, about three years ago there was something wrong with the drains in this house and we had to turn out. Blanche asked Nelly and myself to stay at the Palazzo Fabrini, and begged us to, so we did. While we were staying there, a picture of Blanche painted by Valsan, that French painter, arrived. It was an excitement. It was shown to Guido, but he was having a bad day and he wouldn't look at it, said he hated French art, that he was too ill to be shown pictures, etc. The picture was put in the *salotto* next to his room, and we sat there that night after dinner. When we went to bed I noticed where the picture was.

"The next morning I couldn't sleep and I got up early to go to Mass.

"I had to walk through the *salotto* to get to the corridor. The servants had not begun to dust. No one was up. Everything in the *salotto* was exactly as we had left it the night before – the newspaper on the floor where it had been dropped, the cards lying all untidy on the card-table; the only thing that had been moved was the picture; it was no longer where it had been – nearly, but surely not quite in the same place. I had noticed when I went to bed exactly where the picture was, and now I saw that some one had lifted it to look at it, and had not put it back quite where it was before. It was on the top of a sort of *cassone*, and there were the marks in the dust where the picture had been originally. Nobody had been in the *salotto*. I put it back in its original place. Blanche went to bed when I went to bed, and we stayed up a long time in her bedroom. Xenia was not up. All the servants had gone to bed when we went to bed, which was late.

"The only person who could have moved the picture was Guido, unless Blanche had gone down to the *salotto* in the middle of the night, and this she had not done. I believe that

Guido got up to look at the picture, because when we tried to show him the picture in the afternoon he was peevish, naughty, like a child, and I feel quite certain that he *wanted* to see it all the same, that he was *curious*, only he was too naughty at the start, and then there was nothing to do but to go on."

"But you really think he got up and moved the picture?"

"I am sure of it; of course I have no proof."

"But it might have been one of the servants."

"It could only have been Alfredo, and he told Blanche he had not gone to him in the night. None of the other servants could have been there between the time we went to bed and the time I got up. Their rooms are quite far off. We went to bed late, after twelve, and I got up so early because I had a bad night and couldn't sleep. There is no one else who could have done it."

"But that would show – I suppose – that his illness is different from what the doctors imagine, if they think he can't move."

"I sometimes wonder whether he is ill at all."

"What do you mean – that he is just shamming?"

"Yes; I have thought so sometimes. Sometimes I thought that he started by pretending, and that now it has grown real and that he is frightened. Sometimes I have thought that it *was* real at first, and that he got better later, but did not know how to stop. But I don't know; we never shall know – no one will ever know!"

"But what earthly motive could he have for such a thing? It can't be amusing to spend all your life on a sofa."

"I don't know, but I have always felt that he is a *strange* man, and I think he was *jealous* of Blanche."

"But how would that help? What could that have to do with his jealousy?"

"Well, you see, I remember when they were married. Blanche was so young and lovely."

"More than she is now?"

"In some ways I find her better now. She is far more *beautiful* now, if you know what I mean, and far more interesting to look at. But she was *lovely* then; her face was quite round; she was not so thin – not so much as if her face were carved. Well, Guido was madly in love with her, and Blanche I don't think really understood anything, and married him to please her father, who is now a selfish, worldly old man, and was then a selfish, middle-aged man, charming – my mother likes him – but selfish. Well, as soon as they were married I think Blanche found out exactly what she felt, and that she didn't love him – never would, never could love him; and Guido saw this, felt this; he is what we call in Russian '*Chutki*'; he has *sense* like a – oh! so much – *sense like a doctor's*. Well, I think he never forgave her for having married him, or rather for not loving him, and he was determined she should never love any one else."

"I suppose there must have been hundreds of men in love with her?"

"Well, at first there was a baby and it died, and she was so unhappy, and so ill afterwards, and they travelled a lot. I think they went to Egypt. They used to live at Florence, too, and on the lakes, and later they went to England several times. And directly Blanche made friends with any one, or seemed to be making friends with any one, Guido or his mother – and Princess Julia always knew everything that Blanche was doing – would prevent it. There was a nice man we knew called Sasha Valesky, who would have loved Blanche, but Guido prevented that. He died soon after. Then there was a charming English diplomat, Adrian Tyne. He was musical, a great friend of my mother's; Nelly and I did not know him well. He loved Blanche, but I don't know what happened. Probably Princess Julia did something. The end was, he went away and married some one in England. I saw in the newspaper three days ago that he had died in Copenhagen, where he was minister. They expected him to be Ambassador at Paris. His wife is alive, and a son and daughter, I think. He has never been here since he was here *en poste*, except once, I think, *de passage*. Well, all that time Blanche had always lived a quiet life, and never seen more than half a dozen people, and had always been here in the house nearly every day, and liked seeing musicians sometimes and a few nice English people from Oxford, that sort of quiet people. And then there came a time when suddenly she became *mondaine*. I remember it was the year of the big fancy-dress ball at the Palazzo Sori, and Blanche went, and looked more beautiful than any one else. I shall never forget her, in a sort of Madame de Pompadour dress *couleur de feuille morte* and apricot and silver. She was a vision, an *Erscheinung*. She made a sensation, and everybody was *mad* about her. And then suddenly the day after that ball Guido fell ill, and I sometimes wonder whether he thought that Blanche was going to escape him – escape from his influence, I mean, lead her own life, be independent, and no longer care about her *belle-mère*."

"And was there any one in love with her then?"

"Oh, every one! No one in particular. I think, perhaps, Alfredo Chiaromonte was in love with her; that was just before he met Maria Alberti. But from that day Blanche changed her whole life; she never went out any more; she never looked at another man. She devoted herself entirely to Guido."

"Was it then she became a Catholic?"

"Oh no; that happened before, in England, and it had nothing to do with my mother, as a lot of people thought at the time. You see, converts from the Russian Orthodox Church are not common; it happens every now and then, and it's difficult for Russians, the Government make such a bother about it. But as my mother was a convent and brought us up as Catholics, and as every one knew that Blanche was a great friend of hers, every one in Rome – all the foreign colonies and the people who are not Catholics – said at once that it was mother's doing. As a matter of fact, mother had never said a word about it to her, and was surprised when it happened. But it had nothing to do with Guido's illness; it all happened before, and Blanche has often told me that she does not know herself how it happened; it was all gradual."

"But if what you think is true, that he is or was pretending, shamming, do you think the Princess knew it or knows it, suspected or suspects it?"

"No, certainly not at first; whether she does now I'm not sure."

"It must be awful, always having your mother-in-law so close!"

"Yes; and Princess Julia is such a dominating woman, such a clever woman."

"Is she fond of her daughter-in-law?"

"Oh yes, so far as...in the way that...mothers-in-law are."

"And will it go on like that for ever?"

"I suppose so. Of course Princess Julia is old – over seventy, I think."

"I suppose that would make a difference?

"Oh yes, a great difference, I'm sure. I know that Blanche suffers a lot from her."

"I can't think how she can do it, and then those receptions every day."

"Yes, and such tiresome people. Guido likes all the most bothersome people in Rome."

"I don't think, all the same," Bernard said, after a pause, "that a man could possibly pretend to be ill and lie in a half-dark room for fourteen years if he wasn't really ill."

"Such extraordinary things do happen. Nothing is too extraordinary to happen. And, from jealousy or revenge, a man like Guido would be capable of doing anything."

"But he looks so ordinary, and when one hears him talking politics, or about the topics of the day, it is difficult to believe that he could be doing such odd things."

"You only see the surface. One doesn't know what is underneath."

261

"I think he looks ill, all the same."

"Of course I may be quite silly, and somebody else may have moved the picture. Or he may have been able to get up just that once; that sort of thing happens sometimes; it's like a miracle, or St Peter walking on the sea – he had faith enough to do it for once, for a few seconds. I have felt like that reading at sight sometimes at the piano. I have been able suddenly to read a difficult bar quite well, and then I flounder and call out, '*Gospodi spasi menia*' – 'Lord, save me.' If one only had faith, one could go on for ever. And that may have happened to Guido. But whatever his illness may be, whether it is a real illness, or whether he is ill with jealousy, or ill with a wish to avenge himself, or just ill from imagination, just a *malade imaginaire*, I feel that nothing but a miracle will cure him. And whatever it is, whether he is ill *au moral* or *au physique*, I think he must be pitied. I am so, so sorry for him."

"I'm not," said Bernard impatiently. "I've no patience with the fellow. I'm sorry for her, if you like."

"I'm sorry for Blanche, of course, but that is different. Don't you see, can't you understand, that however bad it is for Blanche, it is not nearly as bad, because she is all right *inside*? She has no *sourness*, no bitterness to feel. But he, Guido, he is suffering from bitterness all the time, from *fiel* – what is it you call it – 'gall'? – all the time."

"Of course he is, if he is shamming, and well he deserves it."

"No, in any case – altogether – whatever it is. If it is a real illness, he *must* feel bitterness, because nobody can cure him, and because nobody knows what his illness is, not even himself. But if it is *not* a real illness, if he is pretending to be ill, then it is *much worse*, because then he is punishing himself every minute of the day, and of the night, and feeding on poison, and suffering *torment* all the day. If it is like that, he is most to be pitied. But I pity him; whatever is true, I feel one must pity him."

"All that is beyond me," said Bernard. "I can't understand you."

Their conversation was interrupted by the entry into the room of Princess Olenev, Mrs Lacy, and the others.

# CHAPTER V

It was after the conversation that has just been recorded that Bernard began to be a frequent visitor at the Palazzo Fabrini during the hours that the Princess received for the entertainment and relaxation of her husband.

There was, as a rule, a crowd of people in the dark sitting-room, but if you went early or late you sometimes had an opportunity of a longer talk with the Princess on the sofa at the other end of the room, while one visitor was talking to Guido. This was Bernard's experience, and in this way he came to know the Princess better, and became after a time more intimate than he had ever expected to be with her, although he was unaware at the time of the progress of the intimacy.

One day, at one of the usual afternoon receptions – only Princess Julia, the Abbé, the doctor, and one or two others were present – they were talking of hunting; this was at the end of January, and Bernard, telling her that his stay at Rome was nearing its end, said to her: "Why don't you come out hunting? All your friends do, and it is great fun."

"I haven't been out hunting for years," she said – "not since I was first married, but I think I *would* rather like to try once more; I used to like it. You see, as a girl I lived so little in the country. My father had no country home, but we used to go and stay with cousins and aunts or friends for Christmas, Easter, and Whitsuntide, or sometimes in the autumn for the shooting, and there I used often to ride, to go out cub-hunting, and sometimes real hunting, and I used to enjoy it immensely. I'm not a good rider – I mean I don't know anything about hunting, and probably call all the things by their wrong names, and make all sorts of impossible mistakes, but I used to enjoy it – I'm not frightened – I used to love galloping over country that looked like a Christmas card, and jumping banks in the West Country; oh, it was fun! And I enjoyed it here too – I hunted when I first got to know Guido. What a long time ago! And then once more, a few winters later. I didn't care for it then so much. I was not well and rather depressed. There was a short moment, too, one winter season when I began again, and then Guido got ill, and I have never hunted, never ridden since."

"Come out the day after tomorrow."

And then one of those curious small coincidences happened which are so frequent in real life, of which writers of fiction fight shy, although they are not afraid of the grand ones. Dr Panuzzi, who had been talking to Guido – he was not a specialist, but the family doctor, the *Hausarzt* – came up to Blanche to say goodbye, and, kissing her hand, he said: "You ought to go out more, Princess. Why don't you take exercise in the open air? Why don't you go out riding or hunting in the Campagna?"

"Yes; why not?" said Princess Julia, who overheard the remark from the other end of the room. She had ears that could hear the grass grow and eyes that could see through the back of her head. "I think that would be an excellent plan, Blanche. I always said it was a pity that you had given up hunting; you used to enjoy it so much and it used to do you good."

Guido, too, assented feebly from his sofa.

"I have always told her I wanted her to hunt" – as if people thought that it might be his fault that she did not.

"Well," said Blanche, "I don't know what I could ride."

265

"There are plenty of horses eating their heads off in the stable," said Guido, and he showed signs of so much impatience that Blanche, to quiet him, promised that she would go to the next meet.

She went, much to the amusement of many of her friends, who were surprised to see her suddenly on horseback, but agreed that it suited her. Donna Laura and Donna Maria chaffed her especially. She had not been out hunting for years – what on earth was the meaning of it?

"Well," she said, "the doctor says I am too much indoors; that I must go out more; that I am making myself ill; that I want exercise; he has recommended riding, and just *riding* bores me frankly, so I thought I would try *hunting*. I used to hunt a long time ago. If I find it too tiring, I shall never do it again, but I thought I would just like to try."

During that month and the next she made a regular habit of it.

And every time she went out hunting she met Bernard, and little by little a curious, an unexpressed intimacy, grew up between them. Bernard looked forward to the next meet, and indeed thought of nothing else, but he never expressed to himself nor admitted that he was looking forward to meeting Blanche.

They had long, swift gallops together, long, slow rides home, and sometimes they would sit by the roadside or on the turf and eat sandwiches, or visit together some little *trattoria* and eat *frittata* and drink some of the local *Vino dei castelli*, with the thirst and hunger that only comes to those who are out hunting when the hour for a meal is long past.

Walter Troumestre was to have come out to Rome for Christmas, but just before Christmas he wrote at some length to explain that this was impossible. Bernard had been annoyed when this letter arrived, and had said:

"Very well; I shall go home at once."

But all at once his mother noticed there was no more talk of his going home, no more railing against Walter. Bernard seemed perfectly content; he said he found Rome so interesting, the people so charming; never had a climate suited him so well.

Mrs Lacy wondered. She thought there must be something, but she did not know what. She did not even go to the meets, so she had no idea what was happening in the Campagna, and Bernard never went with her to the Palazzo Fabrini. If she suggested going there with him, he always had some reason for not going that particular day, at that particular hour. However, whatever the hidden reason might be, and Mrs Lacy was convinced there was a particular reason, she was thankful that her son had no wish to leave Rome, that she had not been instrumental in taking him to a place he disliked, and that he would be sorry to go. And yet – she could not help feeling a vague apprehension.

All this seemed too good; but what was it? He seemed to have no particular friends. Well, she should be thankful that he had recovered from his heart-sickness, for there was no doubt that he had recovered; he had made an unexpectedly quick recovery.

January went by like a flash both for Mrs Lacy and for Bernard. Towards the middle of February, Bernard heard from Walter Troumestre, saying that he was coming to Rome; he was going to stop a few days in Paris and Florence, and then ten days in Rome, and he wanted to travel back to London with Bennard; he understood that Bernard had promised to be in London by the beginning of March.

Bernard showed his mother the letter.

"That's wonderful, isn't it?" she said. "That will be fun for you, but I think it is tiresome of him to stop on the way at Paris and Florence. I think he might just as well have come straight here."

"Yes," said Bernard, "he might." But he did not suggest taking any steps to persuade him to do so.

Walter arrived towards the middle of February. Bernard was delighted to see him, and when Walter asked him if he had made many friends, he said: "Nobody in particular, but there are one or two people I want you to know – Donna Laura Bartolini, who is awfully good-looking, and Donna Maria Alberti, who is charming and great fun, and then there's that Princess Roccapalumba we saw in Paris, but she seldom goes anywhere because her husband's ill."

He asked Walter if he would like to go out hunting in the Campagna, and he was rather relieved when Walter said that he did not come to Rome for ten days to hunt, and that it would take him all his time to see the Forum, the Colosseum, and the Vatican. He, for his part, was not ashamed of being a sightseer. Bernard laughed the laugh of a man who is really pleased, but who is pretending to think that something is ridiculous.

The end of February came – his last days in Rome. He went to the Palazzo Fabrini for the last time. It was incredible to him to think he would not go there again. He had come to enjoy it all: the political discussions, or, rather, the political questions of Guido; the short, dry remarks of the Abbé; the fleecy amiability, with sometimes a sharp silver glint, of Princess Julia; the twitter of stray visitors; the large, high, gloomy, empty rooms; the home-grown old masters; the old-fashioned chandeliers; the friendly, welcoming, shabby servants.

He would not see that any more, nor would he see any more the smiling, pale face, the large, soft, endlessly transparent and endlessly inscrutable eyes of Princess Blanche.

How that name suited her! She could not have been called anything else.

Yes, he would miss her; she had been kind to him, and they got on so easily now. This was odd; at one time he had thought he would never be able to know her; she had seemed to him aloof, far away, and indifferent, almost like a ghost. But now he was comfortable in her society. He thought her so human, such fun; it was, of course, because they both were English, he said to himself.

The day he went to the Palazzo Fabrini to make his final visit, he took Walter with him, and introduced him to Blanche, to Guido, and to Princess Julia, and Walter felt that he was entering and disturbing a precinct of intimacy.

The conversation was general, and dealt with nothing but commonplace topics; and yet Walter felt the whole time as if he were overhearing an intimate conversation, expressed in overtones, and silences, and hints, and reservations. He did not define it more nicely; he did not try to find a cause or a reason; he merely felt that this was so.

When Bernard said goodbye to Princess Blanche, he asked her if she was going out hunting the next day. It would be his last day's hunting; he was leaving Rome on the evening of the day after.

"I don't know," she said. "It depends on Guido."

Bernard then said goodbye, and when he said goodbye to Princess Julia, she said to him in an undertone: "I am so glad you helped to persuade Blanche to go out hunting again. It has done her so much good. She is a different woman since she has taken to hunting again."

"Exercise is good for every one," said Bernard, without paying much attention to Princess Julia's intonations, which were full of intention. They said goodbye, and Bernard told the Princess that his mother would be looking in later.

The next day the meet was beyond Porta S. Pancrazio. Walter Troumestre refused even to go to the meet; he was going to Tivoli with Mrs Lacy. It was a soft spring day. The touch of the early spring is perhaps more subtle and penetrating in Rome than anywhere else. Hidden larks were singing in the light blue sky.

Bernard chattered with the Olenevs at the meet and looked wonderingly at the green, melancholy stretches of flat country.

Their uncle, Prince Potemkin, had driven the two Olenev girls to the meet in a brake and four-in-hand; he was an upright, fine-looking man of sixty, with grey hair and beautifully made boots, and a wonderful whip. He liked Bernard; he liked Englishmen – that type of Englishman.

"Is that what a steppe is like in Russia?" Bernard said to Ira Olenev.

"In a way, yes, but not really. The Campagna is unlike *anything* else; in Russia you don't have those roads carved out of what looks like pieces of dead volcano, nor those cork trees. The grasses later on in May are rather like the Russian steppe when it all blossoms."

"The wilderness blossoms like a rose," said Blanche.

"Yes?" said Bernard. The quotation meant nothing to him; he had never read the Old Testament.

At the end of the plain, on the horizon, the steady clouds looked almost like a range of hills.

There was a crowd of people at the meet – people on horseback, people in carriages – landaus, brakes, cabs, four-in-hands. There was a large luncheon tent; and many cavalry officers in uniform – dark blue, grey and gold; these and the red-coated Master of the Hounds, the hunt servants and a drag-full of hounds, were the high lights of the picture, bold and sharp against the undertoned landscape.

The Olenevs were not riding; they got out of their brake and walked when they arrived at the meet.

Blanche, Donna Maria, and one or two others formed a little group apart. While they were all talking together, an oldish-looking man came up to them, an Englishman, who wore gold-rimmed spectacles. He looked serene, serious, and benign. To Bernard he seemed an old man, but he was only fifty. He said "How do you do" to Princess Roccapalumba, and she seemed surprised and pleased to see him, and introduced him to Bernard as Mr Bretherton.

"Fancy our meeting here!" she said. "You haven't been to Rome for years, and I have seldom been out hunting since you were last in Rome, not till this year. But perhaps you have been to Rome and haven't been near us? If so, it's unkind."

"No," said Bretherton, "I haven't been to Rome for fifteen years. I came here," he said, "because I enjoy these meets so much. I like the Campagna better than anything in the world."

At that moment there was a noise of horns and hooting, and shouts and champing of bits, and plunging of restive horses.

Bretherton looked abstractedly at the horizon and said to himself:

"Over the light blue hills
There came a noise of revellers."

And he handed Princess Roccapalumba a long, branched flower – the little, spiky flower itself a pale pink shot with grey, with grey-green leaves.

"That," he said, "is not for remembrance, but for a forgetting. It is an asphodel. It has a smell of fresh onion. Asphodels and onions are both of them very good things." He said this gravely, and then he took off his hat and said, "It's time for you to start – goodbye."

A moment later they were off.

"What an extraordinary man," Bernard said to the Princess, as he rode by her side.

"Yes; isn't he? He is an English scholar. He knows all about Greek and Latin things. I used to know him here a long time ago, and I have not seen him for years – not since," she said, with a sigh, "Guido has been ill."

It was a delirious day's hunting; Bernard thought the best of all. He had never enjoyed anything more. There was something aromatic coming from the turf – a smell of mint and fennel and spring – he knew not what; there was something intoxicating in the air; his horse went well; there was astounding timber to

271

jump, and soft, springy turf to gallop over. Nature seemed to have caught the mood of the larks that were singing out of sight.

Later on in the day Bernard came across Princess Roccapalumba, whom he had lost sight of for some time. She had broken her stirrup. They both dismounted, tethered the horses to a stumpy cork tree, and sat on the edge of a road alone in the great desolation.

"I wonder," said the Princess, "if there were once streams here. One feels there ought to be."

"I wonder," said Bernard, but he was not really wondering at that. He was wondering that he should be there alone with her, wondering at her, wondering at himself.

"You are really going away?" she asked.

"Yes, tomorrow."

"You have enjoyed being here?"

"Yes, awfully."

"Perhaps you will come back next year?"

"Oh yes; I mean to, if I can."

"But nothing is ever quite the same – quite so good the second time, is it?"

"Do you think so?"

"Yes, I am sure of it."

"You have been kind to me."

Blanche said nothing, but her eyes filled with tears for the moment.

"I felt ill when I first got here, but now I feel quite well. You cured me."

Blanche blushed.

"She can never have looked more beautiful than she does now," thought Bernard.

"Rome is a healing place," she said. "When I first came here, after I married, I mean, I felt ill and thought that I should never recover, but now all that feeling is gone. I got well."

She smiled as she said this softly, and all at once she looked sad – sad with a sadness that Bernard had never come across before. It startled and hurt him.

He looked at her, and she seemed to him to be exactly the right person in those sad surroundings – native to them, the Queen of those desolate rolling plains and brown roads and twinkling grey and pink flowers. The melancholy of the place and the hour was piercing. The great clouds were no longer steady on the horizon; they had rolled away; there was now one black, rather threatening cloud in the east, veiling the sun for the moment, but beneath it there was a shining, golden space; but even that glory was a sad one, as if it came from the underworld. To the left of them there was a fragment of broken masonry, but there was no human being in sight. They were the only live things in an empty, forlorn world. They sat for some time in silence. Bernard looked at Blanche, looked at her as he had looked at her the first time he had seen her, in that *baignoir* at the opera, and once more he thought that she was a stream into which the more you looked the more unfathomable its transparency became.

But now as he looked at her there was a different light in her soft eyes, something he had never seen there before; something infinitely sad, and yet something speaking; something which seemed to open the doors that he had thought would be shut for ever, and which would bridge the immeasurable gulfs; something which filled up all that space and that wide chasm, and destroyed all sense of aloofness and distance, and brought him close, near to her, quite near to her, nearer than anything he could imagine. It was something suffering and human and appealing, something in distress, that wanted pity, comfort, and solace and understanding, and love – above all things, love.

"Don't quite forget me when you go," she whispered.

He took hold of her hand and pressed it, and looked into her eyes, drinking their message as it were to the depths, and then he gave her a long kiss. At that moment the thread of his life

273

crossed and caught that of Blanche's, and the fingers of destiny, with a sudden deft movement, changed the pattern in the cat's cradle of their lives.

The long moment, the short eternity, was broken by the noise of a creaking cart, and presently along the road came a small donkey-cart, with a man walking beside it dressed in skins, and looking as if he had stepped from a picture; he sang – one could not call it a snatch of *song*, but a few hoarse ejaculations – and then he seemed to think better of it and he stopped, and as he passed Bernard and the Princess he took off his cap and gravely saluted them. The cart was followed almost at once by a long string of mules, in charge of some one else.

"We must go on," said the Princess.

And as Bernard began to attend to the question of the stirrup, some friends and one or two grooms – among them the Princess's groom – cantered up. Explanations were made, information was asked and given. A new iron was produced by one of the men. They cantered on, and once more joined the main hunt.

Bernard had another brief and breathless gallop with Blanche, and successfully dealt with two dangerous jumps; but at the third, which looked inoffensive enough, his horse fell.

He was carried unconscious to a little village by people who, as happens when there is an accident, seemed to spring as by magic from the ground. Blanche was riding behind him and saw the accident happen. She turned quite white, but far from losing her presence of mind, she became calmer, more deliberate, and more practical. In the presence of danger she was like ice. She dismounted, called one of the grooms, and gave clear directions as to what was to be done. Bernard was carried into a little battered *trattoria*. A sympathetic crowd assembled and gave advice. They were, as a matter of fact, not fan from Rome, although they seemed to be in the midst of a desert. They were close to Maglianella, and the groom returned with the news that the Princess' carriage was on its way.

Bernard was carefully placed in the carriage and driven slowly home by Blanche. He was still unconscious when they arrived. They were met by a well-known Italian surgeon. The Princess had sent one of the grooms on to call the doctor, who was to warn Mrs Lacy. She, however, was still out, so this had not been necessary. The doctor did all that was needful, and assured Blanche that he would do all he could. He said he thought the accident was serious, but not fatal. One could not say anything definite for at least twenty-four hours. Blanche looked like a person in a dream when she heard these words; and at that moment, to her relief, as she could not wait any longer, Mrs Lacy and Walter Troumestre arrived, and Blanche, skilfully meeting them on the stairs, managed to tell Walter Troumestre first. She beckoned to him, and he ran up the stairs while Mrs Lacy was still dawdling below in the lovely Roman twilight, talking to the concierge's wife. Walter understood in a flash.

"We mustn't frighten her," he said, "or let her think that we are suppressing anything."

They went down the stone steps together and met Mrs Lacy just as she was walking upstairs, with a lange bundle of flowers in her arms. She was surprised to see Blanche.

"Princess Roccapalumba has come to tell you," said Walter, "that Bernard has had a fall out hunting. She has brought him home in her carriage, and the doctor has been and thinks it will be all right, but he is still unconscious from concussion."

Mrs Lacy flew up the stairs without paying attention to them, like a wounded animal, while her superficial self mechanically repeated civil phrases, such as, "Of course, concussion; not serious; thank you so much; how kind of you to come; how good of the doctor; of course he will be all right."

Blanche did not come up again, but she said to Walter before she left: "Tell Mrs Lacy that I arranged with the doctor to send round an excellent English nurse, whom I know well."

The nurse came round later. Bernard did not recover consciousness for forty-eight hours, and even then he did not seem sensible, but the doctor and the nurse assured Mrs Lacy that all was going on well. They could not yet say that he was out of danger. There would, of course, be no question of his leaving Rome for a month or six weeks, but the doctor did not think, so he assured Mrs Lacy, that Bernard had received any serious injury.

One of his eyes was completely red, and two of his teeth had been knocked out, and he had broken three ribs; but the serious feature was the concussion.

Mrs Lacy was profoundly thankful that it was no worse; nevertheless, she lived for four days in an agony of suspense.

Walter Troumestre would have liked to have stayed to keep her and Bernard company during his convalescence, but, as Bernard could not move, it became all the more necessary for Walter to go home at once, which he meant to do as soon as Bernard should be pronounced out of danger. This verdict was at last given to Mrs Lacy, Walter, and Blanche – who called to inquire every day – five days after the accident.

# CHAPTER VI

It was five days before Bernard was pronounced to be out of danger, and ten days before he seemed to be able to talk rationally and recognise people.

During the first days of his recovered consciousness, at one time he would seem to be himself, and then he would doze off and forget everything once more.

He recognised Walter, the first person he was allowed to see. He spent nearly the whole day in sleep. Walter left Rome on the sixth day after the accident.

Bernard was not able to move and go out till the end of March. Princess Roccapalumba lent Mrs Lacy her carriage whenever she wanted it, and she often sent fruit to Bernard and sometimes flowers. Other people were equally kind: the Olenevs, Donna Laura, Sir Hedworth and Lady Lawless, Herbert Napier, and many other English and Roman people, and nearly all the hunting world.

As soon as he was allowed to see people he had many visitors: Blanche came to see him once with Donna Laura; but Guido had not been well, and it was difficult for her to come more often. Nevertheless, Bernard was happy.

When he first regained consciousness the whole of the past weeks at Rome seemed to him like a dream; he did not know what had happened and what had not happened, but he gradually felt that at the back of things there was something new, and something delightful.

And then, little by little, the mists seemed to dissipate. And as they did so, one figure became definite and real in a surrounding world of shadows: Blanche. During his convalescence he only saw her that once, and then not by herself. And yet he felt that she was near him the whole time.

As soon as he was able to get about, the first place he went to was the Palazzo Fabrini; there he found everything going on in the same way, and he met Blanche at the Olenevs' and at Donna Laura's house. Donna Laura saw at once what was happening. She said nothing, but she made things easy. It was Blanche's face and manner that told the story. She was a different woman.

Mrs Lacy knew everything, too; the whole thing had become plain to her suddenly the day of Bernard's accident, or rather when she had thought over the matter after the accident. She grasped the situation, and she refused to face it, or to probe more deeply. She felt she was a coward, possibly a wicked woman, possibly preparing for herself and for everybody else a series of punishments and mortifications in this world and in the next; nevertheless, she could not do anything, nor be anything than simply thankful that her son, who had once been unhappy, was now happy once more.

And then, she argued with herself, what could she do? She could not take Bernard away. She had no influence over him. Again, she would say to herself, what did she know? Oh, what sophistry! She knew everything all too well! However, they would soon be going back to England, and then it would all be over. Bernard would start a new life. That page would be turned over for ever – and then?

But she knew that she was not speaking the truth to herself.

Bernard after his first visit did not go to the Palazzo Fabrini. Blanche had asked him not to. She was afraid, she told him quite frankly, of Princess Julia's scrutiny and of Guido's insight.

"I did not know I was such a wonderful actress," she said one night when they were sitting in Donna Laura's little sitting-room after dinner – Donna Laura was dining out herself and had asked them to wait if she should not be back when they arrived – "nor such a wonderful, calm liar; but I don't think I could keep it up with them. I am not sure that, as it is, my mother-in-law doesn't know."

"It isn't possible."

"I don't think my mother-in-law does suspect any more, or rather I don't think – I am quite sure – she does not *know* anything, but she knows or thinks that you *might* be fond of me, and she is *ready* to suspect."

"I have only been in the house once since I got well," said Bernard.

"It is frightening how much she knows about what is happening everywhere. She asked me the other day why you didn't come in the afternoon so often, and I told her what was true: that the doctor had said it was tiring for you to talk to many people together. I sometimes have a terrible feeling that she might be holding something in reserve for us and is waiting to spring."

"I think it would perhaps be better if I were to come more often," said Bernard. "It looks odd."

"Oh no, I can't bear it; I can't simply face it."

"The result is, I hardly ever see you."

"It can't be helped. We can't be too careful; if we are not careful, scrupulously careful, we may ruin everything."

At that moment Donna Laura came into the room, and presently the whole apartment was full of chattering young men, smoking cigarettes.

It was on such occasions that Blanche and Bernard met. They dared not go much to the Olenevs', for in that camp Princess Julia was able to get information. They dared still less meet at any of the well-known "sights" (galleries, museums), and still less at the lesser-known "sights" (out-of-the-way churches, villas, and gardens). There was no more question of riding and hunting – at least not for Bernard at present.

There were no large entertainments going on, as it was Lent. It was a tantalising situation, and yet Bernard was not unhappy. He was happy to be in Rome, and to feel that Blanche was in the same city.

One evening Mrs Lacy received a note from Princess Olenev, asking her to look in after dinner, as she had some music.

She and Bernard were asked.

So was Blanche, and she was determined not to go. Princess Julia, when Blanche told her that she was not going – and Blanche told all this to Bernard later – expressed disappointment and peevish annoyance. She had so much wanted to go – as Princess Julia disliked music, this was odd – but of course she would not go alone.

Blanche thought that, if she at once offered to go with her, her mother-in-law would cease to want to go, so she at once said that of course she would take her, and that she would like to go herself. Then to her surprise her mother-in-law instead of, as she expected her to do, and according to her usual method on such occasions, saying that she, on second thoughts, thought she would *not* go, jumped at Blanche's offer and made arrangements for their dining together.

At half-past nine they were to go to the Olenevs'.

Blanche wrote a note to Bernard, asking him not to come, and telling him that she would be there with her mother-in-law.

Bernard thought this ridiculous; he thought also that she would be pleased if he *did* come in spite of her asking him not to, and finally – his time at Rome would soon be drawing to an end – that he could not forgo the pleasure of seeing her *in the distance*; they need not even talk to each other. He took no notice of the note and went with his mother.

It was a little concert.

The drawing-room was full of chairs.

When Blanche walked into the room, the first person she saw was Bernard. He looked guilty. Princess Julia greeted him warmly and whispered to him: "Do you like serious music? It's going to be *very* serious tonight."

Bernard said he was not worthy of classical music.

"The unmusical will be able to sit in the next room."

At that moment the musicians walked in at the other end of the room – a pianist and a violinist – and took their places.

The guests sat down with a rustle, and among them Blanche. Princess Olenev made an authoritative gesture commanding silence, and Princess Julia beckoned Bernard to follow her along the corridor into another room, which he did. It was a wide, high room opening on to the corridor. The doors were left open. There they found old Prince Potemkin, Princess Olenev's brother, playing whist with three other old gentlemen, and some of the young people were playing a game like "My bird sings" in a recess.

"You will help me do my patience," said the Princess, and she established herself on a sofa at the end of the room. Bernard fetched a small, vacant card-table for her, and sat down beside it.

"I always do the same patience every night," she said. "It is called 'Metternich,' and it hardly ever comes out. When it does come out, I never feel comfortable, because it always means that something disagreeable is going to happen. I remember it coming out just before the Franco-Prussian War was declared, and once again just before Guido fell ill."

Bernard looked on patiently while the Princess shuffled and dealt, and devised and combined and commented. The patience came out, much to her surprise; she did it again, and that time it did not come out.

"That music is too difficult for me," said the Princess. "The truth of the matter is, I can't bear German music. I like Italian music, and the old-fashioned kind."

"I agree," said Bernard. "German music is too difficult for me."

"But some people like it. My daughter-in-law, for instance."

"Is she musical?" Bernard felt himself growing stiffer.

"Yes, she is musical; she used to play the pianoforte so well, but she gave it up. Such a pity."

"I suppose she hadn't time."

"No, not since Guido has been ill. How do you think he was when you last saw him?"

"I thought he looked a little better."

"That is what they all say. I only hope it's true. I see too much of him to judge. You have a fresher eye. But you never come to see us now. You used to come so often."

Bernard became a little confused.

"The doctor... "

"Told you it was bad for you to see too many people at a time."

"Yes; that's just it."

"It's naughty of you to have come here tonight, but I'm glad you did. I should have been left to myself if you hadn't."

Bernard felt that he had made a mistake; he longed to escape from this conversation before he made another.

"But I hope you don't go out riding or hunting?"

"No; the doctor says I mustn't yet. I think it's nonsense."

"I'm sorry Blanche has given it up *again*. It used to be so good for her. It is good, I think, for any one. I used to love hunting when I was young. One gets to know people so easily, and so intimately. There is nothing quite like it. Especially here at Rome, where it is so difficult to see people except in a crowd. London is so much nicer in that way, I always think. You can see people at home and get to know them intimately without any fuss. However, one mustn't complain, I suppose. One does manage to make friends here in spite of everything."

She gave Bernard a swift look, as quick as the sting of a wasp, as sharp as the prick of a needle.

Bernard felt himself wince under it, but he kept his composure.

He said, with all the calm and indifference he could command: "Yes, I suppose you do," as if it were a question that in no way concerned him. He felt, nevertheless, that there was a strain in his voice.

At that moment Lady Lawless came into the room, to the relief of Bernard.

"I am so late that I didn't dare go into the music-room, and between you and me I was rather afraid" – she lowered her voice into a whisper – "that the music would be beyond me, so I came in here, and it's delightful to find some other friends in the same position. Hedworth couldn't come, poor dear; he has had to go to a man's dinner with the English colony. Chamber of Commerce or something of the kind. Well, Mr Lacy, it is nice to see you again. I think you look better than you did before the fall – *your* fall I mean, not our common fall. Perhaps you would be really kind and come and have dinner with us one night. Have pity on us; we have been so dull and lonely lately, what with Lent and Hedworth's rheumatism. And perhaps I might persuade you to come, Princess Julia, and bring your beautiful daughter-in-law, but it is so difficult to get her. She never will dine anywhere except at Donna Laura's. I was only telling Donna Laura the other day she gets all the young men, all the old men, and all the beautiful women to her tiny little apartment, and it's not fair, because we can't get any one to our empty marble halls. I'm told she had a charming evening the other night – all the youth and beauty. You were there, of course, Mr Lacy?"

Bernard stiffened; it was the evening when he had last met Blanche alone.

"She has always been kind to me," he said.

"Blanche told me she had enjoyed it immensely," said the Princess, "and I am sure she did, for she went so early and stayed so late." She said these words with a soft, cooing voice, but as she said the word *early* she gave Bernard another piercing look as much as to say: "I know perfectly well why you went so early."

He felt he could stand this subtle and protracted examination no longer. It was like being on the rack.

"I think there is a pause or an interval, and I hear them coming out," he said. "I must go and see what my mother is doing," and he got up. "I will come back presently."

The first half of the programme was over, and Bernard met some of the audience in the corridor. Among others, Blanche.

"Have you seen my mother-in-law anywhere?" she asked.

"Yes; I've just been talking to her. She's sitting in there, on the sofa at the end of the room opposite the door."

"I want to tell her I'm going."

"Are you going so soon?"

"Yes; I've got a headache, and I want to look in and see that Guido is all right. He wasn't quite so well."

Bernard was standing with his back to the door.

"I'm sorry I disobeyed you," he whispered. "I couldn't help coming. You are not angry with me, are you?"

"No, of course not," whispered Blanche, with a smile, but hardly moving her lips; "but *do* take care, she can see us."

"She can't see me from here; my back is turned to her. Good night, my darling," he whispered. "Come when you can to Donna Laura's. I'm having luncheon there tomorrow."

He gave Blanche one look of passionate adoration, and then formally and quite clearly he said: "Good night, Princess; I must try and find my mother."

When Bernard said his back was turned to Princess Julia he was right, but when he said that Princess Julia could not have seen him he was wrong; he forgot the large looking-glass that hung in the corridor. There was not much to see, it is true; only a swift, fleeting expression, but what there was to see, Princess Julia could certainly have seen it, and would see it if she were looking. It could have told her little more than what she might already have surmised after her conversation with Bernard at the patience-table – if she surmised anything.

Whatever she saw or did not see, whatever she surmised or did not surmise, she said nothing to Blanche as she drove home with her. She hardly mentioned Bernard, except to say: "I think Mr Lacy is looking better, but I think it is imprudent of him to go to parties so soon, in those hot, crowded rooms. It is not," she added, "as if he were musical."

"I suppose he wanted to be civil to the Olenevs," said Blanche. "Mrs Lacy is a great friend of theirs."

"I suppose so," said Princess Julia, and changed the subject.

It was rather a cold night, and Princess Julia said something as they reached the Palazzo Fabrini to Blanche about the danger of her catching cold by coming out of those hot rooms into the cold air.

But it was Princess Julia, although she had seldom had a day's illness, and in spite of her constitution of steel, who caught cold, and not Blanche; and the next day she sent down a message to say she would come to *déjeuner* with Blanche.

Blanche had arranged to go to Donna Laura's and did not dare say she was going there. She knew that her mother-in-law would be certain to ask her where she was going if she said she was going out, so she sent a note to Donna Laura, saying she could not have luncheon, but would come afterwards, if possible.

Princess Julia arrived, thickly wrapped up, and explained that she felt she was perhaps in for a long cold, and she had not seen Guido properly for some days, so she thought she would spend the whole afternoon with him directly he was awake and cared to see people, and then keep to her rooms the next day if her cold was no better.

Blanche jumped at this idea.

"That will just suit me," she said. "I have ordered the carriage at half-past two. I am going to take Mrs Lacy out

285

driving" (she was going to do this later on), "and I shall be home by the time you will have finished your talk."

"Don't hurry, Blanche darling, as I shall have a *long* talk with Guido today. I haven't seen him properly for days. That is to say, of course, if he wants to talk to me."

"I shall be in by half-past four."

"Don't hurry. Mania Olenev is coming later, and perhaps Lady Lawless."

So Princess Julia remained alone with Guido from three o'clock till half-past four that day. When Blanche came back, her mother-in-law said: "We had a long talk. I really think he is a little better, more cheerful, and he wants to see Mania Olenev and Lady Lawless, if they come, so let him. It will do him good. And now I am going upstairs. I won't kiss you, so as not to give you my cold, and don't be surprised if I don't appear at all tomorrow. I am going to be a mollycoddle and stay by the fire. I feel rather shivery."

She was gentle in her manner and looks – sympathetic, affectionate.

"She can be charming when she likes," Blanche thought, and she shivered.

She was afraid that some one or something was preparing to snatch away her newly found happiness.

# CHAPTER VII

The next day Princess Julia's cold was no better. She stayed upstairs in her room. Blanche went to see her, and she was still in the same soft, affectionate, sympathetic mood. Guido seemed to have taken a turn for the better.

The day after, Princess Julia took to her bed; she had a temperature. The doctor said it was influenza. This was on a Thursday. On Friday she was worse; her temperature was higher, and she had violent pains all over her body, and especially behind her eyes and at the back of her head. On Saturday the situation was unchanged, but on Sunday her temperature went down with a rush to below normal; she was weak and exhausted. Another doctor was called in. Both the doctors talked of her strong constitution. Then, with alarming rapidity, she grew weaker, and when the priest arrived to administer the Last Sacraments, the Holy Oils and the Viaticum, she was hardly conscious.

She died on Monday in the small hours of the morning.

During the last two days Guido had complained more than usual, and Blanche had had to rush from bedside to bedside. Now she had to break the news to him.

He took it calmly.

"I think," he said, "she knew she might die; it is just as well it happened like that. She would not have endured a long, lingering illness. She remained young... "

Blanche looked at him and wondered whether he, too, experienced a sense of escape, as of a weight having been lifted. He certainly had been fond of his mother – so at least she had always thought.

Donna Teresa and her husband were spending the winter in Egypt. They had gone up the Nile. A telegram had been sent them as soon as the Princess' condition was thought to be serious, and now another was sent, but they would not, however promptly they started, and however quickly they travelled, be able to reach Rome for at least six weeks.

The household was in commotion.

Relations arrived in crowds: the Abbé and many other ecclesiastics. Princess Julia's bedroom was turned into a *chapelle ardente*, and for a day her body lay in state covered with roses, with three immense candles burning on each side of the bed.

She looked beautiful in death. All the lines had gone, and there was a smile on her face; but Blanche thought it was an enigmatic smile, as of Mona Lisa, which seemed to say, "Wait, you have not finished with me yet."

Then the undertakers came, and the body was enclosed in a catafalque, and still streams of mourners poured through the palace, and then, after what seemed to Blanche three interminable days, came the Requiem Mass at the Parish Church, which was attended by the whole of Roman society, black and white.

Bernard and Mrs Lacy were there, and this was the first time Bernard and Blanche had seen each other, even in the distance, since the musical party at the Olenevs'.

She had written to him, telling him to be patient, for she felt confident that a new epoch of greater freedom was about to dawn for them, and at the same time all her hope, her great new hope, was shot with apprehension and foreboding.

Bernard was awaiting a summons with impatience, without any doubt, indecision, or trepidation. He was observing the decencies by staying in the background until all the ceremony and business connected with Princess Julia's death should be over. But he was full of hope and happiness. He was untroubled by any fear or anxiety, and happy in the present without thinking of the future.

Bernard had intended to go home at the end of the month, but the doctor told Mrs Lacy that it would be more prudent for him to stay in Rome another month, and to get quite well before beginning his ordinary work once more. So Mrs Lacy settled to stay in Rome till the end of May. It was a lovely spring that year, and Bernard made no objections to this plan. He seemed pleased at staying, and Mrs Lacy knew the reason why, although she soothed her conscience by saying: "After all, there has been nothing in it, and it is all over now."

About a week after Princess Julia's funeral, Blanche, who of course went nowhere, asked her intimate friends, Nelly and Ira Olenev, and Donna Laura, to come and dine alone with her at the Palazzo Fabrini. Guido used to retire for the night just after his early dinner (he dined at seven), and she was left the whole evening alone in the huge palazzo without even her mother-in-law's society. She said it was getting on her nerves, and she begged just those three friends to come and have dinner with her whenever they could, or to sit with her in the evenings after dinner. She asked Bernard as well, and the first time Blanche and Bernard met to speak to each other after Princess Julia's death was with the two Olenev girls. Gradually it became a habit, an institution, that either Donna Laura or one of the Olenevs should dine with her every night. Bernard, too, dined once or twice, or came in afterwards.

Blanche did not talk about her mother-in-law any more, but Bernard felt that for the first time in her life she was no longer living under the eyes and immediate supervision of a gaoler. A weight seemed to have been lifted from her. She was partially free at last.

One evening – it was towards the middle of May – Bernard went to the Palazzo at about half-past nine. Blanche had asked him to come the last time he had seen her. This was two or three nights before. He would find, she said, the Olenev girls. But when he got there he found Blanche by herself.

"I think they will come later," said Blanche; "and perhaps Laura is coming."

They were sitting in Blanche's sitting-room, which was a square, high room with two Venetian pictures hanging on the faded red silk, a large, long writing-table, here and there a *cassone*, and high-backed, stiff chairs. There were a few books lying about on some small tables, and a huge, empty, stone fireplace.

Through the high, open windows came the intoxicating scent of the Roman May evening, and the noises, the many delightful, discordant, and melodious noises of the narrow Roman street – the noises of May in Rome.

They sat in the corner of the room on a long, low sofa, and they spoke little, each of them saying every now and then a commonplace thing.

Blanche suddenly said: "Would you like the lamps? I told them not to bring them."

"No," said Bernard; "I like it just like this."

"When are you going away?"

"At the end of the month. I shall have to go then, as mother hasn't got the apartment for longer than that."

"And then you go to London?"

"Yes; I shall go back to work, to soldiering."

"You will like that."

"I don't mind it. I shan't do it for ever. Is there any chance of your coming to England this year?"

"No chance. Guido can't travel."

"And you can't leave him?"

"Now less than ever; he has not even got his mother."

"His sister?"

"Mario wouldn't let her stay here in the summer. Rome in the summer bores him. They go to Homburg and St Moritz."

There was a long pause.

"I don't think Ira and Nelly will come tonight after all," said Blanche. "If they are not here by ten, it generally means they are not coming, although when they do come they are ready to stop all night. Russians like sitting up late."

"So do Italians, and so do I."

There was another pause. They could hear a rapid chatter going on in the street and a man singing a snatch of song in the distance; his voice was hoarse, but exceedingly passionate. He sang a little flat. This seemed to add to the intensity of the passion. They listened in silence.

"Isn't that delicious?" said Blanche in a whisper, as if she were afraid of disturbing the distant singer.

"Yes; that's just the kind of music I like," said Bernard in a whisper, too.

The song grew louder; the singer was reaching his climax. They could not distinguish the words, although Blanche thought she heard the word "cuore," and then the song suddenly, in the middle of a sustained high tremolo, came to an end; not because, so it seemed, the song had come to an end, but as if the singer had suddenly tired of his song. They wished he would go on again, but although this song was over other noises, friendly noises, came down the street. The *limonaro*, with his shrill appeal of "*Acqua fresca, limonaro, limonaro, chi vuol bere!*" he, too, broke into song presently quite close under the palace windows, and he was accompanied by a violin and a guitar.

He sang a little ditty all about himself which had a light, gallant *panache* about it:

"Ho un capello di paglia, – ma bello!
Un zinale di sopra fino."

"Those songs," said Blanche, "were the first things which reconciled me to living here. I think they are more delicious now in the month of May than at any other time. The beauty of this palazzo is that it is right down here in the thick of the town, almost in a slum. Rome has changed a great deal since I came here. Some of it is unrecognisable, but this part and this street haven't changed at all."

"You must have been lonely when you first came here."

"I was always lonely till I met you. I tried twice to have a friend, but it all came to nothing, and then there were people who liked me, but I did not care for them. Once I grew desperate and nearly ran away with some one – some one I did not care for a bit – but that was stopped by Guido falling ill. It was like the direct intervention of Providence. After that I gave up all idea of ever having a friend, and then I met you."

"When I first met you to speak to, I thought we should never be friends," said Bernard. "The first time I saw you here…but, of course, the first time I ever saw you was in Paris. I thought then we might be friends some day."

"I thought so, too, but I put the thought away from me. I knew then we might be friends, and I knew it again here in Rome, and I put the thought away again. I knew it was wrong really."

"Wrong?"

"Yes, wrong; it *is* wrong. I know it is wrong, and I know it will bring no good to you, nor to me, but I can't help it. It's done and I can't give it up. We *are* friends," she said in a whisper. "Nothing can alter that."

"Yes; nothing can undo that."

They heard the *limonaro* singing farther away in the distance, to the sound of the tinkling guitar.

"What is so jolly," said Bernard whispering, as though he were telling a secret, "is that here I feel as if the people – all those people in the street...everybody...the world was quite close to us, and yet ever so far away. They are there; but we can forget all about them. I think I'm talking nonsense."

"No; I understand. We are like two people in an enchanted tower; we can look down upon the world which is miles and miles and miles below us. We are hidden away in a secret nest right at the end of the world, and yet it, and they, are there, quite close to us, and we can hear the *limonaro* singing, singing for us. Is that what you mean?"

"Yes; that is just what I mean."

They sat on in silence, motionless, hand in hand; they did not press each other's hands, but their two hands seemed to be one hand. It was as if they were afraid; Blanche certainly felt afraid of scaring the wonderful moment, and making it take flight. She felt that one word, one gesture, one breath, one sigh, would be enough to break the charm, to shatter the walls of the fairy castle, to chase away the lovely moment – *the* moment. This was what Faust wanted in exchange for his soul, thought Blanche, and the devil couldn't give it to him. But they had it. They had cheated the devil...they had cheated Providence... it was here...it was here... And so they sat on, side by side, motionless, silent like two statues on a tomb in a dark crypt.

It was getting dark.

"I feel as if we were in another world," said Blanche in so low a whisper as to be almost inaudible.

"So do I."

"I can see you in the dark, and with my eyes shut. I don't have to look to see you."

"I see you, Blanche darling – Blanche – "

"Hush, don't say a word...don't ask me if I love you...don't, don't ask me *how* I love you...let us be happy without words, without any *why*."

Then Blanche softly and gently began to cry – tears of joy.

"Perhaps this is the end of the world," she said. "I hope it is."

"Yes, it is," said Bernard. "I feel as if you and I and the world had all been washed away."

"Yes; and as if – as if all the *weight* had been taken away from me, because everything has gone away...even memory. I can remember *nothing* – it all has melted, all the past, all my sad past, like snow."

"Poor, poor darling," said Bernard; "we will forget it all."

"You see, my dear, dear friend, I'm not young like you." ("Younger than the youngest," murmured Bernard.) "You are young and alive, and have all the world before you, but I am only a dead ghost: you have brought me back to life for a little, but it won't last long." ("For ever, for ever," murmured Bernard.) "But now I feel as if my old sad life had been blotted out, and cancelled...as if there were nothing left now, but you and me. Let us be content with that."

"Yes – content." Bernard's voice seemed to come from a far-off place.

"I feel," whispered Blanche presently, "as if we were dead."

"I am alive… "

They sat for a long time without saying a word, heeding nothing.

"I feel," whispered Blanche, "as if we were in the grave."

"Yes."

"I have loved you, Bernard, ever since I can remember."

"Yes, yes, yes. So have I. Ever since I can remember."

"You have always held my hand just like that."

"Just like that." Bernard's whisper grew softer and softer.

The room grew darker. You could see the shapes of the gaunt, stiff furniture standing out black, distinct, concrete, and yet ghostly in the unearthly dimness of the large, high room. A bat was flitting about the window outside. A church bell chimed the quarter somewhere. Bernard and Blanche paid no heed, and time rushed by them.

"It doesn't matter," said Bernard, "whether it has just begun or whether it has lasted years... It doesn't matter whether we are dead or alive, whether we are in Heaven or Purgatory or Hell...for ever...all that matters is that we are at last together and alone...we two...we shall sleep on and on and on...you and I...together and alone...together and alone... "

There was another long, the longest, silence...the street had become quiet and empty. Some one again was singing – a late reveller with a cheerful, slightly intoxicated voice:

"E, bella, tu non piangera – a – a – a – i,
Sul giorno ch'io sarò mor – or – or – to – o – o – o – o – o."

Time and space had melted and vanished for them: they were absorbed, annihilated in the dream of dreams: passion and peace...peace and passion; like life and death, darkness and light, music and silence. They were like Tristan and Isolde in the unending night of the forest, still intoxicated with the fatal brew, enclosed in wizard walls, floating on the tide of an endless stream, drifting to death...how long had they been there? a minute?...an hour? two hours? five minutes? where were they? on the earth? in Rome?

...Alive?

Suddenly Blanche started.

"Bernard," she whispered, "I thought I heard something."

They both listened intently.

"I don't hear anything," said Bernard.

"Perhaps it was nothing. It may have been only my imagination. I'm sure I did hear something. There! again!"

She withdrew her hands from his and moved a little way from him.

"I am sure I heard something," she said.

They sat still on the low sofa, apart from one another now, with space – infinite space, it seemed – between them, staring into the darkness, listening...listening with all their might...

They heard nothing…and then all at once the door at the end of the room opened, and in walked Guido – Guido upright but deathly pale, carrying an oil lamp.

He looked at them without surprise, put the lamp on the table, and said: "I thought you would like a lamp, so I brought one. I am sorry that I should appear to be inhospitable to Mr Lacy. I can promise him that this will never happen again."

A neighbouring clock struck twelve and three-quarters.

"I'm afraid," said Guido, "all the servants have gone to bed, and there's no one to show you out. But I will show you out if you will come this way."

Guido opened the door, and, taking the lamp, he preceded Bernard to the door, opened it, held it open, and said: "Good night, Mr Lacy; you will find a candle in the hall; the staircase is still lit."

Bernard walked out of the room, along the corridor, into the hall, and down the stairs, which were lit with a great lantern; the door was mechanically opened by the concierge, and Bernard went out into the night.

# CHAPTER VIII

It was difficult for Bernard to believe that the events of that evening were real. It was less difficult for Blanche. She indeed told Donna Laura that she had felt all the time subconsciously that something of the kind would happen. She had felt like a person drifting down a stream to a whirlpool, knowing that the whirlpool is there, but unable to make an effort to stop the drifting.

She knew that she was heading for disaster, but she did not know from what quarter, nor had she thought it would come so soon.

When Bernard had left the house that night, Guido had solemnly escorted Blanche to her rooms without saying a word. He had then gone to bed himself. The next day, life at the Palazzo went on as usual, except that Guido refused to see Blanche or to speak to her, and he sent for his lawyer, with whom he had a long interview.

The same day, in the course of the morning, Donna Laura wrote to Bernard, asking him to come and see her in the evening, directly after dinner. He had heard nothing from Blanche. He went to Donna Laura's. She was alone.

"I know what has happened," she said. "I have seen Blanche. Guido is ill again – that is to say, just as he was before. He said nothing to the doctor about having got up. Whether it was a superhuman miracle, or whether he has been planning this for months and has never been ill as we thought, I don't know; Blanche doesn't know; nobody knows; we shall never know. But it is certain, or Blanche is certain, that he is ill again now, just as ill as he was before – not worse, but the same as he has always been. Guido has said nothing except to ask when you were leaving Rome, or whether you had left. Otherwise he won't speak to her at all. She wants you to go away at once, and not try to see her nor to say goodbye. She says she could not bear it. She sends you her goodbye through me and this letter. I will let you know what happens. You were going soon, weren't you?"

"Yes; next week in any case. I will go at once if she wishes it, but surely I can see her?"

"She *does* wish you to go and *not* to see her. She is frightened, so frightened; she feels she may have killed him, or that he may die of it yet – that she may be a murderess. You know Blanche told me that she never thought Guido was really ill. He was pretending, she thought, the whole time, just to spite her, out of revenge for having married him without loving him. She isn't sure now whether he *is* ill, but she knows he might be – she thinks he has some plan – he is going to *do* something, and that whatever it is, you cannot help. She wants you to go at once."

"Very well," said Bernard, "I will do as she wishes. I will go. What does she think made Guido think…?"

"She thinks Princess Julia opened his eyes just before she fell ill, and told him to be on the look out. She thinks his mother told him this, just to stop Blanche seeing you; but we shall never know, we shall never understand Guido nor Princess Julia; they were not like other people. He is as inscrutable as she was."

In her letter to Bernard, Blanche said the same thing. She begged him not to write to her; but he did not, could not, believe that she really meant it, and he wrote her a long letter, which Donna Laura promised to give her.

That evening, when Bernard reached home, he told his mother that he had been telegraphed for from London by his Colonel, and asked to come home as soon as he possibly could, and he said he must leave the next day. His mother said she would come too. She did not want to stay in Rome. She felt something had happened, but she asked no questions.

They made hurried arrangements to leave the next evening, and they travelled straight through to London.

Bernard had not been many days in London when he had a letter from Donna Laura.

She said that Guido had heard of his departure, but not through Blanche, and that he had not set eyes on Blanche again; that he had sent Blanche his solicitor to inform her that a legal separation had been drawn up; that she would receive an allowance, and that she could live where and how she pleased, but never again did Guido wish to set eyes on her, and he wished her to leave the Palazzo as soon as she conveniently could.

This plan was put into effect at once. Blanche did not answer Bernard's letter, but she sent him more messages through Donna Laura, and begged him once more not to write.

Blanche moved into a small apartment near the *Porta Pia.*

Roman society was, of course, startled and convulsed by the event, and opinion was sharply divided on the subject of Blanche. As usual, there was half Rome, the other half Rome, and the *tertium quid.*

Half Rome, led by Guido's relations and Princess Julia's friends, blamed her severely. They attributed Guido's illness and misery entirely to her: that was what came, they said, of marrying an Englishwoman. Englishwomen always pretended to be better than other people, and often turned out to be worse. It was a good thing at least to see hypocrisy unmasked, for once.

The other half Rome did not blame Blanche at all, but said it was wonderful that she could have endured such a life for so long, and that if she had a lover, small blame to her. It was a wonder that she had not had shoals of lovers. Guido was a lunatic, and what sort of marriage was it to be tied to a man who spent his life on a sofa in a semi-darkened room?

The *tertium quid* said this proved once more that men and women in the long run turned out to be exactly the same. Here was a woman who had always been held up as an exception, a pattern and an example of virtue in the most trying circumstances. Well, she turned out not to be a pattern of virtue after all: to be exactly the same as all other women. Well, so much the better; women, human, weak women, were more lovable than patterns of virtue; besides which, patterns of virtue only existed in the imagination of romancers and sentimentalists. Doctors, lawyers, and, above all, priests knew better. Princess Blanche was a charming woman. It was a comfort some one should have noticed it, and that she should have a little happiness. Nobody blamed Blanche for having a lover, but for being found out so soon after Princess Julia's death...there was something a little tactless, a touch of *mauvais goût* about that...

To sum up, public opinion was, on the whole, slightly unfavourable towards Blanche at first, but it underwent a change, and Half Rome, the Other Half Rome, and the *Tertium Quid* were suddenly brought into line by a little incident that occurred soon afterwards.

There was a Requiem Mass for a certain Princess San Paolo, an old lady who had been very kind to Blanche when she first married. Blanche also knew her son, who was in the Diplomatic Service. Blanche attended this Requiem, and as she went away, when it was over, she found herself on the steps of the church face to face with Mrs Winslope, the American Ambassadress. Blanche said "How do you do" to her, upon which Mrs Winslope turned her back and walked down the steps. The incident had many witnesses, and by the evening all Rome knew of it... The Romans were indignant because, whatever they might think or say about the conduct or behaviour of one of themselves or one of their adopted selves – and they regarded Blanche as one of their adopted selves – they would not bear interference on the part of a foreigner. They all left cards in a body on Blanche the next day, and the general verdict on the whole affair, instead of being unfavourable to Blanche, became favourable towards her. The other half Rome and the *tertium quid* began to say in chorus: "Poor Guido is, of course, *mad*...he may have been the injured party, but he is mad, and what can one do?"

Of course Guido's relations remained uncompromising; but a great many people honestly thought that Guido was mad, and this opinion was held by many of the best physicians.

A little later, Bernard heard that Blanche had gone to spend the summer with the Olenevs in Russia, near Kiev. From Blanche he did not receive a single word. Donna Laura wrote to him from time to time, but after this she could tell him nothing more about Blanche.

As for Blanche, she had been frightened. It seemed to her that the finger of Providence had intervened directly in her life. She was far too frightened, distraught, and numbed to care about the general commotion, fuss, and gossip. Her life seemed to her to have been cut in two, and all that had been connected with Bernard to be over for ever.

There was no reason, of course, why she should not write to him, nor why she should not see him, but she felt it was impossible; that it was over, done with for ever, but she loved him more than ever – more than she had ever conceived it possible to love any one.

Not long after she arrived at the Olenevs' house in the Government of O., in Russia, she received a long letter from Mrs Lacy.

Mrs Lacy pleaded the cause of Bernard. He was, she said, immensely unhappy. She did not blame Blanche for this. She blamed no one but herself. She had done nothing when she might have done something. She did not want to rake up the past, nor to refer to it. She wanted to discuss the future. She was inexpressibly sorry for Blanche, and equally sorry that Bernard should have been the cause of what had happened, but as what happened *had* happened, would it not be better *now* to put an end to everything, once and for all. Not to go on. Bernard was young; he had his life before him. If the present, or rather the past, situation were to continue as it had been in Rome, it would ruin Bernard's life. He would never marry; and was it, could it be, satisfactory? Besides, she, Mrs Lacy, was a believing, practising Catholic, and she believed Blanche to be one too. So was Bernard; unless he were to abjure his Faith, and that would break his heart – and hers.

She didn't want to preach, nor to be heavy-handed, nor to throw stones, or notice the mote in her brother's eye, but was it right? Would it be satisfactory? What would come of it all? She passionately wanted Bernard to marry. He would be the heir of an old estate, and a house both he and she had loved all their lives. She looked upon the position he would inherit as one of responsibility. He would one day be the head of one of the few old English Catholic families. If things went on as they had been, nothing could come of it but scandal and misery for every one concerned. Perhaps, she added, this letter was quite unnecessary, and that Blanche agreed with her already; perhaps she was battering an open door.

She was.

Blanche wrote to her and said that she and she alone had been to blame in the matter, and that she quite agreed with every word Mrs Lacy said, and that the last thing she wished to be was the cause of unhappiness to Bernard, or to spoil his life. She well realised the folly of the whole thing. She would not

302

attempt to see him, nor would she write to him. Mrs Lacy might rest secure.

She kept her promise, difficult as it was. She never even wrote to say that she was not going to write. All he heard was the one short and final little letter she had sent him before he left Rome.

He felt it would be useless to write again: and to go on writing and not to get an answer would be more than he could bear.

Mrs Lacy, Donna Laura, and the Olenevs all thought that the thread that had connected the lives of Blanche and Bernard had been definitely cut. Blanche thought so too.

# CHAPTER IX

Blanche stayed with the Olenevs in Russia until the end of June. She then went with them to Germany, to Ems, where the Princess always took a mild and meaningless cure, and towards the end of the month they went to Gérardmer in the Vosges for the air and the change. This suited Blanche. She had no wish to go back to Rome for the moment, nor to England.

When they arrived at Gérardmer, Blanche was astonished to read, among the names of the visitors on the board of the hall of the hotel, Mr Charles Clifford and Miss Clifford. She wondered whether this could be her Uncle Charles, who to her was almost like a mythical personage.

Charles Clifford was sixteen years younger than her father, and was now in his forty-ninth year. He was a Bohemian version of his brother Henry. He was tall, with sunken, brown, dreamy eyes, and a wistful smile; a high forehead and a round-shaped skull, quite bald in front, with silvery short whiskers and a few wisps of brown hair. He moved about like a ghost, and he would suddenly quietly leave the room, if bored, without your noticing it. He was courteous, and he loved actors, painters, Bohemians, and ne'er-do-wells. Ordinary "good" society bored him to death. He had had an uneventful but strange career. He had started life in the Diplomatic Service, and his career showed promise, at the beginning, of brilliance. He went from Berlin to Madrid, and there he met, fell in love with, and married a Spanish dancer, who, although admirable in many respects, was not looked upon by the Foreign Office, the Ambassador, and his English and foreign colleagues as being the right and suitable wife for an English diplomat. He resigned, and settled down with his wife in Dresden. They usually went to the South of France for a month in the winter and to Switzerland for some weeks in the summer. He was relatively better off than his elder brother, as he had been left quite a respectable little sum by his godmother, old Lady Adrington, who was full of indulgence for the weaknesses of the flesh, and was delighted when she heard that he had married a Spanish dancer. He had a certain talent both for descriptive writing and short stories, and a delicate touch with the brush, and sometimes an inspired sense of colour; and he made a certain amount of money by contributing from time to time to the magazines and by occasional exhibitions and sales of pictures at Cannes and London. He never went so far as to publish a book, for he was an indolent writer, and only wrote under the pressure of need.

Charles Clifford was to the end of her life devoted to his wife. Her name was Mercedes, and she had been beautiful in her youth, with a dazzling skin, large, slow, dark eyes, and magnificent black hair. Later she grew to be rather large. They had two daughters, but they both died. Charles Clifford had shortly after his marriage become a Catholic, which had shocked his relations perhaps more than the marriage itself. However, he cared little for what they thought. He was perfectly happy living abroad, idling and painting, and writing when it was necessary to make money, and then gambling and losing it at Monte Carlo. He liked foreigners, and he was as much at home in hotel life as a fish in water.

Nine years after they were married, Mercedes gave birth to a third daughter. This child, who was called Rosa Maria, according to her mother's wish, was, at the age of nine years, sent to a convent in Paris. The same year, and shortly after her departure, two years before Blanche arrived at Gérardmer, Mercedes died and Charles Clifford was left alone. The death of Mercedes broke Charles Clifford's heart. But this trite phrase, taken literally even, and not as a mere catchword, is an understatement of the effect the death of Mercedes had upon Charles. He was completely lost and at sea. She had done everything for him. She had tended him, nursed him, looked after him like a child, like a baby. He had never taken a step without consulting her. She had managed all his affairs and been instrumental in getting money that was owed to him. But in addition to this he had loved her as a woman and delighted in her as a companion. He had his infidelities: she had overlooked them, and by her good sense and tact she had always made his lady-loves look ridiculous, and always remained dignified, so that his affections seldom roved for long and always came back to roost. Mercedes had been a remarkable, practical woman, with none of the sloth of the South in her. She came from Vigo, and even Henry Clifford admitted she was business-like, and attributed this to her father having been a British naval officer, which may or may not have been true, but there was not a shred of evidence.

When she died, Charles Clifford was like a dazed, stunned child; he did not seem to take notice. Fortunately in his flat at Dresden there was a nice, motherly, sensible, practical *Hausfrau*, who managed the household for him, and he had an admirable Spanish servant called Ramiro, who had been with him for years, and who served him with dog-like fidelity and devotion.

Blanche had hardly ever seen her Uncle Charles, and never seen her late Aunt Mercedes. When she first came out, Charles Clifford was abroad and was making his promising *début* in the Diplomatic Service. Later on, after his marriage, on the rare occasions when he visited London, to arrange for an exhibition to raise money from a publisher or an editor, she was abroad.

Her father talked little of him, and in the tone in which people talk of the irreparably wasted and the irretrievably lost.

"If he hadn't married that Spaniard, Charles would have gone far," he was fond of saying. Or, "No diplomat ever made a more brilliant *début* than Charles; such an admirable linguist, such a good tenor voice...a *real* tenor...so rare, and then he must go and marry that woman."

And when Blanche used to say: "Is she as bad as all that?" he used to answer: "No, not *bad*, but just impossible."

Now she was to see him. How strange it seemed. Perhaps it was another Charles Clifford, and nothing to do with her uncle. But her doubts on this point were settled the first time she had dinner in the hotel. She and the Olenevs had a little table to themselves. The table next to them was empty when they first came into the dining-room, and after they had begun their dinner, and finished the soup, a tall man and a little girl walked into the room. The man, she thought, was unlike her father, and yet there were sudden flashes and hints of affinity one could notice – she would have known him anywhere. There was a look of another strain about him which she could neither define nor trace to its origin – something gentle, wistful, dreamy. As for the girl, she was not at all like the family, nor was she Blanche's idea of a Spaniard, as she had radiantly bright golden hair done in a thick plait. Blanche could not see her uncle properly during dinner, as she was sitting with her back to his table, but directly after dinner, when they went out to sit on the terrace in front of the lake, he came up to her and said: "I think you are my niece. May I introduce you to your first cousin, Rosa Maria?"

They all made each other's acquaintance. Charles was introduced to Princess Olenev and her daughters, and the little girl curtsied and blushed to the roots of her hair. Presently she was sent to bed by her father, who promised he would come and see her directly.

Charles Clifford talked to Blanche as if he were going on with a conversation that had only just been interrupted. He did not refer to Rome, and Blanche wondered whether he knew what had happened. At the same time, she felt that he was one of those people who, even if they knew nothing, would be incapable of saying anything wrong; he would by some divine instinct steer safely through any shoals or quicksands.

He asked Blanche after her father. He, of course, couldn't get away from London just now, with the House sitting. He himself might go to London this year, he said; in the autumn, at the end of September. He talked of Gérardmer. He always came there in July for the air after doing a cure at Vichy.

Blanche was not long in becoming intimate with her prodigal uncle.

He had, she reflected, her father's ease of manner, without any of his worldliness. He had still less ambition than her father, because he was without private as well as without public spirit, and he did not mind if he had money. He was indifferent to discomfort and to food; in fact, a born Bohemian. He suffered from a permanent disinclination to do any work, and even when he had something to do, a piece of work, and he knew that it was pressingly necessary for him to do it, it was torture and agony for him to begin. In this respect he was an artist; he had the artist's temperament, but only just a grain of the artist's power of accomplishment.

For weeks he would do nothing, and then he would sit up all night to finish a magazine story, or get up at five in the morning to paint a landscape, and destroy it when it was finished. But what he liked doing was talking, and especially talking about literary and artistic projects, for the future, the stories he meant to write and the pictures he would paint some day. He made admirable sketches both for stories and pictures, but he rarely finished them.

Sometimes in the dark, cool woods he would, when they drove out for an expedition, tell Rosa Maria a beautifully imagined and exquisitely phrased fairy-tale; but when he did this, Blanche and the Olenev girls would listen with more rapt attention even than that which was shown by the little girl. They would beg him to write it down; he would promise to some day, but the day never arrived.

He told Blanche all about his life. He talked of himself now as a man whose life was over. The only thing which mattered to him, and he said so over and over again, was the future of his daughter. She was at present being brought up in a convent of the *Sacré Coeur* in Paris, where she was not very happy. She didn't like the French. It was at present her vacation. So far so good; she did not mind the Convent and she liked the nuns. "But what," said Charles one day to Blanche when they were sitting out of doors on the terrace, "will happen to her when she grows up? Some one will have to take her out, and I don't feel capable of doing it. Besides, I feel I should do her harm. Her going out with me would do her harm, as I am looked upon by all my family and their friends as a disreputable person – a grey, if not a black, sheep, and an impossible Bohemian. I sometimes believe that if I had done something worse...something in their eyes unpardonable – if I had cheated at cards, or forged a cheque – they would not have minded so much. They would have felt, 'Well, that is done with. We always said it would happen, and there, it has happened.' But it is because I have *not* done anything really criminal in their eyes, because I have just disregarded their standards, infringed their canons, and flouted their conventions, that they are irritated. They feel they have not sufficient excuse for ignoring me."

"But papa doesn't feel like that, I know."

"No; Henry doesn't; he just thinks I have been a *fool*. That's all; but you should see your aunts when my name is mentioned. Mercedes was in their eyes – might just as well have been – a savage. They never saw her, of course, and I dare say you don't know that, judged by whatsoever standard you please,

Mercedes was a *good* woman – at any rate, what I call a good woman, and the only kind of woman I do call a good woman. She was a woman who not only *did* good, but who *was* good. Every one who came into contact with her adored her. She was so generous. You should have heard her play the guitar; it was wonderful. And she was so sensible, too, so practical, so alive. She could do anything; she managed everything, and used to make both ends meet, somehow, when it really seemed impossible. I miss her now so terribly, even more than the first day – I feel it unendurable – and how can I bring up Rosa Maria without her?"

And here Charles broke down.

"I would love to help you to take her out, if you would allow me to," said Blanche.

"Do you really mean that?"

"Yes, of course, but I'm not at all sure that people in England won't think that I am much more than a *grey* sheep – a real *black* one. However, I will do anything I can."

"Black sheep or grey sheep, I shall leave her to you in my will. She shall be your ward, if you don't mind, because, you see, I shan't live long. At least I hope I shan't – my lungs are bad."

"Nonsense, Uncle Charles," said Blanche. "You come from a very long-lived family. You are perfectly well. You are young for your age."

"Yes; but in spite of all that, I know I'm nearly ready for the scrap-heap. I shouldn't wonder if I lived on a year or two, but I don't think I shall ever see Rosa Maria grown up. Anyhow, you will promise me to look after her, and to do anything you can for her?"

"Yes; I promise."

Blanche wrote to her father and told him about her meeting with her uncle and her cousin.

Her father had been a broken man ever since she had first written to him and told him of the catastrophe at Rome. He felt now that the whole thing had been his fault, and he blamed himself; at the same time, he comforted himself a little by saying, "After all, it might have been worse." There had been comparatively little scandal, because so many people had said in Rome that Guido was mad, and this opinion filtered through to London and was fostered by Henry Clifford.

A large section of Roman society had taken Blanche's part, and denied that she had been guilty of anything except imprudence, and after the episode of the American Ambassadress, nearly all Rome, with the exception of a few of Guido's most uncompromising relations and friends, stood up for her, so that English society followed suit, drew a veil over all possibilities, and simply said that Blanche had been ill-treated by a maniac, a man who pretended to be ill, and who was mad.

Blanche got to know her cousin more slowly and less easily than she got to know her uncle. Rosa Maria was the reverse of what you might have expected. She had none of her father's indolence, and Blanche wondered whether the mother, Mercedes, had had any southern, or so-called southern, indolence and characteristics at all; she began to think her father's theory of Mercedes' parentage was correct; she must indeed, she thought, have been an intensely practical and energetic woman. However that might be, there was this girl, who was, to begin with, an athlete; she swam in the lake, she handled a canoe with dexterity, she had a passion for horses, and seized any opportunity for riding. She was ready, too, to ride anything. She played lawn-tennis and any game with real enthusiasm. Her foreign blood and her foreign education seemed to have accentuated everything that was English in her. She seemed a born little John Bull, with a strong vein of obstinate English jingoism.

She liked her Convent and the nuns, but nevertheless she made it quite clear that she hated and despised the French girls, as if they belonged to another race, a lower order of beings. Blanche was sure she dominated them; she was longing (Blanche thought) to go to England.

Blanche did not altogether understand her, and felt shy in her presence. She felt, too, that she, according to Rosa Maria's standards, might be found lamentably wanting; she felt that Rosa Maria would despise her. She would, Blanche thought, be a lovely and most uncommon-looking girl when she grew up – she was reaching the ungraceful age – and she wondered whom she would marry. She felt certain that Rosa Maria would want to marry an Englishman.

"I shall get to know her better in time," she thought, "when I have broken down the barrier of her shyness."

But the time went on, and Blanche did not find that she got to know Rosa Maria any better. It all went well up to a certain point, but no further. She suddenly came upon an impenetrable wall.

"I wonder if she dislikes me, really?" thought Blanche.

She had little reason to, for Blanche went out of her way to be as tactfully and unobtrusively charming to the girl as she could be.

Was it perhaps jealousy? – jealousy of her father? she wondered.

Since the death of his wife, Charles Clifford had been without any regular intimate companion, save his daughter. He made friends, it is true, from time to time, but the fleeting friends that are made at watering-places and at the *table d'hôte* – swiftly made and swiftly forgotten.

But in Blanche, his niece, he made a real friend. They understood each other perfectly, and they enjoyed that best of all intimacies – the intimacy founded on the same sense of fun. They were amused by the same things. Perhaps Rosa Maria felt or guessed this, and was jealous of it. For whether her nature was radically different, or whether it was that she was not grown up, and that her sense of humour was undeveloped, her father found no response in her at certain things, certain phases, lights, certain little silly jokes, observations, and incidents that amused him and Blanche equally. Blanche felt this, and she was careful not to let it be more obvious and palpable than was necessary. But do what she could, she never completely succeeded in winning Rosa Maria. The child was invariably civil and obliging; there was no fault to find with her, but she never entirely capitulated, never quite dismantled her defences, and all the artillery of Blanche's charm and beauty and kindness were launched upon them in vain.

Charles Clifford had suspected this, but he shut his eyes to the truth, saying that "Rosa Maria is, after all, only a child, and she will grow out of all that nonsense."

At the end of the month of August, Charles Clifford and Rosa Maria left for Dresden, and the Olenevs went back to Rome. Blanche went to Dresden with her uncle, and stayed there a fortnight at an hotel, but she left after a fortnight because she thought that Rosa Maria would be disappointed if she did not have her father to herself during the last weeks of her holidays. Besides which, she wanted to catch her father in London; he was to be there for a fortnight in September between two shooting parties. It was strange to Blanche to come back to London after these years, and in these circumstances. It was with an immense relief that she realised that it would not be necessary for her to go to Wood Norton (which Princess Julia had left to Guido), nor any longer to be under the *surveillance* of such a mother-in-law.

She found her father well, and he made every effort at first to behave as if everything had been for the best in the best of all possible worlds; but he could not keep this up, and the first time they had a real talk together he almost broke down, and said, "Forgive me, my darling child; it has been all my fault – nobody else's."

"It has been nobody's fault," said Blanche. "There's nothing to forgive. Everybody in the world has something of the same kind in their lives. The world is made like that. One must face it and make the best of things, and I have a great deal to be thankful for."

She had no hope of seeing Bernard, but she cherished the hope of hearing of him. She thought she might perhaps meet Walter Troumestre, or some other friend of his. She did not mention his name to her father. But the days went by and nothing of the sort happened. There were few people in London and hardly anybody that Blanche knew.

The day before she left London to go back to Rome (she had arranged to meet the Olenevs at Rome at the beginning of October), she thought she would like to go and see Father Byrne at the Oratory. She thought she would like him to hear her Confession, and that he would understand her when she confessed that her whole life and all her heart was still obsessed, possessed, and ruled by one dominating thought, by one absent presence. But Father Byrne was out, and she made her Confession to a stranger, who gave her sound, practical, and most matter-of-fact advice, and told her plainly that, if you incur debts, sooner or later they have to be paid. But, as she left, she met Father Byrne in the street, and he took her back to the Oratory House, where they had a long talk. He asked her no questions and she did not go into the story, but in spite of that he conveyed to her that he knew what had happened, and understood *why* it had happened, and regarded the whole incident as closed. The keynote of his attitude was a phrase he was fond of, and which he had already often made use of to her, "Thank God it's no worse!" Bernard's name was not mentioned by either of them, although Blanche felt certain that Father Byrne knew where he was and what he was doing, and probably knew that she was dying to know.

As she was walking home from the Oratory, dawdling and going as her fancy led her (*so für sich kin*), she happened to pass Ovington Square. She knew that Bernard and his mother had lived there, so she thought she must walk past the house… It was on her way…(it wasn't really)…just to see what it looked like. She passed it, and over it was a board with "To Let, Furnished" on it, "Apply to Messrs So-and-so," who were agents in the Brompton Road. A wild curiosity seized her – more than a curiosity – a longing to see the inside of the house, to see where he had lived, the chairs he had sat in, the pictures on the wall. She walked to the agents, who lived in a furniture shop close by, and asked for an order to see the house. It was at once made out for her.

Then she walked back to the house, and she was let in by a kind caretaker – the housemaid who was the pivot of Mrs Lacy's London household.

"Mrs Lacy," she said, "wants to let the house for a year as she has been ordered by the doctor to spend the winter in a warm place, and he has recommended Torquay, since she has said she did not wish to go abroad this year.

"In the summer she is going to stay in her own little house at Alton-Leigh. She does not wish to spend the winter in London, firstly, because of the doctor's orders, but, secondly" – and perhaps this, Blanche thought, was the real reason – "that her son, Master Bernard, no longer requires a room in London, as he has left the Army, and Master Stephen spends his holidays in the country."

"Oh, really," said Blanche, trying to make her voice sound indifferent and wondering who was Master Stephen.

"Yes, madam; firstly, because of 'is poor 'ead" (she dropped her "h's" directly she began to talk of Bernard. This was a sign of fondness, Blanche thought) "after the fall he had in those outlandish parts, and, secondly, because 'is uncle, Sir Christopher, thought it would be good for him to travel, and he has gone to Africa to shoot the lions on his way to North and South America and the Indies."

Blanche felt stunned, but she was recalled to life and self-control by the caretaker's matter-of-fact voice as she said: "Perhaps you would like to see the rooms – the drawing-room where Mrs Lacy and Master Bernard sit of an evening, but

Mr Lacy never sat there when he was alive; he would be partial to the back room downstairs, what we called the study, that is used now by Master Bernard, when he is at home, to do his writing in, if he has a call to write, but never by Mrs Lacy."

Blanche said she would like to see the drawing-room. They walked upstairs to the drawing-room, which looked on to the square. It was divided into two rooms. Over the fireplace in the front room there was a large portrait of a lady in a crinoline of white muslin with blue ribbons, which Blanche recognised at once as being a portrait of Mrs Lacy, done most probably soon after her marriage. It was not well painted, by an inefficient disciple of Winterhalter, but it breathed *charm*, and Blanche could not help saying as she saw it:

"How like!"

She meant how like Bernard, not how like Mrs Lacy.

"It was said to be a good likeness when it was done," said the caretaker. "You wouldn't recognise that as Mrs Lacy now."

In the back drawing-room there was a large sacred picture – the money-changers being ejected from the Temple – a copy of an old master of the Milanese School. The rooms looked as if the owners had just left them.

On the chimney-piece there were two framed photographs of Bernard. Blanche recognised them at once; one a child of nine or ten, in a sailor-suit, and another a schoolboy about fifteen. There was a larger photograph of another boy, about twelve, who was not Bernard. "That's Master Stephen, Master Bernard's younger brother," said the caretaker. There were some Arundel prints on the walls and some water-colour views of Alton-Leigh – at least Blanche thought it must be Alton-Leigh – evidently done by a painstaking amateur. There was a faint smell of potpourri in the room, and the arm-chairs and sofas were covered with somewhat worn, flowered, stiff, shiny chintz.

"Would you like to see the bedrooms, madam?" the caretaker asked.

"No," Blanche said; "I won't trouble you to take me upstairs, as I think the house is a little too large for me, but I would like to see the downstairs rooms."

They walked downstairs to the dining-room. This was a narrow and rather a gloomy room, furnished with cabinets of red Japanese lacquer, brass idols, and bowls; and over the chimney-piece a large oil-painting of a young soldier with red whiskers in the undress uniform of the Coldstream Guards.

"He is more like his mother than his father," thought Blanche.

"The late Mr Lacy," the caretaker said, "and a speaking likeness, done soon after the war."

She meant the Crimean War.

The caretaker then took Blanche into a room at the back of the dining-room, Colonel Lacy's study. "This," thought Blanche, "must be exactly as he had left it." On one side of the room there was a bookcase, Chippendale with glass doors, which contained the works of Shakespeare, Surtees, and Harrison Ainsworth, all of them bound in calf; the *History of the Peninsular War*, and Lingard's *History of England*. Over the chimney-piece there was the portrait of a cavalier in armour, "an ancestor," the caretaker explained. On the chimney-piece a clock mounted in a nickel horseshoe with a hunting-horn underneath it, the work of Mr Thornbill of Bond Street. On the walls, which were dark and panelled, there were oil-paintings of famous racehorses, hunters, and gamecocks, and one or two sporting scenes. There were two dark-green leather arm-chairs near the fireplace and a leather-covered writing-table opposite the window with drawers on each side of it, and in front of the antique inkstand a small tortoiseshell and brass crucifix. On the wall near the chimney-piece, on the top of the dado, there was a rack full of pipes. The room had an atmosphere of stale tobacco smoke. The curtains were thick and of dark, faded red.

"They always sat here of an evening before the late Mr Lacy died," the caretaker explained, "but never since. They always sit upstairs now, winter and summer."

It seemed to Blanche that Bernard had only just left this room. She could imagine him having just put down that copy of the *Field* which was lying ready next a large ivory paper-cutter on the little round table, covered with a green velvet tablecover, next to the leather arm-chair.

That tobacco-jar in the corner was full of his tobacco; that was the novel (in three pale-blue volumes – one of them had an envelope stuck in it as a marker – with pink labels stuck on them with the name of the Lending Library, Cawthorn & Hutt), called *Greifenstein*, by Marion Crawford, that he must just have been reading.

"Master Bernard went in such a hurry," said the caretaker, as if reading her thoughts, "that he left everything behind him."

"Did he go alone?" asked Blanche.

"He went with Mr Walter Troumestre. He would never desert Master Bernard," the caretaker explained. "But then he will have to be back to duty before long."

"And where is Mrs Lacy now?"

"She is at the Dower House. Would you care to see the basement and the kitchen, madam?"

Blanche said she did not wish to see the basement. She left the house with effusive apologies and explanations, and when the caretaker received her tip, she in her turn became effusive.

# CHAPTER X

That was all Blanche heard about Bernard during her stay in London. She saw nobody else who knew him, and she heard nothing more about him.

Her father saw her off at the station, and, with a husky voice, he promised to come out to Rome at Easter if not for Christmas. Blanche found Rome exactly the same, almost exactly the same, as when she left. Her friends were just the same to her, and if Rome had been divided into two camps on her account, there was little trace of it now. The hostile camp consisted only of friends and relations of Guido, whom she had never seen except on the most formal occasions.

Guido, she was told, went on just the same as usual, and the American Ambassadress took charge of the guests at his daily receptions, although Donna Teresa was the nominal hostess. She and Count Mario had moved into Princess Julia's apartment. Blanche heard the news of her old home from Donna Laura and Donna Maria, who still went there from time to time, and from Princess Olenev and her daughters.

Ira was still doubtful whether Guido was suffering from a mental or nervous breakdown from physical causes, or whether his illness was imaginary or even feigned, but she thought he was iller than he'd been before the break. She

319

thought he had really felt that: that he had suffered in every way – in his heart, in his mind, in his *amour-propre.*

Blanche led the quietest of lives, and seldom went out except to the houses of her most intimate friends. It seemed strange to her to be living at Rome in this manner without having to look after Guido; without having to think of Princess Julia. It seemed all wrong, and, like everything else in life, she thought it had come too late. There was no joy for her in her release, in her new freedom.

She even longed once more for the old bondage – a bondage, that is to say, tempered and rendered fantastically, deliriously exciting by the stolen glimpses of Bernard and brief meetings with him.

At the beginning of January she had the great joy of seeing Walter Troumestre; he was on his way home from East Africa and Egypt. He had left Bernard in Cairo, just starting for India, whence he was going to China, Japan, San Francisco, Chicago, New York, Rio, Buenos Aires, and thence home. He intended to be away two years. It was his uncle who had had this idea.

Sir Christopher Lacy had told his nephew that he intended to leave him everything. It was his wish that Bernard should not only look after the estate, which he would be left, but that he should later on go into Parliament and play a part in the life of the nation. He wanted him to be a leading Catholic representative. He thought he would be better equipped for such a task if he were to see the world first, and he thought it was essential he should have a taste of the East, and of North and South America. On his way home he could stay for a little while in Central Europe, in Germany, France, or, if he liked, in Russia. "If one didn't travel when one was young," he said, "one never did." He could combine this travel with as much sport as he liked. Lion or rhino shooting in Africa, tiger shooting in India, bear shooting in the Rockies, anything and anywhere he liked. He was going to pay for all his travelling expenses. He did not want him to hurry. "Be away two years," he had said, "and make the most of it, and if you get a cable to say I'm dead, say a 'Hail, Mary' for me, but don't hurry home."

As for Walter, he was going back to his military duties. He, too, intended to leave the Army in a year or two, perhaps sooner. He wanted to go to the Near East. He had been studying Arabic; he wanted to learn Turkish, and to travel in the Balkans; those countries and those races fascinated him.

"Does Mr Lacy ever write to you?" asked Blanche.

"Only a post card from time to time with his name scrawled on it. He's not a fluent nor an industrious writer, but I write him long letters, and I will tell him that I have been here."

Blanche looked at Walter with unfeigned thankfulness. This conversation was happening at tea-time in her little apartment.

"Has his mother been ill?" she asked.

"Not really, but the doctors say she ought to be careful during the winter. Her chest is delicate."

Walter Troumestre only stayed a day in Rome. He had stopped there solely to see Blanche. Bernard had asked him to, and although he did not tell her so, in so many words, she understood from what he said, and from what he left unsaid, that this was so. Walter Troumestre's passage through Rome and her interview, her one and only interview, with him at tea-time in her apartment was the sole event of Blanche's winter and spring in Rome that year. She heard from her father constantly. It proved impossible for him to come out to Rome, either for Christmas or for Easter. Travel was becoming irksome to him, and he disliked the expense.

He urged her to spend the summer in England, but Blanche did not quite know how nor where to do this. If she stayed at her father's house, she knew he would feel tied, and she knew that he liked to spend the whole of the late summer in country houses, and that, even if she went to London for the end of the season, it would be an effort for him to have her staying in the house, and she could no longer afford hotel life as before.

321

She decided to stay the whole of that summer in Rome. She had never done this since she had married, never stayed the whole year round in Rome, and she looked forward to it – to the heat, the quiet, and the absence of duties.

One or two of her friends were doing the same thing – Donna Maria, who hated moving, and Herbert Napier at the Embassy, who was saving up his leave for a prolonged spell next year, and who, moreover, would be left in charge during Sir Hedworth's absence.

He was a great resource, and he organised expeditions in the Campagna, to places such as Torre Astura, Subiaco, Vicovaro, Rocca di Papa, Ninfa...sometimes staying the night in a little inn. A new Italian friend of Blanche's, Elena Montanara, would go with them; she was a friend of the English and adored Blanche, but Blanche had never been allowed to know her before, because Princess Julia had considered her to be *too* white, and *too* liberal.

"I'm not black myself," she used to say, "but there are limits."

At the end of the summer holidays Blanche heard from her Uncle Charles, who told her that Rosa Maria had issued an ultimatum: she must, she said, live in England. He was taking her to a convent that he had been recommended, at Oakley Common. He was going to get rid of his apartment in Dresden and settle in England.

"I don't in the least care where I live now," he wrote. "I don't mind if I live in England or abroad – what does it matter? – and I think Rosa Maria has a right to live in England if she wishes to. Only I can't face London. I should like a suburb. I think Chiswick would suit me – the river. Or, better still, a little house about an hour or three-quarters of an hour from London. That is what would suit me best, as the only thing I really care for now, besides Rosa Maria, is gardening."

This was news to Blanche. It was a new hobby. He ultimately found what he wanted: a little house called The Priory, not far from Burnham Beeches and Farnham, only half an hour's journey from London, with the makings of a charming garden. He urged Blanche to come and stay with him, and she promised she would, as soon as she should visit England.

He seemed to be happy; but a few months later, just about Christmas-time, she heard from him again, and this time his tone was different.

Everything was going wrong; he didn't, he said, understand English life nor English arrangements and servants; the cook had given notice; he had got another, a temporary one, but the food she cooked was uneatable; the household books seemed to get larger in an inverse ratio to the quality and quantity of what was consumed; life was four times as dear as it had been in Germany. The English servants quarrelled with Ramiro, his Spanish servant, who had been with him for years. Rosa Maria was home for her holidays. She had become quite English, and had dropped her name (much to his annoyance), giving up the *Rose Marie* version, which she had accepted in Paris, and she now called herself Mary simply. She said it was absurd to have two names. That if she said her name was Rose Mary, people asked, why not Rosemary?

"Why not?" her father had asked.

"Because it's affected," she had answered.

She was being difficult. Instead of making things easier in the house, she made them more difficult; she was most exacting, and expected to find everything in England that she had been used to abroad. He had thought that the Convent would have disciplined her, but she complained to him that the Convent was immeasurably more comfortable than her home, and the food there much better – that she would prefer to stay there during the holidays.

The long and short of it was, he implored Blanche to come to England and help him, to come and live in the house and help him with the housekeeping. He said he was ill; that he had not many years to live; that he was unable to face the situation, and he felt that he was endangering his daughter's happiness.

Blanche, in reading his letter, felt that Rosa Maria was probably right, as she knew how unpractical her uncle could be. Everything at Dresden had been managed and done for him, formerly by Mercedes and lately by the admirable *Hausfrau*, who managed his flat – and several others in the house – cheaply and economically.

Blanche did not hesitate. She changed the pattern of her life; she got rid of the lease of her apartment, said goodbye to her Roman friends, and left Rome for ever.

It would have been a sacrifice, for she was used to Rome now, and strange to England, had she not been buoyed up by the thought that she might one day see Bernard again. Nevertheless, on arriving in England, she no longer felt as before, when she had visited England after her marriage, that she was a tourist, with all the pleasures of a tourist; but she now felt that she was an Englishwoman who had gone astray, an exile in her own country, out of focus, out of place.

When Blanche arrived at The Priory, she found that everything was in a dreadful muddle and mess. The cook drank, and served up the most abominable food; the house was dirty and ill-kept; and the waste and extravagance were indescribable. Ramiro was in a state of morose sulks; Rosa Maria was looking on sardonically and refusing to interfere. She was now thirteen, and was old and tall for her age. Blanche was unable to determine whether she was pleased at her arrival or whether she accepted it as the lesser of two evils.

She was civil to her cousin, and spoke sensibly.

"Father is hopeless," she used to say. "He lets Ramiro do everything he wants, and Ramiro's only idea is to prove to him that life in England is impossible, and that we had better go to Dresden or Vienna, besides which he is so extravagant and unreasonable."

Blanche consulted her, and discussed the situation with her as if she had been a grown-up person.

Uncle Charles was touching, and Blanche thought the one thing which seemed to preoccupy him was Rosa Maria's change of name. He said he understood her not wanting to have a *Spanish* name that nobody in England could pronounce correctly, but he did think she might accept the name Rose Mary, as it had been her mother's wish that she should have that name.

Blanche wrung a consent to a compromise from Rosa Maria that she should be called Rose Mary at home and Mary at the Convent.

Blanche went to London, saw her father, and discussed the matter with her father's butler, Mr Woods, who had been with him for years and put her on the track of good, reliable servants.

"Of course, Charles will spoil any servant in time," said Henry Clifford, "and you can never expect his household not to be extravagant; he is one of those people who, as your poor mother used to say, always thinks a leg of mutton is too little for dinner and a quail too much."

In a week's time Blanche began to get things into some kind of order. She had a long talk with Ramiro, and made it clear to him that his master was not going to live abroad; that, if he found it impossible to live in a house, he would take a service flat, in London; so that Ramiro must either go or make the best of things. Ramiro had no intention of going; the point of honour was the mainspring of his character, blent with a fierce and jealous devotion to his master, whom he cajoled and bullied. Blanche dealt with him tactfully.

In about a fortnight the household was running smoothly. Rose Mary went back to her Convent, Charles Clifford had decent food to eat, the house was clean, the rooms were dusted, and the household books were reduced to a reasonable scale. And all this was managed quietly, unobtrusively, tactfully, so that Charles was unaware *how* it had been done. He was profoundly grateful, and he blessed his niece for having taken pity on him.

A new life had begun for Blanche. Everything that had happened to her in the past seemed like a curious dream, but a dream that had the physical effect of taking from her all desire to begin again, to turn over a new leaf. Her father urged her to come up to London, to stay with him, and to pick up the threads of her old life, or to find new threads, but this she refused to do.

The people she had known as a girl or as a young married woman were scattered all over the world – some of them married, some of them living abroad, some of them dead – all of them different.

Her father's circle of friends had considerably thinned, but he had the gift of remaining young and of making new friends. Princess Solski was still alive – she had white hair now and was a little deaf. Her husband was dead, and since his death she had lived in England. Henry Clifford himself, although extraordinarily young for his age – he was sixty-seven – was beginning to show signs of wear and tear; he, too, was rather deaf, but his life went on as usual. He visited the same country houses at Christmas and Easter; he went to the same shooting parties in the autumn, and he still gave little dinner-parties at his house in Curzon Street. Few of the guests, now, belonged to older generations – his generation; they were mostly, now, considerably younger than himself, some of them quite young, belonging to the rising generation. There would be always some pretty, gay, married women, and a young man or two – Henry Clifford thought "young men" were a necessary appendage at a dinner-party. He deplored their distaste for claret, and their preference for light tawny – which, he said, tasted like chloroform – to old fruity vintage port, but he accepted the tastes and the fashions of the young with the same serene unenthusiastic philosophy that had guided him ever since he had been a young man himself.

He now made a regular habit of spending every other Sunday (the alternate Sundays were spent at Princess Solski's house at Weybridge) with Blanche and his brother, Charles, at The Priory. Blanche had called herself a paying guest in that house, but she was in reality both paying guest and paying hostess – indeed, the only person who ever paid anything in that household. The other members of it simply *spent*.

Henry Clifford understood that this was so in a flash – deplored it, and shrugged his shoulders. The situation, he said to Blanche, as he scolded her one day, would not be a protracted one; he implied, with a downward turn of his underlip and a grave look in his eye, that Charles had not long to live. Charles said exactly the same thing about Henry, and added as an explanation, "Henry will *under*-ice his champagne," and Henry complained with equal bitterness that Charles *over*-iced his champagne, which was wicked if the wine was good; it was frozen; and when he dined on Sunday night at The Priory he would beg Blanche beforehand to see that he had some un-iced champagne. So Blanche had to have a bottle of extra cold champagne for her Uncle Charles – he never forgot to mention the fact: "Not *frozen*, of course, not *frappé*, but *légèrement rafraichi*," he would say – and a bottle of un-iced champagne for her father, who, had there been no controversy, would have preferred it to be *légèrement rafraichi*. In a household that could ill-afford champagne at all, this was something of a tax.

Blanche was interested and amused by the contrast between the brothers who were superficially so much alike at times, and yet so profoundly different.

She felt the most intense pity for her Uncle Charles. He could not get over the death of Mercedes, and he seemed to live in a permanent dazed dream, entirely in the past.

Blanche thought that she had never seen such a wasted life, nor a disposition that was more naturally gifted. He was an artist just gone wrong, a *génie sans portefeuille*. Whatever he touched was right, but he would seldom *touch*; his unfinished sketches were beautiful, but he would so seldom finish them. The same with his writing; he devised the most exquisite things which he never wrote down; he committed nothing to paper except every now and then a pot-boiler for a magazine; but he had long since given up writing; he had never written except for money, and only then when creditors were actually knocking at the door.

His music, too, was a delight. He no longer sang; at least, one could not call it singing; but he spoke the words of German and French songs in tune to admirably played accompaniments. He was one of those singers whom composers seem to have let into the secret of their songs.

But here, again, he only touched the pianoforte at rare intervals; gardening was now, he said, his principal occupation, and with the help of Blanche (and her help was confined to buying the plants and the other necessaries) and a boy, he intended to make the garden at The Priory a thing of beauty; but Blanche foresaw that this passion for gardening would be short-lived.

The spring and the summer passed for Blanche in a new kind of solitude, *solitude à deux*, with this kind, vague, unpractical uncle, with his wasted talents, his passionate hobbies, his fundamental indolence, his absent-minded wit, his permanent sadness. He could be the gayest of all gay conversationalists; fanciful, whimsical, unexpected, with a volubility and accesses of almost hysterical laughter, punctuated by long stretches of silence; but his gaiety broke your heart; in the presence of this agile, gay spirit, and this nimble, careless mind, one was conscious all the time of being in the presence of a soul that had descended into Hell – a mortally wounded soul that was still bleeding, bleeding to death.

Rose Mary came back in the holidays. Every time she came back she seemed to have grown so considerably that Blanche wondered whether she was growing into a giantess. Blanche found her neither more easy nor more difficult to get on with, but just the same.

As she grew older, she was to Blanche more and more inscrutable. Blanche could not make up her mind as to whether Rose Mary liked or disliked her; whether she liked her being in the house, or resented it. She sometimes thought that the child hated her and resented her being there with all her heart, but was ready and even anxious to endure this perpetual mortification for the sake of her father, as she knew by experience that he was not capable of dealing with the household by himself, and that, as it was, he was comfortable.

Blanche discussed the matter with her father. Henry Clifford's verdict was that the Spanish strain in the child accounted for everything, that Spaniards were difficult people to deal with, and that it was a pity Charles had made that unfortunate marriage against everybody's wishes and advice. But the child would have looks, and she would marry in spite of there being no money, and it was to be hoped that she would marry *early*, and settle down.

But then, again, he remarked, there was that unfortunate question of religion, and it was unlikely that a foreigner, a decent foreigner, would marry a girl without a *dot*.

Blanche could not help reflecting that, just as when her marriage was discussed (when she was a girl), this girl's feelings were not taken into consideration even as a possible factor of the most slender importance.

In July Charles Clifford went to the Mont Dore, where the doctor sent him for his asthma, by himself, and in August Blanche and Rose Mary met him at Gérardmer, where the Olenevs joined them.

In September they were back at The Priory, and Blanche thought that a new era of peace had begun for her and for her Uncle Charles. But the winter promised to be a disappointment. It was the first English winter Charles Clifford had experienced for years, and both his health and his spirits began to suffer. There were several bad black fogs in London, and The Priory was damp. It was a cold Christmas, and the doctor told Blanche that it would be wise for her uncle to avoid January, February, and March in England if it was possible.

# CHAPTER XI

It was just after Christmas. Rose Mary was home for the holidays. There was an east wind blowing; the garden at The Priory was full of dead leaves, and the bare trees were dripping in the raw mist; the landscape was desolate and bleak. Blanche was alone in the house. Charles Clifford and Rose Mary had gone up to London for the day. Charles was taking his daughter to *Humpty-Dumpty*, the Drury Lane Pantomime. Blanche was having tea by herself in the little red drawing-room, which was furnished with the flotsam and jetsam of what had survived from her uncle's and her own Lares and Penates.

The walls were covered with red turkey twill. One or two of her uncle's water-colours hung there – those which he had given to his wife – a view of the Lagoon at Venice in the twilight, and of Lake Retourmer just after a thunder shower. Blanche was sitting in front of the fire and trying to unravel the present situation.

As she was brooding in the firelight Ramiro suddenly walked into the room and asked if he might speak to Doña Blanca. He never called her the Señora; that would have meant Mercedes. Blanche was surprised, and wondered what was coming. Ramiro did not beat about the bush.

"Don Carlos will die," he said, "if he stays in England."

Ramiro spoke English in a fluent staccato. He had lived for years at Gibraltar before he entered Charles Clifford's service.

Blanche, after a moment's pause, in which she recovered from the suddenness of the attack, said:

"The English winter is trying for him; I shall try and get him to go south, to the south of France, for the winter."

"And the summer disgusts him yet more," said Ramiro; "it all disgusts him. It is not the climate, although that is bad enough. It is everything – the absence of sun, of people, of noise, of cafés, of talk, of movement in the street."

"I try to make him comfortable," said Blanche.

"It is not your fault," he went on. "Don Carlos likes you as much as he will ever like another, but it is everything else he abominates, and the Señorita cannot bear to live abroad, but now she is at the Convent in England she need only go abroad for the vacation; all the other times she would be here, and maybe sometimes stay in the houses of friends. Now he could go abroad, but not for the winter only – for always. He must never come back here. He will not live here; he will die. He is like a fish on dry land."

"Where could he live?" Blanche said, half to herself.

"Doña Blanca must go with him. He cannot go alone. He must have company; the first year, without any one it was possible." (He meant the first year after Mercedes' death.) "But then he was desperate; he did not notice anything. Now he is better, he is worse; and he is now not well and must be looked after. I look after all his comforts, but I am not enough. It must be a woman as well, and the Señorita is not enough. She is too young, and she loves him too much to look after him well."

Blanche saw that her life was to be once more reshuffled, just as she thought it was becoming normal and calm.

"Where could we go?"

She was afraid he would say Florence, or Portofino, or Bordighera, or Naples, and she felt she could not go back to

Italy now. But she underrated Ramiro's delicacy and his superfine instincts.

"Maybe the south of Spain," he said – "Seville... Don Carlos would like to go to the Señora's country *now*. At first not, but now yes. Or, if not there, the coast of Africa – Tangier – or, maybe, Nice for the winter and somewhere in Germany once more for the summer – Baden – who knows? Don Carlos is fond of Germany. But wherever it is, he must never come back here. He cannot endure it; it is cruel."

"Is this all because he is bored himself?" thought Blanche to herself.

Ramiro seemed to read her thought as by second-sight.

"It is not for me, I say it. I stay where Don Carlos stays till he die, whether at the North Pole or desert of Africa or in England." (That seemed to be the worst possibility.) "And I like English people. It is not that. I think of him."

"I think you are right, Ramiro," said Blanche. "I will see what can be done; but perhaps he would be happier if he went alone or with Donna Rosa Maria; she could leave her Convent if necessary."

"That would be a pity," Ramiro said, "for the Señorita to cut short her education. The Señorita will need all the education possible in her after-life, besides which the Señorita would come out for the vacations and spend them with her father, so she would see as much of him as she does now."

Ramiro seemed to stand before Blanche as the image of fate: stolid, firm, inexorable. His face was white and ageless; his hair dark and curly; his brown eyes seemed to look inwards, like those of a Moor, not outwards. He had a slight air as of a retired bull-fighter: a semi-discarded swagger.

"Very well, Ramiro. I will see what can be done."

Ramiro bowed and withdrew, depositing before he went away a copy of the *St James's Gazette* on the small table next to Blanche. She took it up and began to turn over its leaves, without interest. Suddenly a name caught her eye.

It was the name of Bernard Lacy. It was a short paragraph about the new baronet, the heir of Alton-Leigh. Blanche did not know that Sir Christopher Lacy was dead. She learnt it now. He must have died lately, at the age of seventy-six.

Alton-Leigh and the "quaint Dower House" had been left to his nephew, together with his estate, and his money, with the exception of a few personal legacies and gifts to charities.

A few details were given about the historic interest and the picturesqueness of Alton-Leigh: there were three "priest's bolt-holes" in the house; in one of the bedrooms Charles II had spent a night during his wanderings; a piece of tapestry worked by Mary Queen of Scots was on view, and there was a corridor which was said to be haunted by the ghost of a Lacy who betrayed one of his kinsmen in a moment of peril, and who had been murdered and never buried. And then they spoke of the garden, designed by Le Nôtre, and the park with its lordly oak trees and the walled orchard. It was, they said, indeed one of the stately homes of England.

The new baronet had been popular in the Army, and he had just returned from a prolonged trip round the world. He had come back just in time to see his uncle once more. He would doubtless maintain the best traditions of the family for hospitality. The shooting at Alton-Leigh was famous, and it was not many years ago, the newspapers said, its readers would remember, that Sir Christopher Lacy entertained the Prince of Wales for the covert shooting.

Blanche put down the newspaper. The reading of that short paragraph had a deep effect upon her, and opened a thousand closed doors. A multitude of thoughts buzzed in her mind, but chief among them all was this: she felt she could not leave the country just as Bernard had arrived.

Then there began an internal duologue and a fierce inner conflict between two parts of her self, or rather between her two selves. One self said: "That is just the reason why you should go; it will make things easy. You promised not to see him, not to begin it again…this will remove the temptation."

The other self said: "I don't want to begin it again. He has probably forgotten all about it, and by now he is probably in love with some one else. I should like to be in the same country as he is; and, then, I think Uncle Charles has had enough of me and wants to be free – quite free. Free of any one, however much he may like me."

"Free of you? Are you sure of that? You know quite well he likes being with you."

"And then Rose Mary would so enjoy having him to herself."

"Would *he* enjoy that altogether? Would she look after him? Look after him properly? Could she? Who would manage the household? Who would look after him if he was ill? Rose Mary?"

"With devotion. Who better?"

"Yes, with devotion, no one better, but with experience? What was the experience of a child of fourteen?"

"But there was Ramiro. He was better than a thousand nurses."

"Yes; but Uncle Charles wanted *company*, grown-up company, some one to talk to."

"He would make friends."

"Would he? No, not now."

"Father Michael," one self said in desperation, "told me that I should get into a terrible tangle if I thought that a thing was a duty just because it was disagreeable; that one must do a thing just because one doesn't want to."

"Yes; but this is not a matter of doing a thing because it is disagreeable. It is a matter of leaving a plain duty undone because you wish to follow your inclination which prevents your doing it; and you adduce reasons for following that inclination and call them *duty* reasons; but they are *not* duty reasons, and you know it. You ought to go, and you know you ought to go; and you don't want to go – that's the case in a nutshell; and as to all the reasons you give for not going, Ramiro disposed of them all, you know he did."

"Very well," said the other self, "you have beaten me for the moment, and I give in, and I will discuss it with Uncle Charles."

Charles and Rose Mary did not get back until half-past six. Rose Mary had her tea – a substantial tea – upstairs with Blanche's Italian maid, which she liked doing, and Charles had tea with Blanche downstairs. He looked tired, and he was coughing.

"It was foggy in London," he explained. "I think she enjoyed it – *Humpty-Dumpty*. I did; the pantomime is the best thing that the English stage has to offer. The comic actors – Herbert Campbell, Dan Leno, and Little Tich – are extraordinarily funny, and Marie Lloyd is a *great* artist."

He coughed again and took a lozenge.

"I'm afraid your cough's worse," said Blanche. "Uncle Charles, you mustn't stay here for the winter."

Charles Clifford looked up at her with astonishment.

"I couldn't go abroad now," he said.

"Why not?"

"What should I do with this house?"

"My idea is this," said Blanche (she thought it was best to have the whole thing out at once), "that you should give up this house altogether and live abroad as you used to do. In the winter in some warm place, in the south, where you would get the sun, and in the summer in some nice place like Freiburg or Baden or Heidelberg, within reach of woods and in – pretty, warm country."

"Do you expect me to go and live abroad by myself?"

"There would be Rose Mary."

"Do you want to get rid of me?"

"My dearest Uncle Charles, I would be delighted to come with you and to do anything I could for you, if you would like me to, if it wouldn't bore you."

His face lit up.

"Of course, if you came with me, I should love to go; between you and me, I don't like the English country in the winter, and London depresses me. I'm not used to it, and it's so foggy." He coughed. "But I wouldn't be so selfish as to drag you with me. Selfish as I am, I would never do that."

"It would be doing me a kindness. I want to go away, too. I'm like you. I've lived too long abroad; I can't get used to England. It's too late. I was uprooted too young, and I can't grow again in the old soil. I can only grow in the adopted soil."

"I couldn't make Rose Mary live abroad again. She really hates it."

"It would only be for her holidays, and not all of them; the short holidays she might perhaps spend with friends. She has made some nice friends at the Convent – friends whose parents have country houses and young people constantly to stay with them. I don't think she'd mind coming abroad now she is at the Convent in England, and directly she is seventeen I will take her out in London."

"Yes; we needn't bother about that. I shall be dead by then."

"Nonsense; please don't talk like that, Uncle Charles."

"It's not nonsense. I know I shan't live long, and, for Heaven's sake, don't think I am pitying myself, or that I want pity; that's the last thing I want. It will be a great release. I'm tired, and I do want to meet Mercedes. I know we shall meet again."

"You have absolute faith in that, have you, Uncle Charles?"

"Absolute. Haven't you?"

"I suppose so, in a way. I believe it because I'm told to, and as I know that the other things they tell me are true, and know that many of them are true through my own experience, I accept this too. I accept it with my *will*, if you know what I mean. I make the Act of Faith through my will. But I don't really *feel* it, and what's more, you will think this awful, I'm not sure that I *want* to feel it. I mean, I can't imagine people being the same in another world. I can't imagine anything beginning again. I can't imagine seeing

337

the people I have loved after they are dead – all changed, in different surroundings, spiritualised, in a new world."

"We can't understand that, because we can't *imagine* it. But we must take it on trust that it won't be a disappointment. If it happens, it will happen right. I feel it will be all right. Do you know what it is like seeing a friend suddenly you haven't seen for several years – some one you are fond of, I mean?"

"Yes."

"Well, that always gives me what I think must be an inkling of what the *resurrection of the flesh* must be like."

"Yes; but I'm not sure I'm not rather uncomfortable – I can't remember an instance just at this minute – if I meet some one I haven't seen for a long time."

Blanche's voice trembled; she was thinking what it would be like to meet Bernard suddenly, and she knew for certain that to her it *would* be like the resurrection of the flesh, whatever it might be to him.

"Well, where could we go if we did go?"

"What do you say to the south of Spain – Seville?"

"It is extraordinary your saying that. It is the one place I have been longing to go to. Longing. Her country. I went to Seville once with her for Easter. How we loved it. I couldn't have gone back there till now, but now I feel I *should* like to. It was just after we married. We lived in a tiny little apartment – two rooms like two boxes, just opposite the Cathedral. The bells used to ring us to Mass. It was in April. Oh! the colour and the flowers; the irises in the fields; the magnolia, the jasmine; the orange blossoms in the *alcazar*; the little wild gardens; the syringa; the gay barrel-organs in the streets, and the blinding heat, and the bull-fights. Mercedes adored the bull-fights, especially the end, the *muleta*, to see the man playing so gracefully with death; and the crowd, and the people yelling and throwing their caps and drinking *manzanilla*; the dancing round the image of Our Lady in the homes on the May evenings. I thought at one time I could never go back there, as we, even we, never dared go back; we never dared go back to Spain, that is why we lived in Germany, because we had been so deliriously happy there we wanted to leave that like something precious in a box that one never wants to open again, or a beautiful face that you saw when you and she were young, and that you don't want to see changed, altered, grown old, and different. But now *that* is all over. Now that I'm going to die, so soon, so comparatively soon, I should like to see it once more, to see it with you, because you will understand, and I should like when I meet Mercedes to tell her what it is like now. Isn't that all sentimental and silly? How angry Henry would be if he heard me talking like that! But that's what I feel. I think there comes a time in one's life when the memory of the past – the past of certain things and places – is unbearable, but there still later comes another time, and I think that's a sign of coming death, when you are reconciled, and at the sight of a place that calls up the past and a flood of memories, instead of feeling pain you feel peaceful; and the memories are like those great violet clouds that flood the sky suddenly at twilight in southern places – Algeciras, or Gibraltar, or Seville – and I expect in the Campagna?"

"Yes," said Blanche. "It's like that in the Campagna."

"But you really mean we are to go and live abroad for good?"

"Yes; I really mean it."

"And in summer?"

"Baden or Heidelberg. Let us take a little villa on the Neckar opposite the castle, with vines."

"Ah! Heidelberg. I went there first when I was a boy to learn German. I was a student and learnt their way of fencing, and drank oceans of beer and sang songs." He hummed a tune: "*Es hatten drei Gesellen, ei fein Collegium.*" "Let me see. How does it go?

" 'Es kreiste so fröhlich der Becher
In ihrer Mitte herum.

Da starb von den dreien der Eine,
Der andre folgte ihm nach;
Und es blieb der dritte alleine
In dem öden Jubelgemach.'

"I forget the rest. Yes: *'Es blieb der dritte alleine in dem öden Jubelgemach.'*"

Blanche felt her eyes filling with tears. Nobody could hum music in so melting a manner as her Uncle Charles. He phrased a snatch of song in an unexpected way, and yet when you heard it, it seemed not only the only way, but the simplest way.

Charles had glided to the door while Blanche was still under the spell of his humming.

"Where are you going to?"

"I'm going to tell Rose Mary about our new plan. I must tell her, and tell her at once. I don't think she will mind, and won't Ramiro be delighted?"

Charles did not come downstairs again before dinner. Blanche presumed he had gone straight to rest and dress after seeing Rose Mary. She went up to dress herself at half-past seven. They dined at eight. Blanche was happy in her mind. She felt the question was settled. The sacrifice, if a sacrifice it had been, was now an accomplished fact. No doubt that was the will of Heaven, and it was for the best. She was not meant to see Bernard again.

She dressed for dinner, and before she went down she peeped into Rose Mary's room. It was dark. Rose Mary went to bed at half-past seven. The door was left slightly ajar, as usual, and a night-light was burning on the washing-stand.

Rose Mary was, as a rule, just on the verge of going to sleep when Blanche went down to dinner. Blanche listened at the door. Rose Mary said nothing. If she was awake she used as a rule to call out.

She was asleep or pretending to be asleep. The latter, Blanche thought; she could not have said why. Then she heard the unmistakable heave of a suppressed sob. Blanche went into the room and sat on the bed.

"Rose Mary, darling, what is the matter?"

"Nothing, nothing, nothing," but the sobs were now unsuppressed; she was crying her eyes out.

Blanche took her in her arms and smothered her in kisses.

"What's the matter, my darling? Tell me. Please tell me."

"Nothing, nothing, I promise."

"But there *must* be something."

Then Rose Mary changed her tone.

"Don't, Cousin Blanche," she said. "Go away, leave me, leave me alone, can't you? I am a wicked girl. I hate you, hate you, hate you! You know perfectly well what you have done. You have stolen papa from me, and now you are taking him away for ever."

She broke into sobs once more.

"Rose Mary, darling, listen… "

Blanche poured reassuring words into her ears.

"I promise you not to go with your father if you would rather I did not. I will stay here."

"You say that because you know I *must* stay here now that I'm at this Convent."

"Your father will take you away tomorrow, if you like. You can have lessons anywhere. You shall go alone with him and Ramiro, if you like."

As she said this, she felt Providence was rewarding her for having made the sacrifice, in intention; perhaps now it was not to be made after all. She would not make this girl unhappy, whatever happened; all the more so if Charles was right in thinking he had not much longer to live.

At last she managed to soothe Rose Mary, and left her promising she would try to go to sleep.

"You are late," said Charles, when she came down.

"Yes; I will tell you all about it after dinner."

The first thing that Blanche said when they walked into the drawing-room after dinner was: "I shan't be able to come. It will make Rose Mary too unhappy."

"What nonsense!"

But there was a shade of uneasiness in his tone.

"You know as well as I do that it would make her unhappy."

"I don't think for her sake we ought to give way to that. She will get over it entirely, and soon. It is only at this particular age that girls are like that – that they have these wild fits, these paroxysms of insane, ungovernable jealousy about their parents. In a year's time she will laugh at it, because she really is fond of you."

"I'm not sure."

"She is, really."

"I feel certain, Uncle Charles, that it would be best for you to go with her."

"You mean for me to go *alone*, because how can I take her from the school?"

"She could leave the Convent. She could have lessons at home. She knows, too, about as much now as she will ever learn at school. She is a girl who will teach herself. She knows quite enough book-knowledge now."

"I was right. You have been thinking it over and it bores you. I know I had no right to expect you to come. I don't ask you to come, but let's be sensible. Don't let us waste the child's education and spoil her future. She won't have any money to speak of; she *must* have education. It would be a pity to spoil *that* now, and she is happy at the Convent, happy among her friends there. It would be folly and a cruelty to her to take her away. So much for that. I *won't* take her away. That's settled. Nor will she want to go when she's in her right mind, and not excited after a pantomime. As for the rest, I don't expect you to come, but you mustn't expect me to go alone and begin life again in a strange place by myself. I can't face that.

I can't and I won't. I haven't got long to live. Don't desert me, Blanche. Don't leave me, dearest child."

And here he had a violent access of coughing, and Blanche thought he looked ill and feeble.

"What can we do about Rose Mary?" she said, when he had recovered. "I don't think you understand what she feels – what she is going through, how deeply she feels."

"Yes, I do understand; her mother was like that; she felt things deeply; she took things to heart; she was wildly jealous at times, quite savage, but it passed over, and this will pass over too."

Blanche looked at her uncle; he looked so frail and lonely, so sad and worn – much older than his years. No, she couldn't let him go by himself. It was not possible. Something must be arranged.

"I will come with you on one condition," she said.

"What is that?"

"That when Rose Mary comes out for her holidays – I suppose she wouldn't come out *every* holidays, and we could arrange for her staying with friends, say, at Easter and perhaps Christmas, that will be easy, as they are always asking her...but when she does come out for the long holidays, you must promise me to spend a part of it, or all of it, with her alone, and let *me* go away. I shall go to Russia and stay with the Olenevs. Will you promise me to do that?"

"Yes, for this year, and next year you will see it won't be necessary; she will have got over all that nonsense."

The next morning, Charles had a long talk with his daughter, and Blanche talked to her, too. She found Rose Mary quite calm again, quite reasonable, perfectly satisfied with the arrangement. She had regained her serene inscrutability. Blanche casually let drop the information that she would spend the summer vacation in Russia, after she had established her uncle at Heidelberg, and that Rose Mary must look after him there by herself.

Everything seemed to be settled satisfactorily now, and all parties to be satisfied. The doctor called the next day to see Charles Clifford, and he told Blanche that the sooner she got him to go south the better. Ramiro was triumphant. By the end of January, Rose Mary had gone happily back to the Convent; The Priory was let, and Blanche had disposed of her lease, and she and her uncle and Ramiro had started for Seville, where they stayed at first at the hotel, and where they subsequently took a small house for three years, from an English artist, in the Calle Imperial.

# CHAPTER XII

Rose Mary did not go out to Seville for the Easter holidays, which were short. Her father said it would be too expensive, and she had been asked to stay with the mother of a girl friend, a Mrs Bromley – there was a Mr Bromley, too – who lived in the country not far from Southampton and brought up a large family in a not over-large house. But the house seemed capable of infinite expansion, and they generally had, besides the family, one or two people staying with them. It is true that the children were seldom all at home at the same time.

Seville suited Charles Clifford; suited is a mild term – he adored it passionately. He was ill when he first arrived, listless and weak; but the sun did him good, and, little by little, he seemed to revive. He showed Blanche all his favourite places. He liked taking her to small restaurants where there were barrels of wine in the *patio*, and to the fried-fish shops to await the arrival of the fresh *langustine* from the Guadalquivir. Every morning he would go to Mass in the sombre and splendid church of the Salvador, where, in the brown darkness of the huge pillars and the fantastic baroque decoration and carving, one shaft of amethyst, crimson, and topaz light would fall from a small high window of gem-like stained glass on an acolyte in his vermilion cassock, or a woman at her prayers, dressed all in black, and veiled, kneeling upright and motionless with arms outstretched before a side altar.

Or he would spend hours in a second-hand book-shop in the Calle Sierpes, rolling and smoking cigarettes and discussing the merits of various bull-fighters with the bookseller, or with stray clients who dropped in, or in the Alcazar gardens, talking flowers with the gardener. He was a fluent Spanish scholar.

At the end of June – and Charles Clifford enjoyed the heat; in fact, the hotter it was, the more he enjoyed it – they moved north and went to Heidelberg. They could not afford to take a house there, but they found rooms in a comfortable pension, in which they had a sitting-room of their own. Charles Clifford particularly enjoyed pension life, and he made friends with an American old maid and an English widow.

At the end of July Rose Mary came home for her holidays. Blanche went to Russia to stay with the Olenevs. She stayed with them for six weeks. When she came back, Rose Mary had already left, and at the end of September they went back to Seville.

Rose Mary spent the Christmas holidays with the Bromleys, and she appeared to be, so Blanche thought, happy, judging from the tone of her letters. This is what she wrote:

"OUSELTHORPE, SOUTHAMPTON,
*January* 6, 189 – .

"DEAREST PAPA, – We are having great fun. Five of the boys are here this Christmas, but it's very sad that Elsie and Janie are both away. There are some people called *Lord* staying here – an old man and his wife; they are the parents of Beatrice Lord who was at Roehampton, but she left last year. She is out, quite grown up now, and her hair is done up. Mr Lord is such a funny man. He does marvellous conjuring tricks. We all went over the other night to a concert given in the village. Some neighbours were there – a Mrs Roden with a large party of people. They live near in a large house called Elladon. The concert was great fun. Mrs Roden is very nice; she asked us all to go over and spend the day. There were some boys from Oxford too. – Your loving daughter,

"ROSE MARY."

Charles Clifford got through the winter fairly well. They spent a fortnight at Gibraltar and three weeks at Tangier during the coldest part of the winter, and it happened not to be a severe winter.

They made at Seville the acquaintance of a clever English doctor who looked after Charles Clifford. He told Blanche that he did not think her uncle would live long. Charles Clifford no longer talked about his health now.

At Easter Rose Mary stayed with the Bromleys again, and this time she wrote more cheerfully than ever.

"Nearly all the boys," she wrote, "are at home and the best of the girls, so we are having great fun. There are two old men, as well as a Mr Leveson, who has been called to the bar, and a man called Sir Bernard Lacy, who was in the Army, came down for a night. The Rodens lent me a pony. I went out riding with the Roden girls – they are older than me – and we had a grand gallop."

When Blanche was shown this letter it gave her a slight shock. "But then," she thought, "they would of course seem old to her."

In the summer they again went to the same pension at Heidelberg. Rose Mary came out for the holidays, and Blanche went to England, to see her father, and to stay with her aunts. Her father looked on his daughter's action in leaving England and going abroad with her Uncle Charles as a piece of wanton folly. "If you must look after some one, why can't you look after your poor old father?" he said. But he knew quite well – and she knew that he knew – that he did not really want to be looked

347

after. He was looked after quite enough as it was, and he liked to keep his free time quite free.

At the end of September she returned to Heidelberg, and travelled back to Seville with her uncle. She saw Rose Mary just before she went home. She had grown considerably, but seemed at last to have stopped growing. She was not nearly so tall as Blanche had feared she would be. She was indeed going to be striking-looking; her colour was good, her hair dazzling, her wide grey eyes uncommon.

She was enjoying life evidently, but this time she seemed sad at going back. When Blanche and her uncle got back to Seville, Charles Clifford seemed to be immensely tired. He said he would never go abroad again. His cough troubled him; he had fits of asthma as well, so that it hurt him to lie down.

The doctor told Blanche that the best thing for him to do would be to spend the winter at Madeira; that Seville was too dry a climate for him, in his present condition, and too cold.

Blanche broached the subject to her uncle, but he refused to hear of Madeira; he hated the place – to be cooped up with a lot of invalids; he had never felt better in his life. He was a different being from what he had been two years ago.

Blanche told the doctor what he said, and the doctor said: "Try at any rate to get him to go to Gibraltar, where it is warmer and softer."

But her uncle would not hear of that either. He said the hotel was too uncomfortable and too full, and that it was impossible to get rooms anywhere else, or a house. He was not going to budge from Seville. It happened to be rather a cold winter, and Blanche had the utmost difficulty in keeping their little house, which had a large open *patio*, warm.

She was alarmed at her uncle's state. He was hiding from her how ill he felt, but he did not succeed in deceiving her for a moment.

The doctor said that this summer she must take him to Switzerland, to Davos, or to some place of the kind.

Charles said to her unexpectedly one day – he was lying on a basket-sofa on the roof of the house: "Dr Lingard wants to send me to Switzerland."

"Really," said Blanche. "Did he tell you that?"

"No; but he told you."

Just after Christmas – it was a fine January – he rallied and seemed to be his own self again, and then he rapidly got worse.

Blanche asked Dr Lingard whether she ought to send for Rose Mary, but the doctor said no; he would certainly, he thought, live through the summer.

One morning Blanche was surprised to see a priest walk out of her uncle's room. She asked Ramiro who it was, and he said that the Don Carlos had sent for him.

Her uncle was in bed. She went to see him.

"I have been putting my house in order," he said. "Tomorrow he will bring me the Holy Oils."

"The Holy Oils! but surely, Uncle Charles, you are not letting him give you Extreme Unction *now*?"

"In the early times of the Church you were given the Holy Oils, not because you were a hopeless case, but so that they might make you better. That is why I am having them, but as a matter of fact I feel better today."

Blanche thought over the matter, talked with Dr Lingard again, who still thought there was no need for any immediate alarm.

His lungs were really better. It was true his heart was weak and *flabby*, but there really was, as far as he could see, no immediate danger. In spite of this, Blanche wrote a full account to the Mother Superior, and she told Rose Mary her father was seriously ill, and she thought it would be a good thing for her to come out. It would do him good to see her. It would very likely cure him. She sent her some money for the journey. If he got well, she thought, so much the better. Rose Mary arrived in a week's time.

Blanche said that she had organised this as a surprise for him. She thought it would do him good, and there was an epidemic of measles at the Convent, so that the girls had been sent home. This she invented; there was no such thing.

Rose Mary had not been two days in Seville before her father grew worse. He no longer talked much, but he did say to Blanche one afternoon, as she was sitting by his bed: "You will take care of Rose Mary, won't you? I leave her to you. She will be your ward."

Blanche consulted Ramiro. He shook his head and looked grave. Dr Lingard had found them a nurse.

Charles Clifford's mind had remained clear. He no longer seemed to notice Blanche, Rose Mary, the doctor, nor Ramiro. His mind seemed intent on something, or some one else – some one else who seemed to be there, quite close to him – some one whom the others could not see. He coughed a good deal, and no longer talked, and seemed very weak, but he made all his arrangements. One morning, after a bad night, he sent for Ramiro and told him to fetch the priest with the Viaticum. It was a beautiful day, early in March; there was a touch of spring in the air. The street was echoing with cheerful noises of muleteers, and carts, and women singing.

The houses stood out white and dazzling against the blue sky, in which there was not a speck.

Blanche looked out from the window on the noisy street, and presently, above and through all the business bustle and noise, she heard the sound of a bell and saw a priest walking in his white stole, and by his side was a boy carrying a taper; and the years rolled back for her, and she was once more in a narrow Street near the Palazzo Fabrini, looking on at a procession, just after she married; and how much had happened between then and now. She was a different woman now – the ghost of the Blanche of those days. Her real life was over – all over; her youth had gone; she was middle aged; she felt that she had never really lived, only, that is to say, during those few fatal months in Rome when she had known Bernard. All her friends had either left her or were dead and now this, her last friend, her uncle, was leaving her. She seemed to bring misery and unhappiness to people.

The priest entered the house, and Charles Clifford was shriven, houselled, and annealed. The prayers for the dying were said, and Blanche, Rose Mary, and Ramiro knelt beside the bed. Through the open window came the cheerful noises of a Seville morning. A little boy was playing on a *mirliton*. The umbrella-mender was calling on his gay reed. Life never seemed so fresh, so spring-like, so full of the seeds of fragrance and resurrection. And Rose Mary, kneeling there by the bed, was the emblem and incarnation of spring and youth...Charles Clifford lay with a rosary in his hands and looking straight in front of him.

All at once he smiled and said in Italian, "*Eccoti!*" – it was a phrase from a translated play of Ibsen's which he had seen with Mercedes; Zechetti had said it. They had often discussed how miraculously that great artist had expressed in those three syllables the divine surprise of the expected moment – so anxiously awaited, so long delayed, and so long hoped for against all hope – when at last, in spite of all, it unexpectedly arrives. And he hummed very softly and exquisitely the phrase of a Spanish song, "*Tü me dejaste solito.*"

Then he shut his eyes, and an inscrutable peace and final content seemed to stream from the calm of his face, which was now quiet for ever...

He was buried, according to his wishes, at Seville. He left what he had to leave to his daughter; she was to be Blanche's ward. Blanche was entitled to manage all her affairs till she should marry, or reach the age of twenty-one.

Blanche and Rose Mary went back to London. Rose Mary went back to her Convent, and Blanche stayed with her father and set about to look for a small house – something just big enough for herself and for Rose Mary, when she would come back for the holidays.

She found what she wanted in Kensington – a little two-storied house not far from the Carmelite Church.

The Easter holidays began soon after they arrived, and Rose Mary once more went to stay with the Bromleys. She had taken her father's death strangely: she had shown hardly any signs of emotion, but Blanche was convinced that this seeming indifference was only a mask which concealed a seething whirlpool of feeling, and she was afraid that a part of the foam of this whirlpool was hatred for her. "However," she thought, "there is nothing to be done."

Blanche resolved to be as nice to Rose Mary as she possibly could, and to try and be as little of an obstacle or a hindrance as possible.

Her reports from the Convent were satisfactory. The Mother Superior said she was undisciplined and violent and given to excesses of temper and passion; she was proud; but, on the other hand, she was exceptionally truthful and honest, and loyal to a fault: she did not make many friends, nor did she make friends easily, but those she made she clung to; she did not care for books; she spelt badly and could not write English correctly, but she had a good head for figures, and was first in her class for sums. She was fond of all out-of-door sports and games, and she drew well as long as the subjects were out-of-door subjects – birds and animals which she was passionately fond of, or landscape. She was old for her age, and far older, the nuns said, in mind than her contemporaries. She fulfilled her religious duties in an exemplary manner.

She wished to come out the following year, when she would be seventeen, and Blanche agreed that it would be a good thing.

She thought, indeed she knew from experience, that it was a mistake to marry young. "On the other hand," as she said to Father Byrne one day at the Oratory, "perhaps it is no more a mistake than to marry old, or at any time, as I suppose girls *must* marry."

"Tut, tut," said Father Byrne. "She will make an admirable wife. You must find her a good Catholic husband – "

"That's not so easy," said Blanche. "However, I needn't think of that yet."

Blanche was wondering whether she would hear any news of Bernard, where he was, and what he was doing. Her curiosity was fulfilled in an unexpected way.

Rose Mary came up from the country to spend a few days in London before she went back to Roehampton.

Her friends, the Bromleys, some of them at least, were to be in London too.

Rose Mary had made great friends with the Roden girls at Elladon; one of them was just her age, the other a year older. They were neither of them out.

One day Blanche got a letter from Mrs Roden, saying that her children were having a tea-party. Could she bring Rose Mary? "I don't suppose you will remember me," she wrote, "but I used to know you years ago, when you first married; in fact, I knew you first as a girl *before* you were married, and I remember your dear mother. Francis would so *love* to see you again; he often talks of that night we danced on the lawn when we had Little Warlop and you sat next to him at dinner. He was quite in love with you! Do bring your charming cousin. We are all so fond of her, and my girls rave about her. We will be able to have a talk downstairs while they have tea in the schoolroom."

Blanche took Rose Mary to the Rodens'. Mrs Roden received them with gushing effusion. Rose Mary slipped up to the schoolroom at once.

"You haven't changed, my dear; you look younger than ever. More lovely than ever. Francis will be in love with you more than ever now. He promised to come home to tea today, and I'm sure he will."

They talked of various things, and presently Francis Roden arrived. He looked at Blanche with a twinkling, inquisitive eye and asked minute questions about who was upstairs. He wanted to know who all the guests were, and their ages, and was dissatisfied because Mrs Roden wasn't sure about which or whose boys were there.

Before leaving the house, Blanche was taken upstairs to the schoolroom, where a whole crowd of semi-grown-up children were playing Oranges and Lemons, while in the corner of the schoolroom two governesses, one a Frenchwoman and the other a Swiss, were talking about the sleeves of a new evening-gown.

Rose Mary asked Blanche if she might give a return tea-party for the Rodens and the Bromleys, and it was arranged that the tea-party should be given three days later – the day before she was to go back to the Convent.

Blanche made all the arrangements and prepared an amusing tea with crackers, although this was premature, and chocolate Easter eggs, although these were belated, and she left Rose Mary to receive the guests, saying she would look in before the tea-party was over.

The party was larger than had been anticipated, and quite successful. There were five Bromley children – Elsie, Janie, James, Noel, and Peter; and two Roden girls – Alice and Margaret.

The Bromleys brought with them one of their cousins, who happened to look in at their house that day – Bernard Lacy; and the Rodens brought a cousin too – Caryl Bramsley.

When Blanche came home towards seven she found the two governesses in the little front room downstairs still discussing the sleeve question. In the next room, the dining-room, the tea-table had been cleared away, and an uproarious game of musical chairs was going on.

Blanche went into the room, and there, standing up in front of the fireplace, having taken part in the game, and being "out," was Bernard Lacy.

For the moment Blanche's heart stopped beating. The room swam round her, and yet with a kind of mechanical self-control she walked up the room, and she heard another self, who was not herself, say with a smile that some invisible angel seemed to pin her lips into: "Mr Lacy! I haven't seen you for ages!"

"No," he said, quite naturally; and, as he spoke, Blanche was transported back to those first days when he used to come to the Palazzo Fabrini to Guido's daily receptions. "And I believe I first caught sight of your cousin a year ago when I stayed at Ouselthorpe, and when they told me she had a guardian, and that we were going to her house, I had no idea it was you. I feel I had no right to come. My cousins dragged me here, not even telling me, till we had started, where we were going to."

Blanche had recovered, and she said "How do you do" to the Roden children and to the Bromleys, and then she and Bernard went into the next room, and Bernard began to talk as easily as if nothing had happened, and he had never been away. He lived mostly in the country at Alton-Leigh – he hated London – he wanted to go into Parliament, and he would stand at the next election. Walter Troumestre often stayed with him when he was not travelling.

After Bernard's first flow of talk, there was a pause. Then Blanche said: "I have come back to London for good now, and next year I shall take Rose Mary out."

"She's a lovely girl," said Bernard, "and quite grown up enough to be out. How old is she?"

"Sixteen."

"She is very uncommon-looking."

"Her mother was Spanish."

"Spanish!"

"Yes; it is odd her being so fair, but her mother used to say that her family were *Guanches*, who came from Teneriffe and settled on the west coast. Guanches are fair-haired people, and supposed to be the last remnants of the inhabitants of Atlantis."

355

"Miss Rose Mary looks as if she might have come from Atlantis."

Blanche observed Bernard as he looked across the room into the dining-room, where, at that minute, Rose Mary, crowned with a wreath of paper roses, was taking the leading part in a game. "He does admire her," she thought. She felt wicked, minding his admiration for Rose Mary, and his praise of her, but mind it she did. Every word was like a stab.

"She is at a Convent at Oakley Common," she said.

There was a silence. Blanche thought that Bernard looked older. He was grown up now, and grown up really for the first time. His skin was darker; he was thinner; the bones of his face stood out more; there was more shape about him. His hair was a little thinner. There was a slight scar, she noticed, on his forehead.

But his eyes were the same – those slow, thoughtful, grey, rather sad eyes.

"When does she go back to school?" asked Bernard.

"Tomorrow."

There was another long pause. Incidents of the past were crowding round Blanche in a ghostly herd.

"He has forgotten it all," she thought. "He has *got over it.* He probably loves some one else, perhaps several people. He looks happy; yes, fairly happy. Is he happy? Is some one else, perhaps, making him unhappy? But I don't count for him. And yet I believe he was pleased to see me – just a little bit pleased. His face did light up a little, just like it used to. How absurd I am a woman of forty-three behaving like a schoolgirl."

"You must come and see my mother one day. We live at Ovington Square. She would be delighted to see you."

"I should love to," said Blanche, and she felt herself blushing, and she felt that Rose Mary was looking at her, and she blushed still more. This was intolerable. She got up and said: "Now, children, you can have one last game of musical chairs."

She sat down at the pianoforte and played while they danced. After that the Rodens went away.

"That's the Sir Bernard Lacy that came to Ouselthorpe last year," said Rose Mary. "Did you know him before, Blanche?"

"Yes, yes – I met him at Rome."

"Oh!"

Blanche quailed beneath Rose Mary's scrutiny.

She went upstairs, and she did not have dinner downstairs; she had, she said, a bad headache.

Bernard, she thought, had behaved like a man in real life, and not like a man in a novel; but if she could have read his thoughts as he walked back to Ovington Square, she might have modified her judgment.

"She has quite forgotten all about it," he thought to himself. "She never really cared for me. If she had cared for me, she would have come to me directly the catastrophe happened."

And that moment, and all that he had felt then, and for the last two years, rose before him in a series of dream-like pictures. He remembered that when the catastrophe had happened he had felt stunned and numbed, and as if everything were not really happening at all. He had been, during those first hours, like a man walking in his sleep. He remembered that he had felt like a schoolboy who had got into some tremendous row and who feels that there is looming unseen some horrible retribution, that it is coming slowly on, that nothing can stop it.

And then he had gone home, and when he got home, to England, he seemed to have woken up. It had been a dream. The whole thing had been a dream – a beautiful, enchanted dream, that had ended in a blurred nightmare; and this, mixed with his fall and his concussion, made all his impressions seem still more dream-like. But he went on telling himself that his life was broken, and that he could not live without Blanche; but this was more a dogma he subscribed and accepted than a belief which sprang from his heart. He was not really half as naturally sad as when his engagement with Rose had been broken off.

Then had come his long voyage, the sport, the strange countries and sights and people, the physical fatigue, heat, cold, hunger, excitement, danger, and new worlds: the East; India, China, Japan. And in Japan a fresh brief love affair, a Japanese wife who reminded him a little of Blanche, he thought; and then America, the Rockies, and New York (and a long flirtation there which ended in nothing). This was like a tonic; and then home once more, the death of his uncle, the inheritance, Alton-Leigh with its beauty and its traditions... the gradual settling down into English life...the local interests, English country life and sport which he passionately loved...guests, neighbours, dinner-parties, hospitality...all this had healed his heart, he thought. He would say to himself that he would never *love* any one else...he might have love affairs; he might marry; but he would never *love* any one else...but now he had seen Blanche for the first time after a lapse of four years, he repeated to himself: "No; she never really cared – never cared as I cared. I would have sacrificed everything, and have taken her to the end of the world. I would have been eternally faithful to her, but of course these things only happen in books. And then," he thought, "she is just as beautiful as ever. She hasn't changed one bit. That ward of hers is very good-looking." And Rose Mary's face appeared before him in startling distinctness. It was odd, he thought, that the first time he had seen her at Ouselthorpe he had hardly noticed her. But she was a child then, of course, and he had only seen her for a moment at tea. She had not even come down to dinner. Not grown up. The awkward age. But now she had shot up; she was grown up. She was so young...he put away the thought of her, and thought once more of Rome, and of Blanche, but Rose Mary's grey eyes and radiant hair kept on coming back to the foreground of the picture. When he got home he told his mother he had seen Blanche.

"She is living in London for good now with a cousin who is her ward, the daughter of her uncle and his Spanish wife. She's very striking-looking."

"Really," said his mother. "I should like to see her."

"She's at Roehampton. Princess Roccapalumba said she would so much like to see you again."

"And I should like to see her."

Mrs Lacy said this without a reservation. She thought there was no more danger to be feared for Bernard from that quarter.

The next day Rose Mary went back to her Convent.

# CHAPTER XIII

About a week later, Blanche met Mrs Lacy one Sunday morning coming out of the Oratory.

Mrs Lacy greeted her with genuine warmth and friendliness, and asked her to luncheon. Blanche accepted the invitation, but when she arrived at Mrs Lacy's house, she saw that what she had already guessed was true – Bernard was not there. At luncheon there were one or two people – Father Locke, who played the organ in one of the churches, and a Mrs Lord; but they went away directly after luncheon, and Mrs Lacy begged Blanche to stay on. Bernard, Mrs Lacy explained, had gone back to Alton-Leigh.

"It is impossible to keep him in London for more than a day. I don't know what he will do if he gets into Parliament."

They talked of common friends: the Olenevs – the Lawlesses. Mrs Lacy said she no longer went abroad now. She felt it tiring. She sometimes spent a week or two at Torquay in the winter, but most of the time she was at Alton-Leigh. Bernard entertained, and she helped him as much as she could.

In the autumn he had shooting parties, and there was to be a party at Christmas. They talked of Rose Mary but Mrs Lacy had hardly said a word to Blanche about her before she was conscious of a curious embarrassment, and she dropped the subject. It was, she thought, that she had fancied at the back of her mind that Rose Mary would make an admirable wife for Bernard. Mrs Lacy did not think that Blanche was thinking of Bernard. That, she thought, was all over, and she was happy about Bernard himself. He had, she thought, got over what had been a boyish *coup de tête.*

Indeed, it had all been for the best. The episode had acted like a prophylaxis, as, according to all accounts, Bernard had had several affairs in America and in England, and had come through them all unscathed. He was nearly ripe for marriage, his mother thought, and he had been through the necessary preliminary experiences, and come through them on the whole without much damage. Suffering there had been, but this, in the world such as it is, in a damaged universe, and in the presence of original sin, Mrs Lacy reflected, was inevitable.

Blanche was happy talking to Mrs Lacy; she reminded her every now and then so vividly of Bernard. She was happy to be sitting in the room where he sometimes sat, surrounded by all that had been familiar to him from his childhood.

She stayed talking to Mrs Lacy till nearly four o'clock, and when she went away, Mrs Lacy asked her to come and see her whenever she could.

Henry Clifford tried to get Blanche to come to his little dinners, but she only consented to come if he was alone. She could not, she said, "begin things again" in London. She would have to go out when her ward came out next year, but then that would be normal; she would just be an ordinary chaperon: one of those stiff, stately, and tired figures who sit like waxworks against the walls of ballrooms, and are taken sometimes down to supper by a civil diplomat, or a blushing young man who is told to do so.

Nevertheless, she did accept an invitation to dine with the Rodens one night in the middle of June. She had a presentiment about it that came true. The first person she saw as she walked into the drawing-room was Bernard.

She wondered whether she would be able to exchange one word with him. It was rather a large dinner-party. There were several people she knew: Gabriel Carteret, now Sir Gabriel Carteret, and his wife. She remembered him as a promising young man when she first married. She had met him at Little Warlop the night of the Rodens' dinner, when they had all danced on the lawn, and Adrian Tyne had made love to her. Now he was married, rich and famous, and might one day be President of the Royal Academy.

There was Lady Harriet Clive, whom she had so often met in old times, and who seemed so surprisingly little altered; and one of her former admirers, Cecil White, who looked quite old-fashioned now, as if he belonged to a different epoch – the eighties – but still smart and good-looking. Mr Roden took her in to dinner. She had not been introduced to her neighbour on her other side, but his face seemed familiar to her, although she did not recognise him at first. She looked at the card which was opposite his place, and read Lord Mayfield, and, as she read those words, she felt giddy for the moment, giddy from an emotion which was partly strangeness, a dream-like feeling of unreality.

There, sitting next to her, was the man she had wanted to marry, the man to whom she had been engaged to be married; and there, sitting opposite to her, was Bernard Lacy, the man she had loved, the man she still loved, and would always love.

Bernard, too, was sitting between two people whom she did not know; one was a girl about nineteen, whom she had never seen, but whose face was vaguely familiar to her, and who reminded her of some one, some one, but she knew not who...
She was tall, with soft grey eyes, a dead-white complexion, and a graceful figure and manner. Bernard's other neighbour was a married woman, between thirty and forty, with striking, thoughtful, dark eyes and slightly untidy hair – carelessly dressed...artistic, thought Blanche.

Mr Roden talked to her all through the beginning of dinner. But there came a moment when he turned to Lady Harriet Clive, who was on his other side; and it was then that Lord Mayfield – Sydney Hope that was – turned to Blanche and said: "Do you remember me?"

"Of course I do," said Blanche, but she thought to herself, "It is a wonder I do, considering how much you have altered."

He was not much older than Blanche herself, and now only forty-six; but he looked far older. He was quite bald, and his face still bore the unmistakable stamp of the tropics. He was far more "important"-looking than Blanche could ever have imagined him being.

"Fancy," she thought, "if I had married him!"

But as he smiled at her she still saw what she had liked in him, and she suspected that he felt the same towards her – that he, too, could still reconstruct what he had once found pleasing in her.

They talked of various things. Lord Mayfield, Blanche learnt, was a neighbour of Bernard Lacy's, and he was going to stay with him in the autumn for the shooting.

"I must introduce you to my wife after dinner," he said. "She is sitting opposite you. We've got four children: two boys at school, and a girl coming out next year." He paused. "She is called Blanche," he said, with a smile. That was the only allusion he made to the past. His wife, he said, was musical and literary – "clever, but not alarming, you know"– and went to a great many concerts.

"My eldest boy has inherited all that," he said, a little sadly. "Plays the violin, and goes to the Pops at St James's Hall. Doesn't care for cricket or football, not even for fives. But the girl – Blanche – takes after me. Likes hunting, horses, dogs, and all that. She's just ordinary and stupid, like me. It's a contrary world, isn't it?"

"Yes," said Blanche – "*very.*"

After dinner, there was music in the back drawing-room upstairs, where there was a picture by Burne-Jones, and two Corots. Mr Roden went downstairs to the library to play whist, and begged those who shared his indifference not to go into the music-room, where a violinist, a cellist, and a pianist were to perform. Bernard took Mr Roden at his word, and said to Blanche:

"Let us go into the next room, unless you want to listen. I expect you do; you used to be very fond of music."

"I would far rather talk," said Blanche.

The music went on in one room, the back drawing-room, behind shut, folding doors; but there were two other rooms on the first floor in which there was plenty of space for the non-musical to talk.

Blanche and Bernard sat on a sofa near an open balcony, which looked out upon the square. It was a warm summer night, and a pleasant noise of hansom cabs came from the street. There was a ball going on in a house a few doors off, and from where Bernard and Blanche were sitting, they could hear the music of a valse – a plaintive Viennese tune which was just then the rage, "*Sei nicht böse.*"

"Who was the girl sitting next to you?" asked Blanche.

"She's a Miss Tyne, the daughter of a diplomat, who died about five years ago."

Adrian Tyne's daughter! Of course, thought Blanche, who else, now she thought of it, could it be? There were the same soft eyes, the same grace of manner, the same slightly hectic amiability, the same touch of super-refinement and ultra-civilised finish – which was not affectation – the same exotic charm which would appeal powerfully to some and repel others.

"What a strange evening," thought Blanche. The past was sending her its ghosts, not in single spies, but in battalions. The past was poisoning the present; for all these memories made her feel that her relations, her present relations with Bernard, belonged to the past, and could never again belong to the present. Never again. All that was over. Over? Was it quite, quite over?

"Your father," Bernard suddenly said, "is coming to shoot with us in the autumn. Won't you come with him?"

Blanche for a moment was taken completely aback.

"Well," she said, "I am going to Russia to stay with the Olenevs."

"Won't you be back in October?"

"I suppose I shall."

"Well, we can look upon that as settled. You could bring your cousin, too, of course."

"She will be back at the Convent by October."

"How is she?"

"Very well...and happy...and getting on so well."

"I think she is so pretty."

"Isn't she? I think she will be really *beautiful*: she has elements of real beauty... Of course she is absurdly young."

"Well, you will come...that is settled."

"May I let you know? I must talk it over with papa – and then it depends on all sorts of other things."

"Let me know when you like, to Alton-Leigh. I am going back there tomorrow, for the rest of the summer. Walter is coming in August, and my mother comes next week."

"I will let you know... I should love to come."

"I do hope you will. I hope you won't let those other things interfere with this." Bernard looked at Blanche fixedly. "How extremely beautiful she is," he thought. He had never seen so much grace in human features; a grace that for him, at any rate, escaped definition. He looked at her so thoughtfully that Blanche wondered whether, after all, the past were as dead as she had imagined... A little hope began to creep like a small flame into her heart...if...if, if... But no, it was too absurd, she mustn't think of such things.

Bernard, for his part, imagined in a way that he was just as fond of her as ever, and if some one had asked him he would have said that his feelings for Blanche had never changed...but this was a delusion. He was in love with the memory of what had been, not with the actual present Blanche; but Blanche was in love with the present Bernard, and her love was beginning to give seed to what at first would be hope – hope that so swiftly in its turn begets illusion.

"Do you ever hear from Donna Laura and Donna Maria?" Bernard asked.

"Donna Laura writes sometimes, Donna Maria never. Donna Laura is perhaps coming to London next year, but I rather doubt if she will; it is difficult to get her to move from Rome. She goes to St Moritz sometimes."

At that moment Lord Mayfield came up to Blanche and said to her: "I want to know if I may introduce my wife to you."

Blanche gave Bernard a look, a swift look, and got up. Bernard was caught by some one else as he strolled towards the music-room. Lord Mayfield led Blanche to the other side of the room, where his wife was standing next to the door. She had just come in from the music-room, and seemed to be looking for some one.

Lord Mayfield made the introduction.

"You didn't hear the Schubert?" Lady Mayfield said.

"I missed it," said Blanche. "I was here talking. Are they going to play anything else?"

"Ella Friedmann is going to sing some Schumann songs. Do you like music?"

"Yes; if it's not too difficult. Let's go and listen before they shut the door."

Blanche followed Lady Mayfield into the next room. There were no chairs arranged in rows, as for a concert, but those who were listening sat about the room as they liked, on the chintz sofas and arm-chairs. There were not more than a dozen people in the room. Blanche sat down on a sofa with Lady

Mayfield, and presently Ella Friedmann, looking dark and handsome, and dressed in amber velvet, sat down at the pianoforte and, accompanying herself, sang intimately to the guests. She sang "Mondnacht," "Die Lotosblume," and "Frühlingsnacht." Blanche looked round. There was no Bernard. But Miss Tyne was drinking in the music with evident and rare appreciation; Mrs Roden was listening fervently; Mr Peebles, the Cabinet Minister, was listening with all his matchless intellect; Lady Elizabeth Carteret was listening listlessly, by fits and starts; Gabriel Carteret was listening respectfully, aware that he was listening to an artist, but incapable of the finer shades of appreciation; Lady Harriet Clive was not listening at all. Walter Troumestre – whom Blanche had not noticed at dinner – was there. He had been sitting at the other end of the table.

When the singing was over – and never had Ella Friedmann been in better voice, nor sung better, and she was the finest *Lieder* singer of her generation – the audience were too greatly moved to applaud. Walter walked up to Blanche and said to her:

"I don't know why those songs always remind me of Italy, especially of Florence…cypresses, villas with high walls, fireflies, hot nights, croaking frogs…and yet there's nothing Italian about them; and they remind me," he said, with a laugh – "I don't know why – of *you*. I suppose it's because I met you at Rome. I never met you at Florence; but the first time I ever saw you in my life…at the opera in Paris… I thought of a Schumann song, and I said so to Bernard."

Blanche blushed with pleasure.

"I see what you mean about Florence," she said; "they remind me of Rome, and they remind me still more of Heidelberg. I had an uncle, who is dead now, who was musical, and he used always to sing and hum them, especially the last one, 'Frühlingsnacht' – that was his favourite song."

"How wonderfully she sang it!" said Walter.

"Wonderfully."

"Do you think we could ask for another?" said Lady Mayfield.

"I think she would sing another song if Mr Peebles asked her," said Walter.

"Do ask him to," said Blanche.

Walter walked across the room to Mr Peebles, who was talking to Lady St Cuthbert – a beautiful, pre-Raphaelite vision, with a cloud of golden hair and still, green eyes.

He looked up with kind courtesy at Walter, when the latter delivered the message, and said:

"I must ask my hostess. I am quite willing to act as ambassador if she will give me my credentials."

"Yes, Mr Peebles, do please ask her," said Mrs Roden.

"What shall I ask for?" said Mr Peebles.

"Brahms' 'Winterzeit,' " said Mrs Roden, "if you would like it."

"Very well, Brahms it shall be," and Mr Peebles rose slowly from the sofa and walked up to Miss Friedmann, who was talking to her old friend, Lady Harriet Clive (although unmusical, she respected all celebrities), and proffered his message, with a charming smile.

"Certainly, I will sing again," said Miss Friedmann, "if you are not sick of it; but you would do better to ask M. Franck to play."

"Perhaps," said Mr Peebles, "we may be granted that privilege as well."

Ella Friedmann sang the song, and both the words and the music, with their piercing, intolerable pathos, and the singing with its finished art, and its rich, liquid volume of tone and thrilling high notes, affected Blanche so powerfully that she nearly broke down, and, as soon as it was over, she stole from the room and, finding Mr Roden at the door of the next room – he had finished his whist – accepted his offer to go down to supper.

"I am quite hungry," she said.

"You must be, after all that," he said; and before they started he poked his head into the music-room, and, looking like a slightly ruffled bullfinch, he said, in a high voice: "Rachel, we're going down to supper; bring them down as soon as they've finished."

He talked as if the music were for all of them a tedious task that had to be got through.

Mr Roden then gave Blanche his arm, and other guests followed. The musical audience listened to one last brief Chopin prelude, and then they, in their turn, came down, Mr Peebles bringing Mrs Roden, and with them came the artists.

Bernard had gone, and for Blanche the evening was over. But Walter Troumestre was still there; he had taken down Miss Tyne, and he sat next to Blanche, and this gave her faint joy; he had the reflected glory of being Bernard's friend.

"I didn't listen to the Chopin," he said. "I didn't want to hear anything after that last song."

"That's just what I felt," said Blanche.

"Well, you've all been patient," said Mr Roden. "Rachel never knows when to stop when she gets hold of a musician. They must be famished. But I suppose some of them liked it."

"But, Mr Roden, it was quite wonderful," said Blanche.

"I dare say," said Mr Roden. "I remember you always liked that kind of thing, years ago, when we were at Little Warlop. But I don't believe they are all of them musical, for all that."

At this moment the conversation had been interrupted by the arrival of Ella Friedmann, who had been taken down to supper by Gabriel Carteret and placed beside Mr Roden.

Blanche enjoyed that supper. She succeeded in having a long talk with Walter about Bernard.

"I am going down there later," said Walter.

"It must be a very beautiful place."

"Oh, it's the *most* beautiful place in the world! But I hope Bernard won't spoil it."

"Is he thinking of spoiling it?" Blanche asked, with a slightly nervous laugh.

"He loves the place, and he will never touch the house – never try and improve it, I mean. It is absolutely untouched. But I think he is hankering to tidy up the garden. He hasn't been able to do it yet, because he couldn't afford it – it's expensive already, and Bernard keeps up the shooting, and he hunts, and all that; but you know there's a lovely garden, designed by Le Nôtre; and Sir Christopher, Bernard's uncle, was a crank, and one of his fads was that the garden should not be touched, but be allowed to run wild. He used to say that tidy gardens were an abomination, and that the Spaniards, the Moors, and the Chinese were the only people who understood gardens. Well, that's all very well in Seville or Tangier or Constantinople, or Tientsin, I think, but if you have a garden built on the model of Versailles, with 'trim parterres,' and all that, you do expect it to be tidy – at least Bernard thinks so, and he has, as you know, a tidy mind; he hates frayed edges and dropped stitches. Only as it happens – however right or wrong it may be – at Alton-Leigh it would, I think, be a tragedy if he touched the garden or the park."

"Why?" asked Blanche.

"Well, because by having been neglected, that stiff, prim garden, with its avenues, its yew hedges, and formal beds, and ponds, and little Greek temples, and its stone ornaments, has become an enchanted place. It is all overgrown and wild – and like the palace of the Sleeping Beauty in the Wood. It reminds me of the *Villa d'Este*."

"Is it like an Italian house?"

"No; it is Jacobean, I think – some of it early, and some of it later. There was an older house, which was burnt down; some of that is left, I think, and there's a whole wing by Inigo Jones. It is wonderfully situated, and there's a moat all round it."

"And the inside of the house?"

"Oh! the inside is a dream – wonderful – nothing has been touched since Heaven knows when."

"Beautiful pictures?"

"Nothing extraordinary, just family pictures; but they all look as if they were there by right. They don't look like a furniture shop. Everything seems to have grown there. And then there's a wonderful library which Bernard threatens to sell. There are Shakespeare folios, wonderful books of coloured prints, and old garden books, herbals, missals, and all sorts of things like that."

"But surely he won't sell those?"

"He talks about improving the estate, and a lot about death duties."

"But surely he didn't have to pay death duties? The Bill wasn't passed when he succeeded."

"No, he didn't, but I think he is sure" – Walter stopped abruptly, and then said – "I think he is sure to want to spend money on other things...horses, new stables... "

Blanche felt quite certain that Walter had been going to say, "I think he is sure to marry."

"I have been asked to stay at Alton-Leigh this autumn, with my father," she said simply.

"Well, if you go, you must try and persuade him not to touch the garden."

"I shall try my best, and I will get papa to – papa is an accepted authority."

"And not to sell the books."

Mr Roden, who up to that moment had been pretending to listen to Ella Friedmann's views of Anglo-French politics, but who really had been busily overhearing a conversation which was going on at the other side of the table between Diana Tyne and a young man who was making her laugh, escaped from the toils, and, taking advantage of a slight pause, turned once more to Blanche.

Shortly afterwards the party broke up, and Blanche went home.

# CHAPTER XIV

Shortly after that evening at the Rodens', Blanche left London for Russia. She stayed two months with the Olenevs in their house near Kiev.

After some consultation with her father she decided to accept the invitation which Bernard had not been slow in reiterating.

Rose Mary spent her summer holidays with the Bromleys. Blanche stayed in Russia until they came to an end, and she was back in London just in time to take Rose Mary back to school.

It was Rose Mary's last term at the Convent. It was settled that she was to come out the next year. She had stopped growing, but she was already a striking girl, and her beauty held out promise of still greater possibilities.

Blanche stayed in London till the beginning of October. She had been invited with her father to go to Alton-Leigh in the middle of the month. It was a three hours' journey from London to Alton-Leigh, and when they arrived at the station there was a ten-mile drive. Bernard sent a char-à-banc with two horses to meet Blanche and her father.

It was a wonderful October that year. The foliage was still intact and a blaze of graduated colour – gold, crimson, green, and russet. October seemed to be proving that it could rival the month of April in combinations of colour and rare surprises.

A great stillness seemed to brood over the flat country – the fen country – and the wide, russet-coloured fields with flashes of bright green here and there reminded Blanche of Russia.

She was silent as they drove from the main road into the park which led to the house. Henry Clifford was silent, too. He had so often been there before, and never had he dreamt that the little boy whom he used to see riding a pony, and whom he tipped before going to school, would one day play a part in his daughter's life.

The autumn made him melancholy. He felt his life was nearly over, and he felt, too, that he had made havoc of his daughter's life. He would have liked to have it all over again, and to have managed differently, but he reflected that probably every human being felt the same when looking back.

The park was long and sparsely wooded – with ghostly looking oak trees – it looked deserted, desolate, and strangely ragged; and Blanche felt, as they drove through it on that mellow, still, golden afternoon, catching sight of deer here and there, that there was something unreal about it.

She felt, too, that strange feeling that comes once in a lifetime to everybody – that she had been here before, and had seen all this before…all this, she felt, had happened already, only she couldn't remember when…and when her father said, "We shall see the house in a moment," she felt that was just the remark she had been expecting. Presently the house came into view – it stood in a hollow and in a wide moat – and they drove over the Queen Anne bridge, which was the only entrance to the house. Once more Blanche seemed to recognise the house, although she had never seen a picture of it, and although it was different from the picture she had formed of it in her mind from Walter Troumestre's description.

It was built of yellow stone, which had been tanned and coloured by age like a meerschaum pipe. Blanche gave a slight gasp when she first set eyes on the house. The beauty of the place, the warm walls, the flaming creeper on the square tower, the large mullioned windows with the sun glinting on the square panes, the still moat full of water-lilies, in which one swan was proudly swimming, affected her with a pang of pleasure that was almost painful in its sharpness.

She said, "Oh!"

Her father was delighted at her appreciation.

"I thought you would like it," he said.

The house was a complete quadrangle, two-storied, and the greater part of it early Jacobean. Some of it – the stone gables of one wing inside the quadrangle – was older, Elizabethan; and the front which looked out on to the garden had been built by Inigo Jones a hundred years later than the rest of the house.

When you drove across the moat you reached a large square tower in the middle of the house as it confronted you, and on each side of the tower there was a double row of windows, all of them square and stone-mullioned.

Under the tower there was an arch, which took the whole thickness of it, and a cloister to the right and to the left of it. Over this arch there was a huge mullioned window, with six separate high panes, which formed the centre of a large gallery.

Inside the house nothing, as Walter Troumestre had told Blanche, had been touched; additions had been made, but nothing had been taken away, improved, restored, or spoilt. There was an oak staircase, a low hall, a gallery on the first floor, stretching from one end of the house to the other, which looked out on to the drawbridge. The small rooms downstairs were full of furniture of every epoch: old pictures, old china, old chests, old chairs (on which the *petit-point* seemed fresh and bright), tapestry, musical instruments, harpsichords, harps, great majolica vases, bowls of potpourri, and wide stone fireplaces with wood logs. The whole house was aromatic with the smell of wood and faded spices.

Bernard welcomed them in the hall, which was entirely panelled in oak, and had a huge chimney-piece of white and elaborately carved freestone. He then led them out through the hall through the court of the quadrangle on to the terrace, and the sight here was, Blanche thought, still more wonderful. Behind them the house front was the work of Inigo Jones. There was an elaborately carved doorway in the middle of the wing; three square mullioned windows on each floor to the right and to the left of it, and two large mullioned windows at each end of the wing, taking up both stories, and round the roof a fretted parapet of open stonework.

In front of them stretched a still, formal garden, with a square sheet of water in the middle. On the farther side some elaborate-shaped beds made into patterns and fringed with clipped box, and between an avenue of tall elms; in the farther distance between the elm trees, forming, as it were, the back-cloth and scene of that spacious proscenium, there was a background of green and golden foliage, and in the midst of it a little white temple. The lawns wanted mowing; the grass had been allowed to grow everywhere...it was tangled, there were weeds everywhere...a few flowers in the beds mixed with the weeds here and there, a gorgeous dahlia, a gladiolus, an aconite, a phlox, or a few tiger-lilies stood out. One could see that no gardener had been at work for long, but that the flowers were the remains of the work of other days; and this was true, as Sir Christopher Lacy's wife had been an enthusiastic and skilful gardener, and it was only after her death that Sir Christopher had refused to touch the garden. He used to give other reasons for this, but those who knew him better said it was from sentiment.

The house was full of people; they were all out when Blanche and her father arrived. Most of them had come down the day before, Friday, and Blanche and her father had meant to do the same, but her father had been kept in London.

Walter Troumestre was there, Mrs Lacy, and four other guns besides Henry Clifford and Bernard; some of these were neighbours, one a former brother-officer of Bernard; one was a Scottish peer, and one was "some one in the City." There were plenty of young people, too; some girls, but nobody except Mrs Lacy and Walter Troumestre whom Blanche had ever seen before.

They had tea in the hall, and after tea Mrs Lacy showed Blanche her bedroom. It was a beautiful room, with a large four-posted bed and faded tapestries, telling the story of Jason and Medea, mullioned windows, and a carven chimney-piece, looking out on the garden. Over the chimney-piece there was a picture of a young boy which looked as if it might have been painted by Van Dyck, but it was not even attributed to him. It was a boy with a hawk on his wrist, and wearing a long buff-coloured doublet, long black hair, and soft, melancholy eyes; a Spanish type of countenance.

Blanche was struck dumb by the beauty of the house and the garden. She sat for a long time at her window that evening, looking out on to the terrace. Her window faced west, and she saw the sunset turn the fleecy clouds to a marvellous billowy texture of pearl, grey, and rose, and the burnished trees turned to flame; there was complete stillness in the air, save for the cawing of rooks and the whirring of the starlings' wings. Blanche sat at the window until it grew dusk and the fire had quite melted away even from the afterglow, and only a pale lake of light remained like a stain under a purple bank of cloud. Then she dressed for dinner.

She wondered as she looked in the glass whether people would think she looked old. She felt older than she had ever felt before, in this strange and beautiful house. She would have liked to have stayed in her room that evening, and have remained silent, dreaming, thinking of the past; she felt that to take part in life, in the life of a bustling country-house party, would entirely break the spell, and after she was dressed she sat looking at the logs of her wood fire, which had been lit as the evenings were chilly. She had asked her maid not to draw the curtains, as she liked to see the remains of the fading afterglow, and the first stars through the old casement...the full moon had not yet risen. She sat in front of the fire, looking herself like a Van Dyck picture in her white satin gown with a Medici lace collar round her shoulders and one small row of pearls round her neck, till her father interrupted her reverie by walking into her room, saying: "Come on, darling; we shall be late for dinner."

Blanche found herself at dinner between Bernard and a scion of one of the Scottish Catholic families. It was a large dinner-party, and several of the neighbours had been invited. Bernard talked to her easily and naturally, and at times she felt as though they had never been separated, but at other moments she felt there were boundless seas and unfathomable gulfs between them that nothing could bridge.

She talked to him of the house and the garden.

"I'm fond of the old place," he said, "but the garden is really too untidy – something must be done to it. I can't afford it this year, but some day I shall set about it and get rid of all those weeds and all that mess, and tidy the whole place up."

"I think," said Blanche, "it looks so beautiful as it is."

"You would like it far better if it was tidied up."

"I rather like untidy gardens, like those in Seville."

"That's what my uncle used to say – they're all very well abroad...but here it doesn't do."

After dinner there was whist and music – some one played, and songs and choruses were sung – "John Peel" and "The Midshipmite" – and a round game, Commerce, for the young people...a great deal of noise and talk and laughter.

The next morning Blanche went to Mass in the chapel of the house, and the chapel, which was served from a neighbouring village, struck her as being perhaps the most perfect thing in all that haven of beauty. There was a church in the park, in which many of Bernard's ancestors had been buried, but this church had become Protestant after the Reformation. The chapel was square, simple, and practical. The walls were covered with a faded red silk, and the Stations of the Cross were in mosaic of different coloured woods made by an Italian in the late Renaissance. The chapel looked as if it was there for use. But everything in it was beautiful, from the Spanish silver crucifix and *baldacchino* of stamped dull-red leather, and the small window of stained glass with its deep browns and blues and pale topaz and yellows that the modern try in vain to reproduce, to its small hand-blown organ with its carved wooden case and dull gold pipes. This stood in a little gallery at the west end, where you could hear Mass unobserved. In the course of the morning Mrs Lacy took Blanche all over the house and showed her the pictures, the priests' hiding-places, the historical bedrooms and relics, the library, and everything of interest, and then they walked to the Dower House, which was in the park.

They walked through the wide alleys of the garden, past the stone ornaments, sprawling Tritons and plump Poseidons, that stood over the old ponds and were strewn, just as the walks were, with the leaves from the elm trees, and the sun lit up the stillness, and in the air there was a smell of smoke and burnt leaves, and something that, in spite of the mellow serenity of the level sunshine and the softness of the light blue sky, had a sharp tang in it, the first hint of winter, just as on a fine April day you receive the first hint of summer, maybe in the smell of a hedgerow or the sudden whiff of a breeze; and from a side avenue they walked next into the kitchen garden, which was enclosed by high brick walls and was full of pear trees laden with fruit, and a separate orchard, that had large, wide, grass paths.

They walked through the kitchen garden, past a hothouse that had once sheltered orange trees, stephanotis, and bougainvillaea, and other sub-tropical and tropical plants, but which was now empty and derelict save for a few dilapidated garden chairs and broken tools; past a mossy, overgrown, little Italian temple with a pond in front of it, in which there were somnolent carp and flashing goldfish; through a little gate into another enclosure, a trimmed and ordered garden this time, which Mrs Lacy herself, with the aid of a boy, kept tidy. Here there were beds of snapdragon and roses, and here there had been hollyhocks, sunflowers, and lilies. There were beehives, too. They walked up a stone path to the house, a grey stone building with pointed gables and mullioned windows. It had been built in the fifteenth century, and had remarkable oak doors. Mrs Lacy took Blanche indoors.

"I always lived here," she said, "till Bernard's uncle died."

The rooms were small and low, and were all of them panelled. They were comfortably furnished, and the house looked lived in.

"Does any one live here?" asked Blanche.

"I always used to live here. Nobody lives here just at this moment, but when the house is full, Bernard sometimes puts up people here, people he knows well, and last summer he lent it to an old cousin, an Oxford don, who is writing a book, and who wanted to be quiet. I still look after the garden."

"Do you want to tidy up the big garden, too?"

"Well, no, I am used to it as it is, and I can't bear change."

"But Sir Bernard talked of tidying it up."

"I don't think he ever will; he dislikes change as much as I do. He is ashamed of it in theory; he thinks it is all wrong, but in practice I think he likes it as it is. Happily there are many other things he will do first."

They walked through the house from the garden front to the front door; there was a little stone court outside that, with an old sundial.

"What an enchanting place!" said Blanche. "I should like to live here for ever."

"Yes; it has got a character of its own. I will take you to the church. They will have come out by now."

The eleven-o'clock service was over, and they could see the congregation walking home across the fields. By the time they reached the church the congregation had dispersed, and the venerable vicar, with kindly face and snow-white hair, saluted them from the distance.

"It is an old church," Mrs Lacy said – "Early English. Some of it was rebuilt by Henry VII."

It had a square tower and only one side aisle, in which there were two carved effigies.

"Eight generations of Lacys are buried here in the family vault."

"But I suppose no longer now?" said Blanche.

"No; now there is another church in the village, and a school. Sir Christopher built that. He is buried there. Look at that window; isn't it quaint?"

It was; it represented one of the early Lacys helping to storm Jerusalem and fighting the Saladin.

"Of course it's been a good deal spoilt and restored."

They walked back through the park into the Dower House, and back through the kitchen garden into the long avenue, and here they met other members of the party who were being shown round the grounds by Bernard.

Blanche did not see much of Bernard that day, and the next day the shooting began.

The days passed, and Blanche continued to be on the same easy terms with Bernard, but their intimacy did not increase.

One evening she thought, with trepidation, but not without acute joy, that the situation was about to change. It was the night before she and her father were leaving. They were going the next day, after luncheon. The party was coming to an end. Blanche again sat next to Bernard at dinner, and on her other side there was a country neighbour, who was deaf, interested in topography, and who discoursed easily without waiting for an answer or hearing it if he got one.

Blanche listened, or pretended to listen, to him during the first part of dinner, echoing every now and then the last word he said. But there came a moment when Bernard turned to her, and she was able to talk to him.

"It's sad its being your last night," he said.

"Yes; papa's wretched at going away."

"You must come again soon."

"I should love to."

"Why not at Christmas?"

"Well, there's Rose Mary."

"Why not bring her, too?"

"She generally goes to her cousins."

"There will be lots of young people here. I'll try and get some of her particular friends; but perhaps it would bore her?"

"I'm sure it wouldn't."

"Perhaps" – he said this rather sadly – "it would bore you?"

"It wouldn't," said Blanche, with a smile.

They looked at each other and Blanche thought for a moment that Bernard had lifted a mask and that his old face was there, his old self, the Bernard whom she had known in Rome. Was he, after all, just the same? Was it all just the same?

And Bernard was saying to himself, "Of course she never really cared for me and she never could care for me again, but it would be wonderful if she could and did." But it was the dream he enjoyed – he took no steps to make it come true.

"I have enjoyed your being here so much," Bernard said. Blanche's heart gave a great leap. "And so has my mother." Blanche's heart went down to the depths once more. "She thinks I ought to marry" – Blanche's heart went lower and lower – "but I shall *never* marry." He said this in a calm, matter-of-fact tone without looking at her. Her spirits rose once more, and her heart began to beat quickly again.

The conversation was interrupted, but just before the interruption Bernard said to Blanche:

"Please try and come at Christmas...please, please."

He said the last two words so gently and so sadly that Blanche said to herself... "Perhaps after all..." and she went to bed that night happy, although she had no further talk with Bernard that evening.

She sat up in her bedroom a long time before going to bed. First of all Mrs Lacy came into her room and talked to her for a little while. They touched on no dangerous topic, and Mrs Lacy said how sorry she was, how sorry they all were, that Blanche and her father were going. They must come again. She talked of Bernard naturally, and she gave Blanche the impression that she was welcome in the house, and the further impression that she was not looked upon any longer as a danger. This gave her a pang. "Because," she thought, "a mother's instinct is always right, and if she thinks Bernard could not love me any more, she is right, and he doesn't... but... " and hope sprang up eternal...

Just before Mrs Lacy said "Good night" to Blanche, Blanche asked her, quite apropos of nothing, whether the house was haunted.

"There are the usual stories," said Mrs Lacy. "Swishings of skirts heard on the staircase, and lights seen at the window, and figures in the passage, but no real authentic ghost. Nothing for the Society of Psychical Research. Romantic stories, plenty of them, nothing scientific. I think this house would banish anything scientific, and I think the men of science would scare away the kind of ghost that might haunt this house. They are such romantic ghosts."

"I am sure they are."

"I have never seen anything," Mrs Lacy went on, "but there is a legend that the garden is haunted, or at least that on certain nights of the year a piper walks round the house to serenade a certain Annabel Lacy who lived in the days of the Stuarts. The story is that she said she would love this minstrel if by his music he made her cry, and that in his lifetime he never succeeded, and that he died of grief, and that you still hear him playing on the terrace."

"Did she hear him after he was dead?"

"The story says she did."

"And did she cry then?"

"Some people say 'Yes,' but most authorities 'No.' According to one story, on one night of the year she is punished by being compelled to come back and listen to him."

Mrs Lacy said "Good night," but Blanche felt not at all inclined to go to sleep. She put on her dressing-gown and looked out of the window. It was a wonderful night. There was a full moon, and the large elm trees stood out in the light of it, solemn, and still seemingly full-foliaged, but on the verge of dissolution, like kings arrayed in their robes of state ready for their showy death and gorgeous burial, and the sheets of water and the ponds in the garden were silvered, and there was not a sound in the stillness.

Blanche looked and looked. The night was warm, and the world seemed unsubstantial. She had never, she thought, seen anything more beautiful or more intensely sad. She felt as if not one ghost but a crowd of ghosts, a whole dead-and-forgotten world of plumed cavaliers and court ladies, in soft satins, were walking with plaintive grace along those terraces and in those wide alleys. How still it was! Not a dog barked, not a twig cracked. It must be nearly midnight; yes, there was the church clock in the park ringing out the time in soft and solemn tones, and now the stable clock answered it, and then many more clocks indoors, making a soft hissing noise between each silvery stroke, like the noise a repeater makes when you press it:

"And the press'd watch return'd a silver sound."

384

"What a lot of clocks," thought Blanche, "and not one of them keeping exact time with the others." The stable clock was the loveliest of all; its chimes were so soft, so mellow, so sad. The stables were older than the house, and had never been destroyed.

Now once more it was still again, and then it seemed to Blanche that from the far distance, through that still, clear night, there came the noise of pipes playing an infinitely sad tune...a tune she had never heard before, but which seemed familiar to her. What was it – what was the strange familiar yet unfamiliar music, which she had never heard before, and which she knew so well – "Randall, my son"? No...but something like that. Was this the ghostly piper trying to melt the heart of the proud Lady Annabel? The piping ceased, and in the room itself Blanche seemed to hear the noise of strings, harp strings, and something like a lute, playing a faint, ghostly tune. She started; it was behind her, and she walked towards it, and as if through it; it was a faint, tinkling, metallic sound as of a spinet, a stringed instrument and a whispering voice, and then all at once it stopped and she was not sure she had heard anything at all, but she felt cold and she shivered, and her skin seemed to be all tight. She looked once more out of the window. There was nothing to be seen save the silvered garden and the dark, ghostly trees...and not a sound to be heard. She shut the window and went to bed. She caught sight of her face in the looking-glass on the dressing table. It was white, and yet she did not feel frightened. Then she got into bed and blew out the candle, but she did not get to sleep till it was daylight.

The next morning after breakfast...and Blanche said nothing about her experiences in the night, which now seemed to her like a dream...she went into a little, low, square room on the ground floor which was called, nobody knew why, the Abbot's room, but which was the library, to write a few letters. It was Friday. Blanche and her father were leaving after luncheon. Her father was going on to another house-party in

Hertfordshire. It was a gorgeous day, warmer than ever, almost like a spring day; the grass was wet with dew, many gossamer threads hung on the creepers, and the spiders were busy with their acrobatic feats.

Blanche sat writing by the open window, but she was distracted by the noises of the morning, the birds, the dew, the sun, and by watching a spider spinning its web on the honeysuckle leaves of the wall opposite, which was at right-angles to the window.

Presently she heard voices. Two people were sitting or walking on the terrace – a man and a woman. Blanche recognised the voices…the woman's voice as being that of a Mrs Ebury, a hunting friend of Bernard's, and a country neighbour, who was staying in the house. The man's voice was that of the City friend of Bernard's.

Mrs Ebury was saying: "She is wonderfully good-looking and wonderfully young-looking. They say he was in love with her, but I suppose she didn't care for him."

"No," was the answer; "she was desperately in love with an Italian who wouldn't look at her."

"But the husband nearly killed her?"

"Yes; he was jealous of every one and quite mad – a maniac. But it was the Italian he was jealous of, and not Bernard."

"Did Bernard take a long time to get over it?"

"Yes, in a way; other things cropped up."

"Other people helped him to forget?"

"Yes; that's just it."

"He has quite got over it now?"

"Oh, quite."

"I suppose there's some one else?"

"Yes."

"Let me think. Isn't it that…they were talking of her yesterday, that pretty little American, Mrs Betis?"

"No; I think that's over. She's gone back to America for good. No; for the last year I believe he has been in love with Celia Deacon."

"Really! Well, I don't wonder. She is most beautiful on the stage, but I don't care for her acting."

"She can't act for nuts, and she's very stupid, but she is lovely and young, and Bernard... "

Blanche got up and left the room. She could not go on with her letters.

# CHAPTER XV

Blanche did not see Bernard again till Christmas. During the autumn months she saw few people except her father. The Rodens were in the country, at Elladon, and in mourning for Lord Hengrave, Mrs Roden's brother. Blanche stayed with each of her aunts once, and that was her only dissipation – a mild one. Her only treat was seeing Mrs Lacy and Walter Troumestre; but his visits were few and far between. He never seemed to be in the same place for more than a week at a time, and soon after Blanche left Alton-Leigh she got a post card from him from Constantinople. In December he was back again in London, and he told Blanche that he was going to spend Christmas at Alton-Leigh.

It was now settled that Blanche, Rose Mary, and Henry Clifford were all of them to do the same. Mrs Lacy had urged Blanche to bring her cousin, and Blanche had not the strength of mind to refuse, although she accepted the invitation with reservation, feeling a premonition of disaster and a slight pricking of her conscience. She said to herself: "Why should I refuse? It would be unkind towards Rose Mary to deprive her of such a treat, especially as Bernard has invited some of the Bromleys to meet her." Another voice inside her answered: "She might go without you. But that would look ridiculous. What excuse could I find for not going? And what would my father say?" "You could find all sorts of excuses," said the other voice. And all the time, underneath the plausible reasons and explanations that Blanche gave herself, proving to herself that it would be quite absurd not to go to Alton-Leigh, a still voice kept on saying to her: "Don't go, don't go."

Rose Mary came home for good towards the end of December. She was to come out at Christmas, but when Blanche told her about Alton-Leigh, she seemed disappointed. Mrs Roden had written to Blanche urging her to bring Rose Mary to Elladon for Christmas, and Rose Mary knew of this. The Bromleys were not spending Christmas at home this year. The family was broken up for the moment. The boys were going to Alton-Leigh, but the boys were not Rose Mary's particular friends, although she liked them. Her particular friend, the eldest girl, was going to Elladon, and Rose Mary wanted to go there.

Blanche reviewed the situation with mixed feelings.

(A) She wanted to go to Alton-Leigh. She wanted passionately to be in the same house as Bernard. She admitted this to herself to the full.

(B) She was inclined not to go to Alton-Leigh. She felt, she knew not why, it might lead to difficulties.

(C) She felt inclined in theory, and on paper, to accept Mrs Roden's invitation. She knew Rose Mary wanted to go there, and she knew Rose Mary did not want to go to Alton-Leigh and would think it selfish of her, Blanche, to take her there.

At the same time, she could not get away from another factor which complicated the matter. She knew that if Rose Mary went to Alton-Leigh, do what she would, she would not be able to help feeling jealous of her – jealous of her with regard to Bernard. She felt certain that Bernard would admire Rose Mary. Rose Mary was now almost seventeen; she would be seventeen on the 1st of January. Her hair was done up. She had stopped growing. Her complexion was a dream. She looked as if she had just risen from a clear stream. Her hair shone like spun gold; it was rebellious, too, and curly, and gave one the idea of wind blowing it about. She looked like a creature of the woods and the hills. Her wide grey eyes were grave and still. And then she was young, so young… Blanche felt old and weary and faded beside her. At the same time, she felt this was an ignoble feeling, to be jealous of her ward, and that if this were so, there was all the more reason she should not prevent her cousin going to Alton-Leigh.

Then point D. She knew in her heart of hearts that Rose Mary, whatever she thought now, would, when it came to the point, when she was actually there, enjoy being at Alton-Leigh. She would enjoy it, she thought, more than Elladon. She would ride, she would hunt. There would be every kind of amusement; she would enjoy the people. It would have the charm of novelty. So it was sophistry to say that Rose Mary would not enjoy it.

Then there was point E – a small point, but still a point. She had half promised both Mrs Lacy and Bernard to go. She could easily get out of it. Mrs Lacy, she felt, would not mind much, and as for Bernard, she did not know…but it could be done. She had, in accepting the invitation, guarded herself carefully and left herself a loophole for escape at the last moment. She thought about this all the night after Rose Mary's return. "I wish," she thought, "I knew some one I could consult about it." Father Byrne; he would tell her she was nonsensical, and not to be so foolish. "I am so much worse," she thought, "than he will ever believe." No, there was no one. She must settle it herself. It had to be settled at once. Christmas was in less than a week. If they were not going to Alton-Leigh, she must let Bernard know at once.

The next morning, after a sleepless night, which Blanche spent in wrestling with this question, she said to Rose Mary at breakfast: "I'm afraid, Rose Mary darling, you don't want much to go to Alton-Leigh for Christmas."

"Do you want me to go?" said Rose Mary, and Blanche felt that those grey eyes were looking through her, right to the bottom of her soul.

"I want you to be happy, but I think you would be happy either at Alton-Leigh or at Elladon. But I think you will find Alton-Leigh much more amusing when you get there than you think it is going to be now. I have been thinking it over a great deal, and I have settled to leave it to you. You shall do exactly what you like. It is your coming-out party, and you shall choose. Only there is just this to think of. If you were not out, you could have gone by yourself to the Rodens, and I could have gone to Alton-Leigh, but now that you are out, it would be odd if you did not come with me, and, I think, a mistake. Your father wouldn't have liked it. So you must put up with me whichever you do. Only you can choose. You can do whichever you like."

Rose Mary thought for a moment, and then she said: "I would rather go to Alton-Leigh."

"Are you quite sure, because I must let them know today?"

"Quite sure."

"Well, that settles it. I will write to Sir Bernard today – no, I think I will send a telegram – and say we will arrive there on Thursday. You really are sure?"

"Quite positive."

"Very well."

So the matter was settled, and three days later, Blanche, Rose Mary, and Henry Clifford, all three of them, went to Alton-Leigh, where there was a large party of old and young. The house was so full that Walter Troumestre and another soldier friend of Bernard's were living in the Dower House.

Princess Solski was there, and a number of cousins of Bernard's, some grown up and some not – a lot of girls and boys of all ages.

They arrived late, just in time for dinner, on the Saturday before Christmas Eve, which was on a Monday. They just had time to dress hurriedly, and when they came down into the large hall, in which a roaring log fire was blazing, and where the walls were covered with holly and branches of fir trees, they found the party ready assembled. Bernard and Mrs Lacy welcomed them, and Blanche noticed that Bernard was startled by Rose Mary's appearance.

It was something more than he had expected. Blanche did not sit next to Bernard at dinner that night, as he had Princess Solski on his right and an Austrian lady, Countess Chereni – whose husband was at the Embassy – on his left. Blanche found herself between Walter Troumestre, to her great delight, and on her other side a comfortable country squire, a cousin of Bernard's. Rose Mary sat between two young men, and Walter and Blanche were sitting opposite her.

"Your ward has come on," said Walter; "I think she is quite lovely. She is oddly fair, isn't she? considering she's half Spanish."

"Yes; isn't she fair and lovely?" said Blanche; "and I think she will get lovelier still when she's been out a little time."

After dinner the old people played whist and the young played uproarious games, and some of them sang songs. Blanche talked to an Austrian – Count Paul Chereni – whose father she had known in Rome, the whole evening. Rose Mary was the centre of a laughing group of boys and girls, and Bernard, who played silly games like forfeits, spent all his time – so Blanche noticed – with this group, and not with the card-players or the musicians.

When they went up to bed, Blanche said to Rose Mary: "Are you enjoying yourself, darling?"

"Yes, very much," she said.

The next day being Sunday, many of the guests went to Mass in the chapel. The non-Catholics went to the church in the park.

Bernard Lacy had maintained the traditions of Alton-Leigh, where his uncle had always asked some representatives of the old Catholic families, English and Scottish, at Christmas-time, and always a distinguished foreigner or two, Austrian, French, or Italian, and a large sprinkling of country squires and neighbours. This gave the gatherings at Alton-Leigh a stamp of their own, and made them different from those of other country houses.

Henry Clifford bemoaned the changes that he saw going on around him, and used to say that Alton-Leigh, with the exception of two or three of the big Whig houses, was one of the last bulwarks of civilisation left in England.

It froze hard on Sunday and on Monday, and there was skating on the pond in the garden. Blanche could not skate, but Rose Mary, who took naturally to any sport, skated perfectly, and she and Bernard did figure-skating and danced together on the ice. That evening, Christmas Eve, before dinner, there was a Christmas-tree in the gallery. Each of the guests was given a present of sorts, and children from the neighbourhood, and the school children from the village, attended it.

Blanche sat next to Bernard at dinner.

"I admire your cousin immensely," he said, quite naturally, to Blanche. "I think she is a capital girl, as well as being so good-looking. Aren't you proud of her?"

"Yes; I am indeed."

Blanche felt there was nothing in Bernard's tone to give her cause for uneasiness, nor indeed in his behaviour to Rose Mary. He treated her just as he treated the other young girls there. He seemed to like her frankly, just as he liked the others; that was all; whereas he seemed to be beginning to pay attention to Blanche. He talked to her nearly all through dinner, except when he was obliged to talk a little to his other neighbour, and after dinner he talked to her again. They went to midnight Mass, and afterwards they drank milk punch in the hall. The guests went to bed, but Bernard and Walter sat up late in the smoking-room.

They discussed the guests.

"Princess Blanche looked better than ever," said Walter.

"Yes; didn't she? Far better than any one; younger than the youngest."

"But her niece is good-looking and will be a beauty, I think."

"Yes; I think she will. She's just out of the awkward age."

"But she looks older than she is. That's the foreign blood, I suppose."

"I suppose so."

They talked of other things till they went to bed. Walter was right, Bernard thought, as he went to bed. Blanche looked better than any one there. And what a charming woman! How nice she was to every one! What grace she had! What lightness! There was no one to compare with her, no one to touch her. He would never love any one as he had loved her. "As he *had* loved her," he said, not "*as he loved.*" What a pity it was she did not love him! Because, of course, she did not love him!

If only things had been different...and then, as he switched his thoughts off the past with a violent jerk, a picture arose in his mind, left now to its own devices; but it was not a picture of Blanche – it was a picture of Rose Mary. What a girl! What hair, what a complexion! What life! What youth! How wonderfully well she skated!

The next day there was a Christmas luncheon, and the guests spent the day in the grounds, looking at the stables, and the garden, and walking in the park, and skating in the afternoon. The frost had continued, and the ice was still hard enough to bear, but there were signs of a coming thaw, ominous clouds, a feeling of damp in the air. There were many guests at dinner that night from the County, and after dinner they danced till three in the morning. Bernard danced with Blanche three times and twice with Rose Mary. She, Rose Mary, danced like the wind.

During one of the dances Henry Clifford was sitting with Princess Solski, looking on at the dancers. At that moment Blanche was dancing with Bernard.

394

"She is more beautiful than ever," said Princess Solski; "even more beautiful, I think, than when she was a girl."

"What do you think of her ward?"

"A fine colt, with a bad temper, I should say."

"As proud as Lucifer."

"Yes; that is the Spanish strain." Then she added: "Bernard and Blanche make a striking couple, don't they?"

"Yes, they do, they do," and Henry Clifford sighed.

"It's a pity it couldn't have happened differently."

"Yes, a great, great pity."

"I heard from Rome the other day that Guido was thought to be worse."

"He's always worse, but then he always gets better. I don't believe there's anything the matter with him at all."

"Supposing he died? He must die some day."

"It's all much too late now, even if… "

"I think nothing's ever too late," she said gaily.

"Ah! well, you always were a charming optimist; it's part of your charm."

"And you were a pessimist – a cynic – in blinkers. You couldn't or wouldn't ever face facts."

"Sometimes one doesn't see the facts until it's too late," he said sadly.

"Yes…but let's try and look at things *now* as they are. I think that Walter Troumestre is in love with Blanche's ward, and that Blanche…well, you know better than I do," and here this conversation came to an end.

The next day the thaw set in, and the day after hounds met close to the house, and Rose Mary went out hunting.

Blanche did not go out of doors that day; she sat all day in the library, listlessly looking at the old books. It was a marvellous collection. She had little erudition; she was not a bibliophile, but she had an unerring sense, not only of beauty, but beauty in any shape drew her like a magnet. She looked at the illuminated missals, the old folios, in their dignified

contemporary bindings, the garden books, the early editions of
the Caroline poets, the large portfolios, full of coloured prints,
and from these pages ghosts seemed to rise and crowd around
her. She seemed now to be living in a kingdom of ghosts;
she felt dead to the world, dead to reality, and yet, oh! so
alive...only one nerve really in her system was alive; one string
of the instrument, but that responded, vibrated, cried aloud in
anguish and want. Walter Troumestre had gone out hunting.
There was no one she wanted to talk to. Her father tactfully left
her alone.

As she was sitting by the fire in the square, low library that
afternoon, just as it was getting too dark to read, and before
they had brought the lamps, a footman came into the room and
handed her a telegram on a tray. She took it and opened it. It
was from Rome, forwarded from London. It was from Princess
Mania Olenev. "Guido died quietly last night," it said, "after
receiving Last Sacraments. Teresa with him. Love from all."

Blanche was stunned when she read this telegram. Her
emotions were strangely mixed. The past rolled by her like a
panorama. She saw her engagement, her marriage, Princess
Julia, the early days in Rome, the Palazzo Fabrini, Wood
Norton; all sorts of funny, trivial little episodes and details
surged up to the surface of her mind.

"I was to blame," she said to herself. "Firstly, I ought never
to have married him, and then, as I had married him, I ought to
have behaved differently." She felt profound pity for Guido. "I
used to think," she thought to herself, "that I was being
punished, severely punished; but I haven't really been punished
at all. I have been deliriously happy, and deliriously miserable,
but miserable from the misery that only comes from great,
from ecstatic happiness. All that is no punishment at all. But I
suppose I shall be punished some day, punished properly, and
really – in this world or the next. I certainly deserve it. Poor
Guido." She wondered how he had died. And then, she had
been so unjust. She had thought he wasn't ill; that he never

had been ill. She had been greatly to blame. She had never looked at the matter from his point of view. She had felt no pity for him. "I was too young to understand," she thought; "I should understand *now* better. I shall have to pay for what I did. I feel I haven't paid yet – not to the full – only something on account. It was because I didn't love Guido that he was what he was. I played him false from the start. I ought never to have married him. I married him on false pretences. I killed him. I am a murderess! A murderess! How awful!" She shuddered. The room was now dark. She was afraid to be alone. She left the room and walked along a low, dark corridor into the chapel. There a lamp was burning, as the Blessed Sacrament was reserved.

Blanche knelt down, and prayed, and cried her heart out. The burden of her prayer was that she knew she must be punished, but she prayed that her punishment might not be too hard. Then she prayed for Guido.

"Let him forgive me; let him understand," she prayed. "I was so young. I didn't mean to be cruel. I was too young to know, too young to understand."

She stayed a long time in the chapel. When she walked back to the hall, everybody was in the gallery upstairs, drinking tea. They had come back from hunting. They were hungry and enjoying poached eggs and scones and jam. Rose Mary in her habit looked flushed and excited, and happy. They had had a wonderful day.

Before dinner Blanche told her father what had happened. He took it, as he took everything, with the right shade of composure and understanding.

"Donna Teresa was with him," he said. He laid stress on that comforting detail.

That night Blanche sat next to Walter Troumestre at dinner. She thought he seemed rather sad.

"Did you enjoy yourself out hunting?" she asked.

"Oh yes," he said, but there was a curious strain in his voice, and she felt that his "Oh yes" meant unmistakably "Oh no."

Blanche wondered why he hadn't enjoyed himself. Had any little incident happened to mar the day, or had he just been bored?

"I think," she said, and she said it without any special motive or design, "that Rose Mary enjoyed her day's hunting."

"She did," he answered, and in the intonation of those two words there was a world of meaning.

"He's in love with her," thought Blanche. "Of course he is. What a fool I was not to see it before." Incidents, words, looks, arose in her memory.

Rose Mary was sitting right at the end of the table on the same side as they were sitting. She was out of sight.

"Does she ride well?" asked Blanche.

"I've never seen anybody ride like her."

"She has not had much opportunity, except at her cousins'."

"She's got wonderful hands. She's a born rider. And, then, she's fearless. She's in complete sympathy with the horse."

That was enough for Blanche, but they went on talking about Rose Mary during the rest of dinner, and Walter did not disguise his predilection for the topic, nor did he grow tired of it. After dinner they danced again, but Blanche went to bed early. She said she had got a headache. Mrs Lacy came up to her bedroom and talked to her sympathetically. She had heard the news. She did not refer to it. She mentioned Rose Mary. It had struck her, too, that Walter was attracted by her.

"It's a pity he's so badly off," she said. "He's not badly off for a bachelor, but he's got nothing to marry on."

"There's nothing *I* should like better," said Blanche. "I think he is so charming, and he would be *the* man for Rose Mary; they like just the same kind of things."

"Yes," said Mrs Lacy, but there was a shade in her voice of something; was it doubt, disagreement, or disappointment? "He travels a great deal," she said. "He likes going to outlandish places. That would be rather difficult if they were married, wouldn't it?"

"Rose Mary is used to roughing it. She had an unusual childhood."

"Yes; but I think now she seems to like English country life."

"Yes, she does; but doesn't he?"

"He does in a way, but he's a wanderer by nature – a rolling stone."

"Wanderers end by settling down sometimes, don't they?"

"I suppose they do. But he's only thirty-one – only three years older than Bernard."

"Bernard," thought Blanche, "was not yet thirty, and she was nearly forty-four! An old woman."

The next day Blanche, Rose Mary, and Henry Clifford went back to London.

# CHAPTER XVI

The rest of the winter passed uneventfully for Blanche and for Rose Mary. Blanche was not able to take her cousin to any amusing entertainments. Henry Clifford gave two little dinner-parties for her. They went to the play every now and then, but there was nothing more exciting to do.

Rose Mary saw a great deal of her cousins, the Bromleys; and for Easter Blanche took her to the Rodens' at Elladon, where there was a family party and no other guests. Bernard stayed all the winter in the country, and he then took his mother to Madeira. She had not been well, and the doctors ordered her a warm climate and a complete change. They started in March and stayed there six weeks.

Walter Troumestre, to Blanche's surprise, never came near them in London, and in March they heard that he, too, suddenly left the country for Constantinople; he had been appointed honorary attaché at the Embassy.

Blanche made no new friends, and after Easter, in the summer, the business of taking Rose Mary out began seriously. They were asked to many small dances.

Rose Mary was fond of dancing, and ready to go everywhere and anywhere; to dance all night and to go about all day. She had a constitution of iron and a complexion like dawn. She was much admired, and was soon surrounded by a small train of young adorers.

Blanche wondered why Walter Troumestre had accepted this distant post, if, as she felt confident, he was devoted to Rose Mary. She wondered still more why he had left so suddenly; he had gone without even saying goodbye, as far as she knew. Rose Mary never mentioned him, and appeared to be unaffected by the news. Blanche had no idea what her feelings were towards him; she was inscrutable, and Blanche respected her reserve.

Blanche took Rose Mary to many small dances, but the first real, large ball she took her to was given at Stuart House. It was a lovely sight. The beautiful house was crowded, but it was meant to be a ball for young people – for the Duke of Easthamptonshire's youngest daughter who was just out – and there were no royalties.

The Government had just been defeated, and everybody was talking of the General Election which was imminent.

"It will mean," thought Blanche, "that Bernard will stand for Parliament. If he gets in, he will have to live in London a great deal more than he has done so far."

Just as she was thinking these thoughts, at the same time as she was mechanically talking to a Russian diplomat, she saw Bernard walking through the crowd in the doorway. He seemed to be looking for somebody. Rose Mary was sitting out, but not in the ballroom. Blanche caught his eye, and he walked towards her. At that moment the music began to play, and the Russian diplomat who was sitting next to Blanche rose to his feet, saying he was dancing the next dance, made a bow, and disappeared, while Bernard said to Blanche: "This is ours, I think. Let's get out of the crowd."

They walked through the ballroom, through the crowd on the landing, into a square drawing-room, where they sat down.

"I'm standing for Parliament at home," said Bernard.

"I thought you would. You're sure to get in."

"Well, I don't know. The Liberal candidate is a good man. He got in by a large majority last time."

"Yes; but he had nobody to oppose him."

"It will mean living in London if I get in. Won't that be awful?"

"Yes, awful for you," said Blanche sympathetically; "but you will still have half the year in the country."

"Except when there's an autumn session."

"Your mother will be pleased."

"It's the dream of her life…that – and" (with a laugh) "my marriage!"

"How is she?"

"Not well, I think. She can't possibly stay at Alton-Leigh this winter. It would be much too cold. I can't take her abroad. I don't know what to do."

"Could I take her abroad?"

"That would be kind, but I think she'll probably want to go to Torquay. She doesn't like travelling; it tires her."

There was a slight pause. He changed the subject.

"Is Miss Rose Mary here tonight?"

"Yes; her first *ball* – her first real ball. She was rather unhappy at first, but now she is finding partners. The Rodens have been kind to her, such nice girls, and Harriet Clive has been an angel. I'm afraid I'm not much use to her. I know hardly anybody. I feel not only like a foreigner, but like a ghost."

Bernard looked at her with undisguised admiration.

"A very live ghost," he thought.

She half guessed his thought and blushed.

"It's the first English ball I've been to for years; it makes me feel so old. All my contemporaries are old men and chaperons. The only people I really know well in the room are foreigners, diplomats, and people I met at Rome. I must go back and see what's happening to Rose Mary. She'll think I've deserted her."

They walked back to the ballroom. The last dance was over; the next had not yet begun.

The band struck up once more almost immediately after they walked into the ballroom. Bernard was caught by a politician, who led him solemnly on to a balcony. Rose Mary was brought back to Blanche by a young guardsman.

She sat down next to Blanche.

"Are you dancing this dance?" Blanche asked her.

"Nobody's asked me to yet," she said.

At that moment young Lady Hengrave, an American, who had been told by her mother-in-law, the Dowager Lady Hengrave (whom Blanche had known in her early married days, and who had always been a friend of her father's), to be civil to Blanche Roccapalumba (the Dowager Lady Hengrave pronounced the *a* in Blanche short, like the *a* in hat, not like the *a* in large), and to see that the girl she was taking out "danced" (short *a* here, too), came up to Blanche and said patronisingly: "Dear Princess, I see your charming cousin is not dancing; that's quite wrong." She gave a swift look round the room, and her eye lighted on a boy who was standing up alone against the wall, and who looked shy. "Come here, C.," she said; "I want to introduce you to Miss Clifford."

The introduction was made of Mr Caryl Bramsley to Rose Mary. Mr Bramsley stammered an *invitation à la valse*, and off they twirled, he a little awkwardly; he was busy dancing and had no sense of time; but Rose Mary, with her unerring sense of rhythm and her muscles of steel, steered him, guided him, and danced for two.

Lady Hengrave sat down next to Blanche.

"That young boy is my brother-in-law, Edward's youngest brother but one, Caryl. We call him C. in the family; we have always called him C. He's only just left Oxford; just of age. Reading for the Bar. I hope your cousin will be kind to him. He's not used to going out yet, and, as you see, he can't dance at all."

"It's kind of him to dance with Rose Mary. It's her first real ball; she's only a child."

"Oh, my dear, she'll be all right in time, you needn't worry. She's got looks, and she dances like a bird. Just watch her. She's got what I call real *chic*."

"I think she is graceful," said Blanche, who was provoked by Lady Hengrave's patronising manner.

"My mother-in-law," Lady Hengrave went on, "asked me to be sure and see that your cousin danced. I said I would. She told me she used to know you years ago, when you first came out; I suppose you were contemporaries."

"Almost," said Blanche, with a smile – "not quite. Your mother-in-law was married when I first came out. I used to be frightened of her."

"Really? That is interesting," said Lady Hengrave. "People so often tell me they think her frightening. I find I always get on with people whom other people think frightening. I don't know what they mean. Well, it really means that they don't understand Granny. We always call her Granny. You see, what she likes is people who are *not* afraid of her. But you have lived long enough abroad to know, my dear, that English people are sometimes stupid and kind of *gauche* – awkward, I mean. There! I see that dear Peter – he's such a dear – is all alone, and looking for a partner. I must go to his rescue."

Lady Hengrave sailed away, all the beads and sequins on her light blue ball-gown rattling, rustling, and jingling, to take possession of Count Peter Linsky, First Secretary at the Austrian Embassy, who was looking for some one else. But he was too well-mannered to express anything but unexpected joy when Lady Hengrave accosted him, and he took her down to supper, which was just what Lady Hengrave meant him to do. She was hungry, and she had a keen appetite.

Caryl Bramsley brought Rose Mary back to Blanche when the next dance began.

"Well?" asked Blanche.

"Well, he can't dance, and he didn't say much; but he's Alice Roden's first cousin. They all say he is so funny."

"I expect he was shy."

"All the young men are shy. What is the matter with them?"

At that moment Alice Roden, fair-haired, blue-eyed, high-spirited, led up another young man to Rose Mary.

"This is Mr Wright," she said, laughing; "he can't dance, but he's hungry, and he'll take you down to supper. I'm sure you must be hungry, because I'm starving."

"Yes," said Rose Mary; "I am very hungry."

At the same moment Bernard walked up to Blanche and said: "Will you come down to supper? I have only just been able to get away."

Blanche got up from her chair. As Rose Mary and her young partner preceded them, Rose Mary turned round and looked at them, or rather, Rose Mary looked at Bernard – Blanche was looking at some one else. Their eyes met, and Rose Mary blushed scarlet.

"She looks well," Bernard said to Blanche, as the pair went through the doorway.

"Yes; she's at her best, dancing, because she likes it and does it well."

As they walked downstairs, they passed Lady Harriet Clive on the staircase, who gave them a penetrating look.

"I congratulate you on your ward, dear Blanche," she whispered. "She looks really well in spite of being side by side with such a chaperon! Everybody is asking who *you* are. Everybody is talking about you."

It was true. Rose Mary, striking as her looks were for a girl, passed almost unnoticed in that brilliant crowd of fresh girls and beautiful, young married women; but nobody could help looking at Blanche. She was dressed that night in black satin, as she was still in mourning for Guido, and she wore a long rope of pearls and one camellia. She looked more like a Van Dyck picture than ever.

Many people asked who she was. The replies were, for the most part, evasive and vague: "She's half an Italian – always lived abroad." Or, "She's a foreigner." Or, "My mother used to know her *years* ago" – this a female answer to the question, "Doesn't she look young?" Or else there were the answers of those who knew everybody and everything about everybody; for instance, "She was née Clifford, and her husband was a lunatic, who beat her. She was forced to run away from him. Of course she had many admirers and lovers before that; but the love of her life was Adrian Tyne, the diplomat; she broke his heart."

There the matter ended. Nobody asked to be introduced to her, and the only men she talked to were diplomats whom she had met before, or one or two men of the older generation whom she had known in the early years of her marriage: Cecil White, for instance.

But she was blissfully happy, sitting at supper with Bernard. Rose Mary, with Mr Wright, was at the table next to them, and she seemed happy, too.

Bernard discussed his future with Blanche. Walter Troumestre was mentioned, and when Blanche asked Bernard why he had left England so suddenly, Bernard said he did not know, and changed the subject.

Every now and then Blanche noticed that Rose Mary looked towards their table as if she were waiting for them to get up, so as to follow suit. But Bernard showed no signs of moving; he was interested in his talk, which was entirely personal.

Rose Mary gave one last look towards Blanche's table, then she left the supper-room with her young man.

"I must go, or else Rose Mary will be quite alone," said Blanche.

"Can't you get some one else to look after her? I haven't half finished what I wanted to say."

"Yes, I can. Harriet Clive or Mrs Roden will, I know, if I can find them. But I must arrange it. We can go on talking upstairs if you are not tired of me."

"Yes; and I must have one dance with Rose Mary. I haven't danced with her yet."

"Yes, do. She will be delighted."

They went upstairs, and Blanche released Mr Wright, who evidently wanted to go away. Rose Mary was not engaged for the next dance. The ballroom was much emptier than it had been hitherto. Bernard, seeing Rose Mary partnerless, asked her to dance, and round they whirled. When the dance was over, Bernard led Rose Mary into the next room, and sat with her till the next dance began. Then he brought her back to Blanche, who was sitting talking to Mrs Roden.

"That child dances divinely," he said.

Blanche was longing to dance, and for Bernard to dance with her. She thought he was about to suggest it.

But at that moment the host of the evening, the Duke of Easthamptonshire, who had been told by his wife to see that Blanche was taken down to supper by a suitable personage, when the first procession for going down to supper was being formed, and who had, in his absent-mindedness, done this duty by the wife of the Secretary at the Italian Embassy instead, now came up and apologised. He had, he said, been looking for the Princess everywhere, and, although she had probably had supper, might he at least show her the downstairs rooms the pictures, the library...

Blanche left Rose Mary in the care of Mrs Roden, and followed him. When she came back she found Rose sitting flushed and panting after a dance. She thought she saw Bernard's back disappear in the doorway. The rooms were getting empty. It was late.

"Would you like to stay on, darling, or shall we go?" asked Blanche.

"I should like to go home now," said Rose Mary; "there's no one left I know."

But this turned out to be untrue, for at that moment one of the Bromley boys, who was now at Oxford, came up to her and begged for one more dance. Mrs Roden's girls were still whirling round the room, and the next dance was the Kitchen Lancers, and the occasion of a wild outburst of spirits. The dance was now entirely in the hands of the young.

When the Lancers were over, another young man, a foreigner this time, begged Rose Mary for one more dance, and after that at last they went away.

It was half-past three.

As they drove home in a four-wheeler, Blanche asked Rose Mary whether she had enjoyed herself.

"Yes," she said; "I did, very much. At first I hated it. I thought nobody would dance with me. All the people seemed to be new and different; nobody I knew; and I thought I knew a lot of people, but it was great fun later. Fancy," she went on, "that boy I danced with, called Caryl Bramsley, was engaged to be married, Alice Roden says, to Beatrice Lord, who used to be at the Convent with me, and she's married some one else. Alice says he can't have minded much, because he's got over it so quickly. He didn't say much to me, but they all say he's *so, so* funny."

"People sometimes don't show the things they mind most."

"I suppose not."

"And the world is nearly always wrong about everybody."

There was a long pause.

"Who was your best partner?" asked Blanche.

Rose Mary hesitated a little, and then she said: "That young Austrian diplomat, Sosibrodski, *danced* the best, but I enjoyed dancing most with...well, my friends – Arthur Bromley, for instance."

The next day Bernard came to see Blanche towards tea-time, but he missed her; she was out. Rose Mary, who was at home and surrounded by her girl friends, who were talking over the ball, entertained him and gave him tea, and when Blanche came home she found him laughing at a real, sitting-down tea in the dining-room, with the Roden girls and the Bromley boys.

He seemed slightly embarrassed when Blanche walked into the room.

"I was passing this way, so I thought I might find you," he said. "Rose Mary has been looking after me. I go to Alton-Leigh tomorrow. Everything has been settled. The campaign begins at once. Mother is there. I wish Walter was here, too. He would be such a help."

"I'm certain you will get in."

"Well, I don't know. I'm not so sure. You never can tell. You must put up a candle to St Anthony for me."

"Dozens. Let's go into the next room."

He followed Blanche into the drawing-room. As soon as they left the dining-room, they heard a shout of laughter and talk coming from it. The young people had begun to talk again. They had been silent while Blanche had been there. The loudest voice and laugh of all was that of Rose Mary.

"I'm glad to have just caught you," Bernard said, "because I've got to go at once. I've still a great many people to see."

Blanche reflected that for a busy man, on his last day in London, before an election, Bernard had wasted a good deal of time at a children's tea. But perhaps it was in the hope of seeing her. Was it?

"You must be busy," she said.

"Well, I am, rather."

"I don't think you ought to stay… "

"A few minutes can't matter." He looked at his watch. "I've got an appointment at home, with my agent, at seven. It's only just half-past six. In a good hansom I shall be there in time."

"Goodbye, and good luck," said Blanche.

"Goodbye. I must say goodbye to the children." He opened the dining-room door, put his head in, and called out: "Goodbye, everybody."

Then he went away.

The next morning Blanche got up early, in time for the eight-o'clock Mass.

She put up a candle to St Anthony. There was already one candle on the stand.

When she got home she was surprised to find that Rose Mary was already down.

"I thought you would have a long lie this morning," she said, "as there's a dance tonight, and last night was the only night you've been to bed early for days."

"Oh, I'm all right," said Rose Mary. "It was such a lovely morning I couldn't stay in bed. I have been for a little walk in Kensington Gardens."

This was quite true; but before that she had been to the seven-o'clock Mass at the Carmelite Church, and she, too, had spent a penny on St Anthony of Padua.

# CHAPTER XVII

Bernard was elected for the Division of Fenmouthshire, in which Alton-Leigh was situated, by a large majority.

He invited Blanche and Rose Mary to stay with him at Alton-Leigh as soon as Parliament was prorogued. Blanche went on taking Rose Mary out to dances and other entertainments until the end of July. They then both went down to the Bromleys' and stayed there during the month of August.

Parliament was prorogued at the beginning of September, and just as Blanche and Rose Mary were starting for Alton-Leigh, Blanche got a telegram from Bernard saying that his mother was ill and that he was obliged to put them off. Further details came by post. Mrs Lacy was seriously ill, and the doctors were not hopeful about her. Blanche and Rose Mary went back to London, and thence to the Isle of Wight, where they paid a long-promised visit to Blanche's only surviving aunt, Mrs Walter Clifford. Her daughters were married now, and the eldest daughter, Mary, had married a *parti*, or, rather, some one who was thought to be a *parti*, at the time the marriage took place – namely, Lord Sunningdale, the well-known owner of racehorses. They had now been married for twenty years, and they had a daughter who was just coming out.

During those twenty years their fortune had undergone many vicissitudes; money had been won and lost, lost and won, and the fine estate that Lord Sunningdale's family had owned since the days of the Plantagenets, in Cumberland, had been sold. Nevertheless, they managed to live, and still had a comfortable house at Newmarket and a house in Manchester Square.

Lady Sunningdale and her eldest daughter, Lilian, were staying with Mrs Walter Clifford when Blanche and Rose Mary arrived in the Isle of Wight.

Blanche's Aunt Cecilia, who was now greatly mellowed by old age, was sympathetic with her on the subject of her ward.

"You will have great difficulty in marrying her," she said, "owing to her being a Roman, but I only hope you may find some *satisfactory* foreigner...they do exist, I believe, sometimes; or perhaps a young man from one of the old English Roman Catholic families. The worst of it is that so few of them have any money."

By the end of September, Blanche and Rose Mary were back in London again.

Blanche sent Rose Mary by herself to spend three weeks with the Rodens, while she stayed with her father in London, as he had not been well and wanted looking after. Blanche went to live in his house for a time.

Rose Mary apparently enjoyed herself in the country.

By the beginning of November, Henry Clifford had recovered. Blanche moved back into her own house, and Rose Mary came back from the country.

In the meantime, Mrs Lacy's illness had dragged on; at one time she had been reported to be dying; then she had made a marvellous recovery, and Bernard had been hopeful once more. He kept Blanche informed of the details of his mother's illness; his letters were regular, but formal.

In November, just as Mrs Lacy was thought to be really better and able to move to Torquay, or to some warm place, she had a relapse and died.

Bernard was utterly miserable. He had been devoted to her. He wrote heart-broken letters to Blanche – letters, that is to say, which seemed to Blanche to show he was heart-broken, although they were a shade more formal and stiff than usual.

She was buried at Alton-Leigh. Soon after the funeral Bernard came up to London, on business, and after this he made a habit of coming up every now and then on flying visits, and every time he came to London he made a point of coming to see Blanche and Rose Mary. He was, of course, not going to have any party that year at Alton-Leigh, no shooting-parties in the autumn, and as for Christmas, he did not feel able to face Christmas at Alton-Leigh alone.

Blanche and Rose Mary had been asked to spend Christmas at Elladon, by the Rodens, and Bernard, after consulting Blanche, decided to accept an invitation from his cousins, the Bromleys, to spend Christmas with them. There would be nobody there except the family.

Bernard had now made a habit of consulting Blanche about his affairs; he took her into his confidence and took no step without talking it over with her. He was on terms of easy, intimate friendship with her, and Blanche was not sure whether this was the end of an old situation or the beginning of a new one.

He seemed, so Blanche thought, not to be able to do without her, and yet their intimacy went just so far, and not a step further. Whether Bernard had other affairs going on at this time, Blanche had no idea; whether Celia Deacon, who at that moment was enjoying an immense success – a success of looks rather than of acting – in a drawing-room melodrama, was playing a part in his life, she had no idea.

As a matter of fact, she was not. He had been attracted by her and he liked her, but whatever had been was over. Possibly

Celia Deacon, who, although extraordinarily stupid in some ways, had an instinctive knowledge of how to deal with men, could have kept him if she had chosen, but she did not choose. She was in love herself, wildly, foolishly, blindly in love, with Wilfrid Lockwood, the good-looking actor manager whom she married, and who first of all beat her and then left her, got a divorce, and married an American Vaudeville star.

As time went on, Bernard made more and more frequent excuses for calling at the little house at Campden Hill. He would arrive unexpectedly, and if Blanche were at home he would stay and talk to her for hours, and if she were out and Rose Mary were at home, he would stay and talk to her. He seemed to be on equal terms of friendship, easy, intimate *camaraderie*, with both Blanche and her ward. Christmas came, and at Elladon, where there was only a family party, Rose Mary, so Blanche thought, enjoyed herself immensely. The Bromleys, and with them Bernard, were constantly coming over.

There was a good deal of sport – hunting, shooting, and a little dancing – but nothing pompous and nothing formal.

Rose Mary was improving in looks every day. She looked old – old in expression, that is to say, for her age – and everybody admired her. She was full of life and go; at the same time, there was a dignified gravity about her which was attractive. Bernard thought she was the most attractive girl he had ever seen.

She would, he thought, make an admirable wife.

"Of course," he thought to himself, "I am not in love with her. I have only been in love with one person, really in love with one woman, in my life, and that is Blanche, but as that could never be, and as I ought to marry, why shouldn't I marry Rose Mary? I couldn't well do better. I must consult Blanche."

The more he thought of it, the better the plan appeared to him to be. He resolved to discuss the matter with Blanche at the first favourable opportunity.

Blanche, Rose Mary, and Bernard all came back to London towards the end of January. Bernard went for a week or two to Alton-Leigh by himself. He then came back to London and settled down in the house at Ovington Square for the winter. Parliament was to meet in February. He came to see Blanche more frequently than ever, and stayed longer every time he came. Every time he saw her he meant to tell her about his project of marrying Rose Mary, and every time he saw her he put it off. He got near the topic once or twice, but when the moment came for actually putting the matter in so many words, somehow or other his courage failed him and he talked of other things.

Blanche felt there was something on his mind, or in his mind, that he wanted to tell her, but she was not sure what it was. Never had he been so nice to her, never had he seemed to need her so much, never had their intimacy seemed easier, more natural, and yet Blanche knew that things could not go on like this; either the situation must come to an end, or develop into something different. They seemed, she thought, to be dancing on a tight-rope; it was deliriously delicious, but it could not last. As for herself, she had never loved Bernard so much. She loved him so greatly that she would have done anything, sacrificed anything, dared anything for him, given her soul for him. Bernard was unaware of this. He started from the theory that it had been *he* who had loved Blanche, not she who had loved him, and that she had at once got over it and forgotten it; that he had taken years to recover from what had been an almost mortal wound, and that now they were friends; that she was his greatest friend, and that she was the person he could first confide in, and who would understand him completely when he came to discuss his marriage projects.

And yet there was something at the back of his mind, something which did not find expression, which stirred uneasily, and did not get quite so far as a whisper; to say this was not quite right, not the whole truth. It was perhaps this

415

little hidden shadow that made it difficult for him to come to the point, and discuss his marriage. He had decided that he wanted to marry Rose Mary. He wasn't, he said to himself, really in love with her, but he ought to marry. He liked her very much, liked her enough, admired her greatly, and she would make him an admirable wife. She was a Catholic; there were no difficulties; she was the right age. All the conditions were favourable.

He would not speak to her till he had spoken to Blanche and asked her advice, which he would take. If Blanche were opposed to the marriage, well, he would give up the idea altogether.

It was a cold February afternoon, just before the opening of Parliament. Bernard had written to Blanche saying he would look in at tea-time. He had settled to bring matters to a head. He hoped he would find her alone. He would rather Rose Mary were not there. It would be awkward, he said to himself, to discuss the question if she were there, in the next room.

When he arrived, he found no one at first. Rose Mary was out, and Blanche had left a message with Ramiro (who had looked after her and Rose Mary and managed her establishment ever since the death of Charles Clifford) that she would be in presently; would he wait in the drawing-room.

Ramiro showed him into the little drawing-room. A cheerful fire was blazing. Tea was all ready. Bernard thought of the teas in Guido's room at the Palazzo Fabrini. Over the chimney-piece there was an oil picture of Henry Clifford when he was a young man, and some water-colours by Charles Clifford.

"She's not a bit like her father," he thought.

There was an arm-chair on one side of the fireplace; on the other side of it a small sofa, opposite the tea-table, and then a round table on which there was a lamp, and another arm-chair. On this round table there was a framed cabinet photograph of Rose Mary which had evidently been taken recently. It was just the head; and the classic line of her features, the clear-cut modelling of her face, and her wide, grave eyes, came out with startling distinctness in this platinum photograph.

Bernard looked at it and felt a sharp shock. It was as if she herself had suddenly come into the room. He took up the photograph and looked at it for a long time. Then he put it down suddenly, as if waking from a trance. He was glad nobody had come in then. He didn't say why to himself.

"Yes," he said almost aloud; "she is a handsome girl."

Presently Blanche came in.

"I'm so sorry to be late. I hope you haven't been waiting long; all alone, too. Rose Mary has gone out with the Rodens."

Blanche seemed to fill the room with life and light and grace. It was as if a basket of flowers had been suddenly brought into the room. She was entrancing. She had on a fur toque, and in the fur of her jacket there was a bunch of lilies of the valley. She was rather flushed from her walk in the cold February wind. The weather had given her a look of health and radiance; her eyes sparkled. That, and the pleasure of seeing Bernard, made her look her best. She took off her jacket and made the tea, talking to Bernard all the time.

"What lovely hands!" Bernard thought to himself, as he watched her deft, quick movements.

"I'm so glad you've come," she said, "and that you didn't go away. I got caught, and I was afraid you might get tired of waiting!"

"Oh, Ramiro would never have let me go. I would have waited hours. I particularly wanted to see you."

"Next week you will be too busy to come; I shan't see you any more!"

"Only busy at tea-time."

Blanche handed him a cup of tea and some bread and butter. He drank his tea slowly.

"There's something I want to talk to you about," he said.

"I wonder what it is," thought Blanche. She had no notion what Bernard was going to say, but she liked to rest on a sort

417

of cushion of hopeful daydream…was he going to tell her?…that he…but, no, she mustn't think such foolish things.

"It's this," he said. "I think it is time to make a change. I mean I don't think things can go on exactly as they are now."

Blanche nodded sympathetic assent.

"I know," he went on haltingly, "that you will understand, and that if you feel it's impossible, you will say so."

"Yes, of course," Blanche said softly.

"You will understand?"

"Of course, I shall understand."

"Well, it's this. I should like to be married."

Blanche felt the whole room swim round her. She was dancing on pinnacles of ecstasy; she was far away, at the end of the world, east of the sun, west of the moon, in impossible regions of undreamed-of happiness, in the hues of the sunrise, in crystal castles…

"Yes," she murmured,

"You think it is possible?"

Possible! Blanche couldn't speak. At that moment the front door bell rang.

"Wait a moment," said Blanche; "that may be a visitor, and I'll say I'm not at home. We can't be interrupted now."

She rang the bell. Ramiro appeared instantly. Blanche told him. He gave a swift look at Bernard, and nodded. He came back presently and reported that it was the Señorita, and that she was going out again at once. She had come to fetch something she had left behind.

"I'm not at home to any other visitors," Blanche said, and Ramiro nodded, bowed, and went away.

At that moment Rose Mary put her head in at the door.

"How do you do, and goodbye," she said, laughing. "I've come back to get this." She pointed to the score of a musical comedy she had in her hand – the *Shop Girl*. "I've got a hansom waiting."

As she put her head in at the door Bernard looked at her, and he experienced the same sensation he had felt just now when he had suddenly caught sight of her photograph. Quick as a flash of lightning, a swift look of recognition passed over his face. It lasted less than a second, but Blanche saw it, and it revealed to her a whole world. It was to her fine instincts unmistakable. It was the same look she had seen on her Uncle Charles' face when he was dying at Seville, and had suddenly said: "*Eccoti!*" It was Bernard's "*Eccoti!*" It meant only one thing – Bernard loved Rose Mary; and then she understood. A thousand pictures, incidents, words, facts, silences, rose in her mind. Of course. She had been blind. She saw now. She understood. Her world, her universe, lay shattered at her feet in that one brief second.

Rose Mary had gone. They heard the front door bang and the jingling hansom drive off.

"Well, the only thing," thought Blanche, "is to make the best of it…but I don't believe she loves him, and she never will love him properly, and she's too young to know…

"Well?" said Blanche, determined to face everything bravely, and to give good advice; to be conscientious – to do right.

But Bernard, who up till then seemed to get on quite well with his explanation, felt that the thread was broken. He was disconcerted. The sudden glimpse of Rose Mary had made him feel guilty as of a betrayal. He felt that Blanche had seen through him; he felt like a schoolboy who had been caught stealing. He felt that he was in danger of hurting Blanche, that it was all suddenly difficult.

"Well?" he said. "What do you think?"

And then Blanche felt she was being led by the spirit to the top of a mountain to be tempted – a mountain where she had to make in one second a momentous and final choice.

She knew that Bernard wanted to marry Rose Mary, and found difficulty in saying so. She did not think, she liked to believe, that is to say, that Rose Mary was not in love with him.

419

Even if she were, it could only be, she argued to herself, a schoolgirl's love, not the real thing in her life; she was too young, she couldn't know. It would be like her, Blanche's, love for Sydney Hope. She could conscientiously disregard that factor. How could she, Rose Mary, give Bernard all the love he needed and deserved? *Could* she be the right wife to him? That was the first question. And the answer was: "No, a thousand times, no." The second question was this: Could she, Blanche, give Bernard up? Could she hand him over to Rose Mary without a struggle?

"I suppose I ought to," she said to herself, "and I must decide now, this minute, this second... O God! – "

She answered the second question, as she had answered the first, with a "no, a thousand times, no!" She couldn't give him up.

"I have, after all, the best right to him," she said; "I have loved him, I love him...more than she loves him...more than any one can or could love him."

She looked at Bernard with infinite love, and infinite tenderness, and she said with an accent and a look and a turn of the head that she knew he couldn't resist: "I see no reason why we shouldn't be married, if you *really* mean it... "

And then it was Bernard's turn to readjust his values, to mend and rebuild a broken universe in a minute of time, and to make an irrevocable decision. He made it, too, just as swiftly and just as finally. Blanche thought he had meant her all along. Of course she had thought so. Small wonder! He had really been too stupid. It was entirely his fault; and as she thought this, it was impossible for him to disillusion her now. He could not possibly betray Blanche after all she had sacrificed for him. And could it be possible that she had loved him all this time?

He put his thought into words.

"Is it really true that you love me, can love me, and have loved me?"

"Bernard, my darling, you know I have never thought or lived for anything else, ever since that last night at Rome…but I'm so old and you're so young. How can you like an old woman like me?"

"You are far younger than I am! Will you trust me, then, with your life, and let me try and make you happy?"

"Try? Oh, my dearest, my dearest." Blanche was now sobbing in his arms, and he kissed away her tears. And at that moment he believed once more that Blanche *was* the love of his life, and always had been. In any case, he would never give her cause to think that he had ever *not* thought so, that he had ever thought otherwise…that he had ever been unfaithful for a second.

They remained a long time silent. He held her hand, and they looked into each other's eyes, and Blanche said to herself: "Oh, my God! if I have done wrong I will make it up by loving him in a way nobody has ever loved any one. This can't be wrong. I have a right to him. I love him more than any one else can or could love him. He is mine, mine, mine…for ever, till death, and beyond, and no one can take him away from me… "

They must have stayed like this a long time, hardly speaking, save for a word or a murmur every now and then, and once more time rushed by, and they were recalled to reality by the ringing of the front door bell. It was Rose Mary who had come back…

"Shall we tell her now?" said Blanche.

"Yes; I think we had better."

Blanche called Rose Mary. She came in, and seemed to guess that something had happened from the mere look of the room, which was full, or seemed full to her, of unwonted vibrations, and from the expression on Blanche's face. Bernard was looking fixedly at the carpet.

"Rose Mary darling, we've got something to tell you," Blanche said quietly.

Rose Mary held the score of music that she had in her hands a little more tightly.

"Yes, Blanche," she said in a colourless voice.

"Bernard and I have settled to – "

"To be married? I always thought it might happen. I'm so, so glad. I do congratulate you both," she said, with a frank smile. "I must just go upstairs and take off my things."

She went out of the room gaily, and she wondered whether the little Spartan boy, who had let himself be gnawed by the fox, had worn so natural a smile as she hoped she had managed to produce on this occasion.

"I always knew it must happen," she said to herself. "I always knew that, if ever she saw he was fond of me, she would force him to marry her. I suppose one ought not to blame her – she loved him first; but I can't help *hating* her," and as she reached her bedroom she threw herself on her bed in a paroxysm of tears. "I'm like Queen Elizabeth," she said to herself, and she murmured over and over again, "God may forgive you, but I never can."

A little later she sent a message to Blanche that the Rodens were expecting her to dinner, and she went out without saying a good night again. She had in reality no engagement with the Rodens, but she knew she would be welcome. They were alone. And Bernard and Blanche were both grateful to her for leaving, especially Bernard. Ramiro was told that dinner for two would be wanted if possible. He nodded. He understood the situation, and understood it, perhaps, more fully and more finely than any one else.

# CHAPTER XVIII

The first thing which Bernard did was to cable the news to Walter and to ask him whether he could get home in time to be his best man. Blanche and Bernard settled that they would be married quietly in London as soon as Lent was over. Bernard would then get away for the Easter recess, and possibly for a little longer. Walter cabled back from Constantinople that he would be in England by the middle of March.

They decided not to announce the marriage until just before it took place. Bernard wished to go, directly after the wedding, to Paris for a few days, and then to the south of France.

"We *must* go to Paris," he said, "because it was there that I first met you."

The first thing Blanche did was to tell her father. She went to see him the next day, and found him in the comfortable room on the ground floor in the house in Curzon Street, which she had known ever since she was a child, and which had never been changed.

She found her father sitting in the dark leather arm-chair, and reading a new French novel by Paul Bourget. He was wearing his blue smoking-suit which she knew so well, and a brown smoking-cap that she had herself worked for him before she came out.

He was, she thought, looking old, and he got up and moved with difficulty.

Henry Clifford had not expected to see his daughter that evening. Was it only yesterday…or was he forgetting things, that she had said that she would not be able to look in the next day?

"I've managed to come, all the same," she answered his unasked inquiry, as she sat down on the chair opposite him.

On the table next to her there were some of the small pieces of bric-à-brac, which she remembered since she had been a child; with them some new ones – an hour-glass, a paper-cutter with a twisted handle, and a silver box with an Italian inscription on it. Henry Clifford still collected.

Tea was brought, and to Henry Clifford coffee. He never drank tea, except after dinner, and for a while they talked of the topics of the day.

At last Blanche said: "What I want to tell you, papa, is this – I am going to be married."

Henry Clifford nearly dropped his cup.

"Good Heavens, child, who is it?"

"Bernard Lacy."

There was a long silence. Henry Clifford's eyes filled with tears.

"You think it's a mistake?" Blanche said, with calm resignation.

"No, my dear child; no, I don't. I'm delighted, of course, delighted – but surprised. I can't help being surprised. You see, I wasn't expecting anything of the kind."

"It's no use, papa. I see you think it's a mistake. You think I'm too old."

"Too old! Fiddlesticks. The happiest marriages I have known – perhaps the only happy marriages I have known – have been those where there has been a great difference of age…especially when the wife has been older…than the husband…but you see, darling child, I do so want you to be happy, and I do feel so guilty about everything that happened, that I can't help thinking...well, you know...the fact is, it upsets me," and here he nearly broke down. "I've only a short time to live," he said. "I've both feet in the grave, and I should have liked to see you happy."

"You will see me happy. I have never been so happy, never known that such happiness could be."

This was the literal truth.

Henry Clifford mastered his emotion, and became once more the highly experienced man of the world.

"Well," he said, "Lacy is a charming fellow, and Alton-Leigh is a beautiful place, and he's well off, and he's got into the House, and they say he's doing well."

Blanche could not help feeling that he was making for himself a list of assets in a case of bankruptcy.

"What will you do with Rose Mary?"

She will live with us. She will stay a great deal with the Bromleys and the Rodens, too. They are all so fond of her, but I hope we shall find her a husband soon."

"It's not so easy. You see, she is so badly off, and then there's that cursed religious question."

"She's a lovely girl. She's getting prettier and prettier every day, and she's popular. She's so English. It's curious. In spite of having had a foreign mother, and a Spaniard, too, she's much more English than I am. She puts me to shame in the country."

After her father had asked a great many more practical questions, she left him. He followed her to the door and kissed her tenderly as he said goodbye; but Blanche could not help feeling that, old as he had looked when she arrived, he looked older still when she left.

In spite of all the reassuring things he had said, she felt, she was certain, that her father thought the marriage was a mistake. She was not wrong. That night he dined alone with Princess Solski at her little house in Halkin Street, and they discussed Blanche's second marriage as once long ago they had discussed her first marriage.

It was after dinner, as they sat both of them smoking – Princess Solski a cigarette, and Henry Clifford a cigar – that they broached the matter.

"I don't know why you should be so disappointed...after all."

"You needn't tell me the advantages," said Henry Clifford. "I know them all too well. That's just it. You remember what a mistake I made before about the advantages. What could have been better, more promising, than Guido's advantages?"

"Yes; but Bernard Lacy isn't Guido Roccapalumba." Oh, I know he's an excellent fellow, admirable in every way, and has sown his wild oats, and got through all that, and has settled down now, and likes country life, and is doing well, a rising man in Parliament... It's not that... Don't you see that I'm afraid for Blanche?"

"How?"

"Well, we must face the fact that she's fifteen years older than he is."

"Yes; but they're both young."

"That's all very well *now*, but in ten years' time...that's what I'm thinking about."

"Bernard Lacy will be quite definitely *rangé* by then."

"I wonder. And, then, they are going to keep my niece, Rose Mary, with them. What a mistake! Bernard will fall in love with her as sure as my name's Clifford."

"Why imagine such things? The girl will probably marry. She's only been out a year after all."

"However, there's nothing to be done."

"No, nothing." (The same thought went through both their minds at this moment: "Enough mischief had been done by the first interference.") "Have you seen him?"

"Not since."

And then they went over the same ground once more, but they came to no different conclusion. In her heart, Princess

Solski agreed with Henry Clifford, but she did her best to make him look at the brighter side of the question, and quoted the many happy marriages she had known where the wife had been older than the husband.

One of the drawbacks which weighed heavily on Henry Clifford's mind seemed shortly to be removed, after Walter Troumestre arrived from Constantinople.

Directly he arrived he proposed to Rose Mary, and she accepted him.

This seemed in some ways to be the solution of certain difficulties.

It was not all so easy as it seemed on the surface, as Rose Mary had no money and Walter Troumestre little. But this difficulty was not insoluble. Henry Clifford was so delighted at the idea that he at once announced his intention of making his niece an allowance of five hundred a year. He would have left it to her at his death, so why shouldn't she have it now – at once? Henry Clifford was better off than people supposed, and a great deal better off than he had been in his youth and in his early middle-age, as many of his investments had turned out well, and he had been "put on to" good things by friends who were in possession of good information, besides which he was on many Boards.

This, with the money that Walter and Rose Mary had of their own, gave them about twelve hundred a year to live on. Walter decided not to return to Constantinople as an unpaid diplomatist, but to accept what had been offered to him while he was still at Constantinople – a commission from one of the leading dailies to be their correspondent for the Near East, to make Constantinople his headquarters, or, if he preferred it, Sofia, to travel in the Balkan countries, and to report on the situation. Walter had already, before he went to Constantinople as an unpaid attaché, written several articles on the Near East in newspapers and magazines, and these had attracted attention.

The question of the Armenian massacres was exciting the public and the politicians at that moment, and the Eastern question was just as unsolved as ever it had been before or since.

After he had been out another year or so, then they would see. As it was, Rose Mary, contrary to every one's expectations, jumped at the idea of going abroad, and especially at seeing the East.

Blanche and, still more, Bernard were surprised at this rapid turn in events.

Walter, it appeared, had always been in love with Rose Mary from the first moment he had seen her, but he had thought that there was no chance for him. That is what he confessed to Bernard. He did not also add that, what was true, he had thought Bernard and Rose Mary loved each other, and that Bernard wanted to marry Rose Mary.

As for Blanche, she was relieved, and she soothed her conscience with the thought that there it was. Rose Mary had loved Walter all the time, so she need have had no scruples...but...but... And what was Rose Mary's frame of mind? She was not in love with Walter, but she liked him...liked him...and her one great desire was to get away from Blanche and Bernard, especially from Blanche and Bernard when they were married. That would be to her unendurable. She could get away for a time. She could go to the Bromleys. The Rodens would ask her to stay with them; but, nevertheless, her headquarters would be at Alton-Leigh, and at Bernard's house in London, and Blanche would still take her out. This she felt she could not endure, and she thought she would have accepted almost any one to escape from such a position. As it was, nothing better could have happened. She knew she would never love any one as she loved Bernard. He was her "soul's birth-partner," and, if she *could* not marry him, she did not really much mind whom she married. She preferred him to be a man she could like and respect. Walter was more than that;

she delighted in him as a companion. She liked him in every way. She did everything except love him...that she would never do; but that, she said to herself, he would never know.

Blanche and Bernard were married as soon as Lent was over, quietly at the Oratory. Walter was Bernard's best man. The only friends present were Princess Solski and the two Olenev girls (who were still unmarried). They had come over from Paris on purpose.

Blanche and Bernard left for Paris. They stayed there a few days, and they then spent a week at Cannes and some days at Monte Carlo. They were back again as soon as the recess was over. Rose Mary had been left with her cousins, the Bromleys.

Rose Mary and Walter were married at the Oratory in the first days of June. They, too, left for Paris on the way to Constantinople. Blanche and Bernard settled down in their London house – the house in Ovington Square where Mrs Lacy had lived. Their wedding journey had been a great success. They had had lovely weather; they had been to Nice and to Monte Carlo. Bernard had won at the tables. Blanche, who detested the south of France, had loved being there with Bernard. She came back looking as well and as beautiful as she ever had done in her life, and people began to point her out in public places, as they had once done in Rome, and at the Queen's Ball Blanche made a sensation. They took far more notice of her than they had ever done before.

"That is the beautiful Lady Lacy who was once an Italian Princess," they would say, and when she went to a party or a ball now, people began to flock round her. They had taken no notice of her last year when she had just been a chaperon. But Bernard detested going out, so it was seldom she went to entertainments, and only when he thought it uncivil to refuse or necessary to his political career.

They began to be asked out to dinner, but here again the same principle applied.

Whitsuntide they had spent with some friends in the country. Bernard had not wanted to go back to Alton-Leigh until Parliament was prorogued, as he said it would be unendurable to go there and then to have to come away again as soon as they arrived.

It was at the height of the season, and Blanche was beginning to feel weary of political dinners and the large entertainments Bernard felt obliged to accept; for it was just the large balls and parties that he went to, and it was these that tired Blanche, whereas the small dinners and dances which she might have enjoyed far more he refused. Blanche was beginning to feel London life a strain. All this had come too late for her. What did she care now if people made a fuss about her? It was too late. She smiled when she was conscious of exciting rivalry and jealousies. "If only they realised," she said to herself, "what a short innings I have got left, what a long innings I have already had."

It was just when she was beginning to wonder how she would get through the rest of the London season that the question was solved for her in an unexpected way. Her father caught cold at a party; his cold developed into double pneumonia, and he died after a short illness. He was seventy-two years old. Blanche was with him nearly all the time of his illness, and the last intelligible words he had spoken to her were, "Forgive me, Blanche darling; I didn't mean it."

His love for Blanche had been the one unselfish spot in a selfish life. He had loved her devotedly, and she had returned his love, and now she missed him. She could tell him all the thousand little things that Bernard could not understand, or that would not interest him if he did understand them. With her father's death, almost the last link of her old life went.

Henry Clifford was buried in London, at Kensal Green, and there was a memorial service at Curzon Chapel, which was attended by many members of several generations. The newspapers alluded to Henry Clifford as one of the last of the dandies; as a man who had known how to remain young while growing old with dignity; as a survival of the age of Thackeray; respectful allusions were made to his daughter, and the society newspapers were flooded with paragraphs about the marriage of the beautiful ex-Italian Princess with the heir of the romantic and historic estate of Alton-Leigh.

Parliament went on sitting till late that year; and it was not until the middle of August that Blanche and Bernard left London for Alton-Leigh. Bernard was looking forward to his first visit since his marriage with delight. The tenants were preparing him a great welcome. But there had been a certain amount of disappointment at his having married a foreigner.

Bernard told Blanche that he had arranged a surprise for her at Alton-Leigh, and nothing would make him say what it was. They arrived late on a gorgeous August day; the park and the house looked more beautiful than ever. A triumphal arch had been erected in front of the moat to welcome them, and Bernard had to receive deputations and signed addresses, and to make speeches.

When at last the ceremonial was over, they walked into the house, and Bernard said to Blanche:

"Now for the surprise."

"What is it?" she said. She was as excited as a child.

"It's not here; it's in the garden," and he led the way to the terrace.

On the terrace the gardener was waiting, carrying a large bouquet and wearing a smile of pleased expectation.

"Look!" said Bernard.

It was indeed a surprise. It was more than a surprise; it was a shock.

The garden had been made tidy. It was unrecognisable. The Sleeping-Beauty-in-the-wood element had disappeared completely and for ever.

Every weed had been pulled out. The lawns were close-shaven; the tangles, the thickets, and the undergrowth in the alleys had gone.

The beds were full of ordered red geraniums, with borders of lobelia, and there were also beds of calceolaria and begonias. It was a triumph of neat and bright gardening.

Blanche was so overcome by the sight that her genuine shock might quite well have been interpreted as a shock of delight.

"Oh!" she said.

Bernard interpreted it in that way.

"I knew you would like it when you saw it," he said. "It makes the whole difference to the place, doesn't it?"

"Yes," said Blanche; "the whole difference."

"Tell Roberts you like it," he whispered. (Roberts was the gardener.) "He's been working like a slave to get it ready in time."

"I think it's wonderful what you've done," she said. She had recovered by now, and could lie glibly. "I think it's *quite* wonderful. I can't think how you can have done it. It has transformed the place."

"It is an improvement, m'lady," the gardener said. "It wanted it badly. We had a job to get it done in time. I've already been at Sir Bernard for years to let me tidy up, and he never would hear of it before; but when I said as it would be quite a wedding surprise, a gift like for your ladyship, then he *did* listen."

Roberts presented his bouquet, with another rather flowery speech, and Blanche again thanked him with warmth. Then Bernard took her all round the garden, and she could inspect the damage in detail.

"Of course," she said to herself, "it's absurd to mind. It was meant to be like this. It's right really, *now*; and it was wrong before. In time I will gradually change the flowers and it will be all right…only, only… " It had indeed been lovely as it was, after a prolonged period of Nature's careless treatment, unique, and utterly unlike anything else in the world. And now it was like the garden kept by a municipality, or the garden in the park of a watering-place. Before, it had been the most enchanted of all enchanted places. Nature and accident, the climate, the vegetation, in careless conspiracy had achieved something that was beyond the range of art and forethought. And now, Blanche sadly reflected, the romance, the poetry, had been dissipated for ever from this wonderful garden.

She wondered what Bernard really felt, whether he really sincerely preferred the new to the old state of things. As a matter of fact, he was sorry; he felt a definite pang at the change, not because he thought the garden and the place looked less beautiful as they were, now, but because he disliked change, and he had a half-superstitious, half-sentimental reverence and affection for the idea of his uncle in keeping the place untouched, but at the same time he felt it was right and proper that the garden should be tidied up, and the great thing was that Blanche preferred it. What did it matter what *he* felt? It had been a real surprise for her, successful beyond anything he had dreamt He had always known she would prefer the place tidy, he said to himself, and fit for her, although he remembered her saying she liked it as it was. She would have tidied it herself after a time, if he had not done so, so it showed how right he had been.

"Next year," he said, "you must help Roberts with the flowers."

"Yes, I will," thought Blanche, wondering how soon it would be possible to make a few radical alterations in the composition and colour scheme of the beds.

"And the kitchen garden?" she asked.

"That's not been touched. There was nothing worth altering there."

Bernard said this with concealed relief, and Blanche, too, gave a concealed gasp of relief.

"Let's go and see it," she said.

They walked into the kitchen garden. The wide grass paths were untouched. The walls were rich this year in peaches, nectarines, apricots, and plums. The peaches were ripe. Here in this kitchen garden there was still a remnant of the old charm that had been banished from the garden, but even here, alas, a little mischief had been done; the old, battered conservatory had been "renovated." It was gleaming with fresh paint, and was full of the least attractive of tropical flora. The little temple by the pond was still untouched.

"Let's go and look at the Dower House," said Blanche, hoping and half-confident that at least there nothing had been touched, and yet at the same time half-fearful.

"I told them to leave that alone. There wouldn't have been time with the staff we have at present to have done that, too, and then my mother liked it as it was, and I shouldn't like to make any alterations," Bernard said apologetically.

"He's apologising to me for not having smartened it up," thought Blanche. "Good Heavens!" And the irony of life came to her as never before.

They walked into the garden of the Dower House. Nothing there had been touched. Even the plants in the beds were the same as Mrs Lacy had planted year after year, and had been kept religiously the same by Roberts, the gardener, who knew her (to him) somewhat fantastically old-fashioned taste, her love of sweet-williams, hollyhocks, and sunflowers (the latter were now in flower), mignonette, and petunias.

The sun was now beginning to set through the tall elm trees. There was a mellow richness about the garden and the farther landscape. Presently the moon would rise, enormous and tawny, like the shield of one of the gods in the Trojan War. "Here, at any rate, the old beauty, the old romance, has not been touched," thought Blanche, and at the same time she blamed herself for having felt disappointed at what Bernard had done. He had done it for her, as a surprise. It was absurd, unreasonable, and contrary to Nature to wish that a formal garden which had been designed by Le Nôtre should be untidy and full of weeds. She had been a sentimental goose, like those people she had so often seen at Rome, deploring the destruction of some hideous slum. How they had irritated her! How severe she had been about them, and here she was thinking and feeling the same...and yet a voice answered her: "It was unique as it was; there was nothing like it. Uncle Charles would have loved it, and even papa would have thought it a pity to alter it, as it was like that... "

There was a feeling of harvest in the air, of broad benediction, of something having been accomplished and carried out to its appointed end. Blanche felt that evening, that evening of her home-coming, as she stood in the little garden of the Dower House with Bernard, her husband, as if for her, too, a ritual had been accomplished. She felt as when, at the end of High Mass, she watched the choir walk out from the sanctuary to the sacristy at the Churches in Rome, at the Lateran, for instance...how satisfactory it was! How satisfying...that close...she remembered a phrase from a poem she had first read years ago in a book that Adrian Tyne had given her:

"Ay, like departing altar ministrants... "

What a sense of something accomplished and done in the proper, right fashion, it gave one...and now she felt here, in this calm, rich evening, in this garden of hollyhocks and sunflowers, in front of this old dignified little house, which had been the dwelling and the lodestone of Bernard's mother...here with Bernard standing beside her she felt that an end had come to the tumult, the sorrows, the storms of her life. She had reached the harbour. She was at peace.

All had been for the best. God had been good to her. He had given her far more than she deserved – she was happy. The sky was all gold, that soft rich umber that only comes with the approach of autumn. Blanche felt a sense of peace descending upon her.

Then Bernard said suddenly: "I say, Blanche, I've got a wonderful idea! What a fool I was not to think of it before!"

"What is it?"

"Well, you know I heard from Walter this morning, and he's longing to come back to England next year and to settle down here and write. She wants to come back too. His book is coming out in January – a short one – sketches he has written in the last few years; but he wants to write a long book. The difficulty is, can they afford to live in England with houses so expensive? Well, he thought they couldn't – at present. Now, I've got it. Why shouldn't they live here in the Dower House? It would be just the thing for them, wouldn't it?"

"I think that would be perfect," said Blanche.

They went home. It was getting chilly.

# BOOK III

# CHAPTER I

Walter Troumestre's book came out in the spring of the following year. It was read, talked about, well reviewed, and went through three editions. It was a collection of sketches and magazine articles that he had written during his travels in the Near East and in other places, during the last years.

The book made his newspaper anxious for him to stay in the Near East, and they raised the scale of the terms they were offering him. The reviews said his descriptions of Eastern life were the best things of their kind that had appeared since *Eothen*.

In the meantime, Bernard had written to him, suggesting that he should come and live at the Dower House and settle down there to his book.

Walter had, during the last five years, collected material about the East; he wanted to write a long book about it – something more important than mere sketches of travel and *choses vues* – a suggestive, half-historical, half-philosophical book. To do this he would have to settle down in a quiet place for some time. Bernard's offer was ideal.

He consulted Rose Mary. She was longing to come back to England, but at the same time she did not much like the idea of living so near Blanche and Bernard, or, rather, the idea frightened her...in some ways she liked it too much. But she

439

had no reasonable objection to make. She had up till then been longing to go back to England, and had said so. This changed the situation altogether, and when Walter's editor begged him to stay out in the Near East until the end of the Parliamentary Session, he, with the encouragement of Rose Mary, consented to stay till the middle of June. He was writing a weekly letter to his newspaper, the *Morning News*. His headquarters were at Constantinople, but he visited Athens and Sofia with Rose Mary. He rode from Sofia to Uskub and Monastir soon after they arrived in the East. At the beginning of the following April, Rose Mary gave birth to a child. It was a boy, and they called it Bernard; Bernard was godfather by proxy.

Walter refused to stay out longer than June. He wanted to see the Jubilee festivities and procession.

"After all," he said, "we can always come back here if it is necessary, to make the pot boil, and if we live at Alton-Leigh we shall be able to save money. Even if we don't, which I dare say is improbable, we shall have enough to live on."

They were back in London by the middle of June, and they stayed in London for the Diamond Jubilee festivities. They stayed with Walter Troumestre's mother, Lady Alice Troumestre – a widow with one married daughter and still one unmarried daughter to take out – who had a small untidy house in Mansfield Street. They had been invited to see the procession from Whitehall House. They had been asked to the fancy-dress ball at Wessex House, and Blanche and Bernard were going as well. It was the second fancy-dress ball that Blanche had been asked to in her life, and she had no wish to go to it, but Bernard wanted her to, so she said she would go. She and Bernard and Walter and Rose Mary were all dining with young Lady Pevensey (the old Lady Pevensey, the friend of Princess Julia's, had been dead for some years), who had a dinner-party at Pevensey House, at which every one was to be in fancy dress before the ball.

A few days before the ball, Blanche's Aunt Cecilia, Mrs Walter Clifford, died, and this put them in mourning. Blanche said it would be impossible for *her* to go; it would hurt her cousins' feelings, but she insisted on Bernard going, and they could both dine with the Pevenseys. Mrs Walter Clifford was Rose Mary's aunt as well as Blanche's aunt, but Rose Mary had never seen her in her life, nor her cousins either, so it was settled she should go, and it was at that dinner that Blanche, Bernard, Rose Mary, and Walter met together for the first time since their marriage...

Rose Mary went to the fancy-dress ball as a Spanish lady in a dress copied from a picture by Goya, which had recently been bought by the National Gallery. It was a picture of a fair lady in rose-coloured satin and black lace, with a mantilla of black lace hanging from a tall comb. This suited Rose Mary's fresh beauty, and she knew – it was her Spanish blood – how to wear a mantilla.

Blanche was dressed as an ancestress of Bernard's, but she had not taken much trouble about it. Her dress was copied from a picture that was at Alton-Leigh, of the Annabel Lacy who had lived in the days of Charles I, and about whom there was the romantic story of the ghostly minstrel. She was presented in the picture in sea-green satin, that watery blue-green with high lights in it (the colour of the Greek seas) that you often meet with in Van Dyck's pictures; she wore a pearl necklace and large pearl ear-rings, and one large pink carnation, and her hair was done Henrietta-Maria fashion, with a small chaplet of pearls at the back.

At Pevensey House there was a crowd of costumed guests, old and young – but all of them on the more conventional side – handsome and distinguished more than beautiful. Rose Mary and Blanche, without any comparison, won the most marks for beauty, and Rose Mary was thought the most beautiful person in the room, and she was enjoying this certainty – till Blanche and Bernard arrived. Bernard went as a Venetian nobleman, in a dress copied from a Venetian picture, of black satin, embroidered with gold fleur-de-lis – a figure of great distinction and picturesqueness.

When the couple walked upstairs into the large, decorated drawing-room, where Lady Pevensey received her guests, they both of them made an impression. They neither of them seemed to be dressed up, but to belong to the house.

Rose Mary tried, but failed, to stifle a pang of bitter envy.

"How does she manage it?" she thought. "She puts me and every one else out, like a candle. She has no business to look like that. After all, her features are nothing wonderful; plenty of people have got finer eyes; she's got an extremely graceful figure, but, then, so have lots of people. She's over twenty-five years older than I am, and yet I feel slovenly and common beside her, as if I were made of some coarser texture and substance."

Some of the guests at this dinner were relations of the Pevenseys, who formed a large clan, and they were all of them Catholics; but there were other guests, too.

Blanche met an old friend and an old acquaintance, neither of whom she had seen for a long time. The old friend was her contemporary, Maud Dallington, who was a widow now and lived nearly all the year round in Italy. Blanche had not seen her since Roman days; and the old acquaintance was Sir Gabriel Carteret, ARA, who was there with his wife. Blanche did not recognise him at first, which was not surprising, as he was dressed in gold brocade, with a cape fastened by large turquoises, and a scarlet close-fitting cap with two Himalayan pheasant's feathers, copied from a figure in "The Marriage of Cana," by Veronese, at the Louvre.

They were a picturesque procession as they walked downstairs into the Italian dining-room, with its white-and-gold walls and yellow marble pillars: Lord Pevensey, young, distinguished, a little bit deaf, and dressed in brown velvet and satin, with a white ruff, leading the way with Blanche; and the hostess, in Medici clothes, at the end of the procession, on the arm of Count Peter Linsky, the Hungarian diplomat, magnificent in his national costume of fur, black velvet, and real emeralds. He looked like an old picture.

At dinner, on the other side of Blanche was a young Irish peer, Lord Laracor (in an eighteenth-century uniform), whom she found easy and gay.

Opposite her sat Rose Mary, between Bernard and Gabriel Carteret, and on Gabriel Carteret's other side was Maud Dallington, brilliant as a Venetian Court lady, in white and gold, with olive-green, gold-embroidered sleeves.

At the beginning of dinner those who were sitting immediately opposite to Blanche could not help looking at her. They discussed her beauty.

"How wonderful Blanche is looking," said Rose Mary to Bernard.

"Yes; isn't she? That period suits her." There was a tinge of absent-mindedness in Bernard's voice as he said this, as if he were used to saying it, and he talked of other things.

Rose Mary detected the shade of absence of mind in his intonation, and wondered.

Every now and then, whenever he could, without her noticing it, and without seeming to stare, Bernard took a surreptitious look at Rose Mary – a look of admiration.

He was used to Blanche's beauty, but Rose Mary's came to him as a fresh surprise every time he looked at her. It was the kind of beauty he admired most. Rose Mary did not know this, although she felt he admired her; and this increased the bitterness she was feeling – the bitterness against Blanche. She felt she was going to have a miserable evening. Her misery was nothing to that which Blanche herself was experiencing. Blanche could not bear to see Bernard sitting next to Rose Mary. She saw the way he looked at her, and stole a look at her every now and then, when Rose Mary was unaware of it; she saw the frank, unmixed admiration in his eyes. She knew that look. She knew that he was feeling perfectly happy. She thought that Rose Mary must be making her look old...she felt a great wave of bitter, black, burning jealousy rising in her.

While all these thoughts were surging through her mind she was carrying on a civil interchange of platitudes and topics with her partially deaf host, and, on the other side of the table, Maud Dallington was saying to Gabriel Carteret: "Yes; I have known her all my life; we came out together. I agree, I think she's almost better-looking now than she ever was – but perhaps we see her with the eyes of the past. It really is despairing; when she first married she made me feel dowdy, like a housemaid, and now she makes me feel like a housekeeper."

"She ought to have put on more rouge tonight *for the ball*," said Gabriel Carteret. "It suits her white skin and brings out her eyes."

"You ought to paint her."

"She's not paintable. You would lose all the charm in a picture; she's not a classic beauty with regular lines and features. All her beauty is in her atmosphere, and her grace, and her light, that shining light that seems to stream from her...it is intangible, like the scent of a flower, or the quality of a tune. One couldn't, at least I couldn't, get it on to canvas...it's much too illusive. Another thing, I think she has perhaps too much distinction to be as beautiful as she might be, to be a *paintable* beauty."

"Oh! But surely that's her great, great point; that's why and how she puts us out...makes us look dowdy."

"Yes, here – in a room – at a dinner, next to all those" – he gave a swift look round at the more conventional figures – "but on *canvas* it's different. You see Lady Lacy's beauty isn't a *footlight* beauty. It would never get across the footlights, as the actors say. I doubt even whether she will be much noticed at Wessex House tonight. Now I could paint her cousin, my neighbour," he said, lowering his voice, and giving a quick look at Rose Mary. "She would get across any footlights; the more the better."

"Do you admire her the most of the two?"

"Oh no! I admire my *vis-à-vis* most; but she is beyond my reach – she is too rare, too *absolute* – for brush, pencil, paint, or canvas."

"I agree."

While this conversation was going on, Lord Pevensey was saying to Blanche: "What a remarkably beautiful person Mrs Troumestre is; she's your cousin, isn't she? She's so uncommon."

"Isn't she?" said Blanche. "Her mother was Spanish."

"Ah, that accounts for it. Bernard seems to admire her; you'll have to be careful," he said, laughing.

He was a contemporary and an old school friend of Bernard's.

"Yes," said Blanche, joining in with his laughter, and feeling that her laugh was dreadfully hollow and artificial.

Towards the end of dinner, Bernard seemed absorbed by Rose Mary's presence, quite unconscious of any one else. He gave up any attempt at talking to his other neighbour, with whom he had exchanged a few civilities at the beginning of dinner, and gave himself up to the enjoyment in which he seemed to be swimming. Blanche was acutely conscious of what was happening.

After dinner she had a long talk with her old friend, Maud Dallington, who told her all the Italian news and gossip; and when the men came up from the dining room, Walter Troumestre (who was rather incongruously dressed as an Elizabethan and managed to be as untidy in sixteenth as he was in nineteenth-century clothes) came and talked to her.

"Do you admire Rose Mary's get-up?" he said. "Do you think it's a success? It was my idea; she wanted to go as something quite different – an orange girl, or something. I happened to see that picture a little time ago at the National Gallery, and it struck me as being exactly the thing."

"It suits her quite extraordinarily well," said Blanche.

"You're not coming to the ball?"

"No; I'm going to be Cinderella tonight. Bernard's going."

"Will you arrive at midnight?"

"I'm afraid not."

"I think it's a great pity. It will be an historical sight. And, then, it's only your aunt-in-law."

"Yes; but, you see, I know the daughters very well, and they might be hurt, I think, if they saw in the newspaper that I had been there. But I think there is no possible reason why Bernard shouldn't go. He doesn't know my aunt."

"I suppose Rose Mary oughtn't to go really?"

"Oh! that's all right; she doesn't know her cousins."

Presently some friends arrived who were not going to the ball, and other dressed-up people as well, and towards eleven o'clock the party broke up.

Bernard and Blanche went home. As they drove home, Blanche said to Bernard: "Didn't Rose Mary look well?"

She hoped he would say: "Not as well as you do!" Instead of which he cordially agreed.

"Yes," he said; "I thought she looked *lovely*."

"You didn't like my gown?" she said.

"Of course I did. Every one did."

"Did they really?"

"Of course they did. They always *do* admire you."

Blanche had the horrible feeling that she was being taken by Bernard as a matter of course; something established and ordinary, as established and as ordinary as the Marble Arch. But as for the tone of voice in which he spoke of Rose Mary, there was something new in it, and something unmistakable, which caused her acute pain.

Blanche was to drop Bernard at Wessex House and then go home by herself, but when they got into the carriage – into the comfortable brougham – Bernard said to Blanche:

"I will drive you home first."

He thought she was feeling sad at not going to the ball.

"No," said Blanche; "you had better not...it will make you so late. You ought to see the people arrive."

Bernard pulled the string, and, putting his head out of the window, just said "Home" to the coachman.

"I don't think I want to go without you," Bernard said, after a pause.

"Oh! you *must* go. It would be too silly to miss it...besides which, you will enjoy it."

"No; not without you."

Blanche gave a little laugh which had a note of bitterness in it. She had meant and tried to keep this note out, but she had failed.

"You don't believe me."

"Of course I do," she said, without conviction.

Bernard was hurt and angry.

"Very well, then, I shan't go."

"Really, Bernard, I promise you, I swear I believe you; I know you would like me to go... I know you don't like leaving me... I know you are sorry for me."

"Sorry for you! Why?" he asked suspiciously.

It was an unfortunate phrase.

"Sorry for leaving me behind like Cinderella. Alone and dressed up, too."

"But I'm not leaving you dressed up and alone. I told you I'm not going; I meant it," he said rather sharply. He was getting angry.

His anger annoyed her and flicked her on the raw.

"When you would enjoy yourself so much," she went on, taking no notice of the interruption. "There will be so many people there you like and admire."

447

Bernard said nothing.

There was a long pause while they drove down past Knightsbridge into the Brompton Road.

"You mustn't be silly, Bernard; you must go. You needn't bother about me. I've got a headache and would like to go to bed. I want to go to bed."

Bernard looked at her with compassion, and all might have been well and ended happily, only Blanche unfortunately said: "Besides which, my gown is a failure. You don't like it."

"How can you say such a thing? That's really too unfair," he said abruptly.

"You didn't say a word about it."

"That's not true, Blanchie dear," he said savagely. "I told you I admired it immensely. What more could you want me to say?"

"It's not what you *said* – it's the way – I could see you didn't admire it really."

"Oh, Blanchie!"

"You were quite right. It's a failure. I look awful. I look old. I could see everybody thought so."

"What nonsense! They all said you looked better than any one. Rose Mary said: 'She's making us all look like frumps.' "

"Did *she* say that?" There was a tinge of satire in the question.

"Yes; she did." A pause. "And every one else did, too."

"It's no use saying that *now*; it's too late."

"Blanchie, Blanchie, don't be so unreasonable, please." He said this imploringly.

"Well, then, you must go to the ball."

"I don't want to go without you."

"I know you want to go. It's a great shame if you don't go; you make *me* feel so selfish."

"Well, I *won't* go without you," he said firmly, with a set jaw.

"Please do, Bernard; I really do want you to."

Do what she would, she could not put a note of real conviction in her voice. She could not help there being just something a little bit hard, just a little tiny grain as hard as crystal, in her intonation.

They had arrived home by now. They got out of the carriage. The footman opened the door of the carriage.

"I shan't want you any more," Bernard said to the coachman, who touched his hat. "Don't ring," he said to the footman. Bernard opened the front door with his latch-key.

"Yes, yes, we shall want you," said Blanche to the coachman. "Wait a minute."

The coachman touched his hat again.

"Come in for a minute; I want to say something," said Blanche.

"You needn't wait," he said again to the coachman.

The coachman touched his hat again, and drove off. Blanche was now white under her rouge.

"You are cruel. You *are* unkind to me," she said.

The carriage had now driven off with the footman. She sat down on the wooden, old-fashioned, high-backed chair that was in the front hall, next to the table which was littered with visiting-cards, turned down at the corners, and on which Bernard's several top hats, beautifully brushed and ironed, were put out in a serried order. She looked at the picture of the Battle of Alma which hung over this table, and she burst into tears. She felt that she had destroyed the palace of her happiness, and was sitting among the ruins. Bernard was at once melted by the sight of her tears.

"Don't cry, Blanche darling, don't cry. *Please*, don't cry."

"Will you go to the ball, then?" she said, through her tears.

"Well, it's too late now; I've sent away the carriage."

"You can go in a hansom."

"Not dressed like this."

"Why not?"

"Well, it's impossible."

"In a four-wheeler, then."

"I should never get one *now*; it's too late altogether, and, besides which, I honestly, really and truly, don't want to go, and one would have missed everything by now."

"Very well," said Blanche; "then I shall go."

"Dearest, darling Blanche, don't be so silly."

"I mean it."

"You will hurt your cousins' feelings."

"What do I care? And, besides which, it's late, as you say, and we shan't even be announced. They'll never know, and I don't care if they do."

"Don't be so unreasonable, Blanche," he said in a calm, matter-of-fact tone.

"You mean you would be ashamed of me – of my looks."

"You know I don't mean that."

"You do. You *are* ashamed of me. You are afraid of being laughed at...of people saying, 'There's that poor Bernard Lacy who's married a woman much older than himself, and she looks it... Poor fellow!' "

Blanche was carried away by her nerves now, and was beginning to talk recklessly.

"Very well," said Bernard. "I'll go if you insist."

"And will you take me?"

"If you want to come, of course I will."

"Of course I want to come. Do you think it's amusing for me to... " She stopped and burst into another paroxysm of tears.

"Blanchie, Blanchie, dearest, darling Blanchie!"

He took her in his arms and kissed away her tears.

"I'm so sorry, Bernard," she said, sobbing. "I have been horrible."

He kissed her, soothed her, and comforted her.

"I'll do anything you like... I'll go with you or without you."

Blanche smiled once more.

"I should like you to go without me."

"No," said Bernard; "I know you want to go – you *must* go."

"How shall we get there?"

"It's quite easy in a four-wheeler."

"How shall we find one? The servants have all gone to bed."

"I'll find one in a moment. There's a rank just outside the square."

"Don't, Bernard...well, for *you*...but not for *me*."

Bernard went out, and returned presently with a fourwheeler. Blanche knew he minded going out dressed up as a Venetian nobleman to fetch a cab, while passers-by made facetious comments, and she felt now she *must* go.

"Very well, I will come," she said, "only I must tidy first, or every one will see that I have been crying. I shan't be a minute. I don't think it will matter my going now, because we shall be much too late to be announced."

"No, of course; it's all right," Bernard said meekly.

Blanche went up to her bedroom and washed her eyes with rose-water. Her maid came – re-did her hair, and she powdered her face and rouged it, and tidied up generally, and preened herself before a tall looking-glass. The process took over half an hour. Bernard waited in the hall and tried manfully to master his impatience. He smoked cigarette after cigarette.

At last Blanche appeared.

"You look wonderful," said Bernard.

"Do I really?"

"You will look far better than any one there, I promise you, darling."

It was past half-past twelve, nearly one, when they arrived at Wessex House, and the hostess was no longer on the staircase. Quadrilles were being danced; supper had begun some time ago.

Bernard caught sight of Rose Mary almost at once, and asked her to come down to supper with him. She accepted with alacrity.

Rose Mary stood out among these surroundings, in that glittering crowd of dressed-up people... Her beauty and her fancy dress went straight across these particular footlights; the surroundings acted on them like footlights, and supplied her with exactly that which was needed. She looked as brilliant as a stage figure. She had blackened her eyebrows and put an extra coat of rouge on her face just before the ball – she had not dared do this before dining at Pevensey House – and this, combined with her very fair hair, her wide grey eyes and high black lace mantilla, made of her an unforgettable figure.

Sir Gabriel Carteret, with the instinct of an artist, had guessed this. He had guessed right about Blanche, too. At Pevensey House, at that dinner of stiff, handsome, distinguished, and aristocratic people, Blanche had shone out radiantly; among the distinguished she was the most distinguished; she would put every one out in a match for distinction *now* – in former years she had done far more than this – but here, in this motley crowd, in this galaxy of brilliance, stage-finery, and real jewels, among these Cleopatras and Theodoras, and Hebes and Charlotte Cordays, she, in her blue Van Dyck gown, did not look as if she were dressed up at all. She looked as if she were wearing an ordinary evening-gown, and her particular beauty suffered for the first time in her life a definite eclipse.

She was aware of this herself the first moment she reached the top of the staircase. Nobody took much notice of her. She sat on a gilt chair on the landing, with her back to the staircase, and said to herself:

"What a fool I was to come!"

She saw Bernard walk downstairs with Rose Mary on his arm – Rose Mary, her eyes sparkling, laughing, talking, shining, effective, young; and every one turned round to look at them as this couple passed... They didn't see Blanche...they went down on the other side of the staircase. "After all, he wouldn't have come without me," Blanche said to herself. "It would have been selfish not to come, to deprive him of this... "

Sir Gabriel came up to her.

"There's an Italian quadrille just beginning; shall we go and look at it?"

"Yes," said Blanche.

They went, not actually in the ballroom itself – it was full – but they stood in a semicircular space outside the ballroom; this space had a series of three doorless doorways formed by pillars, which opened on to the ballroom. They got a beautiful view from where they stood, just behind the row of chairs where sat those who were looking on. Blanche thought of the ball, the fancy-dress ball, at the Palazzo Sori. How long ago that was, and how different! It was more beautiful than this, although here there were, perhaps, more beauties. This was like a Drury Lane pantomime in comparison, in spite of the beauties. The dresses were most of them tawdry in comparison, especially the men's... And what an effect she had made then! What nonsense it was for people to say that one grew better-looking as one grew older! "I'm done for now," she thought... "nobody looks at me... "

Sir Gabriel made comments. "There is some one who knows how to dress up and who looks like an Italian picture...that lady in Venetian red and silver. Let me see...it's Lady St Cuthbert. Yes; she does look picturesque."

Blanche heard two people talking Russian behind her. This reminded her of Rome. The couple who had been sitting just in front of them went away, then Blanche and Sir Gabriel went into the ballroom and sat on the chairs which had just been left. They were now in the front row for seeing. Behind them Blanche heard some one, a lady – a voice she had heard before and knew well, but couldn't place for a second – asking some one else the following question: "What was it those two Russians were saying?"

"One of them," was the answer – it was a man speaking – a voice she knew ("It is Herbert Napier, of course," she thought. It was; he was just home on leave from St Petersburg) – "asked who she was... "

"That?" said the other voice, in a low undertone, almost a whisper; but Blanche could hear the grass grow, and she felt the lady was almost imperceptibly, either by look or gesture, indicating some one...she felt, she knew not why, it was she herself who was being pointed out.

"And the other," he went on in an undertone, "said *'Bwivshaya krasavitsa.'* That means a *past* beauty...some one who has been a beauty. Just fancy!"

Blanche longed to turn round, but she didn't. She felt sure now it was she they meant, and, yet, why?

A little later she did turn round. The young man – he was about thirty – was dressed in *Henri Quatre* clothes, and the lady was a dazzling vision in gold and silver and covered with pearls; she was "the Queen of Cyprus." She looked as if she had never worn anything else.

"I think," she said quite loudly, as Blanche turned round, "that Daisy Fennmouth is more beautiful now than she ever was... "

"Well, they didn't mean me after all," thought Blanche. Yet Herbert Napier seemed to be tacitly receiving an unexpressed telegraphic signal, and he said hurriedly and loud: "Yes, yes, of course."

"She thinks I heard," thought Blanche, "and she is making it all right." And then the Eastern potentate in question seemed to notice her for the first time.

"Dearest Blanche, how are you? How lovely you look! What a wonderful gown! Who made it? Foucet? Copied from a picture, isn't it?"

It was Lady Agincourt, whom Blanche had met in Paris and sometimes in Rome.

"You know Herbert Napier, of course." Blanche remembered him well, and shook hands with him. "Do come and see me some time."

Lady Agincourt and Napier walked off, and Blanche heard Herbert Napier's ringing laugh coming through the crowd. "I'm sure," thought Blanche, "they're laughing at the *gaffe* they might have made – they *nearly* made."

Sir Gabriel offered to take Blanche down to supper. She accepted. Never had she felt more miserable, but she had made up her mind to endure it to the end. It was her own fault.

They went downstairs and took two empty chairs at a round table in the dining-room, where there was a laughing crowd. At the next table Blanche saw that Bernard and Rose Mary were still sitting. They must have finished supper a long time ago... They were talking, talking, unaware of the world, unaware of time. Blanche felt as if a sharp sword had been plunged into her. She felt almost sick.

Gabriel Carteret was hungry, and accepted hot soup, a hot quail, and strawberries and cream, as they were offered to him. Blanche had no appetite, but she drank, almost unconsciously, a glass of champagne, and toyed with a strawberry. She was unconscious of what Gabriel Carteret was saying, but she answered him mechanically. After a time her attention was caught by her other neighbour, who was disguised as a Napoleonic soldier. She did not recognise him at all, and then it flashed on her – he was talking to her as if they knew each other quite well – that it was Sydney Mayfield.

"You know," he said, "I had no idea who you were at first."

"No; I suppose I have altered a lot."

"Oh yes," he said; and then, correcting himself, "fancy dress does make every one look so different."

"I suppose it does," said Blanche, and she got up and said she must be going.

As she passed the table where Rose Mary and Bernard were sitting, she said to Bernard: "I am going home. I have got a headache. Can I have the latch-key? I will leave it under the mat."

"But why?" he said. "I'll come with you."

"No, please don't," she said. "Please," and there was so much imperative anguish and insistence in the syllable that Bernard felt obliged to obey it.

"Very well," he said, giving her the key. "Will you really be all right?"

"Yes," she said, "perfectly. Sir Gabriel is getting me a four-wheeler."

Sir Gabriel led her out to the hall and saw her safely into a four-wheeler. Blanche, when she got home, went to bed, but not to sleep. She cried till her pillow was wet; but when Bernard came home two hours later he did not notice that anything was amiss. He looked into her room and said "Blanchie." There was no answer. "That's all right," he thought, "she's asleep." But Blanche did not get to sleep at all that night.

# CHAPTER II

The day after the ball, Walter and Rose Mary left London, and went to stay with some friends of Walter's in the country. Blanche and Bernard stayed in London till the end of the season, at the beginning of August. They then went to Alton-Leigh, where Rose Mary and Walter soon joined them, and established themselves in the Dower House.

Walter settled down to write his book. There was a stream of guests at Alton-Leigh – first of all, in September, for the partridge shooting, and, later, for the pheasant shooting.

Blanche had begun to improve the garden; she had, at least, chosen what should be in the beds this year. She had put a check, too, on further trimmings, cuttings, and clearings, with the result that the garden looked well, but it could never, she thought, have the charm it had possessed when she first saw it. But the Dower House looked at its best. Rose Mary arranged it well, and Blanche envied her for living there.

Rose Mary at first came seldom to Alton-Leigh. She always waited to be asked. This irritated Blanche. She knew she was being unfair to Rose Mary in resenting this, but it irritated her none the less. She would have preferred – so she told herself – Rose Mary to be constantly walking in and out of the house. As it was, she (Blanche) felt she was to blame.

In spite of this, they all saw a great deal of one another, as Bernard was always asking them to dinner or to luncheon, or to come and play lawn-tennis in the afternoon.

Bernard would often stroll round to the Dower House to see how they were getting on, and to ask after the baby, who was Bernard's godson and called after him; but on these occasions Rose Mary would fetch Walter immediately, or, if Walter was busy, she would go to the nursery and send word that she could not come down.

Bernard was aware, after the first month, that it was difficult to see Rose Mary alone for a moment. Blanche was conscious of this, too. But, instead of its calming her, the situation annoyed her. It excited suspicion in her – suspicion that she kept on repeating to herself was ignoble, unfounded, mean, and unworthy of her, but which she nevertheless could not help harbouring. It was as if Rose Mary divined this suspicion; and she seemed to take pains by every means at her disposal to defeat it. It was as though she were determined that Blanche should have no cause for complaint. Blanche was puzzled by her. Inscrutable as she had been as a schoolgirl, she was more inscrutable now.

"She hates me with all her might," thought Blanche, "and for that reason she is determined that I shall never have anything tangible to complain of. She thinks I have robbed her of everything that had been most dear to her; first of all of her father, and then of Bernard. The first charge is untrue. As to the second…he was mine… But there is nothing to be done. It is irreparable," she reflected. "I must simply endure the situation as it is. Nothing can make things any better. It is my fault."

Rose Mary seemed anxious, too, that Walter should not be unhappy. She did everything she could to make him happy. Blanche thought he was happy. He was devoted to the baby; he was engrossed in his work; he liked being at Alton-Leigh; he enjoyed seeing Bernard, and Blanche thought he liked her company without being in the least in love with her.

It was pain and misery for Blanche to see Rose Mary with her child, and the thought that she herself had no children, and never would have, was doubly painful because she knew Bernard would have given his eyes to have a son; that he would never have one was a source of an almost intolerable sadness.

In the month of September an event happened which tended to solidify and to crystallise the situation.

Bernard's mother, Mrs Lacy, was the niece of an old Lord Windlestone, who possessed a Tudor house and a small estate in the country of Southeastshire.

The estate was entailed. Lord Windlestone died at the age of seventy-three, shortly after the death of Mrs Lacy, and left the estate to his only surviving son, who was at that time forty-seven years old. He was married and had several children, but he outlived them all, and his wife as well, and now he himself, at the beginning of this very September, died without issue. The title, the house, and the estate went to Bernard. He was the son of Lord Windlestone's niece, and the heir.

So Bernard became Lord Windlestone – (Blanche changed her name for the third time) – and the heir to Chalgrave House and the estate in Southeastshire. Bernard went up to London to interview lawyers and to get through such business as was necessary; he then sent a telegram to Blanche, asking her to come and meet him, and together they travelled down to Chalgrave, which was a two hours' journey from London, and, although on the way to Alton-Leigh, easier to reach from London than from any station in Fenmouthshire. Bernard wanted Blanche to see the house and to hear her opinion about it.

They arrived at the village, had some food in the inn, and drove in a fly to the house. It was a red-brick Tudor building, with a fine gateway, fine windows, and stone sculpture. Inside, the rooms were high and dignified, but the house was in shocking need of repair. Old Lord Windlestone had allowed nothing to be touched, and his son had apparently inherited his prejudices.

"It would need at least four thousand pounds spending on the house alone," said Bernard.

Inside the house there was a fine collection of armour, and one or two interesting pictures, among them a Raeburn.

Beyond the house, the garden and the lawns were in a state of greater untidiness than Alton-Leigh had been when Blanche had first seen it. An old housekeeper showed them over the house, in which the only habitable rooms seemed to be the immense kitchen and the panelled housekeeper's room. The bedrooms, with their hanging tapestries and four-posters, were mouldy and damp.

"It would need a great deal more money-spending on it than I thought," was Bernard's comment.

Blanche, who welcomed a chance of getting away from Alton-Leigh, made little of the disrepair, and took an optimistic view of everything. After half an hour she had almost persuaded Bernard that it would be a pity to sell such an interesting place, and that the repairs would really cost little, when Bernard said: "Of course, we could never live here."

"I thought perhaps – " said Blanche.

"Of course, I could never leave Alton-Leigh, especially now that Walter and Rose Mary are there…but in any case I should never dream of leaving it."

"Of course not, but I thought perhaps we might come here sometimes, for some part of the year, perhaps in the spring or at Easter."

"My dear, we couldn't afford to keep up both these establishments; as it is, I have got to pay enormous death duties. We must either let it or sell it."

Once it was laid down – and she saw that it had been laid down – that they were not going to live there, Blanche cared little whether it was let or sold; in fact, if anything, she preferred that it should be sold, as she thought it would make

Bernard more comfortable. So she gave up making out a case for keeping it, or for repairing it, and took the ultra-sensible view that the sooner it was sold the better.

"I knew you would be sensible about it," said Bernard.

As a matter of fact, it was the last thing he had thought. He had been convinced that Blanche would cling to this place with all her might, and that he would have a desperate battle to persuade her even to let it. He was surprised, but relieved.

They went back to London, and the next day Bernard put the whole thing into the hands of an agent, with instructions to offer Chalgrave for sale. He decided, if this proved to be difficult, to let it.

It did not prove difficult. An American who was over in England for the fall, and who, in addition to being rich, was a man of culture and knowledge, saw it in company with his wife, and they both fell in love with it. He bought it at once, lock, stock, and barrel, and subsequently spent twenty thousand pounds in making it more liveable.

It meant, of course, that Bernard ceased to be a Member of Parliament, and determined to let the London house during the next season. He detested London. He had never really cared for politics, and now he had enough of them. He settled to devote himself for the future entirely to looking after his estate and to farming.

Blanche's feelings on the subject were conflicting. She had looked forward to another London season with positive dread, feeling incapable of dealing with London life any longer; on the other hand, life at Alton-Leigh, with the constant neighbourhood of Walter and Rose Mary, or, rather, with the constant juxtaposition of Bernard and Rose Mary ever before her, was a nightmare, too. She did not know which was worse, and she could not help feeling that the presence of Rose Mary at Alton-Leigh had in some measure affected his decision.

Perhaps it had, subconsciously – but not consciously. Bernard thought that he had reached with Rose Mary a relationship of easy, natural intimacy; that they were excellent friends and perfect neighbours, and perfect "in-laws"; that everything was as it should be; that he felt towards her just as it was right and proper for him to feel towards the wife of his best friend.

Blanche knew what he felt, and knew that it was not really true, that the true situation was really different – how different she did not know – and the thought stung and exasperated her, and she despised herself for feeling this sting and this exasperation.

They got back to Alton-Leigh in time for Bernard's first shooting-party, and Blanche was too busy entertaining and looking after her guests to think of much else. They found when they arrived that Rose Mary and Walter were not there. They had gone off for a little holiday. Walter had suddenly been seized with a desire to see Venice, and they had gone off to spend three weeks in Italy, and perhaps a day or two in Paris on the way home. They were back again by the first of October, and they all settled down for the winter.

Bernard had urged Walter to stand as a Member for the constituency he had just vacated, and had offered to pay his election expenses; but Walter had refused to have anything to do with politics. He abominated politicians of all shades, and he was delighted that Bernard was no longer in Parliament.

He was happy now at Alton-Leigh. He was getting on with his book and enjoying the writing of it, and he felt that Providence had been unusually considerate to him, having steered him, after a certain amount of tumult and troubles, into such a clear, calm, secure backwater. He was heartily thankful, and every day he enjoyed being at Alton-Leigh more and more, and he little guessed at present, although he was a man of unusually fine intuition, that his presence there was being indirectly the cause of suffering to Blanche. The autumn passed without any untoward incidents.

In October, Bernard had a large party for a week's covert shooting, the guests consisting mostly of neighbours, with one or two London political friends.

At Christmas there was another large party, also of neighbours and relations, and this was painful to Blanche, as it recalled to her the Christmas party she had spent there before she was married to Bernard. There was a Christmas-tree as usual, and dances, and a servants' ball. There was hunting, but Rose Mary was not hunting just now, for she was to have another baby. Blanche knew it. Rose Mary had not said a word to her. But Walter had said to her one day, "Of course, Rose Mary has told you."

"Of course," said Blanche, who, indeed, had needed no telling, and had instantly divined the fact long before Walter had been aware of it.

Walter told Bernard, too, and Blanche noticed now that Bernard was always taking steps to see that Rose Mary should do nothing injudicious. The baby was not expected until the following June.

After Christmas, Blanche proposed that they should spend a little time in London. Blanche did not mind being in London during the winter-time. Indeed, she would prefer it now, as things were, to Alton-Leigh.

Bernard said "Certainly." There was no reason why she should not go up to London whenever she liked, and stay as long as she liked. She would not need a whole establishment, and a kitchen-maid would be enough to look after her.

"I shan't be able to come up much myself, but you can get on without me," he said.

Blanche was just beginning to think of packing, when one morning at breakfast Bernard said to her: "Oh, I forgot to tell you that I have let the house."

"Yes; for the season? You said you were going to – "

"No; for the whole year, from the first of February. It was such a good offer I couldn't refuse it, and if you go to London you can always stay with some one, or, if the worst came to the worst, go to the hotel."

"There's no one I could possibly stay with," said Blanche sharply, her eyes blazing. "It really is too tiresome of you. I think you might have told me."

"Well, you see, I had to settle at once, by telegram, and you were out when Jackson came to see me about it."

Jackson was the agent.

"That settles London," said Blanche. "I shall never be able to go there again."

"What nonsense! I'm sure Alice Pevensey would put you up in that huge house."

"Nothing is such a bore as staying with other people in London; it's a bore for oneself and a bore for them."

"What about the hotel? You could have rooms at… Smith's."

"Don't talk of it."

"I'm very sorry, but I never dreamt you would feel so strongly about it. I thought you were happy here."

"Of course I'm happy here, Bernard. That's nothing to do with it. I like going to London every now and then – to get clothes and see the shops, to see people, streets, plays, cabs – life."

"So you shall. I shall take a flat for you, if necessary."

But, in spite of this, nothing was done, and life at Alton-Leigh went on in just the same rut as before.

Rose Mary took to country life seriously. She was made for it. She liked the country, and especially the English country. She was fond of fields, birds' nests, cows, animals of every kind, and everything to do with a farm. She at once started a chicken farm, which was, so Bernard said, far better managed than his. Bernard gradually realised that Rose Mary was an expert in farming, and first of all he began by discussing matters of that kind with her, and he ended by consulting her and taking her advice. He never asked Blanche's advice on any practical matter. "Blanche," he thought, "takes no interest in that kind of thing." This galled her.

"I'm not such a fool as he thinks I am," she thought; "and I do wish he would sometimes tell me what he is doing."

She was as yet not aware that he consulted Rose Mary, as she made a point of never seeing them when they were together if she could help it. That is to say, she saw Rose Mary when she and Walter were asked to a meal, or she saw her when she went to see her at the Dower House by herself; but she never strolled into the garden of the Dower House with Bernard.

Bernard strolled in "to see Walter" more often than ever, and he found a way of seeing Rose Mary which she could not well avoid. He came to consult her on business. He had given Walter the chicken farm, and as Walter knew nothing about farms, or chickens, and cared less, Rose Mary was the person who undertook the management, and so it became imperatively necessary for him to see her. He used to ask her to look in at his dairy and the home farm, and to see the dairymaid, but this Rose Mary refused to do. It was Blanche's province, and if she did not take any interest in it, well, so much the worse for her, but that was no reason why she should interfere.

Bernard could not understand this; could not understand her refusal. Rose Mary did not tell him the reason of it.

One day Bernard said to Blanche – it was towards Easter-time; the skies were getting soft, the clouds feathery, and the trees red with sap, and they were sitting out of doors on the terrace looking at the hyacinths and the tulips: "It is astonishing what a capable woman Rose Mary is, and how much she knows about farming and animals …astonishing…and to think she had a Spanish mother."

"Some Spaniards are passionately fond of outdoor life and farming, and know a lot about it."

"But you would have thought that, having been brought up as she was...your Uncle Charles didn't, I fancy, care much for agriculture... "

"Probably her mother's relations did. It's fortunate, as she has to live in the country."

"Jackson told me he had never met a woman who had such a grasp of practical farming."

"Really!"

"I was wondering whether we couldn't let her manage the dairy."

"Oh no!" said Blanche; "that would never do. Mrs Potter would give notice at once."

"I don't think she would, and if she did – "

"What's wrong with the dairy? I went there yesterday. I thought everything was going well, and don't you think the butter and the cream are good?"

"Excellent; only Jackson says we spend three times as much as we need on it, and I really don't think that the results are such as to justify – "

"Very well; if any one else interferes with the dairy, I shall go to London and stay there. I mean that, Bernard."

"My dear, I had no idea you felt so strongly as that about it." (This was becoming a frequent phrase of Bernard's in talking to Blanche.) "Of course no one shall interfere. I did not know you even knew there was a dairy."

"You never asked me about it," said Blanche. She began to cry, and Bernard took her in his arms and tried to comfort her. "I go there every day," she said, between her sobs. "That is all the thanks one gets for trying to make you happy and comfortable, to be told I spend ten times as much money as I need, that I am ruining you, and that the dairy is bad – the butter nasty. Get some one else – you had far better. Any one would do it better than I can. I know I'm a fool and incompetent, and that you despise me. It's a pity you didn't marry a practical woman."

Soothe and comfort her as he might, Blanche went on sobbing. He promised her that the dairy should not be touched, that she could spend double as much as she already did, if she liked. That he had been a fool and a brute. Still she went on sobbing.

"What more can I say? What can I do?" said Bernard.

"It's not about the dairy I'm crying," she said. "I don't care a pin about the dairy. I'm crying because you no longer love me, and because you're sorry you married me."

"Blanche, Blanche, Blanchie, don't be so foolish; you hurt me. You make me quite wretched and miserable. What am I to say and do? I tell you what we will do for Easter. I'll take you to Paris for a fortnight. It will be a change for you, and you shall buy some clothes. We'll choose them together, and you shall spend money like water. Do stop crying, there's a darling. You have been here too long at a stretch. We have all been here too long. It will do us all good."

"What, just you and I?" Blanche said, drying her tears.

"Yes, just you and I…it's no good asking old Walter, he would never tear himself away from his book just now. But perhaps it would bore you just going with me."

"Bore me!"

"Very well, that's settled, isn't it? We will start next week, and get there in time for Holy Week and do our Easter duties there, and we will stay at the Westminster, and go to all the cafés and the theatres, and you shall go to all the shops you like, and get what you like, and it will do us a world of good."

Blanche smiled.

"I'm sorry to be such a fool," she said. "Would you really like to go to Paris with me?"

"Nothing I should like better."

"And you won't be ashamed of being seen with me?"

"What do you mean?"

"I mean of my looking so much older than you?"

"Oh, Blanche! don't talk like that. Only yesterday Roberts said you seemed to get younger every day, and you know how brutally frank he can be. He said you and Rose Mary were the two 'bonniest lassies' he had ever seen."

"Oh, did he?"

"Yes; he did…and I think so, too."

"Think what?"

"That *you* are the 'bonniest lassie' I have ever seen."

"Do you really think that?"

"Of course; you know I do."

"How can I know if you never tell me?"

"Oh, Blanche, don't be so silly! You make me angry."

"I mean it. I thought you thought me hideous – a hideous old frump."

"Blanche!"

"Do you really think I look nice sometimes?

"I think you are the most beautiful woman that has ever happened, as the Americans say."

"More beautiful than any one else… "

"Yes; than any one else."

"More beautiful than Celia Deacon?"

"My dear, how can you say such things? She's not to be compared with you. Celia Deacon, indeed!"

"But you used to be in love with her."

"Never."

"Oh, Bernard!"

"I liked her, and thought she was a good sort…and I admired her in her way; who didn't? But I *never, never* was in the least bit *in love* with her. She would be the first to tell you that is true. The whole truth."

"Well, I think her beauty is blinding."

"Yes, on the stage, I agree."

"And off the stage?"

"Well – but you would put her out – put her out like a candle."

Peace was now quite restored, and it was settled that they were to go to Paris.

That afternoon Bernard strolled round to the Dower House and found Walter and Rose Mary having tea. He told them of the Paris plan, and he said to Walter: "Why don't you and Rose Mary come too? It would do you good to have a holiday. You would stay with me at the hotel."

"It would be great fun," said Walter.

"My dear, it's quite, quite impossible – out of the question," said Rose Mary.

"Why?" asked Walter.

"Because" – she blushed – "because it's impossible."

"Oh, I forgot."

That evening after dinner, when Blanche was doing needlework and Bernard was smoking a cigar in the library at Alton-Leigh, he said to her: "I suppose Rose Mary couldn't very well travel now?"

"Well, it would be a mistake, and she wouldn't enjoy it. Why?"

"I was only thinking it would have been great fun if Walter and she could have come with us...only, as you say, it's impossible."

"What a pity!" said Blanche.

# CHAPTER III

The visit to Paris was a great success. Blanche enjoyed it immensely, and Bernard seemed to enjoy it too. Blanche bought a lot of clothes and hats, and she was admired by the French. One night they went to the opera, and there, sitting in the same box, was Madame d'Aurillac, who had in that box introduced Bernard to Blanche ten years ago.

There, too, was her husband, and the same old academician. Madame d'Aurillac had changed in these ten years, and, although she was still beautiful, her nine years of extra youth gave her no pull over Blanche, who still annihilated her. She was still her equal, and so far from suffering from the comparison, she still made Madame d'Aurillac look like a lady-in-waiting.

Madame d'Aurillac was charming to them both, and showered compliments on Blanche.

"It's not fair," she said to Bernard. "Blanche gets younger every year, and makes us all look old."

She asked them to dinner the next night *en petit comité*, and they went, and met at her house a middle-aged man about Paris, the academician, a playwright, one of the secretaries of the British Embassy, and Madame d'Aurillac's daughter, who was just out.

Bernard asked them all to come to Alton-Leigh, and M. d'Aurillac, who was fond of shooting, accepted for the pheasant shooting in October.

The next day they went back to London, and there Blanche found that Bernard had a fresh surprise in store for her. He had taken a small furnished flat in Mount Street for two months.

"I shall have to be a good deal in London this year," he said. "I knew you would enjoy having a bit of the season in London."

Although the season was the last thing that Blanche was hankering for – the thought of it nauseated her – she was immensely touched, and she was glad to spend a little time in London once more.

Bernard no longer felt obliged to go to political dinners, and the flat was too small for them to entertain, so that question was solved.

Blanche just saw a few old friends, and Bernard went a good deal to the House of Lords, and spoke once or twice. Blanche refused to go to balls, and as Bernard had no wish to go either, this was easy.

In the middle of May, Rose Mary and Walter arrived in London. They stayed with Walter's mother, Lady Alice Troumestre, in Mansfield Street. Rose Mary had come up so as to be in London when her baby arrived.

Bernard and Blanche spent three days at Alton-Leigh at Whitsuntide, and then they came back to London. Blanche's pleasure at Bernard having taken this flat was spoilt for her by the arrival of Rose Mary. She knew this was unreasonable. She kept on saying to herself that Bernard would have taken it anyhow; that it was the most natural thing in the world for Rose Mary to come to London; that it would have been madness on her part not to have done so, and yet…it took away the little, sharp pleasure that his act had given her.

The thought that Bernard looked in to see Walter and consequently Rose Mary every day was torture to her. She did not know he did this, and she never asked him a question about where he had been or whom he had seen. But he would quote Walter constantly, and he would often quote Rose Mary, so Blanche was certain he did see them every day, or nearly every day.

Bernard was unconscious of what was going on inside Blanche's mind. It never entered into his head to think she could be jealous of Rose Mary. He adopted the theory that they were the best of all possible friends. He would make plans for Blanche to go out driving with Rose Mary – Bernard's carriages, his brougham and victoria, were in London – and Blanche used to suggest it, but Rose Mary always happened, on the day Blanche suggested a drive, either not to be going out that day, to have a headache...or to be driving with some one else. Not that they didn't see each other sometimes. Blanche often went to luncheon with Lady Alice Troumestre, and sometimes Rose Mary came to see her, but it was nearly always with Walter; and when she went to Mansfield Street she would find either Walter or Lady Alice there as well as Rose Mary. They appeared to be friendly – in reality, each felt guilty where the other was concerned. Rose Mary felt that she had been accusing Blanche unreasonably of having taken Bernard away from her. She did not know what had really happened. She simply felt that Bernard might have cared for her if Blanche had not been there. She said to herself: "I know this is unreasonable, only I can't help it." She knew the whole story of Blanche's relations with Bernard while Guido was still alive. Walter had told her all about that, but she had always known before she was told.

As for her present feelings...nobody knew what they were; she did not even know herself – at least, that is what she would have said.

As for Blanche, she, too, accused herself of blaming Rose Mary for taking Bernard away from her now. But here she had no evidence, no real evidence. Bernard was charming to her – kind, thoughtful, generous, unselfish... he couldn't have been better...and yet there it was, gnawing at her like a canker. She was unreasonably, wildly jealous of Rose Mary. She could not help it. She felt that if it had not yet happened, it would happen one day. One day Bernard would cease to love her and would love Rose Mary.

"It is only natural," she thought.

And then there was Walter. She liked Walter extremely. Walter was just blindly, whole-heartedly in love with his wife, and thought of nothing else, and it never occurred to him to question anything that concerned her. Moreover, Rose Mary gave him no chance. She was an admirable wife. But Walter looked upon Blanche as their best friend, and Rose Mary played up to this and never let him suspect for a moment that this was not so. He delighted in Blanche's company, took pains to see her often, and consulted her frequently about Rose Mary. He quoted her to Rose Mary just as Bernard quoted Rose Mary to Blanche.

This was the situation when Rose Mary's second child was born one morning at the beginning of June. And then the unexpected happened, with all the suddenness and violence of a thunderbolt out of the blue. Rose Mary looked, seemed, and to all appearances was, extremely healthy. She had had her first baby under unfavourable and uncomfortable conditions at Constantinople without difficulty, and with comparatively little suffering, and now, directly the baby was born – it was another boy, and an enormous baby – she was taken ill, and was at once pronounced to be in great danger. Two of London's best known doctors were called in (by Bernard), and there were two nurses, a day and a night nurse, besides Mrs Charlesworth, the nurse who had been in charge all along.

Walter was distraught and as one demented, and he begged Blanche and Bernard not to leave him for a moment. They stayed at Mansfield Street all day. Lady Alice had given up the whole of the drawing-room floor to Rose Mary. She had sent her unmarried daughter, Hester, to stay with some friends in the country. Walter slept on the ground floor in what had once

473

been her husband's bedroom, while as a living-room they all of them used the study, a square room on the ground floor, and when the doctors came they would leave this room and sit in the dining-room.

The whole day passed in waiting for bulletins, in waiting for the doctor to come, in waiting for what the doctors would say after they had had a consultation, and then in waiting for them to come again.

Lady Alice used, during these first days, to tell Bernard to take Walter out of the house for a walk, to do anything with him to distract him. Bernard used to obey and do this, but directly they got as far as the Club, Walter, after taking up and throwing down several newspapers, would say they had better be going home again. He would keep indoors, as he did not like meeting Lady Alice after he had been told to go out. He looked haggard and white; he was on edge, but the more anxious he was the more good-tempered he became. He was consumed with anxiety, and clutched at each hopeful straw, at any tiny thing that could be construed into a hope, or an improvement, into anything that was not a definite sign of the contrary.

Lady Alice looked on at them all and said little. She had been brought up in the school of an old-fashioned generation of Catholics, who were taught to master their feelings and to efface "self," but she was devoted to Walter, none the less. She was ten years older than Blanche, the younger daughter of an impoverished peer and one of an immense family. She had been battered, but never defeated, by the world. She had never had enough money and always rather too many expenses; a poor but extravagant and careless husband; a son in the army; a daughter who hadn't married as well as she had been expected to; another daughter still unmarried; and two other sons who had died in childhood; but, in spite of all, Alice Troumestre had managed somehow to float upon the tide. In spite of her poverty, which was notorious, she had succeeded in making two ends meet. Her father had helped her while he was alive, and her brothers and sisters, some of whom were well off, after he was dead. She was not thought to be a clever woman, but she was brimful of tact and intuition. While her husband had been alive – he had been a clerk in the Foreign Office, with a passion for racing and écarté,, and an expensive taste in claret – she had managed to keep his affairs in order. Fortunately, he consulted her before making investments, and, although she knew little of such things, she was generally right. She always knew what it was best to leave undone, and in spite of a superficial gentleness, noiseless movements, soft grey eyes, a cooing voice, and a pretty manner, she had an inflexible will, and had not only been brought up in a school of high discipline at home, and for two years at a convent, but she had spent all her life in disciplining herself.

Her unselfishness was complete. Both her daughters were charming, but she was fondest in her heart, although she manifested impartiality, of Walter. He was the apple of her eye, and now she watched his misery with intense pain, but unflinching courage and determination. She did most of the nursing. She was an ideal nurse. She had the nurse's touch that is born and cannot be acquired. She was quiet and deft in her movements, minutely thoughtful and far-seeing.

Blanche used to wonder what she thought of her. She would never know. No one would ever know. Alice Troumestre had no confidants; you knew what she told you; you might guess by what she said or left unsaid, by what she did or left undone, but that was all.

The days passed in alternate hope and fear, and Rose Mary got no better. Walter became more distracted. Bernard's face was, Blanche thought, quite grey, his eyes were as if veiled, but he was outwardly calm.

Lady Alice, who sat up all night and only snatched sleep on a sofa every now and then, was perfectly serene.

She used to say every day, in her quiet, silken voice: "I believe Rose Mary is just a *little* bit better today; nurse thinks she had a slightly better night." Then she would say to Blanche: "Blanche dear, I think it would be perhaps a good thing if you were to take Walter for a drive this afternoon. Just round the park. It's good for him to have some air."

And Blanche would always find herself doing what Lady Alice told her.

"But, dear Lady Alice, hadn't you better rest?"

"I shall be all right, dear; don't worry about me. I had a beautiful sleep early."

What exactly "early" meant, nobody knew, as Lady Alice had certainly not undressed, and she had been to early Mass at half-past seven. She did this every day.

All this time, Blanche was going through what was perhaps the greatest spiritual crisis of her life. She was fighting a battle with herself. She was trying to conquer an overmastering temptation. She was trying hard, with all her might, not to wish for the death of Rose Mary. She went and sat in a church every now and then. She went to Mass. She tried to pray for Rose Mary's recovery. She prayed for it with her lips, but she felt, like Hamlet's uncle, that her thoughts were not with her words; that her prayer could not be heard, for the simple reason that it had not yet been made.

She hated herself. She despised herself. But she could not help it.

She felt that if she were finally defeated by this temptation she would have no more peace in this world, no more happiness, no chance of happiness in this life or the next. She did not expect to be happy again, but she felt now she was in danger of an infinite unhappiness, of being more lastingly unhappy than she had ever been. She saw all this clearly, but she felt helpless. Her heart was dry. She felt she had lost her faith. She acted as if she had not, but she felt inside her that she had not a grain of faith.

Rose Mary was thought to be worse. Although nothing had been said, it was felt that the doctors, who had talked so much hitherto about her marvellous vitality, about her strong, healthy constitution, were beginning to give up hope.

They came in the morning, held a long consultation, and said that nothing more could be done; it would be a question whether she could get through the next twenty-four hours. If she could, well and good. If not...they would come again in the evening. They told Lady Alice in private that they had hardly any hope.

The family met at luncheon, and Lady Alice talked naturally about the topics of the day, and looked as serene as if the bulletin had been optimistic. Her calm was infectious, and it soothed Walter's ragged nerves.

He was a piteous sight, and Blanche was touched by his appearance, and then she looked at Bernard, and she was alarmed. Bernard had a healthy skin and complexion, so that he always looked well, even if he was ill. But now, today, he looked ill, as it were, under his skin, like a woman who turns pale under rouge, or a coloured Eastern who turns pale in spite of his bronze complexion. Again, she felt the anguish at her heart, the sting, the moral toothache, the gnawing canker of jealousy.

After luncheon, to Blanche's surprise, Lady Alice came up to her and said: "I have sent Walter out for a walk with Bernard. I have told him to take him to the Zoological Gardens. Walter is so fond of the Zoo, and knows many of the keepers. There is an elephant called Jessie that always recognises him. They are going there in a cab. Bernard has kindly said we might have the victoria, and I am going to drive you down to the Convent at Oakley Common to see Mother Superior and Sister Mary Annunciation. They would like to see us. Of course they have all been praying for Rose Mary every day. But I think they would like to see us, and I think," she added gently, "that it would do us good too."

"But do you think we can go so far?…that we can stay away so long safely?" asked Blanche, who, although she really did not know the worst, divined the seriousness of the situation.

"Yes," said Lady Alice gently but decidedly. "It will be all right. We shall be back before the doctors come. There is nothing we can do here. Nurse Edwards is here, and Mrs Charlesworth. They both had some sleep last night, and Nurse Mason is sleeping. A little fresh air will do us both good, and you need it, Blanche dear, as much as any one."

Blanche was astonished that Lady Alice should choose this day of all days for the expedition. It was, she thought, the day of final crisis, the critical hour; and yet she calmly sent Walter out to the Zoo… Walter had no idea how serious the situation was; his anxiety had got to the pitch of being numbed…and she calmly suggested this long drive to the Convent at Oakley where Rose Mary had been at school.

Nevertheless, she found herself as usual doing what Lady Alice suggested.

"If anything happens," she thought to herself, "Walter will never forgive her."

In a quarter of an hour's time the victoria drove up to the door, and Lady Alice came down, dignified and with a look of great prettiness that is so engaging in the old when it occurs, and charmingly dressed in her black lace gown with a white rose pinned in her lace fichu, and her pretty, dignified black toque and veil, which rested naturally on her hair – once all golden and now nearly all grey – and her black parasol. Blanche was astonished at Lady Alice being able to look so fresh after all she had been through lately, and she looked at the ivory face and the soft grey eyes with admiration. Lady Alice was as pretty, Blanche thought, as an autumnal flower. "That is what people will soon be saying about me. But, will they? Shall I be as pretty as that in ten years' time, or shall I go to pieces suddenly?"

"You see," said Lady Alice, as they started, "they were all so fond of Rose Mary at the Convent. I had a letter from Mother Superior directly the baby was born, and I wrote to her as soon as we were anxious, and since then I have had a word from her every day. She is a remarkable woman."

"Mother Superior?"

"Yes; and so is Sister Mary Annunciation."

"She is an angel. The children were always all of them so fond of her."

After they had driven a little way, Blanche said to Lady Alice: "Do tell me what you really think. Do you think there is *any* hope?"

"There's always hope, my dear. If it's God's will that she is to live, she will live. We must pray."

"I do, only – "

"I know it's difficult," she said gently.

Could she, thought Blanche, have guessed? No; it was impossible.

"Difficult to have faith...just when one wants to. But one must pray for faith."

"It's a wonderful gift."

"That's why it's a good thing to see people like Mother Superior and Sister Mary Annunciation, who have got it. It's like having one's batteries charged."

"Oh, they are wonderful. I envy them."

"Rose Mary liked being there, didn't she?"

"Yes; very much."

When they arrived at the Convent, Mother Superior and Sister Mary Annunciation were expecting them. They went out into the garden, and Mother Superior, after talking to them both together for a little, led Lady Alice away and left Sister Mary Annunciation with Blanche. Sister Mary Annunciation had a wonderful countenance: there was a radiant good-sense about her; one felt she was made of the salt of the earth.

She asked after Rose Mary.

"We are all praying for her," she said. "I feel confident that she will get well; and if it is God's will that this should not happen, she will die after a happy and well-spent life. She was, she has always been, a *good* child. I'm afraid she has not a *happy* nature. But if she lives, her children, whatever happens to her, will be a source of happiness."

Blanche thought it odd that she should say nothing about Walter.

"Her husband is distraught," she said.

"Poor man, we have all been praying for him too. Such a clever man. We read his articles in the newspaper. They are so interesting. Rose Mary brought him here when they were engaged, before they were married."

They did not stay long at the Convent; they had a cup of tea and then they drove away. Blanche felt the better for having seen them both. It had been like a draught of mountain air. At the same time, she felt as if she had been looking through the bars of a shut gate into an unattainable Paradise.

On the way back they stopped at the Oratory.

"I thought we might both go to early Mass tomorrow," Lady Alice said; "and I thought I would like Father Byrne to hear my Confession."

"Yes," said Blanche; "and while you are doing that, I will go to one of the other Confessionals."

Blanche dealt with the situation in this manner because, although she was desperately anxious for some one to hear her Confession, she felt that in her present mood she could not face the penetrating moral scrutiny of Father Byrne. He knew her too well. Lady Alice, she thought, seemed surprised, but she accepted the situation, and after she had sent in her name, she was taken by a boy up into one the little waiting-rooms on the ground floor.

"I will wait for you here," Lady Alice said to Blanche, as she went upstairs.

Blanche asked for a priest, and was told that one of the Fathers was in his Confessional in the church. She made her Confession to a stranger and received Absolution, but all the time she felt she was playing a part, and in reality telling a lie. She did not feel an atom of *real* contrition.

When Blanche went back to Lady Alice in the waiting room, Father Byrne was with her; he greeted Blanche warmly. He was sympathetic and comforting.

"We must hope for the best. Give my love to Bernard and to Walter."

They drove home, and when they got there they found the situation the same as when they had left – neither better nor worse. The doctors had not yet been. Lady Alice went up to Rose Mary and stayed there some time. Bernard and Walter came in soon after they did.

The doctors came at nine o'clock in the evening. They did not stay long, but when they came down they looked grave. If Rose Mary could live through the night, all would be well, but there was hardly one chance in a thousand…they would not like to say there was a hope.

It had been already arranged by Lady Alice, Blanche discovered, that Rose Mary should receive the Last Sacraments that night. But Bernard and Walter were unaware of this. Lady Alice told them. She said it as if it were a matter of course.

"And you know," she added, "people have often been known to recover after receiving the Holy Oils – people who were at the point of death."

They were all standing in the little study when Lady Alice said this. The room was untidy. It had a grey Morris wallpaper and a bookcase full of the most miscellaneous books: St Augustine, Jorrocks, Ruskin, Walter Scott, *Les Mémoires d'un Âne*, Alfred de Musset, Ouida's *Strathmore*, Lord Lytton's *Lucile*, Lingard's *History of England*, Newman's *Grammar of Assent*, Miss Broughton's *Doctor Cupid*, Pascal, and the Poems of Crabbe.

There was a chintz-covered sofa along one of the walls, a large writing-table at right angles to it, between the door and the wall with two windows, which faced the street. Over the chimneypiece there was an engraving of Millet's "Angelus." On the other walls there were some coloured prints of Old London, and mixed with photographs of pictures in Florence and Venice... Titian and Giorgione, and a framed photograph of the interior of St Sofia. The curtains were not drawn; it was not yet dark. A pleasant noise of jingling hansom-cabs came from the street.

London was gay just at that moment. It had been a hot day. It was a delicious evening.

Bernard and Walter were both of them standing up when Lady Alice made this remark. They were both of them smoking – Bernard a cigar, and Walter a black Algerian cigarette. Bernard was staring at the window. In the street a barrel-organ was playing "Star of my Soul" from the *Geisha*. Walter was standing in front of the fireplace, looking down at his feet. Blanche noticed that his shoe-lace was undone. His white tie, too, was crooked. He was not aware of his surroundings – he was like a man in a dream. She herself was sitting on a little sofa on one side of the fireplace. Lady Alice was sitting opposite her on the big sofa against the wall, doing crochet. She was making a sock for the baby. The picture imprinted itself in every detail indelibly on Blanche's mind. On the hearthrug Walter's Airedale terrier, Sultan, was asleep.

As Lady Alice made the remark, which no one had expected, Blanche caught sight of Bernard, who was standing on her right, in profile between her and the window. As Lady Alice said the words, his whole face changed. It seemed suddenly to freeze, to be touched by an invisible frost, a stealthy, mysterious blight. He seemed to age in a second, to be drinking a cup to its lees; to be suffering real, hopeless, unrelieved, inconsolable anguish – a grief beyond all expression and all solace. Blanche felt a sharp stab of pity...she no longer felt the gnawing canker, and in that second she realised that up till this minute her love for Bernard had been an entirely selfish love. She had in loving him thought only of herself. In this supreme minute she thought of him, and she felt that her love for him was so great she would be willing to face anything that would make him happy, that she would do anything in the world, that she was prepared for any sacrifice, so long as *he* should be happy. In that second she offered a silent prayer: "Please, dear Lord, let Rose Mary get well, and make Bernard happy." At the same time she felt that she had been wrong all the time; that she had been the artificer of mischief and havoc; that she had devastated the lives of Bernard and Rose Mary, possibly of Walter. "Let me be punished, not they," she said.

At that moment the front door bell rang. Lady Alice smiled. "That is the priest," she said. She walked up to Blanche and took her arm. "We will go upstairs," she said.

They went upstairs, and Rose Mary received the Last Sacraments. She was conscious, and smiled at Walter. An hour later they thought she was dying, but she did not die; two hours later she slept. The next morning she was better; at seven o'clock she was still asleep.

Lady Alice called Blanche at a quarter to seven, as she said she would do, and they walked to Mass in a church in Langham Street. On the way there, Lady Alice said to Blanche: "It's all right; she will get well. The doctor said if she could live through the night she would get well. I thought she would."

It was the Octave Day of *Corpus Christi*. Blanche went to Confession again, and confessed a bad Confession – her Confession of yesterday. She felt calm.

As they left the church, Lady Alice said: "We mustn't forget to thank Our Lady," and she put up a candle in front of the image in the Lady Chapel.

"Do you really think it's a question of *thanking* yet?"

"I am sure of it."

When they got back, they found Walter and Bernard both of them down and dressed. They, too, had been out.

"They say she really is better," said Walter, but he was still too dazed to take it in, and Bernard looked white and drawn.

When the doctor came at nine o'clock he was delighted.

"The one chance," he said, "in a thousand has come off."

From that moment Rose Mary began to mend. In a week's time she had begun to be convalescent.

# CHAPTER IV

Bernard and Blanche left London soon after Rose Mary was pronounced to be out of danger, as the lease of their flat came to an end in the month of June.

They went back to Alton-Leigh. Rose Mary, as soon as she began to mend, made a quick recovery, and she and Walter were back at the Dower House by the end of July.

Bernard was radiantly happy when they arrived, and Blanche no longer felt the old bitterness. She had by one supreme act of self-sacrifice killed that...only she felt that the act would kill her, slowly perhaps, but surely. She already felt half dead. And now, day by day, she had to watch the spectacle of Bernard being happy with Rose Mary, of his being unhappy without her. He was charming to her – Blanche – considerate, kind, generous, but she felt now that she no longer counted in his life. She was a thing of the past. It was only natural, she said to herself. As for Rose Mary, she certainly did not seem to give Bernard any encouragement.

Her line of conduct now was the same as it had always been ever since she had come to live at the Dower House. She went to Alton-Leigh when she was asked. She never proposed herself to a meal. She sometimes went with Walter to see Blanche. She never went to see Bernard. She was busy with her own affairs. Bernard went to see her as often as he could, but

485

he seldom found her, and he never found her alone. When he came Walter was always there; often at tea-time he would stroll round to the Dower House, find Rose Mary and Walter having tea, propose a walk to the farm, and discuss farming on the way with Rose Mary. She was always just the same to him – open, frank, and friendly. She seemed to take pride in not attempting to be more, to take pride in sedulously avoiding all the arts of coquetry. And so the situation lasted all through the summer and the autumn. Walter had almost finished his book when he came back with Rose Mary to the Dower House. He finished it before Christmas; he hoped to get it published, and sent it to his publisher, who accepted it without hesitation, and sent it at once to the printer. It was included in the publishers' "Spring List."

Towards the end of November, Monsieur and Madame d'Aurillac and their daughter came to stay at Alton-Leigh for the pheasant shooting. At one moment it looked as if they would put off coming, as the political relations between France and England were strained, but everything quieted down, and Monsieur d'Aurillac was determined not to miss his shooting. Blanche thought at one moment that Madame d'Aurillac might cut out Rose Mary in Bernard's eyes, but almost at once she realised that this would not happen. M. d'Aurillac made love to her at once, as a matter of course, and she had some difficulty in curbing him, as he thought her resistance was merely an example of British hypocrisy, and was there only superficially, for the sake of form. And when he saw that he could do nothing, he simply came to the conclusion that Blanche had a lover already, and he soon made up his mind that it was Walter Troumestre.

Walter Troumestre was asked to the shooting, and Bernard had asked them both to come and stay in the house and to help Blanche with her guests, but Rose Mary had settled to be away for that week and to stay with her old friends and cousins, the Bromleys – one of the girls was married now. It would bore

Walter, she said, to go there, and he would enjoy the shooting. She would merely be in the way, so she went away for a fortnight. She didn't come back till Christmas. There was the usual Christmas party at Alton-Leigh, but Blanche and Bernard saw little of Rose Mary and Walter, as Lady Alice Troumestre and her unmarried daughter, Hester, were staying at the Dower House.

Among the guests at Alton-Leigh there was a young man who had just come down from Oxford, called Horace Crane. He had been at Magdalen College and was a good scholar, but had not done as well as was expected. He had enjoyed life too much, and, although neither sporting nor athletic, he had had friends in both those camps, and in those camps only. He preferred them to the more serious or the more artistic. At the same time, he was a great reader. His friends suspected him of writing verse, in secret. He was untidy and short-sighted, and he had a round, good-natured face like the moon, and an infectious laugh.

There was also staying at Alton-Leigh a certain Eustace Lee, who was a private secretary in one of the Government offices. He was just over thirty, good-looking, and active. He looked like a Lawrence or a Raeburn. His parents were dead and he lived with a widowed uncle, who, it was thought, might possibly leave him money, unless the whim took him to leave it to a perfect stranger, which was possible. Bernard had known him for some time, and Blanche had sometimes met him in London.

The rest of the party consisted of a neighbouring squire and his wife, an old brother-officer of Bernard's, Sir Frank Wigmore, one of the Under-Secretaries in the Foreign Office, and his wife, two of Bernard's female married cousins and their husbands, and one unmarried cousin, and Blanche's cousin, Mary Clifford, who was now married and was Mrs Legge, the wife of Captain Arthur Legge, in the 60th Rifles. There was also a priest, Father Rendall, whom Blanche had heard of, but whom she had never met.

These guests furnished the supers and the setting for a curious little drama.

Eustace Lee, as soon as he arrived, fell violently in love with Blanche. He thought that he had never met any one so charming or so beautiful in his life. He had always admired her at a distance in London, and had always heard of her charm, but he had never experienced it. Blanche at first was flattered, pleased, and amused, but she soon began to be alarmed. Eustace Lee was a violent man, sudden in his moods, and exacting in his claims. He was undisciplined.

The situation saddened her, for, she said to herself, "Why do I have the power of apparently fascinating everybody except the only man in the world I care for?"

Bernard, she was convinced, never gave her a thought – not in the way she would have wished. His whole mind and soul were absorbed by something else. He still admired her; she could still *make* him do anything, but that was all that could be said, and Blanche thought, as she dressed for dinner on Christmas Eve, and took great pains to make herself look nice: "As long as my looks last – "

She looked at herself in the glass. "It is all right still," she thought. "I may be eclipsed at a fancy-dress ball, and even then it was because I did not take enough trouble and did not wear the right clothes, but I have still got my looks." She was dressed in white satin and silver, with an emerald green velvet train hanging from her shoulders. "Tonight, at any rate," she thought, "I do look well."

She had been out of doors all the afternoon with the shooters, and the sharp air had given her the faintest touch of colour and had brightened her eyes.

She walked down into the hall, knowing that she was going to make an effect, and conscious, as soon as she reached it, of the critical eyes of her female cousins, who at once, she felt, dismissed her emerald green train as eccentric and hideous, and aware, too, that the men looked at her with admiration, and one of them – Eustace Lee – with more than admiration; but Bernard, as usual, took her appearance as a matter of course.

The party from the Dower House were dining that night, and even when Rose Mary arrived, a vision of health, youth, and beauty, she still felt able to keep her own. She still felt that nobody could compare with her there, that night, and that was indeed the universal verdict of every one present, except Bernard. Bernard was, as she guessed, so used to his wife's appearance, that he no longer really noticed it, although, if you had mentioned it, he would have abounded in praise.

She was taken in to dinner by Sir Frank Wigmore, and on her other side sat Eustace Lee, who, directly he got the opportunity, began to upbraid her.

"Why have you been so beastly to me all day?" he said in a sulky, irritable undertone.

Blanche was startled.

"What do you mean?"

"You watched all the others shoot. You talked to the others all through luncheon. You never said a word to me."

Blanche smiled at him.

"That was only an accident."

"But it's always an accident. That's what you always say. Why is it always an accident that you leave me out and talk to the others? Why is it always an accident that you never leave Horace Crane out?"

"Don't be so silly. I hardly said a word to him, and, please, don't talk so loud; every one is looking at you. You mustn't really talk to me like that, or else we shall have to stop being friends."

"Friends!" he laughed bitterly.

Blanche turned to her neighbour, who she saw was not talking, and had become isolated, and she began to talk to him feverishly.

Delighted at being taken notice of by his charming hostess, Sir Frank Wigmore launched into reminiscence. He beamed on Blanche through his spectacles, and Blanche, who up to that moment had thought he looked rather like Mr Squeers, was struck by the extraordinary blueness of his eyes – not a light blue, or a grey blue, but a deep blue, like a sapphire – and instantly two sayings flashed through her mind: one was what Gabriel Carteret had once said to her, that all men of action had grey eyes. The other was what Hedworth Lawless had often told her about an Arab, who, on meeting a famous Englishman, had said: "He's a cruel man; he has blue eyes."

"I recollect Lord Derby saying to me in 1866 – no, I'm wrong, it was 1867 – that Bismarck had said to him at the Paris Exhibition, that the Théâtre Français was the only permanent institution in France. It had survived all the Revolutions, and Napoleon had taken notice of its organisation even while Moscow was burning. Bismarck was a charming man in many ways. I recollect that at the Peace Congress at Berlin... "

Blanche's attention had drifted away like a balloon, although she seemed to be listening intently. She had been looking down. As the stream of reminiscence gathered strength and volume, she shifted her position slightly and looked across the table. Horace Crane was sitting opposite to her, between Walter's sister, Hester (on whose other side sat Father Rendall), and her cousin, Mary Legge. He seemed to be getting on with Hester, who, although she had not got all her mother's charm, had a marked personality of her own – frank, independent, and amusing. She wasn't pretty, but she had one of those faces that make you happy: grey eyes, a turned-up nose, and a way of letting out funny things, as if she couldn't help it, and she was always making disastrous mistakes – moral malaprops which were just to the point.

Blanche wondered what Horace's future would be. She thought he seemed intelligent – she knew him little, so far; she guessed in him a passionate love for beautiful things – landscape, music, poetry...how long would that last? Perhaps all his life...only it would be mixed with other things... He was enthusiastic, she could see. She had talked to him that day at luncheon, but without thinking about him, without thinking what he was like; what he did, what he felt, what his future was likely to be... As she was thinking of this, he suddenly looked at her across the table, and the look startled her...it was as if he had guessed by some telepathic process that she had been thinking about him. She felt uncomfortable, and repeated the last word which she heard Sir Frank say, which happened to be "office." There was a pause, and then Sir Frank said: "And that was the last time I ever set eyes on him."

"How *very* interesting," Blanche said. She had not the remotest idea who the subject of the discourse had been. Eustace Lee, she saw, was just about to return to the charge, so she quickly caught Lady Alice's eye and gave the signal for the departure of the ladies.

They were going, those of them who were Catholics, to Midnight Mass in the chapel. They spent the time until then in games and music, just as in former years. All this brought back to Blanche a host of memories.

She did not take an active part in things.

When the men had arrived upstairs into the gallery, both Eustace Lee and, to Blanche's astonishment, Horace Crane as well, made a dart for Blanche, and almost climbed over the furniture in a race to meet her; but she observed the first symptom of the manoeuvre and defeated it by asking Father Rendall, who was standing up between herself and the young men, to come and talk to her.

Captain Legge was sitting at the pianoforte, playing all sorts of popular tunes, ancient and modern, by ear, and every now and then some one would sing a song. Eustace Lee sat scowling

491

by himself in one corner of the room. Horace Crane leant over the back of the grand pianoforte, apparently listening to the music, but not joining in either the talk or the song.

Father Rendall was over fifty, and his hair – what was left of it – was grey. He had originally been a convert. His parents were well-to-do, North-country people in Lancashire, and after he had left Shrewsbury, where he was educated, they had sent him to learn French in France, thinking that it would be a valuable asset for him. They had destined him to be a schoolmaster. In Angers, where he went to learn French, he was converted, and almost at once he became conscious of a vocation for the priesthood. He was now a secular priest in London, attached to a special Mission.

He had a countenance in which the ascetic and rather drawn lines of the face and features were contradicted by the twinkling eyes. He was, as people found out when they came to know him better, an observer whom few things escaped, and an acute psychologist.

His life had been difficult. He had incurred criticism and met with much misunderstanding. He was continually falling between two stools; among radicals he was considered a reactionary; among conservatives, a radical. He was an eloquent but an over-suggestive preacher, and his preaching pleased some, but irritated others. To those who knew him well he was a mine of solace and sympathy. Bernard had known him for many years, but Blanche had only met him latterly. For years she had only known priests professionally, and had had no friend among the priesthood. Father Byrne she was fond of, but him again, outside his professional capacity, she only knew slightly. The only priest whom she had known really intimately – Father Michael Gardiner – was still in Rome.

Blanche led Father Rendall to a sofa at the end of the room, and they sat down.

Just then Captain Legge broke into song and sang the "Love Song of Har Dyal."

They listened in respectful silence, and when it was over Blanche said: "Are you musical, Father?"

"No," said Father Rendall; "but I'm inured to it."

The song was followed by some dance music. They could talk safely through this without interrupting.

"I wonder they don't dance," said Blanche.

"Young men are so shy about dancing; they're afraid of dancing badly."

"I think I shall have to go and do something soon."

"I think they are quite happy as they are."

"But those two young men are out in the cold."

"Perhaps they prefer it."

"But it's not fair on the girls."

Father Rendall sighed. "No, I suppose not. But you can't make them both happy." He looked at her with a twinkle.

Blanche blushed scarlet. She got up with the intention of walking to the other end of the room, but she sat down again. To any one else she would have said: "Don't talk such nonsense"; but she couldn't say that to Father Rendall. She felt he knew the truth, whatever it was, and that he had the right to tell it. She had always remembered Father Michael saying to her that priests were put into the world as into a pen, separate from other men, in order to tell people the truth.

"You don't mean *both* of them?" she said.

"Yes; *both* of them."

"I know that Eustace Lee is being foolish, but not the other one too. Not Horace Crane? I hardly know him. I never set eyes on him before he came here. Today at luncheon was the first time I have talked to him since he has been here."

"But when you were looking at him at dinner tonight when Sir Frank was talking to you, weren't you thinking of him?"

"Yes; I was. I wondered what he was like, and what would he do in life. I was day-dreaming."

"It's a dangerous thing to think of people...even if they're not there. If they are there, it's worse still. It only takes perhaps one thought to do the mischief – one thought of a particular kind. You thought of him with interest. That, for him, in his present disposition, was enough. Now the mischief has been done. It doesn't take more than a second to catch scarlet fever. The microbe is a small one, and it does its work quickly, quicker than thought."

"I'm so sorry you think that."

"I do think it."

"You must think badly of me. I didn't do it on purpose."

"I know you didn't…but it's not… "

"Please don't say what you were going to say…you were going to say I don't dislike it… I suppose I don't in a way; that is to say, I like people to be kind to me, to be nice to me, to praise me, to flatter me, if you like. I can't help that, because sometimes I feel starved and cold, and I am cold and hungry and long for warmth and food; but I promise and swear that I would never lift a finger to try and make any one fond of me, that when those two boys came here, I never gave them a thought. How could I? I'm old enough to be Horace Crane's mother. After all, Bernard asked them. I didn't. I have often seen Eustace Lee before, and he has never paid the slightest attention to me… I thought he put me among the people who are over. If you knew the whole story of my life, you would understand. I shouldn't mind telling it to you some day if it didn't bore you too much."

"But now I think you must do a little mixing."

Father Rendall was right; the guests at the other end of the room wanted looking after. Some had suggested dancing, and both Eustace Lee and Horace Crane had said with one voice that they did not know how to dance, and Hester Troumestre and one of Bernard's unmarried cousins, Elsie Hayward, were being left to themselves. Walter Troumestre was talking to Lady Wigmore, a dignified figure in black velvet and lace, with white hair and amethysts; and Bernard was talking to Rose Mary. The other guests were standing helpless, as if they expected to do something and did not know what to do, or rather as if they expected to be told what to do; as if they were soldiers waiting for orders.

Blanche at once put order into the chaos. She settled some of them down to a letter game at one table – word-making and word-taking – and she started a game of "My bird sings" at another table, and a four of whist was made up with the Wigmores, Lady Alice Troumestre, and a Colonel Wallace, a neighbour, the M.F.H. Rose Mary joined the "My bird sings" table. Bernard went downstairs, saying he would come back presently; he must see Jackson a moment.

That disposed of every one except Walter and Father Rendall. The latter went to look at the pictures with Mrs Wallace, who knew all about them.

Blanche was left with Walter.

"Do you know Father Rendall, Walter?"

"Not well, but I like him, and I admire him enormously."

"He preaches well, doesn't he?"

"I believe he does, but that's not what I admire most about him. What I admire is his knowledge of human nature. He is the most acute psychologist I have ever met. Talk of the French psychological novelists! He would wipe the floor with them."

"Really, that is interesting."

"He knows exactly what one's thinking…his intuition is almost like second-sight, and yet one feels that it all comes from experience, that he has learnt the rules of a difficult game."

"That's rather frightening, isn't it?"

"It is; one couldn't lie to him with any comfort."

"But I feel he would understand if one did – "

"Oh, he's charity itself."

Blanche had arranged that Eustace Lee should sit at one table, and that Horace Crane should sit at another, thinking that would ease the situation, but she had not been talking long to Walter before Horace Crane left his table where they were playing the letter game and walked up to her, saying: "I'm no good at that game; in fact, they've turned me out. I can't spell, and I can't think quick, and I can't see. I'm too short-sighted and too stupid. May I come and sit down here?"

"Of course," said Blanche, inwardly annoyed; it was just what she had wanted *not* to happen, and what added to her annoyance was that Walter at once said to Horace: "I'll go and take your place; I love the letter game." Horace Crane sat down next to Blanche.

"What a lovely house this is, Lady Windlestone," he said. "How you must love living here. And the garden – I have never seen anything like it! It's so unspoilt. Every room is perfect, and that library! Those books! Those folios – "

"I believe they are good. I know nothing about books," said Blanche, hoping to put him off.

"I suppose you don't need to; you know it all without books."

"I know nothing; I'm a complete dunce, and always have been."

"But you've known how to arrange the house."

"It's always been like it is now."

"Many people would have spoilt it… "

"The garden is – " She stopped.

"Mrs Troumestre told me you had improved that enormously; that when you first came here it was like a wilderness."

"So it was… "

"It's lovely now."

"Bernard and the gardener do all that. I have nothing to do with it," she said, lying glibly.

"Mrs Troumestre says you do everything."

Blanche felt foolish, as if she had said this on purpose to provoke contradiction.

Horace Crane laughed.

"It's no use," he said; "some people can't hide their talents. If you denied that you had good taste and liked beautiful things, on the stake or on the rack, I shouldn't believe it. People have atmospheres, and they can't get away from them."

"Do you think people are always what they look like?"

"In one sense absolutely. I mean I think all beautiful people are good."

"Oh!" ("He is very young," Blanche thought.)

"Or rather that you can't have a particular kind of beauty without being good."

"But what about all the Cleopatras, Guineveres, Mary Stuarts, Borgias? They weren't good."

"I don't expect they were beautiful. The pictures of Mary Queen of Scots and Cleopatra are hideous."

"They must have had great charm."

Eustace Lee had been watching this conversation, and now he could bear it no longer. He suddenly flung down his cards on the table, and said: "I can't play this game; I give it up." And he walked across the room to where Blanche was sitting.

The people he had been playing with thought he had gone off his head. Rose Mary looked at him with annoyance. He was white in the face, and he walked up to Blanche and said: "You promised to show me the library. Will you show it to me now?"

"Yes, certainly," said Blanche, hoping that Bernard might be sitting there. "We'll go and see it. Won't you come too, Mr Crane?"

Eustace Lee looked at Horace as if he could kill him.

"Certainly," said Horace.

They all three walked out of the room in silence. On the landing they met Father Rendall, Mrs Wallace, and Bernard.

"They both want to see the library," said Blanche, giving them an imploring look. "Do come and help me show it to them."

"I have promised to go and play 'My bird sings,'" said Bernard. "And you must play too," he said to Mrs Wallace.

Father Rendall smiled benignly on them and understood the situation.

497

"Yes; let us go and see the library," he said. And he filled up the gaps in the conversation, which was not being done by either of the young men.

They found the library empty, and Father Rendall forced the young men to look at the books, and as they were doing this, Blanche, saying she must see if everything in the chapel was ready, made her escape.

# CHAPTER V

There was so much happening the next day that Blanche managed, with the help of Father Rendall, to get through the day without much bother. There was a large luncheon-party; a general walk in the afternoon. Blanche took Sir Frank Wigmore with her, and showed him the garden, the farm, and everything there was to be shown, in detail.

At dinner she gave herself up to the elderly, and after dinner, when the young people danced in the gallery, she sat the whole evening with Colonel Wallace, listening to his stories, which she knew well, and refusing to dance with any one, on the ground that she had a stiff knee.

The next day there was shooting, and Blanche had a bad cold and stayed indoors. In the afternoon she was alone in the house with Father Rendall. Every one else had gone out, either with the shooters or for a walk. She asked Father Rendall to come and talk to her, and they went to her sitting-room, which was downstairs. It formed one of the corners of the terrace front, the opposite end to the library, and it had a large mullioned window. It was panelled and comfortably furnished with chintz chairs and sofas. There were a few pictures, which had belonged to her father and to her Uncle Charles, on the wall, and some other water-colours. Blanche disliked photographs, and loved colour, however humble. The books in her bookshelf were characteristic. They consisted of *The Imitation*, *Tom Jones*, *Undine*, *Barchester Towers*, *Jackanapes*, *Happy Thoughts*, Zola's *Une Page d'Amour*, and the poems of Herrick.

There was a wood fire burning in the stone fireplace, and the low December sun shining through the mullioned window made the dark panelled room glow like a pre-Raphaelite picture. She made Father Rendall sit by the fire, and gave him some cigarettes.

Blanche felt that the opportunity had come for telling Father Rendall the story of her life, and yet she felt it impossible to begin.

She was longing to consult him about the present situation. She could not do that without telling him so much. They talked about Alton-Leigh, its date, its architecture, about Sir Christopher Lacy, about Walter Troumestre's book, his new book, his future, his children, about Lady Alice.

"What a wonderful woman she is!" said Blanche. "She's so quiet, and yet she's got a will of iron. I always feel with her that she is reading me as a watchmaker reads the works of a watch."

"With one of those funny little tortoiseshell magnifying glasses screwed into one eye?"

"Yes."

"Do you mind that?"

Blanche laughed.

"No – not so long as people understand."

"You have found that rare?"

Here was an opening, but Blanche did not take it.

"I've nothing to complain of. I've known many under-standing people all my life. I've got two Russian friends who understand everything."

"You met them in Rome, I suppose?"

"Yes – in Rome." And instead of going on to talk of her Roman life, Blanche changed the subject. She felt she could not begin at the beginning, and, then, if he wanted to hear her story, surely he would just simply ask her to tell it him…but what would she say? Yes or no? She did not know herself. What she actually said was, "I think it's going to freeze."

"I suppose they skate here on the pond?"

"Yes; I can't myself, but Rose Mary skates beautifully; so does Bernard."

"You spent most of your winters abroad?"

"Yes; either in Italy or, when my Uncle Charles was alive, in Spain. Did you know my uncle, Charles Clifford?"

"No; I never met him, but I heard about him. He must have been a charming man."

"He was."

"Is his daughter like him?"

"I don't think she is – nor like her mother; I think she takes after some ancestor or ancestress of her mother's."

"But her mother was Spanish. She doesn't seem to me Spanish."

"No – she's a regular John Bull."

"*That* often happens when there's foreign blood. It creates reaction."

"I suppose it does. I had never thought of it."

"I greatly prefer Spain to Italy, although I have only been there once."

"So do I." Here again was a chance to talk about her life in Italy. Instead of which, Blanche said, "I think Russia's such a fascinating country. I went there every summer at one time."

"It must be. The Church music must be wonderful."

"It is."

"The Eastern Liturgy is very fine. Especially the *Panichida*, the requiem."

"I never heard that in Russia. I heard one in… Rome."

Again the conversation had come back to Rome quite by chance, but Blanche said: "I used to enjoy listening to the peasants singing in the village in the evening in the distance."

They talked a little about songs. Father Rendall talked of folk-songs and told some of his experiences in Scotland and the outer islands where he had been at one time. Suddenly, vividly, there came into Blanche's mind a song she had heard in the streets of Rome sung by a limonaro one May evening. She remained pensive and brooding and silent, looking into the fire.

"I suppose," she said slowly, "people always know much more about one than one thinks they do, and that when one is taking great pains to avoid a topic or a fact, or to hide it, one is really being like the ostrich? There is an opportunity for *him* to ask me a leading question if he wants to," she thought.

But Father Rendall did no such thing.

"The majority of human beings are self-centred," he said.

"And yet how much they talk about other people! Perfect strangers always know all about one's income and one's most private affairs."

"But rarely about the soul."

"Yes," said Blanche nervously; "I suppose that does not interest them."

"No." Blanche was glad now he had not asked a question.

There was a long pause. Then Blanche said: "The shooters will be back presently."

She felt that now the opportunity had gone. It was, for one thing, too late; she had just heard the clock strike the quarter – a quarter-past four.

"That's a beautiful clock," said Father Rendall.

"Yes; isn't it?"

"This house is full of beautiful sounds and chimes. And that little organ in the chapel has a beautiful soft tone."

"There is a ghost, too, that makes music." And Blanche told him the story of the ghostly minstrel. By the time she had finished the story, Bernard walked into the sitting-room. "Well?" said Blanche.

"Not a bad day – sixty brace. They want you to give them tea. Come down, Father, will you? Tea's in the hall."

They went downstairs. Blanche felt that the opportunity of telling her story to Father Rendall, and of consulting him, had gone for ever. She must do as best she could without advice; and, after all, what advice could he give? Perhaps that was why he had not encouraged her to talk. He certainly had not encouraged her. But Blanche felt certain that he had guessed that, although she wanted to talk in theory, she felt unable to do it in practice, and she now felt certain that, if he had asked her point-blank to tell him her story, she would not have been able to do so. She knew this by the way she had fought shy of one opportunity after the other as they had presented themselves.

"After all," she thought, "I hardly know him, and he knows nothing about me. If ever I get to know him well, it will be different."

But the question was how to get through the next few days.

Eustace Lee and Horace Crane were being a great difficulty. They were both of them staying till the New Year. Rose Mary was looking at her with no good eye, and Blanche felt that she was being blamed by her, and that Rose Mary thought it was Blanche's fault.

"Life *is* difficult," she thought.

It was to appear more difficult still.

She avoided Eustace and Horace as much as she could; Bernard noticed it, and said she was being rude to her guests – to his friends; he did everything to throw them together.

He complained that night as she was dressing for dinner.

"I wish you would be a little kinder to those two young men. I know they're young, and perhaps not very interesting, but I have known Eustace Lee ever since he was a little boy, and Horace's mother was always so good to me, and I never could repay all her kindness. You simply ignore them."

"No, Bernard; I don't. I like them both; only as they are young, I do think it is more amusing for them to talk to the young people than to me."

"Well, do be a little bit nice to them to please me."

Blanche laughed. "I promise I will," she said.

She wondered what Father Rendall would have said if he had heard this conversation.

After dinner that night she started a table for "Up Jenkins," at which she made all the young people play, and Father Rendall as well.

"Bernard," she whispered to him, with a smile, as they walked to the table, "says I am *neglecting* the young men."

Father Rendall nodded and his eyes twinkled.

It was not a great success. The young men had to bear it. There was no escape, and the result was neither of them had the ghost of a *tête-à-tête* with Blanche that night.

The next day they all went out hunting, and the evening again passed as usual, only Blanche was obliged to have Eustace Lee on one side of her at dinner, to his great delight, and he looked forward to a treat. He was disappointed. Colonel Wallace, her other neighbour, monopolised her throughout nearly the whole of the meal, and when she finally turned to Eustace when the mince-pies came round, he was so sulky that he would only speak in monosyllables. From the other side of the table Horace Crane looked on reproachfully. After dinner, as they once more settled down to games – Clumps, this time – Eustace was still mute with rage.

Blanche began to feel callous about it. What was she to do? It was Bernard's fault; he insisted on her talking to these boys. She had done everything she could not to encourage them; she couldn't help what Rose Mary thought; and, after all, what Rose Mary was doing, or rather what she had done, was surely worse. She was taking away her husband. It was true she saw little of Bernard and appeared to make no effort to encourage him, but that was the most dangerous of all policies. She felt she was beginning, in spite of everything, to hate Rose Mary again. All this passed through her mind while she was engaged in an active cross-examination in a game of Clumps.

"Did you say mineral?"

"No, not exactly" (from Hester Troumestre).

And then a chorus of "No," "Yes," "No, no, no, of course it isn't."

"Vegetable?"

"No."

"Animal?"

"Yes."

"Animal?"

And then the chorus again: "Yes, of course it is," while Blanche was thinking: "Is all this misery going to begin again? Am I going to be a prey to that demon of jealousy, that terrible envy, that black poison?"

"Is it found in Europe?"

"Yes."

"In England?"

"Yes."

"In the north of England?"

"No."

"Yes, yes" (from the chorus). "No, no."

"In the south of England?"

"Yes."

"Why was Rose Mary so severe, so hard? What more did she want? She had taken Bernard away from her. She was young. She was pretty. She was admired. She had all her life before her. And yet there she sat, frowning inwardly, Blanche felt, at her, although smiling outwardly. Was it her fault that these two boys were being silly about her? Weren't all boys foolish? Besides, if she only knew… "

And meanwhile the questions went on.

"Can one touch it?"

"Not now" (from some one).

"Could one ever touch it?"

"Yes."

"Last year?"

"No."

"A long time ago?"

"Yes."

And Blanche reconstituted to herself what she imagined Rose Mary was thinking. "It is too bad of Blanche. She is too old for that sort of thing; and to turn the heads of those two wretched boys who have done her no harm. And that's the way she neglects Bernard! No wonder he looks elsewhere – she's nothing but a heartless flirt! She has always flirted all her life, and that's what Papa thought, although he never said it. She even flirted with him. She took him away from me. It's a shame! However, whatever happens, she shall never have the chance of blaming me! That's what she's thinking," thought Blanche.

Was she right?

There sat Rose Mary upright, calm, and gracious, as usual, smiling and inscrutable. What was behind those grey eyes?

The next day it froze. Most of the guests skated, but Eustace Lee said he did not know how to skate. Was this true, or did he say it because he knew that Blanche didn't skate either? However this may be, in the afternoon, when they had done luncheon, Bernard said to Blanche: "Eustace Lee so much wants to see the farm, and I can't take him there this afternoon, as I must go to Alborough. Will you take him?"

Blanche was about to make some excuse, but she saw an irritated expression cross Bernard's face, and thought the only thing to do was to comply. After all, perhaps she had better have things out with him. Horace Crane had asked her in the morning to let him wheel her about in a chair, on the ice, and she had half said she would. She had first to break the news to him that this could not be.

"But surely you might come and see us skate on your way back?" he said.

"Yes," said Blanche; "we will."

Eustace Lee had no intention of doing this.

They walked to the farm, and at first they kept to safe topics, but soon Eustace broke out into an indictment of her conduct to him – a bitter list of his grievances.

Blanche pretended to be angry.

"It really is silly of you to talk like that. You do make things *quite* impossible."

"I don't make things impossible. I only want you to treat me as you treat any one else."

Blanche felt tired. She felt she knew so well the lines on which the whole conversation would proceed. It brought back to her the days when Adrian Tyne used to make love to her in Rome.

"I'm old enough to be your mother," said Blanche wearily.

"I don't mind if you're as old as 'She.' What has that got to do with it? The point is, *you* are *you*."

"Alas! alas!" said Blanche, with a sigh.

"It's not as if I asked for *much*," said Eustace. How familiar the words seemed to her. "I only ask – "

To Blanche's relief she saw Mr Jackson, the agent, walking towards them, looking red and comfortable, in his grey tweeds and brown gaiters, smoking a pipe.

"Here's Mr Jackson," said Blanche; "I don't think you've met him."

Eustace made a resigned gesture. Mr Jackson came up to them and Blanche introduced him to Eustace.

"Mr Lee so much wants to see the Home Farm," she said. "Can you come with us, Mr Jackson? You would show it to him so much better than I should. Or are you too busy?"

"Not at all," he said. "I was going there myself. Quite a change from the other day, isn't it? More like Christmas at last. I thought it was going to be a second green Yuletide. I suppose the young folk are all skating on the pond. Don't you skate, Mr Lee?"

"No; I'm afraid I don't know how to."

"Prefer hunting, eh? I hear they had a good day last Tuesday over Lowton way."

They reached the farm and inspected everything in detail: the cows, the pigs, the poultry, the dairy, the new silo. The conversation became technical.

At last, to Eustace's relief, Mr Jackson said he must look in at the office, and, after walking a little way back from the farm with them, he said goodbye, and took a turn to the left.

"Now, at last," thought Eustace. But at that moment, at the end of the long alley along which they were walking, a figure in knickerbockers was seen swiftly advancing in the distance. It was beginning to get dark, and Blanche could not see who it was.

"Who is that?" she said.

"You know perfectly well," said Eustace; "you probably told him to meet us."

"I can't see who it is. Oh! Horace Crane!"

There was a note of genuine surprise in her voice, which Eustace thought, or chose to think, a masterpiece of simulation.

Horace Crane walked up to them at a fast stride. He was swinging a pair of skates in one hand.

"Where are you going to?" said Blanche.

"I was going for a walk."

"Come back with us."

There was a heavy silence. They all three began to walk home.

"Well," said Blanche, "did you have a good skate?"

"I didn't skate at all."

"Oh, did the others skate?"

"Yes; *they* did."

There was a curious strain in his voice. What made Eustace angry made Horace sad. They walked on, Blanche making conversation, and the two men answering in monosyllables. Blanche pretended to be unconscious of the situation, and from time to time she made a remark and forced an answer. But she felt it was tiring.

As they reached the garden they met other members of the party, and among them Rose Mary, who looked at Blanche coldly. "She has never looked at me quite like that before," she thought, wondering whether it was fancy or not. They went in and had tea.

Before dinner Blanche went up to her sitting-room to have a rest. Bernard came and asked her how she had arranged the table for dinner.

"I haven't done the table yet; I'll do it later," she said.

This was not true. She had done it carefully, on an envelope, which was at present in her blotting-book, and the table had been arranged with care.

"Let's do it together."

"Not now, Bernard. There's nothing to fuss about."

"Who is sitting next to you?"

"Sir Frank takes me in, as he is going away tomorrow."

"And on your other side?"

"I had thought of putting Father Rendall. He wants to talk to me, I know."

"He sat next to you at luncheon. I want you to put Horace Crane next to you."

"Certainly, but why?"

"Because I think you have hurt his feelings."

"Really, Bernard, how can I have done that?"

"Well, I think you have. You know the young are sensitive. And Horace is shy. I do so want you to be nice to him for his mother's sake. I do so want him to tell her he has enjoyed himself here."

"Very well; of course he shall sit next to me."

He did. Blanche's nerves were on edge. Rose Mary was sitting next to Bernard, and looked more aloof and more unbending than usual.

Sir Frank was wallowing in anecdote. His high, prim voice went on like a musical box. Every now and then Blanche was conscious of the words "Foreign Office," "Salisbury," "Mr Gladstone," "Lord Pairnerston," "Cavour," "Crispi."

Suddenly Horace Crane gave her a long look with his moon face and round eyes. He was red in the face and looked as if he had swallowed a hot potato. She saw that he was trying to suppress a sudden surge of laughter. She was just in a state when the infection of laughter is irresistible.

Luckily at that moment Sir Frank Wigmore quoted a *bon mot* which had been made at Berlin about the Shah, to the effect that *"la nuit tous les chats sont gris."* Blanche rocked with laughter. Sir Frank, who had expected nothing more than an appreciative smile, was surprised, but pleased. Blanche, feeling that her laughter was excessive, and knowing that it was not going to stop at once, for she had lost all real permanent control of herself, managed to say:

"And I believe the Shah, when he stayed at Windsor, killed a sheep" (her voice trembled over the word "sheep") "in his bedroom. Imagine the Queen's feelings!"

She looked at Horace, roping him into the conversation, and they both of them doubled over the table with laughter, and fortunately at that moment Sir Frank's attention was engaged by Lady Alice, who was sitting on the other side of him. She saw what was happening, and came to the rescue. Blanche looked at Horace, and once more she was dissolved in a long, low peal of almost hysterical, wild, uncontrollable laughter. So was Horace. He sympathised with her so thoroughly. He enjoyed the painful ecstasy of this involuntary outburst to the full. They each of them tried to say something, but at each fresh effort they only each of them gave way once more. And every time that Blanche looked at Horace's moon face and round eyes, she felt inclined to laugh more and more hysterically. Tears were pouring down her cheeks. She was not making any noise, but her shoulders were shaking, her body was swaying backwards and forwards.

She looked at Horace in an imploring way, as much as to say: "Do help me to stop if you can." But his need of help was as great.

After a little while she managed to stem the volcanic deluge of laughter, and she began to talk to Horace.

"I haven't laughed like that for years," she said, drying her tears. "I didn't know I could. I didn't know it was still in me."

"It hurts, doesn't it?" said Horace. "But it's highly enjoyable, all the same."

"Do you think he thought I was rude?" She indicated Sir Frank, who was busy pouring out a new flood of anecdote to Lady Alice.

"On the contrary, he never had such a success in his life."

"Bernard will be so angry with me."

"I don't think he was looking."

Blanche knew that Rose Mary had been looking, and Eustace, too. He was sitting with a face like thunder on the other side of the table. She and Horace talked of other things, but every now and then a word, a smile, a look, started one of them off again, and as soon as one of them began to laugh the other caught the infection, and they would silently bend over the table and rock and sway, utterly out of control, but as quietly as they could.

Dinner at last came to an end, fortunately for Blanche, for she felt that if she had had to have another conversation with Sir Frank it would have been beyond her power either to keep her countenance or to provide the necessary jokes to excuse the volume of laughter.

That night there was a servants' ball, which simplified matters. Blanche was kept busy till they all went to bed, but Eustace would hardly speak to her, and Rose Mary, for the first time in her life, treated her with open coldness.

Up till then Rose Mary had always smiled at her; Blanche had guessed at a hidden disapproval, or aversion, but tonight it was more than that. She seemed to have taken off the mask and revealed a face of ice.

"It's not my imagination," thought Blanche. "She really does *hate* me."

# CHAPTER VI

The frost was followed by a gradual thaw. Bernard sent the young people out hunting; there was another day's shooting; and so the days passed till the last day of the old year, which was a Thursday. The guests left Alton-Leigh, and Lady Alice left the Dower House. Both the young men left on the same day. Blanche had managed to keep them in hand until the end of their visit, but only by humouring each of them, by giving each his innings, which, in the circumstances, was complicated.

Horace Crane left, feeling sad, but the richer – the richer for a new and possibly a lasting factor in his life; and Eustace Lee, dissatisfied and furious, feeling that he had been cheated.

They each of them wrote to Blanche.

This was Eustace Lee's "*Collins*":

> "189 RYDER STREET, LONDON,
> *January 1.*

"DEAR LADY WINDLESTONE, – I believe it is usual for people who have enjoyed the hospitality of their friends (if I may still call you by that name!) to write and thank the hostess when the visit is over. Although I do not suppose for one moment you would notice the omission were I to neglect to do so, I feel compelled to write to you all the same, and to thank you for your great kindness in having asked me to spend Christmas with you.

"When I was at school we used to read in the work of a man called Homer about a charming lady, a demi- or semi-goddess, I think she was, called Circe, whose name is, I am sure, familiar to you. She lived on an island. And she was a charming hostess. She entertained the guests and bewitched them by her beauty and her manners, and as soon as they were thoroughly charmed she turned them into pigs, boars, or any other appropriate shape.

"I don't know why I was reminded of the story during. my visit. But seriously, and all joking apart, don't you think it is ι ιfair and cruel to lure people gently on to a cold doom? Do you think it is fair to lead people on, to be charming, to be sympathetic, and then to throw them away like so much waste-paper? To throw them away, to treat them like the back number of an illustrated newspaper one finds in the waiting-room of a doctor or a dentist?

"*It's not fair.* Why did you ever begin it? Why did you ever take any notice of me? What harm had I done you? Why did you go out of your way to pick me up from the roadside, which was my proper place? Was it to make me realise that my real proper place was the ditch? It was not long before you threw me back there, and I'm there now *for good*, at the bottom of it.

"Well, let me stay there; don't bother about me any more. I think, though, a signpost ought to be put somewhere near the place where I was thrown, as a warning for others. Oh, it was cruel of you! Don't, please, say you couldn't help it; *you know that isn't true*! You know that you did what you did quite deliberately, with your eyes open.

"Well, I've got no more to say except that I wish I could hate you, as *you deserve*, but I can't – I can't. Oh, I long to see you if only for a moment! But that only makes what you have done worse and worse, and I hate you as much as I can. I mean it.

"Please remember me kindly to Bernard. – Yours very sincerely,

"EUSTACE LEE."

This was Horace Crane's letter:

"WALNUT CLUB, LONDON.

"DEAR LADY WINDLESTONE, – Ever since I left Alton-Leigh I have been thinking of all the things I should have liked to have told you, and of all the things I did say which I wish I hadn't said! It was a marvellous Christmas. Thank you for it very much. It was wonderful seeing you in that setting. I hope that you and Lord Windlestone will perhaps let me come again. I travelled back in a very full railway carriage with talkative fellow-passengers; one of them was a photographer, and the other was a man who knew all about safes, and explained to me the dangers of unsafe safes. I don't want to make a joke, but can't see how to help it! They talked to me the whole time, and I talked to them, but I'm afraid I didn't listen, and they must have thought me very absent-minded. Eustace Lee went in another carriage. I'm at home now for a few days, and then I go back to London to read for the Bar. It is quite useless; I hate the law and everything to do with it, and now more than ever. How shall I be able to pay any attention to all those knotty points and all those cases? I forgot to ask you whether you like Meredith's books; some of his characters remind me of you. If you have never read *The Egoist* and *Richard Feverel* and *Rhoda Fleming*, may I send them to you? I should love to talk over them with you. You are the only person I have ever met who understands what one means when one talks about these things. I shall never forget that last talk we had, the morning before I went away, on the terrace, and I thank Heaven that I sprained my ankle skating. Never did an accident happen at a better moment. I can't express myself, but you will know what I mean. I don't expect an answer to this, of course, but it would be wonderful to see your handwriting on an envelope. I should guess it was there even if it was hiding under a mound of legal documents and bills. Please thank Lord Windlestone for everything for me. Is there any chance of your coming to London this winter? I do hope so. Please let me know if you do. – Yours sincerely,

"HORACE CRANE.

"PS – Do you know these lines?

" 'You are at first hand all that's faire and right
And others' good reflects but backe your light.
You are a perfectnesse, so curious hit,
That youngest flatteries doe scandall it.' "

When the two young men had gone, Blanche thought that the incident was over. It had not been of her asking, nor of her making, and when they were there it had been Bernard's fault more than her own that she had seen as much as she did of them.

"Well," she thought, "I'm sorry if I did wrong, but it's over. They will forget me in a week or two, and all will be well." But whatever the result of the incident on them might be, and it was different from what Blanche foresaw, it had other results as well, which were not without their effect on her life. This is how it came about. The incident profoundly modified the attitude of Rose Mary. It was about two days after the New

Year, and Bernard, after a day spent riding with Jackson, strolled into the Dower House, and found Rose Mary downstairs, having tea by herself.

"Walter is upstairs; he is in the middle of the last chapter of his book and doesn't want to be disturbed. He's having his tea sent up to him."

"May I have some tea with you?"

"Please do. I'll send for some fresh tea."

"No; let me have that. I don't like tea that's too hot."

Rose Mary handed him a cup of tea and gave him some buttered toast.

She sat without saying anything, looking into the fire. The lamps had not yet been brought, and the firelight from the wood fire lit up her bright hair and her colouring.

"I wanted to see you, Bernard," she said.

"Yes?" Something in the tone of her voice made him slightly apprehensive.

"Yes; I wanted to see you particularly. I have been thinking over things, and I have come to the conclusion that… "

"That what?"

"That things can't go on like this…as they are now."

"What do you mean?"

"Oh, Bernard, please don't make me explain. You do know perfectly well."

"Honestly and truly, I swear I haven't the slightest idea what you mean."

"Well, I mean this life… You…you know… you occupy too big a place in my life…and I can't face it any more – and we shall only bring misery to everybody – to ourselves, to Walter, to Blanche… "

"Has Blanche said anything to you?"

"Not a word; she never would."

"And Walter?"

"Walter is unconscious of everything, and thinks everything perfect."

"Well, then, what's the matter?"

"I'm only thinking of the future. I mean, I think we ought to take things in time before it's too late…to nip the disagreeable things in the bud."

"But what disagreeable things?"

"Well – I see too much of you."

"I never heard such nonsense. I hardly ever see you. Never alone."

"Alone or not, it doesn't matter. You have made a habit of coming here, of talking to me, of consulting me – "

"Well, why shouldn't I? It would be rather odd, wouldn't it, if I couldn't come and see my best friend and his wife, when they are my neighbours, and live a few hundred yards from my front door."

"Bernard, please don't make it difficult for me. You know. You must know."

"But I *don't* know."

"Well, there are others besides ourselves."

"What others?"

"Well, Walter's mother thinks it a pity."

"Did she say anything?"

"Not directly, but she talked about the danger of giving *scandal*. How important it was for Catholics not to give scandal. I know exactly what she means."

"Well, what do you propose to do? What do you propose that I should do?"

"Well, it comes to this…if we can't manage to live a little differently, Walter and I will have to go away."

"To leave the Dower House?"

"Yes; for good."

"I'll do anything you like to prevent that."

"You see, as soon as Walter's book is published, he will get restless, I think, and want to travel."

"When will it be published?"

"Not before May. It can't go to the printer before the end of the month."

"Well, what do you want me to do, exactly?"

"I want you not to come here so often."

"I thought I came so seldom."

"Every day, and sometimes twice a day...but it's not that. It's your way of treating one as if nobody else existed. A way of consulting one before everybody, which people must think so odd."

"But surely no one thinks – "

"I don't think any one does think anything, and I don't really care what they think, what the outside world thinks, but I *do* care what Walter thinks, what Lady Alice thinks, what Father Rendall thinks."

"Did he say anything?"

"No; not a word. Of course he talks of detachment in the abstract. He thinks all 'friendships' are a mistake...between men and women, that is to say...and I don't think he believes that they can exist."

"Well, do you want me never to see you again? What nonsense! How can we help seeing each other?"

"It's not the actual seeing one another that I mean. It's the *way*. Well, I ask you to do this for my sake. Even if you think it mad, even if you think...whatever you think. I can't go on living here unless you do. That's the long and short of it. I have thought over it thoroughly, and I have quite made up my mind."

"But I still don't understand what you are asking me to do."

"I want you not to come and see me when Walter is not here; not always to consult me before people...not to come here so often, not to ask us so often to Alton-Leigh."

"I see what has happened."

"What?"

"Oh, nothing."

"Nothing has happened except inside myself. You know, Bernard, that I have a vile character in many ways. I am selfish, obstinate, bad-tempered, jealous, but I have one good quality. I am honest. I don't think what we are doing is fair – not fair on Walter."

"And on Blanche?"

"No, nor on Blanche, of course." As Rose Mary said this, her expression hardened; but Bernard did not notice it.

"Well, I think it's madness."

"Even if it is, will you do it to please me?"

"I'll do anything you like."

"Because, you see, otherwise we would have to go. I really mean it."

"I'll do anything you like, only it will look so silly – if I suddenly – if we suddenly begin to avoid you. What will Walter think?"

"Don't bother about Walter. I understand Walter, and that will be all right. I promise you."

"But you will still come to Alton-Leigh?"

"Of course, whenever you and Blanche ask us…only it's just the way…and if you ask us and I say, no, please don't insist, as you always do. That does make it so difficult."

"Very well. I'll try not to."

"That's it; let's try – and if it doesn't succeed…well, Walter and I must go, that's all… "

"You shan't do that," muttered Bernard.

At that moment Walter came in, and a shade of disappointment passed over his face when he saw Bernard, and a tiny shade of relief when Bernard said, "I must be going home." He was just going to say, "You'll come and dine, won't you?" but he checked himself. He thought the whole thing was nonsense, but it was better to humour Rose Mary for the moment, as long as she was in this strange mood. He said good night, and went home.

Directly he went, Walter said to Rose Mary:

"I want to read you my last chapter. I want to know what you think of it."

"I'll ring for the lamp," said Rose Mary.

The lamp was brought. Rose Mary sat down on the sofa, on one side of the fire, Walter in an arm-chair on the other side. The tea was taken away. He began to read. Rose Mary had been for a long walk that afternoon by herself. It was a sharp, windy day. It had made her sleepy.

The last chapter of Walter's book was called "The Charm of Byzantium."

She thought the opening sentences sounded well.

But soon, strive as she would, she fell asleep. Walter read on, absorbed in his work, without noticing. As he reached the last page he looked towards her, and said: "I believe you're bored. I believe you're asleep."

She was deep in that sound, irresistible sleep which comes to one sometimes in public places: in church, during a sermon; at theatres and concerts, when one is straining every nerve to keep awake.

She opened her eyes mechanically.

"Oh no," she said; "I was just shutting my eyes because of the light. I think it's excellent."

Walter read on to the end.

"That's all," he said. "Well?"

"Well, I think it's *excellent*." She could think of nothing more particular to say. She had heard so little of it. "I liked that last bit about the walls."

"Is there anything you think wants altering?"

"Nothing."

"You don't think it's too long?"

"Not a bit. I must run up and see the babies."

"Are we dining at Alton-Leigh tonight?"

"No; not tonight."

"Thank God! I don't want to go out again." But Walter reflected that Blanche was a more helpful critic than Rose Mary. Whenever he had read her anything, she had always had some suggestion to make – a word she thought better away, a paragraph which was too long or too short.

Rose Mary, as she went up to the nursery, thought she had indeed been right in launching her ultimatum to Bernard. But the motive of it had not been fear of what Walter might feel, for she felt safe on that score, nor any criticism on the part of her mother-in-law. She had exaggerated that in talking to Bernard.

The motive had been her pride. Rose Mary had been watching Blanche's conduct with Eustace Lee and Horace Crane. She considered that Blanche had been leading them on, and playing one against the other. This was, in reality, unfair, as Blanche merely dealt with the situation as best she could; that she exercised a fatal fascination over both these young men was her misfortune. No doubt it pleased and flattered her, but chiefly because it made her feel she had something still left to please Bernard. But she did not lift a finger in encouragement, and she had been spurred on to be more civil to them by Bernard.

But Rose Mary, in observing the episode, made up her mind that she would never behave like that. If she had a lover, she would have a lover, but there would be none of that subtle coquetry – none of those insidious flirtations masked under the names of interest and friendship. "Then," she reflected, "perhaps people are saying the same thing about me and Bernard now!" A word that her mother-in-law said to her strengthened her suspicion, although it was but the slenderest hint.

"Well," she thought, "if that is what they think, they shall never think it again. Whatever happens, Blanche shall never have to complain of me."

As for Bernard, he had been at first bewildered. He then thought it was a passing mood, a fitful whim on the part of Rose Mary, due to some little cause which he was unaware of. Then he thought to himself, "I suppose the real reason is that Blanche has not been kind to her lately." He reviewed Blanche's conduct in his mind, and remembered occasions when she had talked of Rose Mary in rather a sour way.

"The worst of Blanche is," he thought, "that she's so infernally jealous in small things, and about things that don't matter. I wonder what she would do and say if I really were to give her cause for jealousy, if one day I really were to get more fond of some one than of her?"

When he got home he went straight up to Blanche's sitting-room and threw himself into an arm-chair.

"You're late," she said, with a lovely smile. "Will you have some tea?"

"No, thank you. I've had tea."

"At Jackson's?"

"No; I just looked in at Walter's. Walter has nearly finished his book. We shall have to celebrate the event."

"Yes; we must, indeed."

"Talking of Walter," he went on, "I do wish, Blanchie dear, you could be just a little bit more friendly to Rose Mary."

"More friendly to Rose Mary? You must be out of your mind. My dear child, what could I possibly do for Rose Mary more than I am doing at present?"

"It's always I who have to do all the asking."

"On the contrary, I asked Walter to luncheon yesterday."

"You ask Walter, but not Rose Mary."

"I ask whichever I happen to see first."

"I don't believe you like her, and I think she feels it. You've no idea what a sensitive child she is. Of course I know you don't think there's much in her, and that I see more in her than there is. But she is sensitive. You must admit that. Every one agrees about that. Lady Alice was only saying to me the other day how sensitive she thought Rose Mary was."

Blanche felt herself getting hot with rage, but she controlled herself.

"I promise you, Bernard, you're being too, too foolish for words. I'm always asking both of them here, only I think when people live so near, and have interests of their own, it doesn't do to be always bothering them. Besides, they both know that they can come here as often as they like and whenever they like. They don't need asking. They understand that perfectly well."

"Ah! That's just it! That's just where you are wrong! They need asking more than if they lived fifty miles off. And it's *you* who ought to do the asking, not always me. If you don't do it, they of course think that you don't want them to come."

"Oh, my dear Bernard," Blanche said, with a weary sigh, "what has put this into your head? Has Rose Mary said anything to you?"

"Oh no, of course not; she never would."

"Has Walter?"

"Is it likely?"

"Well, then, who? – what?"

"Nobody has said a word, but one can't help noticing things, and seeing, too, that other people notice them, and I could see that everybody at Christmas thought you were not being over-amiable to Rose Mary."

"Who's everybody?"

"Well, Lady Alice, for instance."

"Did she say anything about it?"

"No, nothing; but I could see that she was astonished."

"Astonished? At what?"

"Oh, well, at your general attitude."

"My general attitude?... But, Bernard dear, what more could I do? What more *can* I do? They were here every day and all day."

"It's not the quantity, it's the *quality*. It's the way of doing things. If you could only look a little more pleased to see her."

"Do you think she looks pleased to see me?"

"Yes; that's just it; she does, and then you freeze her off."

"Well, I'll try and do better in future. Only I do think it's absurd. Rose Mary is independent and knows quite well what she wants, and when she wants to come here."

"You don't mean to say you think that she thrusts herself upon us?"

"No; I mean she would tell me if she thought I was being unkind to her."

"She *is* frank, that's true; but then she's got immense delicacy."

"Well, Bernard, I promise I'll try to do better. I'll send her a note and ask her to come and dine tomorrow night. Colonel Wallace and Kitty are coming, and so is Dr Warley."

"No; not tomorrow. Wait a little. You're so impetuous."

Blanche smiled sadly.

"I can't do right," she said.

Bernard left the room, and Blanche reflected that he was behaving just as Guido used to behave about Mrs Winslope.

"History repeats itself," she said to herself.

And she sat a long time in front of the fire, brooding over the difficulties of the situation.

"It's insoluble," she said to herself, "unless one cuts it. I haven't the courage to do that."

# CHAPTER VII

Blanche carried out Bernard's instructions, and Bernard, so far from paying any attention to what Rose Mary had told him, thought that "all that nonsense was over." It was simply, no doubt, owing to Blanche not having taken quite enough trouble. Walter and Rose Mary were asked more and more frequently to Alton-Leigh. Bernard looked in at the Dower House regularly every day, and, whether he saw Rose Mary or not, he always saw Walter.

Rose Mary understood that it was useless to say any more. But she did not accept defeat. Walter's book was finished, and had gone to the printers. She suggested that they should go to London. It would be more convenient for him to correct the proofs there, and Lady Alice had asked them to stay with her. Walter, who, now that his book was finished, had begun – as Rose Mary had foreseen – to be restless, was pleased with the idea, and it was settled that they should go to London in February.

It was Walter who told Bernard they were going. He talked of it as just a short visit. Bernard felt no real alarm. Rose Mary had made him no further reproaches; indeed, he had not had any intimate conversation with her since that afternoon when she had made him her strange request. He had seen her more often than ever, but never alone.

Walter and Rose Mary left the Dower House at the beginning of February, and Blanche and Bernard were left to themselves in the country.

Blanche was blissfully happy. She had not been alone with Bernard for such a long time. Ever since the preceding August there had been a succession of guests in the house, and she was tired, tired of being the hostess, tired of ordering dinner, tired of making arrangements, tired of looking after people and things – deadly tired. Now she felt she could have a rest. She was so sensitive to moral atmospheric conditions that the mere sense of this temporary freedom made her spirit expand. As the spring began its slow, stealthy invasion that year, she seemed to grow younger. She saw this rejuvenation reflected in the way Bernard looked at her.

"He is," she thought, "still a little bit fond of me still just a tiny bit proud of me."

Bernard watched Blanche and thought he had never seen her more beautiful than she was that year. What grace she had! What charm! Who was there the least bit like her? He ought indeed to consider himself lucky.

He asked Blanche one day if she would like to spend any time in London.

"The house is there, if you would like to go. I don't mean to let it this year."

"Let's stay here," said Blanche; "it's so delicious. I do love watching the early spring. What should we do in London?"

Bernard agreed that it would perhaps be a pity to go to London.

"I thought you might be bored here," he said, "alone with me."

"Oh, Bernard, if you knew."

February and March went by, and those months seemed to Blanche almost unreal in their happiness. It was uncanny, she thought, and too good to last.

They were expecting Walter and Rose Mary back for Easter. Walter had corrected the proofs of his book. It was to come out at the end of May, just after Easter.

Bernard had asked a few people to spend Easter with them, and amongst others he had suggested to Blanche that Eustace Lee and Horace Crane should be asked.

"I don't think Eustace Lee could come," said Blanche. "I think it would be useless to ask him."

"Well, what about asking Horace Crane?"

"I think that he will go home for Easter. I don't think we ought to encourage him not to go home. It's probably the only time his relations set eyes on him."

"Very well; just as you like."

Blanche, as a matter of fact, knew that Horace Crane had no plans for Easter. He wrote to her constantly and kept her fully informed of his doings. From Eustace Lee she heard nothing directly.

Shortly before Easter, when Bernard was looking forward to seeing Walter and Rose Mary back at the Dower House, Bernard heard from Walter again. Walter told him that they had changed their plans. They had been asked to spend Easter in Florence, with Walter's married sister, Marian, who had taken a villa there for a month, and after that they were going to stay on in London. His sister Hester was engaged to be married to a nice sailor, and they were going to stay in London to help Lady Alice with the trousseau and with the wedding arrangements. The sailor was the eldest son of the well-known Admiral, Sir Clement Houston. He was a young man about twenty-five. He was doing well and was sufficiently well-off to marry, so everything was satisfactory. Hester was radiantly happy. Blanche was secretly delighted by the news. Bernard concealed his disappointment. He did not admit that he was disappointed.

Blanche and Bernard were having breakfast in the small library.

"I suppose we ought to go up to London for Hester's wedding," he said.

"Well, I don't think it's necessary."

"I think it would hurt Walter's feelings and Lady Alice's if we didn't."

"When is it?"

"The first week in June."

"I think *you* ought to go in any case."

"And so must you. They will all be hurt if you don't. It would look odd if I went and you didn't."

"Very well."

"James Langton" (one of Bernard's House of Commons friends) "can't come after all," Bernard said, handing Blanche a letter. "But I have had a letter from Eustace Lee, asking whether he could come just for Easter, so you see I was right. That will do beautifully, won't it?"

The only other guests who were expected so far were Mr and Mrs Roden and Margaret, their second girl; the eldest daughter, Alice, was married.

"It's fortunate," said Bernard, "that he's proposed himself, otherwise we should have had nobody to talk to Margaret Roden."

"Well, as a matter of fact, I have had two letters from people asking to come, this morning," Blanche said – "one from Horace Crane and the other from Father Michael Gardner, whom I used to know very Well in Rome. He was a friend of your mother's. But that would make us too many men, wouldn't it?"

"Not at all. Of course, they must all come."

Blanche felt immensely weary. She had thought that that situation was over. "It will begin all over again," she thought. "However, they will have to get used to each other. Nothing ever stops in this world."

"Very well," she said. "I will write to them today."

529

"Father Michael will be a help," she thought. "He will understand."

The Rodens, Jane, Eustace Lee, and Horace Crane, all of them, arrived just before Easter. Eustace Lee was furious when he saw Horace Crane. Horace Crane was resigned. Eustace made Blanche a scene as soon as he had the opportunity, and she told him she could not face these scenes any longer.

"I haven't the strength," she said. "If you choose to come here, you must put up with the guests. You must put up with Horace, otherwise either you or I must go. I mean it in all seriousness. If you want to be friends, you must be sensible. You know quite well that I have done nothing to encourage either you or Horace. If it weren't for Bernard, neither of you would be here."

There was something in her grave seriousness that calmed Eustace, for the time being, at any rate. He promised to "be good." In spite of this, and in spite of the attempts which he did make to carry out his promise, his presence was a strain on Blanche.

Father Michael Gardiner arrived on Easter Monday. Blanche was delighted to see him again. She had not seen him since she had left Rome for good. She did not find him much altered. He was whiter and thinner, but she thought he looked on the whole just the same, although he was now nearly seventy.

The morning after he arrived they went for a walk together.

Blanche told him a great deal of what had happened to her.

They walked through the long brown alleys, in which here and there there was a green tree, into the wood. The grass was starred with daffodils, and the hedges were full of primroses and white violets.

"It's nice to smell an English spring again," said Father Michael. "I never thought I should again." There was a pause. "I was delighted when I heard about your marriage," he said, after a time.

"Were you, Father Michael?"

"Yes. Hadn't I every reason to be delighted?"

"I'm not sure...not if you knew the whole truth."

"What do you mean?"

"I mean that I'm nearly sure, quite sure in fact, that Bernard wanted to marry my cousin, Rose Mary. He came one day to tell me this and I misunderstood him...misunderstood him deliberately, so that he thought *I* thought he was proposing to me, and he hadn't the heart to undeceive me."

"Are you sure? It seems to me fantastic and improbable."

"No; it's quite true. He was fond of me then still in a kind of way. I mean, I could make him do anything. I almost can still! – only it's a question of *making*. But he was really in love with Rose Mary, and I couldn't give him up. I couldn't. Only I am, of course, being terribly punished...he is more and more in love with Rose Mary every day."

"My dear child, what are you telling me?"

"She hates me, Father Michael, with all her soul, but she's so proud, that she is enjoying feeling superior. She doesn't encourage Bernard; she hardly sees him; she's gone to London now to get away from us."

"Well?"

"But she loves him all the same. She's eating her heart out with love of Bernard and with hate of me."

"I can't help thinking you're imagining things."

"I'm not. After you have been here a few days – no, one day – you will see that I mean nothing to Bernard now, nothing really. His heart and mind and soul are somewhere else. He is still proud of me, as I suppose I'm still rather nice-looking; but that won't last long, and there he will be a young man with an old woman tacked on to him, an old woman who bores him, and the worst of it is that I am fonder of him than ever. I adore him, Father Michael; he's my *whole life*. I am only a small part of his. And I'm being punished in other ways, too. Bernard asked two boys here for Christmas. They are both fond of me. I am making both of them unhappy, without meaning to.

I haven't encouraged them. I've done nothing, and there it is. They each of them proposed themselves. Bernard insisted on asking them. He says I'm not nice to them. He sees nothing. After Christmas I thought it was all over, instead of which – "

"You find it is just beginning."

"Well, I hope it's not quite as bad as that. It's extraordinary how everything happens at an unexpected moment, just when one thinks all is safe."

" 'Just when we're safest there's a sunset touch.' You know the poem?"

"Yes; Robert Browning, isn't it? A friend I knew years ago in Rome used to quote it to me when Browning was quite unknown – when we called him 'a *Mr* Browning.' Papa knew him only as a man who liked music and dined out. That's always what has happened to me. It's always when I've felt perfectly safe that something unexpected and catastrophic has happened. I suppose it really means that the temptations that one thinks one has successfully resisted were really not temptations at all. One is proud of a victory when in reality there has been no battle. All through the most difficult years of my life, when Guido was ill, everything seemed so easy. I felt safe and settled, and never gave a thought to other things and people who used to take notice of me – and make up to me – and there were dozens. It seemed so easy not to pay attention to them. The reason was, I suppose, I hadn't even an inclination to pay attention to them. Directly I felt the real inclination, the real temptation, directly I met Bernard, the walls of my defences fell like the walls of Jericho – you remember – only *before* the trumpet sounded, and I suppose that's exactly what will always happen to me."

"God sends us temptations to humble us, and when we are tempted we must fly, as our Master fled, to prayer. We must be humble. We must be humbled. It is good for dust and ashes to know that it is not fine gold. What better hope for heaven than a fierce temptation overcome?"

"Yes; a temptation *overcome.* But what I find, Father Michael, is this. The temptations I can overcome turn out afterwards not to have been temptations at all, and when they really are temptations, I cannot overcome them."

"Never?" He gave her a searching look. "Did you pray?"

"Well, now you come to say that, I didn't when I had the first great temptation of my life, but then *I didn't want to.* I didn't look upon the temptation as a temptation, but as the greatest of all gifts and blessings. I was carried away on a tide, on a wave. It was as if I had drunk of a potion – a love philtre. I didn't think it awful – I wasn't like *Phèdre* in the play. I thought it wonderful. I had no remorse. I felt no twinge of conscience. But last year I had quite a different kind of temptation, easier to fight and yet far more difficult. It was mental and moral; a question of hating Rose Mary. When she was ill I did pray to resist the wish that she might die, and at the critical moment I did get the better of it."

"There, you see!"

"Yes; but I am afraid it will come back – that it has come back."

"Well, you must pray incessantly and insistently, not just once and leave it, but *always* – every day – every hour – and then very likely, at the darkest moment, you will see the glimmer that means everything."

"Pray that I may, because I feel so utterly helpless."

"We all feel like that. We are of ourselves helpless."

"It's so easy to believe those things when one is 'safe,' so difficult when the ground begins to totter."

"Don't think of the ground tottering."

"And, then, I do such a lot of involuntary harm – those boys."

"I know what you mean. Don't talk about it. Do what you can; don't do what you know is wrong, and nobody can blame you. That may be all a punishment, or a part of a punishment for something else, an expiation."

"I expect it is. I certainly deserve it, all of it, but it seems hard on them."

"Their life is another thing altogether... There's Bernard. He's coming our way."

"Well, I'm glad we've had this little talk. I've nothing more to say. You understand it all. I only ask you to pray for me, because I sometimes feel that my misery is more than I can bear. I feel that human life is *unendurable*."

"It is almost, but not quite. It is to be endured. Think of the Agony in the Garden."

Blanche remembered Lady Mount-Stratton saying almost the same thing to her in the *Podere* in Florence.

"I feel, too, that I have done irreparable things."

"You can feel remorse to the verge of despair, but not one inch farther."

Bernard shortly met them.

"Horace Crane has never seen Enderby Abbey," he said. "We might all drive there this afternoon. I will take the Rodens, and you and Eustace and Horace might go in the pony carriage."

Blanche felt happier after this conversation with Father Michael, and better able to face the situation. She found that her increased confidence made her readier to deal with the matter. It was as if Eustace and Horace, by some strange telepathy, were aware of this. Eustace made no more scenes, and Horace was meekness itself. But Blanche trembled to think what this superficial quiet might conceal. She was not worried about Eustace; although he was by far the more violent of the two, and seemed to have the disease in its most virulent form, she felt certain that he would get over it the soonest. It was Horace Crane who worried her more. He was quieter. He never made scenes. He only looked at times reproachful and infinitely sad. But she felt that in him the malady went deeper. She felt it would take him longer to recover. He reminded her in a way of Sasha Valesky, whom she had known when she was first married at Rome. She hoped he would not share the same fate, but she felt an uncanny presentiment that he might not live long.

One evening she was talking to him on the terrace. It was the night before he was to leave, and during the whole of his visit she had hardly exchanged two words alone with him. It was a lovely April evening. The trees were red with sap, and most of them were still bare. A faint and exquisitely clean new moon had risen in the silver twilight. The house behind the terrace looked more beautiful than ever, but there was something ghostly about it.

"I'm glad to have seen this again," he said, looking round.

"I hope you'll see it often." He smiled sadly.

"Won't you?"

"I don't know. Perhaps – I doubt it."

The sentiment so exactly fitted in with what Blanche was feeling herself that she felt frightened.

"That shows," she said smiling, "how young you are! When one is quite young, one thinks everything must be coming to an end almost at once…it seems so funny afterwards when one looks back right down the long, long corridor of time. You have got the corridor in front of you."

"I think when the door is open at the end one feels the draught. It's unmistakable."

"That's just what one often makes a mistake about."

"Do you think so?" he asked, a little wistfully.

"Yes, I do, really."

"Well, whether you are right or wrong, I am glad to have had this little moment. It can never come again. Don't say the usual comforting, sensible things. You know what I mean."

"I used to think things could never happen twice, but I found they happened over and over and over again."

"Not the kind of things I mean," he said gravely, and he looked at her with a look of infinite sadness and tenderness. Blanche shivered.

"Let's go in. That's a new moon. You ought to wish."

"I have already seen it, only, unfortunately, through the glass window."

"That doesn't matter. I have often done that. It makes it all right if you turn a coin in your pocket."

They went indoors.

That night, the night before the guests were leaving, the Wallaces dined.

Of all Blanche's neighbours, Kitty Wallace was the only one who was a friend, although she was fifteen years younger than Blanche. As a girl she had been not only greatly admired – she was still handsome – dark with flashing brown eyes and rather sharp features – but had been thought brilliant and clever. She was an exquisite musician, and she was fond of books, pictures, and verse; and a good linguist. Then, to everybody's astonishment, after being out several years and having refused many seemingly attractive offers, she became engaged to a Colonel Wallace, a country squire, who had left the Army, and who had no ambition except to live in the country and hunt. He was Master of Hounds. Margaret settled down in the country and became the mother of a large family. She never went to London.

This evening after dinner Bernard went up to her and said: "Do play us a tune."

"I shall be delighted," she said; "but I haven't brought any music. I shall only be able to play what I remember."

The party sat down in pairs.

Bernard sat next to Margaret Roden, whose fair hair, blue eyes, and silent gaiety reminded him, so Blanche thought, of some one else. Colonel Wallace and Mr Roden walked right to the other end of the gallery and plunged into hunting shop. Horace Crane talked to Mrs Roden, and Blanche was left with Father Michael and Eustace. Father Michael went and sat next to Mrs Wallace at the pianoforte. They found some music, and he turned over for her.

She played various things – some Chopin, a valse by Brahms, some dance music, some Schumann. She had an exquisite touch.

Eustace, having been "very good" during the whole week, thought the time had come when he could be allowed a little relaxation, and he began to pour out his grievances. But Blanche checked him: "It's rude to talk through that beautiful playing."

"Every one else is talking."

"They are farther off, and she can't hear them."

At a quarter to eleven the Wallaces went away and Blanche said good night to everybody.

"At any rate we shall see you both in London," said Mrs Roden to Blanche.

"Yes," said Bernard. "I may have to stay some weeks in London this summer, on business."

That was the first Blanche had heard of any such arrangement.

Horace Crane and Eustace Lee were leaving early, and said goodbye.

When Horace Crane said goodbye to Blanche, he said:

"That Schumann music reminded me of you."

As he said this, Blanche felt the presence of many ghosts.

# CHAPTER VIII

Blanche and Bernard went up to London in the middle of May. Hester's wedding was fixed for the second week in June. Blanche wanted to go back to Alton-Leigh as soon as the wedding was over, but she knew now that Bernard had determined to stay the whole summer in London "on business." She wanted to leave him in London and to go back to Alton-Leigh by herself.

Blanche had read Bernard's mind accurately when she said to Father Michael that he was unaware himself of his love for Rose Mary, and probably still considered himself just as devoted to her, Blanche, as ever. Bernard did not realise his own feelings. If any one had said to him, "You are in love with Rose Mary," he would have thought they were talking nonsense. He would have thought it in all sincerity.

He considered that he had never loved Blanche as much as he did at present. He had certainly never been more attentive. He consulted her wishes about everything. He refrained from doing many little things that he thought might cause her the slightest pang of annoyance. Alas! they were not the right things. They were just the things she didn't mind.

He went to Mansfield Street every day, as a matter of course, and reported his visits to Blanche.

He often asked Rose Mary and Walter to dinner, but they were so busy helping Lady Alice with her relations and the new "in-laws" that they were not able to come during this period.

Eustace Lee and Horace Crane were both of them in London, and they each of them were frequent visitors at Ovington Square. Father Michael had gone back to Rome. Father Rendall sometimes came to see Blanche, but she dreaded intimacy with him; he knew too much.

At Whitsuntide, Horace Crane, who was going into the country with his father and mother, fell ill with typhoid fever.

Hester was married at the Brompton Oratory, and the bride and bridegroom left London for Paris and the Italian lakes.

Blanche thought of her first wedding and her first wedding journey; it seemed to belong to another life.

Before her now was the prospect of spending the rest of the summer in London, and of witnessing Bernard's growing infatuation for Rose Mary. She did Rose Mary entire justice. "She is not encouraging him," she thought; "she is blameless; but that makes it worse. I don't really know that she cares for him, but I am *sure* he cares for her. He doesn't know it; doesn't know that he loves her yet, but when he does…"

She did not know what excuse to make to go back to the country by herself, but Providence came to her rescue unexpectedly.

Nelly and Ira Olenev arrived in London. Their mother, Princess Mania, had been dead a year, and they still lived in Rome and spent the autumn in the south of Russia. They had come to London in the hope of seeing Blanche, and what they wanted more than anything was to see something of the English country, and, if possible, Blanche's home. Blanche jumped at the opportunity.

No sooner had she read Ira's letter, which arrived one morning when she and Bernard were having breakfast, than she said: "Ira and Nelly Olenev have arrived in London and they are staying at some odd hotel near Leicester Square; isn't that like them? They are longing to see the English country."

"We must ask them down for a Sunday to Alton-Leigh."

"Only a Sunday, when I have stayed at their home in Russia for weeks and months at a time!"

"Yes; it's a pity we're not there!"

"Well, I might go back and take them with me – "

"But then you would miss all our London fun."

"I wouldn't mind that."

"But I don't think *I* could come. You see, this business – "

"You mustn't come, of course; you must stay in London; that would not be in the least necessary."

"Wouldn't they think it rude?"

"No, of course not."

"I could come down for Sundays, or some Sundays, while they are there... How long would they stay?"

"I should like to try and make them stay till the end of July."

"That's when they go back to Russia. You will want Mrs Stokes." (Mrs Stokes was the cook.)

"Oh no; she can stay here with you. The kitchen maid will do for us."

"No, of course not. You shall certainly have Mrs Stokes. What shall I want her for? It's not as if I were going to entertain. I'll stay here with Lockwood" (Lockwood was his servant), "and you can take Ramiro."

"I think that's unnecessary."

"No; I wish it...and I shall come and spend Sundays with you."

Bernard now seemed to be delighted with the idea.

"But are you sure you really don't mind leaving London?"

"Really and truly."

"I thought you were looking forward to having a little bit of season."

"I've had my season. Quite enough," she said, with a smile.

"Well, you must do what you like best."

Blanche went round that morning to see Nelly and Ira Olenev, and it was settled that they were to come down to Alton-Leigh on the following Saturday. She herself decided to go down before, so as to get everything ready for them. Bernard acquiesced in the arrangement, but he was uneasy. He did not understand what was in Blanche's mind. He felt relief at her going, and he did not like admitting this to himself. He did not admit it, but it was there nevertheless.

"I hope she is not unhappy," he thought to himself. "She certainly has no reason to be unhappy. Nobody in the world has ever received so much devotion."

That afternoon he went to see Rose Mary and Walter. He found them both at home.

"Blanche is going back to Alton-Leigh," he said.

"For good?" asked Rose Mary.

"Yes – for good. She is taking two Russian friends – two Princesses Olenev – back with her. They are great friends of hers and of mine – charming people – and Blanche has often stayed with them in Russia."

"I rather wish we were going back," said Walter.

"Unfortunately it's impossible just now."

Walter's book, *East of Suez*, had been out about three weeks, and had been well received by the Press. It had at once gone into a second edition. It was said to be an advance on his first book, better written, and more mature in judgment and outlook.

On the strength of it he had been offered the editorship of the *Foreign Review*, a new organ, which dealt with questions of foreign policy, and chiefly with Eastern foreign policy. It had a literary side as well. It was a well-paid job, and Walter thought it would be folly to refuse it. The work kept him in London.

"We must all go back soon," said Bernard.

"Walter won't be able to get away for a long time," said Rose Mary.

"But surely he'll get a holiday?"

"Not till August."

Blanche went down to Alton-Leigh; the Olenevs arrived, and were delighted with everything. Bernard came down for the first Sunday they spent there, but had to leave on Sunday night so as to be back in London early on Monday morning. He was busy.

He went away happy. "Blanche is enjoying herself," he thought. "She looks tired, and the country air will do her good. London is stuffy just now."

Nelly and Ira Olenev found Blanche singularly unchanged. But they did not think she was happier than she was before. This was a disappointment to them.

"Poor Blanche," said Nelly to Ira, one night in her bedroom, after they had been there a few days. It was the Sunday night that Bernard had left. "Poor Blanche, she is not happy."

"No; she is not happy."

"He does not love her."

"He is looking at some one else the whole time – some one who is not there."

"And Blanche knows it."

"Blanche knows it, of course."

"But she loves no one else."

"She loves Bernard only. He is nice, but he does not deserve all that."

"I find him nice, but a disappointment. He looks so nice, and then there is...nothing."

"Of course there must be *something*."

"She thinks so."

"She is still very, very beautiful."

"More beautiful than when she was quite young. Do you remember her? One didn't notice her at first...but I think she looks ill and tired."

The morning after Bernard left, Blanche read in the *Times* a short paragraph to the effect that the Honourable Horace Crane, the second son of Viscount Walmsleigh, had died of typhoid fever, after a protracted illness. Blanche had received news of him from time to time from his sister, who was helping her mother to nurse him, and the crisis, she had heard at the twenty-first day of the illness, had been tided over, and they hoped for the best. He was weak, and if only he could make an effort, so his sister wrote, all would be well...evidently he had not made the effort.

Blanche cried her eyes out, and Nelly and Ira wondered. Blanche told them she had lost a friend, but her grief was really impersonal. She had been fond of Horace, but it was the sadness of things in general, of life in general, that made her feel so wretched. A few days later she heard from Lady Walmsleigh. She gave a business-like narrative of the facts, and added that at the end, during the last days, he asked after several of his friends, and said he would like to be remembered to Blanche. "He sent you this." She enclosed an envelope directed to her. It contained a few faded white violets, picked at Alton-Leigh, but nothing else.

"So his presentiment came true," thought Blanche.

The month of July passed peaceably for Blanche, with her two friends. At the end of July, Bernard came back – he had not been able to come down any other Sunday. Walter and Rose Mary were not coming till the end of August, as Walter could not get away. Bernard was disturbed by the political situation in South Africa, which he thought was serious.

He and Blanche persuaded Nelly and Ira Olenev to stay another month.

"Why not stay here till you go back to Rome?" said Blanche one day.

"That would be too long; we must go to Russia."

"Why?"

"Well, it's not necessary really."

"Please stay," said Blanche to both of them. "I do want you so much," and suddenly she burst into tears.

"Very well," they said, "we will stay." And it was settled that they should stay till they went back to Rome in September.

As time went on, Bernard grew more and more restless. He would not have admitted it, but what made him restless was the absence of Rose Mary: the sight of the empty Dower House. He admitted to missing Walter, and he kept on saying that he thought it was foolish that Walter should stop in London during the month of August.

He had suggested that Eustace Lee should come, but Eustace was kept in London by his chief, so Blanche was spared that. Towards the middle of August, Nelly and Ira said they would have to leave England at the end of the month. Blanche told Bernard one evening before dinner, when she was in her sitting-room, and thinking about beginning to dress.

"They mustn't go before Walter and Rose Mary arrive," he said; "that would be too silly, wouldn't it?"

"Yes. I don't see why they should go. It's too early for them to go to Rome. I think they think they have stayed here too long."

"They've hardly been here any time. I should like them to stay here for ever. I never knew more charming, easy people...people who get on with every one. Jackson thinks them charming, so does Wallace."

"Well, you must persuade them. I have done all I can."

"I'm sorry if they go without getting to know Rose Mary and Walter...If they do insist on going... I mean if they really have to go...then couldn't you ask Rose Mary to come down before Walter comes, as he can't get away till the end of the month? She might stay here if it is more convenient, although I suppose the servants are at the Dower House. I think she would like the Olenevs, and it would be a pity if she just missed them."

Bernard was looking out of the window at the August sunset, so calm, so peaceful, such a glory of golden dust, wheeling birds, and full-foliaged trees...the ponds and every sheet of water glinting in the sun; the beds (now under

Blanche's direction) a blaze of dahlias, sunflowers, tiger-lilies, marigolds, aconite, salvias, phlox, and poppies.

He seemed to be looking beyond the garden, beyond the golden sky...

"You would like her to come?" said Blanche in a toneless voice.

"Yes, I should."

"How you do love her!" said Blanche, biting her lips, and her voice quivering.

"Love her? What do you mean?" Bernard looked round, startled.

"I mean you love her – love her; that you are in love with her; that you think of no one else – of nothing else; that the sight of any one else is too like so much dust, especially the sight of me."

Blanche talked in a quick, low voice. She was panting, and she looked on the ground. She tore her little handkerchief.

"My dear Blanche, I really think you are off your head."

Bernard was stunned.

"It's true, all the same...it's not your fault... I don't blame you...you can't help it... If it's anybody's fault it's mine, but it's true...you love her... Rose Mary – and small wonder."

"Blanche, you really are talking wildly. I'm very, very fond of Rose Mary... I like her... I enjoy seeing her and enjoy her being here, and Walter is my best friend, and I enjoy seeing them both, seeing them both together, enjoy their being both of them here together, but that's all...otherwise there is nothing... nothing more. I can't think what you mean...what can have put that into your head?... "

"Don't, Bernard; it's no use. You love her, and you know it, and I know it, and now you know that I know it."

Bernard got red in the face. He began stamping up and down the room like a caged animal. He tried to light a cigarette; the match went out; he lit another.

"It's really *too* unfair," he said, "and too unreasonable! The fact is, Blanchie dear, you're spoilt; nobody in the world has ever had such devotion as you have had given you, and you treat it all as nothing…it's too unfair. If I had ever dreamt you thought such absurd things, I should never have mentioned Rose Mary's name. I should never have let them live here; but I treated you as a reasonable, rational, human being."

"I'm human, Bernard," she said. "I'm not reasonable."

"I wonder what you would do if I really were to care for some one else?"

"I wonder," she said, with a sad smile.

This made Bernard all the angrier.

"I never heard such a thing!" he said. "All right. I tell you what I will do. They shan't live in the Dower House any longer – not an hour. I will tell them I had promised to let it after this year a long time ago, or say it has to be repaired, or I will pull it down. After all, it's useless, and the garden and the farm would be improved without it; but I swear you shall not have the excuse for saying such things to me. I will not stand it."

He was shouting now.

"Oh, Bernard, don't talk like that. Ask her down. I would like her to come, I promise…ask her here…don't listen to me… I am foolish… I am distraught… I am overtired, but tell me, do you still love me a little?"

"Of course I do."

He calmed down at once. The scene took the turning these scenes usually took. He tried to soothe her with kisses. She cried. She sobbed her eyes out.

"I wish I could believe it," she said through her sobs.

"It is so difficult to believe…so…so difficult to believe."

"But I swear it's true – swear – promise…what can I say to make you believe it? What can I say to drive such things out of your head?"

"You do love me a little?"

"Of course I do… "

"More than you love Rose Mary?"

"My dear!"

"Swear?"

"Of course."

"Well, you will ask her, won't you, or let me ask her?"

"If you like."

"I'll write to her tomorrow, but I don't think she'll come."

"Why not?"

"Well, I think she won't leave Walter."

"It only means a fortnight without him."

"I know, but all the same – "

"Well, you won't think such foolish things again, will you?"

"I'll try not to."

"Promise?"

"I promise…but, were they so foolish?"

"Oh, Blanche, you'll drive me out of my mind if you begin that all over again…what more can I tell you?"

"Very well. I won't be foolish any more. I promise." She smiled. "Run away now, as I must dress."

But, before she began to dress, Blanche had another long cry. Then she went to bathe her face. In spite of all that Bernard had said, she was still convinced that she was right. She knew it all too well; only she thought, "I really don't believe he does realise it – not even yet."

That night when she came down to dinner, in spite of having treated her face with care, her eyes with rose-water, and her cheeks with powder; in spite, too, of having had a long, hot bath before she dressed, both Ira and Nelly Olenev noticed that something had happened.

"*Ona plakala,*" Ira whispered to Nelly, which meant, "She's been crying," and then she whispered, "Bernard?"

And Nelly nodded assent.

They went in to dinner. During dinner Bernard said to Ira:

"You really mustn't go before Walter and Rose Mary Troumestre come here. They would never forgive us if we let you go before they arrived. We expect them at the end of the month for sure, but Blanche is going to write to Rose Mary tomorrow and ask her to come here *at once*, before Walter comes. He has to be at his office till the end of the month, but we were talking it over before dinner, and we neither of us see why Rose Mary shouldn't come at once; he can stand being left alone for a fortnight – don't you think so? And we are going to ask her to stay *here*, so she won't be alone at the Dower House."

Ira and Nelly exchanged a quick look, and Ira said to Bernard: "I hope she will come. I remember Mr Troumestre a long time ago."

"But you don't know her, do you?" said Blanche.

"No; I have never met her."

"You will admire her. She is *most* beautiful."

Bernard said nothing. He seemed embarrassed.

"But why shouldn't you stay on another month?" he said briskly. "It's surely too soon to go back to Rome. Rome will be empty, and hot and dusty and smelly; positively unhealthy. Stay here with us. It will do you good to stay as long as you can in the country, and it will do *us* good. We get rusty from not seeing anybody but country neighbours; don't we, Blanche? And you will be doing Blanche a service; you can imagine how bored she must get here alone with me."

"We should like to stay," said Ira, "only I'm afraid we really must go. We are not going straight back to Rome; we are going to stay with some cousins on the way, at Berchtesgaden. We have promised to."

"Well, you must put them off. I'm sure I am right. I shall leave it to Blanche and you to settle."

That night, after dinner, when Blanche was alone with them, she begged them to stay on a little longer.

"Please, please do," she said. "You have no idea what a service you will be doing me."

She looked so unhappy and so forlorn as she said this, that Nelly and Ira were pensive.

"Do you really mean it?" said Nelly.

"Yes, I really mean it. It's not a civility. I never meant anything more seriously in my life. Life here looks simple, doesn't it? Life always looks simple, doesn't it? But, you know, nobody knows better how deceptive that can be; and I want friends, friends just like you, who understand without one having to explain anything, and who never *ask* anything."

Her eyes filled with tears again. Nelly and Ira, who knew her whole history, and understood her through and through, were filled with pity. They promised to stay.

# CHAPTER IX

Bernard was profoundly affected by what Blanche had said to him that evening. Her words had the effect on him of a revelation.

Scales had fallen from his eyes. He would never, could never, be quite the same man again. He had crossed a moral Rubicon. At first he was stunned, and then he seemed gradually to come to, to think over the matter, to puzzle it out...to unravel a tangle of threads, and through all this, in all this conflict of shadows and echoes, the face of Rose Mary shone out in startling distinctness, and the accents of her voice rang in his ears with persistent unblurred iteration.

Blanche wrote to Rose Mary and asked her to stay with them at Alton-Leigh, but she no longer could advance the last days of the Olenevs as a pretext, as they had decided to stay on. Rose Mary refused. She could not leave Walter; she said she must travel down with the babies. They would all come together at the end of the month.

They arrived at the end of August, and the old routine of things began once more.

They dined at Alton-Leigh the night after their arrival. The Wallaces were asked to meet them, and two young men who were staying with them: one of them, Lord Laracor, the Irish peer, whom Blanche had met the night of the fancy-dress ball at Wessex House, and the other a nephew of Colonel Wallace, also called Wallace, a good-looking, shy boy, who was still at Sandhurst.

After dinner Mrs Wallace played to them, and some of them listened. Bernard, the Colonel, and Walter had a long and serious conversation about the political situation in South Africa. Bernard felt convinced that war was inevitable. Walter was more doubtful; the Colonel was pessimistic...they were all three of them preoccupied.

"If there's a war?" said the Colonel.

"I shall go," said Bernard.

"So shall I," said Walter.

"What will Blanche and Rose Mary say?" asked the Colonel.

"Yes, yes, there's that," said Bernard.

He did not look forward to the prospect of announcing this decision at all.

"I should like to go too," said the Colonel; "but I'm too old, and I fear useless. I suppose it will be soon over, if there is a war."

"I'm not so sure," said Walter. "I don't suppose for a moment we're ready; we never are...and then it's an awkward situation. Bismarck said that South Africa would be the grave of the British Empire. I don't like the saying. I hate the whole thing, you know."

"It's all Gladstone's fault," said the Colonel. "Majuba's got to be wiped out some time or other."

"I don't suppose the Boers are any worse marksmen now than they were then."

"Let's hope for the best," said Bernard. "We're disturbing the music. What was that?" The last remark was addressed to Mrs Wallace.

"That was a little French song – Breton – I was trying to remember."

Rose Mary talked the whole of the evening to Lord Laracor, with whom she got on easily. Blanche devoted herself to the young man, Hedworth Wallace, who was shy, but who looked at her with surprised, admiring eyes. He thought he had never seen any one so beautiful.

"That is a jolly woman," he said to his uncle, as they drove home after dinner.

"Ah, there's no one like Blanche," said the Colonel; "but you should have seen her five-and-twenty years ago. She was a dream."

"I think she's almost better-looking now," said Mrs Wallace.

"Ah, well! Nothing makes up for youth…and when I first saw her she had been married at least three or four years. It was at Vichy I first saw her, not long after the Franco-Prussian War. She was a vision then."

Ira and Nelly, after they had said good night to Blanche, discussed the evening, and the guests, while they brushed their hair.

"She is beautiful," said Ira – she meant Rose Mary – "there is no doubt about it – far more beautiful than I expected. Her beauty has that tiresome quality – tiresome for us, I mean – of making one feel *old*. I felt a hundred when I was near her. She is so *fresh*."

"So did I," said Nelly. "And everybody looked old near her except Blanche."

"Blanche is saved by that great dazzling whiteness and her great distinction."

"But I find the girl has more real beauty…less distinction, but more beauty…plain *beauty*…and I feel that… "

"Bernard feels that."

"Yes; he loves her; there is no doubt."

"Poor Blanche! how she must suffer."

"He is nice."

"Troumestre?"

"Yes – comfortable."

"I wonder what he thinks."

"He thinks nothing...he sees nothing...he just adores his wife."

"And she?"

"That is much more difficult; she is deep. I don't know what she feels. I am only sure of one thing: she does not like Blanche."

"You feel that?"

"Yes; didn't you?"

"Well, I thought so at one moment, and then I thought it was my fancy."

"No; I feel sure of it. I felt sure of it when she said good night to Blanche."

"Why should she dislike her?"

"If she loves Bernard."

"But we don't know that she does."

"No; we don't know. If she does, she keeps it to herself. Poor thing, perhaps she suffers, too."

"She is young."

"I'm sorriest for Blanche. She has had enough unhappiness in her life already."

Ira and Nelly stayed at Alton-Leigh till the end of the month, and during that time life there went on as usual. Nothing extraordinary happened. Some people came for the partridge shooting; guests came and guests went. There were rumours of war in the air, and yet nobody realised that war was really there, in the offing. Blanche did not think about it seriously. It never occurred to her that Bernard or Walter would go if there was a war.

At the end of September, Ira and Nelly left England. Blanche was sorry to say goodbye to them. They went straight back to Rome. Their presence made a great difference to Blanche, and tided her through a difficult month. Walter went to London at the end of the month, and left Rose Mary and the babies at the Dower House. Bernard had not seen much of Rose Mary. He dared no longer go to the Dower House. He felt almost uncomfortable in her presence now, and yet, without her, he felt lost. He simply longed to see her every moment of the day. He knew this now. He had faced the fact that he loved her, and his sole effort was to conceal it from Blanche and to spare her suffering. But he was no longer under any delusion.

Blanche did not notice any difference in him, but she was aware that he saw less of Rose Mary than he used to do, and after Walter had left for London he did not seem to see her at all. Blanche left the situation alone. She tried not to think about it – not to probe. She lived from day to day, feeling that she was being like the ostrich that hides its head in the sand, and feeling, too, that she was drifting towards some catastrophe.

And then, at the beginning of October, came the war.

When the news of the ultimatum issued by the Transvaal Government reached Alton-Leigh, Bernard said to Blanche: "Nothing can stop war now. Of course, that means that – "

"Not that you'll go?" said Blanche.

"The Reserves are not called up, but I shall go, all the same, and join something out there; South African irregular cavalry or something. So will Walter. He is going with me."

And then all at once it seemed to Blanche quite inevitable, although up till then she had never dreamt of his going... It seemed to her natural, as another last and final nail in the coffin of her happiness.

"Yes, of course, I suppose you must...you will... it's stupid of me. I forgot. I never thought...and Walter."

At that moment Ramiro brought in a telegram for Bernard. He read it.

"It's from Walter," he said. "He's coming down this afternoon. I shall have to go to London tomorrow."

"And I'll come too, of course."

"Yes," said Bernard.

And then they discussed the prospects of the war and their immediate arrangements.

Walter came down in the afternoon and brought them the latest news.

It was settled that they should all go up to London the next day. Walter and Rose Mary would stay with Lady Alice, who would have everything ready for them. This, then, would be their last day at Alton-Leigh for a long time – perhaps the last day they would ever spend there. It was a beautiful day. The foliage was pale green and golden, bright yellow and crimson. So far it was all untouched. The sun shone brightly on the cabbage fields, and turned them to emerald. The flowers still made a brave show in the garden. It was so still that the air seemed to be in the arms of some calm, implacable fate.

Blanche felt that the end of the world might be coming. She expected as she stood on the terrace to turn round and find that the house had vanished. Bernard spent the day in making arrangements for his absence, in interviewing a quantity of people. At five o'clock Walter strolled up to the house and said to Blanche: "I've come to say goodbye to you, and have a talk. I feel we shan't have time in London."

"You had better go and see Rose Mary," Blanche said to Bernard.

"Yes, do," said Walter, "please; you will find her in."

Blanche could not have explained why she asked Bernard to do this. She felt as if some spirit outside of her was compelling her to act in that way, and had prompted the words, had whispered them into her ear – a voice that could not be disobeyed.

And Bernard felt, too, that he must obey; he must go and see Rose Mary. He strolled through the garden, and as he looked at the well-ordered beds, still a blaze of colour, although here and there slightly dishevelled, he regretted the sight of the garden as he had remembered it in his childhood, and then he reflected: "Blanche likes it like this."

When he got to the Dower House he found Rose Mary walking in the garden.

She did not seem surprised to see him.

"Would you like some tea?" she asked.

"Yes; I would like a cup, but it's such a lovely evening, it seems a shame to go in."

"Yes; it is."

They went in, all the same, and Rose Mary gave Bernard some tea.

"Is Blanche going up to London with you tomorrow?" she asked.

"Yes; I suppose we'll all go up together by the ten-thirty. Walter is saying goodbye to Blanche *now*; he told me I should find you. He wanted to have a talk with Blanche; as he rightly says, there won't be time for anything in London. I wanted to say goodbye to you."

"Did you expect it?"

"The war? Yes and no. It's always difficult to believe a war is really going to happen until it happens."

"Do you think it will last long?"

"Longer than people think. Wars always do."

"Walter's wild with excitement at going."

"It's a pity he can't write about it."

"I think one of the things that pleases him most is that he won't have to write about it."

"I thought he liked writing."

"He likes it when he's finished, and he likes going somewhere so as to write, but he hates the actual writing."

"He'll probably write about it afterwards."

"Yes; if he comes back."

"Are you frightened?"

"Not very…not *this* time…but some time or other, sooner or later, he'll go away and not come back… I'm sure of it. I've faced it. It's better to face things at once."

"Yes; it is. I feel optimistic as far as we are concerned. I feel as if we would both come back all right."

"It's so far…we shall never hear."

"Oh, we'll write"

"And I suppose letters will be censored?"

"Sure to be...but I think one will be able to get them franked."

"I hope you will both of you write often."

"We will. I will see that Walter writes to you."

"That will be kind."

"But you must write to us, and tell us all the news, all the little things."

"I write such bad letters. Blanche writes such good letters, doesn't she? My father used to say she did."

"Yes; she does. Shall you stay in London for a bit, or come back here?"

"I shall stay in London, at first at any rate, with my mother-in-law. I'm afraid she will mind Walter going."

"She won't show it."

"No. She never shows anything. She's marvellous in that way. What's the shortest time it could last?"

"I don't know...nobody knows."

"Walter is pessimistic."

"Is he?"

"Yes;...he thinks everything has been going too well lately...and then... I don't think he approves of the war."

"He doesn't like Kruger, does he?"

"No; but he hates the Uitlanders, and he says the whole thing has come about because of the mines."

"I suppose it has...only there must always be an ultimate cause to everything."

"I suppose it had to come sooner or later. I am a fatalist about that sort of thing – wars, railway accidents, fires, and earthquakes."

"Yes. One must accept them."

There was a pause.

Then Bernard said, "I have no presentiments, and, as I told you just now, I feel *quite* happy about ourselves – about Walter and myself. I feel we shall come home all right, but I may, of course, be wrong, and in spite of what I feel, it may be the last time I shall ever sit in this house talking to you like this – alone."

"Yes; it may be."

"I have been thinking all day whether to tell you something, or not."

"Is it something I know already?"

"No; you don't know it. I don't think you can possibly know it. Perhaps I ought not to tell you, and yet I do so want you to know…after all, the truth is the truth, whether one tells it or not, whether one faces it or not…if one hides it from others and from oneself, it is still there…laughing at one."

"Yes."

"Life is so strange…so much stranger than anything one reads of in books, isn't it? It is so improbable, so fantastic in its little incidents. Things happen that no writer would dare invent. And when they do get hold of a true story, I believe they often have to tone it down to make people believe it."

"Yes; I believe that is true."

"It's all so puzzling and sad. The worst of it is one hurts people so without meaning to – people one is fond of."

"Yes; I know."

"I am entirely to blame in all the difficulties I have had. Only I myself am to blame – nobody else. But if I had to live my life over again, I don't know how I could have behaved differently."

"I understand that."

"Yes, you understand…you understand everything…you probably know it all already…you must have guessed. You know the main things, the most important things…but you don't, I expect, know the little things. You know what happened, but you don't know *how* it happened."

"Walter said the other day that our lives are like the pattern in a game of cat's cradle, as if some one was playing cat's cradle with us…as if we were the threads… "

"Yes…it's a funny pattern they make. I think that's rather true; the same threads get changed into different patterns and combinations. I wonder what made him think of that."

"Walter often has original ideas."

"I wonder what I ought to do, whether I ought to tell you, or not? I think I will, because I couldn't bear the idea that I might be killed, or die out there of some disease, and that you would never know."

"Perhaps you had better *not* tell me. You know one guesses a great deal."

"Yes; but, all the same, I must tell you. I must make you my confession…it's only during the last month that I have understood myself, that I have seen into myself. For years I have been living in a dream. My eyes have been sealed; I see everything plainly now. You know the beginning. You know Blanche's history, and what happened at Rome, and Guido's story, and all about her life with him."

"Yes; I know all that."

Rose Mary stared in front of her. She felt as if all this were unreal – happening in a dream, or that it had happened already.

"I expect nobody will know what she must have gone through. And then you know he turned her out of the house. That was my fault. Blanche wasn't to blame. And then the years passed. I travelled…and I inherited Alton-Leigh, and that changed my life. Then I met you at Ouselthorpe, at the Bromleys'. The first time I saw you…it was only for a moment – I hardly noticed you; and then I met you again in London, at the Bromleys' house. You were not out; you were only fifteen or sixteen, at the most. But you were tall – grown up. And, do you know, Rose Mary, I believe… I honestly believe that I fell in love with you then and there, and at that moment, suddenly…at first sight."

Rose Mary shivered and turned white.

"I didn't know that at the time. I didn't get to know that till years afterwards, not really till the other day. And then you came to Alton-Leigh for Christmas. And the next summer you came out regularly, in London. In the meantime Guido had died, and Blanche was free. But I thought she had given up caring about me years before this, and I didn't think she gave me a thought. And then, Rose Mary, my mother was always bothering me to marry, and I never wanted to, never thought it conceivable, till I met you; but at the same time, if any one had said to me then that I was in love with you, I should probably have said it wasn't true. But I wanted to marry you, all the same, and that shows how one can deceive oneself. I didn't think it all out, but I was determined that, if you accepted me, I would marry you, and I had made up my mind to propose – to try. I didn't know what you felt – I thought you might laugh at the idea.

"Walter was in love with you. I think he fell in love with you directly he saw you, but he thought I was fond of you, and so he said nothing, and in fact went away. That was just like him.

"Then I was elected to Parliament, and soon after that my mother died. If she had lived, I think things might have been different – at least, I expect they would have been different.

"I used to see Blanche a great deal during all this time. I looked upon her as my best friend. I consulted her about everything. I would probably have said she was the love of my life, but that she had entirely ceased to care for me, except as a nice, easy, comfortable friend. That's what I thought was true.

"Well, then, I came to London for the opening of Parliament, and I had settled then to propose to you, and to marry if you accepted me. I had no idea whether you liked me, whether you would accept me-what you thought – and I decided to tell Blanche all about it. I went to see her, and I told her that I wanted to be married. And just as I was telling her, you came home – you were out doing – I don't know what – and you put your head in at the door. You had come to fetch some music.

"Well, I asked Blanche what she thought about it. And Blanche... I hadn't mentioned your name... I hadn't mentioned any name...thought I meant *her*... "

Rose Mary gasped and said "Oh!" and then checked herself. She still felt like a person in a dream.

"And I suddenly saw that she *did* care for me, that she cared for me just as much as ever. I couldn't undeceive her...Well, you know the rest. At first all went well. I thought that she was right, that I had been right, that we all had been right, especially when you were engaged to Walter. I then thought that all was for the best, in the best of all possible worlds. Only when you came to Alton-Leigh, then from that moment, or rather from long before that moment, a slow, long process went on inside me, and it was only a month ago I realised how far it had gone. I knew then that I loved you, and you only. That is the whole sad, sad story. Of course I suppose I oughtn't to have told you this. 1 wouldn't have told you if I hadn't known that you knew, that you *must* know the *big main fact*. You did know that, didn't you?"

Rose Mary nodded. She couldn't speak. She looked fixedly on the ground.

"But I thought you couldn't know *how* it had all happened." She shook her head.

Indeed, all that Rose Mary thought she had known was that Blanche had made Bernard marry her, and that if Blanche had not been there, Bernard might have married Rose Mary. About that she had felt bitter. Her feelings were intensified a hundredfold now, because when Bernard told her that Blanche had made a mistake, she did not believe that part of the story. She felt certain that Blanche had known the whole time from the very beginning; and there she was mistaken, for at the beginning, as has already been told, Blanche *did* make a mistake, but she realised her mistake almost at once. Rose Mary did not give her the credit for even one second's mistake.

Rose Mary thought that Bernard had simply been taken in, and a great wave of bitterness surged up in her.

"Of course, now, the only thing to do is to prevent Blanche ever guessing, and to prevent her from suffering."

Rose Mary nodded.

"You see she has never guessed – never really – she has been jealous, once or twice, but then she has always been jealous about little things, and it's always been perfectly easy to convince her. But, Rose Mary, promise you will never mention this again. We must go on living exactly as we have done, if I come back alive, and neither Walter nor Blanche must ever dream that anything of the kind has ever happened."

"You want me to go on enduring all this?" Rose Mary whispered in an agonised voice.

"We must each endure it. It's difficult, but it must be done. If we do anything else, they would see. We must go on exactly in the same way as before. That is our only course."

"I suppose it is."

"And in spite of the utter misery, and the hopeless tangle of the whole situation, I have given thanks and will give thanks that we are together, that at least I can see you. Don't say anything to me. Here's Walter coming. Goodbye, Rose Mary."

"Goodbye, Bernard."

They sat in silence a few moments, as though they expected something to happen. It was growing dark, but nothing happened, except that Walter walked in and said a few ordinary things, and presently Bernard walked back to Alton-Leigh and found Blanche in her sitting room. She was writing letters.

She looked up from her writing-table and gave him a quick look. She felt certain that he had told Rose Mary something, and she felt the pang, as of a sharp wound, for now for the first time she was convinced that Bernard no longer loved her, but loved some one else. She had said this to herself for a long time, and frequently, but she had never believed it. She had never had the proof of it. She felt now she *had* the proof, a silent, intangible proof, more plain and more convincing, more irrefutable than if it had been written across the sky in letters of fire.

# CHAPTER X

They all went up to London together, and to all of them, except to Walter, the journey was like the worst of all possible nightmares. Walter was radiantly happy – radiantly happy, not at leaving, but at going to the war, and it was pathetic to watch his pretending to be miserable at going away; he felt his spirits were indecent.

He was sorry to be leaving Rose Mary and the babies, but the joy of going to the war obliterated everything else.

Blanche watched this spectacle with a sad, amused interest, and Rose Mary saw that Blanche was watching it with sad, amused interest…and hated Blanche all the more. She hated Blanche. She hated Blanche, not as Iseult of Brittany, Iseult the lily-handed, had hated Iseult of Cornwall, although logically, if priority of claim were to be considered, this would have been right; but she hated Blanche, as Iseult of Cornwall hated Iseult of Brittany, because she felt that priority and time had nothing to do with it. She felt certain that her right was the greater, not because she loved Bernard more, although she thought that, too, but because she knew that Bernard loved her and did not love Blanche, and had never really loved Blanche. That was the main fact for her.

Blanche had loved Bernard, had *seduced* Bernard, in fact, but Bernard had never really loved Blanche. It had been for him

564

a passing fancy, a *coup de tête*; he had given in to her love – the love of an older woman at the height of her dazzling beauty for a young man. This, given the circumstances, and his youth and temperament, was irresistible.

But it was nonsense to think of Bernard's love for Blanche, so she thought, as one of the great loves of the world. It had been a mistake. She admitted that Blanche loved Bernard, but then she thought of Blanche as a born and incurable flirt, a coquette, who couldn't help enslaving every man she came across.

Such were Rose Mary's reflections. And Blanche, during all these days, knew that they were her reflections.

"And, after all, she has taken away Bernard from me…what more can she want?" Blanche kept on repeating to herself, but she knew that Rose Mary might, and, in fact, did, want a great deal more.

And so the days dragged on, till, towards the end of October, Bernard and Walter sailed.

Eustace Lee sailed by the same boat. He was going out to South Africa as one of Reuter's correspondents.

He came to see Blanche before he sailed, but he found her in a whirl of packing, with people coming in and out of the room every moment, with Bernard and Walter perpetually interrupting, so there was no chance of one moment's intimate talk. Blanche was profoundly thankful for this.

And then the last hours. Lady Alice's goodbye to Walter at Waterloo. She did not go down to Southampton; she thought that might spoil Walter's goodbye to Rose Mary. And then came the journey down to Southampton in the train…the soldiers singing, "Goodbye, Dolly, I must leave you"…the noise, the chaff, the songs, the laughter, the tears…the final whistle…the band…the waving handkerchiefs…the desolation at the end.

Blanche broke down – she wept floods of tears; but Rose Mary looked on self-possessed and dry-eyed till the end, although she was deathly pale, which was all the more remarkable in a person who had, as she had, so much colour and so much freshness.

Blanche, Rose Mary, and Hester travelled back together, and throughout the journey Rose Mary did not utter a single word.

Blanche had decided to spend the winter in London at Ovington Square, so as to be within reach of news, and Rose Mary was going to stay with her mother-in-law.

When Blanche got home that night she found Father Rendall waiting for her. He had come to ask her help in the organisation of a bazaar, and they talked about this in detail, as well as of many other matters of the same kind, for an hour. Then he went away, and Blanche found that she was the better for the visit, and realised that she had not broached any topic that fringed intimacy.

She asked him to come again, and indeed it would be necessary for her to see him often about this bazaar.

She felt miserable. Her life was over. She felt that somehow or other, even out of the circumstance that she had herself been instrumental in bringing about, she ought to know how to extract some profit, or at least some solace; but she felt unable to do that; she felt unable to consent to the scheme of things.

All she knew was that she had ruined three people's lives, and there was no help for it.

She felt, too, that Rose Mary blamed her – that everybody blamed her except Father Rendall, and that he did not know.

"If he knew the truth," thought Blanche, "he would blame me as much as the others."

Then came the news from the front – the first inkling of bad news that nobody made much of; Nicholson's Nek, Talana Hill, Elandslaagte, conveyed no particular message to the public. But to Blanche, this news, the way it arrived, and the comments that were made on it reminded her painfully of the comments that her mother-in-law's friend, the Abbé, used to make at the beginning of the Franco-Prussian War, when the news of the first Prussian victories came dribbling in.

"Of course, we weren't ready, but it will be all right soon," was the general verdict.

Late in November the battle of the Modder River was fought, which was an eye-opener as to the leadership and discipline of the Boers. Bernard and Walter were both in this engagement – as well as at Belmont and Graspan.

Then came the black week, in December, and Blanche found herself, to her astonishment, buying newspapers at every street corner. But both Walter and Bernard came through all that dangerous time safely.

The newspaper posters, and the cries of the men shouting, "Special, another great defeat in South Africa – heavy casualties," were a great trial and a great strain.

Blanche heard from Bernard regularly, and his letters seemed cheerful and hopeful.

One day, early in 1900, she received a long letter from Eustace Lee. He wrote cheerfully, too. He had made many new friends, and he mentioned especially a certain Caryl Bramsley, who had gone out as a correspondent for a newspaper called the *Northern Pilot*. Blanche remembered the name. He had been one of Rose Mary's partners the first year she came out.

The day after she received that letter she read in the *Times* that Eustace Lee had died in hospital at Cape Town of enteric fever.

Then came news of Spion Kop, and shortly after this the news that Walter had been wounded and was in hospital. At the same time came the news of Paardeberg, the Relief of Ladysmith, and the turn in the tide. Walter was kept for some time in South Africa, and did not reach London till the end of June. He brought Blanche reassuring news of Bernard, who, he said, was in splendid health.

And at the end of the summer Blanche broke down and was seriously ill.

It was no doubt the strain and the anxiety which had made her receptive to illness. She was vaguely ill for some weeks before a definite diagnosis was arrived at. She saw several doctors, and suddenly it was said that she had got peritonitis and must be operated on without delay. She was sent to a nursing-home, and the operation was successfully performed. But it left her weak. She was sent to the seaside to recoup, and in the winter she was back again in London. She could not bear to be far from the news.

At the beginning of the next year Bernard was down with enteric, and after being kept for some weeks at Cape Town he was invalided home.

Blanche expected him back at the end of the summer, and they were to go to Alton-Leigh together. Walter and Rose Mary were to join them. Rose Mary's third baby – a daughter – was born in London soon after Christmas. Walter had not resumed his work for the *Foreign Review*, but he was writing a book on his South African experiences. Blanche was looking forward to Bernard's arrival with a passionate dread. Although she had recovered from the effects of her operation, she felt that she was now definitely an old woman, that she had lost her radiance for ever, and that it would be a terrible shock for Bernard when he saw her.

She exaggerated the effects of her illness. Blanche was one of those people who look ten or twenty years younger than their real age all their life. This explains why that, pretty as she was as a girl, it was not until many years after her marriage that her beauty dawned on people in Rome; that she was not really appreciated until then, and it was not till many years later that the same thing happened in London. And now that she was in reality fifty years old, she looked thirty-five at the most, even after her illness, and her beauty was still thought striking by those who had never seen her before, and, although bereft of its old dazzle, charming to those who had, if no longer the miraculous thing it had been. It was just the loss of that wonderful blinding quality that Blanche deplored, and she had no illusions about its being a temporary result of illness. She knew it had gone for ever.

She dreaded reading that fact on Bernard's face. "He won't be able to hide it," she said. The nearer the day of his return approached, the more frightened she became.

He reached London at the end of July.

She went down to Southampton the night before to meet the boat the next morning. "He won't recognise me," she thought.

As the liner steamed in, Blanche caught sight of him on the promenade deck. She was shocked by the change in his appearance. He looked thin, white, and ill. That was her first thought. They met on the quay. Her second thought was that all her worst forebodings were true.

As he first caught sight of her in the crowd there was something in his expression, something that passed swiftly over his face, as if he had suffered a pang, and had then immediately been intent on concealing it.

"He thinks I am an old, old woman…it was a real shock to him," she thought.

"Yes; we had a lovely voyage," Bernard was saying, "and a nice lot of passengers…quite a lot of friends. It was sad about Eustace, wasn't it? Just as he was doing so well, too."

"He can hardly bear to look at me," she thought.

But in reality Blanche was mistaken. Bernard was so used to Blanche's looks that he noticed no change in her whatever. He simply thought, "Considering she has been ill"– and Blanche had given him bowdlerised accounts of her illness – "she is looking remarkably well."

"You are looking wonderfully well," he said. "Are you quite fit again?"

("He is trying to *act*, but he can't," Blanche thought. But if she had realised the truth: to what extent Bernard was used to her looks, how incapable he was of *seeing* her, she would have been still more humiliated.)

"Yes, Bernard; I'm perfectly well…but I don't think you look well."

He was not feeling well, and the pang that Blanche had noticed and thought was due to the shock of seeing the change in her was a passing twinge of physical pain.

They reached the station and got into the train.

"And how is everybody?" asked Bernard.

"Everybody's just the same."

"Walter – I suppose you've seen a lot of him?"

"Yes; he's busy writing another book."

"And Rose Mary?"

"She's very well."

"Well, I suppose we'll all go to Alton-Leigh directly."

"Whenever you like."

"By the way, I've asked some people I met on the boat to come and stay. A fellow called Renfrew. You'll like him. He's a Canadian."

"What – directly?"

"No, not directly, in a week's time. You see, he's sailing soon. His wife's over here, and I've asked him to bring her, too. I know all about them; they're capital people."

"Will they stay long?"

"Oh no, not more than a fortnight. And then, later, for the shooting, I've asked some other friends, called Heinholdt. He's in business out there…a capital fellow, and you'll like his wife, a clever, cultivated woman – musical, too."

Blanche asked him about the war, about his experiences, about his illness, about Walter's wound, and a hundred other things, but she soon saw that it bored him to talk about that. He had really forgotten it…or, she thought, more probably, she was not the right person for the conversation. She felt he wanted some one whom he could really talk shop with. Then, she felt, he would let himself go, and talk of South Africa for ever. As it was, he soon lit a pipe, and plunged into the *Strand Magazine*.

"When will the war be over?"

"It's practically over now; it's only a question of rounding up. It's rather a long, slow business, but it ought to be over by Christmas, I should think." He read on for some time, and then he said, "What shall we do this evening?"

"Anything in the world you like. Would you like to go to a play, or to Earl's Court?"

"Earl's Court! That's just what I should like, and we'll go on the switchbacks and the water-chute. Let's ask old Walter and Rose Mary."

"Very well. Any one else?"

"No; just we four. That will be great fun."

Walter and Rose Mary were disengaged that night, and they were to dine early at Ovington Square, and after dinner go to Earl's Court.

Blanche and Bernard were ready to receive them in the little room downstairs at a quarter-past seven – in that little room where Blanche had been through so poignant a drama, so decisive and momentous a battle. They were a little bit late. They arrived in day clothes. Rose Mary was in white, with a cherry-red belt, and a transparent "lisse" hat, the folds of which were accentuated with a tiny line of straw, and a great bunch of red roses at her waist. Blanche saw that Bernard, as she came into the room, gave a gasp of surprise.

Rose Mary had altered during his absence. She had come on. She was now twenty-three and a half, and she had not yet reached the full bloom of her beauty. He hardly recognised her as she came into the room. She seemed to have expanded, to have gained in height and authority, although this was only fancy. He had left her looking like a frail and delicate flower; he came back and found her a goddess – Artemis stepping from the woods – Atalanta ready to run a race. There was something proud and regal about her. Blanche felt and knew that it was her turn to be put out, her turn to look old. She could not vie with this triumphant vision of youth and colour and freshness.

"You *are* looking well," said Bernard. "The war must have done you good."

"Yes," said Walter; "isn't she looking splendid? I hardly recognised her at first. Gabriel Carteret has been painting her. People are beginning to rave about her. I am getting quite to feel like the jealous husband. But I can't get her to go out much. She's an obstinate girl, as you know."

"Don't be so silly, Walter," said Rose Mary.

"But it's not silly, it's true."

Ramiro opened the door of the dining-room.

"Dinner's ready," said Blanche. "Shall we go in?"

As Blanche had foreseen, as soon as Bernard and Walter found themselves together, they began to pour out volumes of South African shop, and this lasted all through dinner.

When afterwards they got to Earl's Court, Walter and Blanche, who were together, lost the other two, and did not see them for the rest of the evening.

Blanche felt tired, old, and miserable. Walter was charming to her, but in spite of that she could hardly listen to what he was saying.

"Yes," she thought; "it's all over. It's all finished. I'm old and she's young, and he loves her, and will always love her now... and he'll be *kind* to me...and I must just look on. I must bear it. I must show nothing. I must never, never make another scene...never, whatever happens, say a word which will make Bernard think I am jealous, or that I mind, or that I am feeling anything out of the ordinary. It's my fault... I have brought all this about, and now I must bear it, but, oh! oh! oh! how difficult it will be!"

"Bernard isn't looking at all well," Blanche said.

"No; but he'll be fit again after he has been a few weeks here. Think how quickly I got well, as soon as I got back."

"Are you coming to the Dower House?"

"Yes; the day after tomorrow. Rose Mary wanted to go abroad, to Switzerland. She has got it into her head she wants to climb, but I refused to go just the moment Bernard was arriving. He would have thought it extraordinary; don't you think so?"

"He would have been disappointed."

"And, besides, I want to see him myself."

"He's asked some South African friends to stay."

"Oh, has he?"

"Yes; I don't know who they are; people I have never heard of."

"He must have been glad to see you."

"Do you think he missed me?"

"I'm sure he did. I know he did."

"I don't think he is a man who misses people for long. I think he soon gets used to missing one...soon fills up the gaps."

"You talk as if you were just the same as any one else."

"Well? I think most people end by being rather alike."

"Oh, Blanche, you know you are different."

"I don't think any one thinks so...except you, and that's only your kindness, and your good nature, and your loyalty...you like me for old acquaintance' sake."

But Walter felt there was a great deal of truth in what Blanche said about Bernard. He felt that he did get over her absence with surprising easiness, and he thought that Blanche was neglected. Walter looked upon Blanche as one of the rarest of human beings, the most charming companion, the most sympathetic and understanding of women, so amusing to be with, too, and so beautiful; to his eyes she was just as beautiful as ever...and he wondered whether Bernard appreciated this; whether he appreciated it as much as he ought. "If I were her husband I should treat her so differently," he thought. "I don't think I would ever get over the great, great privilege that such a gift had been given me." And then he thought of Rose Mary, and the way he treated her. He felt he had nothing to reproach himself with there. He worshipped her. "And she knows it," he thought. "I missed her every moment I spent in South Africa, interesting and exciting as it was. How funny to think that I once thought Bernard was fond of Rose Mary and wanted to marry her! It's all turned out for the best, and we're all friends, and everything has happened right, which is so rare in real life. 'And they lived happily for ever afterwards.' We are doing the 'lived happily' now. And it will be our own fault if it doesn't go on just as well as it has hitherto. But it will."

Just then they met Bernard and Rose Mary.

"You must come on the water-chute with us," said Bernard.

They went together to the water-chute, and went down it twice running. Then they went home.

When Blanche got home that night she found on the front hall table a large envelope directed in a handwriting she knew. It was from Horace Crane's mother. It contained a little book of private printed poems which were all the "literary remains" he had left behind.

There were a few sonnets, and a few short lyrical and elegiac poems, on classical subjects. They were still rather derivative, and bore traces of the influence of Rossetti and other of the modern poets, but there was, nevertheless, a note of originality in some of them. But Blanche was quite indifferent to the merits or the defects of the poem that appealed to her. It was called, "To – ":

I saw you standing near the ivied wing,
Between the terrace and a classic bower;
Forget-me-nots and tulips were in flower,
And daffodils made here and there a ring.

Hark! to the birds how wantonly they sing!
I feel the presage of an April shower!
Of all the year I love this swift-winged hour,
The first soft sigh of half-awakened spring.

When you spoke thus to me, I quite forgot
Fragrance of wallflower or forget-me-not,
The blessing of the firmamental blue,
The longed-for music of the blackbird's note.
I heeded rarer scent, a softer note,
Another, a diviner glory: you.

# CHAPTER XI

Blanche and Bernard went down to Alton-Leigh the next day, and Rose Mary and Walter followed them.

Life there began to go on once more as it had done before. Bernard's new friends arrived. First of all, the Renfrews – friendly, cheerful people, who were no trouble to entertain; and then the Heinholdts – he, a sharp and good-natured man of business; she, quiet and cultivated, and an exquisite musician.

In the evening they played bridge.

Walter was busy with his new book, but they saw a good deal of him. He came to see Blanche continually. He came to consult her about one point and another. He read every chapter to her as soon as he finished it. He had hitherto read his chapters to Rose Mary, but he was convinced now that this bored her, so he no longer did it. She had suggested it once and he had evaded the question, so she never asked him again. She felt mortally hurt, all the same.

"He thinks I'm too stupid to appreciate what he writes," she thought. She felt, too, that he consulted Blanche – which was bitterer still – but she was too proud to mention it.

Bernard was intoxicated by the presence of Rose Mary, but she held aloof more than ever, and gave him no opportunity for any approach to intimacy. The more intimate she saw Walter was becoming with Blanche, the less intimate she let herself become with Bernard. But she suffered all the same.

The Renfrews came and went; the Heinholdts went; new guests came, first for the partridge and then for the pheasant shooting. It seemed they had only just got back when Christmas was upon them.

The house was full of people for Christmas – Bernard's cousins, Blanche's cousins, the Legges, the Cherenis. Lady Alice stayed at Alton-Leigh this time, as Rose Mary and Walter had Hester and her husband at the Dower House. An unexpected guest arrived in the shape of Bernard's younger brother, Stephen, whom Blanche had always heard of, but never seen. He was ten years younger than Bernard, and on leaving school he had gone to Ceylon in a tea-planting business. This had happened just before Blanche paid her first visit to Alton-Leigh, and he had been there ever since – seven years. He had done well, and was prosperous, and now Bernard suddenly heard from him that he was married and was coming home with his wife. Bernard asked them to Alton-Leigh, and they arrived just before Christmas.

He was unlike Bernard, being tall, thin, and dark, although certain intonations in his voice, and certain shades of his expression, reminded you of his elder brother. He was good-looking and looked older than his age – slightly thin and tanned – but this was due to the tropics.

His wife was the daughter of an Indian judge and the niece of a Shropshire squire. They had met at Simla. She was pretty, round, and small, with dark, beady eyes, a delicate skin, and a purring manner. She was proud of her county connections, and immensely particular. Her name was Elizabeth, but her friends called her "Bessie." She considered that she had conferred a favour on Bernard's family in having married a Papist. She thought, too, that it was a come-down for one of her family, for her father was a Logan-Knayston (one of the Shropshire Logan-Knaystons).

But so far she had not given any expression to what she thought about these things. She gave the impression at present of being a soft, pretty, demure little thing, as playful as a kitten, and a little tremulous.

Her father was well-to-do, and she had expectations from an uncle, and she had settled as soon as she arrived in England not to go back to Ceylon. Stephen must find some other job. She could not be expected to live in Ceylon the rest of her life. She had not yet informed Stephen of her irrevocable decision.

Stephen had always been considered to be the black sheep of the family, although he had done nothing outrageous except to be lazy at school – he was said to be clever and quick – and to have shown indications of a rather precocious taste for racing. In Ceylon he had wiped out the bad impression, and now he had crowned his career by marrying some one who was almost an heiress. Bessie's uncle had no children, and one day she looked forward to inheriting a house and estate in Shropshire.

"What do you think of Stephen and Bessie?" Bernard asked Blanche, the night his brother and his new sister-in-law had arrived, when every one had gone to bed.

"I don't think he's at all like you," said Blanche.

"No; he's not like my father or my mother, but he's rather like Uncle Christopher, and like my Uncle James, who died a long time ago. He was an unsatisfactory boy – plenty of brains, but lazy, and always getting into scrapes. I really do believe that Ceylon has made a man of him. She's pretty, isn't she?"

"Very," said Blanche; "but I don't think she is as soft as she looks."

Stephen made friends with Blanche at once. He made friends easily, and had always liked people who were older than himself. He told her all about his life in Ceylon. His marriage, Blanche gathered, had been a sudden affair. He had met Bessie at Simla, where he had gone for a holiday, and they had become engaged in three weeks. They had been married a month later; as it was not possible for Stephen to leave Ceylon for at least six months after his engagement, they settled to get married as soon as they could, and to go to England after their marriage.

Soon after Christmas Stephen and Bessie went to stay with her relations in Shropshire. She was looking forward to showing her husband what a real English country home – unpolluted by foreigners – should be like. Stephen found the demonstration trying.

Bernard's guests left after the New Year, and Blanche, Bernard, Rose Mary, and Walter were left alone once more.

Bernard soon heard from his brother that Bessie thought it unwise to go back to India. The doctor said she would not be able to stand the climate.

"She's one of the most robust-looking people I have ever seen," said Blanche.

"Do you really think so?" said Bernard. (Bernard thought her attractive.)

"Yes, I do."

"But Stephen says she's expecting a baby."

"I thought she was."

Blanche wondered whether the wedding had had to be hurried on; the idea opened the door on many possibilities.

"Well, the long and short of it is, he's not going back, but a fellow who's had business dealings with his firm in Ceylon is going to give him a job in his London business, so all is for the best."

"Yes, if he doesn't want to go."

"You think he wants to stay?"

"Not now; but I think he may want to go later."

Walter was now constantly in the house. He consulted Blanche more than ever about his book, and not only read her every chapter as soon as he had finished it, but he consulted her beforehand on every new phase and point. Bernard, on the other hand, was a frequent visitor at the Dower House, and yet he seldom seemed to see Rose Mary. She kept resolutely to the line of policy she had laid down before the war. Hester's husband had received an appointment in the Mediterranean Fleet, and had gone to join his ship. Hester had seen him off, and then Rose Mary had insisted on her coming back to the Dower House and staying there for a time.

So things went on till Easter.

At Easter there was no party at Alton-Leigh, but two South African friends of Bernard's came down for a few days.

Rose Mary and Walter had gone to London before Easter. They settled to stay on in London for the season. Walter had finished his book and sent it to the printer. It would come out in the autumn. He wanted to see the Coronation festivities.

Rose Mary consented. She put no spoke in the wheel. She was glad to remain away from Alton-Leigh, although she feared Bernard's presence almost more in London than in the country.

One morning, when Blanche and Bernard were having breakfast, he said to her: "I shall have to go to London this summer, after all."

"Oh!" said Blanche.

"Yes. You see, since I've been on those boards" (Bernard had become interested in finance and was on several boards) "it is absolutely necessary for me to be in London – that is to say, every now and then…not always, of course."

"Yes, I see, but I think you won't want me, and I would rather on the whole stay here."

"Stay here by yourself! I never heard such a thing! If you don't come, I shall stay here and go up once a week for a day or two, which will be expensive and inconvenient."

"If you really want me to come, of course I will come. I thought you wouldn't want me."

"Of course I want you. How can you think I don't want you? I always want you. I don't really know what puts such things into your head."

"It's only my foolishness."

She saw it was a mistake to say anything of the kind; it only annoyed him and did no good.

They went to London and settled in Ovington Square. Blanche did not feel well, and she got the doctor to say that she was not to do too much, not to overtire herself. This was not difficult for him to do, as he thought it.

She made it an excuse to refuse invitations to dinners and to country houses, but she begged Bernard to go by himself, which he now began to do.

Rumours from the outside world reached Blanche, although she mixed as little as possible with it. Walter came to see her almost every day, and told her all the news of his family. "We have been leading rather a gay life this last week. I have got Rose Mary to dine out twice," he said to her one day. "Rose Mary is admired, and I don't wonder, when she goes out. She has never looked so well in her life since Beatrice was born. Everybody admires her, and her picture has been a great success."

"I'm so glad; she deserves it," said Blanche.

"It's funny," he went on, "she seems to enjoy going out when she does go, but I can hardly ever get her to go anywhere."

"Perhaps she doesn't like London?"

"Well, she was all for coming, this summer."

Stephen came to see Blanche frequently too.

Blanche thought he was a different Stephen from the Stephen who had come to Alton-Leigh. Bessie, who was expecting her baby, was evidently, and naturally, rather peevish. The weather was hot and trying. They lived in a small house in Hill Street, Knightsbridge.

"I hate London," said Stephen one evening – he used to drop in about two or three times a week. "The fact is, when one's lived long enough in the tropics, one isn't fit for anything else. I simply long to be back."

"Perhaps you will go back some time or other."

"No; Bessie will never go back. She hates India, Ceylon, and everything to do with it."

"Does she like London?"

"Yes and no – " Stephen hesitated. "She likes…well, all sorts of things I don't like," he laughed. "I suppose that's bound to happen when one's married."

"Oh, bound to…marriage is a long compromise; it's all give and take."

"But you and Bernard seem to like the same things."

"I'm glad you think so," she laughed; "but we do like many of the same things."

"But Walter and Rose Mary! They are a funnily assorted couple!"

"Do you think so?"

"Yes; he seems to me a wanderer by nature. I can't imagine him sticking in the same place for long, and she's a regular country girl, isn't she? Now I think Bernard ought to have married her, and you ought to have married Walter!" He laughed at the idea.

Blanche laughed too, and to her surprise her laughter sounded natural.

"But do you think I would have been a good wife for a traveller or a wanderer?"

"Oh yes. At least I can imagine you in the tropics. I believe you would adore that kind of life. I imagine you in the East or in the South Seas…as a sort of Queen."

"But that's a lazy life, and Walter likes movement and travel, and going from place to place."

"You would fit in everywhere; besides which, he won't always travel, and I don't see Rose Mary fitting anywhere except in England. She is so English."

"And you know her mother was Spanish."

"Yes, I know; I think it's so odd."

"Everything's odd."

"Yes; everything's arranged wrong," he said, with a sigh. "Everything is at sixes and sevens; and I, who was meant by Providence to be a tea-planter, am sitting all day on an office stool. It's awful."

"But you won't have to do that all your life?"

"It would be much worse to live in Shropshire with Bessie's relations. You've no idea what they are like."

"You must be patient; something will turn up."

"Is that your experience? Have you ever found in your life that things turned up at the right moment?"

"They turned up, but generally at the wrong moment!"

"That's just it," said Stephen, and he laughed. "Well, I mustn't worry you with my grievances. We are dining out tonight with some awful people – Bessie's cousins. They think, you know, she has married beneath her, and are always what they call 'putting me in my place.' "

Blanche laughed.

"They are afraid, too, of my converting Bessie, and as to the thoughts of the baby's spiritual future, if there is a baby, well, they don't go so far as thinking about that yet." He paused. "Come and see Bessie soon, will you? Come one afternoon early, before I get back from the city. She will like that."

"I will. I will take her out driving, if you like, in the carriage. I will come and arrange it with her tomorrow."

"That would be kind."

He went away, and Blanche remained pensive. She saw one thing clearly, that Stephen was bitterly regretting his marriage – repenting at leisure. England evidently had focussed it differently, even if it had appeared desirable in Ceylon, which she doubted; and the post-marriage Bessie was probably different from the pre-marriage Bessie.

"However," she thought, "there's nothing to be done... nothing."

The next day she went to see Bessie at tea-time. She found her at home. The drawing-room upstairs was crowded with furniture. There were a great many small tables through which one had to thread one's way, as each table was laden with knick-knacks and silver photograph frames. On the chimney-piece there were many framed photographs as well, and china animals. An Irish terrier lay in front of the grate.

Bessie was smartly dressed in orchid mauve muslin, with a lot of bangles and chains that jingled, and rather an imposing white picture hat. She presided at the tea-table, which was heavily loaded with silver.

"So kind of you to come, dear Blanche," Bessie purred. "I know how busy you are…you go out a great deal, do you not?"

"Well, not much now. Bernard goes out and I stay at home."

"Do you mean he goes out *without* you?"

"As much as I can make him. Going out tires me, and then people like getting a husband without a wife – it's more convenient."

Bessie bristled.

"Nobody that I know," she said, "would ever dream of asking Stephen without me, nor should I dream of letting him accept such an invitation."

"No; but, you see, you are both so young, and only just married."

Bessie smiled indulgently. She could afford to be indulgent. And yet Blanche looked provokingly young today, and so cool, and dressed – well, fantastically dressed – thought Bessie, and too young in that white muslin, black sash, and sailor hat, it was absurd, of course, her dressing like that, too young for her age, perfectly ridiculous…she had no right to, but, still, it was annoying it should suit her so well. What did she do to preserve her looks? Some people said she rested all day; that must be it.

"I suppose you find going out tiring?" said Bessie.

"Well, I do, rather," said Blanche. "I had a bad operation two years ago, and I have never felt quite so strong since."

"Ah! that is why you rest a great deal. I did the Academy this morning." Bessie thought it tactful to change the subject.

"I haven't been. Is there anything interesting this year?"

"Well, the picture everybody is crowding to see is the portrait of your niece, Mrs Troumestre."

"My cousin."

"How stupid of me, of course, she's your cousin."

"It's by Gabriel Carteret, isn't it?"

"Yes, and wonderfully good. So like, although it hardly does justice to her beautiful, fresh complexion. I was telling my cousin, Elsie Logan-Knayston, who went with me, that Mrs Troumestre makes us all look old; doesn't she?"

"Yes, she does; she is lovely, isn't she?"

"And is it true that her mother was a ballet-dancer?"

"Oh no. She was a Spaniard – a charming woman, I believe."

"I suppose you remember her well?"

"I might have seen her, but I never did. My uncle used always to live abroad, and I never saw anything of him till his wife died."

"Stephen says you were so good to your niece – I mean your cousin. You did everything for her, and practically brought her up."

"I sent her to school – that was all."

"To school? Really. Just fancy." Bessie smiled the superior smile of those who have never been to school.

"Yes; she went to the Convent at Oakley Common."

"Oh!" Here a frigid look, to show she didn't approve of convents. "Was her father born a Roman, or was he a pervert?"

"My uncle was converted after he was married. A great many of my family are Catholics."

"You won't think me rude, dear Blanche, as I know *you* are not bigoted, but I must say I think your Church is most unreasonable – fanatical – about the question of the children in mixed marriages. I do think they might consult the mother's wishes a little. If at least they allowed the girls to have the same religion as their mother."

"Yes; it is hard. I agree, but one does that with one's eyes open, doesn't one? One knows one will have to make the sacrifice."

"I suppose when you first married the old rule was still in force."

"No; do you know, it wasn't. It was the same then as it is now."

Bessie again tactfully changed the subject. She knew that children was a topic to be avoided with Blanche.

"I'm so looking forward to the Coronation. We have been promised seats in the Abbey, but I doubt if…whether I shall be quite well enough to go…and then the Astley-Clintons have asked us to see the procession from their stand at the Corinthian Club in Piccadilly. I think we may go there. You will, of course, go to the Abbey?"

"Yes; Bernard is going…he must go, and I am not sure whether I shall go. It will be tiring."

"But surely it would look rather strange if you let your husband go without you on such an occasion. It would look so marked, especially as he is a Roman. I always say, I'm sure, dear Blanche, you will forgive my frankness, but I always tell Stephen that Romans must be careful to do nothing that implies any laxity in questions of loyalty to the King or Country, as they have a bad reputation on that score, and much lost ground to make up for."

"I don't think anybody has ever suspected either Bernard or Stephen of being disloyal," Blanche said, laughing.

"Nobody who knew them would ever dream of such a thing, but outsiders might get a wrong impression."

At that moment Stephen entered the room. He had meant not to come in till he thought Blanche's visit would be over, but at the last moment he had not been able to resist coming in. He wanted to see Blanche, if only for a moment. He found the sight of her rewarding indeed. What a contrast she was, he thought, to Bessie. She looked positively younger than Bessie today! So cool and distinguished in her black and white, so easy, whereas Bessie looked so elaborate, so fussy, so complicated. Of course it wasn't fair to judge Bessie just at this moment, but, still, he couldn't help making the comparison, and Bessie felt that he was making it, and she hated Blanche from that moment.

"Well, you are late," she said. "The tea is quite cold; we shall have to ring for some fresh."

"No; don't do that. I like it cold."

He sat down.

"How hot it is, isn't it? But you look deliciously cool," he said to Blanche.

"Blanche is the fortunate possessor of a carriage," Bessie said sharply.

Blanche smiled, but thought to herself: "Oh, foolish Stephen, to say that before Bessie!"

"It is deliciously cool here," she said. "I like your outside blinds so much; I wonder where you get them."

"The Stores, I think," said Bessie; "but I really don't know. I leave all that to the butler."

This was untrue. She knew not only the shop, but the exact price and the discount.

Blanche said goodbye, and in spite of Stephen's urging her to stay, and saying it was quite early, she said she must go home.

"You must come out driving with me, Bessie," she said. "What day will suit you?"

"Well, let me see, tomorrow I am driving with Susan Delamere, and the day after I am driving with Elsie Logan-Knayston, and the day after with Mrs Astley-Clinton, so, as you see, I am rather busy, but I should be delighted to drive with you on Friday, if that would suit you, Blanche."

"Yes; that will do beautifully for me. I'll call for you here at three."

Bessie gave Blanche a refined peck, and Blanche left the house. When she had gone, Bessie said to Stephen: "It's a pity that she wears such thin muslins; one sees her stockings."

# CHAPTER XII

Bessie's baby was born on the day on which the Coronation was to have taken place. It was a girl, and she was called Veronica Elizabeth. Stephen asked Blanche to be godmother, and Blanche could not well refuse, although she felt it annoyed Bessie. The baby was baptized at once, but the full rites were not celebrated until some weeks later.

During all the time that Bessie was laid up, Blanche visited her continually, and the more she saw of her the more difficult she found her to deal with. She had a curious system of tactics in her intercourse with Blanche. She would send out a cloud of amicable scouts on both flanks, and, according to the old Scythian tactic, she would withdraw her centre, making it appear as if there were nothing there, and then, just when the enemy or friend felt safest, she would fall on him, or her, with a pitiless hail of javelins. Blanche felt that one had to be on one's guard the whole time not to offend her, as Bessie was perpetually on the defensive.

The baptismal service in church, when it took place, was a source of friction. The beauty and glory of the service, its antiquity and sublime symbolism, were as lost upon Bessie as a Greek tragedy would be on a Hottentot, and she said pointedly that it was a shame to maltreat the poor child by putting salt into its mouth, and that she disliked candles in church; they were messy besides being pagan.

Blanche not only went to see Bessie, and took her out driving when she could, but Stephen came to see Blanche, and before Blanche had had time to realise it, she felt that she was on terms of complete intimacy with him. At first she thought to herself, "It can't matter, because he really is so young, and I am now old enough for these things not to matter." But one day, when he came to tea and had been there a considerable time, Father Rendall looked in, and Blanche introduced Stephen to him. Stephen stayed on a little and then went away. When he had gone, Father Rendall said to her:

"I see you have made another victim."

"Not Stephen?"

"Yes, Stephen."

"Do you really think so?"

"Don't you?"

"I'm sorry you think so…it's so – "

"I *do* think so; I am sure of it."

Blanche quickly reviewed a whole series of episodes and sayings in her mind, and said:

"It's tiresome if it's true. What am I to do?"

"Stop while it is still not too late. Don't let it go any further."

"But, Father Rendall, how can I stop it? I can't help seeing him. Even if I did everything I could to leave off seeing him, I can't prevent his being Bernard's brother. Bernard would still ask him here, and to Alton-Leigh, and it does seem silly when I am twice his age. It would have been absurd of me to think *beforehand* that such a thing could happen, you must admit."

"But it has happened. Age has nothing to do with these things. I always look upon it as one of the strangest lessons that life teaches us when one first learns and realises the surprising fact that age has nothing to do with these things. And you, as you know, are younger, years younger than your age. Some people are born like that. Stephen, for instance, is years older than his age. Is he fond of his wife?"

"I'm afraid not. I'm afraid she irritates him...she is – "

"Jealous?"

"She might be, very...and then she's on the defensive."

"Why did he marry her?"

"Ah, why? That's just it."

"Well, the only thing you can do is to try and not make the situation worse. Try and let things remain as they are... "

"As they are?"

Blanche sighed, and then she laughed.

"Isn't it dreadful, Father Rendall? I do really feel that it was not my fault, not *this* time... Oh, how complicated life is! I wish I could be a nun. However, we shall be going to the country soon. They won't be coming – not yet, at any rate. Bessie takes Stephen to stay with her relations when he has his holiday. She doesn't like Alton-Leigh; at least I don't think she does. She can't bear Catholics, for one thing."

"And yet she married Stephen... "

"And yet she married Stephen...in India, you see – "

"Yes."

And then Bernard came, and they talked of other things.

Blanche went to Alton-Leigh at the end of June. She left Bernard in London. She spent three weeks at Alton-Leigh entirely by herself, as Rose Mary and Walter stayed in London till the middle of August. Walter wanted to see the Coronation. He was fond of pageants, and anything historical had glamour for him.

Bernard went to Alton-Leigh in July, but went up to London in August for the Coronation. He tried to persuade Blanche to go with him, but she said that it would tire her too much, that the doctor had warned her not to overtire herself. Walter and Rose Mary came to the Dower House when the Coronation was over.

Bernard had been awaiting their return with impatience. He could not live without Rose Mary now – without the sight of her, that is to say. She still refused him a grain of intimacy; she still maintained her policy of aloofness, and all her bulwarks and defences intact and unpassable.

But, in spite of this, Bernard wished to be near her, to see her. It was an obsession that grew as time went on. Blanche was aware of it, and resolved, too, on her part, however she might suffer, she would never now as long as she lived show a trace of jealousy or annoyance, or do or say a single thing which should or might make Bernard think that she was giving the matter a thought.

Rose Mary gave her no credit for this. She put it down to subtlety. She thought Blanche was letting things be, and having her revenge by taking Walter away from her. Blanche did see a great deal of Walter. At least Walter insisted on seeing a great deal of her. He was not in love with her, but he found in Blanche a perfect friend. Again, Rose Mary did not appreciate this fact.

As time went on she felt her resentment against Blanche was attaining such proportions that one day there was bound to be an explosion. Blanche was unaware of this, as Rose Mary was outwardly so calm and so inscrutable, and looked so serene and so beautiful. Blanche envied her radiance. She thought her one of the most beautiful people she had ever seen. "That ought to satisfy her," she said to herself, "that and her youth, but it doesn't."

It did not, indeed. Rose Mary hardly gave her looks a thought. She knew she was beautiful and accepted the fact. But what good did it do her? Her beauty was not the beauty she would have desired. She envied Blanche her rarer beauty, her subtler, ageless charm.

Stephen spent his holidays with Bessie's relations and then went back to London. Walter was offered and accepted a commission by one of the daily newspapers to write a series of letters from Spain. Rose Mary was going with him for a part of the time; she did not want to be away from the children for too long. They were to start at the end of August, and Walter expected to be away for about three months, perhaps longer.

Bernard was distraught when he heard this news.

Walter's book came out in September, but, although it was praised, it was not so successful as his two former books.

Life at Alton-Leigh went on uneventfully till Christmas, when Rose Mary came back. Walter had been asked to stay on in Spain until Easter. His articles had been successful, and his editor had asked for more, and offered tempting terms; but he was uncertain whether to accept. He decided to come home for Christmas and discuss the question with Blanche, and of course with Rose Mary.

There was to be a party at Alton-Leigh at Christmas, and Stephen and Bessie were asked. Bernard had suggested that Rose Mary and Walter should come and stay at the big house, but Rose Mary said this was impossible, as both her mother-in-law and her sister-in-law, Hester Clouston, were coming to stay with them.

Besides Bessie and Stephen, the guests at Alton-Leigh consisted of the usual relations, the usual foreigners, this time a Spanish Secretary and his wife, who were at the Spanish Embassy, and Sir Hedworth and Lady Lawless. Sir Hedworth Lawless had just been appointed Ambassador at Paris.

Walter arrived just before Christmas, and lost no time in consulting Blanche about his future. He seemed always to be wishing to go away, to travel, and yet as soon as he got away he seemed to long to come back again. He would suddenly walk into Blanche's sitting-room, and say, "Shall I go away or shall I stay?" and Blanche would say:

"What does Rose Mary think?"

"That's just it," said Walter. "I don't know what Rose Mary thinks. She won't tell me. I can't understand Rose Mary. I can never make out whether she likes being here or not. Sometimes

I think she can't bear being anywhere else, and sometimes I think she is longing to go. You see she loves the country, and she understands the country, there is no doubt about *that*; everybody is agreed about that. Jackson says she would make a fine practical farmer. At the same time, she seems to want to go to London every now and then."

"My dear Walter, there's nothing extraordinary about that, is there? We all like change. We all must have change or we would die of stagnation."

"Yes; but it's not that…it's different. Rose Mary is different. I don't know what's happened to her, or at least I don't understand her. I don't know where I am."

"I can't advise you; I don't know. You must settle it with her. If you tell her what you have decided one way or the other, you would probably be able to tell whether she approved or not, wouldn't you?"

"No, not with Rose Mary; she's as inscrutable as the Sphinx, when she chooses."

This was typical of their conversations.

Walter was at Alton-Leigh all day. Bernard, on the other hand, if he went to the Dower House, always found Lady Alice or Hester there. It was as if they did it on purpose.

Stephen sought Blanche in the same way. It seemed as if it was a relief for him to be at Alton-Leigh. The day after he arrived he said to Blanche, as she was showing him the garden: "You don't know what a relief it was when you asked us here for Christmas. Bessie had planned to go and stay with her uncle, and I believe she would have insisted on going if it had not been for that letter which Bernard wrote to her. Your letter wasn't enough. Bernard's flattered her, and also the thought of the Lawlesses being here. Bessie thinks there is something sacred about an Ambassador, especially the Paris Ambassador. She can't forget that one of her cousins was minister to Brazil, and she is very proud of that; she talks of him as 'my cousin who was in diplomacy.' She never mentions the spot; she gives you to believe it was an embassy somewhere."

"You oughtn't to say those things about Bessie."

"No; I know I oughtn't, but it's no use, Blanche. I may as well tell you the whole truth, because I know you know it already, and what's the use of disguising it or pretending it's different; the only way you can help me to rumble on somehow is by knowing the truth. My marriage is, of course – as you know – a failure, a dead failure, the greatest failure. I hate Bessie, and she hates me, and yet would be jealous if she thought I cared for any one else. I had no illusions at the beginning. I mean before we were married. I was in love with her when we first met, but no longer in love with her when we were married. I know you guessed why that happened. You guessed that, although no one else did, You were right. I had to marry her. There was an awful row; her father, who is violent-tempered, and her mother, who is ultra-refined and rather second-rate, both of them made the most awful shindy. You can imagine in the heart of the official world, the burning heart of Simla, a scandal of that kind, and they called me every kind of name, and yet they were secretly pleased that it was not, after all, so bad a 'match,' a good family at least, and all that; also I'm supposed to have done well, but they aimed higher. Bessie is an heiress, or supposed to be, or hopes to be; they aimed high, and yet Bessie's mother was shrewd enough to know that out there they were not likely to get anything much better. And then they made a great fuss about the religious question. They wanted me to change my religion, said it was only fair, and, when I refused, the old judge cursed me. It was quite alarming. I was adamant, and when he said I wasn't a gentleman, and all that, I admitted it freely. So there it was; they had to take it or leave it. It was all hushed up – nobody knew. Nobody guessed the marriage was hurried on. Of course I did behave abominably, only she wasn't so damned innocent as all that, and I am sure she had gone to almost all lengths before, but never quite...and now she is happy here because she thinks Bernard is in love with her."

"Bernard does think her attractive."

"She is attractive, but he'll get over that."

"I'm not sure; Bernard is easy to please, and once he's pleased he goes on being pleased."

"Yes; he's pleased with you, and so he ought to be."

"My poor child, he's forgotten all about me years ago," she laughed.

"Rot! I don't believe it."

"It's only too true. You forget, Stephen, I'm an old woman."

"You old!" He laughed.

"It's true, all the same. I know I look nice, for my age, but soon the time will come, it may come any minute now, when all that will have gone; it will be all over, just as the moment comes in the life of a flower when the petals turn brown and fall off..."

"But that means the flower dies; we all die, of course."

"Yes; but before a flower actually dies, it fades...it lives a long time faded – at least people do. I'm not saying all this to make you contradict, to soothe me with compliments. But it's the truth, and I have faced it. As far as Bernard is concerned, it has happened already. I don't believe it would make much difference to him if I appeared tomorrow in a white wig, and all wrinkled. I don't believe he would notice it. He has got beyond that. He is so used to me that he doesn't notice me. I have only just realised this. It takes one a long time to learn one's lesson – all of it. When he came back from South Africa, and saw me for the first time after my illness, I thought my appearance had been a shock to him. I was looking ill then. But I realised only the other day that this had nothing to do with it. He told me casually a little time ago that he thought when he came back from South Africa that he had never seen me look so well, and that it was a pity I didn't look so well now, and I could see he meant it. Bernard is as honest as the day, as you know. He can't deceive any one, poor dear. However, such is life."

Stephen had been right. Bernard was attracted by Bessie in a slight degree. He thought her pretty. She was pretty, and she was insinuating, and clever enough to know what *not* to say. She concealed her ignorances. She gave the impression of being quiet and cultivated and refined. The surface was perfect.

Lady Lawless guessed what was under the surface at once, and took pleasure in drawing Bessie.

She watched the situation with interest, and one day, after Christmas was over, and she was talking to Blanche in her bedroom before they went to bed, she said to her:

"Blanche dearest, I feel…you won't mind my saying this, I know, as, although I'm younger than you are, you make me feel so much older. Well, aren't you frightened?"

"What about?" Blanche was alarmed. She trusted Lady Lawless's perspicacity.

"Well, about Rose Mary?"

"Rose Mary?"

"Yes, my dear; can't you see you're making her very, *very* jealous?"

"I…am…making… *Rose Mary jealous*?"

Blanche had never thought such a thing could be possible; she had been so preoccupied by her jealousy of Rose Mary, with Bernard's love of Rose Mary, although she admitted that Rose Mary did nothing to encourage it, that she had never given a thought to any other possible phase of the situation.

"It's impossible!"

"It's more than possible. It's true. Can't you see that that child thinks you are taking away her husband from her? And I must say she has some excuse for thinking it. I know you don't mean anything by it, and I dare say you have never given the matter a thought; but you see, my dear, he is here from morning till night, and he obviously consults you about everything. He goes to you first."

"I promise you, Elsie, on my word of honour, by everything I hold most sacred, that Walter is not, and never has been, in love with me."

"I quite believe that. But that makes it worse, in a way."

"What am I to do? You see what is happening. You see how it all happens. What can I do? I should have thought that if any one had the right to be jealous I had. Bernard is so sick with love for Rose Mary that he can hardly see straight. He is ill, distraught with love... "

"Really? Do you think so? But she doesn't encourage it... "

"I know she doesn't, that's the maddening thing and yet you say that I encourage Walter!"

"I don't know if you encourage Walter, but she thinks you do."

"Well, Elsie, what am I to do? There they are, there they live! Here am I, and here's Bernard! What is one to do? I can't go. If we go to London, it's no better, it's worse. Walter is all day at Ovington Square, and Bernard is all day hovering round Mansfield Street."

"Quite a case of 'elective affinities,' isn't it?"

"It's not a joke, Elsie. Don't laugh at me, please. It is *so* awful...and if Walter were only in love, things would be easier."

"Walter isn't in love with you; you are a habit and a comfort to him. It's not flattering, what I am saying to you, is it? But I tell you what, my dear, Stephen is in love with you!"

"Stephen! What next? He's twenty-five years younger than I am!"

"That's the dangerous age...the dangerous age for him. He's in love, and what's more, that little minx of his wife sees it, and she hates you, hates you, Blanche, and she is waiting for an opportunity to pay you out. She will wait for years, if it is necessary. You must be careful. I can't help laughing, because God made me like that; a person who sees the funny side of things, and if I didn't laugh I should cry myself to death, I assure you; but you must be careful, or else all this will end in a tragedy."

"Oh, don't, Elsie; surely I have had enough tragedy in my life as it is."

"One never knows; one's not safe till one dies, as the Greek optimist said. Was he an optimist or a pessimist? Both, probably, if he was wise."

"Advise me, help me. What am I to do?"

"Well, I think that with just a little management and care you could make Walter more reasonable. I mean – as you say he isn't in love, and I agree – I should have thought it would be possible to manage that he shouldn't so obviously, so publicly, so shamelessly, turn to you, as his guide, philosopher, and friend."

"I'll try; but that is largely Rose Mary's fault."

"Is it? I believe it is always *our* fault; the trouble is we won't admit it, and it's so nice not to be neglected. You see I know it all so well from experience. I was wildly in love with Hedworth when we were married, and he was in love with me then. And you must admit it, I was lovely. Do you remember the party at the Rodens', when we danced on the lawn to the tunes of the Hungarian band? Oh, what times those were! And then all went well till he met Madame San Paolo, and then, oh dear, oh dear! Well, you know what it is like…the terrible attentions when one's husband's unconscious conscience makes him not 'neglect one'; when he first says, 'Do you mind this cigar?' Or even goes so far as to throw away the cigar. All the little attentions he never paid before when he was really in love…and then the excuses, the absent-mindedness, the daily, hourly, inside, hidden humiliation; and then one's own pitiable part, the way one plays up, helps him out, helps him to tell as few lies as possible, invites the other woman, makes it all easy…oh dear, dear! If you knew what I have been through, and how I hate that woman, whom Hedworth has hardly ever seen, as we are nearly always in different posts. But the excuses he has had to make to fly half across Europe to see the end of her nose! And she's got a fearfully jealous husband, mind you, and one day there will be trouble. Oh dear, oh dear! Sometimes I feel as if I couldn't bear it, and then people wonder why I'm flippant, and why I flirt, and call me heartless!"

And to Blanche's surprise, Elsie Lawless burst into tears.

"I'm a silly goose, a ninny," she said, laughing through her tears. "What would they think if they could see me? Hedworth would think it so unworthy of a woman of the world to give way, to behave like that... Forgive me, Blanche dearest, but all I want to say is, Walter is all right. I know you can deal with him; it's comparatively easy; but what is more serious and more difficult is Stephen. I should not encourage him; I should nip that in the bud at once, as I'm sure Bessie will give you trouble, and it might all end badly. Good night, darling. I'm a silly woman, ain't I?"

Lady Lawless left her.

# CHAPTER XIII

The Christmas party went off well on the whole. Bessie was enchanted with Bernard's attentions, which, to do him justice, were only due to civility. He never gave her a thought, but he thought her attractive, and took pains to be civil to her. He never ceased thinking of Rose Mary for a moment, and the less she would have to do with him the more he thought about her.

Sir Hedworth Lawless seemed to be in the same mood as Bernard. He was charming to every one, civil and agreeable, but he moved as one in a dream, and his heart and soul seemed to be elsewhere and far away.

Blanche diagnosed the case clearly. Walter was the only happy member of the party. He was the only one who was not in love, except with his wife, which proved, Blanche thought, the platitude, that if you want to be happy you had better be good.

When the Christmas party was over, after the New Year, Walter and Rose Mary went up to London. He had not yet decided whether to return to Spain, or to go somewhere else...the newspaper had suggested several other places if he had had enough of Spain.

Bernard and Blanche stayed on at Alton-Leigh, and once every fortnight, sometimes oftener, Bernard was obliged to go up to London on business.

Walter settled after some deliberation to go back to Spain. Rose Mary stayed in London. Stephen was settled in London and went to the City every day, and Blanche thought that all was well with Walter and Stephen. There was no cause for anxiety or alarm about them. The Rose Mary situation was a different thing. She minded it acutely, and more and more every day.

Bernard decided to spend two or three months in London, after Easter. He said it was necessary. Blanche thought he was bored at Alton-Leigh, and only happy now when the house was full of people. He was more restless than he used to be; altogether, she thought, he had changed.

It was true Bernard was obsessed by Rose Mary. He could think of nothing else. He would not have admitted it, but it was true, nevertheless. Blanche and Bernard went up to London after Easter, and everything began again. Walter was constantly at Ovington Square – every day, in fact. Bernard hovered round Mansfield Street, and Stephen came to see Blanche whenever he could.

"After all," thought Blanche, "there is nothing to be done. I have been placed in this situation, and I can't get out of it, nor do I think it much matters; if they want to be friends with me, well, let them be. I don't see that anything tragic need come of it."

Blanche refused to go anywhere. She said she was not well, and the doctor bore out what she said, and ordered her to rest as much as possible.

And now the whole situation underwent a change in the changed attitude of Rose Mary.

She did nothing deliberate. But the result of her broodings was that almost unconsciously she changed her whole line of conduct.

Her inward brooding had for a long time been to this effect: That Blanche was behaving abominably – inexcusably; that Blanche was false to the core; that she was a flirt, and nothing else; that she professed virtue and did worse than practise vice; *she did not even practise vice*; if she did, she would have been a better woman; as it was, she led people on and left them high and dry...she threw them away when she had done with them; she was heartless, she was vain, jealous, exacting. She had ruined Bernard's life, and then, when she had done with him, she had cast him away; she had ruined Horace Crane's life and Eustace Lee's, and the lives of how many more that Rose Mary had never heard of; she did not like to think of how many... And now, to crown all, she had taken away Walter, her husband, from her, and she was busy ruining the life of Stephen, her brother-in-law...this was too bad.

She had no pity for her.

The result of all this incessant brooding on this one subject was that Rose Mary began to take the stage. Instead of keeping in the background, and in the shadow, she advanced into the glare of the footlights.

Walter wanted her to go out, so she would go out. She went out and she was admired. As so often happens in life, people who had seen and known her for several years now suddenly began to take notice of her beauty, and to praise it up to the skies. She had been just as beautiful before, perhaps more beautiful, but no one seemed to have noticed it, except once at the Wessex House ball.

It was now as if a *mot d'ordre* had been given, as if a general order had been circulated to society at large, that Rose Mary Troumestre was a beauty. Even those who did not admire her, or who did not want to admire her, had to accept the fact and conform to the fashion; they had to obey the order. And with this increase of appreciation her beauty seemed to increase and to expand. She had never looked so well in her life before. Everybody talked of her. As for Blanche, she was completely forgotten; nobody mentioned her, She lived in her corner, seeing nobody but Walter and Stephen. Stephen was infatuated with her. He thought she was ten times more beautiful than

Rose Mary, but he kept this to himself. He felt as if he were in possession of a rare and secret chest. So was he, he thought, in the words of the sonnet:

> "as the rich whose blessed key
> Can bring him to his sweet up-locked treasure."

In the meantime, while Blanche remained at home, Bernard went out, and the world, without malice or forethought, but naturally, because it was convenient – because it seemed to fit so well – began to ask Rose Mary to meet Bernard and Bernard to meet Rose Mary. This was not discussed, planned, or conspired; it was just done. It happened as naturally as the sunrise. When a hostess asked Bernard, she naturally asked Walter and Rose Mary. Blanche was asked too, but Blanche refused so consistently that people began to stop going through the form of asking her; they would say to Bernard: "We wish Blanche could come, but she never will go anywhere *now*, will she?" And Bernard would assent and make excuses.

Rose Mary was the person most admired, most talked of, most discussed, most prominent, that year.

Gabriel Carteret's picture was now said to be insipid, and not to do her justice. She was to be painted by Delmar, the Frenchman. The picture was to be exhibited the following year. He was over in London and asked to paint her; he made the sittings as protracted as he could. Nobody saw the beginning, except Bernard, and he disliked the picture and said it was like a street-poster, and altogether a crude caricature. Next year he said she must be painted by some decent English painter. But Rose Mary had had enough of sittings, and was determined to be painted no more.

Blanche heard rumours of all this. Bessie would come and see her sometimes, and tell her what people were saying...people who did not know either Rose Mary or Bernard, and who got everything at second or third hand, and wrong. But this showed Blanche how far the ripples made by the stone of Rose Mary's beauty extended.

Bessie would say:

"They say Delmar's picture is so *clever but so cruel*. So *crude*. He never flatters any one, does he? He is quite merciless. He seems to bring out everybody's hidden secrets. I think it's so brave of Rose Mary; but, then, she is brave, and of course as she's not well off she will always be able to *sell* the picture if she finds she can't bear to live with it. I wonder she can afford it, but then Walter is so clever, and makes such a lot of money, they say, writing. They say they give him £50 a letter; do you think that can be true?"

"I haven't any idea; I hope it is."

"Well, if *you* don't know, I'm sure nobody else can know."

Bessie would insert little insinuations like these every now and then.

But, oddly enough, she had no idea at this time that Bernard was devoted to Rose Mary. She lived, in reality, in another world. She envied Rose Mary from the bottom of her heart, but she thought that Bernard would always be her devoted slave.

She had no idea that Bernard went out at all. She rather looked down upon him for not doing so. He didn't seem to go to any of the functions or entertainments she read about in the *Morning Post* and in the society newspapers. He didn't go to Ascot or the Court Ball, or the State Concert, or the large political receptions, or the big dinner-parties or garden-parties... She thought he wasn't important enough to be asked to these... Catholic peers were not important.

The entertainments he did go to were just those which were never mentioned in the newspapers. And it was there he met Rose Mary. People asked them together, to the same country houses, to spend Saturday to Monday, and Blanche would help Bernard to find some excuse for his going and for leaving her at home. She did it exceedingly well. She never showed that she minded, and yet she minded more and more every time it happened. The iron entered deeper every day into her soul, and she wondered sometimes how long she would be able to go on bearing it.

"I suppose one gets used to everything," she thought to herself.

Bernard took pains to be nice to Bessie. He gave this no thought, but he did it naturally, and he always accepted when she asked him to dinner. Bessie laid it down as an axiom that Blanche, of course, was too delicate now to dine out and didn't even ask her, although she made an apologetic phrase when she saw Bernard. Nor did she in the least realise that Stephen was on terms of ever-increasing intimacy with Blanche. When he came back late from the City, and said that he had been to the Club, she believed it. It was as a rule partially true. He did look in at the Club either before or after his visit to Blanche, and Bessie used sometimes to have corroborative evidence of the fact.

She was satisfied herself to be keeping quiet, as she was expecting another baby, and this gave her a sense of superiority over Blanche. But Blanche had cared enough about that in her life, had minded too much to mind any additional pin-prick that Bessie or any one else could inflict upon her now.

As Rose Mary advanced to the footlights and into the limelight, Blanche seemed to recede into the background. Indeed, Blanche felt now that her part had been played; that she was a useless super on the stage, and that if she left it for good, nobody would notice her absence.

She did not think she was really ill, but from pretending to be ill, and telling the doctors that she felt ill, and from being told sympathetically by them to take care…it was obvious she had some worry, mental if not physical…she was beginning to be ill in real earnest.

She lived through all that summer in a dream. She was unconscious of Walter's voluble daily visits full of plans and projects. He was writing or going to write a new book now, another kind of book.

Walter was one of those people who are obliged if they write anything to air their views to a friend beforehand. If he smoked cigarettes, whether ordinary cigarettes or the *cigarettes enchantées* (the name which Balzac gave to talk about the books one means to write)...he had to do it in company. He could not smoke by himself, with any enjoyment; Blanche was now the person he had chosen to smoke with. He had tried Rose Mary at the beginning of his married life, but she, although full of sympathy and interest, had not ever convinced him she was interested, although she had been more interested than he had imagined.

But now, in Blanche, he found a perfect listener, and not only a perfect listener, but a contributor, a collaborator, some one who could not only object, but suggest. She was a constructive listener and she enjoyed the work. She had no pretension to literary or artistic knowledge. On this account, her help and advice were doubly valuable, because they came straight from the mint. There was nothing second-hand about them. Blanche gave him her opinion, such as it had been formed by life; her own experience, interests, and her own rare tact and taste.

He found he could talk easily to her, and at any length about any project that interested him, and he always found that her advice was right, even if he did not agree with it at first.

Rose Mary, on the other hand, felt vaguely that something was going on which she was being left out of, and she resented it. Walter had been offered by the *Morning News* to go to Japan, to stay there a year, and to report on what was happening; to travel in the Far East, to go to Port Arthur, to report on the likelihood of war between Russia and Japan. He was tempted to accept this offer, but it meant staying away for more than a year, and he did not think he could take Rose Mary with him. He certainly could not take the children, and he knew she would not leave them behind.

As usual, he consulted Blanche, and Blanche, as usual, asked what Rose Mary thought about it.

"Oh, she'll always do what I want to do," he said. "I want an independent, unbiased opinion. Rose Mary is too unselfish. If she thinks I want to go, she will say it is splendid, whatever she really thinks."

"Well," said Blanche, "I think it would be rather long for you to go without Rose Mary, and you say it would be impossible for her to go with you."

"Quite impossible...quite impossible to take the children, and, of course, she wouldn't leave them."

"You couldn't go and come back, and then go out again?"

"No; it would take too long. If I go there I must stay at least ten months, or a year, on end."

"Well, then, I shouldn't go."

"And you see, if I went I should have to give up writing my book on Spain, which would be a pity, as I have got the foundation for it already, in the articles I have written, and the publisher is offering me good terms for it, and I want to do it. I think I could make an interesting book of it. And I don't always want to be doing reporter's work, interesting as it is; and much as I should like to go to the Far East – "

"I understand that... I should think over it a little longer."

"No; now that you have helped me, I see quite clearly. I *have* settled. I shan't need to think over it any longer. I shan't go."

"You'd better not take my advice."

Blanche thought her advice had been good, and she tried to think it was impartial...but she knew in her heart of hearts that if Walter were to go away for a year, to the end of the world, she would feel as if her life had been devastated, and as if she were being left utterly desolate.

Walter went home and found Rose Mary getting ready to dress for dinner.

"Are we dining out tonight?" he asked.

"Yes; don't you remember? With the Hengraves."

"Oh yes," he said wearily. "By the way, Rose Mary, I've settled about Japan."

"Already? You told me you were going to think it over for several days."

"Yes; but since then I've settled... I've written."

"To go?"

"No; *not* to go."

Rose Mary was pleased; at least she would have been pleased if she had felt that he was staying because of her, or that she had had any part in the decision; that it was owing to her advice and in deference to her opinion that he was taking this decision. She felt this was not so; indeed, she was certain he had taken other advice – Blanche's advice.

"Well, I expect you are right. I think I should have thought over it a little longer. I believe I could have gone out to Tokyo quite well and taken the children."

"Think of the expense."

"I thought they paid your expenses?"

"So they do, but not my wife's and children's expenses."

"Well, I expect you are right."

There was a pause. Then Walter said: "I thought you would be pleased."

"So I am; that is to say, if you are pleased. I want you to do what is best for you, for your career."

"I know you do, but what does that all matter? I want to do what makes you happiest."

"By the way, how is Blanche?"

"Has she been ill?"

"Not ill; but Bernard says the doctor is rather anxious about her. She has had that horrible neuralgia again."

"She seemed all right this afternoon."

"Did you have tea there?"

"I just looked in on my way back from Prince's."

"Yes. Well, you had better go and dress; you will be late."

Rose Mary was inwardly consumed with rage and jealousy. She could not possibly look at the matter from Blanche's point of view. She was only aware of one solid, bitter fact – Walter consulted Blanche constantly about his life, and not her. If some one had said to her: "But what about you and Bernard?" she would have answered: "I have never lifted a finger to encourage Bernard," which was true. And she would have added: "Bernard comes to me because Blanche neglected him; she is so busy with every one else that he had to look for a friend somewhere. It is entirely her fault."

While she was thinking this out, Blanche was talking to Stephen. He had arrived late, after Walter had gone. He found Blanche in the room downstairs.

Blanche asked after Bessie, and they talked of various things for a moment, and then she said suddenly: "I have been thinking things over, Stephen, and I have come to the conclusion that I am not a good friend for you, and that all this great intimacy must stop."

"I don't know what you mean."

"I don't know that I can explain. I couldn't explain without telling you the whole story of my life. I'm not going to do that, but I only know this, that if everything goes on as it is going on now, one day Bessie will – "

"Do what?"

"Well, she'll mind."

"I don't care a damn what Bessie thinks. Let her mind."

"Yes, but I do, and it's impossible – then Bernard will mind."

"Bernard?"

"Yes, Bernard. And, then, it's ridiculous – ridiculous, Stephen. You are too young, and I am too old. At any rate, whatever the reason is, and you must think what you like, think I am an old, mad, hysterical woman – if you like – I can't go on like this any longer; it is making me ill. I haven't the health. You must really believe me. I mean it!"

"But what in the world do you want me to do? I can't help being Bernard's brother, and your brother-in-law."

"You can help coming here every day of your life."

"I could, but I won't."

"Oh, Stephen, please... I knew it would end like this. I knew I should be a bad friend for you."

"Friend or no friend, I can't and won't live without you. That's all. And it's too late now to alter things."

"Oh, Stephen, don't, please, please don't... "

"Well, what am I to do or to say? You should never have begun it, if you hadn't wanted this to happen! It's far too late to do anything now."

"I entreat you not to say these things. I am seriously ill, and I can't stand it. You can ask the doctor; he will tell you. You don't want to kill me. You must leave me to act as I think right."

"It's all very well to say that, but what about me?"

Blanche buried her face in the cushions of the sofa. She felt utterly miserable.

"Don't cry, Blanche darling, don't, please."

"You see, I have only brought misery to every one I have ever known all my life, and the sooner I die the better."

"Don't talk like that; you make me quite, quite miserable."

Blanche said nothing, but went on crying silently. Then she stopped and dried her eyes.

"I am being absurd," she said. "We are both being absurd. Now, Stephen, I'm going to be a sensible woman. We can be good friends, but you must behave in an ordinary, normal way, and it's no use your coming here every day, because I shan't see you. Here's Bernard, and he'll be late for his dinner if he isn't quick."

"Who is he dining with?"

"The Hengraves."

"Who are they?"

"She's an American."

"And are you dining there too?"

"No; I said I wasn't well enough – which is true. I shall have a poached egg on a tray in my bedroom. Good night, Stephen."

# CHAPTER XIV

Bessie's baby, a boy this time, was born at the end of July. It was called Bernard Stephen Alfred. When she was well enough, she went down to the seaside for a month, and Bernard told her she and Stephen could come to Alton-Leigh whenever they liked. He expected them for Christmas whatever happened. But Bessie did not much want to go there for Christmas; she preferred Christmas at her uncle's house, where she queened it over every one, and where she was considered more or less as the hostess; but she consented to go to Alton-Leigh for the pheasant shooting. Stephen put off his holiday until then. Blanche and Bernard went back to Alton-Leigh at the end of the summer. Blanche felt tired and worn out, and she looked ill. Rose Mary looked fresher and younger than ever.

Walter had begun his new book. Rose Mary plunged into farming; she got up at five in the morning, went for long rides, and led an independent life. She saw neither more nor less of Bernard than she had done before. At Alton-Leigh there was the usual trickle of guests; people who played lawn tennis in August, then guns for the partridge shooting in September. No particular friends of Blanche came, and no one whom she cared for.

Stephen wrote to her often, but she answered seldom, and then only briefly.

Bernard's first covert-shooting party was at the beginning of November. Besides Stephen and Bessie, there were the Wallaces, the Hengraves, the d'Aurillacs, and the sixth gun was Walter, but he did not stay in the house.

Bessie treated Mrs Wallace as an equal, as she belonged to a county family. She was amiable to Lord Hengrave and to Colonel Wallace, arch with M. d'Aurillac, who tried to kiss her in the passages, patronising to Blanche, condescending to Madame d'Aurillac, icy to Lady Hengrave – she tried to give the guests the impression that Bernard was her lover.

Stephen looked on half-amused and half-irritated. He quarrelled now with Bessie almost daily. They spent their life in small bickerings.

Bernard was careful at this party not to neglect her, as he thought she might feel neglected, and he begged Blanche to see that this should not happen. Bessie purred approval at Bernard's attentions, and confided to him with a look at Lady Hengrave that she thought all Americans a little bit – well – not quite…

The shooting was successful. M. d'Aurillac enjoyed it. He enjoyed the house and the company too. He was a connoisseur in pictures and objects of art, and he found Alton-Leigh extremely interesting, although it was not the period he preferred. His favourite period, he said, was *Régence*. He admired the female beauty in the house too. When his wife asked him what he thought about the lady guests, and their looks, he summed them up as follows:

"*Lady Windlestone a été très belle; elle a de la ligne et de la branche…la petite Lacy est vulgaire mais elle est bien faite. Madame Troumestre n'est pas laide mais elle n'a aucun charme. Lady Hengrave sait s'arranger, mais elle n'a pas de tempérament; Madame Wallace est très sympathique, très intelligente, mais comme femme elle n'existe plus.*"

Bessie enjoyed encouraging his attentions and treating him as a Don Juan, and Stephen looked on cynically, begging her now and then ironically not to make herself ridiculous, upon which she turned round on him and said nothing, but smiled pityingly.

The party began on a Monday and ended on a Friday. The guests spent their last morning in looking at the stables, the farm, the garden, the hothouses, the Dower House, and all the sights of the place. They left in the afternoon, but Stephen and Bessie remained behind. They were to stay till the following Monday, when Stephen had to go back to London.

Saturday was a lovely day. It had been arranged that Bessie, Stephen, and Blanche should go over to the Wallaces' house and spend the day there. Bessie, however, had a cold and said she would prefer to remain indoors.

Bernard was busy and was spending the morning with Jackson.

Bernard came in from his rounds with Jackson about a quarter to three, and had some cold luncheon by himself. Bessie was not yet down. She had stayed in bed all the morning, so he was told, and had some food sent up to her; she would come down for dinner.

After he had finished his luncheon Bernard strolled on to the terrace to smoke. Presently he saw Rose Mary walking towards him through the garden.

She looked as if she had been taking exercise, fresh and pink, in her tweed coat and skirt, with a fur tippet round her neck, and scarlet berries in her cap. She was followed by Sultan, Walter's dog.

She walked straight up to him.

"Walter wants to know if you can lend him the volume of the *Encyclopaedia* dealing with Velasquez. He wants to look out something," she said.

"Of course. But I will send it down by a boy. It's too big for you to carry."

"I can carry it perfectly."

"Is he in a great hurry for it?"

"Oh no; any time during the next few days will do. Is Blanche in?"

"No; they've all gone over to Altersham except Bessie. She's not well – only a cold."

"Well, I'll go and fetch the book from the library and then I must go home."

"Sit down here for a minute."

Rose Mary sat down on the seat against the ivied wall.

"It's been a lovely day," she said, "so soft…not like an autumn day."

The sun was low in the sky and shone like a great red ball through the ragged leaves of the trees in the avenue. They sat for a little time in silence. The rooks were cawing; a robin was hopping about in the bed in front of them. In the bed yellow, white, and russet chrysanthemums still made a brave show.

"Rose Mary," Bernard said, all at once.

"Yes, Bernard."

"I have been thinking lately that this year, or this last summer, at least, when in a way I have seen more of you than usual…more than ever before…it seems to me as if I had hardly seen you at all."

"In London? It's always like that in London, isn't it?"

"Oh, here… I never see you at all…you might just as well be at the North Pole."

"Perhaps it would be better if I was at the North Pole."

"I wonder what will happen next year? I suppose everything will go on just the same as before…it always does, but I am not sure I can bear it."

"When Walter has finished this book he is certain to want to go away somewhere."

"You won't go with him?"

"I might – unless he goes to Lhassa, or some place like that. I can't leave the children now for long. You see, Bernard's getting a big boy."

"Yes; time does fly."

"Soon I shall have to be thinking about a school for him. Just fancy!"

"Not for a long time yet."

"In about three years' time. Three years is nothing. We have been here six years, and it seems like a day."

"Didn't the war make things seem a little longer?"

"While it lasted it seemed to be an eternity, and every day of it was like a month, especially at the beginning, but as soon as it was over it seemed to have passed in a flash."

"Yes; I felt the same thing."

"Were you glad to get back?"

"I didn't think I should come back. I thought that was going to be the solution of everything...only in a way that would have been *too* good to be true."

"I knew you would both come back."

"There won't be another chance of such a good solution again."

"Perhaps the solution will come from my side...you see things happen to *us* too – to women, I mean; although we don't go to war, we have babies. There was my illness – I thought everything was going to be settled then."

"Don't talk like that. Did you feel you were going to die then?"

"I don't know what I felt. I felt as if everything had been taken out of my hands. I minded leaving the babies. I wondered what would happen to them...otherwise I felt calm."

"They were awful days for us. I think I grew years older in one week. Walter's mother was wonderful. Without her – "

"Yes; Lady Alice was wonderful, but I don't think she approves of me."

"I thought she was devoted to you."

"No; she *knows*, you see. She thinks I ought never to have married Walter. She is quite right. What right had I to marry Walter when I never loved him? And when I not only didn't love him, but loved some one else. It was wrong."

"You have made him happy."

"He doesn't know any better. He's like a boy when he first goes to school. He thinks that *is* happiness. Of course, I've tried to be a good wife, a good mother, and all that, and to behave decently...but at the bottom of it all he must feel there is something wanting. Just imagine if it were different, and just imagine if he knew!"

"I don't believe you could make Walter happier than he is at present. I believe he is perfectly happy. You see, you've never given him cause for a moment's jealousy."

"I tried not to, at first. I tried to be honest! Honest! But how can one be honest in such a situation? It is all wrong, and sometimes I feel as if the flowers and the trees and the stones of the house were all shouting out the truth, were all saying, 'Hypocrite! liar! deceiver!...you're not a good wife! you're not a good mother, because all that is pretence and play-acting and a sham! You would throw everybody and everything to the winds for one word from Bernard.'"

"Is that true, Rose Mary?"

"Yes," she smiled; "it's true. It's my whole existence, and it has to be trod underfoot, kept out of sight, never even mentioned. Even this talk we are having now is a mistake. It will only make things more difficult when it's over."

"It's all so different from anything any one else dreams, isn't it?"

"Yes, yes... I sometimes wonder whether they guess or suspect. And what does Blanche think or know? – besides hating me."

"She doesn't hate you...that's nonsense."

"She has always hated me...because she knew...she guessed...not about you, but about *me*."

"She doesn't know anything really. If she did, I should know at once. However secret she tried to keep it, she couldn't help showing it. She always tells me the slightest little thing that makes her jealous, and if she doesn't I see it. I know everything she thinks. She can hide nothing. I read her like an open book."

"What is to happen?"

"What do you mean?"

"I mean to us. What is to happen to us?"

"I don't understand."

"Well, you remember before the war I asked you not to come and see me so often, to behave differently, and all that."

"I remember."

"Well, it did little – no good...and then came the war, and that day when you told me...everything...and then I felt as if the whole world were different. My world was broken to pieces, into a thousand million pieces. I thought that nothing worse could happen. Yes, there was one thing worse, you might have been killed. And then I had to live through all those months and pretend...not pretend I didn't care, but pretend I cared more for Walter than for any one else, when all the time you were all I was thinking of. I prayed... I did everything I could think of – I prayed not to love and not to hate, but it was no use. And then you came back, and the reaction was so great I nearly died of it...and then life began again, and it was like a dream. It wasn't real to me at first, and I felt as if we had both died, and were beginning to live again in another world...and as if there were now some unbridgeable gulf between us. You will think that all this is nonsense. You won't understand. You can't possibly understand, but things seemed no longer real to me. I was determined not to let you become a real person to me again, only a ghost from a former dead life. And then – "

"And then what?"

"Oh, I can never explain to you nor to any one what happened...what happened to me, inside of me...never, never, never. Oddly enough it was to do with Walter and with Blanche. It happened through them...it was absurd...and then I thought to myself – yes, I *will* live, and I *will* be a live person for Bernard again. I *will* live and love and be loved. That is why when people asked us to go out in London I went, and when they asked us to meet I went, and I *let* you talk to me, and although I felt the gulf was still there, yet you, on your side, were alive; you weren't a ghost any more, and I wasn't a ghost either, and that is why – what happened – happened; and I thought for a moment I could be happy – we both could be happy. But now I feel I can't go on. I can't, Bernard. It's killing me."

"It's killing me too. Let us leave it all, go away and begin again somewhere else."

"How can we? There's Walter and there are the children…and there's – "

"Blanche."

"Yes; there's Blanche."

"But, after all, things like these have happened before. The whole of history, not to mention fiction, is full of nothing else. Why should we put ourselves upon a pedestal as being better and nobler or stronger than other people?"

"It's not that; it's that we can't help ourselves. You know it as well as I do. If we are to live at all, we can't…oh, it is useless to talk of it – all over again – we have thrashed it out so often. I must go."

"Don't go; we may not have another opportunity for who knows how long."

"It would be best if there never is an opportunity."

"It will make it easier for me if you tell me now what you want."

"I want to go…only I want it to happen naturally, for Walter to settle it, not for him to race abroad to China or somewhere like that, but to settle down somewhere else in England…not in London – to get me a farm."

"You know he won't do that."

"He won't *now*, but I want you to help me. I think I could manage it, if you help."

"He would think it odd if I encouraged him to go. And, then, Blanche is fond of him."

"That's just it…that's just what makes it so difficult."

"But, apart from that, I can't – I can't – I won't – I can't live here if you go. If you go, I shall… I shall… I don't know what I shall do, but I don't care what else you do, if you hardly ever see me, if you never talk to me, if we hardly ever meet, only just let me know and feel you are here. I can't live without you, Rose Mary; I can't really – it's too late."

"Living here like this is just what I find so unbearably difficult. It is killing me."

"But it will kill *me* if you go."

"Oh, Bernard, are you as fond of me as that? Are you sure you don't just love me as you have loved dozens of others – just because I am young and fresh-looking? My looks are nothing really, and they will soon be gone. I'm not a beauty. I never was – all that will go – and then one fine day you will wake up and think you have been mad."

"Rose Mary, you don't understand. But surely you *do* understand – you must understand. Surely you know…you have known ever since that day I told you everything, before I started for the war, that it's quite different from all that. Yes, it's true I've had other affairs in my life, God knows, and they were real, but, as you know, in a man's life there is always one thing, and only one thing, *which is the real thing…which counts more than all the others…*well, I thought…you know what I thought, and the mistakes…the mistakes we all made. It was nobody's fault. There it was – there it is. Nothing can change it now. But that doesn't prevent the truth from being here, above and beneath and beyond everything else, and what is the truth? The truth is that I love you more than myself, more than all the world, more than my immortal soul, although I made a great, a fatal mistake, and couldn't and can't change that now. I lived in a dream after your marriage and mine, like a man who had been drugged, and from time to time I came to, for a moment – had lucid intervals, seemed to awake – and then I would be sorry that you were not my wife. But I tried to hide my feelings as best I could, here, in public with every one round us...and I was glad all the same that we should be together. That was at first – until South Africa – I thought I might be killed – and that would finish it. Then I came back – and knew things couldn't go on as they had done; and they didn't – but now, as things are, it's worse than ever – if you go away now – you can't, can't leave me. I don't know what I shall do."

"I want you to help me to *endure*."

"I know everything was my fault from the beginning – I am entirely to blame."

"I don't see that you are to blame."

"Of course I am to blame. I should never have got into that position."

"But, Bernard, you loved her."

"Yes, I did...but then, you see, I was – "

"Oh, I know. I understand. Don't let's go into that. But the question is, *can* we go on like we are going on now? Won't it all end in some hideous catastrophe?"

"Why? In a way it can't be worse than it is. I don't see what else could happen...unless – "

"Blanche or Walter?"

"They will never know. If the worst came to the worst I am ready. I would go with you to the end of the world."

"Do you think I would let you...ruin your life?"

"As if it wasn't ruined already!"

"Yes; but that would mean a different ruin. However, it's no use talking about that; we've talked of all that so often before, over and over again. You know what I feel, you know what I can do, and what I can't do."

"I know. All I ask and beg of you now is not to go now, not to go *yet*."

"Perhaps it will all be settled for us. Things often are settled for one, just when one is in despair about ever settling them oneself. You see nobody can help us. We must help ourselves."

"I can't – "

"Hush, Bernard, don't…don't let us make things worse than they are. I'm so frightened, so frightened; sometimes, sometimes I feel a dread, an apprehension, just of the unknown, not because of anything that has actually happened, but a vague apprehension of what may happen. It is like feeling the approach of a wave that is far away, and that one hears slowly rolling towards one. One knows that nothing can prevent its coming, and that when it does reach you it will mean – "

"What will it mean?"

"Disaster – the end."

"Do you feel like it now?"

"Yes; now and always – particularly now – since we came back from London this summer."

"But what could happen?"

"So many things. Does one ever know? I feel we are as helpless as pins on a pincushion."

"But you oughtn't to feel like that."

"Oh, I know… I know it's wrong…but it's fear that makes me feel like this – not remorse. I regret nothing, Bernard. I would do it all over again, but all the same I know it's the devil. He knows how weak I am, and attacks me in my weakest spot."

"Well, it seems to me there is only one thing that is certain, and it's this. Whatever we do, we must not let Blanche and Walter suffer. You see, if Blanche were to know, it would kill her."

"And I don't know what Walter would do."

"Well, then, it seems to me clear that you *mustn't* go. If you leave Alton-Leigh, Blanche is sure to suspect."

"You do make things difficult. You never will listen to my solutions. How often have I asked you to let me do what I feel is right."

"Yes; it would be right if there were only you and me to consider. But there are the others. We can't help it, and we are obliged to think of them. You can't go. Perhaps it was a mistake your coming back here...after... You can't go *now*. It's too late. There is no escape from the situation; we must simply go through with it. Let's try and get through with flying colours."

"It's so easy to say that, but just think what it means!"

"I see no other solution, unless you would like me to go away with you. I am willing, but it would kill Blanche."

"No; that's impossible."

"Well, then, we must just carry on."

"I suppose so."

"I hear wheels, I think. They're coming back; let's go and meet them, and I'll fetch you the book."

They walked down from the terrace through a small gate which led to the courtyard on the other side of the house.

While this conversation was going on, Bessie had been sitting by her open window in her bedroom, which overlooked the terrace. It was the bedroom that Blanche had occupied the first time she had been to Alton-Leigh.

The voices drifted up. She could hear almost every word, and she listened with all her might. She did not understand all they said. She did not grasp the whole situation, nor understand what had led up to it. But she understood enough to feel almost certain that Bernard and Rose Mary were lovers...had always been lovers... Even if they weren't, it was every inch as bad – perhaps worse; but she was sure they were.

Bessie did not make up her mind what to do with this precious weapon that had been put into her hands, but for the time all her feelings were concentrated in her hatred for

Bernard. He, she felt, had played a double game and had pretended to make up to her when all the time he was making up to some one else. How could she best punish him? That would need careful thought.

# CHAPTER XV

Bessie spent that night devising the best means of avenging herself on Bernard. She would like a punishment that would hurt Blanche, if possible, as well, although it was Bernard whom she was the more angry with. She could, of course, tell Blanche, but that, she reflected, would not necessarily punish Bernard. The only way of really hitting Bernard was to do something that would mar, or, if possible, end, his relations with Rose Mary. That was the only thing he would really mind.

She must try and open Walter's eyes. It would probably be difficult to do this at once. She had little time to do it in. They were going back to London on Monday. She did not know when she would see them all again. Walter was capable, she knew, of going to the end of the earth at a moment's notice. She must act promptly.

As it was, circumstances favoured her. Bernard had asked Rose Mary and Walter to luncheon. After luncheon, Bessie asked Walter to show her the Dower House, and Bernard at once seized the opportunity of arranging that he, Rose Mary, Stephen, and Blanche should walk to the farm. This would give him, he knew, an opportunity of talking to Rose Mary, while Blanche looked after Stephen.

"I don't want Bessie to see it without me," said Rose Mary. "I'll come with you."

"I told Mrs Jackson you would have tea with her today," said Walter, "so you had better go with them. We shall still be there when you come back, and I won't show Bessie your sitting-room till you come."

The truth was, that Walter, if he had to spend the afternoon with Bessie, would rather spend it with her alone than with her and Rose Mary. A talk of three together he could not endure with Rose Mary, as he felt she would make mental notes of his conversation, which with Bessie would be necessarily not a real one...but alone with her he didn't care what he said; he would be shameless, and get on with Bessie perfectly well. He knew what pleased her, and the line to follow, but he could not do that before Rose Mary. So she had to give in.

"I think it's most officious of you," she said.

"If they're expecting you," said Bernard, "you had better go, as Mrs Jackson is certain to have prepared a tea for you; won't she, Blanche?"

"Yes; she takes great trouble over her teas; they are excellent."

So they went off, and Walter took Bessie to the Dower House. First they inspected the kitchen garden, and then the Dower House garden. Bessie cared little for gardens, but she knew exactly what to say, and her memory was so retentive she even remembered the names of plants.

Bessie wasn't at all sure how she ought to broach the subject. Not sure whether she would be able to. She relied on the inspiration of the moment. On the way they met Walter's children out for their afternoon walk with their Nanny – the two little boys, Bernard and Basil, walking, and Catherine, the baby, in the perambulator.

"That's a sight that makes me long to get home to my babies," Bessie said. An inaccurate statement, as she was not overfond of children, especially if they were small.

"Yes," said Walter; "you must miss them."

"Are you fond of children?"

"I'm fond of my own children."

"Now that's just what I feel. I adore my own children, but other people's rather bore me. But I thought your children looked lovely. They take after their mother. I suppose she is fond of children?"

"Rose Mary? Oh yes."

"It's sad for poor Blanche, not having any children, isn't it? I suppose Bernard feels it?"

"Yes; I think he does. I think he did... "

"You have known Bernard a long time, haven't you?"

"Oh yes, for years – all my life. We were at school together, and then in the Army."

"Was he always just the same as he is now?"

"Yes...in what way?"

"Was he always such a dreadful flirt?"

"Do you think he's a flirt?"

"Well, of course I do. Stephen is bad enough, but nothing like Bernard."

"I shouldn't have said that."

"He makes up to everybody. Didn't you notice how he made up to that Frenchwoman?"

"I can't say I thought he did...particularly."

"Men never notice anything. Why, he made up to me even! Of course, only in fun, but I had to be careful, because I shouldn't have liked Blanche to have thought there was anything of that kind going on, even in fun."

"He always admired pretty women. There surely is no harm in that?"

"And then, of course, he flirts with Rose Mary," Bessie went on imperturbably. "I wonder it doesn't make you jealous."

"No; I'm not jealous. They can flirt as much as they like. I have the utmost confidence in Rose Mary."

"Of course we understand those things, but, you know," she said slyly, "I couldn't help thinking the foreigners thought it *odd*."

"Do you think so?"

"Yes; but then the French are so extraordinary, aren't they? They have such curious minds...such...nasty minds sometimes. They always think the worst of us. One day, during the week, they were sitting on the terrace, on the seat, in the morning, after breakfast, discussing the party. It was the morning of the day they left. I could hear every word they said. They little knew that. Of course, I wasn't *trying* to listen, but I couldn't help hearing what they said. I was having my hair done, and the window was open. I was thankful they were talking *French*, so that my maid couldn't hear what they said."

"Did they say awful things about us?"

"Not so much awful as ridiculous. She told him all our most intimate histories! For instance, that Stephen had married me for my money – just fancy, my poor money, as if I had been a millionairess! Then that you were Blanche's lover, of course. They seemed to take that as a matter of course."

"You don't really mean it?"

"Yes; they didn't even discuss that. They mentioned it, agreed, and went on to something else."

"What else did they say?"

"Well, they told a long story. They said that Bernard had never wanted to marry Blanche, and that she had made him promise to marry her years ago in Rome when all that...all that sad story happened...that if ever she were free, and that horrible Italian were to die, he would marry her, and that she kept him to his word, although he didn't want to – although he loved some one else all the time."

"What rubbish! And who did they say was his love?"

"Can't you guess?" – this with a slight laugh.

"I haven't an idea."

"You are dense."

"Not Celia Deacon?"

"Oh dear, no, not an actress. They had never heard of her."

"I give it up."

"It's some one you know quite well."

"Kitty Wallace?"

"No."

"Well, I give it up."

"Well, Rose Mary, of course."

"Rose Mary? That's funny. I thought at one time before he married Blanche that he wanted to marry Rose Mary, but I was quite wrong."

"Yes, quite wrong; and then she said that Bernard was, of course, madly in love with Rose Mary *now*, and although I know she talks nonsense, and that foreigners are like that, it made me think that perhaps it *is* a little imprudent of Bernard and Rose Mary to go on like that before foreigners."

"To go on like what?"

"Well, for him to *seem* so devoted."

"I don't agree at all. They seem to me hardly ever to see each other. It is extremely difficult to persuade Rose Mary to go to the big house."

"Yes; and in the eyes of the French people, that of course seemed to prove it."

"What nonsense! I never heard anything so silly! And did they think that Rose Mary" – he laughed nervously – "was in love with Bernard?"

"Oh yes! They thought that…but, you know, about Bernard, I do agree with them to a certain extent. I mean I think he is rather in love with Rose Mary, so much attracted, shall we say, as to be *almost* in love, and, if she were any one else, I should think it dangerous. As it is, if I were Blanche I should mind. I shouldn't mind if I were *you*, because, you see, you *know*…but if I were Blanche, I should mind. I couldn't help minding."

"Why?"

"Well, because, you see, Rose Mary is so much younger, and Blanche, beautiful and charming as she is, is at least fifteen years older than Bernard. That makes a great difference, doesn't it? Madame d'Aurillac said she remembered Blanche years ago in Paris, and that she was so lovely then."

"I think she is beautiful now – most beautiful."

"So do I. But youth is youth, isn't it? and one can no longer expect when one is getting on for sixty to be quite like what one was when one was twenty-five or thirty. And, you see, Bernard is so susceptible to youth and beauty, that of course a foreigner, seeing all that goes on, would only draw one conclusion."

"But, seeing all *what* go on?"

The way Bernard treats her...talks to her...looks at her... Of course she takes no notice – no notice at all. I dare say she doesn't even see it...but it's quite obvious to the outside eye that Bernard admires her more than he admires Blanche...far, far more."

"You don't really mean it?"

"You see, it's not only the French people it strikes in that way, but in London, in the summer, everybody said Bernard was perfectly crazy about Rose Mary, and that it was so cruel, as she never gave him a look. So you have no cause to be jealous, which is always something."

"But if they say I was Blanche's lover, they would say anything."

"They never said that in London! That was only the French people here who said that. They are obliged to think things like that; they are made that way. In India they used to be just the same; they thought it *rude* to suppose one hadn't lovers, if one was married – almost an insult; and they would certainly think it an insult in the case of a beautiful woman like Blanche. And then, you see, you are always there; you always consult her about everything. People can't help noticing it."

"Yes; we have always been great friends, and always shall be."

"What they don't understand is that the circumstances are peculiar, are they not?"

"I really don't see anything peculiar about them."

"Well, the whole history is an odd one. Bernard having known Blanche such years ago, and then having married her, after all, years later, when no one expected it."

"But we all of us expected it – at least I did."

"Ah, you and his intimate friends, of course, but I was thinking of the outside world; it was a surprise to them. And then, you see, your marrying Rose Mary directly after, and coming to live here, and you all living together here, almost under the same roof, and…"

"What?"

"Well, then you and Blanche becoming such great friends, and then Bernard admiring Rose Mary – so obviously admiring her…and she looking younger every day, and Blanche becoming a little older looking, and gradually beginning at last to show some signs that she is no longer quite, quite young – which is only fair. You see, it was an unusual set of circumstances, you must admit."

"Yes; but if one knows the facts, the truth – there is nothing odd about it."

"No, of course not…that's just what that French lady did say. She said, 'If one knew the truth there is probably nothing odd about it all,' and her husband said to her, '*Ma chère*,' he said, 'we *never* shall know the truth.' And she said, 'About Blanche? She seems to me transparent.' And he said, 'No, not about Blanche, about the other one; she is deep.' And Madame agreed. 'Yes,' she said, 'still waters run deep.' 'But there is no doubt about it that he loves her,' the husband said. 'And no doubt about it,' she said, 'that Rose Mary loves him. Only men are so stupid, they see nothing.'"

"She meant Bernard saw nothing?"

"No, no; she meant that her husband saw nothing. Wasn't it amusing? I told Stephen, and at first he was amused, and then he agreed with me that Bernard ought to be more careful before foreigners. 'But it's no good any one saying anything,' he added, 'as Bernard is as obstinate as a mule.' "

"Well, it's extraordinary what people will say, isn't it?"

"Quite extraordinary. And they always seem to know everybody's most private affairs."

"Yes; don't they? Always. And those French people discussed to a penny exactly how much money I had when I married. All wrong, of course; and exactly how much money you and Rose Mary had, and how much you made by your books – fabulous sums they said – and then, this will make you laugh – they discussed whether you were jealous, and he said you were so busy running after Blanche that you noticed nothing, and she said that you never would know; that you were the kind of man who was blind about certain things."

"They are right there – I am; especially when the things don't exist."

"They made dear Rose Mary into such a romantic figure. She had, of course, according to their version of the story, always been in love with Bernard, long before he married Blanche."

"It can't have been so long, as she was only just out when we were married, and she had only just seen Bernard once or twice then."

"They had heard all the story abroad from some of Blanche's old *Roman* friends…and they said Bernard had met her when she was quite a child – sixteen – and had fallen in love with her at first sight – it was a real case of that – and then that Blanche, of course, scenting the danger, had kept him to his bargain before anything went any further."

"How absurd!"

"And now they made out she was dying of love for him, and he for her. And Madame actually said…it shows you what lies people will tell…that she had overheard them having what they called an *'explication,'* and that Bernard had said this had gone so far that he could bear it no longer, and talked of running away… "

"What rubbish!"

"Yes, and that Rose Mary had said it was impossible because of you, the children, and Blanche. And Bernard had agreed that it would *kill* Blanche, and that was all Madame said she had heard."

"And where did they have this public discussion on this private matter?"

"Oh! on the terrace, of course. I must say that terrace *is* dangerous. If the windows are open in the bedrooms the people up there hear every word you say. But I couldn't help thinking it was so lucky *I* overheard that, and no one else. Other people might have believed it, or thought there was something in it."

"I don't think so."

"And, then, so lucky they were speaking *French*. Just fancy, if my maid had heard all that! Luckily she doesn't understand a word of French."

Bessie now thought she had said enough. She had invented the whole scenario of the French people's discourse. The only remark she had heard them make was something about an *explication* that one of their French friends had had with another of their French friends – all the rest was fiction. Bessie did not know what effect her words had had. But she felt sure of one thing: Whether he thought it all nonsense or not, and however vehemently he might declare it to be all nonsense, she was certain that he henceforward would look upon the situation with a new eye…he would begin to notice what he had never noticed before. Bernard and Rose Mary would do the rest by themselves. She felt that whatever happened, things could never be the same again, unless Walter were a stupider man than she thought. "He will watch her, and she will notice it," she thought, "and that will make the situation impossible for her; and then she will tell Bernard, and then Heaven knows what will happen; there, Master Bernard, I think I've arranged a nice little pie for you, and it will be a good lesson to you not to trifle with the feelings of those who have never done you any harm."

They went into the Dower House now, and Walter rang for the tea. Bessie admired the room, the pictures, the chairs, with a look of silent reservation on her face. It meant she was only admiring out of civility. She wished this to be felt and recognised.

Just as some people have such subtle good manners that they make others feel comfortable without their knowing they are being made to feel comfortable, the goal aimed at and successfully reached by such manners being the care for other people's feelings, so others have equally subtle *bad* manners that make others feel uncomfortable; the goal aimed at here and equally successfully reached being the gratification and expression of self-importance at the expense of other people's feelings. Bessie's manners were of the latter kind. If, for instance, she had luncheon with the Jacksons (Bernard's agent, and Blanche had taken her there one day), she would look at the food on her plate with an air as much as to say, "This is not what I am accustomed to, but I am such a lady that I am concealing the fact," and yet she made the distaste, the disapproval, and the concealment of the distaste excruciatingly clear, and meant to do so, meant her hostess to observe and to feel it. It was all the more unnecessary as the Jacksons' food was simple, but excellent. But Bessie prided herself on never having been rude; she was proud of her "manners."

Presently Rose Mary came back.

"I haven't shown Bessie your sitting-room," Walter said, "nor mine. Rose Mary is proud of hers, and I am proud of mine," he explained.

"I hope you haven't let Walter make the tea," Rose Mary said, giving a glance at the tea-table. "He has no idea of making tea."

Bessie smiled condescendingly and reassuringly.

"Oh no!" she said, "the *parlour-maid*" (Bessie stressed the word, as in her house there was a footman) "made it." Walter's household consisted, besides the cook, of two parlour-maids and an Italian servant whom Walter had picked up during his early travels, and who had remained with him ever since.

In Bessie's eyes this was a combination of two unpardonable categories – the middle-class and the Bohemian, and not only the Bohemian, but the foreign.

They had tea, and Bessie rejected the offer of scones, tea-cake or cakes, and fastidiously nibbled a little piece of plain bread and butter, with a look as much as to say: "One can safely eat that…in the country."

They talked of the Jacksons.

"A nice, well-brought-up little woman," said Bessie patronisingly.

"She's a clever woman," said Rose Mary.

"Oh, clever, indeed? Just fancy."

"She manages the whole farm."

"Oh, I see, clever in that way."

"She's clever altogether, I think; practical, sensible, isn't she, Walter?"

"Yes," he said absent-mindedly; "I like Mrs Jackson."

"Bernard says that Jackson could do nothing without her," said Rose Mary.

"Really? Does Bernard say that?" And as Bessie said the word "Bernard" she used a particular intonation, and gave Rose Mary a meaning look. Rose Mary felt it, and flushed slightly, and then felt annoyed with herself at having flushed, and Walter began to think of what Bessie had told him, and of Madame d'Aurillac's gossip.

Rose Mary went on bravely, determining to leave no awkward gap in the conversation, for she felt Bessie was dangerous, and did not understand what she was driving at, nor what was the cause of this sudden insidious undercurrent.

"Yes," she said; "Bernard thinks highly of her. He says she has such good judgment."

"Bernard and Stephen both are fond of relying on *others* for advice. I suppose it is a family trait." Bessie purred.

"I don't think Bernard and Stephen are at all alike," said Walter. "Let's show Bessie the sitting-rooms."

There was nothing much to show. They went into Walter's sitting-room first. It possessed two shabby armchairs, a large writing-table, littered with papers, pipes, photographs, snuff-boxes, tobacco tins, bills, letters, all in indescribable confusion. Over the chimney-piece there was a large photograph of the temple of Sunium, on the walls some water-colours of the Golden Horn, the City of Constantinople – pink, white, and opalescent in the haze of the early morning, with a few minarets indicated in the distance and some dark cypresses in the foreground. A large bookcase occupied one whole wall, in which there were books in many languages and a complete set of *Punch* and of Zola's works.

Bessie cast a look of disapproval over the whole, and said to Rose Mary: "It is a comfort when one's husband has a room where he can smoke pipes and cigars, isn't it?"

"Walter smokes all over the house, I'm afraid."

"Oh, really, I should never allow Stephen to smoke a pipe in the drawing-room. It is so dreadful for the curtains, but – " She stopped, but her expression meant, "With curtains such as you have, it wouldn't much matter."

They then went up to Rose Mary's sitting-room, which was on the first floor. It was almost austerely simple, with a plain deal table, everything on it tidy and well arranged, some bowls of chrysanthemums, a large crucifix on the chimney-piece, and some Arundel coloured prints on the walls, and an oil painting of a grey cart-horse. A sofa and a few chintz-covered chairs, and no books except a large French cookery book and some manuals on agriculture and gardening; a great many catalogues of roses, lilies, bulbs, and seeds.

"Very nice and fresh," said Bessie; "and so tidy. So much tidier than your room." She looked at Walter, with a smile of mock scolding.

"Well, I must be going," she said. "We shall meet tonight. You are coming to dinner, I believe?"

"Yes, we are," said Rose Mary.

Bessie went home. After she had gone, Walter and Rose Mary sat downstairs in front of the fire. It was quite dark out of doors now; the curtains were drawn, and the lamps had been brought in.

"Before you came," said Walter, "she told me a long rigmarole about the d'Aurillacs."

"What about them?"

"A long and preposterous story about the way they gossiped; what they said about all of us."

"How could Bessie know what they said to each other? She doesn't even understand French."

"Well, she says that she was in her bedroom having her hair done and the window was open, and that d'Aurillac and his wife were sitting on a seat on the terrace, and that she could hear every word they said, and they were saying all sorts of silly things about all of us."

Rose Mary felt herself blushing scarlet to the roots of her hair. She understood what had happened. Bessie had overheard her conversation with Bernard.

The story of the d'Aurillacs' conversation, she knew, was an invention. Bessie had small French. This was her way of telling Walter. She couldn't say anything. She looked straight before her into the fire, and prayed that Walter might not notice.

Walter did notice. He couldn't help it. But he pretended not to; he, too, stared into the fire, and at that moment he realised in a blinding flash that what Bessie had said was true; the d'Aurillac story may have been – no, was certainly – an invention, but the fact was true – the fact about Bernard and Rose Mary. He saw the whole truth – a thousand forgotten episodes, words, sights, slender shreds – atoms – of evidence, stood out before him as in letters of fire. He saw the whole truth, and, what is more, he understood it. He misunderstood nothing. He saw the whole story as it had happened. He understood the situation as it was now, exactly as it was.

There was a long silence, and then Walter said: "It was only nonsense, you know. I believe Bessie invented it. She hates foreigners."

"Yes," said Rose Mary, in a voice which she hoped in vain might sound natural "she hates foreigners."

# CHAPTER XVI

Bessie and Stephen left Alton-Leigh the next morning. Bessie went away thinking she had done some fine work, and had achieved her object. As a matter of fact she entirely misread the situation. She had, it is true, been successful in opening Walter's eyes to the truth, but she little knew what the effect of this operation would be on Walter, as she was not only completely in the dark about his character, but she would have been incapable of understanding it, however carefully it might have been explained to her. She thought that Walter would behave as she would have behaved in the same circumstances: make violent scenes of jealousy, forbid Rose Mary to see Bernard, or take her away from the Dower House. Instead of which Walter's only object was to prevent Rose Mary from ever guessing that he knew.

Life went on at Alton-Leigh and the Dower House just as usual, and so quietly, and in so ordinary a fashion that Rose Mary could hardly believe anything untoward had happened. She felt convinced that Bessie knew the truth, and had tried to make as much mischief as she could, but she had no idea what Walter thought; what he knew, what he had guessed…she left things as they were, and tried not to think about them. She avoided seeing Bernard alone.

Walter finished his new book before Christmas. His eldest sister, Marian, whose husband, Sir Daniel Lowe, was in the City and prosperous, asked them to spend Christmas at their country house in Norfolk. Rose Mary accepted this invitation with alacrity. She dreaded the Christmas party this year at Alton-Leigh, although Stephen and Bessie were not to be there. Rose Mary intended to stay away as long as she could.

At Alton-Leigh there was a smaller family party than usual, but Bernard's South African friends, the Heinholdts, were there, and Blanche's cousins, the Legges, and Father Rendall.

Stephen, when he first left, wrote to her often and fully, but Blanche answered his letters so briefly and at such long intervals that he gave up writing in despair. He saw it was no use; she was determined not to write.

Stephen's married life was becoming more thorny, and his relations with Bessie more strained. He began to spend more and more time at the Club, and less and less time at home. He played cards now regularly – bridge and écarté.

After Christmas, at the beginning of February, war broke out between Japan and Russia, and Walter at once approached the editor of the *Northern Pilot*, whom he knew, with a view to going out as correspondent on the Russian side. The editor was delighted. It was arranged that he should go. Walter seemed radiantly happy at the prospect, and Rose Mary did nothing to dissuade him, She felt she had not that right. But she felt that when Walter was gone she could not go on living at the Dower House by herself. She did not know what to do.

Lady Alice came to the rescue, and helped her out of the difficulty. She seemed instinctively to guess Rose Mary's problems, although Rose Mary had not said a word to her about them.

Lady Alice suggested that she and Rose Mary should take a house together; she knew of a house in Sussex which she had had her eye on a long time; it was too large for her by herself, but for her and Rose Mary and the children it would be perfect.

If they took this, she would let her house in London for a year, at any rate. Rose Mary could stay in the country with her as long as Walter was away, and then, when he came back – he wouldn't be away for long – they could go back to the Dower House, or, if they preferred it, stay in Sussex. He would see. She wanted to go and live in the country and had really no use for a London house, now that Hester was married; at the same time, she felt it would be lonely to live in the country by herself, and she would like to be with the children; she was so fond of them.

Walter was delighted with the idea, and wondered what Rose Mary would say; she jumped at it, and the matter was settled at once. Walter wrote and told Bernard of the new plan, and Bernard was not able to realise it.

"We must, of course, go up to London and say goodbye to Walter," he said to Blanche.

He had not contemplated doing this before. He thought, although this was not the reason he gave himself for going, that, if he were to see Rose Mary, he might persuade her to reconsider her decision. He felt that if she once left the Dower House she might never come back.

Walter was starting for St Petersburg at the beginning of March, laden with letters of introduction.

Blanche and Bernard went up to London to see him off. They arrived in London the night before he started. There was no farewell dinner, or anything of the kind. Each one of those concerned tacitly felt that would be unendurable. Walter dined with his mother and Rose Mary at Mansfield Street, and Bernard dined alone with Blanche.

Lady Alice had found a tenant for her London house, who was to move in at the end of March. He had taken the house for a year.

They all met the next morning at Charing Cross Station. It was a cold, raw morning, and there was a cutting east wind blowing. Lady Alice looked frail in her fur tippet. Rose Mary looked calm as ever, fresh and beautiful, in her neat blue serge with a small fur collar, lilies-of-the-valley at her waist; and Blanche felt cold, and she shivered. Bernard was like a somnambulist; he did not seem to hear a word that was said to him.

"I suppose you will still find snow when you get there?" said Lady Alice.

"Yes; I think so," said Walter, struggling with a large leather bag. "I have got far too much luggage," he said. "A saddle, too, takes so much room."

"That's registered, isn't it?" said Rose Mary practically.

"Yes; but in spite of all that is registered, there is still this luncheon-basket, this bag, this little bag, and this hand portmanteau, which has got all my 'civilian' clothes in it!"

"You can leave all that behind at St Petersburg," said Rose Mary.

"Shall I leave the luncheon-basket behind? I don't believe I shall want it?"

"Not if it's got a kettle in it," said Blanche, "to make tea; a kettle is always a comfort."

"I always envied any one who had a luncheon-basket in South Africa," said Bernard.

"Yes," said Walter; "that is really why I have taken it with me, and, after all, it's quite light. It's got a spirit lamp in it and a small kettle."

"Have you got books?" asked Blanche.

"Yes; mother has given me some very nice train books – Sherlock Holmes in the *Tauchnitz*, *Bleak House*, and a book called *The Napoleon of Notting Hill*, by a new man called Chesterton. Then I've taken a small Shakespeare, and a Browning in one volume, and I've got all the magazines."

"I think you will have a good crossing," said Lady Alice. "The forecast is quite good."

"Is it? I didn't see it today."

"Have you got plenty of tobacco?" said Bernard.

"Yes; I saw to that," said Rose Mary. "Walter always leaves his tobacco behind."

"And matches?" asked Blanche.

"Boxes and boxes; but shan't I have to declare them?"

"I think you will, if they are wax matches."

"They are fusees."

"What time will you get to Ostend?" said Bernard.

"About half-past three, I think."

"You will telegraph directly you get to St Petersburg, won't you?" said his mother. "I shan't expect anything till then."

"I'll telegraph, if I can, from Ostend and from Berlin, and I'll send you a picture post card from Berlin, if I can get one."

Walter got into the carriage, and the others followed him.

"Tickets, please." The ticket-collector opened the door of the carriage. "Are you the only gentleman travelling?" he said, taking the solitary ticket offered.

"Yes," said Walter.

"Well, you'll have the carriage to yourself now. Do you know any one else who is going?" said Bernard.

"No; I don't. They say there's a man going for the *Daily Record*, and the *Morning News* have got some one out there already."

"The *Times* haven't got any one, have they?"

"No; the *Times* have quarrelled with the Russian Government."

"I suppose they will end by having some one?"

"I suppose so."

The guard appeared and said: "The train will be starting in a moment, sir."

They all got up.

"You must go, mother darling, or else you'll have to come to Dover."

"Well, we must say goodbye."

Walter threw his arms round his mother's neck, and she gave him what she felt was a final kiss – she gave a little gulp.

"God love you, my darling!"

She got down – Bernard helped her.

"Goodbye, Rose Mary. Goodbye, Blanche." Walter kissed Rose Mary. She and Blanche got out. "Goodbye, Bernard. Goodbye, everybody; goodbye."

The guard blew his whistle. A flag was waved.

"Take care of the *Hun-Hutzes*," said Bernard.

Walter leant out of the window, waving his hat. There was a chorus of goodbyes.

Lady Alice looked, her eyes full of tears, at the receding train. She couldn't speak. "It's the last time I shall ever see my darling son. God guard and love him," she thought.

"Come, darling," she said to Rose Mary, "we must go home."

They went out of the station, waving goodbye to Blanche and to Bernard. Bernard had not had a word with Rose Mary, but he saw by her face and felt by her manner that her decision was irrevocable.

"She will never, never come back to the Dower House," he thought. "All that is over…over for ever… "

"How he loves her!" thought Blanche. "It's extraordinary to be able to love more than one person at a time, because it is not as if he didn't love me; he does."

"Poor Walter," thought Rose Mary. "I have been a bad woman, a bad, bad woman. I deserve to be punished. Let *me* be punished, but not the children. It was not their fault." And awful instances of the sins of parents being visited on the children raced through her mind.

"Poor Walter!" thought Blanche, as the train steamed out of Charing Cross, "I shall miss him the most; how bleak and lonely he must be feeling now! Up till this moment he has probably felt excited. Now I think he must be feeling as he felt the first time he left home to go to school. But it is worse now! He probably feels there is now nowhere in the world where he is really wanted! His mother? yes; but she has learnt to do without him. Myself? Yes, but he probably is saying to himself,

'She will miss me a little but… The only thing for me to do is to go away, and, if possible, to die…even that won't happen, it would be too good.' Poor, poor Walter – I shall miss you, I promise!"

At the end of March Rose Mary and Lady Alice went down to their new house in Sussex, a charming old brick house with rambling rooms and passages, a garden enclosed by a high brick wall, and a little chapel, where the priest from the village, which was only a mile off, could come and say Mass.

Rose Mary felt that a solution of some kind had been reached.

"I was wrong to think," she said to herself, "that Walter's mother hates me. She doesn't hate me. She either doesn't know or she understands and wants to help. I think it's that she knows and understands."

Blanche went back to Alton-Leigh and stayed there alone for a little while. Bernard had business in London. She was not sorry to be alone.

At Easter, Bernard came back to Alton-Leigh, and brought some of his City friends with him. After Easter he proposed going back to London, and suggested that Blanche should come with him. Blanche felt she could not face London. And yet she felt she had no excuse for not going with him, and that it was hard on Bernard if she did not go. After thinking it over carefully she felt obliged to go.

They went up after Easter. It was for Blanche a quiet summer. She got the doctor to say that she must keep quiet, and not sit up late, although really she felt better than she had done for a long time. She urged Bernard to go out as much as possible. She knew he enjoyed it, and knew he enjoyed going out alone.

She felt he needed distraction, something to take his thoughts from Rose Mary and the empty Dower House, and yet never had he been more gentle to her, more considerate, and more loving.

"The funny thing is," she thought, "that I really do believe he does still love me, but...but ... "

Stephen came to see her fairly often, but she did not encourage his visits; and she saw a certain amount of Father Rendall. He, she felt, understood the whole thing so far better than any one else. He understood it and her so well, she felt, that she did not dare talk about it with him...she was afraid of the depth of self-revelation it might lead to, and she kept on impersonal topics, although she would have dearly liked to have discussed certain aspects of the situation with him and to have asked him for his opinion, if not for his advice.

Then, towards the summer, just as she had felt she had made in him one reliable, impersonal, impartial, and detached friend, he received orders to go to America. She received a message from him on the telephone one evening that he was going, and the next day he had gone. She had no idea when he would come back. Her life was now a desert. There was Stephen, but she did not want Stephen's intimacy and friendship. She felt it was all wrong, and that she was simply making trouble between him and Bessie. It was difficult to make that situation worse than it was. Stephen cleverly concealed from Bessie that he ever saw Blanche, while she was in London.

Rose Mary remained resolutely in the country and did not come up to London for a single day.

At the end of July, Blanche and Bernard went back to Alton-Leigh, and the usual routine of their autumn life there began once more.

Elderly financiers, young soldiers, their wives, neighbours, guns, consisting partly of neighbours, like Colonel Wallace, and partly of foreigners, like the Cherenis, came to stay. There were a few small shooting-parties in September for the partridges, and one large shoot for the covert shooting later.

Bernard seemed to feel the emptiness of the Dower House acutely.

He asked Bessie and Stephen for Christmas so long beforehand that it was difficult for them to refuse, but Bessie declared that they must go to her uncle's; that he would be offended if she refused.

"We went there last year," said Stephen, "and I don't much care if we do offend him."

"No; that's just it, you don't mind how rude you are to *my* relations, but you expect me to be polite to yours, whatever I may think of them or feel about them myself, and, after all, my relations are quite as good as yours… "

"Oh, I know, I know, but we went there last Christmas, and Bernard does really want us to go, but you can go to your uncle's by all means; *I* am going to Alton-Leigh."

Bessie stormed a great deal, but she saw there was nothing to be done, and she preferred going to Alton-Leigh with Stephen to his going alone, besides which, she looked forward to being able to pay out Bernard again, possibly. At any rate, she would "put him in his place."

They ended, after many discussions, arguments, and rows, by going, both of them, to Alton-Leigh, where there was a small family party.

Blanche seemed tired and listless, and not able to do much.

Bessie felt that any shafts of hers were powerless to reach her. Bernard was unconscious of any hostility on the part of Bessie – unconscious that he was in disgrace. He was just the same to her; he still thought her attractive, and was ready to be amused by her, and took pains to please her. Bessie received all this ironically, but he didn't notice the irony. He had no idea there was anything wrong anywhere. And so the visit went off well, for, in spite of everything, Bessie was flattered by Bernard's attentions, although she pretended to be indifferent to them.

Bernard had made Blanche ask Rose Mary and Walter's mother for Christmas, but Lady Alice was not well; she had a series of chills and bronchitis, and it was impossible for her to travel.

Walter, having found it impossible to get any matter of importance over the wire, had decided to come home. He started home just before Christmas, and he was due back early in January. In the meantime, Lady Alice's bronchitis grew more serious, and developed into pneumonia. The crisis passed and left her exhausted and weak. She was old, she was frail, and the doctors shook their heads. Nurses were sent for, and Rose Mary nursed her with the utmost devotion, but it was all of no avail. She died in Sussex on the Feast of the Epiphany, quietly, after hearing Mass.

Walter arrived in London just too late to see her. He was in Sussex two or three days after the funeral. She had only let her London house for a year, and had only taken this Sussex house for a year. In her will she left her London house to Walter.

So, at the end of March, Rose Mary and Walter left Sussex and went to London, and Walter announced his intention of going back to Alton-Leigh, either after Easter or at the end of the summer. He wanted to write a book about his Manchurian experiences.

Bessie and Stephen left Alton-Leigh after the New Year, and went back to London. Stephen had found the society of Blanche more than a relief after a long period of bickering with Bessie. It was to him intoxicatingly delightful.

As soon as he got home, after his first day in the City, finding nobody at home, he sat down to write Blanche a long letter in his little sitting-room – the only room in the house, he thought, which a human being could sit in.

Bessie was out, and had not come home.

After he had written about three pages, he heard the telephone bell ringing. The telephone, the only one in the house – there were no extensions – was in a little box at the end of the hall passage.

He went to answer it. It was some one from the Club who wanted him to dine and play bridge. The call was a prolonged one, as at first Stephen refused, and then began to let himself be half persuaded, and finally said he would see, and ring up later. He meant to find out first what sort of mood Bessie was in, and whether she had anything on foot. While he was telephoning, Bessie came home and let herself in with her latch-key. Seeing Stephen's hat on the hall table, she went straight into his sitting-room. She saw the unfinished letter lying on the blotting-paper, and, at first, she glanced at it, and then she read it. She did not take long to master its contents. It was the manner, rather than the matter, of the letter that she thought important.

It was a letter that implied a greater degree of intimacy than it expressed; it was a letter that showed Bessie, although she was not mentioned in it, that in Stephen's eyes Blanche evidently belonged to a plane to which she, Bessie, could not aspire.

It filled her with envy, hatred, and malice. But she said nothing and did nothing. It was Blanche she hated more than Stephen. She resolved to have somehow or other her revenge on Blanche, to hurt her really, if she could, and she felt that she could. After all, she had precious weapons in her possession; the only question was, how could they best be used?

The situation must, she thought, be dealt with scientifically. She felt too angry to do anything just at once; she must think over it until she regained the full possession of her wits. She would need, she felt, all her presence of mind, all her wits about her, and complete calm; just at this moment she was far from calm. She was seething with rage. Just as for poets poetry is said to be emotion remembered in tranquillity, so for a spiteful, envious, mean nature, an act of revenge is spite remembered rather than spite actually experienced. She must wait; she must regain her serenity. For the moment she felt she had lost all self-control, and yet, when Stephen, unsuspecting, walked into his sitting-room and said: "Oh, you've come back, have you, Bessie dear," she smiled at him sweetly, and asked him if he had had a tiring day. She stood in front of the chimney-piece and didn't even seem to notice the writing-table.

"I've just come in, and I must go upstairs," she said, walking towards the door, to Stephen's relief.

"By the way," said Stephen, "are we doing anything tonight?"

"No; why?"

"Well, Tommy Rashleigh has just rung up to ask me to dine with some friends of his – a man's dinner he's got tonight. I told him I didn't know what you were doing, and that I would let him know."

"By all means go," said Bessie, delighted at having the evening to herself to work out her plans. "I've got rather a headache, and I'm not going to come down to dinner. I shall just have a little something on a tray." Stephen wondered why she took the matter so calmly, but he did not give it much thought. He simply said: "Oh, very well; I hope your head isn't bad?"

"Oh no. I'm a little overtired, that's all."

She left him, and Stephen finished his letter and posted it himself. Bessie from her bedroom heard him go out to post his letter, and heard him come back.

"Poor fool," she thought.

# CHAPTER XVII

While Stephen was enjoying a gay dinner with some friends at the Palmerston Club, and winning money at cards, after dinner, Bessie wrote a letter. It took her a long time – from eight-thirty till ten. She then posted it herself.

"It is too late for the country post," she thought. "It will reach Alton-Leigh by the second post, or possibly not till the day after tomorrow."

The letter was written to Blanche.

Bessie put in this letter all that she could imagine would be most hurtful, most venomous, and most deadly; all that suggested itself to be wounding to the angered instincts of a malicious and angry woman. She said to herself, as she finished the letter: "Only a woman could have written that, only a woman would know exactly how to wound in such a way!" She was satisfied with her work.

She was so frightened of the letter going astray, and of not being able to recapture the exact phrases she had used, that she made a fair copy, and so the letter, like many other works of art, while it had the appearance of being unpremeditated, was in reality the result of calm deliberation, steady retrospect, and collected presence of mind.

"I think," she said to herself, "that Blanche will really mind this letter."

She had told Blanche many things...about her relation to Stephen, and especially the conversation she had overheard between Bernard and Rose Mary. But she had cleverly managed to leave it in doubt who had overheard this conversation. It might not have been Bessie at all, from her letter, and yet it was not definitely said that it was anybody else.

The letter arrived at Alton-Leigh, according to Bessie's calculations, by the second post the next day. Blanche found it on the hall table at five o'clock, when she came in from her walk. She was feeling particularly serene. It had been a lovely spring day. The first manifestations of early spring were in the air. She had picked some snowdrops in the garden. The winter jasmine was out on the walls of the house.

She took up Bessie's letter. She did not open it at once. "It will keep," she thought. She recognised the handwriting, and she was astonished at Bessie writing her what seemed to be a long letter.

She had tea with Bernard. Bernard seemed in a happy, lazy, contented mood. He was smoking a pipe, and he had got hold of a new book that pleased him, a new Wells, that had just come out, and which was keeping him so tightly bound that he could not pay attention to anything else.

When she had done tea, Blanche went up to her sitting-room to write her letters.

Then she remembered Bessie's letter.

"I'd better read that now," she thought, and she sat down in her arm-chair near the fire.

She read the first page rather absent-mindedly, and she did not at first catch the drift of it. She turned the page...it was more than an eight-page letter – the handwriting was characteristic; it was revealingly common. On the grey writing-paper the direction was heavily embossed in white capitals. She saw words and sentences that she did not quite believe in; she did not for a moment believe that she had seen what she had read. She dropped the letter on her lap. Then she took it up, turned over the leaves; and phrases which belonged to a further part of the letter caught her eye...they were burnt into her mind at once, as by a red-hot iron. Then she took the letter and tore it up into shreds, and threw the bits into the fire.

The effect of the letter on Blanche was not at all what Bessie had expected...it was in a way greater than anything she had expected, greater than anything she could have understood: it reached Blanche's soul, and wounded that. Bessie's aim had been a lower one.

All that there was about Stephen in the letter, Blanche agreed with, sympathised with.

All that there was about Bernard she knew already, only there was this vast difference: You may know a disagreeable, a tragic, a horrible fact; you may *fear* it has happened; you may have guessed it has happened; you may by intuition and in your inner self be quite sure, morally sure, it has happened...but that is all; you have, having reached that intuitive certainty, put the matter away from you. There is, between this inner intuitive knowledge and the brutal announcement of the fact by a third person – enemy or, worse still, friend – all the difference in the world. When this inner, undefined, intuitive certainty is confirmed from the outside by an enemy, a friend, a stranger, or a casual acquaintance, or, perhaps, a paragraph in the newspaper, then the effect of it is immense – shattering – overwhelming.

So it was with Blanche. It was to her the final blow, the final knock-out blow, that is delivered by the victor of a fight, after he has really won the fight, after the decisive, the fatal blow has been dealt; when, after the defeated man has perhaps risen to his feet, and can still spar in a dazed fashion, then a last seemingly superfluous blow is dealt which finishes the whole thing.

Blanche knew well – she had known for years – that Bernard loved Rose Mary, but that others should realise it to that extent, that Bessie should know it, that was the sting...and greater, bitterer far than that, there was a further sting. Blanche had up to now always said to herself: "Bernard loves Rose Mary, and small wonder, considering how young and lovely she is, and considering I am old, and so much older than he and she, but, all the same, I played a greater part in his life than she did... I meant more to him, and nothing can alter that... "

But now there was the phrase in Bessie's letter about Bernard having said to Rose Mary that in every man's life there was one thing, only one thing that really counted, one thing different from all the others, and that in his life it was she, Rose Mary. Blanche knew that Bessie could not have invented that phrase, with the best will in the world. She knew, too, that Bernard could never have said it if the contrary had been true; if, for a moment, in reality she, Blanche, had been what had counted most in the past to him, however much he might have forgotten her since, however much better he might have loved Rose Mary afterwards, later.

No; it was true. That was the fact that she had never faced before. She, Blanche, was not the person – she *never had been* – who had counted the most in Bernard's life (although Bernard may have thought so). She was an accident. She...and other phrases that Bessie had used to accentuate this fact in her letter rose before her in hideous distinctness.

Oh, how horrible! how bitter! how hideous it all was! And how richly she had deserved it! This was her punishment... Did she deserve all this punishment? She had surely been punished already...yes, but then she had always done wrong, always gone on doing wrong. Punishment was not meted out to mortals as by an irritable governess or a tyrannical schoolmaster; you were not sent to Hell as a child is put in the corner, or sent into a dark cupboard, arbitrarily, because you are getting on the nerves of a grown-up person, because you have been inattentive, or idle, or stupid – no, punishment is the logical result and consequence of ill-doing.

Goethe's poem came into her mind... How fond Adrian Tyne had been of quoting it:

> "Dann überlasst ihr jim der Pein;
> Denn alle Schuld rächt sich auf Erden."

The Nemesis is in your acts. Every sin avenges itself, carries its vengeance with it, just as a seed carries its fruit. You are made over to retribution, because all ill-doing necessarily bears its fruit, and its fruit is pain, retribution, compensation, punishment, whatever you like to call it. And even those who did not admit this had to submit to it. Even those who said there was no such thing as sin, or that sin is no different from measles or neuralgia, or those others who confidently looked on remorse not only as a weakness but as a positive evil, a crime rather than a medicine. They, too, had to submit. They could not avoid their retribution, although they might call it by some other name.

Farinata degli Uberti disbelieved in Hell while he was alive, and despised it, so Dante tells us, when he was dead, and in it, in a burning tomb...but despise it however much he might, with a *gran dispitto*, there he was, in it...it was there, the result, the inevitable fruit of his deeds, misdeeds, disbelief.

And now Blanche felt that for the first time she was reaping the reward of everything she had done, and she said to herself: "No; there is nothing *unjust* about it. It is quite right, and I shall bear it. And whatever happens now, I shall do nothing to make it worse...or shall I? It is rash to speak like that. Help me, dear God, dear Lord, not to, because I know how easy it is. Help me to pay the debt that I owe, that is already there to be paid, without adding to it. Otherwise, it will be a greater sum than I can ever meet."

She felt that around her there was a great emptiness, an arid, endless wilderness, a long, long, wide, wide loneliness – "It is all my fault," she said. "I have been selfish all my life, and I have done nothing but make others unhappy, because I have always thought of myself and not of them. I have always thought of myself with regard to Bernard, of myself with regard to Walter, of myself with regard to Guido, of myself with regard to Adrian, of myself with regard to all of them – Horace Crane, Eustace Lee, Stephen – even as far back as Sydney Hope. It has always been the same story…self, self…self, vanity…vanity…thirst for appreciation…and yet I never meant to do harm… I suppose that is the worst of excuses, and it is not as if I had been really bad – vicious. I suppose that makes it worse too…the worst things I did were in a way the best; they were the most honest and the most easily forgiven. But now, oh, what shall I do? How can I go on living? Why should I be there, chained to Bernard like a cannon-ball chained to a galley-slave, a drag on him, simply making him miserable… Why? Because I myself forged the chain. That is why. I made the situation."

She remembered a little French proverb she had seen acted in her father's drawing-room – "*Comme on fait son lit on se couche.*"

Those little proverbs had a way of bringing the truth home to one quicker and sharper than anything else.

Blanche remained sitting before the fire that night till it was time to dress. The whole of her past life seemed to pass before her in a series of pictures.

"I am not to be pitied," she thought. "All the others are far more greatly to be pitied – Arthur, Guido, Serge, Adrian, Bernard, Walter, Horace, Eustace, Stephen… If I had not made the initial mistake, all this would not have happened.

"The mistake was marrying Guido. I knew it was wrong at the time, and I did it; everything else proceeded directly from that, nothing wiped out that first blunder. It is like making a mistake at the beginning of a game of bridge…however well you play afterwards, however brilliantly you recover, you will not make the odd trick unless your opponents make some still greater mistake; and in life the opponent never makes a mistake. You can never count on that. The adversary is inexorable and infallible. I have made myself unhappy, and others more unhappy still, and so will it go on until I die. Oh no! Not that, dear God."

She walked into her bedroom and knelt down on her *prie-Dieu* in front of the crucifix. "Not that," she prayed. She prayed to be saved from herself for what remained of her life, not to do more harm, not to cause further unhappiness...and scalding tears poured down her cheeks. And it was then the wound caused by the whole situation seemed to pierce her soul, and, as it pierced it, it healed it.

The poison suddenly left it...the venom disappeared. It was as if God had suddenly touched Bessie's poisoned arrow while it was still deep in the quivering wound, and, without lessening its power and pain, changed the nature of it, took away the venom and left instead of it, balm; a sense of medicine and healing and peace. Blanche felt at that moment that she would for the rest of her life be able to sacrifice herself. She made the supreme act of self-sacrifice; she knew now, that from henceforth she would never grudge Bernard his love for another; she would be able to live without help, without friends, without love; without Walter, without Stephen, without any one. And from the act of inner self-sacrifice and renunciation she made, came balm; just as, hitherto, from every act of self-indulgence she had ever made, had come a sense of scorching ashes. "*Entbehren sollst du, entbehren,*" she said to herself, and she realised that although she had often repeated these words with her lips, it was the first time she had ever said them with her heart. Thus it was that Bessie wounded and healed Blanche's soul.

She dressed for dinner and dined downstairs. The Jacksons came to dinner, and Bernard was glad to see that Blanche seemed to be in unusually good spirits, and Jackson paid her jocose compliments, and said to Bernard over the port and the nuts: "Her ladyship is looking like a queen tonight."

Bernard agreed.

"The air here does her good," he said.

Whether it was the result of Bessie's letter and of the spiritual crisis brought on by the receipt of it, or whether it was merely coincidence, it was about a week later that Blanche, having been unusually energetic, and after having been busy at all sorts of local affairs, and having dined with some neighbours and entertained others every day, suddenly fell seriously ill. The local doctor, who was a clever man, and whom Blanche preferred greatly to the London doctors (his name was Warley, and he had had an interesting career in his youth in Germany, but had slightly not ruined but lessened his prospects and career by marrying an expensive wife), was puzzled; she had a temperature for no ostensible cause...she was weak, anaemic, like a person who is suffering from a sudden shock.

"Keep quiet and rest for a few days," he said. "Perhaps you have been overdoing it."

The weather had been unseasonably warm, too...but the days went on and she grew no better.

Dr Warley felt at a loss; he frankly said that he did not know what was the cause of this disease, and he advised her to go up to London and consult the London doctors.

Bernard took her up to London, and she saw not only Bernard's doctor, but a famous physician in consultation. They neither of them said anything definite. They advised rest. She must drink Burgundy...she wanted *tone*. They prescribed tonics... So matters went on till Easter.

Blanche had a slight temperature almost every day. The doctors recommended change of air, and at the end of May, Bernard took her to Aix-les-Bains, where they spent a month in baking weather.

Bessie's letter had exactly an opposite effect on the relations between Blanche and Bernard than what she had anticipated when she wrote it. She thought it would cause a final breach between them, instead of which it brought them closer together – closer than ever, to all outward appearances. Never had Bernard been more attentive, more considerate, more unselfish; and although the agony was to Blanche the same, for she felt that all the time, although his affection was with her, his heart was leagues away...she knew she could bear it.

Walter and Rose Mary were back at the Dower House. Walter was writing his book. Rose Mary was leading a sane, busy, practical, outdoor life, as before. She was fully occupied. She seemed never to have time to come to Alton-Leigh.

Aix-les-Bains did Blanche no good.

Bernard took her to Paris, where they consulted French doctors with reputations and lucid powers of exposition, and later to Germany, to Marienbad. But the doctors – French and German – were baffled.

They went home. At the end of July they were back at Alton-Leigh. Blanche begged Bernard to go on just as usual, to invite his friends. Even if she were not well enough to play an active part, others would help him; she would like to feel that everything was going on just as usual.

Stephen and Bessie were asked, but they refused. Stephen was busy. He did not know what had happened, but he guessed that Bessie had done something which made things more difficult. He had written to Blanche, and received a note from her nurse saying she was not well enough to write. And this made Stephen hate Bessie all the more. He neglected her as much as he dared. She had lasting influence over him, all the same. He spent all the time he could at the Club; he played cards; he won money; he lost money. He was careless; he grew fat and bloated. He insisted on cutting down expenses. Bessie refused to. They had scenes. She told him he had married her for her money. He retorted. They said unforgettable things to each other which were not lived down, but which they had to live down, and yet their life went on, and a sort of compromise was maintained. Stephen still did visit her relations with her from time to time – not often, and not for long, but he did it. He still let Bessie give little dinner-parties, where bridge was played afterwards, and still dined out with Bessie occasionally at pompous dinner-parties in Eaton Place and Wilton Crescent. But they never went to Alton-Leigh.

Blanche saw few people. She no longer came down to meals, and there was a nurse now looking after her permanently. More medical advice was taken, but the doctors all said the same thing: there was nothing to be done…rest, air, no worry, good food, attention.

Gradually, as happens, every one began to get used to the fact that Blanche was ill.

Bernard no longer had large parties, but he asked a few men friends for the shooting. Blanche used to come down when it was fine and be wheeled about on the terrace in a bath-chair. She never came down to dinner now. There were days when she was better, days when her temperature went down, but she was a bad sleeper and had to be given sleeping draughts. By Christmas-time, although she had hardly been ill a year, her appearance was sadly altered. She was getting dreadfully thin and was losing weight. She looked extremely frail, her skin seemed almost transparent, her eyes unnaturally large.

After Christmas, which they spent quietly – (Bernard only asked two friends) – and the New Year, Blanche seemed to rally, and she went to London again. For a week or two she seemed to improve; a new treatment had been recommended which seemed to do her good. Bernard thought that the English climate was too cold for her, and he took her – at the advice of a new doctor – to the south of France. He took a villa near Cannes. But there she fell ill again – so ill that at one moment her life was despaired of. However, she rallied and got better, but she was left exhausted, and extremely weak. She had lost several stones, and now she weighed almost nothing. She was the shadow and ghost of what she had been. She passionately wished to go back to England, and as soon as it was thought possible for her to travel, she was allowed to go back. She reached London in June, and after a day or two they went down to Alton-Leigh, and there her invalid life began again, but she seemed to be a little better. The rest of the year went by without bringing any change in her condition. Sometimes she would be better, and sometimes she would be worse, but she was always ill. She was terribly thin.

At the end of July the two Olenev girls came from Rome on purpose to see her, and at Bernard's urgent request they stayed at Alton-Leigh till they went back to Rome at the end of October.

Their visit did Blanche good, but they were shocked at her appearance and condition. "Blanche," Ira said to Nelly, "is dying of starvation – heart starvation." Nelly agreed. They were the only friends she had left in the world – the only people she felt she could talk to. From time to time Blanche would see Walter, when she was well enough to see any one, but she never saw him for long. That friendship was over. She had cut it out of her life.

Stephen came to Alton-Leigh that autumn for the shooting by himself. Bessie had taken her children to the seaside.

But his visit coincided with one of Blanche's bad weeks, and he was not allowed to see her, not even for a moment.

Christmas came and went, and Bernard did not think that Blanche would live through the winter. The doctor was constantly in the house, and she had to be given drugs.

In January, just as in the previous year, she had another bad relapse, and once more all hope was given up, and once more she rallied, and at Easter she seemed better than she had been for a long time. She felt a wish to go to London. She wanted to see Father Byrne, who was getting old; she felt that if she did not see him soon, she would never see him again.

Father Byrne was getting old, but he came to see Blanche. He was shocked at her appearance when he saw her. They had a long talk both about religious and secular affairs, but Blanche no longer felt any need to consult any one any more about her intimate affairs. All that, she felt, was over. What was happening now was the quiet, sad harvest of her unfruitful life – the twilight – the end. She told Father Byrne she thought she had made those around her unhappy all her life, and that she had caused a great deal of misery, but he swept this aside and told her she was suffering from *accidia*, which was a sin one should be careful to guard against. He left her with many blessings, and said she ought to be thankful for the many graces she had received.

Blanche, having made this effort, felt she could not make another. The doctors and nurses were more hopeful about her now; they said that, if they could gradually get her used to leaving off the heroin which she had been given, she would recover her strength. They gave her diminishing doses, but every time they left it off entirely she got ill, and they had to begin to give it once more. She was ill in June, in London, and as soon as she made a slight rally she begged to be taken back to Alton-Leigh. She suffered from racking headaches now, sleeplessness, and neuralgia.

That year Rose Mary and Walter had spent the summer in London. Walter worked for a weekly review; indeed, he helped to edit it. His book on his Far Eastern experiences had enjoyed considerable success, and editors and publishers began to run after him. But he wrote no more and no less than before, and he was determined to travel again as soon as he had the opportunity. He still felt that he was in the way and not wanted, in spite of Rose Mary's admirable behaviour, in spite of the great love he had for his children; they were fond of him, too, but fonder of their mother.

During all this time Bernard behaved with restraint. He never tried to see Rose Mary. He did everything that was possible for Blanche, and he looked after her with the most delicate and unflagging devotion. Blanche was touched, but the greater his attention, the sadder it made her. Her sadness never diminished for a moment.

It was a warm Christmas – a green Yuletide. There was no party in the house. Walter and Rose Mary were staying with Walter's sister, Marian, who had a large children's party. They took the children with them. Bessie and Stephen were staying with Bessie's uncle.

At Alton-Leigh there was nobody except the Wallaces. Bernard had asked them to come and stay, because he thought it was good for Blanche to have some one with her, and Kitty Wallace was a woman she was particularly fond of.

Blanche seemed to be a little better, and on Christmas Day she was wheeled into the gallery of the chapel to hear Mass. But after Christmas she had a relapse. She was weaker. Mrs Wallace thought her condition serious. So did the nurse, and so did Dr Warley. They prepared Bernard for the worst.

Bernard sent a telegram to Walter saying that Blanche was seriously ill. This was on the morning of 6th January, the Epiphany, exactly four years to a day after Lady Troumestre had died. It was a lovely, still day. Mass was said in the chapel in the morning, but Blanche was too ill to attend it. The priest heard her Confession and brought her Holy Communion, and she asked him herself for the Holy Oils.

When the nurse arranged the little table by her bedside as an altar, with a crucifix and two candles, and made his preparations, she thought of three things: the procession of the Viaticum she had seen years before in Rome, the death of her Uncle Charles in Seville, and his last words, and the evening when Rose Mary was given the Last Sacraments in Mansfield Street. She wondered whether she too would get well...but this, it seemed, was a side issue, a speculation that no longer concerned her any more than the winner of next year's Derby...whether she did or not, she felt that everything was settled...she was perfectly lucid, she just felt tired, utterly exhausted, and yet at peace. The priest talked of a "sick call":

she felt it was a call that had been sounding all her life: she was now answering it. "I have never," she thought, "answered it before."

In the afternoon she was better. Bernard at once became optimistic again, and when the doctor said she really had taken a turn for the better, Bernard said there was no doubt she would recover. He cited the case of Rose Mary, and went out with Jackson.

There was a lovely sunset that evening – still and grey and pink, the first faint presage of spring. It was warm for the time of year. When the sunset faded, the night was lovelier still; the moon was in her first quarter; there was one star in the still, luminous darkness.

Blanche's bedroom was hot. Mrs Wallace was sitting by her bedside; she had just left the men in the dining-room to their port.

Bernard came in presently, and said, with a look of unfeigned happiness: "Walter and Rose Mary are coming back tomorrow."

"I'm so glad," said Blanche, and she smiled.

"I'll come back presently," he said, "as soon as Jackson goes."

Jackson and Dr Warley had been dining at the house. Dr Warley thought he would perhaps stay the night. He was uneasy about Blanche, in spite of her apparent improvement.

"What a lovely night it is!" said Blanche.

The curtains were not drawn, as Blanche liked to be able to see out of the window.

"Do you think we could open the window a minute?"

Mrs Wallace asked the nurse next door. She said yes, the window could be opened a moment if Blanche wrapped up well. Kitty wrapped Blanche up in a white shawl, opened the window, and from outside came the noise of music – strings and whistling, a flute, a harp, and violin. Farther off some one was singing a carol.

"There's a dance going on tonight," said Mrs Wallace, "in the stables."

"Doesn't it sound lovely?" said Blanche. "Twelfth Night... Epiphany music...shepherds...the kings...the star...it's all there."

The music stopped. There was evidently a pause between two dances; but in that pause a fainter music, as of distant pipes, came stealing through the air, clear and distinct – a sad, plaintive tune: a lament.

"He's calling Lady Annabel," Blanche said in a whisper.

She closed her eyes; and then she smiled and called: "Giovanni!"

"I think I'd better shut the window now," said Kitty. She got up and shut it.

But Blanche did not answer her. She was lying back on her pillow with closed eyes, looking, as she looked many years ago, like a beautiful white flower – her skin whiter than any camellia now, with an almost unearthly radiance, and smiling, as people smile when they hear soft music.

# CHAPTER XVIII

Blanche was buried at Alton-Leigh. She was greatly missed in the neighbourhood. It was, people felt, as if a rare, an exquisite scent had been taken from the atmosphere. Bernard was said to be inconsolable.

He went up to London directly after the funeral. Walter and Rose Mary went up as well. Walter was busy with his newspaper, which was not proving a financial success. It was doubtful whether it would last long.

In the spring the "trouble in the Balkans" was more virulent and more ominous than usual, and Walter decided to give up the editorship of the *Review*, which nobody seemed to want, and to go to Constantinople for the *Northern Pilot* or the *Morning News*, or for any one who would send him.

Now that Blanche was dead he felt more in the way, more unnecessary, more superfluous than ever. He was certain that Bernard and Rose Mary loved one another more than ever; although they seemed to be worlds apart, and hardly saw each other, Walter was convinced of it.

"If only I could be got out of the way," he thought, "they could be happily married, and all would be well. How badly the world is arranged! However, one must carry on as best one can."

In April, exciting events happened in Constantinople, and it was not difficult for Walter to get sent there. The *Morning News* jumped at the suggestion.

He went there and wrote a series of vivid letters about the counter-revolution against the young Turks, the deposition of the Sultan Abdul Hamid, and the accession to the throne of Sultan Mehmed V. Walter narrowly escaped being killed by a stray bullet in the main street of Pera, one day when bullets unexpectedly began flying about. He was wounded in the head, and had to stay in the hospital for five weeks.

He was back in London by the beginning of June.

Bernard spent the whole summer in London. He had by this time considerable financial interests in the City. He was busy. He had many friends.

"Poor Windlestone," people said. "He will never get over his wife's death."

Bessie's uncle had died in the meantime, and she had inherited the property in Norfolk. This made her hold over Stephen greater than ever. Their cat-and-dog life went on just as before, except that now Bessie had definitely the better of the situation. She had a strangle-hold on Stephen, and she made the most of her advantage.

Stephen escaped to his Club whenever he could.

In the summer, Bernard went for a prolonged tour in Canada and the United States, and he did not come back to Alton-Leigh till after Christmas. He felt he could not face a Christmas there this year. "There would be," he said to himself, "too many associations of Blanche for me."

Walter and Rose Mary were settled once more at the Dower House. Rose Mary would have preferred to have gone somewhere else, but Walter pointed out that they couldn't afford it, with the children growing up. The eldest boy was going to Downside in September; the second boy was at a private school at Eastbourne.

Walter was busy writing another book – a work of fiction this time, based on what he had seen in the Near East.

When Bernard came back from Canada in January, after Walter had come back from Constantinople, life at Alton-Leigh soon began to be the same as before Blanche died. That autumn there were guests for the partridge shooting, guests for the covert shooting in November, and, later on, a Christmas party.

Rose Mary, too, took pains to have her spare room occupied as often as possible. She invited Walter's sisters, and asked Walter to invite friends of his whenever he liked.

Their household seemed an ideally happy one; so much so, that when people who were staying at Alton-Leigh would see Rose Mary surrounded by their children, and a friend or two, they would say: "There is a happy marriage!"

Walter missed Blanche dreadfully. It was as if his one playmate had been taken away from him.

He wanted to go abroad again, but there was nothing sufficiently interesting happening anywhere to give him an excuse for going.

But before Christmas that year there was a General Election. Bernard persuaded Walter to stand for Parliament, for the local seat, which he had once stood for. He would pay his expenses.

Walter refused to admit that he was either a Liberal or a Conservative, but finally a compromise was reached, and he stood as an Independent Conservative, and got in.

The next year Walter and Rose Mary settled down in London for the opening of Parliament.

Bernard came up to London; he, too, was busy.

They all stayed in London through the summer. A few people came to Alton-Leigh in the autumn, and in November Bernard sailed for India to see the Durbar at Delhi. He sailed from India a few months later.

Rose Mary stayed in London as long as Parliament was sitting. They spent the recess at Alton-Leigh. In October, war broke out between Bulgaria and Turkey and Servia, and Walter declared he must go out and see what was happening. He promised not to be away for more than a month. Rose Mary thought it foolish. She tried to persuade him not to go.

"You had better let him go," said Bernard. "He will be so restless if he doesn't go, and the sooner he goes, the sooner he will come back."

He went to Sofia, to Monastir; then back to Sofia, and from Sofia *via* Bucharest to Constantinople. There, after having visited the Chatalja lines, he had an attack of dysentery, to which he bad been liable ever since he had been in the Far East, and he died at an hotel at Pera, after a short illness.

Rose Mary received a cable from the British Ambassador, telling her the news. She was shocked, stunned, and relieved that at least she had tried to persuade him not to go. She sent the cable to Bernard, and she broke the news to the children, and wrote to the boys at school, and telegraphed to the headmaster.

All that night Rose Mary reviewed her past life and her life with Walter. She felt no remorse, and she blamed Blanche. It was Blanche who had upset their lives, who had entangled the threads of the legitimate pattern on the loom of their lives; she could not forgive her.

That Blanche had suffered, that Blanche was dead, did not affect her. She was unchanged and implacable in her judgments. Perhaps it was the Spanish strain in her that made her so unrelenting.

Whatever the reason, there it was; and whenever people talked to her about Bernard not having got over the death of his wife, she felt her heart freezing; she had to exercise an effort not to let people notice it.

Bernard was frankly and genuinely miserable. He felt that it was his fault that Walter had died; that he had been the obstacle to Walter's happiness; and he had, in fact, ruined his life. However, there it was. It was now all over.

Rose Mary left the Dower House for good. She settled to live henceforth either in London or with her sister-in-law, Hester, whose husband was nearly always away. They took a little house together in Dorsetshire. Hester now had four children of her own.

Bernard felt intolerably lonely at first at Alton-Leigh. He invited any one he could think of for Christmas, and now that Blanche was dead, Bessie had no objection to going there with Stephen. They both spent Christmas there that year.

The next year Bernard went up to London and spent March and April in the south of France, and the summer in London. Then he went back to Alton-Leigh, where he stayed during the autumn and the winter in the usual way.

He did not see Rose Mary again till just after the following Easter. He tried to see her, but she was never in London when he called. They met accidentally in Kensington Gardens. There she was, walking by herself, looking just the same – radiant, proud, and beautiful – young. She looked younger than ever.

He acted on the spur and impulse of the moment, and before he knew what he had done, he had asked her to be his wife. She was taken aback, and said: "No, Bernard; it's impossible."

"Why is it impossible? They would both be pleased."

"No, no."

She ran away from him.

"Think it over," he called after her.

Rose Mary went home in a state of great perturbation. She had not thought such a thing could possibly happen. She didn't sleep at all that night. Bernard had taken her so much by surprise that she had answered before she really knew what she thought about the matter.

She had answered automatically. Now that she began to think about it, she said to herself: "Is it so impossible after all? Can it be possible that he still cares for me after all these

671

years?" Or was he acting on a sudden impulse? Wasn't she too old? Well, she was not so old as Blanche had been when Blanche had married Bernard. She, Rose Mary, was now thirty-six, whereas Blanche, when she had married Bernard, had been at least forty-four, possibly older. Rose Mary looked at herself in the glass and decided that she looked young enough.

She would not put him to shame; and, then, she was younger than Bernard. She did not know his age, but she knew he was more than ten years older than she. From that point of view, then, it was not absurd after all. But there were other considerations. Could she make him happy? He had made one mistake, would he not now be making another? Yes…make him happy? did he really love her enough? She loved him enough; she had no doubt of that. She loved him just as much as ever. Perhaps he would never allude to it again; perhaps it was just the impulse of one mad moment.

But it was not so. Bernard came to see her the next day, and found her in at tea-time. He returned to the charge.

"I love you more than ever," he said. "I can't love you more; no one else can ever love you as much; you know it. You always have known it – all these years. Well, now, this seems to me the hand of Providence… "

"Supposing it's a failure?"

"It won't be a failure; we will make it a success. You know me now, you know my faults, and we know that we understand one another better than any other two people. We have always known that. I see no drawback."

"The children… "

"I have always loved your children, and I'm sure there's no one Walter would rather have had to help to bring them up instead of himself than me."

"Yes! I don't think Walter would have minded that."

"Do you think he would have minded anything?"

"No; I don't think he would, but ought we to snatch this happiness?"

"Why not?"

"Well, in a way it seems too good. I don't think we deserve it. At least, I know I don't."

"If it comes to that, nobody deserves anything; but if we all acted on that principle, nobody would do anything."

"It seems so soon."

"If you want me to wait, I'll wait. I'll wait for years – but haven't we waited long enough? Don't you think if we are to do it, the sooner we do it the better?"

"I wonder what Lady Alice would have thought about it?"

"I'm sure she would have said, 'Do it.'"

"Have you talked to anybody about it?"

"No; not to a soul."

"I should like to ask Hester what she thinks."

"Ask Hester, by all means."

"I should like a fortnight to think it over."

"As long as you like."

The fortnight passed – slowly to Bernard, quickly to Rose Mary. She passionately wanted to marry Bernard, but she was not sure whether she was doing a perfectly wise thing. Nobody could say there was anything wrong in it, but she had a superstitious fear of the future if she married Bernard. She was afraid for him. But she now knew that unless some unforeseen catastrophe happened she would do it.

When Bernard came to see her at the end of the fortnight, the discussion was brief. His first words were:

"Well, have you made up your mind?"

She smiled at him, and nodded.

She was standing in the little downstairs room in the house in Mansfield Street, the room in which Bernard and Blanche, Walter and Lady Alice, had waited the night Rose Mary had been so ill.

She was dressed in white. He thought he had never seen her look so beautiful. Her face was transfigured with happiness. He took her in his arms. There was no further discussion.

They were married quietly (not by Father Byrne; he was dead) at the beginning of June, so as to avoid May, and they went away for a month to a little house in Normandy that Madame d'Aurillac kindly lent them, and at the end of June they went back to Alton-Leigh.

This was a strange homecoming for Rose Mary – to find herself now living in the big house, and no longer at the Dower House. The marriage surprised some people, but most people found it natural, and every one said, "It is such a good thing."

They arrived at Alton-Leigh on the last day of June. The weather was perfect. The place looked at its best. The garden was a blaze of flowers; the Madonna lilies, which had been planted by Blanche, were all out. The house looked as if it belonged to a fairy-tale. It was so serene, so mellow, so still, so dignified, in its quiet, romantic beauty. Bernard and Rose Mary made a fine couple as they walked across the courtyard into the hall, where Ramiro had tea ready for them. Rose Mary wondered what Ramiro thought. He never showed his feelings; only in the drawing-room he was careful to put Blanche's favourite flowers.

They had travelled straight down to Alton-Leigh when they arrived from Havre to Southampton, and so absorbed were they in themselves, and so oblivious of everything else, that they did not even bother to buy newspapers, and when later on in the evening Rose Mary saw Bernard looking at the *Times*, and she said to him, "Is there any news?" he said to her, "No; nothing very interesting. They've shot an Austrian Archduke, and the fleet has been well received at Kiel."

Bernard felt that after many troubles and vicissitudes, after having been buffeted on stormy seas, and blown about by merciless winds, they had at last reached a quiet haven.

"Now we can at last be happy...and quiet," he said.

"Yes; it is peaceful, isn't it?"

They were so contented, and so absorbed in their happiness and in each other, that they paid little attention to what the newspapers said about foreign news.

But one day Bernard, after reading the *Times*, said: "I say, Rose Mary, things do look serious about Austria and Servia."

"Yes; I have just been looking at the newspaper. If Walter had been alive, he would have started by now for some outlandish place. But I suppose the Austrians will accept the apology."

"Sure to. The Powers would intervene. We couldn't all go to war about Servia."

"Austria could go to war, I suppose?"

"Well, if the Servians do everything they want... "

But two days later Bernard received a letter in a buff envelope.

"I shall have to go to London. The reserves are being called up."

"I'll come too."

They went up to London, and found every one in a state of excitement, although nobody seemed to know what was happening. But one fact stood out clearly: Austria was not satisfied with the Servian answer, and refused to listen to any offer of mediation. It seemed certain that there would be war between Austria and Servia, and what might that not lead to?

One night Rose Mary and Bernard went to the Russian opera and heard Chaliapin sing in "Boris Godounov," and one night they went to a dance they were asked to at the Thames Hotel by a friend of Bernard's.

People were talking of the situation as grave. It was certain there would be war, but war between whom? That was the question.

Rose Mary had not been to an entertainment for a long time – not for a long time before Walter had died. She looked beautiful in night-blue tulle, with a large red poppy at her waist.

She did not find it difficult to find partners. She danced every dance. Supper was served at little tables. She was sitting at supper with Lord Ayton, who was a Parliamentary Under-Secretary.

At a table not far from where she was sitting, Mrs Wallace was having supper with Herbert Napier, who was now First Secretary at the Embassy at St Petersburg. She had known him years ago, but they had not met for years, not since she had married. She had been one of his partners when he first came out, and they had had the greatest fun together during his first London season. He had gone abroad, and she had married, and they had never met since.

"And now you've got a daughter out?" said Napier.

(Kitty Wallace had had five sons, who were now all grown up, and one daughter.)

"Well, she's not supposed to be out till next year. She's been for the last six months at Paris at a *pension*, polishing up her French, and I went over to fetch her last week; but they begged me to bring her tonight, and as she has already been to a *bal blanc* in Paris, and as she was longing to go, I thought she might as well come. There she is, dancing with that tall, fair boy."

"She looks as if she were enjoying herself."

"She may as well, while she can. What do you think of the news tonight?"

"I don't think it looks good. It's war between Austria and Servia, whatever happens."

"I saw in the *Westminster* that the crowd in Berlin shouted 'Hoch England!' What did that mean?"

"I suppose they think that if there is war between Germany and France we should be neutral."

"But we couldn't be, could we?"

"I hope not."

"Are you going back to Russia?"

"Yes; I'm starting tomorrow…or else it may be too late."

"It's like the ball the night before the Battle of Waterloo, isn't it?"

"Yes; just like that. The lines in *Childe Harold* about that always give me a lump in my throat."

"So they do me. If there's a war… I think we are sure to be in it, don't you?"

Kitty looked across the room: one of her boys, just twenty-three, tall, good-looking, fresh, in the Guards, was dancing with a pretty girl.

"Sooner or later. I only hope if we are to be in it we shan't be too late."

"What do they think at the Foreign Office?"

"I saw Vauban, one of the French Secretaries, who is pessimistic. He thinks there's bound to be a war, and he thinks we shan't come in till it's too late."

"I think Grey will do well."

"Yes; I'm sure he will."

"Who is that dark lady sitting at that table over there talking to Sir Frank Wigmore? That is Sir Frank, isn't it?"

"Yes. It's the Italian Ambassadress, Madame San Paolo."

"Oh, really! Not the one… "

"The one Sir Hedworth Lawless…yes. Did you know the Lawlesses?"

"Yes; a little. They used to come and stay in the country near us with Bernard and Blanche Windlestone. They're both dead now, aren't they?"

"Yes. She died last year; he, of course, died three years ago."

"She is handsome, isn't she?"

"Madame San Paolo? – yes, and so charming."

"Is he here tonight?"

"Yes. He's sitting over there talking to Lady Trafalgar. Apropos of Bernard Windlestone – you know him, of course, very well?"

"Yes; we are neighbours. I see them constantly."

"And now he's married again?"

"Yes; he married Walter Troumestre's widow. There she is, talking to George Ayton."

"Do you admire her?"

"Yes; I think she's radiantly good-looking, but nothing like Blanche."

"I quite agree; she *was* lovely, wasn't she?"

"Yes, quite, and what charm!"

"I remember seeing her when I first went to Rome, when she was Princess Roccapalumba. I couldn't take my eyes off her."

"She went on being beautiful till she died."

"What did she die of?"

"I don't know what they called it, but I can tell you what it was…plain misery; what used to be called a broken heart."

"I see… Bernard…"

"Yes."

"Poor thing!"

"Is Bernard here tonight? I haven't seen him."

"He's at a table right over there having supper with his back to us."

"I can't see who that is with him."

Bernard was sitting next to some one who was screened from Mrs Wallace's view, although Napier could see her. She was a beautiful and extremely finished-looking person, with drooping, soft violet eyes, and long lashes, exquisite lines, shoulders and hands, and graceful movements. She was dressed in pink satin and tulle – several shades of pink, like the heart of a rose – and wore no ornaments, except a cluster of stephanotis on her shoulder. She was looking down, and seemed to be listening to Bernard with grave and rapt interest.

"It's Mrs Bucknell," Napier said.

"Leila?"

"Yes."

"Is she just as pretty as ever?"

"Just."

"She has never been a friend of Bernard's, has she?"

"No, not yet, that I know of."

"Tell me who some of the other people are. I have been away for so long, and lived such a hermit's life, that I don't know a soul by sight. Who is that fair-haired man sitting at the table just in front of us?"

"I believe he's at the German Embassy."

"Well, if the Germans are here, relations can't be so strained."

"No, not yet. But things happen so quickly."

"I believe a war would be unpopular up in the north. What do people in your part of the country say?"

"I don't think they have realised it at all. They don't understand why we should go to war about Servia."

"Of course, it wouldn't be about Servia."

"No; but that's what's so difficult to make them understand."

While this conversation was going on, Rose Mary was sitting at supper with her partner, George Ayton. She was saying to him: "But, if there is a war, would Bernard be able to go?"

"I think he would find it difficult to go at once. Everybody will be wanting to go, and they can't all go."

"No; but Bernard was a soldier, you see, and he was in South Africa, and he's in the Reserve…he's got his papers."

"Oh, he'll get some job – but it might be in England."

"But it's not certain there will be war, is it?"

"There'll be a war, but it's not certain we shall be in it, by any means."

"Bernard's sure to go – "

"By the way, is Bernard here? I haven't seen him."

"Yes; he's over there having supper with some one. I can't see who it is because of the pillar."

"It's Mrs Bucknell."

"Oh!"

"Do you know her?"

"Very little; just to say 'How-do-you-do?' to."

"Pretty woman."

"Yes, very."

Rose Mary and Bernard were both silent as they drove home in their motor-car. Rose Mary had a strange sense that this drive had happened before. Bernard felt strange as well. There was something in the carriage – what was it? – a slight, subtle fragrance of cherry-pie and jasmine that reminded him softly of Blanche. It was like a whisper. When they had almost reached Ovington Square, Rose Mary said to Bernard: "Was that Mrs Bucknell you were having supper with?"

"Yes – and looking well, I thought."

"Very; do you know her well?"

"No; I have always just missed knowing her somehow, but she was telling me tonight how fond she used to be of Blanche."

There was a note of reverence in his voice, which was more noticeable when he said the word *she* than in the word *Blanche.*

"Oh," said Rose Mary.

As they walked to their front door a strayed reveller passed them on the pavement. He was singing a snatch from a song which had drifted from the Music Halls *via* the Pantomime, into the popularity of the street.

"Goodbye, Piccadilly,"

he sang cheerfully,

"Farewell, Leicester Square;
It's a long, long way to Tipperary… "

# Maurice Baring

## 'C'

Baring's homage to a decadent and carefree Edwardian age depicts a society as yet untainted by the traumas and complexities of twentieth-century living. With wit and subtlety a happy picture is drawn of family life, house parties in the country and a leisured existence clouded only by the rumblings of the Boer War. Against this spectacle Caryl Bramsley (the *C* of the title) is presented – a young man of terrific promise but scant achievement, whose tragic-comic tale offsets the privileged milieu.

## The Coat Without Seam

The story of a miraculous relic, believed to be a piece of the seamless coat won by a soldier on Mount Golgotha after Jesus of Nazareth's crucifixion, captivates young Christopher Trevenen after his sister dies tragically and motivates the very core of his existence from then on, culminating in a profound and tragic realization.

# Maurice Baring

## The Puppet Show of Memory

It was into the famous and powerful Baring family of merchant bankers that Maurice Baring was born in 1874, the seventh of eight children. A man of immense subtlety and style, Baring absorbed every drop of culture that his fortunate background showered upon him; in combination with his many natural talents and prolific writing this assured him a place in literary history.

In this classic autobiography, spanning a remarkable period of history, Maurice Baring shares the details of an inspirational childhood in nineteenth-century England and a varied adulthood all over the world, collecting new friends and remarkable experiences. It has been said that Baring's greatest talent was for discovering the best in people, that he had a genius for friendship, and in this superb book his erudition and perception are abundantly clear.

'A classic autobiography' *Dictionary of National Biography*

## Tinker's Leave

Reserved and unworldly, young Miles Consterdine and his epiphanic trip to Paris is Maurice Baring's first bead on this thread of a story based on impressions received by the author in Russia and Manchuria during wartime. From here Baring allows us to peek through windows opening onto tragic and comic episodes in the lives of noteworthy people in remarkable circumstances.

# Maurice Baring

## Daphne Adeane

Barrister Basil Wake and his arresting wife Hyacinth lead a well-appointed existence in the social whirl of London's early 1900s. For eight years Hyacinth has conducted a most discreet affair with Parliamentarian Michael Choyce, who seems to fit into the Wakes' lives so conveniently. But an invitation to attend a Private View and a startling portrait of the mysterious and beautiful Daphne Adeane signifies a change in this comfortable set-up.

## In My End Is My Beginning

This historical novel tells the tragic story of Mary Queen of Scots, from her childhood until the beginning of her end, whose unwise marital and political actions provoked rebellion among Scottish nobles and forced her to flee to England, where she was beheaded as a Roman Catholic threat to the throne. The clash of opinion over whether Mary was a martyr or a murderess is perfectly represented by four eye-witnesses (The Four Maries – her ladies-in-waiting) who narrate this captivating story with distinctive conclusions.

## OTHER TITLES BY MAURICE BARING AVAILABLE DIRECT
## FROM HOUSE OF STRATUS

| Quantity | | £ | $(US) | $(CAN) | € |
|---|---|---|---|---|---|
| ☐ | 'C' | 8.99 | 14.99 | 22.50 | 15.00 |
| ☐ | THE COAT WITHOUT SEAM | 8.99 | 14.99 | 22.50 | 15.00 |
| ☐ | DAPHNE ADEANE | 8.99 | 14.99 | 22.50 | 15.00 |
| ☐ | IN MY END IS MY BEGINNING | 8.99 | 14.99 | 22.50 | 15.00 |
| ☐ | THE PUPPET SHOW OF MEMORY | 9.99 | 16.50 | 24.95 | 16.50 |
| ☐ | TINKER'S LEAVE | 8.99 | 14.99 | 22.50 | 15.00 |

ALL HOUSE OF STRATUS BOOKS ARE AVAILABLE FROM GOOD BOOKSHOPS
OR DIRECT FROM THE PUBLISHER:

**Internet:** www.houseofstratus.com including author interviews, reviews, features.

**Email:** sales@houseofstratus.com please quote author, title, and credit card details.

**Hotline:** UK ONLY: 0800 169 1780, please quote author, title and credit card details.
INTERNATIONAL: +44 (0) 20 7494 6400, please quote author, title and credit card details.

**Send to:** House of Stratus Sales Department
24c Old Burlington Street
London
W1X 1RL
UK

Please allow for postage costs charged per order plus an amount per book as set out in the tables below:

| | £(Sterling) | $(US) | $(CAN) | €(Euros) |
|---|---|---|---|---|
| **Cost per order** | | | | |
| UK | 1.50 | 2.25 | 3.50 | 2.50 |
| Europe | 3.00 | 4.50 | 6.75 | 5.00 |
| North America | 3.00 | 4.50 | 6.75 | 5.00 |
| Rest of World | 3.00 | 4.50 | 6.75 | 5.00 |
| **Additional cost per book** | | | | |
| UK | 0.50 | 0.75 | 1.15 | 0.85 |
| Europe | 1.00 | 1.50 | 2.30 | 1.70 |
| North America | 2.00 | 3.00 | 4.60 | 3.40 |
| Rest of World | 2.50 | 3.75 | 5.75 | 4.25 |

PLEASE SEND CHEQUE, POSTAL ORDER (STERLING ONLY), EUROCHEQUE, OR INTERNATIONAL MONEY ORDER (PLEASE CIRCLE METHOD OF PAYMENT YOU WISH TO USE)
MAKE PAYABLE TO: STRATUS HOLDINGS plc

**Cost of book(s):** —————————— Example: 3 x books at £6.99 each: £20.97

**Cost of order:** —————————— Example: £2.00 (Delivery to UK address)

**Additional cost per book:** —————————— Example: 3 x £0.50: £1.50

**Order total including postage:** —————————— Example: £24.47

Please tick currency you wish to use and add total amount of order:

☐ £ (Sterling)   ☐ $ (US)   ☐ $ (CAN)   ☐ € (EUROS)

VISA, MASTERCARD, SWITCH, AMEX, SOLO, JCB:

☐ ☐ ☐ ☐ ☐ ☐ ☐ ☐ ☐ ☐ ☐ ☐ ☐ ☐ ☐ ☐ ☐ ☐ ☐ ☐

**Issue number (Switch only):**

☐ ☐ ☐

**Start Date:** ☐☐/ ☐☐          **Expiry Date:** ☐☐/ ☐☐

**Signature:** ———————————

**NAME:** ———————————————————————

**ADDRESS:** ———————————————————————

————————————————————————

**POSTCODE:** ——————————

Please allow 28 days for delivery.

Prices subject to change without notice.
Please tick box if you do not wish to receive any additional information. ☐

House of Stratus publishes many other titles in this genre; please check our website (**www.houseofstratus.com**) for more details.